PRAISE FOR *HUNTRESS*:

"Lo's storytelling and prose are *masterful*, and her protagonists will fascinate, particularly Taisin and her relationship to death and its accompanying rituals, her visions, and the way she can occupy another's mind."

—*Publishers Weekly* (starred review)

"Most notably, the inclusion of gay characters in a young adult fantasy, and the natural unfolding of their relationship, comes as a refreshing change."

—*The Horn Book*

"*Heartbreaking sensuality*... blossoms between the female leads. Beyond romance, however, stunning action sequences abound, including one literal cliffhanger and a breathtaking confrontation with the villain. Fans who found themselves entranced by Lo's previous work will be pleased to know that the magic has returned to the Wood."

—*Bulletin of the Center for Children's Books*

"The lovely thing about this fantasy . . . is the completely natural sweetness of the attraction between Kaede and Taisin, which is unremarkable in their culture."

—*Kirkus Reviews*

"Lo has created a *wonderfully detailed world*, and this dynamic and moving story of love that must find a way against nearly insurmountable odds will be as well received as *Ash*."

—*School Library Journal*

Huntress

MALINDA LO

LITTLE, BROWN AND COMPANY
New York   Boston

Copyright © 2011 by Malinda Lo
Map illustration copyright © 2011 Dave Stevenson

"The Fox" © 2011 by Malinda Lo
Originally published in www.subterraneanpress.com in April 2011

Little, Brown and Company
Hachette Book Group
1290 Avenue of the Americas, New York, NY 10104
Visit us at LBYR.com

Little, Brown and Company is a division of Hachette Book Group, Inc.
The Little, Brown name and logo are trademarks of Hachette Book Group, Inc.

The publisher is not responsible for websites (or their content) that
are not owned by the publisher.

First Paperback Edition: June 2012
First published in hardcover in April 2011 by Little, Brown and Company

Library of Congress Cataloging-in-Publication Data
Lo, Malinda.
Huntress / Malinda Lo.—1st ed.
p. cm.
Prequel to: Ash.
Summary: Seventeen-year-olds Kaede and Taisin are called to go on a dangerous and unprecedented journey to Taninli, the city of the Fairy Queen, in an effort to restore the balance of nature in the human world.
ISBN 978-0-316-04007-5 (hc) / ISBN 978-0-316-03999-4 (pb)
[1. Fairy tales. 2. Love—Fiction. 3. Voyages and travels—Fiction. 4. Fairies—Fiction. 5. Hunting—Fiction. 6. Lesbians—Fiction.] I. Title.
PZ8.L773Hun 2011
[Fic]—dc22   2010038827

Book design by Alison Impey

To Amy Lovell

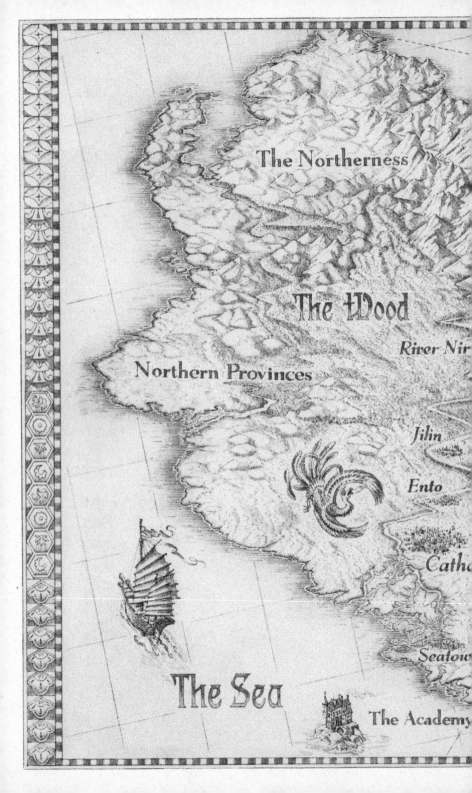

Elowen's
Island

The Glacier

Taninli

Mona's
Cottage

River Kell

The Kingdom

Southern Provinces

AUTHOR'S NOTE

Huntress is set in the same world as *Ash*, but it takes place many centuries earlier. There are some significant cultural differences between the time periods.

PRONUNCIATION GUIDE

In multisyllabic names, the emphasis is on the italicized syllable. In some cases, both syllables should be given equal weight. In human names, the letters *ae* are pronounced like the *a* sound in *mate* and *skate*; the letters *ai* are pronounced like the *i* sound in *kite* and *site*. Xi names (designated with asterisks) have different pronunciation rules.

Ailan: *Eye*-lahn
Anmin: *Ahn*-min
Cai Simin Tan: Tsai Sih-*meen* Tan
Con Isae Tan: Con *Ee*-say Tan
Ealasaid*: *Ay*-lah-*sed*
Elowen*: *Ell*-oh-*when*
Farin: *Fahr*-in
Kaede: *Kay*-dee
Kaihan: *Kye*-hahn
Maesie: *May*-see
Maila: *My*-lah
Maire Morighan*: Mare *Mor*-ih-*gahn*
Mona: *Mo*-nah
Nara: *Nah*-rah
Niran: *Nee*-rahn
Noa: *No*-ah
Ota: *Oh*-tah
Parsa: *Par*-sah
Pol: Pole
Raesa: *Ray*-sah
Raiden: *Rye*-den
Shae: Shay
Sota: *So*-tah
Suri: *Soo*-ree
Taeko: *Tay*-ko
Taisin: *Tie*-sin
Tali: *Tah*-lee
Taninli*: *Tan*-in-*lee*
Tanis: *Tan*-is
Tulan: *Too*-lahn
Xi*: Shee
Yuna: *Yoo*-nah
Yuriya: *Yoo*-ree-ah

PART I

Clouds and thunder arise:
The sage brings order.
Those who chase deer without a hunter
Lose their way in the Wood.

—*Book of Changes*

Chapter I

he saw a beach made of ice, and she felt her heart breaking.

The ground where she stood was frozen white, but twenty feet away, cold blue ocean lapped at the jagged shore. Someone there was climbing into a rowboat, and she knew that she loved this person. She was certain of it in the same way that one is instantly aware of the taste of sweetness in a drop of honey. But she was afraid for this person's life, and the fear raised a cold sweat on her skin and caused a sick lurch in her stomach, as though she were on a ship during a violent storm.

She opened her mouth to call the rower back—she couldn't bear the loss; it would surely cripple her—and at that moment she realized she could hear nothing. All around her was an eerie, unnatural silence. There was no sound from the ocean. She could not even hear herself breathing. She felt her tongue shaping the syllables of the person's name, but she did not recognize what the name was until the rower turned to face her. *Kaede.*

The rower was Kaede, and she looked back with dark, troubled eyes. Loose strands of black hair whipped around her pale face; there were spots of red on her wind-roughened cheeks. Her lips parted as though she would speak. But then Kaede reached down into the boat and lifted out a long oar, dipping it into the azure sea to propel the small craft away from the shore. The droplets of water falling from the blade of the oar were tiny stars, extinguished as quickly as they burned into being. The boat cut through the water, leaving the shore behind, and just before the destination came into view, the vision ended.

She was wrenched out of the icy landscape and back into her body, where she was sitting in the empty practice hall, alone on her cushion.

She opened her eyes, blinking against the light of the single candle she had lit on the altar. Her heart was pounding, and there was an acrid taste in her mouth. Her hands, folded in her lap, were trembling and chilled. A trickle of sweat ran from her temple down her cheek.

She drew her knees up and hugged them close, burying her face in the crook of her elbow, and because there was no one to hear her, she let out the sob that reared up in her throat. The sound echoed in the vaulted ceiling of the practice room, and for once she gave in to the overwhelming feelings rushing through her. She felt gutted. She felt powerless.

She had never seen so clearly before, and her teachers would praise her for it. But she felt no satisfaction, for she could not rejoice in the vision of someone she apparently loved departing on a journey to her death.

4

Chapter II

aede was working in the cliff garden when she received the summons. This was her favorite part of the Academy—the crescent-shaped patch of earth carved out of the edge of the island, facing the mainland. On a clear day, she could see the brownish-green hills behind the crooked roofs of Seatown. But there had not been a clear day in a little over two months; only this constant gray light and scattered drizzle. Yet, as much as she hated it, it was better to be outside in the brisk sea air than trapped indoors behind the Academy's suffocating stone walls.

She continued down the row of stunted carrots, working in the rich fertilizer that Maesie, the Academy's cook, had given her at the start of her shift. A hard winter had been followed by no sign of spring, and Maesie had delayed planting at first, hoping for sunshine and warmth before she subjected her seedlings to the cold earth. But one morning she announced that she would wait no more, and the seeds went into the ground that day, followed by biweekly applications of the thick black fertilizer she concocted in the evenings. And despite the lack of sunlight, the seeds sprouted, though they were thinner and weaker than usual.

Kaede had just finished the row and was about to drag the jug of fertilizer to the next when Maesie came out of the kitchen, an odd look on her face. She held a wooden spoon in her hand as if she had come straight from the stove. Kaede straightened, brushing off her dirty hands on her cotton trousers. "What is it?"

"I've just had word from the Council," Maesie said. "They want to see you."

Kaede was puzzled. What would the Council of Sages want with her? She was hardly one of their favorite students. "What? When?"

"Now. You'd better leave your things there. I'll have someone else finish up for you."

She blinked at Maesie. "Now?" She wasn't sure she had heard correctly.

"Now. But you should clean up before you go—you don't want to track mud all over their chambers."

⁓

Kaede had not been to the Council chambers since her first visit to the Academy of Sages when she was eleven, to apply for admission. In the ensuing six years, there had never been a reason for her to make the long trek to the North Tower, for the only students invited into that inner sanctum were those who could perform the rituals they were taught. Although she had read the *Book of Rituals* several times, Kaede had never successfully completed even the simplest of blessings. She knew she had only been allowed to remain at the Academy because her father was the King's Chancellor, and her mother—before she married him—had been a sage. Now she wondered if her time at the Academy was finally coming to an end, for why else would the Mistress have called for her, if not to dismiss her at last?

To reach the Council chambers, she had to climb a lengthy, circular flight of stairs. Carved in every step were the words to a different verse from the *Book of Changes*. She knew that if she read each step in order from the ground floor up, she would find the entire first folio there, comprising the core teachings that every student was required to learn during her first year. But Kaede only glanced down at random, and the verses made little sense out of context.

In disorder, misfortune.
In sincerity, fear gives way.
Dragons battle on the plain: yellow and black blood spills.
Fire in the mountain lake: grace brings success.

The phrases irritated her, reminding her of countless hours spent huddled over her books, feeling as though they were only mocking her. By the time she reached the landing outside the iron doors to the Council chambers, she was eager to be done with it. Whatever form her dismissal might take, she would welcome it.

She reached for the rope hanging from the mouth of the iron dragon embedded in the stone wall, and pulled. Several minutes later the left-hand door was opened by Sister

Nara, the youngest of the three Council members. Her black hair, which was normally coiled in two careful braids tucked against the nape of her neck, was coming loose as though she had rushed through her morning rituals. Two small vertical lines appeared between her brown eyes as she said, "Come in."

Kaede followed Sister Nara through the circular antechamber to the inner redwood doors. Each was hung with a round gold shield. On the left was a phoenix, its tail feathers curling toward its beak, wings extended: the sign of harmony. On the right was a unicorn, the symbol of justice; its deerlike head was lowered so that its curving horn pointed down, while its goatlike tail curled up.

Sister Nara opened the doors, and the moment that Kaede entered the Council chamber, she knew something was wrong—she could not have been called there merely to be dismissed. For there were two men seated at the long wooden table along with the Council members and the Mistress of the Academy: One of them was her father, Lord Raiden, the King's Chancellor; the other was King Cai Simin Tan himself. What could have possibly brought him all the way from his palace to the isolated Academy?

Out of long habit, she folded her hands and bowed to the King, but she did not acknowledge her father. The last time they had spoken, they had argued heatedly, and the memory of it still made her face burn with suppressed anger.

At the head of the table, Maire Morighan, the Mistress of the Academy, said, "Kaede, please sit down."

As she walked to the table, her cloth shoes making no

sound on the cold stone floor, her pulse quickened with curiosity. She saw the three Council members: Sister Nara, who was just pulling out her chair; Sister Ailan; and Sister Yuna. She saw Maire Morighan, her hands clasped on the table before a small wooden box. And, unexpectedly, she saw another student seated beside Sister Ailan. Kaede recognized the girl's face, but she couldn't remember her name. They had arrived at the Academy the same year, but after that first year, they had never had any classes together. She was supposed to be extraordinarily gifted, and she took all her classes in private with Sister Ailan. Kaede had never given much thought to her, but now she wondered why she was here. The girl's cheeks darkened a little under Kaede's gaze, and she turned deliberately toward the Mistress. And then Kaede remembered: Her name was Taisin.

Maire Morighan said: "You must be wondering why you have been called here. But before we can tell you that, you should know a bit more about why His Majesty has visited us so unexpectedly." She inclined her head toward the King. "Would you like to tell the tale, Your Majesty?"

King Cai glanced at Lord Raiden before turning his attention to Lord Raiden's daughter. He had seen her before, of course, when the Chancellor brought his family to the palace, but the King had never done more than keep track of her as a potentially useful tool. She was not the beauty her mother was, though she resembled her in spirit, at least, for she raised her eyes to him boldly. He ran a hand over his triangular beard, considering where to begin.

"One month ago," the King said, "a visitor arrived at the palace in Cathair. He demanded an audience with me, but he was in a wretched state—looked as if he'd been traveling for months, clothing all torn up. I thought he might be mad. Of course, I refused to see him. I couldn't risk it. This year alone my guards have uncovered three assassination attempts—those southern lords are getting more brazen by the day. So I waited until Lord Raiden—until your father returned from his visit to the South. That was about two weeks ago."

Kaede finally let herself look at her father, whose face was carefully blank as he regarded the King. He was wearing the plain black cap and robes of his station, but they were made of the finest silk, embroidered all over with phoenixes in black thread. The last time she had been home in Cathair, her father had been preparing for the trip to the southern provinces that the King had mentioned. The past two years had delivered extremely harsh winters followed by particularly poor harvests, especially in the South. This year, the strange, lingering winter, combined with the unexpected spoilage of much of the Kingdom's food stores, had led to growing panic among the people. The Academy was largely insulated from such things, but Kaede knew that some in the Kingdom were already going hungry, and hunger led to unrest—especially when the wealthy continued to eat well.

The King continued: "Your father met with this visitor as soon as he returned. He—I could hardly believe this when I first heard it—the man claimed that he had been given something by the Fairy Queen, and she had ordered him to deliver it to me. We have heard nothing from her people, the Xi—at least nothing *official*—in generations." He leaned forward, stabbing a heavily ringed finger against the table to emphasize his point. His blue silk sleeves ballooned. "I thought it was a hoax at first."

Kaede asked, "What do you mean, nothing official?"

Irritated by the interruption, the King answered brusquely, "There have been some sightings—nothing definite, mind you—but it seems that some of the Xi have been coming across the borders into our lands."

"It may not be the Xi who are crossing over," Maire Morighan said.

"Then who—or what—are they?" the King snapped. "They're unnatural, these creatures, whatever they are, and they don't belong here."

Lord Raiden said mildly, "Your Majesty, perhaps we can discuss the identity of these creatures later. Let's continue."

The King relented. "The man brought a box with him; he said it had come from the Fairy Queen herself. Inside the box there was a medallion and a scroll. The scroll was written in the language of the Xi, which we could not read. Lord Raiden informed me that the scroll appeared to be genuine, and in that case, we had no choice but to bring it here. This morning, the Council deciphered it. It appears to be an invitation to me to attend the Fairy Queen at her palace in Taninli at midsummer."

"This is the box," Maire Morighan said, gesturing to the small rosewood container before her. She placed her finger in the center of it, and the top opened like the petals of a flower. From within, she removed a tiny scroll and a medallion on a long silver chain. "We have read the scroll, and it is indeed an invitation. It seems that the Fairy Queen, at least, still abides by the laws of our treaty."

Kaede was puzzled. "What treaty?"

"Many generations ago, our kingdom negotiated a treaty with the Fairy Queen that established the border between her lands and ours," said the Mistress. "It was also agreed that we would each keep to our side of the border, and that no one—human, Xi, or other races of fay—would cross it without an invitation from the other land's sovereign. It has been so long since the Borderlands Treaty was signed, and no invitations were ever issued, I believe, until now. So this is quite unexpected."

Everything Kaede had been taught led her to believe that the Xi had no interest in humans anymore. Some traces of them remained—especially here at the Academy, where each Mistress took on a name in the Xi language—but Kaede had always had the impression that the Kingdom was better off without the Xi. "Why do you think they're contacting the King now?" she asked.

The Mistress's eyes flickered to the gray sky outside the windows. "We believe that the unchanging seasons—and even those creatures who have been crossing into our lands— we believe that these are all connected. You have learned, in your lessons here, that we are all part of one vast motion of energies. Something is disrupting the natural flow of things. The meridians that run across our world have been…bent… somehow. We suspect that the Fairy Queen may be aware of this, too. It is very important that we accept her invitation." Maire Morighan's lips narrowed briefly, as if in disapproval. "However, the King is not able to go on the journey, for it will take many months and may be quite dangerous. He will send his son, Prince Con Isae Tan, in his stead."

"I remind you that my hands are full dealing with the chaos in the southern provinces," the King said defensively. "They're nearly ready to launch a civil war. I cannot leave my kingdom for months just to gallivant off on an invitation to the Fairy Queen's court—an invitation that says nothing about why she's inviting us after all this time, I might add."

"With all due respect, Your Majesty," Maire Morighan said, "it is the Council's strong belief that the Fairy Queen may know why the seasons haven't changed, and *I* remind *you* that all the storms and droughts and food spoilages have been the primary cause of all that unrest. We need to reestablish relations with the Xi; it is a matter of supreme importance."

"His Majesty and I agree that we must answer the Fairy Queen's invitation," Lord Raiden put in, trying to smooth both King Cai's and Maire Morighan's ruffled feathers. "But he cannot travel now. Not only are we on the verge of war, the Queen is pregnant."

"I dare not leave her," the King said stiffly. "She has had a difficult pregnancy." Kaede remembered that the King's first wife had died more than a decade ago, but he had not remarried until last year, when he chose a much younger bride. It had been something of a scandal, for the new Queen was the same age as Prince Con, the King's son from his first marriage.

"We understand," Maire Morighan said, as though they had argued over this many times already. She looked at Kaede. "We have also consulted the oracle stones about the invitation, and they called for Taisin, your classmate, to accompany the prince."

13

Kaede shifted in her seat, confused. "But what does this have to do with me?"

The Mistress leaned forward slightly, her dark eyes focused on Kaede. "You have been called, as well."

Kaede stared at her for a moment, dumbfounded. "Me?" It made no sense to her.

And then Taisin, who had been silent until now, said: "I had a vision. I had a vision, and you were in it."

Chapter III

ord Raiden watched his daughter's face as Taisin spoke. Kaede was startled, curious, but guarded. She lifted a hand to tuck a strand of hair behind her ear. He had noticed the minute she entered the Council chambers that she had cut off her hair at chin-level since the last time he had seen her. She should be wearing it in a cylindrical roll at the nape of her neck in the manner of a proper sage-in-training—like Taisin. It was a small rebellion, but an unmistakable one, and Lord Raiden felt a familiar frustration rising in him. He had thought the Academy would discipline his daughter, force her to act in accordance with her station. But instead, it seemed to have only encouraged her to run wild. He could see traces of dirt on her hands, and he frowned.

"Taisin is a true seer," Sister Ailan was saying, "and we consulted the oracle stones. They confirmed what she saw. Kaede must also go on this journey."

"But the stones are not always clear," Lord Raiden objected.

"There are hundreds of stones with thousands of marks on them. Perhaps they've been read incorrectly. And Taisin is so young—"

Sister Ailan said crisply, "I have not read them incorrectly, Lord Raiden. And Taisin may be young, but she is our most gifted student in a generation."

Lord Raiden looked pointedly away from Sister Ailan to Maire Morighan. "Mistress, I must question the wisdom of sending my daughter on such a mission. You yourself admitted it might be dangerous. I know the state of our kingdom right now, and I can assure you it is not a place of peace. I refuse to risk my daughter's life."

"Raiden," the King said, "you know we would send as many guards with them as necessary."

"Of course, Your Majesty, but you know as well as I do that Kaede is not gifted in the way that Taisin apparently is. Nor is she trained to defend herself as your son is. And Kaede is only a child; she is not yet eighteen." Lord Raiden glanced back at Maire Morighan. "You should be sending an experienced sage, not a couple of students. You heard my daughter—she isn't even familiar with the Borderlands Treaty."

Kaede's cheeks burned at the dismissive tone in her father's voice. Resentment seethed inside her, acidic and sour. She wanted to lash out at him, but Maire Morighan gave her a warning look, and Kaede reluctantly bit her tongue.

"Lord Chancellor," the Mistress said, "I understand your concern for your daughter's safety, but the matter is no longer in our hands. Taisin's vision was exceptionally clear, and when we consulted the oracle stones about Kaede, they were decisive. Kaede is meant to accompany Taisin, and no other sage may go. That is the word of the stones. Even if we don't always understand why the oracle stones say what they do, there is a reason. They have never steered us wrong. We must trust in them."

"Wait," Kaede interrupted, frustrated. She turned to Taisin, whose brown eyes were shadowed as though she had not slept well. "What was in this vision?" Kaede asked. "What was I doing there?"

Taisin glanced at Sister Ailan as if to ask permission, and when her teacher gave an almost imperceptible nod, she said haltingly, "I—I saw you on a beach—a beach made of ice." The memory of it washed through her; she felt the same loss and fear she had felt that night in the practice room, and beneath it all, she remembered the deep ache of love. It was disorienting, for in her life at the Academy, she had rarely noticed Kaede before, and now, sitting there across the table, Kaede was simply another girl in a black Academy robe, the plain stone buttons marching across her left shoulder as they did across her own. Taisin was sure she had no feelings for her—not here in the Council chambers. The emotions in the vision seemed to belong to someone else, and Taisin couldn't reconcile them with the present.

"What were we doing on this beach?" Kaede asked.

Taisin took a deep breath. "The vision was very clear, but it was also quite limited. I only saw the beach, and the ocean…and you. You were important." Taisin colored, and she lowered her eyes to her lap. "I had the vision the night

17

after the Council told me the oracle stones called for me to go to the Fairy Queen. I knew that the vision was about this journey, and I knew it was telling me that you must be a part of it."

"Kaede," Lord Raiden said, addressing his daughter for the first time that day. "You know that you have duties that you cannot shirk." Kaede's stomach dropped; she should have known he would bring that up. "This is not the best time for you to be absent."

"When would be the best time, Father?" Sarcasm twisted her words. "Should we ask the Fairy Queen to wait until you're finished with me?"

The Chancellor's face darkened with suppressed rage. "You disrespect your King, and I will not tolerate that," he snapped.

"I think you are the one who is disrespecting *me*," Kaede countered, hot with anger.

The King frowned, but before he could speak, Lord Raiden pushed his chair back from the table, the legs scraping loudly against the stone floor. He stood, towering over the table. "You are behaving like a spoiled child, Kaede, which only goes to show that you are not prepared to take on the responsibility that this journey would entail."

"If I'm so irresponsible, why do you want to marry me off to some lord from the South?" Kaede demanded. "Why would you trust me with a political alliance if you think I'm such a child?" The words seemed to echo in the room, and she heard her own heartbeat thudding in her chest. When her father had first presented her with his plan last winter, they had argued over it for hours. He wanted her to marry a complete stranger just to keep the man's province under the control of the King's Guard. The idea of it sickened her.

"We are trying to prevent a *war*, Kaede," Lord Raiden said coldly. "Surely you are not so selfish that you would send your kingdom to war just because you don't wish to settle in the South?"

"It's not about where I wish to *settle*, and you know it. And who's the selfish one? You only want me to marry him because it would be good for *you*."

Maire Morighan rose abruptly, cutting into their argument. "Enough," she said. "Lord Raiden, please sit down."

"Mistress—"

"*Sit down*," the Mistress ordered. The Chancellor's face was nearly purple with frustration, but he sat, the chair legs scratching across the floor again. "Lord Raiden, with all due respect, this is not your decision to make."

For one brief, glorious moment, Kaede felt vindicated, but then her father said, "She is my daughter. She is not of age. She does not go where I do not permit."

Kaede fumed, but before she could rebut him, the Mistress said coolly, "Undoubtedly that is true. But this journey is every bit as important—perhaps even more important—than your plans for her. You must give her up to us. She has another duty that comes first now."

"Don't I have any say in this?" Kaede asked. She looked at Maire Morighan, who seemed exasperated with both her and her father. "Mistress, you can see that I have no desire to do what my father wants me to do. But you aren't giving me a choice, either." Maire Morighan frowned, but before she could speak, Kaede rushed on. "I have been a student here for almost six years. Not the best student, but I have paid attention. And the one thing that has always made sense to me is the teaching that every individual has the right to make choices about their lives. Every minute of every day, we make choices. Why would you take that away from me now?"

Kaede knew she was taking a risk by speaking so forcefully to the Mistress of the Academy. But the anger she felt at her father boiled within her, driving away any fear of offending Maire Morighan.

The Mistress was not surprised by Kaede's willfulness. That had always been the one quality that hampered Kaede's ability to work through the rituals. But she was taken aback by Kaede's appeal to the Academy's teachings. From across the table, Sister Yuna said softly, "She is right. She deserves to choose her own path."

Maire Morighan looked at Kaede, whose face was filled with desperate determination. At last the Mistress said, "All right. You have until the evening meal to make your decision."

Chapter IV

aede's entire body was tense as she hurried down the stairs away from the Council chambers. The unexpected encounter with her father had rattled her, and she needed to shake it off. Her teachers would have advised her to go to the practice hall, to sit quietly, but she wanted to go outside and breathe the fresh air.

She took the empty corridor behind the kitchens, avoiding the students at their work shifts. The kitchen cat, curled in his basket by the back door, stretched lazily as she unlatched the door and slipped outside. The rain had lightened to a drizzle, but the cobblestones of the path down to the beach were slick, and she walked carefully. The sea, visible ahead of her in a gray swathe only a few shades darker than the sky, moved in giant, undulating swells. She could hear the crash of the surf below.

When she reached the edge of the kitchen garden, she went down a narrow stone staircase toward the sand. A stream of smoke curled up from the groundskeeper's workshop huddled against the retaining wall ahead. Fin was in. Kaede hesitated only a moment before heading for the workshop. She knocked on the wooden door, and hearing a gruff answer from within, she pushed it open, the hinges creaking slightly.

Inside, the workshop was a warren of crates and sandbags, wood scraps and tools. A lamp was lit in the back, where Fin called out, "Who is it?"

"It's me," Kaede replied. She threaded her way through the shop toward the sound of Fin's voice.

Fin was seated on a stool at her workbench, mending a gardening tool. Her short gray hair curled over her ears and forehead, which was marked with black oil as if she had pushed her hair aside with dirtied fingers. She had once been tanned dark from the sun, but without a clear day in months, her skin had paled. She was still as vigorous as ever, though, despite the fact that she had celebrated her half-century mark the previous winter. She glanced at Kaede with quizzical brown eyes. "What are you doing down here? Your work shift with me isn't until tomorrow. Maesie has you today, doesn't she?"

Every student at the Academy spent several hours each day working in the kitchens or the library, cleaning the practice hall or sweeping the corridors. During Kaede's first year, she had been assigned a task suitable for a Chancellor's daughter: sitting in the library and marking down the names of every student who came and went. The duty had left her so restless that she had soon been reassigned to Fin, the Academy's groundskeeper, who set her to work sweeping the Seawalk or filling sandbags. On slow afternoons, Fin would take her out to the North Beach and set up a target, teaching her how to toss the knives she kept in a tooled leather case, evidence of her former life with the King's Guard.

Fin saw the nervous energy in Kaede's stance, and she asked, "What happened?"

Kaede took a deep, shaking breath. "My father is here. And the King. When did they arrive? Where is their ship?" She hadn't seen or heard any ship in the harbor that morning, and she knew it would have caused an uproar, for the only ships to come and go were scheduled months in advance.

Fin put down the tool, wiping her oily fingers on a rag. "They came in the middle of last night. The ship sailed back to Seatown as soon as the King disembarked. They wished to keep it secret." But there could be no secrets from Fin; she had been roused by Sister Nara herself, bearing a candle and urging her to come down to the dock. She looked at Kaede's agitated expression and said, "We should take a walk out to the North Beach."

Startled, Kaede said, "Now?"

"Now is as good a time as any. I could use a break." Fin levered herself up from the stool, reaching for a long leather case on the shelf bolted to the wall above her head. She slung the case over her shoulder. Her joints were a bit stiff from sitting still in the damp air, yet she moved with the measured gait of the former soldier she was.

Kaede followed Fin out into the misty afternoon. "Did you know they were coming?" she asked as they walked across the wet sand.

Fin shook her head. "I didn't. They sent word by carrier to the Council, but only an hour or so before they arrived. You've spoken to them?"

"Yes. The Mistress summoned me to the Council chambers."

"Ah. What did they want?"

Kaede explained what had happened, and recounting the argument with her father caused her anger to flare again. "I can't do what my father asks—I just can't," she said vehemently.

"Are you—" Fin hesitated, glancing sideways at Kaede, who had a fierce scowl on her face. "Are you in love with someone else? Is that why you refuse to marry this man?"

Kaede almost laughed. "No. I'm not in love with...anyone." She wasn't sure if she ever had been in love, although she remembered the rush of emotions that accompanied her first kiss, with her classmate Liya, up in the crescent garden. It had been almost two years ago, on a sunny early summer afternoon. They had been clumsy and shy at first, but the giddiness that flooded through her after the kiss had plowed through all those nerves. She had felt exhilarated—free. But had she been in love? She didn't think so. There was no heartache on either side when their little romance ended a few months later.

Kaede and Fin rounded an outcropping of rock that jutted from beneath the Academy's iron foundation and stepped onto the North Beach, a crescent of unmarked, light brown sand cradling the sea. About a hundred feet out, waves crashed against submerged rocks that created a breakwater. When it had been warm, Kaede had often come here with classmates to swim in the sheltered cove. Fin set the case down on the sand and unlatched it, asking, "Who does your father want you to marry?"

Kaede paced back and forth, her footprints sending long trails across the sand. "One of the lords in the South. Someone named Lord Win."

"Is it a political alliance?"

"Yes."

"Your older brother made a political marriage, didn't he?" Fin unfolded the wings of the leather case; within it were about a dozen knives. The smallest—an ornately jeweled dagger—could fit into an ankle holster; the largest was more accurately a small sword.

"Kaihan? Yes. He married the King's niece."

"And how is that marriage working out?" Fin straightened, carrying a square target toward the stony cliff wall that sheltered the cove. Years ago, she had affixed hooks into the wall and punctured holes in the target to hang it.

"I don't know. I haven't heard anything out of the ordinary." Kaede stopped pacing and squatted down by the knife case. She was about to select her favorite throwing knife—a bright steel dagger with a black leather grip—but Fin bent down and pointed to a different one.

"Why don't you try this one today?" Fin suggested.

Kaede was surprised. "Why?"

Fin shrugged and moved off. "It's time for a change, I think."

So Kaede picked up the dagger that Fin had pointed out. The blade was just shorter than the length of her forearm, and though it was made of a darker metal than the other knives, it was simple, straightforward, and ground very sharp. Her fingers slid over the nubbly surface of the grip, and it fit comfortably enough in her hand.

She rose, counted out twenty paces from the target, and shifted the hilt in her hand so that the blade was pointing backward toward the sea. Then she flung it, extending her arm in the direction of the target. This dagger flew differently than the ones she was accustomed to. It was heavier, and she hadn't adjusted her technique to the weight yet, so it struck the very edge of the target and tumbled to the sand.

Fin went to pick it up and asked, "Do you think Kaihan objected to his marriage?"

"I don't think so. His wife—we've known her since we were children. But even if he did object, it wouldn't have made a difference. My father doesn't take no for an answer."

Fin handed the dagger back to her. "Again. The flight of the blade was unsteady last time. Be centered in your body when you throw it."

Kaede curled her fingers around the grip again, and this time, she felt the core of her belly engaged in the movement of her arm. When the knife left her hand, she felt her fingers reaching after it, and the dagger struck the center of the target.

"Good. It's not so different from the other knives, you see."

Kaede sighed. "I can't marry this Lord Win."

"Why not?" Fin's expression was blandly curious.

Kaede pulled a face. "Fin, I could never marry any man, you know that."

Fin gave her the dagger again. "Kaede, you should realize that the chances of your making a political marriage with another woman are—well, it is unlikely. It has happened before, but you know that it's rare."

Kaede reddened. "I don't want to make any political marriages with anyone."

"That is your birthright, and it is your burden." Fin stepped out of the way. "Try it again."

The dagger clanged against the cliff, several inches off the target.

Fin asked, "Did you talk to your mother about it?"

Kaede grimaced. "Yes. She said that I should be open to the possibility that I could love a man. That I was being too narrow-minded." She pushed her hair behind her ears as the wind came up, blowing a salty, wet breath across her face. "And beyond that, she said that plenty of married women have lovers—and sometimes their husbands die young, especially in a time of war. Can you believe that?"

"Well, your mother is a politician's wife," Fin said, smiling slightly.

"Yes. But I don't want to be a politician's wife."

"What do you want to do, then?"

Kaede held the knife in her hand again, feeling the weight of it. It was made of iron, she realized. Solid iron. "I don't know," she said slowly. "I don't want to be a politician, either. Marrying this man is just a way for me to establish myself at court. It cements an alliance, and I would be expected to do my best to make sure it stays strong. I'd have to be pregnant within a year. I don't want that. I want to do something else with my life. I'm not like Kaihan, who just wants to have a family and stay in Cathair. I want to see the world."

"You could see it. If you go with Taisin to answer the invitation of the Fairy Queen."

Kaede had never even considered the possibility of seeing Taninli, the Fairy Queen's city. It was only a legend to her. A thrill ran through her as she thought about it: What would it be like to set foot on those streets? They were supposedly built of diamonds. But a nagging worry tugged at her. "Fin, I don't understand something. Yes, the idea of going on this journey—it's exciting. At the very least, if I go I can put off the marriage my father wants to arrange. But the vision that Taisin had..." She trailed off, struggling to put her finger on what was bothering her. "I think she's hiding something," Kaede said at last. "I have no talents as a sage, but Taisin said that I'm important. Why? It doesn't make sense to me. But visions—I don't think they can be avoided. I'm not even sure if I truly have a choice."

Fin studied her student, with her serious expression and windblown hair. She noticed Kaede's fingers cradling the hilt of the iron dagger as if it had always been hers. After a long moment, Fin said, "The teachers here know much more about visions and fate than I do. But what I know is that in every moment of your life, you have a choice. Every choice leads to another, and another after that. You can only make a decision based on what you know now."

Kaede laughed. "That's almost exactly what I said to Maire Morighan. But what if what I know now is not enough?"

"Making a decision isn't about knowing every potential consequence. It's about knowing what you want and choosing a path that takes you in that direction."

Kaede shifted the knife from her right hand to her left,

and back again. "I guess I know what I want, then." She lifted the knife; it was heavy, dependable. She felt every muscle in her arm engage as she threw it. The dagger struck the very edge of the target and clung there, quivering slightly. She sighed, opening and closing her fingers. "At least, I know what I don't want. And I'll delay that marriage as long as I can."

Fin put her hand on Kaede's shoulder and squeezed it gently. Then she went back to the target and retrieved the knife, bringing it to Kaede. "This is for you," Fin said. "It's forged from one piece of iron. I have had it since I left my mother's home; it used to be my father's dagger. It will now be yours."

"I can't take your father's dagger," Kaede objected, trying to give it back to Fin.

"Yes, you can. This dagger is as powerful a thing as I have ever had." Reluctantly, Kaede took it. "If you go on this journey, you're likely to encounter the Xi. They don't like iron. Most blades these days are made of steel, but this one is all iron. And it has survived for many generations. You should keep it on you."

"I thought the idea that the Xi don't like iron was only an old wives' tale. Is it true?"

"This Academy would not be built on iron if it were only a tall tale. Do you realize how much effort—how much magic it took to raise this place?"

Kaede looked at the Academy's iron foundation, sunken into the top of the rocky cliff. Above the dark gray iron, stone walls formed the North Tower.

"No Xi will ever set foot on this island," Fin said. "That's proof enough for me."

"Have you ever seen the Xi?"

Fin nodded. "When I was with the King's Guard in the Northerness. I was young. The Xi came out of the Great Wood one afternoon while we were securing one of the villages up in the hills, and they watched us." Fin voice was urgent. "You keep an eye out, Kaede. They're not like you and me. Bear that in mind."

Her words reminded Kaede of something else the King had said. "Have you heard the news of creatures coming out of the Wood in recent months? The King spoke of them, but Maire Morighan did not explain. Is it the Xi?"

Fin furrowed her brow. "I don't know. Your teachers have told you nothing about it?"

Kaede shook her head.

"What I know is only hearsay," Fin said. "Some strange bodies have been found in the villages bordering the Wood. Some folk have said they're the bodies of monsters. All I know is that the Xi don't look like monsters, and that's why they're so dangerous. If you're going into the Wood, it won't be an easy journey. You must keep that dagger with you at all times."

The intensity in Fin's tone was sobering, and Kaede said, "I will."

She stepped back, lifting her arm, and threw the knife again and again, until all she could hear was the iron ringing as it flew through the air, the sharp strike as it hit the wall, and behind her, the rising-and-falling groan of the sea.

Chapter V

aisin saw Kaede arrive late at the dining hall for the evening meal, and she knew it meant that Kaede had just come from Maire Morighan's chambers. They did not speak, for all meals were taken in silence, but they looked at each other from their opposite corners of the sixth-form students' table. There was a new sense of intention in Kaede's demeanor, and Taisin was certain that Kaede would be coming on the journey. It made her nervous all over, anxiety and anticipation prickling across her skin.

After the meal, a servant was waiting for her in the corridor with a message: Sister Ailan wished to see her in her study. Taisin went immediately, hoping to avoid Kaede for as long as possible. She didn't know what to say to her; she didn't know what she *could* say to her.

She had barely knocked on Sister Ailan's door before it opened. Her teacher ushered her into a beautifully appointed room lit with two globe-shaped oil lamps, one on the desk, one resting on a dark wooden stand carved with lotus flowers. One wall of the rectangular room was lined with windows, but umber-colored curtains were pulled across them to block out the night. Beside the windows, two simple, elegant armchairs faced each other across a low round table on which a tea tray rested. A black earthenware pot of tea steamed there, and Sister Ailan gestured to Taisin to take a seat while she poured the tea.

"Tomorrow morning, you will depart," Sister Ailan said.

Taisin lifted the warm teacup in her hands, inhaling the scent of jasmine flowers. It had been many months since she had smelled such fragrance; the jasmine, these days, was reserved for special occasions.

"I have one item to give to you before you go," her teacher said, and she went to retrieve something from top drawer of her desk. She placed it on the table before Taisin: the wooden box that had come from the Fairy Queen. "Go ahead and open it."

Taisin set down her teacup and leaned forward to look at the box. The carving was exquisite; the lid looked exactly like a chrysanthemum. She had never touched anything made by the Xi before. Until the King's arrival she had never thought the Xi would come into her life at all, except through the pages of history books. The idea of going to their land was strange and wonderful—and frightening, if her vision was true.

As Maire Morighan had done, Taisin placed her fingertip in the center of the carved chrysanthemum and felt the wood give slightly, like a bed of moss. She lifted her hand away and the petals folded back smoothly. Within the box she saw the scroll and a black velvet pouch.

"That is the medallion," said Sister Ailan. "Take it out."

Taisin emptied the pouch into her hand, and the medallion tumbled into her palm. The links of the chain gleamed in the lamplight. There were faint colors in it: slight streaks of azure and emerald coiling through the silver. The same colors were repeated, though faintly, like a watercolor, in the silver metal that held the stone, and symbols were engraved around the rim. When she touched the symbols, the stone seemed to shimmer as if there were something living within its depths. "What do these symbols mean?" she asked in a hushed voice.

"We are not sure. It is not the language of the Xi—or if it is, it is something more ancient than we can read. But you shall take it with you."

Taisin was surprised. "Me?"

"Yes. It will be entrusted to you. It may be a talisman of some sort—to mark you as a proper guest of the Xi."

Taisin slid the chain around her neck, and when it touched her skin it was cold for only an instant, and then it felt as though she had always worn it. She cupped her hand around it in astonishment, and looked at her teacher. "It feels like it's mine."

Sister Ailan's brow wrinkled just slightly. "You must keep it safe, Taisin."

"I will."

Sister Ailan sat back in her chair, lifting her own teacup. As her right arm rose, the dark green silk of her robe's wide sleeve fell back, exposing the sage's mark on her forearm. Every sage who took the vows was given a mark just above her wrist: a stylized symbol slightly larger than a gold coin.

Though it was tattooed in black ink, Taisin had always seen colors in it, as she did now in the lamplight—shadow colors, as indistinct and shifting as dusk over the sea.

She had looked forward to receiving the sage's mark on her own skin since she was a child, but remembering her vision, her face burned. "Teacher," she began in a hesitant voice, "I must ask you something." When she had first told Sister Ailan about her vision, she omitted the feelings that had been so upsetting, fearing they were a sign of weakness or inexperience. But they had come back to her again and again, and now she could not ignore them.

Sister Ailan regarded her gravely. "Yes?"

"In my vision, I felt something." Taisin clutched the teacup with both hands, as if that might hide her self-consciousness, but she was afraid it was written plainly on her face.

"What did you feel?"

"I felt—I think that I"—she looked away, biting her lip, and finally she blurted it out quickly—"I think that I was in love with Kaede. In my vision. But that is—that can't happen, can it? I want to be a sage, and I know that all sages take vows of—of celibacy. Does this mean that I—that I will never become a sage?"

Sister Ailan heard the anxiety in Taisin's voice. She answered carefully: "Your vision is not the same as a fortune foretold by a traveling mystic. It is not a prediction of the future, Taisin."

"No, but visions—the one I had—isn't it a glimpse of the truth? A truth that exists already within the energies of the world? Everything I do—everything that Kaede does—will bring those energies into the form they took in my vision. Isn't that what you taught me?"

"You are thinking about this too analytically. Your vision is the truth, but it is not the future. It may be that you don't yet understand what you saw."

Taisin put down the teacup, curling her fingers into fists. "Teacher, I want to be a sage more than anything I've ever wanted in this world. I don't want to jeopardize that by falling in love with anyone."

Sister Ailan considered Taisin's flushed face, her renitent posture. She asked, "How did it make you feel, this... love?"

Taisin was taken aback by the question. "I—I have been trying to forget it."

"Why?"

"Because it can't happen," she said miserably. "It can't. If Kaede comes on this journey—if my vision comes true—then—" She broke off, remembering the dreadful fear roiling in the pit of her stomach when she saw Kaede leaving the beach behind. At last she said, "I don't want her to die."

Sister Ailan leaned forward and took Taisin's hands in her own, curving her warm, dry fingers over Taisin's fists. She looked into her student's dark brown eyes. "Love is not what you fear, is it? You fear the loss of it."

Taisin's eyes filled with tears; she was mortally embarrassed. She should not cry in front of her teacher. She wanted to pull her hands away, but Sister Ailan held them fast.

"It is true," her teacher said in a low voice, "that sages

take a vow of celibacy. If you wish to be a sage, you will have to walk that path alone. It is a wondrous path, Taisin, and I know that you wish to follow it. That is a choice you will make later, when you are ready. You are not a full sage yet. Now you have a different path to take. Don't let your fear of the future overshadow your decisions in the present. You must remember that."

She let go of Taisin's hands, and Taisin folded her arms across her stomach, looking uncertain. "What should I tell Kaede, then?" she asked in a small voice. "How can I tell her what I felt?"

"Why do you need to tell her?"

Taisin shrugged. "I don't know. I thought—she is the only other person in my vision. Shouldn't she know?"

Sister Ailan leaned back in her chair, running her hands along the armrests. "Taisin, sometimes it is better for others to not know what we have seen in our visions. You see how much it has distracted you. Think of how much it will distract Kaede."

"Then you think I should not tell her?"

"You must determine that on your own. Just know that whatever is meant to happen will happen, whether she knows what you saw or not. It might be better for her to make her decisions without the additional…suggestions that your vision would give her."

Taisin nodded. "I understand."

"Good." Sister Ailan gave her a rare smile. "Then shall we continue? I have a few other things to tell you."

"All right." Taisin listened as Sister Ailan gave her instructions on what she would need to do when she reached

Cathair, but beneath it all she felt an upwelling of emotions that threatened to engulf her. How could she keep her feelings secret? Was there any way to prevent what she had seen from happening?

She resolved, at least, to try.

PART II

A tree grows on the mountain.
The wild goose flies near:
It seeks the flat branch.

—Book of Changes

Chapter VI

he next morning, the King's ship came to ferry Kaede, Taisin, the King, and his Chancellor to Seatown. Kaede remained out on the deck for the three-hour crossing, preferring the salty sting of the wind in her face to the cramped warmth down below. The spray soaked through her cloak, but she didn't mind. She wanted to remember this day: when she left behind the life her parents had built for her. She watched the Academy diminishing as they sailed away until it was only a small gray speck, indistinguishable from the vast dark sea.

In Seatown, a contingent of the King's Guard was waiting to escort them through the crowded, noisy wharves. It stank of fish and seawater, but all Kaede saw were the black uniforms of the guards around her, their thick leather boots splashing through slimy puddles. They soon arrived at two black carriages, their doors emblazoned with the mark of the King, and Kaede and Taisin were quickly ushered into the second one. The carriage lurched as it turned away from the wharves and began the ascent up the steep road into Seatown proper.

Kaede watched out the window as they drove past an open-air kitchen with an old woman ladling out steaming broth to a line of young men—sailors, with their hair tightly plaited in single braids. They passed long brick walls dividing the compounds of Seatown's wealthy traders from the common folk who did the work of the city. And soon enough, they left Seatown behind and struck out onto the King's Highway.

❧

The journey to Cathair would take a little over a week, and every mile of it was carefully scripted. Every place they stayed was first secured by the King's Guard, and every meal they ate was first tasted by the King's chief taster to ensure that the food was not poisoned. Kaede and Taisin rode in the fifth black coach in a line of eight. Lord Raiden and the King rode separately in the third and fourth carriages; two were reserved for the King's servants and were loaded with his wardrobe trunks; and they were all preceded and followed by guards.

Neither Kaede nor Taisin had traveled with the King before, and at first all of it was strange and overwhelming: the guards who rode with their hands on their swords; the rituals of greeting each evening when their hosts prostrated themselves before the King, holding their empty hands out to him for his blessing. And they ate better than they had in years, for no landlord would serve the King anything less than his finest offerings, even if that meant butchering a tenant farmer's last suckling pig. The King, who wore a different silk robe to each meal, ate it all with gusto, but Kaede, who had grown accustomed to the simpler food at the Academy, found all the rich sauces and succulent meats to be excessive. The King's appetite turned her stomach.

During the day, she and Taisin sat mostly in silence within the cushioned confines of their carriage, each staring out her window at the countryside. They passed a farmhouse burned to the ground, its roof about to collapse. They drove through a village that was empty but for a few hollow-eyed beggars lurking in the abandoned market street. And they passed many people in torn cloaks walking down the side of the road toward Cathair. Sometimes the travelers ran after the coaches for a short distance, but the caravan stopped for no one.

"Where are they going?" Kaede wondered aloud.

"To search for food," Taisin answered, startling Kaede. Taisin rarely spoke, and Kaede had not yet determined whether it was because she was disinterested in conversation or merely shy.

"How do you know?" Kaede watched Taisin struggle to contain some kind of emotion, fidgeting with the edges of her cloak.

"It has been a difficult year. Two difficult years. My family's farm—we have done better than some. My family has received travelers for some time now, seeking food. We send them on to Cathair, for we have heard that there are provisions there for the needy."

"Your family has a farm?"

Pink crept up the curve of Taisin's cheeks. "Yes."

Kaede realized that Taisin was self-conscious about it,

and that made Kaede feel tactless, clumsy. She changed the subject awkwardly. "Do you have any brothers or sisters? I have three brothers. They're all older than me."

Taisin seemed surprised by the question. "I have a younger sister, Suri. She is twelve."

"Is she as gifted as you are?"

Taisin turned red, the color streaking across her throat and face, and she stammered, "M-my sister is gifted in her own way."

Kaede was taken aback by Taisin's reaction. She wanted to tell her she hadn't meant to embarrass her, but her classmate had turned away to stare out the window, her eyes fixed on the changing landscape. Kaede didn't understand why Taisin seemed so uncomfortable around her. Had she done something wrong? She tried to find something to distract herself in the carriage, but there was nothing new to see in that small, dark space. She suppressed a sigh. It might be a very long journey indeed.

❧

On the fourth day, it rained. It was a heavy, unwelcome downpour that turned the dirt road into a muddy mess. At a crossroads that had seen better days, the caravan had to stop entirely while the drivers climbed down and dug the first carriage out of a rut that had trapped the wheels in several inches of sludge. Taisin had almost nodded off to sleep in her seat, the sound of the rain soothing away the bumpy discomfort of the King's Highway. When Kaede cried out in alarm, Taisin jerked awake, her head knocking against the window.

There against the glass was a man's angry face, his mouth

open as he shouted at them, raising his fist to bang against the door.

Taisin screamed; she scrambled back as the force of his blows caused the coach to sway. Her shoulder slammed against Kaede, who was also pushing herself away from the door. In their haste they tumbled onto the floor, their bodies pressed together in the narrow space between the seats.

The man outside raised his hand again, and this time there was a rock in it, and it smashed against the glass so hard that it cracked. But before he could strike again, a guard grabbed him, pulling him away with a force that yanked his shoulder back at an unnatural angle. Another guard joined the first, who pinned the struggling man's head in the crook of his leather-armored elbow, and the second guard struck him full in the face, blood flying out as the man's nose was crushed. A third guard appeared, and the man, who was thin and weak from hunger, had no chance at all. One of the guards drew his sword, and before the man could take another breath, the guard slit his throat. He doubled over, his life spilling down his chest, mingling with the rain that still fell, unceasingly, from the sky.

It was a crime punishable by death to attack the King, and the royal mark was painted on every one of the coaches in that caravan.

Inside the battered carriage, huddled on the floor, Taisin felt her heart pound from shock. Kaede was crowded so close to her that Taisin could feel the other girl's muscles as tense as a drawn bowstring. Suddenly the door was wrenched open, and Kaede's father was standing outside, the rain running down his face. He hadn't bothered to put on a cloak. "Are you all right?" His voice was rough with panic. Behind him three guards stood with their swords drawn, and beyond them the body of the attacker was slumped on the muddy road.

"We're fine," Kaede said, her voice shaking.

"Blasted idiots!" Lord Raiden shouted, and spun toward the guards. "You paid no attention!" he snarled. "This cannot happen again. Next time it will be one of you who is dead." He slammed the door of the carriage shut, and the cracked glass shattered completely, letting in the rain. Lord Raiden threw up his hands and ordered, "Fix this!"

Kaede began to get up, and Taisin realized that she was gripping Kaede's hand with white fingers. Heat rushed through her and she dropped Kaede's hand as if it were a live coal. Kaede turned to her, a strange look on her face, and then the guards came to sweep the glass out of the carriage. Taisin pulled herself onto her seat, avoiding Kaede's eyes. A man had just been killed scarcely ten feet away, and yet all she could think of was the jolt that went through her when she felt Kaede's hand in hers. She had reached for her without any awareness of what she was doing. Was it already happening? Was her vision already coming true?

Taisin set her jaw stubbornly to prevent it from trembling. She deliberately gazed out the broken window, where the guards were carrying the body of the dead man toward the side of the road. Others approached with shovels, and they began to dig a grave in the soft ground. None of them had any idea who he was, and they would never find out. After the guards rolled him into the earth, they marked the grave with a circle of stones, and the caravan departed.

Eight days after they left the Academy, the road widened and flat paving stones replaced hard-packed dirt. The coaches picked up their pace, and the King's guards were able to relax just slightly. After the attack, there had been repercussions all around. The guards had been ordered to increase their vigilance, and now no one was allowed to leave the caravan unprotected. Kaede and Taisin were sent off with two female guards if they needed to stop at the side of the road, and though the guards turned their backs, Taisin especially chafed at the indignity of it. Kaede, who was more accustomed to being followed by servants, still had never experienced this level of interference in her daily life. She did her best to pretend as though it was entirely ordinary: traveling with the King, being surrounded by armed guards at every moment, riding in a carriage with a window covered by an oilcloth where it had been broken by a starving bandit. If she paused to think about it too closely, the significance of it all frightened her, and she would rather go blindly forward than dwell on what it all meant.

By the time they saw the stone walls of Cathair in the distance, Kaede had almost convinced herself that this new existence was normal. After all, the crenellated guard towers of the city were as tall and warlike as ever. Nothing had disturbed them, so far. But then they encountered a sight that she had not anticipated: a growing collection of tents pitched on the barren fields on either side of the road. As they drew closer to the city walls, the tents appeared more and more like permanent fixtures, the canvas walls dirtied with grime from fires burning in hastily dug pits. Kaede realized that the people camped closest to Cathair had been there the longest. They stood up as the King's caravan passed, but though some children ran toward the coaches, most remained still, gaunt as specters, knowing that nothing would come their way.

The sight of all these desperate people overwhelmed Kaede. The world had changed so much since she had last been outside the Academy walls six months ago. She hardly recognized this city that she had grown up in. The streets were thick with guards, and all the guards carried weapons. Half the shops seemed closed; the ones that remained open had new bars over their windows. When the carriage rolled to a halt outside her family's compound, Kaede was absurdly relieved to see that her home was the same as ever—red gates and dark red tiled roofs rising behind the wall.

Taisin was continuing on to the palace, where she would stay until they departed a week from now. Kaede looked back at her before she exited the carriage, feeling oddly reluctant to leave her. She said, "You can send word if you need anything."

Taisin was surprised by the offer, but also a tiny bit pleased, and it was the pleasure that made her feel awkward. "Thank you," she said formally.

Then Kaede heard the red gates open, and her mother's voice calling her. Giving Taisin a small smile, she climbed out of the carriage, carefully closing the door with the oil-cloth tacked over the broken window.

Chapter VII

here was a strange man in her father's study. Kaede paused in the doorway, her hand on the latch. He was tall, and he wore an uncommonly fine dark blue silk tunic embroidered with white-capped waves, but his hair was as short as a guard's. He turned at the slight creak of the door that Kaede pushed open, and broke into a smile. A single dimple creased his left cheek.

"Kaede," he exclaimed. "It's good to see you."

"Con?" she said, recognizing him at last. He had been a regular guest in her parents' home when she was a child, for he was close in age to her brothers Taeko and Tanis. She bowed to him. "What did you do to your hair?" The last time she had seen him had been at Kaihan's wedding last year, and Prince Con Isae Tan—like all young men of rank—had worn his long black hair in a topknot.

The prince grinned, running a hand over the prickly ends of his black hair, now barely half an inch long. "I cut it off."

She laughed. "Why?"

He shrugged. "I wanted to look ordinary."

Behind her, Kaede's father said, "Ordinary? What did your father think of that?"

Kaede stepped aside as Lord Raiden entered his study, carrying an account book under one arm. He set it down on his desk and took his seat behind it, flicking back the wide sleeves of his black robe. "Kaede," he said, glancing perfunctorily at his daughter, "the prince and I have business to attend to. You may leave us."

The smile that had lit Kaede's face upon seeing Con disappeared. The prince glanced from father to daughter and said, "Lord Raiden, perhaps Kaede might join us."

"What? I don't think so."

"Lord Raiden, she is part of this business." The prince's voice was gentle but firm.

Lord Raiden met the prince's gaze. There was a brief silence. "Fine," he said gruffly. "Kaede, close the door when you come in." He did not wait for her to sit down before opening the account book and paging through to a section marked with a ribbon. "As I was saying earlier, the King has ordered a contingent of guards to accompany you, as well as several wagonloads of supplies. I've no idea how long this trip will take; all the maps are confoundedly inaccurate."

Kaede realized they were discussing the journey she was about to embark on—and that her father had had no intention of telling her anything about it. She bit back the flaring anger inside her and sat down in the empty chair next to Con. The prince said, "Lord Raiden, I know that my father always travels with a large number of guards, but I think we would be better served by a smaller party."

"It is dangerous out there, Your Highness. The people are restless. Our caravan was attacked on the way back from the Academy."

Con nodded. "I know. But I think we would be more likely to slip by, unnoticed, if we were fewer in number. Consider this: If we travel with one guard each, we can stay at inns along the way instead of requiring shelter from my father's loyalists. It will allow us to gain information, as well. I can send word to you by carrier or messenger if necessary."

Lord Raiden frowned. "One guard each is not much. The King will not support it."

Con leaned forward, putting a flattering smile on his face. "Lord Raiden, my father will support anything that you recommend."

Kaede's eyes flickered from Con to her father. She could see that he wanted to believe what the prince said.

"Your Highness, that is kind of you to say, but I'm afraid it will be too dangerous." Lord Raiden glanced at his daughter, who was watching him with a stony expression. "And besides, my daughter is traveling with you. I want her to be safe."

Kaede choked back a laugh; he had never been so concerned for her safety before she was called to go on this journey. When she was a child, he had rarely seemed to notice her at all. She was convinced that his worry, now, was only a pretense; he was just frustrated that she was not doing what he wanted. When her father saw the disbelief on her face, he glared at her, and she glared back.

Con saw the exchange but made no mention of it. "No one will know who we are if we travel lightly, Lord Raiden. But if we travel with a caravan of guards, we will be a slow-moving target."

"What about the Xi? They aren't to be trusted. It would be better to send more guards with you."

"The more people we send, the more the Xi can turn with their glamours. We should bring only the guards we can trust."

Lord Raiden tapped the tips of his fingers together. "Whom would you propose to take with you? Which guards?"

Con relaxed a bit. He could sense that Lord Raiden was about to give in. "Tali, of course," Con said. Tali had been his personal guard since he was a boy, and he was trusted by both the Chancellor and the King. "He is completely loyal to me."

Lord Raiden nodded. "Tali would be going with you anyway. I agree he is a good choice. Who else?"

Con had already consulted with Tali on this, and he had two names ready. "Pol should go. He is one of Tali's favorites and has been in the King's Guard for ten years now. He is from the Northerness, and he is a skilled hunter. He would be a valuable asset. And I think we should also bring Shae, from the Third Division, though she is fairly new to the Guard." Tali had suggested the woman, who had only been a guard for two years. "She's from the village of Jilin;

grew up near the Great Wood. She'll know it better than any of the other guards."

"So there would be six of you," Lord Raiden said. "You, Taisin, Kaede, and three guards."

"Yes."

"You'll need six horses?"

"I would suggest four riding horses, and two to pull the supply wagon."

"No servants?"

"Tali will do the cooking," Con said with a grin.

Lord Raiden let out a short laugh. "You won't eat well."

"We don't need to eat well. We just need to survive the journey."

Lord Raiden nodded slowly. "All right. I'll speak to the King about your wishes."

"Thank you." Con looked over at Kaede, who had listened to their conversation in silence, and asked, "Does that sound all right with you?"

Kaede blinked. "With me?" She hesitated. Her father was watching her. Hearing the prince and her father discuss the details of the journey had made her feel largely irrelevant. Six years at the Academy behind her, and she was utterly unprepared for this sort of thing. She felt both useless and irritated by the uselessness. But she would never allow her father to see her misgivings, so she said nonchalantly, "Of course. It all sounds fine." But the palms of her hands were clammy, and Con's words rang in her ears: *We just need to survive the journey.* What was he expecting? She began to wonder, seriously, what she had gotten herself into.

The night before their departure, the King hosted a private banquet in their honor, and even Queen Yuriya, her belly swollen in the seventh month of pregnancy, joined them in the dining room. In addition to the King and Queen, Taisin's family was present: her father and mother, with somewhat awed expressions on their faces; and her sister, Suri, with large dark eyes that seemed to look right through a person.

Kaede's family had been invited, as well. Her mother, her hair twisted into the shape of a spiraling shell, sat at the King's right hand. Her father sat next to Prince Con, who suffered the good-natured ribbing of Kaede's three brothers for cutting off his hair. Kaede was between the prince and her middle brother, Tanis, who had recently returned from the South and only wished to discuss politics with the prince. Caught between them, Kaede fell silent, watching Taisin across the table. She was seated next to Kaede's brother Taeko, who was the closest to her in age and had become something of a flirt in the last few years. Taisin had a small smirk on her face as Taeko attempted to impress her, and Kaede liked Taisin the better for it, as few were immune to Taeko's charms.

The broad, circular table was laid with a cloth of pale gold silk printed with twining crimson and green flowers, and there were eight courses. There was cold salad and clear soup, with translucent mushrooms floating within the broth in cloudlike clusters. There was roast duck and sweet, brined pork and tender, spiced lamb. There were tender

54

cabbage leaves sautéed with ginger; there was an entire river fish with its mouth propped open on a carrot; and at the end there were bowls of sweet bean soup, with candied plums sinking to the bottom like treasure. Kaede couldn't help but feel as though it were a last meal of sorts, and the forced joviality of it all made her uneasy. It seemed wrong to eat like this when people were going hungry in that tattered tent city outside Cathair's walls.

At the end of the evening, the King stood up and toasted them as if they were about to depart on a holiday, and Kaede almost winced as she was forced to raise her glass along with everyone else. When she glanced at Con and Taisin, she saw that they, too, had sober looks on their faces as they listened to the King's booming, slightly drunken voice. She was relieved when the toast was over. She did not know what lay ahead, but she was ready to find out.

Chapter VIII

aisin lay awake on the platform bed, gazing up at the wooden canopy. The silk sheets were cool and slippery beneath her, and when she shifted, her skin slid across them with a whispering noise that sounded abnormally loud in the hush of her chamber. Her family had been given rooms adjoining hers, but the palace was so large that she could hardly believe they were sleeping under the same roof. The last few days with them had been precious, though. She would see them in the morning once more, but she already missed them.

She tried to relax; she knew she should get as much sleep as possible, because tomorrow would be a long day. But she was anxious and unsettled, and the palace was too grand to be comfortable. When she first arrived, she had stared wide-eyed at everything. She had never seen furniture as fine as the dark red lacquered armchairs and tables in these rooms; she had never slept in a bed as magnificent as this one, with a frame carved into the shapes of singing birds on branches. At night, there had been a phalanx of servants to bathe her in jasmine-scented water, and in the morning, more servants came to dress her in clothing so exquisite she was almost afraid wear it.

But all the luxury in the palace did nothing to dull the sharp clarity of the emotions that gripped her every time she remembered her vision.

Since the first time she had envisioned that beach of ice, she had seen it twice more in dreams. Each time she awoke feeling torn up with loss, the sight of Kaede departing as painful as a fresh wound. Tonight in the palace, she was still awake when the vision began to pull at her, like fingers gently tugging her toward a deep blue pool. Part of her did not want to go, but part of her experienced this tugging with a kind of intellectual detachment. She had never encountered this kind of Sight before; it was like there was someone or something leading her forward. It was not unpleasant or frightening; it was merely quietly insistent. She knew it would win eventually, and so she gave in, allowing her mind to open up to what it wanted to show her—and then she was there: standing on the beach as always, her feet planted on the snow, looking out at the boat that Kaede rowed away from the shore.

For the first time, she sensed another person with her. She knew, somehow, that if she turned around, Con would be standing behind her. And she realized that she could feel some of what he was feeling: pain, physical pain, and beneath that a knotted rope of worry. He was moving toward her, and his fingers wrapped around her shoulder as if to restrain her. She saw Kaede leaving; her stomach twisted with dread.

But this time there was more: a hot wash of guilt, spreading a bitter taste in her mouth.

The Taisin lying beneath silk sheets in the palace twisted her body, curving it as though she were running after Kaede, but the one standing on the beach did not move beneath the press of Con's hand. Instead she looked up, past Kaede's receding figure, and there she saw something that took her breath away. In Cathair she gasped out loud, crumpling the sheets into her fisted hands. There before her in her mind's eye was a fortress rising up from the frigid sea like a mountain of snow. It was as though an iceberg had been carved with a giant knife, shaped into towers and walls; and cut into those walls were glass windows that winked in the brilliant sunlight like a thousand sparkling diamonds.

The fortress was on an island—or perhaps it was simply a particularly large ice floe—and Kaede was rowing toward it. Each stroke took her farther from the beach Taisin stood on, her feet growing colder by the second, and now she heard a sound for the first time: Con speaking in her ear, an urgent tone in his voice. *Come back*, he was saying to her. *Come back.*

❧

Taisin awoke well before dawn, the vision still clear in her mind, her nightgown soaked with sweat. She shivered; the silk sheets held no warmth. She sat up, shaking, and climbed down from the platform bed to retrieve her knapsack. She pulled it open and rifled through it in the dark until she found her woolen traveling cloak. It had been laundered by the palace servants, and now she wrapped it around herself, the scratchy fabric a welcome contrast to the cold silk.

What had Con meant? Come back from what? The image of the ice fortress loomed in her memory, monstrous and beautiful. Who—or what—could have built that? The only thing she was sure of was the way her heart constricted every time Kaede left, and every time she felt it, she was more determined to make sure it never happened. But now the guilt confused her. Why hadn't she felt it before? She was bewildered; she was frustrated. She didn't understand the version of herself in the vision. That Taisin had emotions that the present-day Taisin—the one clutching her cloak to her chest in the King's palace—couldn't relate to. Was she fated to become that other Taisin?

Restless, she went to the windows overlooking the courtyard and unlatched them, curling up on the window seat. She tried to remind herself who she was right now, at midnight, in this grand, noiseless palace. She was a student at the Academy of Sages; she was in her sixth year, nearly ready to receive the mark. She was the daughter of two farmers; she was an older sister to Suri. She was not in love with the daughter of the King's Chancellor.

She repeated these facts to herself over and over as if they were a mantra until she fell asleep, her head leaning against the window frame.

Chapter IX

aede awoke the morning after the banquet with a thrill of excitement inside her: Today was the day. She couldn't wait to leave Cathair behind. Her earlier misgivings were forgotten; now she tasted the allure of adventure.

Three guards were waiting with Con and Taisin in the palace stable's south courtyard when Kaede and her father arrived. Though a few stable hands were standing nearby with the horses, no one else had come to see them off, and the small group was dwarfed by the vast expanse of carefully raked gravel around them. Even Taisin had arrived alone, having already said good-bye to her family. Kaede supposed they were already following Con's plan to draw as little attention to themselves as possible.

The prince introduced Kaede to Tali, a burly guard with a salt-and-pepper beard and hair shot through with gray. The second guard, Pol, moved with the stealthy grace of a dancer. He was older than Con but younger than Tali, and he spoke with a northern accent. The third guard, Shae, was Con's age or perhaps a year or two older, and like the other guards and Con, she wore her black hair cut very short. She had expressive dark brown eyes, and there was a liveliness in her that Kaede liked immediately.

There were four riding horses, and two hitched to a supply wagon. Taisin would ride with Pol on the wagon seat; Con, Tali, and Shae would ride their own horses; and Tali led a chestnut mare to Kaede. "Con tells me you can keep up with us," the guard said.

She had to crane her neck to look up at him. "I can."

"Good." Tali gave her an unexpectedly encouraging smile. "The mare's name is Maila." He left her with the horse and went to talk to her father and Con.

When everything had been checked one last time, Kaede's father came to kiss her formally on both cheeks. The press of his lips was so dry and light that she might have imagined them. "Go safely," he said.

She felt a twinge of disappointment at how distant he was. She did not see that he turned his face away to hide the worry that lined his forehead.

They exited Cathair through the North Gate, passing a short line of travelers waiting to be admitted into the city. There was no encampment outside this gate, only brown fields with patches of moss growing over the ground. Every so often they passed a family walking toward Cathair, their belongings dragged behind them on a handcart or piled onto their backs. At noon they stopped by the side of the road to eat steamed bread stuffed with salty pork.

"From the palace kitchens this morning," Tali said as he

passed around the buns. "We won't get much of this from now on, so enjoy it while it lasts."

Kaede took a bite as a gust of wind blew around them. The horses stamped. In the distance she saw smoke rising from a farmhouse chimney, and two figures moved slowly in the empty field as if cataloguing their losses. "The road wasn't so empty south of Cathair," she observed.

"The winter was much harder north of the city," Tali said. "I think that those who wished to seek shelter in Cathair have already come; most of the rest refuse to leave their villages."

Con squinted up at the sky. "It's going to rain." He looked at Kaede. "North of here is the Great Wood. People believe that the trouble comes from that direction—I don't think anyone wishes to seek it out. With few people coming or going, it makes for an empty road."

"Then won't we be highly noticeable?" Kaede said. "What about maintaining some secrecy?"

Tali frowned. "We'll be all right. There are travelers on the road—just not many. And we're such a small group that we shouldn't attract too much attention."

"What will we say is our purpose?" Taisin asked. The damp wind whipped back loose strands of her hair.

"Sir," Shae said to Tali, "if I might make a suggestion?"

Tali gestured with his half-eaten bun. "Go ahead."

"If we are asked, we could say that we're going to visit my family. That will take us to Jilin, and beyond that is the Wood itself—we won't need a story then."

"It's a good idea," Tali said. "We can do that if we need to, but I don't think we'll need to tell much of a story." He turned to Con and added, "Let me do the talking, Your Highness, and no one will ask."

"All right," Con said. "But you don't need to address me so formally. None of you do—in fact, you shouldn't while we're on the road. What happens to one of us happens to us all. We are all equal in this."

As if to underscore his words, at that moment the sky opened, and Kaede stuffed the last bite of her bun into her mouth as they all scrambled for their rain gear.

჻

It rained for little more than an hour—not heavily but steadily, sliding down their oil-slicked cloaks and dripping onto chilled hands. When it stopped, there was no sun to dry them off, and they were still damp when they arrived at the hostel they planned to sleep at that night.

It was in a small village built right up to the road, a way station for merchants. The hostel itself was tiny, and all but two of its half-dozen rooms were taken. After a supper cooked over the shared stove in the courtyard, they separated to go to their rooms for the night, Kaede with Taisin and Shae, Con with Tali and Pol. Each room had a single platform bed that looked particularly hard and unyielding.

"There's not much space," Kaede said. Gauging the width of the bed, she judged that there was just enough room for the three of them. She guessed that in Con's room, one of the men would have to sleep on the floor.

Shae lit the murky oil lamp on the wobbly bedside table and said, "There's no heater, either. We may as well get to know one another."

Kaede laughed. "I'll take the side closest to the wall." She began to spread her blankets out.

"I'll be closest to the door," Taisin said quickly.

Shae shrugged. "That's fine with me—I'll be the warmest one." She and Kaede grinned at each other, but Taisin seemed to color a little and would not meet their eyes. She turned her back on them to unlace her boots and pull off her outer tunic. As Taisin lifted her hands to her hair to unpin her braids, Kaede caught herself watching. She looked away and saw Shae observing her with a small smile. Kaede flushed. "So," Shae said, "you have brothers. Three of them, I understand?"

Grateful for the change of subject, Kaede answered, "Yes. All older than I am."

"I have an older brother myself, and an older sister."

"Are they both still in Jilin?"

"Yes. My entire family is."

Taisin tried to ignore them, setting up her bedroll on the edge of the platform. Kaede asked Shae, "Did you grow up there, then? What was it like?"

Shae pulled a leather-bound flask from her knapsack and sat down on the dusty wooden floor, cross-legged. "It was a good childhood," she answered, taking a swig from the flask and offering it to Kaede. "You're not too young for this, are you?"

Out of the corner of her eye, Taisin saw Kaede sit down, leaning her back against the cold wall. "Do you think I'm too young?" Kaede said.

"One never knows. Would you like some?"

"Not for me. At the Academy, we don't indulge."

"You're not at the Academy anymore."

"True," Kaede agreed, but she did not take it.

"Taisin," Shae called. "None for you, either, I imagine?"

"No, thank you," Taisin answered, feeling uncomfortable. She didn't know what to make of Shae. They had said very little to each other all day, and they didn't seem to have much in common. But she could tell that Kaede liked her, and that made Taisin feel oddly jealous of the guard. Annoyed at herself, Taisin pulled out the *Book of Rituals* from her knapsack, telling herself that she should review it. She climbed onto the bed and opened the book in her lap, squinting at the page in the dim light.

"There are stories about the Great Wood," Kaede was saying.

"What have you heard?" Shae asked.

"I've heard that things work differently in the Great Wood. That people get lost, even if they have a map. That magic goes awry there; rituals go bad. That sort of thing."

"I've heard those things, too."

"Are they true?"

Shae did not answer immediately, and when she did speak, her words were measured. "Every story, I think, has a grain of truth to it. But sometimes, people are misled by what they believe, and they see what they think they should see, not what is actually there."

"That could be said of almost anything in life."

"That doesn't mean it's not true." Shae paused for a moment. "I'll tell you this much. The Wood is a special place. It was difficult for me to leave it. Every day I spend

66

away from it, I miss it. For me—for my family—things make more sense when we are at home there beneath the trees."

"Then why did you leave?"

"There was nothing for me to do at home. My family is not rich, and King Cai offers a steady wage to his guards."

There was no shame in her voice, only a matter-of-factness that made Taisin wish she could be as easy about her own family background as Shae was about hers. But Shae was a guard in service to the King; it didn't matter who her parents were. Taisin wanted to be a sage, and few of them were lowborn. Taisin knew she was lucky that the Academy had taken her, for her family could not afford to pay for her education. It was a compliment to her talent, yes, but it was also a reminder that she owed the Academy a great debt.

"Why did you decide to become a guard?" Kaede said.

"I like action," Shae said, a smile in her voice. "I had no talent for the sagehood, and besides, the King makes it easy to join his Guard. When the recruiters came to Jilin two years ago, it seemed like a good thing to do." Shae shrugged. "I've liked it well enough so far, though I didn't think I'd be away from home for so long." There was a pause, and Taisin heard Shae putting the flask away, lacing shut her knapsack. "How old are you, then?" the guard asked.

"I will be eighteen at midsummer," Kaede replied.

"You'll celebrate your birthday at the Fairy Queen's palace."

"I suppose so."

Shae yawned. "I'm exhausted. There are many nights ahead of us; we can talk more later. I'm going to sleep."

"Would you like me to turn down the lamp?" asked Taisin, blushing when she realized her question showed that she had been listening.

Shae smiled at her, and it was such a friendly smile that Taisin was ashamed for feeling jealous. "I can sleep in broad daylight," Shae said, getting up and gathering her bedroll. "Don't bother to stop your reading for me. But perhaps Kaede has a preference?"

Kaede shook her head. "Stay up as late as you like," she said, and stood to change out of her traveling clothes.

Taisin looked away, trying to focus on her book. She shifted over to make room as Shae and Kaede climbed onto the creaking platform and settled in for the night. At home, Taisin always shared her sister Suri's small bed; indeed, she probably had less space there than she did tonight, but it was not the same. She could have curled up against Suri's back, sharing her warmth. Here, her body was tense, trying to avoid inching too close to Shae's slumbering form.

Taisin sat up past midnight, feeling awkward and self-conscious, staring at the page before her but not reading a word. Her ears rang with the sound of Shae's and Kaede's breathing in that small room, and beneath it, the flutter of her heartbeat seemed as loud as a drum.

⁂

Kaede awoke very early, eager to get back on the road. Her eyes opened to dim light coming through the small window, and beside her she felt the warmth of Shae's body. She sat up too quickly and winced; she was not used to riding a horse all day, and her muscles were paying for it. The hard bed hadn't helped, either, and she gingerly eased herself out of it, trying to avoid waking Shae and Taisin. She dressed as quietly as she could, and after a moment's hesitation she buckled the dagger that Fin had given her onto her belt. It made her feel a little self-conscious to wear a weapon like that, but the guards—and Con, too—were all armed. Feeling the hilt pressing gently at her ribs, she picked up her boots and took them outside to put them on. It was chilly in the courtyard, and from the color of the sky above she could tell that it was just barely after dawn. She decided to head to the stable and look for breakfast among their provisions instead of waiting for the others to wake up.

Just as she was rounding the corner of the hostel she heard the swift passage of an arrow followed by a thud as it struck its target. She flinched. Pol was standing in the stable yard and shooting at a tree. He looked over his shoulder at her and said, "You're up early."

"So are you."

He went to pull the arrows out of the tree. "It's too cramped in that room. Tali's a big man."

She smiled. He shot again and again, sending a series of arrows fleet and sure to the center of the trunk, just below a branching limb. She marveled at the way he made it seem so effortless: lifting the long bow, nocking the arrow, loosing the string so that his right hand arched back gracefully, echoing the flight of the arrow itself. She wanted to be able to do that.

"Will you show me how to shoot?" she asked.

He looked at her as if gauging her potential. "The bow is a bit long for you."

"Let me try. At least it'll be something to do while we wait for the others to wake up."

"All right."

The bow, made of a springy, yellowish-brown wood, was as tall as she was. Pol took off his shooting glove—an odd, three-fingered leather glove with a bulging, padded thumb—and showed her how to strap it onto her right hand. The first time she tried to pull back on the string, she could feel the muscles of her neck and shoulder straining at the effort. The arrow she had nocked slipped and fell, flailing like a downed bird, to the ground at her feet. It was not, she realized quickly, like throwing a knife. Pol seemed amused by her attempt, but said kindly, "My father gave me my first bow when I was a boy of six. It'll take some time before you get the hang of it."

He corrected her stance and told her to breathe in as she raised the bow; to press that breath down within herself as she stretched the string; to allow the arrow and her breath to loosen simultaneously. But the more she tried, the less she succeeded, and she began to sweat from the effort.

"You are too willful," Pol said, observing her latest failed attempt. She reminded him of a young bird flapping her wings, unable to gain the lift needed to take off.

"What do you mean?" Kaede's arm and shoulder ached, and the bowstring had snapped loudly and painfully against her left forearm enough times that she was sure it would leave a red welt there.

"If you think about it too closely, you will choke the energy of the arrow. Your body—and your thoughts—are getting in the way. Try to let go of your thoughts when you shoot. You do not have to force the arrow to fly; it wants to fly."

His words reminded Kaede of her teachers' instructions at the Academy, but hearing them applied to archery was like hearing those lessons in a different language—one that was maddeningly familiar but as elusive as a slippery fish.

Pol saw the growing frustration on her face, and he took the bow from her and showed her, again, the smooth rhythm of the draw, the arrow in flight, his hand in the air. "Stand like this," he told her, spreading his feet wider. "Put your hand here." He moved her left hand down on the grip.

Bit by bit, the bow began to seem less foreign to her, though she knew she was far from being as skilled as Pol was. By the time Tali came out to the stable yard to fetch their breakfast supplies, Kaede was sweating and famished, her right shoulder aching, and still the arrow had not struck the target.

Pol said, "We'll practice every morning—how about that?" He seemed excited by the prospect.

"Delightful," she said, smiling weakly, and he laughed at her. But she handed the bow back to him with some reluctance.

Before she left the stable yard, she couldn't resist unsheathing her dagger and tossing it at the tree, just to remind herself that she wasn't completely inept. It flew out of her hand so easily—she didn't have to think about it—

and struck the tree with a solid thunk. She flexed her fingers thoughtfully. Her hand knew what it was doing. Perhaps it was her body that needed to learn this new language, not her mind.

She went to retrieve the dagger from the scarred tree trunk and went inside for breakfast.

Chapter X

wo days after they left Cathair, the road curved east as it followed the bend in the river Nir. In better times, fishing vessels trawled the river, but now there was little to catch, and what could be caught was better left uneaten. Word had spread through the roadside hostels of a fisherman who had brought in a giant carp—a rarity in any season, but especially abnormal now—only to discover that the fish's belly housed hundreds of tiny stinging eels.

There were other rumors, too. One traveler, a thin man with a nervous black horse, told them he had seen a strange creature lurking behind one of the riverside taverns: half woman, half animal, with a fox's red-gold tail and sharp teeth. A young man had been found dead nearby, his body bruised and bitten.

"All of this trouble comes from upriver," the thin man said, jerking his thumb toward the Nir. He ran his eyes over the group of travelers and their gear—their wagon still full of supplies, the fine workmanship on their horses' saddles—and suspicion flickered over his face. He glanced at the burly, gray-haired man, who was clearly their leader, and asked, "Where are you headed?"

"To Jilin," Tali answered, his tone not inviting further questions. Jilin was at the southwestern edge of the Great Wood, where the Nir originated.

The thin man eyed the group's wagon; the wheels were especially well made. There weren't many travelers heading north, and even fewer who were so well outfitted. But a kind of unspoken camaraderie had developed among travelers on the King's Highway in the last two years, for dark times gave cover to dark deeds, and it was better to pass on one's news without learning too much about anyone else. So the thin man said only, "I've heard that something's not quite right at Ento. I haven't been there recently, but as you're headed in that direction, you might ask about it."

Tali said, "We will."

 ∽

Two nights later, they lodged in a tiny village perched on the banks of the Nir, and Ento was the only subject of conversation in the village's lone tavern. Crowded with out-of-work fishermen, the dark, low-ceilinged room smelled of river water and spirits. The locals had glanced at the six travelers when they first entered, but made no effort to lower their voices to keep their gossip private.

"A man came through the other day," a fisherman was saying. "He told me people are deserting the place as quick as they can."

Built on an old crossroads, Ento had once been home to

a major marketplace. But now there was little to sell, and the town had fallen on hard times.

"That family who was here last week said the same thing," said another man.

"I hope whatever's happened in Ento doesn't move south to us."

"Not likely to be so lucky," said one man bitterly. "Wind blows south from the Great Wood—we're right in the line of it."

Tali turned in his seat and said casually, "We're headed in that direction. What happened?"

Taisin kept her eyes down, but she was curious, too. The more they heard about Ento, the more she was convinced there was something there that she should see. Her instincts were tugging on her in a way she had never experienced before. She turned slightly toward Tali, hoping he would ask the right questions. Earlier in the day, he had told them he would find out as much as he could about what was going on in Ento, and Taisin twitched with impatience.

The fishermen all swiveled around to stare at Tali, and one of them—a man with a long, scraggly gray beard—said, "You'd be better off avoiding that place."

"Why?"

The fishermen looked at one another uneasily before one of them spoke, his missing front tooth flashing like a dark eye. "It was little things at first—goats gone dry, wells turning bad."

"Same things have been happening all over the Kingdom," said the gray-bearded man.

"That was bad enough, but now folks are saying that the Xi are taking our children," said the man with the missing tooth. His voice was harsh and loud, and the common room fell silent.

Taisin glanced up in surprise; she had never heard of the Xi having much interest in human children before. Across the table, Tali just barely shook his head at her, and she swallowed her question.

"It's only one child, and no one knows if it's true," objected a man from across the room.

"Has a child been taken or not?" Tali asked bluntly.

The man with the missing tooth scowled. "The mother says it's still her babe, but the father came through here just yesterday. Looked as though he'd lost everything. He said the child is a monster, and his wife has gone mad."

"It's dark magic," said the graybeard. "If you can avoid Ento, you should. Take an alternate route."

The room erupted with men arguing whether the town was safe to travel through. "Thank you for the information," Tali said, his voice nearly drowned by the din.

Taisin tried to focus on her meal, but the fisherman's words rang in her mind. What kind of dark magic? Her pulse raced. She wanted to know.

༄

The rumors came more quickly as they approached Ento. The child was one of the Xi, cursed to inhabit the body of a human to atone for a crime; the child was the reincarnation of a legendary sorcerer; the child was a demon who had eaten the human child. After hearing the tale of the demon, Tali suggested, "Perhaps we should bypass Ento altogether." They were in the stable yard of another inn in another fishing village, unpacking their gear for the night.

"It will lengthen our journey by several days," Pol said.

Taisin, who had just finished feeding the horses, came around the corner of the wagon. "I think..." She hesitated as they all turned to look at her. She took a breath and said: "I think we should continue the way we planned. The rumors are...they're just rumors."

"They're rumors, yes," Con said, "but, Taisin, I traveled north with Tali last fall, before the worst of the winter storms. The things we saw there were—well, they make me inclined to believe these rumors."

"Nobody seems to have been hurt by this child," she said with studied nonchalance.

"That's true," Tali agreed.

"Then we might as well travel through Ento," Taisin said. "It will be inconvenient to avoid it, and there is no guaranteed benefit." She saw Kaede watching her with interest. She could tell that Kaede wondered why she was so adamant about this, for she had never indicated her opinion on their route before. She still couldn't explain it; she only knew that she needed to see this creature, whatever it was. She lowered her eyes, trying to hide her excitement. Tali would be suspicious if she appeared too eager.

Shae said: "She has a point, Tali. And we'll only be there one night."

He relented. "All right. Ento it is."

∾

A little over two weeks into the journey, the rhythms of travel had settled into Kaede's body. She woke early, met Pol in a stable yard or at an empty patch of dirt near their hostel, raised the bow, and loosed arrows until breakfast. Her arms and shoulders grew stronger, but still she could not strike the target. They rode all day, stopping only for a noon meal at the side of the road, eaten cold. She came to know her horse, Maila, who was both sweet-tempered and energetic. She grew accustomed to falling asleep with the sound of others breathing nearby, and at times she wondered how she had ever lived another way. She thought of her small chamber in that great stony Academy, and her parents' luxurious Cathair home, where she had entire assortments of rooms to herself, but she did not miss them. She realized that she loved the road: Every day was new and unexplored.

Kaede especially enjoyed talking to Shae, who told stories about her training as a guard; about learning to fight and to ride with a sword. Her life was so different from Kaede's years at the Academy that she was always eager to hear more. She began to wonder if she could join the King's Guard when she returned from this journey. Then she would never have to face the dreary politics of court life; she could be on a horse all day, going to places she had never been before.

Shae always included Taisin when she told her tales, even if Taisin was pretending to study, as she often did. It was noticing Shae's kindness that caused Kaede to gradually become aware that Taisin watched her, often, with hooded eyes. She would look away as soon as Kaede glanced at her, so initially Kaede wondered if she were imagining things. But as the days passed, she began to watch Taisin, too. Her classmate was quiet, reserved; she spoke when spoken to, but rarely entered into any conversations on her own. Con tried to draw her out by joking with her, and sometimes Taisin seemed to appreciate it, but she quickly retreated back into a state that seemed to hover between anxiety and frustration. Once, when Kaede caught Taisin looking at her, she had the odd impression that Taisin thought of her as a problem to solve, but she did not know how to do it.

The day they were due to reach Ento, Kaede spent nearly the whole afternoon puzzling over the enigma of her classmate. She had just resolved to speak to Taisin about it directly when they caught sight of the town gates in the distance. They hung open as though abandoned, and as they approached they saw there was no one in the gatehouse.

"You're sure you want to stay here tonight?" Pol said from his perch on the wagon seat.

Tali said: "We'll just sleep here and make an early start in the morning. Let's go."

❧

They were the only guests at the hostel that night, which meant that, for once, there were enough vacant rooms for each of them to sleep alone. After supper, Tali, Con, Pol, and Shae went upstairs, but Kaede lingered behind in the common room waiting for Taisin, who had taken their empty bowls to the innkeeper in the kitchen. When Taisin returned several minutes later, she was startled to see Kaede still there.

"I thought you went upstairs," Taisin said, picking up her cloak from where she had left it, slung over a chair.

"I wanted to talk to you." Kaede stood up, but hesitated. What should she say? All her words seemed to flee from her; she felt awkward.

Taisin suddenly looked nervous. "Now? Now is not—I can't talk now."

"Why?" Kaede eyed Taisin's cloak. "Where are you going?"

"I'm going to see the child."

A chill rushed through her as Kaede realized which child Taisin meant. "The child—the one they say is a monster?"

Taisin began to move toward the door, pulling the cloak over her shoulders. "The innkeeper told me where the mother lives."

"You're going now?"

"Yes."

Fear prickled across Kaede's skin. "I don't think that's a good idea. Tali wouldn't like it."

Taisin stopped and looked back at Kaede. "I haven't yet seen any of these strange creatures that people keep telling us about. Don't you want to see what we're dealing with?"

"What do you mean, 'what we're dealing with'? Why are you so eager to go?"

"It's all related," Taisin insisted. "The weather. The

rumors we've been hearing about these…creatures. The Fairy Queen's invitation."

Kaede remembered Maire Morighan's theory that these disparate events were all connected, but Taisin spoke with an assurance that was surprising. "How do you know?" Kaede asked.

"I can feel it. Every day on the road—I feel something pulling me. I don't know what it is, but I have to find out. I know it's important."

Kaede was doubtful. "I don't think you should go alone. Let me get Tali, or Pol—"

"They won't let me go," Taisin objected. "They barely even agreed to stay in Ento for one night. They certainly won't let me go look for the child. You can't tell them."

"But—"

"I have to go. Now." Taisin's hand was on the doorknob as she added, "Do you want to come with me?"

Kaede glanced at the empty stairs uneasily. She knew she should tell the others, but Taisin was right. Tali would never allow her—or Kaede—to go, and Taisin's urgency had sparked Kaede's own curiosity. She wanted an adventure. Perhaps now was the time to get it.

Just as Taisin was pulling the door open Kaede said, "Wait. All right. I'm coming with you." She ran back to grab her own cloak from where she had left it at the table, and pulled it on as they left the hostel.

Chapter XI

hey took the lantern hanging at the entrance to the hostel courtyard, and it shed a small pool of light as they went down the road. "The innkeeper told me that she lives in a house on the edge of town," Taisin said, but beneath her briskness was a note of trepidation.

The buildings they passed on either side were dark, and some of their courtyard gates were wide open. There would be nothing inside to tempt any thieves; Ento had been deserted as if it were the host of a plague. At the end of the paved road they turned left down a rutted dirt lane; only the last house seemed to be occupied. A dim glow emanated from a curtained window, and from within they heard a baby crying.

Taisin strode up to the front door and raised her hand to knock, her knuckles ringing on the wood. The door was pulled open by a woman with haunted eyes and thin, oily black hair. "What do you want?" she asked defensively.

"May I see your child?" Taisin asked.

The woman's eyes flicked back to Kaede, who was standing behind Taisin. "Who are you?"

"I may be able to help," Taisin said. "Please, let me see your child."

"I won't let you take him away from me," the woman warned her.

"We are not here to take him," Taisin reassured her.

"What can you do? You're only a girl."

For a moment Taisin wavered. What exactly was she planning to do, anyway? The baby cried again, and the sound of it jerked at her gut. She forced down her self-doubt and said: "I am training to be a sage. Please—I've come a long way, and I want to help you."

The woman eyed the two girls on her doorstep. They were both young and obviously inexperienced. The girl who had spoken was so eager to prove herself, while her silent companion seemed reluctant to be there at all. These days, the woman was suspicious of almost everyone who came to her door, but these two girls, with their artless faces, made her feel hopeful for the first time in weeks. Perhaps this girl really was a sage in training, but even if she was lying, what harm could a couple of girls do? She stepped back and allowed them to come inside.

The house, consisting of one room, was small but clean. A fire burned on the stone hearth, and nearby was a rocking chair and a cradle. There was a platform bed against the far wall, its blankets mussed as though someone had slept there recently. A little shrine was built into the corner;

Taisin saw the scroll listing ancestors' names, a spray of dried flowers, a small pot of incense. It did not look like the house of a madwoman.

"When was your baby born?" Taisin asked.

"Three months ago." The woman's eyes darted toward Kaede, who said nothing. "He is healthy," she insisted.

"Where is your husband?" Taisin asked.

Tears filled the woman's eyes, and she began to rub her left arm nervously, as if it were a lucky stone. "He has gone," she answered, and her voice broke. "He has gone."

"Why?" Taisin asked.

"He—he believes I have betrayed him." She rubbed her arm more quickly.

"Why would he think that?"

"He says the baby is not his." As she spoke, the baby opened his mouth and wailed. She knelt down and picked him up, rocking him in her arms until he quieted. "But I never betrayed my husband. I was with him every night. This is our baby." Tears trickled out of her eyes, leaving shining rivulets on her cheeks.

Taisin walked to the woman and put her hand on the baby's blanket. "Let me see him."

At first the woman clutched her baby closer, but as Taisin waited calmly, she slowly relaxed and allowed Taisin to pull back the blanket. The child looked perfectly normal: a sleeping baby boy, fine new hair in a black cap over his head, a small nose, a bow of a mouth.

Kaede approached them, unease rising in her. The mother's eyes were skipping about the room, looking everywhere but at Taisin or her son. The boy let out a small coo as he awoke, reaching for Taisin's hand. He wrapped his little fingers around her thumb and tugged. Taisin's eyes widened; a shudder went through her.

"What is it?" Kaede asked. This did not feel right.

"How wondrous," Taisin breathed. The baby's eyes were black as coal, without a glint of light in them. They were unnatural.

"Taisin," Kaede said warningly. She could see the boy's eyes now, and a knot of horror clenched in her belly. No human had eyes like that.

"It's all right," Taisin said, but Kaede didn't know if she was talking to the baby, his mother, or herself. Taisin seemed entranced by him.

He let go of her thumb and reached up with chubby fists, trying to grab the strands of Taisin's hair that had come loose from her braids. She leaned closer, and the medallion that Sister Ailan had entrusted her with tumbled out over the collar of her tunic, as if it had been pulled. It was shiny and bright, and the stone was like a magnet to the child's hands. When he touched it, he and his mother and Taisin shone for an instant as long as one blink—and then Taisin was clutching at the child's fists, which were firmly clasped around the medallion.

"Let go," Taisin hissed, and the child would not obey. There was an eerie smile on his face as if he were mocking her, his black eyes wide and staring.

"What are you doing to him?" the mother demanded,

trying to back away, but he would not let go of the medallion, and it tethered the both of them to Taisin.

"Let go!"

"He doesn't understand you. He's only a baby!" the
mother pleaded.

"He understands," Taisin said, and the baby's mouth
yawned open in a soundless cry.

Kaede wanted to intervene, but she didn't know what to
do. Panic raced through her frozen body.

Taisin put her hands on the baby's forehead and said,
"Reveal your true spirit—I command you to come forth!"
The baby let out a growl, raising the hairs on Kaede's
neck.

The child strained toward Taisin while his mother tried
to pull him back, and it was almost as though he was suspended in the air between the two of them. Kaede wondered if her eyes were playing tricks on her, for he seemed
to be lengthening. Taisin said again, her voice harsh and
deep, "Reveal your true spirit! I command you to come
forth."

And then the child began to change. His hands were
growing, his head was enlarging, and where baby fuzz had
once covered a pale new scalp, now long tentacles were
emerging. Parts of his body were dissolving into mist and
then re-forming into a greater thing: a creature made of
scales and feathers both, as if it could not decide exactly
what kind of being it should be. Its hands were still pulling on the medallion around Taisin's neck, and the woman
was still trying to hold this creature that had moments

before been her baby but was now kicking back at her with clawed feet that tore gashes into her arms. Blood erupted on the woman's skin, and the creature screamed, fury distorting its face.

Kaede was rooted to the spot, stunned by what was happening in front of her. She felt useless; her limbs would not obey her. She saw the creature's taloned hands stretch toward Taisin's throat. Kaede realized that it was going to rip that medallion from Taisin's neck, and her neck would come with it. Instinctually, Kaede felt for the dagger that Fin had given her. The touch of the iron hilt seemed to unstick her feet from the floor at last, and she moved through what felt like thick mud toward the monstrous child.

The woman was clinging to the thing that had erupted from her baby; she was screaming at Taisin; Taisin was still trying to pull the medallion out of the creature's hands; and Kaede took the last few steps, her muscles straining against unseen weights, and plunged the iron into the monster's chest.

After the viscous density of the air, there was little resistance; it was suddenly like carving through fog or mist. But the monster felt it. It turned its horrible black eyes toward her, and for a moment, Kaede lost her breath looking into those bottomless depths. They were as dark as a thousand starless midnights, and she was dragged down with despair; she was sure that she would sink so far into the earth that her body would be crushed at any moment by the mass of the world above it.

And then she felt something give. Warmth seeped over

her skin, and time sped up again with a great whoosh like a blast of winter wind, and the monster shriveled up until there, in the woman's bloody arms, was a baby with an iron knife protruding from its still belly.

Along the side of the baby's face was an iridescent fringe of feathers, grown out of its skin like a strange mane, the only sign that it had ever been anything other than a plump little boy.

Chapter XII

he woman collapsed onto the floor, and the lifeless creature rolled out of her arms, leaving a glistening crimson trail down the front of her dress.

Taisin's body hummed with a jumble of emotions—awe at witnessing the child's frightening transformation; terror that it was going to kill her. But Kaede had saved her. She was alive. And then the full force of what had just happened—what she had barely avoided— swept through her.

She sank to her knees, taking a deep, ragged breath. She was as cold as if she had been submerged in icy water. She wrapped her arms around herself; she was shaking. She became gradually aware of the heart-wrenching sound of the mother's sobs: She was crying. And Kaede stood as still as stone, her face ashen, her right hand streaked with the creature's blood.

Taisin pushed herself up; her knees wobbled. She touched Kaede's arm. "Kaede, it's over."

Kaede's dazed eyes flickered to Taisin. As if she were coming awake after a disorienting dream, awareness flooded into her. She saw Taisin's face, drained of color; her dark, anxious eyes. Taisin could have been killed. Kaede reached for her, cupping Taisin's face in her hands, pulling her closer as her thumbs pressed into Taisin's cheeks. "Are you all right?" she asked urgently.

Taken aback, Taisin said, "Yes."

"It didn't hurt you?"

"No."

Kaede's face was tight with worry, and Taisin realized that the worry was for her. All at once, she wasn't cold anymore. She backed away, flustered, and Kaede's hand left a smear of red on her left cheek.

They heard a voice behind them: "What's going on?"

They spun around to see Con standing in the open doorway.

"Are you all right?" he asked, taking in the sight of Taisin and Kaede, the queer little body on the floor, the keening mother.

Taisin swallowed; she tried to gather herself together. The strange pull she had felt before was gone. Had the child been the source of it? Had it called to her? And what was that creature? She had certainly never heard of anything like it at the Academy, and her lack of knowledge frightened her.

She saw Con still watching her, waiting for an answer. "The child that we have been hearing about—it was not human," she said. Her voice was steadier than she expected it would be. "We must destroy it." Saying the words turned the horror into a task, an assignment.

"Why?" Kaede asked. She still felt a bit muddled, and seeing the iron dagger still protruding from the creature's belly made her shudder. She went to it and pulled the dagger out. The blood was bright on the blade, and it made her stomach clench. She could have thrown the weapon into the fire, never to see it again, but Taisin came to her side and held out a torn rag.

"Use this," Taisin said. Kaede hesitated, but finally took the rag and ran it over the edge of the blade. The blood came off in long dark streaks. Taisin knelt down beside the tiny body. The eyes were still open, reflecting the firelight with an eerie liveliness. She shivered. "We must burn the body."

"Can't we just bury it?" Kaede asked.

"I don't know what kind of magic created it. Burial will only allow it to take root and spring up again."

Kaede imagined tiny, gnarled fingers reaching up through the soil like a strange new plant. "Fire, then," she agreed quickly. "Where?"

They wrapped the body in a canvas cloth that had been discarded in the corner, and Kaede tucked the bloodied rag inside. The mother lay like a broken doll on the floor, paying no attention to them. Con saw Kaede's worried expression and said, "We won't leave her alone; I'll tell the innkeeper about her."

Behind the woman's small house there was a bare dirt yard, and in the light of the lantern that Con held, they found the woodshed. He helped Kaede assemble the funeral pyre, and then they laid the small, wrapped body on top of it. It was light as a feather.

Kaede had taken flint from inside the house and was about to light the fire when Taisin said, "Wait. Let me bind the body to the earth first." She went back inside and returned a few minutes later carrying a saltcellar.

Con saw her fingers tremble as she fumbled with the coarse white grains. "Have you done this before?" he asked, not unkindly.

She wouldn't let herself look at him; she didn't want to see the doubt that must be in his eyes. "I know how it is done," she said. At the Academy she had learned about the appropriate rituals for a funeral, but only from books. And her knowledge of binding a malevolent being to the earth was entirely theoretical; she had never before encountered such a creature. She began to circle the funeral pyre three times clockwise, trying to quell the apprehension bubbling inside her. She didn't want to think about what could go wrong if she performed this ritual incorrectly.

She sprinkled the salt on the earth; she breathed deep into her belly. The night smelled of dampness, mud, and smoke from the small house's chimney. She halted at the head of the shrouded body, completing her three circles, and set the saltcellar down on the ground at her feet. She folded her hands together just below her breastbone and felt the rapid thrumming of her pulse, her whole body taut with nerves. She tried to slow down her breathing, to calm herself, but her voice still shook a little as she said, "As earth calls to earth, we bind you here: May you rest in peace and disturb us no more." She repeated it twice, then stepped back and said to Kaede, "You can light the fire."

The wood was slightly damp from the rain, and Kaede had to kneel down to blow on the spark until the kindling caught fire. Ever since she was a child, she loved to watch the flames dance; she and her brothers would build giant bonfires on the beach outside Seatown in the summer, adding driftwood until the fire roared like a dragon. But as these flames licked at the shrouded body, it turned her stomach to see it eat away the cloth. When the creature's skin began to catch fire, she turned away, pressing her hand over her nose to block out the smell. She felt a deep pain within her. Even if that creature had been a monster when she killed it, she had still killed it. The knowledge of it was oppressive; her heart felt like iron.

❧

It was past midnight before the fire consumed all the remains. Taisin's eyes stung from the heat, and she felt weak, exhausted—as though something wild had been dragged through her body. "When the ashes have cooled, we'll have to bury them," she said.

"I'll stay," Con said. He saw the weariness on Taisin's face and the dull remains of shock on Kaede's. "You're both worn out. You should go back to the hostel and sleep if you can."

"Are you sure?" Taisin asked.

He squeezed her shoulder. "Yes."

Kaede rubbed at her eyes and asked, "What about the mother?" They hadn't heard her crying in some time.

"I'll bring her back with me if I can," Con said. "Just go back with Taisin. You look as if—well, you need some rest."

Kaede blinked. Her eyelashes felt clogged with smoke. "How did you know where to find us, Con?"

He seemed surprised by her question. "I noticed when you didn't come upstairs—I promised your father I'd look out for you. So I asked the innkeeper if he knew where you'd gone, and he told me."

Taisin touch Kaede's elbow. "Come on. Let's go."

Con's brown eyes reflected the embers of the funeral pyre. He nodded at her gently. "You should go. I'll see you in the morning."

Kaede and Taisin walked back to the hostel in the dark, having forgotten to bring the lantern with them. Kaede felt confused and tired; she felt guilty. Whenever the dagger at her side brushed against her thigh, it sent a shock through her.

She was startled when Taisin spoke, her voice only slightly louder than the sound of their footsteps on the dusty road. "Thank you. I owe you my life."

"You don't owe me anything." Kaede was overcome by a wave of despondency. If the night were not so black already, she would have closed her eyes to block out any light. The smell of the funeral pyre seemed to be burned into her nostrils.

"Kaede, you did the right thing—you did the only thing you could."

She knew that Taisin was trying to comfort her, but it only made her feel worse. "Let's just go back. I'm tired."

They walked the rest of the way in silence.

※

Kaede could not fall asleep. The bed was hard and cold, and she missed the sound of Shae and Taisin breathing nearby. All she could see, over and over in her mind's eye, was the hilt of her iron dagger protruding from the still form of that creature. It looked disturbingly like a human baby. She wondered if she would be haunted by that image forever.

After what seemed like hours, she threw off her blankets and packed up her bedroll, dressing quickly. She went downstairs and out to the stable. It was still dark. She rifled through the wagon until she found Pol's bow, taking it out to the courtyard. She nocked an arrow and let it fly at the wooden hitching post.

She missed.

It made her angry. Her skin flushed at her own incompetence. What good was she? She would never be a sage, and she had no other skills. Why was she even trying to shoot a bow? Did she actually expect to become a guard like Pol or Tali or Shae? Her father would never allow it. And she couldn't even kill a monster—a *monster*, she told herself—without feeling like a monster herself.

She jerked the iron dagger out of its sheath at her waist and threw it savagely at the post, but as soon as it left her hand, she knew it was a bad throw. She heard it clanging to the ground beyond the post. She let out a frustrated groan and stalked across the dirt yard to retrieve it. Her knees shook when she squatted down to pick it up. Her whole body was worn out, but she was too tightly wound to rest. She shoved the dagger into its sheath and went back to the bow.

When she had shot all the arrows, she went to where they lay and picked them up, stuffing them back into the quiver. Then she returned to where she had been standing at the opposite side of the courtyard and raised the bow again. She couldn't keep feeling this way. It would drive her mad. She breathed in, trying to loosen the knot of frustration and self-loathing inside herself.

The arrow's feathers brushed against her gloved hand as she pulled back on the string. She told herself that the only thing in the world was this arrow. There was no stable yard; there was no village of Ento; there was no Kaede, even. Everything melted away like fog in sunlight. She was riding on the sharp point of the arrowhead itself; she was flying through the predawn stillness.

The thud as it struck the hitching post surprised her.

She pulled another arrow, and another, and sent them all, more or less, into the post. Some shivered a bit before tumbling down, not having been sent with enough force. When she saw one fall, she pulled back harder on the next one. She felt emptied of everything; she only existed to hold the bow and to ready the arrow for its task.

She did this repeatedly until the sky brightened into gray. She did it until her shoulders and arms were aching and her eyes stung from staring so fixedly at the target. She did it until the gate to the stable yard opened behind her and she heard Con's voice say, "You're getting pretty good at that."

She turned to look at him, and it all came back to her: the woman, the child, the dagger in its belly. "My father asked you to look out for me," she said.

He was taken aback by the sharpness in her tone. "Yes. And your mother. And your brothers."

"They think I'm incapable of taking care of myself," she said bitterly. "They must think I'm a child." Her arms burned from holding the string taut, and the bow that had felt so light moments before now became heavy in her hands.

He frowned, shaking his head. "That's not it. They want you to be safe."

She looked down at the ground. The numbness inside her was being pushed away by hot emotion: resentment at her father, a sudden ache for her family—she missed them, she realized. There was a sludgy black sadness at the bottom of it all. She yearned for the clarity, the nothingness that had flooded her when she was shooting. She tried to draw some memory of that into her now, to smooth away the rawness. She remembered the creature's human mother. She asked: "What happened to the mother?"

"I brought her back with me. She inside. She's—she's had a shock." When Kaede only stared morosely at the arrow clutched in her hand, he said, "Come inside and eat some breakfast."

She nodded. There was an emptiness inside her, but she did not think it was due to hunger.

Chapter XIII

veryone told Kaede that she had done the right thing, but she felt hollow inside. When Fin had given her that dagger, it had been like a toy to her. Now she knew what a weapon was.

Two days after leaving Ento, the road narrowed and became packed dirt instead of paving stones. They had reached the end of most of the farmland, and now low hills began to rise in the distance. They were far from Cathair, and yet they still had more than a week of travel before they would reach Jilin and the Great Wood. Kaede felt the lack of sun with a brutal sense of futility: The whole world was gray, colorless. Her fingers were cold where they gripped the reins, and though she rode beside Con, who had been trying all morning to engage her in conversation, she felt alone. She knew he meant well, but he had no idea what she was going through. In the distance the road curved around a hill, and she was overcome by the desire to run, to leave them all behind.

She leaned over the neck of her horse and urged her into

a gallop, pushing past Shae and Pol. She heard them calling after her, but she didn't answer. On the left the road sloped down toward the river Nir; on the right it curved up a brown hillside. She caught sight of a lone tree at the top, stripped bare of its leaves, and then she was rounding the hill and there was only more road.

She loved the whip of the wind in her face. It was cool and faintly wet. She remembered the first time she had ridden a galloping horse: She had been a child, barely eight or nine, trying to keep up with her older brothers. They were at a family friend's country home, and her brothers had taken their host's horses out for a run in the morning. Her mother had told her she was too young to go with them, but she hated being left behind. She had sneaked down to the stables and taken out a fat little pony and somehow forced him into a gallop, chasing those boys down to the riverbank. When she arrived, flushed and proud of herself, only their host's son was surprised; her brothers laughed and chided her for taking so long.

Now she let her horse gallop at full speed until she felt her begin to tire, and then she gently slowed her down to a walk. When the road curved close to the river, she turned Maila toward the water, leaning back in the saddle as they went downhill the short distance. She dismounted at the riverbank and watched as Maila lowered her head to the water. The Nir was wide and deep here, sliding with a dim roar south toward Cathair. At this time of year, it should have been full of fishing vessels and ships carrying goods from the north—woolens, lumber, stone from mountain quarries. But the river was empty. Not even a waterbird floated on its surface. Trade had halted last fall when the storms began, and business had not returned to normal. The empty river should have been a peaceful sight, but instead it drove home something that Kaede hadn't fully understood until now: The Kingdom would die if the seasons did not change.

She sucked her breath in sharply. This was why she was here, standing on the banks of the Nir so far from the protection of the Academy walls and her family's influence. She was here because the Council of Sages believed the Fairy Queen knew something about why their kingdom was turning into a wasteland—a place where crops spoiled overnight, where farmers couldn't replant because there was no sunlight. Where monsters crawled out of their dark places and were found dead in northern villages, or were somehow reborn in the soft little bodies of human babies. She was here because the oracle stones said she was part of this journey to discover what the Fairy Queen knew. Did that mean that what she had done in Ento was meant to be?

Behind her she heard a horse on the road. When it began to descend the hillside to join her, she turned to see that the rider was Shae.

"Did they send you to bring me back?" Kaede asked.

"No." Shae dismounted and came to stand beside her. "To keep you safe."

"Safe. I don't think we've been safe for a long time."

"Does that worry you?"

"Should it?"

Shae shrugged. "I don't believe in worrying. It's a waste of energy."

They stood for a while in silence, gazing out over the river. Dried grasses rustled as a wind gusted down the barren slope, raising several strands of Kaede's hair. She tucked the ends behind her ears and looked at Shae, whose face was open, waiting. "Shae," Kaede said, and she felt the words come tumbling out of her: "When I chose to come on this journey, I thought—I thought it was going to be an adventure." Kaede grimaced at her own foolishness, but Shae gave her an encouraging smile.

"I like a good adventure myself," Shae said. "Why else do you think I wanted to join the King's Guard? I needed a living, yes, but I could have done something less...life-threatening. Some of us need adventures."

"But in Ento—" Kaede stopped, rubbed her hands over her face as though she could wipe the memory away. "It's not an adventure anymore. If it ever was."

Shae reached out and squeezed Kaede's shoulder. Several heartbeats later, she bent down, pulled up a dry stalk of grass, and began to shred it with her fingers. "I killed someone once," she said in a low voice.

"As a guard?"

"Yes. It was in one of the southern provinces, my first year as a member of the King's Guard. There was trouble at a border village, and I was sent with a contingent of guards to...to quell the resistance." Though her tone was calm, there was an undercurrent of tension in her words. It was clear that the memory was not an easy one. "At first it seemed as though the villagers would comply with our orders. Everyone was obeying. But then several men attacked us just as we were preparing to depart, and there was a—a scuffle. It turned out later they were sent by a neighboring lord to protect his stores, and they had been given the order to keep us out of the village for fear that we would take his grain." She paused, and plucked another long brown blade of grass from the ground. "Grain was never on our list."

"What were you sent to do?"

"We were supposed to make sure that the people of that village accepted the lord whom King Cai had instated as governor of that province. Because they were complying, there was no need to use force."

"But you did."

"Ultimately, yes. The men who attacked us were well armed and strong, and they took one of our guards quickly. I saw him beheaded not a foot in front of me. That's not a sight I'll ever forget." Shae let go of the torn shreds of grass. They fluttered out over the hillside like dandelion blossoms on the wind. "After that, the men who attacked us smelled a potential victory, and they—they charged us. I reacted before I could think." Her eyes were fixed on the distance as though she were seeing that day again. "One of them came at me, and all I knew was that if I did not kill him first, he was going to kill me. So I did."

"You were defending yourself."

"Does that make it all right?" They looked at each other, and the guard's dark brown eyes were troubled. "I knew that to be one of the King's Guard meant that I might have to kill. But I wasn't prepared for it when it happened. I wasn't prepared for the way it changed me. It was weeks before I could talk about it, though all my fellow guards praised me for what I had done. On the battlefield, they said, there is no time for anything but instinct. And yet, I can't help but wonder if perhaps our instincts are sometimes wrong."

"Do you regret it?"

Shae sighed and looked away. "How can I regret what I did, when it kept me alive?"

Chapter XIV

hat night, they camped on the side of the road for the first time. There would be no hostel for another two days' journey. Taisin and Shae tended to the horses as usual, rubbing them down and feeding them. Taisin enjoyed the work; it reminded her of home. When she was a little girl, her father had given her the task of brushing down the farm horses at the end of the day, and she had loved being in the barn at twilight, the smell of hay and horses all around her. Those were things she had truly missed at the Academy: the warmth of animals, and the simple honesty of their energies.

Focused on the horses, the feel of their muscles beneath her hands, she was startled when Kaede appeared by her side, a cup of tea in her hand. "Tali says supper will be ready soon," Kaede said, offering her the warm drink. Kaede seemed more relaxed now than she had been earlier in the day; Taisin wondered what had soothed her.

"Thank you," Taisin said. She began to tuck the brush under her arm, but then Kaede held out her hand.

"I'll trade you," Kaede said, smiling.

The smile made Taisin's cheeks burn. She was glad it was dark. "All right." She handed the brush over in exchange for the tea. It smelled of barley, nutty and hot, and it tasted wonderful.

"It's the last of it. I didn't want you to miss out." Kaede tilted her head briefly at the campfire, where Con and Pol were sitting on their bedrolls, joking with Tali as he prepared whatever concoction they would be eating tonight.

"What about Shae?" Taisin looked at the guard, who was working on the wagon horses several feet away.

"I already brought her a cup."

"Oh." Taisin raised the tea to her lips again, the steam wafting into her eyes. It reminded her of wintry nights at the Academy, curled up in her tiny room with her bed strewn with books. She felt a deep tug of homesickness inside her.

"I wanted to tell you something."

"You did?" Taisin's stomach fluttered. She often felt nervous around Kaede. It frustrated her, but she didn't know what to do about it. She was doing everything she could, she told herself, to avoid the fate in her vision—but she was afraid she was losing that battle.

"Yes." Kaede took a deep breath, steeling herself. "I didn't really understand, until today, even, what was at stake on this journey. Now I do. You were right, in Ento—we need to know what we're dealing with, or as much as we can know. So I have to ask you: What did you see in your vision, Taisin? You haven't told me—not exactly. But the way you look at me sometimes, I have to know: What did you see me doing?"

Taisin clutched the battered metal teacup with both hands and swallowed. All she could think was that Kaede had caught her staring at her. She was mortified that she had been so obvious; she was terrified that she would have to tell her the whole truth.

Kaede saw Taisin's distress. Even in the dark, the way her shoulders had stiffened betrayed her. "Is it so bad?" Kaede's own anxiety began to rise. "What did you see me do?"

Taisin shook her head swiftly. "No—no, it's not anything— you didn't do anything awful. That's not what I saw."

"Please. Please just tell me."

She knew she had to tell her something. "I saw you—and I—we were on a beach. An icy beach." Her voice shook a little, remembering. "You stepped into a rowboat, and you rowed away. I saw you leaving." She stopped, hoping that Kaede would ask for nothing more.

"A rowboat?" Kaede was puzzled. "And I was leaving? That's all?"

"Yes," Taisin said, and pressed her lips together.

As Kaede mulled over her words, Taisin saw that she didn't seem to realize that anything had been held back. But why should she? Taisin knew she had done her best to keep her emotions hidden. She had even tried to keep them hidden from herself, though it was becoming increasingly difficult.

Kaede asked, "Where is this beach?"

Taisin was startled. It had never occurred to her to wonder about that at all. "I don't know. I just saw it. It's part of this journey—that's all I know."

They heard Tali calling to them; supper was ready.

"You go ahead," Taisin said, taking the opportunity to change the subject. "I'll be there in a minute. I just want to put away the brushes." She held her hand out for the brush Kaede had taken from her, and for a moment Kaede didn't seem to want to give it to her. She was looking at Taisin closely, searching her face. Taisin tried to school her expression into one of calm blankness; she had the irrational fear that Kaede could see right through her.

But Kaede only said, "All right," and handed over the brush. "Don't be long. The food will get cold."

Taisin clutched the brush with one hand, the teacup with the other, and told herself that she shouldn't be so silly. It was dark, and besides, Kaede couldn't read her mind.

⁓

Around the campfire that night, they told stories. What had happened in Ento had left them all unsettled, and taletelling was a welcome distraction. Con, it seemed, had heard every story ever told, and he regaled them with the legendary exploits of King Rin Tai, who traveled to the clouded mountain to face the sinuous green dragon who had terrorized the people of six provinces.

"And when he returned, I suppose he married the most beautiful highborn lady in the land and had a dozen children," Shae said drily.

Con shrugged. "You object to a happy ending?"

Shae leaned forward, poking at the fire with a stick. The flames roared. "I'd like to hear a tale about an ordinary person for once. Not all of us are born princes." She softened the sharpness of her words with a smile, but Con was chagrined.

Tali laughed. "She has a point. Do you have a story in your head for us common folk?"

"Is that a challenge?" Con asked.

"Yes," Tali said. "A challenge."

"All right, then." Con flexed his fingers and thought for a moment. "Have you heard the tale of Farin and Anmin?"

Taisin smiled. "I have."

"Good. Then you can correct me if I get it wrong. Farin was a blacksmith—a noble enough profession, to be sure, but one that kept him hard at work day and night. His village was located near the King's Highway, and his smithy was adjacent to the town's best inn, which was always busy with travelers. One autumn, a wealthy merchant and his family were passing through Farin's village and boarded at the inn. The merchant had a daughter, whose name was Anmin. She, they say, was as beautiful as a spring morning."

Tali whistled. "I haven't seen one of those in a while."

Con gave him a stern look. "Anmin, as I was saying, was a beautiful girl. Her father had aspirations for her. He was a merchant, but he hoped to marry her to a wealthy lord and thereby increase his standing in the court."

"Here come the nobles," Shae said.

"Wait until you hear the whole story," Con objected. "Anmin was more than beautiful; she was also intelligent, and she knew what her father's plans were. But she had other goals in life. She had heard from her father that there were other lands across the sea, and she wanted to explore them. She knew that to become an explorer she would have to learn how to ride and defend herself—talents that no lord's wife needed—so every chance she had, she would practice swordplay or horsemanship. One afternoon while she was in the village, she discovered that her sword had a knick in it, and she decided to bring it to the blacksmith nearby. When she and Farin saw each other, they knew immediately that they had found their one true love."

"How did they know?" Shae asked. "Sparks flew from the anvil?"

Con grinned at her. "Don't you have any faith in the power of love?"

"Do you, Prince Con?" she teased him, and the tone in her voice made a tingle run through him. She was watching him with her head half-cocked, and he noticed a sly smile turning up the corners of her mouth.

He responded, "You're avoiding the question." The expression on Shae's face changed just slightly—he wondered if it was self-consciousness—and she ducked her head and poked at the fire again.

"Tell the story, Con," she said lightly, but she avoided his gaze.

"As you wish," he said, feeling a little surge of anticipation. Shae had always been friendly with him, never anything more or less, and for the first time Con became aware that he might like it if there was something more. While she prodded at the burning coals, he continued: "As I was saying, when Farin and Anmin first saw each other, they fell in love. They resolved to marry as soon as possible, but when Anmin told her father of her intentions, he flew into a rage and told her he had already arranged her marriage to the King's nephew. When she saw that he had no intention of backing down, she decided to elope with the blacksmith. However, the following morning, she awoke to discover that her father had been robbed during the night. All of the goods he had been transporting to Cathair had been stolen, and because soot had been found in the room where the goods had been stored, her father believed that Farin was the thief.

"Farin was brought to the village magistrate, who listened to the merchant's suspicions and found Farin guilty. But Farin insisted he was no thief, and he also knew that the magistrate could be easily bribed. With Anmin's help, Farin appealed to the provincial magistrate, who also sided with the merchant. Farin was about to be thrown into prison when the King's Magistrate agreed to hear his case—thanks to Anmin's hard work—and Farin was so convincing that the King's Magistrate told him that if he could face the judgment of the unicorn and survive, then he would be set free. Of course, if the unicorn found him guilty, he would be gored by the beast and die."

"No one ever survives the judgment of the unicorn," Pol said. "We are all guilty of something; the unicorn never finds anyone innocent."

"In some of the tales they survive," Taisin put in.

"Really? Which ones?" Pol asked.

"Hang on," Con said. "Let me finish this tale first. So: Farin was taken into the Wood to seek out the unicorn."

"In the version I heard, the unicorns were kept in a special enclosure at the palace," Taisin said.

Con blinked. "An enclosure?"

"Yes. There was an enclosure, adjacent to the King's Magistrate's office," she said. "The accused would be brought there and judged."

"I can't imagine the creatures would submit to being enclosed," Pol said.

"Because you've seen them before?" Tali said skeptically.

"No, but they're not horses to be trained. You might as well keep a phoenix as a songbird."

"I'm sure that's been attempted by some king or another," Shae said. "Con, please continue."

When she spoke his name her eyes flickered to him, and warmth spread over his skin. He swallowed. "All right. So, Farin was taken to the unicorn to face his judgment. Of course, Farin was innocent, but his heart was so pure and his love for Anmin so true that the unicorn not only let him live, he showed him who the real thief was: Anmin's own father, who had sought to incriminate the blacksmith to prevent him from marrying his daughter. When Farin returned to his village, he immediately told the merchant that he knew his secret, and he threatened to tell Anmin as well. But the merchant knew that if his daughter found out, she would never again acknowledge him as her father. Faced with the loss of his only daughter, he agreed to drop his accusations, and Farin and Anmin were soon married. Afterward, they both became explorers and lived long and happy lives."

Tali clapped, and the others laughed and joined in. Shae said, "That is a sweet tale, Con. But what's the moral of the story?" She watched him, her face half in shadow.

"Magistrates are generally corrupt," Pol quipped.

"Fathers shouldn't attempt to marry their daughters off to noblemen when there's a handsome blacksmith nearby," Kaede said, pulling a face.

Con smiled. "Those are a couple of ways to think about it." He looked at Shae as he said, "Or, perhaps the lesson is that true love will always prevail."

"How romantic of you," Shae said, and she might have meant for her words to sound wry, but Con heard a thread of wistfulness in her voice.

"I think it's true," he said. "Love knows no limits; it sees no distinctions based on birth or any other characteristic. A prince may love a seamstress as much as any princess."

"But would the seamstress be allowed to love the prince?" Shae asked.

"Love will always prevail," Con said. He thought he saw the hint of a blush on her face, though he couldn't be sure, for she stirred the embers in the campfire again, and the light flared reddish-gold over her skin.

૭

They sat up late telling stories, and by the time Taisin rolled into her blankets by the fire, she was so tired she fell asleep immediately. She didn't know how much later the vision came, but when it began, she could still feel the hard ground beneath her body, softened only slightly by the blankets she had folded into a thin pallet. But she could also feel the cold breath of winter on her face, and she could see the fortress of ice again. This time, she had left the beach behind entirely; she was floating, hovering up high, ascending toward the glass windows set into thick, frozen walls. She had never known that ice could take on so many shades of blue: sharp lines of indigo like the deepest sea, aquamarine shadows, even the glint of blue-green where the sun struck just so.

For the first time, she realized the significance of that. The sun shone here. Wherever *here* was, it was not locked in the unchanging clouded gray that blanketed the Kingdom. She wanted to look up at the sky, to gaze into the sun's brilliant white-gold eye, but she had no control over her movements, and she had arrived at one of the windows. The glass was like a mirror reflecting the light, and what she saw in the window made her jerk in surprise. A tiny person was hovering there on little feathered wings, like a hummingbird, and Taisin heard the creature speaking some kind of language she did not understand.

A moment later the window opened, and the creature fluttered inside. Taisin was pulled along with her, as if riding in the draft of her wings. The creature flew so quickly that all Taisin could do was follow. She only caught glimpses of what passed: walls of white, glacial floors, and every once in a while, a torch burning with a cold blue flame. She became aware, slowly, that the flying creature's heart was beating as quickly as a tiny war drum, urgent with some kind of duty. And then all of a sudden the way opened wide, and Taisin now understood that they had been flying down a corridor and had just emerged into a great, echoing space. She heard more sounds like the words that the winged creature had spoken. She could not make out the distinct syllables, but they made her heart ache, for they were all sounds of yearning—each being who cried out was crying out for freedom.

Taisin saw the creature's bright orange and emerald wings flutter as she twisted in midair to look down, and Taisin reeled at the sight below her. There were cages, hundreds of them, stacked like crates. She saw golden bars; she saw eyes of different colors peering up at her. The voices she had heard came from within those cages.

The flying creature turned to look back, but she did not seem to see Taisin. She had a tiny, delicate, girl's face, and she wore an expression of dread. Her glittering golden eyes widened with alarm, and then Taisin was thrust out of the vision as though someone had pushed her aside, and she was lying on her back on the hard ground beside a fire that sent golden sparks up into the black night sky. She saw Pol sitting up nearby; he had taken the second watch that night.

Her breath came as quick as that creature's wings had been beating. She knew she had been close to seeing something important. What had pushed her aside? Who was trapped in those cages? The memory of the imprisoned voices made her shiver. Who, she wondered, was their jailer?

PART III

Dragons battle on the plain:
Yellow and black blood spills.
Where frost is underfoot,
Ice cannot be far.

—*Book of Changes*

Chapter XV

heir first glimpse of the Great Wood came nearly three weeks after leaving Cathair. It was a dark smudge against the distant hills that blinked in and out of sight as the road curved. And then one afternoon as they rounded another bend, there it was, spreading its fingers out into the valley below, brushing up close to the river, extending to the horizon in waves of brown and green. Kaede had never before seen so many trees.

They camped within a copse of oaks that night. The weather had turned the leaves brown, even though it was midsummer, and a cold wind gusted through the gnarled branches, making the dried leaves rattle.

"We should get to Jilin sometime tomorrow," Shae said, squatting down to warm her hands at the fire while Tali cooked the rice. "Hopefully before dark."

"When was the last time you were there?" Con asked, sitting down beside her.

"Two years, one month ago," Shae answered. "It's been too long."

Shae's eagerness to reach Jilin caused them to push the horses hard the next day. The road took them through the outer reaches of the Great Wood, winding through clumps of oaks and bay trees. As dusk fell, shadows deepened beneath the branches. The road widened ahead, but the murky twilight made it difficult to see.

Shae, who was riding in the lead, called them to a halt. "Something's wrong," she said in a low voice. Beside her, Tali drew his sword.

Kaede felt a prickle of apprehension run down the back of her neck. It was too quiet; they couldn't even hear the sound of insects.

Suddenly a torch flared twenty feet ahead of them, and behind that torch, a half-dozen more burned into life. In the smoky light, Kaede saw men and women approaching with weapons in their hands; some held swords, while others carried long wooden staffs or axes. Fear raced through her. She heard the loud, ringing scrape as Con drew his sword, and she reached for her own iron dagger.

A man stepped out of the crowd of torchbearers, his black beard obscuring half his face, his eyes glittering in the torchlight. "Who goes there?" he called out in a harsh voice.

Shae had drawn her sword as well, and Tali and Pol flanked her. "Noa, is that you?" Shae called out. "What is going on? It's me, Shae."

The bearded man took a step forward, but he still brandished his sword before him. "Shae? Niran's sister?"

"Yes! Don't you recognize me?" She dismounted and sheathed her sword, approaching him with her hands outstretched. "Noa, I'm back. It's me."

For a long, tense moment, Kaede was sure the man was going to deny that he had any idea who Shae was and strike her down, but then he lowered his sword and closed the gap between them, crushing Shae into an embrace. "Shae," he said, his voice heavy with relief. "Why didn't you send word in advance?"

The other torchbearers gathered around Noa and Shae, their voices rising as they pelted Shae with questions about why she was back. She answered with rising concern in her voice: "I will tell you all—I will tell you everything, but where is Niran? Where is my brother? Why isn't he with you?" The crowd fell silent, and Shae turned to Noa and demanded, "Tell me, Noa. What has happened?"

"Your brother, Niran, is fine," he said, but his tone suggested that he was holding something back.

"Noa," Shae said. "What do you mean?"

"I'll take you to him. He's fine," Noa said again.

"Now," Shae said firmly, and Noa nodded.

୧◦⁀◦

The village of Jilin was surrounded by trees, and trees marched down Jilin's few streets. The buildings seemed to have been situated to make room for giant trunks and root systems, and in the wavering torchlight, they looked almost as if they had grown out of the trees themselves.

Noa led them to a massive oak outside a long dark

building and said, "You should leave your horses here. It'll be easier."

Shae knew the village of Jilin intimately, and she knew immediately that Noa was not taking her to her brother's home. "Where are we going?" she asked him.

"Into the Wood." Most of the other villagers had returned to their homes, but two remained behind, carrying torches. "Let's go," Noa said, and struck off down a small trail.

In the daylight, the path would have been an easy walk, but in the dusk—brightened only by the flickering torches—it was an obstacle course. Even Tali tripped once, cursing under his breath. Kaede kept her eyes on Noa's torch ahead, trying to ignore the strange sensation that there was something out in the dark, watching her. It made the hairs on her neck stand on end, but she told herself she was imagining things.

After they had walked for about a quarter of an hour, Noa paused and called out, "Niran!"

Moments later a man came running down the path; behind him someone followed more slowly, bearing a torch. "Shae?" the man cried. "Is that you?" Niran was a tall man with a closely cropped black beard; his hands and face were streaked with dirt, but it could not disguise his surprise and joy at seeing Shae. He crushed her in an embrace, asking, "What are you doing here? Why didn't you tell us you were coming?"

"I'll tell you everything later," Shae said. "But why are you out here? What's going on?"

"We've found something," Niran said.

The torchbearer who had followed Niran came forward;

she was a woman, her black hair hanging in a long braid over her shoulder. "Shae?"

"Parsa," Shae said, and threw her arms around her brother's wife. When they parted, Shae asked, "What have you found?"

"Come and see for yourself," Niran said, and stood aside. There was a clearing just past him, and a long rectangular hole gaped open in the ground. Shovels were leaning against a nearby pine tree, and Kaede realized that she was looking at a grave. A chill ran through her. Beside the grave was a shape wrapped in a sheet. A body.

Niran bent down and pulled back the sheet. They saw the corpse of an inhuman creature, its arms wrapped around bended knees, its head lolling sideways onto the ground. It had long hair that resembled hundreds of tiny vines, some of them smashed and brown. The eyes had been covered by a torn piece of cloth, like a blindfold, and the mouth was stuffed with a black stone. From its fingertips, nails like long green blades of grass extended, curling over mottled, barklike skin. They were the only living things on the creature: It was as if the grasslike nails had sprouted out of a seed and were determined to make a new life out of what had already expired.

Taisin edged past Niran to take a closer look, curiosity vying with aversion. She wondered if it was some kind of fay. There were fay races other than the Xi—she thought the winged girl she saw in her vision must be fay—but she knew little about them. This one looked like it could have grown from a tree. She asked, "When did you find it?"

"Yesterday morning," Niran said.

"Did you place the stone in its mouth?" Taisin asked. It was traditional to put a stone in the mouth of a person who had been murdered, to prevent him from speaking to the living if he returned as a ghost.

"I did," Parsa said. "It is marked with the sign for peaceful rest."

Taisin couldn't see the mark; the stone was wedged in too deeply. The creature's lips were cracked and dry, reminding her of parched earth after a drought. "You were going to bury it?"

"Yes," Niran said.

"It should—it would be better if it were burned," Taisin said.

"We can't burn it," Niran objected. "We would set the Wood on fire."

"And we won't carry it into Jilin; it is polluted with death," Parsa said. Her eyes narrowed on Taisin. "Who are you? What would you know about this?"

Taisin shrank back, feeling stung. Shae said quickly, "We're here for a reason. I didn't send word because, well, our reasons mustn't become widely known. But I will tell you the truth." She glanced uneasily from the body to Taisin. "First, though, I think we should finish what you have started here."

Shae's brother looked them over skeptically, but he nodded. "All right."

He bent down to pull the shroud over the face of the dead creature again. Taisin said nothing. She hoped that the stone and the blindfold would do their jobs and take the place of a funeral pyre. She told herself that if the ghost of the creature could not speak or see, then no real harm could be done. But still, she was uneasy. She had no idea if those traditions would work on something so clearly inhuman. She wanted to know more about it: How had it died? And where had it come from?

Niran and Parsa picked up their shovels, levered them under the body, and tipped it over the edge of the grave, where it fell with a dull thump. Taisin flinched. Beneath her breath, she muttered a blessing ritual meant to keep a body in its grave.

☙

Niran, like his father and grandfather before him, was a blacksmith, and his family's home had been built adjacent to the smithy over the course of many generations. Kaede had the impression that additional wings had been added at random, creating a maze of connecting rooms that opened here and there into sky wells and broader courtyards. Niran led them through the main gate and past the smithy, the forge still smoldering, and then into the main hall, next to a kitchen where a fire burned in an open pit.

Shae's older sister, Raesa, who had heard news of Shae's arrival, greeted them warmly. "The children are asleep," she said. "You must come and eat."

Raesa's husband, Tulan, had brought back two hares from his traps that afternoon, and the rich fragrance of braised meat made Kaede's mouth water. They gathered together in the hall, sitting around two square tables pushed together, and ate salty flat bread and rabbit stewed with aromatic spices. A brown-and-black hound nosed his way around their feet, sniffing for fallen scraps. Raesa poured them hot, bitter tea in small earthenware cups, and Shae told her brother and sister why she had brought five strangers with her to Jilin.

"Please, don't tell anyone else what I've told you," Shae said when she finished.

Niran nodded, and glanced around the table at her companions. "How long do you plan to stay?"

"Not long," Tali answered. "I'm sorry."

"Stay through tomorrow," Parsa insisted. "You have to at least give us time to welcome you back."

"All right," Shae assented with a smile. "As long as nobody else objects."

"I'm happy to have a roof over my head for one more night," Con said, and no one disagreed with him.

"You're traveling into the Wood?" Raesa asked.

"Yes," Tali said. "We're headed north of the river Kell."

Raesa glanced at her husband, who had been mostly silent. But now he said, "When I was a boy, my uncle said he traveled that far, but when he returned there was something off about him. I never could get the whole story out of him."

Tali had brought their map case inside, and now he opened it, pushing aside empty bowls to unroll a map of the Wood onto the table. Kaede scooted her chair closer, wanting to get a better look. Tali had never shared them with her, though she had heard him discussing their route with Pol and Shae. Jilin was clearly noted on the map, and trails splintered off from the village and led into the Wood. Some of them ended abruptly only a few miles in; the longest followed the river Nir north, and then ended just south of where the Nir intersected with the Kell, which flowed east. Above the Kell, the Great Wood continued unabated to the northernmost edge of the map, which was marked with mountains: the Northerness. Tali looked at Tulan and asked, "Is there a way to cross the Kell? A bridge? It is unmarked."

Tulan leaned over the map to examine it, but he shook his head. "Not that I've heard of. I suppose there are stories of folks who have crossed the Kell."

"Where did they cross it?" Tali asked.

"They're stories, not directions," he said mildly.

Tali seemed disappointed.

"I think this map is as good as you're going to get," Tulan said. "It's accurate enough around here. I don't know about the northern part; I imagine that's all a guessing game."

"So how would you advise that we find our way to the Kell?" Shae asked.

"Follow the Nir. I'm fairly certain it does meet the Kell. You'll find it that way. That's as best as I can tell you." Tulan frowned, tugging at his beard. "You're going off the map. No one knows what's up there."

Chapter XVI

hey slept in their bedrolls on the floor of the main hall, pushing the table and chairs to one side, next to the family shrine, to make room. Kaede found the stone floor as comfortable as a feather bed after days of sleeping on lumpy ground, and she fell asleep so quickly she barely had time to enjoy the flatness beneath her back. She was awakened in the morning by the shrill voices of children—Shae's nieces and nephew—who ran into the room and pounced on Shae's sleeping form, startling a yelp out of her.

At breakfast, Raesa and Tulan announced that they were going hunting, for they planned a celebration that night and hoped to bring back a deer. Pol volunteered to go with them, and when he asked Kaede if she'd like to come along— "You should see the bow in its natural environment," he said—she was surprised but pleased, and said yes.

The hound, whose name was Ota, came with them, his ears perking forward as they left Jilin behind and entered the Wood. It was another cool morning, but the Wood held none of the menace it had the night before, and Kaede wondered if she had imagined the sensation of something watching her. Now there were only trees, their gray-brown trunks scaled with lichen, and every so often the sound of a squirrel or rabbit bounding through the underbrush. Raesa and Tulan, like Pol, had quivers strapped to their backs and hunting knives at their waists; they carried their bows and moved with a stealth that Kaede knew she could not match. Her footsteps sounded like a herd of giants compared to theirs, and she feared that Pol had been wrong to invite her. She didn't want to scare away their supper.

But as they walked, Tulan said to her, "Raesa is a much better shot than I. When we find the deer it would be best if she and Pol move downwind, and then you and I can nudge the deer toward them."

"So you'll take advantage of my clumsy footsteps," Kaede said, smiling.

"You'll get better," Raesa said.

Kaede tried to limit the noise she made. She set her feet down as lightly as she could, imagining that she was a cloud, a mist, snaking slowly but surely around the gnarled oak trees. The Wood smelled of damp things: rainwater soaking into fallen logs, softening the bark until it crumbled back into the ground. In the distance, she heard the caw of a crow, over and over.

It was nearly an hour before Ota scented the deer; when he did, his entire body pointed northwest, his legs quivering in excitement. They had long ago left the well-maintained paths behind and were now picking their way down a tiny deer trail. As soon as Ota gave the signal, Raesa and Pol melted into the trees, moving as quietly as they could to avoid startling the deer. Ota vanished after them, and Tulan and Kaede continued on. Soon afterward Kaede saw the flash of a white tail just off to her left. All her senses came alive, and a thrill rippled through her. It was awe-inspiring to be so near to this animal. And yet—her breath caught in her throat—they were going to kill him. Her knowledge of the buck's imminent death seemed to magnify everything: the beauty of the animal, the smell of the forest, the beating of her heart. Time seemed to slow down. The caw of the crow echoed through the trees like a bell.

Beside her, Tulan crept forward, and the deer began to back away from them. Kaede followed, her pulse racing, and they pushed the deer ahead for some time, always moving in the direction that Pol and Raesa had gone in. With every careful step, Kaede was aware that death was coming closer, and she began to wonder if the buck knew it, too.

And then an arrow struck the deer in his side, and he bolted.

Ota leapt after him, baying, his nose soon dropping to the ground to follow the scent of spilled blood. The deer had been wounded, but it would run in panic for some distance. They could only hope that the arrow had landed deep enough, or else it would be a long and potentially fruitless chase.

Pol and Raesa came out from their cover, and Tulan asked, "Who sent the arrow?"

"Raesa did," Pol said. "You're right—she's a good shot."

"Don't speak too soon," she cautioned him, and they began to follow Ota on a jagged path through the trees.

But they were lucky; the arrow had been true, and it was only another half mile before they found the deer collapsed on the ground, his flanks heaving. Tulan unsheathed his long hunting knife and went to the deer, and before Kaede could catch her breath, he slit the buck's throat.

Raesa held Ota back from the stream of blood while the deer died.

Kaede halted several feet away. The sight of the dying animal brought back the memory of the creature she had killed in Ento, and for a moment she thought her stomach would turn itself inside out. Cold sweat beaded her forehead. Pol saw the expression on her face and said, "The buck will feed many of us tonight, and more tomorrow. It was a necessary death."

She swallowed. She knew that Pol was right. But never had the word *necessary* seemed so cold.

❧

They strapped the deer's legs to a long fallen branch and hoisted it up on their shoulders, each taking turns to bear the weight on the way back to Jilin. Ota ran between their legs excitedly; he had been given a piece of the warm liver, but he smelled the meat and was eager for more.

When they reached Niran's home, Kaede slipped away. She felt bruised somehow, as though someone had smashed a fist into an old wound, and she wanted to be alone. There was a garden behind the smithy, and when she saw the rows of low green shoots, a pang went through her as she remembered working with Maesie. There were some things she missed from the Academy: the sea, and Maesie and Fin, and her friends. Beyond the garden, a small path led into the Wood, weaving between bay trees. It was gloomy now, but seeing the way the branches arched overhead, Kaede suspected it would be beautiful beneath the sunlight. She imagined a green tunnel, the leaves whispering in a warm breeze. She ached for the warmth of summer. Though it was now nearly midsummer, it was still as cool as late winter.

The path ended in a small clearing with a stone bench. Opposite the bench was a statue that appeared to have been shaped out of the oak stump rooted there in the ground: a deer's head. She sat on the bench and stared at it, wondering who had made it, who had imbued such life into the way the ears tilted.

She heard the footsteps some time later, and glanced up to see Taisin coming down the path. She looked a bit nervous, and she held out something wrapped in a white cloth. "I brought you some bread," she said tentatively.

"Thank you," Kaede said. It was flat bread fresh from the pan, still warm.

Taisin sat on the far edge of the bench beside her. "They're eating, if you want to go back."

The flat bread was good, slightly charred and salty. "I'll go back in a little while," she said between bites.

"They're butchering the deer. I think that Parsa intends to invite all of Jilin here tonight." Taisin glanced sideways at Kaede. "How was the hunt?"

Kaede's fingers were smeared with salt and lightly greased

with oil from the bread. She wanted to lick them, but thought it might be impolite. She scrubbed them on the cloth and said, "It was successful. No help from me." She grinned, but there was no joy behind it. "I just followed."

Taisin could feel the forced cheer coming from Kaede, who regarded her with serious brown eyes, her mouth slowly turning down at the corners as the grin faded. Taisin asked, "Are you all right?"

The question caught Kaede off guard. "All right? I'm—" She hesitated, the words stuck in her throat, and she looked down at her hands, twisting the cloth into a knot. "I didn't like seeing the deer die," she said at last. "It is—I thought hunting would be...normal, somehow. But something has to die."

Taisin wasn't sure what to say. She thought about telling Kaede that she had seen her first pig butchered when she was a baby; that she had helped every autumn—until she went to the Academy—when her father harvested their meat for the winter. She could say that the deer had died so that they might live, or that its spirit had been released into the world and it would return, again and again, transformed each time into a different being. But it did not change the fact that death came and took things that were not yet ready to leave the world of the living.

She reached out and covered Kaede's hands with her own, and Kaede looked at her in surprise. Taisin felt Kaede's fingers loosen on the cloth; her hand turned upward into Taisin's. Their fingers interlaced. Taisin's heartbeat quickened; a flush crept across her neck. She saw, as if from a distance, that her feelings were changing whether she wanted them to or not. She sensed that she was about to tip over the edge, and at some point, she wouldn't care if she was doing the right thing anymore.

But today, she was still in control. She pulled her hand away, taking a quick, determined breath. "We should go back. I told Parsa I would help her."

Kaede nodded, seemingly unfazed. "Yes. Shae's family has been very kind to us." They stood, and Kaede pocketed the cloth. "I don't think we'll eat so well once we leave."

"We should enjoy it while we can," Taisin said, and immediately felt ridiculous trying to make small talk about surviving the next leg of their journey. But Kaede didn't seem to notice her discomfort. She had started back down the path and turned to wait for her. Kaede was always polite; she was the daughter of the King's Chancellor, after all. Taisin suddenly felt every inch the farmer's daughter—clumsy and foolish.

Taisin balled her hands into fists at her side and followed, keeping her eyes on the ground to avoid betraying her self-consciousness. The path was well maintained, though narrow; the dirt was hard packed in the center, and tufts of brown grasses grew along the edges. And then she saw something that made her stop and turn back. She knelt down on the trail. There was a limp flower bud there, tucked behind a clump of grass—the only splash of purple anywhere in sight. Normally at this time of year, the Wood should be dotted with them, and the sight of this solitary blossom was almost as saddening as it was miraculous.

"Look at that," Taisin whispered. Kaede turned to see what she had found.

Taisin stroked the flower with one finger and bent her

head down close to it, trying to breathe in the air around the tiny growing thing. For as long as she could remember, she had been sensitive to all the shifting meridians of energy around her, and her years at the Academy had sharpened and honed her awareness of them. The last two years, with their summer droughts and winter storms, and now the unending grayness, had been heartbreaking. Before, she had been able to sense the life all around her—in the waving sea grasses that grew on the beach below the Academy; in the oak trees that climbed so slowly toward the sky on her parents' farm. It had been a steady hum underlying everything; a feeling of constant renewal. But in the last two years, the hum had faded; the lines of energy had become increasingly sluggish. Even the plants in the ground seemed to have given up. It was like seeing all the color leeched out of the world bit by bit. So, given the faintest whiff of rebirth in the form of these wilted, half-opened petals, Taisin could not resist.

She cupped the flower in her hand and called to it, and as Kaede stood over her, watching, the flower grew plump; the stalk lifted itself from the earth as though sunlight poured from Taisin's breath into its green leaves. The petals opened one by one, each a perfect violet teardrop, and at the center, the flower's black eye gazed unblinkingly up at Taisin, whose face glowed with the energy unfurling through her.

Kaede could have chastised her, for their teachers at the Academy had taught them from day one that such a display of power was reckless. It was the equivalent of lighting a signal fire on the tallest mountain to announce one's presence during a war. But at the same time, Kaede understood why Taisin had done it, for it was written clear as day on her face: It made her whole.

Afterward, when Taisin was too weakened to walk back immediately, Kaede sat with her on the forest floor, watching as the purple flower, gloriously open to the air, bobbed in the wind.

∾

That night it seemed as though everyone in Jilin stopped by Shae's family home. Parsa and Niran seared thin slices of venison and served it with onions cooked until they were sweet. Other villagers brought more of the flat bread, some stuffed with pickled greens or mushrooms culled from the Wood; and one family brought two jugs of home-brewed spirits. Kaede avoided them, for the fumes alone made her eyes water. There was no talk of bad harvests or strange creatures; it was as if everyone had tacitly agreed to pretend that nothing was wrong, and the only thing on their minds was celebrating Shae's brief return home.

Kaede was grateful for the holiday feel; it drove away the shadows that had clung to her since Ento. She played a game of tacks with Shae's nephew; she joked with Tali about how much venison he could eat; she watched Con flirting shamelessly with Shae, who laughed at him and said loudly—so that everyone could hear—that he had no chance with her. But the way she turned her eyes back to him gave a different impression, and Kaede suddenly wondered whether there was something between them. The thought was surprising to her, but also a bit funny. Kaede simply couldn't imagine Shae in court dress at the palace with Con. She grinned to herself and glanced around the room, taking in Pol talking with Tulan, Parsa's two daughters racing out the door with rock sugar in their fists. Taisin was seated at the table chatting to Raesa, a smile on her face. The smile transformed her. Her cheeks were pink from the warmth of the room; her eyes were shining. She was a young woman still unaware of her own beauty, and Kaede could not look away.

Con pushed his way onto the bench beside Kaede and said, "She's lovely, isn't she?" He threw his arm around her shoulders with a brotherly squeeze.

"What?" she said, startled.

"Shae," he whispered in her ear. "Look at her!"

Kaede gave him a sidelong glance. "Are you being serious?"

"I'm always serious," he said, ruffling her hair. It had grown long enough now that she usually tied it back, but tonight she had had the opportunity to bathe, and it fell loose, still slightly damp, to her shoulders.

"Stop it," Kaede said, swatting his hands away and tucking the ends behind her ears. He reminded her of her brothers, and all of a sudden she missed them fiercely.

"Do you think I have a chance with her?" Con asked.

It took a moment for Kaede to remember what he was talking about: Shae. She tried to swallow her homesickness and said with forced lightness, "You have every advantage. Who wouldn't fall in love with you?"

His eyes sparkled as he gave her a mischievous grin. "Do

I detect a hint of jealousy? Are you going to fight me for Shae's love?"

Kaede gaped at him. "Now you truly must be joking. Why would I do that?"

"You don't want her for yourself?" He elbowed her. "I know you enjoy her company."

Kaede shook her head. "I take it back," she said, laughing. "You're too much of a fool—Shae will never love you."

He pulled an exaggerated frown. "You wound me, Kaede. Your brothers told me I could trust you—I shouldn't have believed them."

"That's good. I never believe them, either." They laughed together, and Kaede felt the tightness within her relaxing. She would see her brothers when she returned, she told herself.

Con's arm was still around her shoulders, and he whispered in her ear, "I saw you looking at Taisin. She's especially pretty tonight."

A flush spread over her face. "You must have been looking at her, too, then," she said, and Con raised his eyebrows at her in a sly smile.

She glanced away, her eyes seeking out Taisin almost automatically. Taisin was watching them, a thoughtful look on her face. When Kaede's gaze met hers, Taisin colored as though she had been caught stealing sweets. Kaede broke into a smile, and Taisin quickly turned away, ducking her head as if she wanted to hide. But scarcely a moment later she glanced back as though she couldn't help it, and Kaede felt a tremor inside herself as the blush on Taisin's cheeks deepened.

Con squeezed her shoulder. "I see I won't have to fight you for Shae," he said in an amused tone.

She gave him an exasperated look. "She's not going to fall in love with you if you stay here all night with *me*."

He grinned at her. "Good point." He stood up and straightened his tunic. "We must take advantage of tonight, for who knows what shall come tomorrow?"

Kaede watched him head toward Shae, but she did not make a move to go to Taisin. She finished her tea, one ear tuned to the conversations around her, occasionally glancing out of the corner of her eye at Taisin, who had pulled a little boy onto her lap to play a game of peekaboo with a red wooden ball. Kaede hadn't felt that tug toward another person in a long time. She certainly hadn't expected to feel it for Taisin, who was usually so distant and self-contained that any possibility of a deeper connection had seemed impossible from the beginning. But this afternoon, the sight of Taisin's face after she urged that flower to bloom— she had been luminous. It was as if a door had briefly opened, and behind it there was sunlight, warm and rich and seductive.

But Taisin was going to be a sage, and sages made vows of celibacy. Kaede had learned this in her earliest days at the Academy. Students were not permitted to form romantic attachments to each other—at least not officially, though Kaede had not been the only one to break the rules. But Taisin had always adhered to those guidelines. No one had even whispered about her in the dormitory.

Kaede told herself that what she felt was only a little seed; she would simply not water it. It wouldn't grow any larger than this tiny prickle of attraction. She wouldn't let it.

But that night after everyone had left, and they had all spread their blankets on the floor of the hall, Kaede lay awake for some time, trying to make out the sound of Taisin's breathing in the dark.

Chapter XVII

t began to rain scarcely an hour after they left Jilin. They pulled out their oilskin cloaks, but as the day wore on with no sign that it would let up, Kaede began to feel the wet weight of it like a burden on her back. That morning, Shae's family had seen them off with as much good cheer as they could muster, but it was obvious they had a difficult time fighting their fear that Shae would never return.

Niran had convinced Tali that their wagon would never make it through the narrow trails carved into the Wood, and he traded them two sturdy packhorses for the wagon itself. Pol and Taisin rode the two wagon horses, outfitted with saddles that Tali bought from one of Niran's neighbors. As they picked their way through the dim, drenched Wood, Kaede peered out from beneath the hood of her cloak at the surrounding trees. She felt, again, the eerie sensation of another presence. The farther they rode into the Wood, the more she noticed that there was a peculiar awareness to this place. The oaks might be half dead, but something else was distinctly alive out there.

When it began to grow dark, they set up camp just off the trail; downhill, the river Nir was pregnant with rain. Tali and Pol struggled to set up their tents in the downpour, staking them out between trees as best they could, while Shae and Con took the empty water skins down to the river to be filled. Taisin volunteered to search for bits of dry wood, and Pol called, "You'd better take Kaede with you." He stuck his head out from one of the half-constructed tents. "I don't have a good feeling about this place."

Even though the day had been one long, wet slog through an increasingly muddy forest, Kaede was absurdly pleased about the prospect of taking a walk through the Wood with Taisin. Taisin herself looked momentarily alarmed at the prospect of Kaede accompanying her, but the expression vanished almost instantly, making Kaede wonder if she had imagined it. As they struck off down the trail, Kaede glanced at Taisin, but Taisin kept her eyes to the ground, seeking out sheltered places that might have kept fallen wood dry.

They found a few branches here and there, and piled them into their arms beneath their oilskin cloaks. As Taisin pushed her way through thickets and into hollows, Kaede was surprised by her classmate's apparent disregard for mud. Taisin had always seemed so neat and orderly, not a hair out of place. Now she pushed back a stray lock with dirty fingers, leaving a dark streak on her face.

They came to a clump of hollyberry trees sheltered by a giant overhanging oak, and they bumped shoulders and hips as they reached for kindling beneath the brush. Taisin backed out a bit breathlessly. "You go first," she said, her face flushed. Kaede tried to stuff down the warmth that flared in her when Taisin's body had snaked past hers, and she began to haul out handfuls of twigs, handing them to Taisin.

When their arms were full, they headed back to the camp, and Kaede said with a grin, "You're covered in mud."

Taisin pointed out, "So are you."

Kaede glanced down at herself and laughed; the entire front of her, from her chest down to her knees, was smeared with dark brown. Taisin began to giggle, and then they were both bent over double, clutching the twigs and branches to their chests as they guffawed, their voices ringing in the twilight Wood. Kaede felt a little delirious; she was soaked through, muddy, and darkness was falling. The whole situation should be terrifying, but she felt a kind of helpless surrender to it. Here she was on this journey to a place that didn't exist on their maps, and all around unseen things seemed to stare out at them day and night. But there, not two feet away from her, was a girl who made her feel light-headed.

As their laughter faded they looked at each other, and there was an openness in Taisin's face—a kind of camaraderie—that Kaede had not seen before. It made her skin tingle. She did not think she was doing a good job of letting the seed die.

⁓

The rain clung to them for several days. Sometimes there would be a break in the middle of the afternoon, or the rain would turn to mist for a while, but their belongings began to have an exasperating dampness that could not be burned off by their smoky campfire.

On the morning the rain finally stopped, they awoke to a world covered in fog so thick it was difficult to find one another in their small camp. It curled around the trees in ghostly white, seeping through their clothes and into their bones with its chill. But the fire burned hot that morning, and they drank their tea standing up, turning around slowly to warm their backsides. The fog clung to the river Nir all morning, making the trail difficult to see, and it did not burn off until afternoon. That evening, her teeth chattering from cold, Kaede stood so close to the campfire that when the wind gusted, it sent flames dangerously close to her face. She jumped back in alarm, and Tali laughed at her as he eased the iron kettle into the fire.

"Watch out," he warned her. "This wind is not like any I've encountered before. Sometimes it seems to have a mind of its own." The two of them had stayed to set up camp while the others went to gather more wood and refill their water skins.

Shae and Con returned from the river as Tali spoke, and Shae set her heavy water skin down on the ground and sighed, stretching her arms. "I'll take the wind over the rain any day—or night."

"At least the rain drowns out the sound of the wind," Tali said. "Sometimes I swear I hear it calling my name." He shuddered. "I don't like it."

Con looked at him curiously. "What do you mean? Are you hearing things, Tali?"

The guard squatted down and stirred the pot with a long-handled wooden spoon. "I must be. This Wood gets to me; I don't think it wants me here."

"Don't be ridiculous," Shae said. As if her words were an invitation to prove her wrong, the wind whipped around them, ruffling Shae's short hair and making the flames roar.

Kaede felt it like a silken scarf sliding quickly around her neck. She shivered.

Shae glanced at her sharply. "Did you feel something?"

Kaede put her hand to her throat, touching her skin with cold fingers. "I don't know. It was so fast."

They didn't notice, at first, that Tali had cocked his head a little, as if he were listening to someone whisper in his ear. His eyes were slightly glazed, and his entire body seemed pulled in a direction even he was not aware of.

"Tali!" Con called, alarmed.

Tali blinked and let go of the wooden spoon in surprise, and it fell into the fire. "Blast," he said, standing up. "I don't have another one."

"What did you just hear?" Kaede asked.

He looked confused. "Just now—did you hear it as well?"

"I don't know," Kaede said, disquieted. "I felt something, though." She looked at Shae and Con. "Did you hear anything?"

"No," Con answered.

Shae seemed worried. "Not really. The wind seemed a little...odd, but I don't know why."

Tali said grimly, "It's only talking to me, then."

"Who's talking to you?" Taisin asked. She was coming

back toward the fire, Pol following her. She dropped an armful of wood on the ground.

"The wind," Tali said. His broad shoulders were stiff with tension as he added, "The Wood itself."

Taisin's eyes widened. "You must not listen. Do you understand? Whatever you hear—whatever they tell you—you must not listen to them."

Tali was taken aback by her intensity. Pol, laying his firewood down, asked, "What's going on?"

Tali said gruffly, "We're just hearing noises in the dark."

Taisin's forehead wrinkled. "Has anyone else heard anything?"

They all looked at one another, anxious faces turned gold by the firelight. The black night beyond the camp had never felt so heavy; the branches of the trees leaned above them like ghosts. For a moment, the only sound was the crackle of the fire. The strange wind had left them.

Kaede finally said, "I felt something."

"What?"

"It—it felt like the wind was tightening around my neck."

Taisin stared at her, fear plain in her eyes. She turned to Tali. "Tell me what you heard."

"It wasn't speaking our language," Tali said, scrubbing a hand through his gray hair. "But it wanted—it wanted me to follow it." He had broken into a nervous sweat, and he wiped his forehead on his sleeve.

"You mustn't follow it," Taisin said.

He seemed a bit affronted. "Of course I'm not going to follow it."

"I just—I'm just trying to keep you safe," she stammered.

"Taisin," Con said, seeing the distress on her face, "have you felt something, too?"

"Yes," she said reluctantly. Whatever it was had been increasing in strength the deeper they traveled into the Wood. At first it had been merely a whisper, as if a feather were lightly brushing against her, but now it came more insistently, like a child pulling at her hand.

"What is it?" Tali asked.

Taisin hesitated. She hadn't known what to make of it in the beginning, for the Wood was full of energies she had never encountered before. It was difficult to separate out this presence from the others, but she was increasingly convinced that this spirit—if that is what it was—had a goal. It reminded her of something she had felt once, but the memory eluded her, like an itch in the middle of her back that she couldn't quite reach. It was irritating and frightening all at once, for she sensed that this presence was not benevolent.

She said carefully, "It is intelligent. There is a purpose to this creature—or this presence. I don't know what it is. But it seems…it wants something. It seems malicious."

"Is it the Xi?" Pol asked.

Taisin thought back to what Sister Ailan had told her and what she had read. It was so bizarre to apply those dry teachings to the eerie reality of this Wood. "Sister Ailan— my teacher—she always described the Xi to me as possessing a presence of great purity. Powerful, of course, but pure. Not hot or cold; not emotional; simply *there*. Pure. This presence that I feel is not pure. I don't think it is the Xi."

Tali asked, "What do you think it wants?"

"I don't know."

"How can we protect ourselves, then?" Con asked.

Taisin turned to Tali, expecting him to answer, but the guard was looking at her with a reluctant expression on his lined face. "Taisin, you know the most about this of any of us."

Taisin realized he was relying on her now, and she felt paralyzed. She hadn't even been marked yet. She might be the most gifted in her class, but she was still a student. All at once the gaps in her knowledge seemed too great, and a cloud of panic engulfed her. How could her teachers think she was ready for this? She was only a frightened schoolgirl. She felt faint, and pressed her fingers between her eyes. She took a deep breath, and another. She could not crumple into a puddle of fear—that was not why her teachers had believed in her.

"We must stay together," she said, her voice wavering at first. "If you hear anything speaking to you—in the wind, in your ear, whatever—just ignore it. And tell someone. Don't leave the camp alone." She looked over her shoulder at the dark. It was alive with energies she hadn't yet teased apart, but one of them was waiting and listening. Taisin turned back to the others. Her mouth was dry as she said, "Promise me. Don't leave the camp alone."

They all agreed, and their nodding shadows rippled across the trees.

❧

Wrapped in her bedroll that night, the chilly air seeping through the thin canvas walls of the tent, Kaede longed for the dry heat that used to bake the streets of Cathair in the summer. She dreamed of sunlight spreading like honey over her skin; she dreamed of sweat sliding down between her shoulder blades as she ran down sweltering alleyways behind the palace. She dreamed of Taisin, standing in the shade of a stone building at the end of a maze of narrow streets, a bouquet of flowers in her hands like the prize at the end of a race. But no matter how fast Kaede ran, she couldn't quite reach her. The muscles in her legs groaned with the effort; her lungs heaved; she woke with a jerk, gasping.

Beside her Shae shifted, turning her back to Kaede. It was the middle of the night. Kaede's heart was pounding, her skin flushed as if she had truly been running. She flung off her blanket, feeling overheated. What had awakened her? She wanted to go back into that dream world. She wanted to reach Taisin, take the flowers out of her hands, touch her. A wave of longing rushed through Kaede's body.

She turned over, looking past Shae toward Taisin. She could barely make out her silhouette in the dark, but she could hear her breathing. It was uneven. Was Taisin awake, too? The thought made Kaede's skin prickle all over with excitement. It seemed impossible that Taisin could sleep through this—every nerve in Kaede's body was screaming for her to notice—but there was no answering sound or movement from Taisin.

Kaede lay awake for some time. She was tense from her dream. She counted her breaths, attempting to make them regular. She lost count. She listened to the sound of wind in the trees, remembering Taisin's warnings, but she heard nothing out of the ordinary. She did not realize she had fallen asleep again until she was awakened by shouting outside. Someone was calling for Tali.

Shae scrambled up first, pushing aside the tent flap and stumbling into the dim morning, pulling on her boots as she went. "What is it?" Shae asked, and outside Con and Pol were standing, dazed, near the ashes of the fire.

"Tali is missing," Con said, panic thick in his voice. "When we woke up this morning, he was gone."

Chapter XVIII

t was Shae who found him. He was lying in a clearing barely fifty feet from their camp on the other side of the trail. Dried leaves encircled his body as if blown by a great whirlwind. He lay on his back, arms and legs spread-eagled, his face expressionless. A strange gray dust was trapped in his salt-and-pepper beard, and a thin white film had crawled over his open brown eyes. He was cold to the touch, and there was not a mark on him.

Con knelt on the ground next to Tali's body and lifted the older man's hand. His fingers were stiff. Con was stunned; he couldn't believe that Tali was dead. He had survived so many military campaigns; how could he have been taken so easily, so silently, by—Con didn't even know what had taken him. "Who—what did this?" he demanded.

All the color had drained from Taisin's face. She knelt beside Tali's head, stretching her hand out over his eyes. She felt nothing. There was no life energy left within him;

his body was only a shell now. And she did not know whether his soul had safely traveled to the other side. The thought chilled her to the bone, and she muttered to herself, "I should have done it."

Con looked at her. "You should have done what?"

Guilt washed over Taisin, hot and sour. "I could have—I should have done a protection ritual. Around the camp."

Con's mouth opened, but he couldn't speak. A torrent of emotion battered at him: disbelief, grief, anger. Was Taisin saying she could have prevented this? He felt like he had been punched in the gut, and he had trouble breathing.

Shae squatted down beside him and squeezed his shoulder. She asked in a carefully measured voice, "Why didn't you?"

Taisin gulped, her heart pounding. She said in a rush: "My teacher told me that I shouldn't use that ritual except as a last resort. I didn't know this could happen. I thought we would be safe enough if—if we didn't leave the camp." Tears pricked at the corners of her eyes, and she blinked them back fiercely.

"Can you do that ritual now?" Pol asked. He stood at Tali's feet, his arms crossed.

"I can do it tonight when we set up camp. I can't protect us as we are moving."

"Wait," Shae said, frowning. "Taisin, why did your teacher warn you about the protection ritual?"

Taisin drew in a trembling breath. "Because it—it might draw attention to us."

"What do you mean?" Pol asked.

"Weaving a protection ritual around our camp would… rearrange the natural meridians. Those who are sensitive to the lines of energy would—if they are near enough or powerful enough, they would notice."

"The creatures we've seen," Con interjected, struggling to make sense of what she was saying. "Can they sense these things?"

"I don't know. I suppose…it's possible."

Kaede understood, suddenly, the reason for the hesitation in Taisin's voice. "You think that by doing the protection ritual, you'll draw them to us."

Taisin met her eyes somberly. "It has occurred to me."

"But what's the alternative?" Con asked. "Tali was—" His voice broke, and Shae slid her arm around his shoulders. Con wiped away the tears that burned down his face. "Tali was stronger, I thought, than all of us. For this to happen to him…We can't let it happen again." He looked across Tali's still form at Taisin, and he noticed how young and vulnerable she looked today, with purple shadows beneath her eyes and her narrow shoulders slumping. He realized that he had been on the verge of blaming her for Tali's death, but he couldn't. She was only seventeen. She had done the best she could. He felt a yawning ache inside him as he said to her, "You have to do it tonight, Taisin. Whatever protection ritual you can. We'll deal with the consequences when they come."

Taisin's lips trembled, but she squared her shoulders. "All right. I will do it tonight. But first, we must leave this place. And we must bury Tali."

"Here?" Con said.

"No. This place is—it isn't right. We must take him with us, but we have to bury him before nightfall."

None of them disagreed. It was the worst kind of luck to leave a dead body in the open overnight—especially when the person died of unnatural causes. And though there were no signs of struggle on Tali's body, there was no doubt in any of their minds that his death had been far from natural.

❧

When they broke camp, they strapped Tali's body, shrouded in his woolen blanket, onto his horse. Tali had always ridden in the lead before, but today Shae took his position and his map case. Con followed her, leading Tali's horse, and Taisin and Kaede came after him. Pol went last as usual, keeping one hand on his sword.

As they rode, Taisin stared at Tali's body, hanging face-down over his horse's flanks. Part of her still couldn't quite grasp it. How could *Tali*, of all people, have been lured away so easily? He was so solid, so dependable. Why had the Wood—or whatever was in the Wood—chosen to take him? And if it could take him, what would it do to the rest of them? The questions made her increasingly nervous, and the queasiness in her stomach rose until she abruptly pulled her horse to a halt and dismounted, running off the trail to bend over, retching. Nothing came up, but she felt like she was turning inside out, and her throat burned.

A moment later she felt a hand on her back, and Kaede was leaning over her. "Are you all right?"

"I'm fine," she gasped.

"Here," Kaede said, handing her a water skin. Taisin tried to breathe more slowly. She was panicking. She knew she had to calm down. She heard Kaede saying to the others: "Just give us a minute."

Taisin straightened up, feeling woozy. Her face was flushed, and her hands shook as she raised the water skin to her lips. The liquid trickled into her mouth, and she swallowed carefully. "I'm sorry," she muttered.

Kaede shook her head. "There's nothing to be sorry about."

"Yes, there is. If I had done the protection ritual, Tali would still be here." Taisin spoke without thinking, and now that the words were out, she was both ashamed and relieved.

"You don't know that," Kaede objected.

Taisin turned to face her. The dull gray daylight carved deep shadows beneath Kaede's eyes and darkened the hollows in her cheeks. She didn't look like the same girl who had argued with the King's Chancellor in the Council room, demanding that she be given a choice. She looked bruised. She looked sad. "What are we going to do, Kaede?" Taisin whispered. "This wasn't supposed to happen. What if Maire Morighan was wrong? What if I can't do whatever it is I'm supposed to do? What if I don't know enough?"

Kaede heard defeat hovering at the edge of Taisin's words, and it tore at her. "You know enough," Kaede insisted. "The oracle stones would not have chosen you if you didn't know enough. And what's 'enough,' anyway? You don't know everything, but nobody can." She heard herself repeating what Fin had told her on the beach at the Academy: "All you can do is make your decisions based on what you know now."

"What I know now," Taisin repeated. What she knew now was that this journey was much more dangerous than she had anticipated. Perhaps she had not wanted to acknowledge that before. In Ento, she had called that creature out of the baby's body, but it was Kaede who had faced the consequences. Now Tali's death had driven home the fact that there was a malignant force out there, and she knew she had to open her eyes and look it in the face. It frightened her, but she had never fled from something because she was afraid. Going to the Academy alone when she was eleven, leaving her family behind, had terrified her. The vision of Kaede on the beach still scared her. But she knew what to do with fear: She fought it.

"You're right," Taisin said to Kaede. "Thank you."

Before she could doubt herself again, Taisin headed back to the trail, ignoring the panic that still churned in her stomach.

༄

Just before noon, they found a roughly rectangular clearing a few feet off the path, with soil that looked like it could be broken with their makeshift tools. Taisin fitted one of their few remaining candles into a lantern and lit it, setting it on the ground where the head of the grave would be. The light was meant to guide Tali's soul to the land of the dead. Usually sages did not perform funerary rites; that responsibility typically fell to village greenwitches or, in the cities, to specialists. But there were no specialists here. Everyone did their part.

Taisin helped Shae and Kaede dig the grave while Con and Pol wrestled with Tali's body, dressing him in his cleanest clothes. The mysterious nature of his death was unlucky enough, but it would be even worse for him to be buried in the clothes he was wearing when he died. They lugged water from the river and washed his hands, but they could not remove the dirt from beneath his nails. They sponged off his face and neck, closing his eyes and covering them with a blindfold torn from Tali's cloak. And then Taisin found a stone on the riverbank that had a particularly peaceful energy, and she handed it to Con.

"His death was not...natural," she said awkwardly. "It would be best to place this in his mouth."

He looked sick to his stomach, but he nodded. Tali's body had stiffened by now, and it was difficult to pry his jaw open. Con feared for one awful moment that he might have to break it, but then, at last, Tali's mouth opened just enough, and Con slid the stone between his cold lips.

Afterward, Con had to sit still, holding his head in his hands, trying not to throw up.

It was late afternoon by the time the pit was deep enough, and the light was becoming dim. Dirt smudged all of their faces where they had wiped away sweat that had risen while they dug. Tali's body had been wrapped into his blanket again—the closest they could come to a shroud—and Con and Pol rolled it as gently as they could into the grave. The candle flickered within the lantern as if a breath had blown against it.

Con sat back on his heels and looked at the rest of them. "It's time."

They each scraped up a handful of dirt and, beginning with Con, sprinkled it into the grave. The sound of dirt pattering onto Tali's body reminded Con of rain on the roofs of Cathair: hard and cold. A wave of loss threatened to engulf him; he curled his fingers into fists, feeling his nails pressing into his palms. The others began to push the loose soil back into the grave. In the background, he heard Taisin murmuring. The words were familiar; he had heard them before, at funerals. As she repeated them, Kaede echoed her, and then Pol and Shae. Their voices, low and sorrowful, lifted the words of the lament into the heavy stillness of dusk in the Great Wood.

This fleeting world:
Life passes as quickly as the morning star,
As a rumble of thunder,
A gust of wind over the grasslands.
This fleeting life:
Brief as a spark,
Ephemeral as a dream.
Soon enough we are ghosts upon the cloud.

Chapter XIX

hey left the lantern burning at Tali's grave while they set up camp. Taisin walked in a circle around the perimeter, marking it with stones or branches. "Bring everything we'll need into this circle," she told them, "because after I set it up, no one will be able to leave without breaking the boundary."

"What about Tali?" Con said. "I want to sit vigil with him tonight."

Taisin had taken out her small brassbound trunk and opened it, but now she paused with her hand on a glass vial. "It's not safe, Con."

"Tali was like a father to me," he said. "I owe him that respect."

Taisin saw the sadness that dragged at his shoulders; his ashen face, drawn with grief. She knew that he would do it whether or not she agreed with him, so she said, "Then I will sit with you."

"Will you extend the circle of protection to the grave?" Con asked.

"I can't. The space around it must be open, so that Tali's soul can travel freely." She didn't tell him that she suspected that Tali's soul had departed long before any of their burial rituals.

Con eyed her closely, as if he guessed that she was holding something back, but he didn't question her further. "All right. We'll sit vigil together. Let me know when you're ready." He went to help Pol set up their tent, leaving Taisin kneeling on the ground.

Her fingers shook slightly as she took out the herbs that she would need for the ritual. Sister Ailan had given her these supplies for this very reason, but Taisin had never actually believed she would need them. Milk-vetch root, dried and ground up in yellowish-brown crystals, for strength. Fox nut, pounded into a pale powder, for life energy. The barest sprinkle of dragon bone scrapings, like minuscule white petals, for power. Taisin combined them all in an iron bowl, stirring them together with her index finger. The powders seemed to glitter a bit, just as Sister Ailan had told her they would. The mixture was ready.

She asked Con to stand just outside the perimeter, and she placed Shae, Pol, and Kaede at three places along the interior of the circle. It would have been better if there were a fourth person, so she could create a full compass, but they would just have to make do with three points tonight. Holding the iron bowl in her hand, Taisin walked to the northernmost edge of the circle and closed her eyes, standing still. She had performed smaller protection rituals before, but never one this major, or as important. Sister Ailan had explained it to her and assured her that she could do it, but this was no Academy examination, where she might be forgiven for making a mistake or two. Taisin's heart raced as her nerves nearly got the better of her, making her hands clammy. She took a deep breath and tried to calm herself.

First, she had to find the way in. That was how her teachers always described it: being sensitive to all the currents of energy around her until she discovered the one that called to her—the one that was her own special path into the unseen world. Meridians of energy ran through every human being and animal and plant; they lay in limitless lines in the earth and the air like a vast web. Every living thing had its place in this field of energies. The protection ritual would reshape portions of that field, reweaving the net into a barrier around their camp.

If only she could do it. Every time she thought she had found the way in, it slid away from her. She was like a fisherman trying to reel in his catch, but it leapt away from him time and time again, splashing back into the sea.

And the wind that had whispered in Tali's ear was everywhere, distracting her. It slipped beneath her collar, tickled her earlobes, caressed her skin in cool, lingering breaths. It took every effort to ignore it, to focus instead on the elusive thread of energy that had come so easily to her when she had seen that purple flower. The thought of the flower helped, and she envisioned it in her mind's eye; she could feel the life of it, pulsing. And then she had it. She felt the humming threads of life all around her, and they were different here, deep in the Wood. There was still something not quite right about them, but they were a thousand times more vibrant than they had been in Jilin. She plucked one strand out—easy as tucking a lock of hair behind her ear—and began to weave it around their camp as she walked, eyes closed, for she didn't need to see the ordinary world when she could see, instead, the extraordinary one.

At the north, south, east, and west points of the circle, she sprinkled some of the powder on the ground. She said, "Peace within, darkness without." The powder burned into the ground like fox fire. Taisin walked around the perimeter of the camp three times, and each time she felt the web of protection tightening. It was exhilarating. She felt all of the energies she controlled at her fingertips: such incredible power. She was connected to the heartbeats of every living creature in the Great Wood; everything wanted so fiercely to live, even the trees that seemed half dead.

On her third circle, Taisin stopped before each person. She opened her eyes, looking directly at them, touching her fingers to their hearts, murmuring, "Peace within, darkness without." Pol's heartbeat was strong within him. Shae was worried; her breathing was quick and anxious. Kaede was tense as well, and when Taisin reached out to touch her, she felt a jolt pass between them. Taisin was so startled she almost faltered in the ritual.

To her surprise, Kaede reached up and covered Taisin's hand with hers. Taisin pressed her palm against Kaede's heart. She felt it speeding up until it matched the pace of her own. She was breathless. Kaede's eyes were light brown; Taisin saw her pupils dilating as they looked at each other, dusk spinning out around them, cloaking them in shadow. She wished she could stay there forever, the space between them freighted with possibility.

But she had to complete the ritual. She whispered, "Peace within, darkness without."

And then, reluctantly, she closed her eyes again. She saw Kaede, Pol, and Shae bound within a circle of energies like creatures caught in a spider's web. She pulled herself away from Kaede, feeling the link between them stretching like a gossamer thread. She made her way back to the place where she had begun, and she set down the iron bowl, pressing it into the ground.

When she straightened, she folded her hands before her lips and bowed first to the circle, then to the dark Wood beyond. It was done.

∽

At the head of the grave mound, the candle still burned. Taisin sat on one side of it with her hands folded in her lap, and Con sat across from her. She had never kept overnight vigil at a grave before, and she knew she was not in the best condition for it. She was drained from the protection ritual and from the day itself. The hard, cold ground pressed sharply into her shins, and the dreadful wind was worrying at her hair.

Con shifted in the dark, uncrossing his legs and trying to find a more comfortable position. As time passed, he began to nod, weariness overcoming him. "Con," Taisin whispered, and he jerked himself awake.

"I'm sorry," he said. His tongue felt heavy and thick; his senses dulled.

"It's all right," Taisin whispered. "Just—don't fall asleep." She spoke as much for her own benefit as for his, for the air here was ripe with magic. Some of it was residue from the circle of protection she had woven, but some of it was darker, more malevolent. She was not certain, but she thought she recognized a thread or two of this other magic. It had a very distinct, unusual scent: like winter. It was the smell of that fortress of ice.

The visions had come more often since she entered the Wood, and sometimes they came at particularly inopportune moments. When she was riding, sometimes she would suddenly glimpse dark brown skin, mottled like lichen. Or when she was gathering firewood, she would catch sight of that winged creature again, flying high against icicles hanging like teeth from a cavernous ceiling. It would only be the briefest glimpse, and then she would snap back into reality, knocked slightly off balance, and Pol or Kaede or Tali would ask her if she was all right. Her heart sank at that memory. Tali would never speak again.

She looked across the grave at Con; his body was rigid, and his wide-open eyes reflected the flicker of the candlelight. He no longer seemed in danger of falling asleep. He shivered as if someone had run a finger down his back, and for a moment, he cocked his head to the right, listening. "Con," Taisin said, her voice a whip crack in the stillness.

He jerked. "What?" he said hoarsely.

"Look at me." Taisin was almost certain that something was trying to lure him away, just as it had done to Tali. "Are you hearing something?"

"I don't know." He felt a caress on his cheek; he wanted to turn his face into it. It was as seductive as the sleep that had dragged at him earlier. But he struggled against it, trying to fix his eyes on Taisin. The tiny light of the candle only served to make the Wood beyond seem blacker, a spill of ink on black paper. How could it possibly be enough light to guide Tali's soul to the other side?

Taisin could sense the energy around Con; it was charged with frustrated desire. She felt it gathering in strength, like massing thunderclouds, and then it turned its attention, abruptly, to her.

She was nearly knocked over by the power of it: a gale-force wind, ice-cold, biting into her face and pulling at her clothes. Long, wordless screams buffeted at her, and she clapped her hands over her ears to protect herself from the sounds. She stared in horror across the grave, trying to anchor herself to Con, who was gaping at her. He said something, but she could not hear him. She wanted to run, but she did not dare leave the light of the candle, and she would not leave Con.

She remembered, suddenly, what had been so familiar about the wind that had come teasing at her hair earlier. Now she had only a younger sister, but there had been a time when she also had a younger brother named Sota. He was Suri's twin, and when Taisin was ten years old, Suri and Sota fell sick. Suri recovered, but Sota did not, and died. After his death, her father and mother sat vigil beside his still little body all night. Four-year-old Suri hadn't understood what was going on, and Taisin had been charged with taking care of her. She crawled into bed with her, listening while Suri mumbled the name of her brother in her sleep: *Sota, Sota, Sota.* The word was a hypnotic rhythm. It lulled Taisin into an uneasy sleep of her own, cuddled next to her little sister.

She woke later that night to hear voices—despairing, yearning voices. She felt fingers running along her arm, touching her. If the wind could form itself into hands, that was what it felt like. She went rigid with fear, goose bumps rising all over her body. Suri was still asleep, but sweat dampened her brow as if she had broken into a fever. Suri's hair was being lifted as though someone were running their fingers through it, smoothing it back from her face. Taisin was terrified. She muttered her sister's name; she gripped Suri's shoulder and shook it.

Suri opened her eyes, and the wind ceased. Warmth flooded into the room, and Taisin realized that it had been freezing before—how could Suri be sweating?

"Sota?" Suri whispered.

Taisin put her arms around her sister, trying to rock her back to sleep. "Shh," she murmured.

"Ghosts," Suri said. "Ghosts."

Those ghosts, frightening though they were, were nothing compared to what circled Taisin now. These were different. These were much more powerful. They had been wronged.

But now that she understood what they were, she felt calmer. She knew what to do.

She removed her hands from her ears. They shrieked at her, their voices pounding into her head. "Stop it!" she cried.

"Taisin!" Con was calling her name. He was trying to stand up, but he could not move. Something was pinning him down.

"It's all right," Taisin said. "It's all right." And then she said to the circling ghosts: "I will listen to you."

Instantly, the Wood disappeared; she plunged into a world of vivid color. Everything was richly green: the color of newly budded leaves, of luminescent moss, of every possible shade of pine needle. And then she was in the middle of the ocean, carried by warm currents, the water changing from sea green to midnight blue as she sank from the surface into the depths. She had fins; she was as slick as a porpoise. She broke into the air; she was on top of the tallest tree; she was the tree itself.

The images were confusing at first, until she finally understood that she was experiencing the lives of each of the ghosts speaking to her. These were not the lives of humans, and she knew with absolute certainty that they were not the lives of animals, either. These were fay, creatures who inhabited the trees and the rivers, the seas and the hills. They had lived lives that were full of wonder, and now their lives were over.

She was thrust into darkness. When she could see again, she was cold all over. She saw golden bars. She heard the dragging shuffle of someone pacing in a tiny cage. She had never wanted to be free so badly. She wanted to strike at the bars with her bare hands, but the metal cut her skin. Black blood dripped from the wounds in her side. Something had been torn out of her. She bent over, falling onto her knees, feeling the icy floor beneath her.

They had been wronged.

∽

Taisin's eyes flew open. She was still standing beside Tali's grave. The night was not over. She gasped for air as if she had been underwater.

Con had moved; he was now standing directly in front of her. His hands gripped her shoulders.

"Taisin," he said. "Taisin."

"I'm here," she whispered, dazed.

He loosened his grip on her just slightly. "Are you all right?"

She shuddered. "Yes."

"Did you see something?"

She realized he had no idea what she had just experienced. "They're ghosts," she said.

A shiver ran down Con's spine. He looked beyond Taisin, but there was nothing but darkness.

Taisin reached up and pulled his hands from her shoulders, holding them in hers. "It's all right," she said. She felt the energy of the ghosts dissipating. She had satisfied them for now, but ghosts always returned until their wrongs had been righted. She only hoped they would not return tonight.

"Is it safe here?" Con asked.

She almost laughed. "Safe? No. But we must stay. We must stay with Tali until dawn." He began to pull away from her, but she did not let him go. "Sit here, right here, with me."

And so they sat together until the dawn light came, pallid and gray, and they saw that the soil of Tali's grave was newly rimed with frost.

Chapter XX

hen Taisin and Con returned to camp, Shae had brewed strong black tea for them, and Kaede and Pol had already disassembled the tents. While they waited for the rice porridge to cook, Taisin told them what had happened the night before.

"Ghosts," Pol muttered. "Just what we need."

"There are many of them," Taisin said. Her legs ached from sitting all night in the cold. "It's still not safe for us out there. We have to stay together at all times."

"Is that what took Tali?" Pol asked.

"I don't know," Taisin said. "Maybe. They were not happy spirits."

Before they departed, Taisin had to release the space where they were camped back to the Wood. She retraced her steps around the perimeter of the camp three times, grinding the remaining powders into the forest floor. She felt the meridians of energy springing back like strings snapping into position; it made her skin feel red, chapped, as though she had been scoured by a dry wind.

The days that followed were gray and heavy, as if Tali's death was a dark cloud surrounding them. They decided to set one of the packhorses free; Shae believed he would find his way back home to Jilin. They transferred the supplies to the wagon horse that Pol had been riding, and Pol rode Tali's horse instead. On the mornings that Kaede found time for target practice, Pol pushed her harder than he had before. She understood why: The bow was a weapon, and without Tali, they were one guard less.

For Kaede, the one bright moment in each day came at the end, when Taisin wove the circle of protection around their camp. Every time Taisin put her hand on Kaede's heart, warmth bloomed between them, pushing back the dark night just enough to give them room to breathe together. Kaede found herself waiting for Taisin's touch all day, turning the memory of it over and over again in her mind as they rode through the wild Wood. Every night, she felt the link between them thickening, ripening: at first a slender shoot, and then a vine that curled around them, strengthening each day. She began to wonder if Taisin might feel it, too, but Taisin never said a word about what happened between them during the ritual.

Taisin was afraid to acknowledge it. From the very first time she performed the ritual, she had known that the connection between the two of them was different than what she felt with the others. As the days passed, she became gradually aware that Kaede knew it, too. The realization thrilled her, but it also raised the specter of her vision. It shook her to know that this ritual that should protect them all was also doing the one thing she wanted to avoid. And yet, part of her—a growing part of her—wanted only to nurture the delicate bloom between them.

Sometimes that desire would subside, and Taisin thought she might succeed in preventing her vision from happening, but then her feelings returned at the most unexpected moments. When Kaede brewed tea for everyone, she took care to hand a cup directly to Taisin. Their fingers brushed together against the hot metal, and the thread between them drew tight. Taisin turned away with studied casualness, trying to hide the rising color on her cheeks. She tried to remember that she did not want to fall in love with Kaede, but more and more, she forgot. She forgot to avoid lingering near Kaede when they paused to rest during the day. She forgot to put space between them when they sat by the campfire at night.

One morning Kaede awoke to discover—her head still full of the mustiness of sleep—that Taisin had curled up beside her in the tent they shared with Shae. The warmth of her body was comforting, for the dawn air was cool and slightly damp. As she turned onto her back, Taisin moved, too, burrowing her head into Kaede's shoulder, and Kaede blinked her eyes open, feeling suddenly, acutely aware of Taisin breathing so close to her. And then Taisin shifted, stretching as she awoke, and her entire body slid against Kaede's side. At first, still half asleep, Taisin levered herself up on one elbow and looked at her, and at that moment

Kaede could have reached up and pulled her back down again—but then Taisin woke completely, and she blushed so deeply that the tips of her ears went pink.

She scooted away as quickly as she could, mumbling something apologetic, and almost tripped over Shae as she stumbled out of the tent.

Shae, who was just waking up, rubbed her face and muttered, "What's going on?"

"Nothing," Kaede whispered, closing her eyes. Maybe if she didn't get up right away, she could slide back into those delicious moments before Taisin awoke. Her whole body was tingling. What would she have done if Taisin hadn't left so abruptly? She would have kissed her. Even with Shae right there beside them, she would have done it. The thought made her feel like fire had erupted over her skin.

She threw off the blankets. She needed to get out into the cold morning. She crawled out of the tent, ignoring Shae's protests as she climbed over her.

Outside, her breath misted into the air; the whole camp was surrounded by fog. There was no sign of Taisin.

Con was stirring the fire. He looked up at Kaede's abrupt arrival. "Good morning." His brows drew together. "Are you all right?"

"What? I'm fine." She shoved her feet into boots, bending over to lace them as she asked, "Where did Pol and Taisin go?"

"To get more water."

"Oh."

Con grinned at her. "She'll be back soon enough. Would you like a cup of tea?"

Kaede turned red. But she accepted the battered metal cup with as much dignity as she could.

∽

Pol and Taisin took much longer than expected, and by the time they returned, Con, Shae, and Kaede were standing nervously beside the fire, staring down toward the river and thinking uneasy thoughts. "We were beginning to worry," Con said, unable to hide his anxiety. Taisin set down the heavy water skin she was carrying, and her eyes flickered immediately to Kaede, who looked relieved to see her.

"I apologize," Pol said, kneeling to pour water into the kettle. "I saw something, and I had to find out what it was. Taisin wouldn't let me go alone."

"What did you see?" Con asked.

"Something is following us," Pol said.

"Something?" Shae repeated, eyeing the trees warily.

"Yes. I don't know what it is. But it's not human."

Chapter XXI

On the third night after Pol's announcement, their followers finally showed themselves.

It had been drizzling all afternoon, and lighting the fire was an ordeal that put everyone in a bitter mood. They ate their supper in silence, huddled beneath oilskins as the rain dripped down, hissing, into the fire. They slumped over their food, tired and vulnerable. Even Pol, who had been so vigilant, did not notice that they were slowly being surrounded. It was Kaede who looked up after finishing her meal and saw the eyes in the dark. She stiffened just like a deer noticing he was being hunted.

"Pol," Kaede said in a harsh whisper.

He looked around sharply. Several pairs of yellow eyes glowed in the dark, reflecting the light of the fire. Shae and Pol reached for their weapons at the same time, standing up to face the dark.

"What are they?" Taisin asked in a small voice.

"Wolves," Pol said. "Will the circle of protection keep them away?"

"I don't know," Taisin said. "The circle is meant to keep out harmful magic, not—not wolves."

"But it's also meant to protect us," Pol said. "Isn't it?"

"Yes. We should stay within it while they're out there."

They sat up all night, looking out at the eyes looking in at them. Their initial fright turned inevitably to weariness, for the wolves did not seem to be interested in advancing. Kaede had the eerie suspicion that they were merely there to watch them, to assess their strengths and weaknesses. Sometimes one of them looked directly at her, and she was startled by how intelligent the gaze was.

As morning approached, the wolves began to melt away, and when dawn finally broke and there was light enough to see beyond their campfire, there was no sign of them. But all around the circle of protection that Taisin had woven were long paw prints in the rain-dampened ground, where the wolves had paced.

⁊

They had barely been in the saddle for an hour that morning when Kaede caught sight of the wolves running through the trees about fifty feet away, roughly paralleling the path. They stayed downwind of the horses, who had not yet noticed them. Pol, who was bringing up the rear, sped up briefly to ride alongside her. "Take this," he said, handing her his bow and quiver.

"What about you?" Kaede said, slinging the quiver onto her back.

He drew out his sword. "I'll need more mobility. You stay with Taisin."

Kaede nodded, trying to ignore the fear that bubbled in her stomach as Pol dropped back again. The trail was so narrow that they were riding single file. Shae was first, followed by Con, who was leading one of the packhorses. Next came Taisin, also leading a packhorse, and then Kaede; Pol rode last, his sword resting on his thighs.

As the morning wore on, Kaede began to suspect that these wolves were not entirely ordinary. They were practically flaunting themselves now; every once in a while one of them would break away from the pack and come closer to the path, either to get a better look at them or to demonstrate how bold they were. Kaede counted at least a dozen wolves, though she could not be sure, for they blended into the mottled brown of the Wood as if their coats had been made for this purpose.

Being constantly on guard after a sleepless night was a good way to render one's muscles stiff and clumsy, and that was the way Kaede felt when the wolves finally moved in. She wasn't sure what she had expected, but she knew she had not thought they would go after Pol first. He was clearly their strongest member, and he was riding Tali's horse, a great black stallion trained for battle. When she heard his horse cry out, she was so startled that she almost dropped the bow. By the time she fumbled an arrow out of the quiver and twisted in Pol's direction, he was already slashing his sword down at the wolves that had surrounded him in a ferocious, snarling wave, isolating him from Kaede and the others. One wolf sank his teeth into the horse's neck, and another bit into Pol's thigh, releasing a thick stream of red blood. He screamed, but he kept fighting, clinging to the back of his horse.

Kaede's fingers trembled on the fletching of an arrow. The wolves' brindled backs were a sea of matted fur and muscle between her and Pol. She knew that all those mornings in empty stable yards came down to this instant: the instinctual motion of hand to arrow to string—and release—and the arrow plowed into a wolf's chest, knocking him down. Kaede's blood pounded in her ears. There was no time to think; the wolves did not stop coming. She nocked another arrow, and another. Her nostrils filled with the beasts' stench.

Out of the corner of her eye she saw the packhorse tied to Con's saddle tear free from his lead rope, fleeing into the trees. Two wolves sprinted after him, and he never had a chance. They brought him down as easily as they might bring down a much smaller deer, and they howled their victory.

Con's stomach reeled as he watched the wolves tear into the packhorse; they had split into two mobs, one surrounding the horse, the other surrounding Pol. Kaede was trying to pick off the wolves around Pol, but she couldn't shoot too close to him. Con's fingers were sweaty on the hilt of his sword. Pol needed help.

"Stay with Taisin!" Con shouted at Shae, and doubled back through the trees parallel to the trail, heading toward Pol. As he approached the melee, a wolf charged him. Yellow teeth bared, she launched herself at Con's horse, who reared and struck at her with his iron-shod hooves. Con's own blade whistled in the air. He held on to his horse with his knees and slammed his sword into the wolf's shoulder. The beast's snarl turned into a whimper; Con ripped his weapon out and struck again, drops of hot blood stinging his hands. The creature collapsed, her rank scent filling the air. When Con looked up to find his next target, he saw two wolves yanking Pol from his horse onto the ground, and the guard's body disappeared beneath the pack.

"Pol!" he screamed.

Taisin heard him, and she twisted in her saddle to see Con trying to fight his way closer to the fallen guard. Terror engulfed her. Kaede was shouting at her; she was raising the bow, and an arrow flew frighteningly close to Taisin, making her flinch. It lodged in the flank of a gray wolf scarcely twenty feet away. That was when she noticed more of the beasts emerging from the trees and loping almost casually in her direction.

She could feel them: They were all hunger and vicious need. They were meant for this—to hunt and to kill—and there was a frightening beauty in their sharp golden eyes and powerful jaws. It was the beauty of a creature fulfilling her exact purpose in the world, being the precise thing she had trained her whole life to be.

The moment the first wolf leapt at her, Taisin acted entirely out of instinct, driven by panic. She had never used her knowledge of magic as a weapon before, and she knew there were proscriptions against it. None of that mattered when faced with a slavering wolf.

She forced her way into the fields of energy around her, tearing out fistfuls of the power that lived in every plant and animal, and she flung it at the wolves, knocking them down like paper dolls.

It was as easy as plucking ripe fruit from a tree. She felt like she had been born to do this. Her entire body thrilled with the power running through her. All the meridians of energy that ran across the Great Wood buckled beneath her touch. And the wolves began to run from her, yelping in fear.

Kaede stared at Taisin in amazement as she slid down from her horse, striding off the path toward the wolves. She raised her arms, flinging something at them that Kaede could not see. Whatever it was, it struck them like great punches, and Kaede saw one wolf's rib cage collapse, while another's snout was smashed, blood arcing through the air.

Taisin's eyes were shining, her hair coming loose. White light pulled at the ends until they swirled around her head in a black cloud. She looked like she was possessed by something as ferocious as the wolves themselves, and Kaede was chilled by the expression on her face. Taisin looked inhuman—powerful and frightening and hard as ice.

The wolves outside the radius of Taisin's power lifted their heads, looking in her direction. They backed away with deep-throated growls. It was as if a lightning storm had settled over her, and they wanted no part of it.

As the wolves retreated, Shae left the path to ride back toward Con and Pol, her blade dark with blood from the wolves that had left the fallen packhorse to find new prey. She did not see the ones who ran silently out of the trees east of the trail, and within an eyeblink, dragged her off her horse.

Shae screamed as the wolf bit down on her ankle; she tried to kick at him. Her horse reared, but it only loosened her from her saddle. She slid awkwardly, one foot caught in the stirrup, one hand tangled in her reins, and she tried to drive her sword into the wolf who had bitten her. It glanced off his shoulder, and then she was on the ground, her free hand scrabbling in the slightly damp earth, her cheek scraping against the soil. The wolves, their saliva dripping from hungry jowls, came for her.

Shae was fifteen feet away from Kaede when she was attacked. The space between them was a straight shot, and as one of the wolves raised his head to look at Kaede, she sent an arrow directly into his yellow eye.

He collapsed, but his pack mate turned in Kaede's direction and growled. She shot again, and the arrow lodged itself in the wolf's shoulder. He yelped and abandoned Shae, bounding toward Kaede instead. She loosed another arrow, but it only glanced off his flank. Then he was less than ten feet away from her, and before she could think she pulled out the iron dagger and hurled it squarely into his throat.

Finally he fell, his jaws nearly touching Maila's hooves when he slumped onto the forest floor. Hot relief flooded through Kaede's body. Her lungs heaved.

Through the buzzing of blood in her ears, she heard the wolves howling. When she looked up from the dead wolf, she saw his pack mates fleeing. The path toward Pol was clear at last, and Kaede saw that the guard's neck was bent at an unnatural angle, and his left thigh had been torn into a mass of bloody flesh.

But Shae was still alive, and as the wolves' howls faded into the distance, her gasps of pain filled the air. Con slid from his horse, dropped his bloody sword on the ground, and ran to her. Kneeling beside her, his face turned gray at the sight of her wound. Shae looked up at him, reaching out for his hand, muttering something that he could not understand.

"You're not leaving us, Shae," he said fiercely. "You're not leaving us."

Chapter XXII

aede ran toward Taisin, who had collapsed on the ground surrounded by dead wolves. Her lips were faintly blue, and she was breathing shallowly, her forehead glistening with sweat. Kaede was afraid Taisin had been injured, but she couldn't detect any physical wounds. She knew that Taisin might have sustained other, less visible, injuries, but she had no idea how to treat them. In all the years she had studied at the Academy, she had never heard of anyone doing what Taisin had just done, and she was fairly certain that it was forbidden.

But she would not let herself think about what that meant. All she wanted right now was to make sure that Taisin was not hurt. She knelt on the ground and lifted Taisin's hand. Her pulse raced within her wrist. Kaede leaned forward, pushing back damp strands of hair from Taisin's forehead. Her eyes suddenly opened, her pupils so huge they made her brown eyes seem black. She began to shake violently, and Kaede gathered her into her arms to quell the tremors, concerned that she would harm herself. At last the shaking subsided and Taisin asked in a hoarse voice, "Are the wolves all gone?"

"Yes." Kaede was relieved; Taisin sounded mostly normal. "Are you all right?"

Taisin squinted up at her. "I don't know." Her whole body felt bruised, and the pain was excruciating. But she also remembered the way she had held all of that energy in her hands: as muscular as a snake, as powerful as a fistful of iron.

Her stomach heaved with the memory, and she scrambled away from Kaede, doubled over on her hands and knees as she threw up. She might have been invincible against those wolves, but now she was weak as a newborn, shuddering her way into a strange new world.

When she had breath to speak she asked, "How are the others?"

"Shae is wounded. Pol—I don't know—"

Her voice broke off, and Taisin looked at Kaede and saw the fear on her face. Taisin took a deep, uneven breath. She pushed herself up onto her feet, wobbling like a colt taking his first steps. She surveyed the scene: the wolves' bodies splayed in a circle around them; the mauled packhorse, with their gear strewn across the forest floor; their four skittish mounts huddled together; Con bent over Shae on the ground. Down the trail she saw Pol's body; his horse had been dragged off by the wolves.

"We should go to them," Taisin said. She had to keep moving, or the gravity of what she had just done would overwhelm her. "We have no time to lose."

Shae was seriously injured. Her leg was in horrible shape, and she had sustained some ragged slashes on her side. They bandaged her wound, but there was nothing else they could do until they set up camp, and none of them wished to remain here, surrounded by the stinking corpses of dead wolves. Kaede retrieved her dagger and most of the arrows she had shot, but she didn't have the stomach to pull out the one lodged in the wolf's eye.

There was no saving Pol. They wrapped his broken body in his blanket and slung him as gently as they could over the back of the remaining packhorse, redistributing their supplies across all the horses. Con helped Shae climb back onto her own mare; she stubbornly refused to faint and instead had to grit her teeth over every bump in the road. They managed to put an hour's slow walk between themselves and what remained of their attackers before Con insisted they stop to tend Shae's wound. The bone in Shae's shin was exposed where the wolves had torn out her flesh, and Con had to hold her down while Taisin and Kaede wrapped her leg with a clean cloth. The cuts on her side where a wolf's claws had dragged across her body were jagged, and although they cleaned them as thoroughly as possible, Taisin had a bad feeling that the wounds would become inflamed. She brewed a bitter tea that would send Shae to sleep for the time being, which was the best she could do for the pain, and then they measured out just enough space for another grave.

Con broke up the ground with his sword while Kaede and Taisin dug with their battered metal bowls. Every time his blade bit into the ground, he remembered the way it had cleaved into the wolf's shoulder. He had killed that one, but he had been too late to save Pol. He had been too late to prevent Shae from being attacked. Seeing her on the ground, bleeding, had ripped him open, too. It made him realize that he had so much to say to her. Sweat broke out on his skin despite the cool air. He did not want to even consider the possibility that Shae wouldn't survive her wounds. He rammed his sword into the earth, making Taisin and Kaede jump out of the way.

"I'm sorry," he said. They kept digging.

Night fell before the grave was deep enough. The candle they had lit for Pol's soul did nothing to push back the dark. Taisin suggested they light a fire so that Shae would not get chilled. "You two will have to gather firewood," Taisin said. "I should stay here with Shae and Pol."

"Alone?" Kaede said. She straightened, standing in the grave itself. "Con should stay with you; I'll go alone."

"No." Taisin rubbed her eyes wearily with the back of her hand. "I'll be fine here. I can protect myself, but it's not safe for either of you to be alone in the Wood."

"Come on," Con said, offering his hand to Kaede. "Let's get it over with. We should have done it earlier."

Kaede frowned, but she took Con's hand and scrambled out. The lip of the grave crumbled beneath her foot as she climbed, sending clods of dirt tumbling into the pit. Taisin began to climb in.

"You shouldn't do that," Kaede said, her skin prickling. "Wait till we return."

"There's not time," Taisin said, picking up her bowl to dig. "We have to bury Pol as soon as possible."

Con and Kaede did not stray far from the path as they foraged for fallen branches. The Wood seemed particularly malignant that night. Kaede could have sworn she saw the eyes of wolves peering out at her from the cover of darkness. And it was so cold. She had been warmer when she was digging, but now she felt the wind on her face, and it smelled sharply of snow.

When they returned to their camp, they could hear Taisin chanting to herself as she dug. She didn't stop when they returned. Kaede built the small fire as quickly as she could, and Con pulled Shae's sleeping form toward it, pillowing her head on a rolled-up blanket.

As soon as the grave was deep enough, they rolled Pol's body into it. There had been no time to wash him or to change him out of the clothes he had died in. Taisin knew it was bad form, but she didn't know what else to do—it was already too late at night for proper burial rites—and she was so exhausted that she could barely say the words of the funeral lament. But Kaede and Con helped her, and together they laid Pol to rest.

∽

In the morning, Shae awoke feverish and in pain. Taisin had learned some rudimentary healing practices at the Academy, but she was not trained as a healer, and Kaede had never reached that far in her studies. Con refused to give up; his stomach churned at the thought of losing Shae. "We'll just keep going," he said. "We'll find the Xi in time. They'll help." He heard the desperation in his voice, and he turned away so that he didn't have to see the awful sympathy in Kaede's face.

They were nearly packed and ready to go when the dog came trotting down the trail toward them. At first Kaede thought it was another wolf, and her dagger was in her hand before she realized it was not a wild animal. Though he was tall as a wolf, he moved differently, and his brown eyes lacked the feral sharpness she had seen in those beasts. He barked at them, and Taisin and Con jumped at the sound. When they were all staring at him, the dog began to wag his tail.

Behind him, coming down the trail, was a white-haired woman. She walked with a slight limp, leaning on a horned staff, and as she approached she called out, "Good morning, travelers! That's my dog, Cavin; he's harmless enough." When she was standing at the edge of their camp she paused and smiled. "On a little journey, are we?" she said lightly.

The three of them were silent. Con did not know what to make of the strange old woman. She looked innocuous, but he knew that a helpless old woman could never survive on her own in the Great Wood. Tali would not trust her. Con could almost hear him warning them: *Don't be fooled by the appearance of weakness.*

Con stepped forward, putting himself between her and the others. "Who are you?" he asked.

The woman cocked her head at him, hearing his defensiveness. "I am only here to help. I saw the wolves yesterday, running past my cottage. I thought that someone might be in need of my assistance."

"What kind of assistance?" Con asked.

"One of your party is injured, I see. Perhaps I can help."

Despite his doubts, hope flared inside him. "How?"

"Let me see her, and I will tell you what I can do."

194

Chapter XXIII

er name, she told them, was Mona. She was blind in her left eye, but she seemed to have no trouble examining Shae's injuries. Con watched her carefully, noting the practiced way she handled the bandages, her touch light and quick. When Mona suggested they bring Shae back to her cottage where she could treat her, he agreed.

Taisin, who had said nothing during the exam, now asked, "Are you a healer?" A note of skepticism could be heard in her voice.

Mona looked at her out of her one good eye—it was startlingly blue compared to the filmy white covering the other—and said, "I am a greenwitch."

Taisin was surprised. "And you live here in the Wood, alone?"

The old woman smiled crookedly. "Solitude, young one, teaches many things not found within the walls of your Academy."

Taisin stared at her, startled, for she had not mentioned the Academy of Sages. But it was obvious that Mona had guessed Taisin was a student there. Before she could ask how Mona had known, the woman got up. "We'd better go," she said. "Your friend must not wait any longer."

Mona's cottage was about an hour's walk into the Wood, away from the river Nir. It was a roughly built log cabin with mud plastered into the cracks, and there was one door and one square window covered with greased paper. But the interior was unexpectedly cheerful, with a colorful quilt thrown over the bed in the corner and dried herbs hanging from the ceiling. On one wall was a fireplace in which the remains of a fire glowed; on the other wall was an iron-bound trunk surrounded by stacks of leather-bound books. The sight of them astonished Taisin. A cottage like this one was the last place she would have expected to find so many books. They were costly items and difficult to obtain.

Mona told them to put Shae on the bed, and then asked them to build up the fire. "There's wood out back, behind the lean-to," she said. "And I would much appreciate it if one of you could bring me some water. You'll see the well by the woodpile. And you"—she motioned to Taisin—"I could use your help."

❧

Shae was shivering. Mona had built up the fire until it roared, but though the heat of it sent sweat trickling between Taisin's shoulder blades, it seemed to have no effect on the guard, who was lying on the bed beneath several heavy quilts. Mona had given Shae something to make her sleep before she treated her wounds, but even asleep she was restless and agitated. Her face was white, her lips almost blue, and she breathed shallowly.

"Will she recover?" Taisin asked, watching the old woman touching Shae's forehead and cheeks with the back of her hand.

"She has a fever. There is poison inside her."

"From the wounds?"

"From the wolves. They're dirty beasts."

"Can you save her?" Taisin was afraid to know the answer, but she had to ask.

"I don't know yet." Mona left the bedside and went to the stack of books piled near the trunk. She pulled out a thick volume bound in black leather and propped it open on the mantle above the fireplace, holding it in place with a heavy pewter candlestick. Taisin came closer to look; on the page was a recipe listing at least two dozen ingredients. She recognized a few of them—milk vetch, aralia root, sage. But she didn't know many of the others: goldthread, blue aralia, skullcap.

"What is this for?" Taisin asked.

"Your friend is very weak. She has suffered a great shock." Mona opened the trunk, and inside there were dozens of little boxes and vials stacked one upon the other. "Her energies have been severely depleted. She has bled quite a bit. Her body could overcome the injury to her leg on its own if she were strong and healthy, but the wolf's bite has drained her." Mona began to pull out a number of boxes and handed them to Taisin. "Put them on the table by the clay pot."

"Are you making a tonic?" Taisin had learned about healing tonics at the Academy, but her knowledge of them was limited to the relatively harmless brew she had made for Shae the night before. It had not kept the pain away for long.

"It is a kind of tonic," Mona said, pushing herself up from the trunk to set down two more vials on the table.

"What will it do?"

"If it works, it will restore her vigor and strengthen her blood, and drive out the infection." Mona opened one of the boxes and pulled out dried flowers, rusty brown in color, and dropped them into the clay pot. She added little round seeds and the scrapings of a gnarled, flesh-colored root; furry, blue-gray leaves and pale orange blossoms. When all of the ingredients had been combined and crushed into a fine powder, she drew a small knife from her pocket and bent down to hold it in the hottest part of the flames.

"What is that for?" Taisin asked.

"There is another ingredient," Mona said, and a moment later she straightened, waving the knife in the air to let the blade cool off.

Something in Mona's voice made Taisin recoil. "What is it?"

"Your blood."

Taisin stepped back, her foot banging into the trunk. "What?"

Mona did not move; she held the blade lightly. It was only a paring knife. "Your blood," she said again. The woman's blind white eye moved as if it could see. "The tonic will not work without it."

"No tonics require human blood," Taisin objected, her skin prickling.

"Do you know every tonic?" Mona asked mildly. "What a scholar you are."

Taisin flushed. "No, I—" She clenched her fingers into fists. "I'm not saying I know everything. But I have never heard of blood as an element in healing rituals."

"Blood is the water of life. Your friend has been drained of too much of hers." Mona took a step closer to her, and Taisin had the impression that the old woman could see right into her mind. It was unnerving. "You are young, and I know that the energies run strong within you," Mona continued. "I felt it yesterday, when you defended yourself from those wolves. I felt the way you pulled and stretched the meridians to do your bidding. That is not something the Academy teaches its pupils, is it? And yet you knew how to do it."

Taisin stared at her, shocked. "You—you felt that?"

Mona gave her a shrewd look. "You should know better, Taisin. You know that when you do something like that, others can sense it."

"The wolves would have killed me—"

"And your friend will die if you don't give her your blood."

Taisin's heart pounded. She glanced at Shae, at her white face and heaving chest. When she turned back to Mona, the woman was watching her with a patient expression. "How much do you need?"

"Not so much. You are strong enough that a little will go a long way."

Taisin took a deep breath. "All right."

"Come here, then, and give me your arm."

Taisin went to her, knees shaking, and rolled up her left sleeve. Mona held her arm steady over the bowl of herbs, their bitter scent wafting up to her nostrils. Mona placed the knife against Taisin's skin, and with a short, quick move, sliced into her forearm. Taisin gasped; it stung. She watched as blood welled up in the cut, and let out a short moan when Mona wrapped her fingers above it, squeezing. The blood dripped, hot and red, onto the herbs.

Mona was saying something, but Taisin couldn't understand her. The words were in another language—something brutal and dark, like a knuckle scraping against stone. She felt light-headed as her blood drained from her, making a slight hissing sound when it struck the mixture in the clay pot. She couldn't look at the cut anymore; it was a mouth on her arm; it screamed at her.

She turned her eyes away, feeling sick. She stared at the fire, at the hearthstones, at the candlestick holding the black leather book open, the words crawling like worms across the page.

And then Mona was smearing an ointment over the cut, and she pressed a cloth against it. "Hold it there," Mona ordered, and began to crush the herbs into the blood. She poured in water from a black bottle; she knelt before the hearth and shoved the pot into the coals. She made a sign in the air—a circle—and she folded her hands together and touched them to her forehead, her mouth, her heart. A log fell with a crash, sending up sparks.

After several moments Mona stood again, and Taisin asked nervously, "Is it ready?"

"No, not for at least another hour. The herbs must absorb the blood fully." Mona looked tired, and she sat down in the rocking chair. "Let me see your arm."

Taisin had almost forgotten about it, but now she peeled back the rag. The ointment had left an oily residue on the cloth, which was now stained red, but the cut itself had stopped bleeding. She didn't resist when Mona wrapped a strip of linen around it, tucking the ends into place firmly. Her arm throbbed a little, and Mona said, "You should sit down. You've lost blood now, too."

Dazed, Taisin sank down to the floor. As Mona rocked nearby, Taisin stared at the iron pot in the fire, wondering if she had been right to let the greenwitch take her blood.

Chapter XXIV

Con paced back and forth in the clearing outside the cottage, his shoulders taut with worry. Earlier, they had heard Shae crying out in pain, but hours had now passed with no sounds from within. Taisin was still inside with Mona, who had shooed Con and Kaede away once they delivered the firewood and water. "You'll just be in the way," the old woman had said. "You'd best wait outside."

So they tended to their horses. They built a small fire in the stone-lined pit in the middle of the clearing, and they boiled water for tea. They cooked a cup of rice to eat, but neither Con nor Kaede had much experience with cooking, and the rice began to burn. They added more water, and then it became too wet. They ate it anyway, feeling gloomy and tired.

Afterward, Kaede pulled out her bedroll. She was so worn out she was sure she could sleep in broad daylight, but Con was too wound up, and he began to pace. His agitation was contagious, and she was about to give up on sleeping when he sat down on one of the logs beside the fire pit, demanding in frustration, "Why haven't they come outside yet? This woman must not know what she's doing. I was too eager to believe in her."

Kaede rolled over, pillowing her head on her bent arm to look at him. "She said she's a greenwitch."

He put his head in his hands. "But what do we really know about her?" he asked, his voice muffled. "Mona, is that her name? Who would want to live out here alone?"

"She has a dog," Kaede pointed out drily. Cavin was lying just outside the cottage door, apparently asleep.

Con let out his breath in an exasperated sigh. "You're making jokes, Kaede?"

She groaned, lying back again and blinking up at the gray sky. It seemed unusually bright today. "I'm sorry, Con. You know I'm worried about Shae, too."

He nodded briefly. "She seems unusual, though. This greenwitch."

"Do you know many?" Kaede rubbed her hand across her eyes. Yes, she was positive: The cloud cover was thinner today.

"A few. I met a few when I went up north last year. Aren't they women who never passed the tests required to become sages?"

"Some of them are. But I've heard of others, in recent years, who have rejected the sagehood and chosen to call themselves greenwitches instead."

"Why?"

She glanced over at the cottage. The door was still closed.

"There are some greenwitches who claim that the Academy—and the Council—are too distant from the people of this kingdom," Kaede explained. "They believe that sages should be among the people, not removed from them."

He was surprised. "I haven't heard anything about this."

"I don't think the Council wants it to be widely known."

He quickly understood. "It would stir up trouble if people knew that some are resisting the Council's orders."

"And there are fewer sages made every year," Kaede pointed out. "They don't want to lose anyone."

"What about you? Aren't you due to join their ranks?"

"I will never be a sage," she said, and she realized that the idea of it no longer made her feel inadequate. It felt, instead, perfectly ordinary.

"But you've been a student there for six years."

"I've read the classics, but I'm not meant to be a sage. I don't have the skill."

"Why didn't you leave the Academy earlier, then?"

She turned back onto her side, propping her head on her hand, and gave him a tiny smile. "I have a powerful father, Con. He—and my mother, who would have been a sage if she hadn't married him—wanted me to be there. I'm sure they hoped I'd develop the abilities, but...I don't think it's something you can learn."

"What are you going to do, then? When we return."

The question startled her. They had been on the road for almost five weeks now, but it felt like years. Her life before—the Academy, her family, her obligations—was a different world, one she could barely believe she had ever lived in.

The real world was here and now: this clearing, where the clouds overhead were thin enough to remind her what a blue sky might look like. The dirt under her nails, the healing scars on her hands, the ache in her shoulders and back from digging Pol's grave. Returning to her previous life seemed impossible. What would she do?

"I don't know," she said at last. "My father wants me to marry someone."

"Who?"

"I haven't met him." She grimaced. "Someone named Lord Win."

His eyebrows rose. "Really? I've met him. He's—"

"Don't tell me," she interrupted, sitting up. "I don't want to know anything about him. I don't intend to marry him."

Con's lips twitched as though he were amused, but he only said mildly, "I didn't expect you would."

Kaede sighed. "Tell that to my father."

"All right, I will."

She gave him a skeptical look. "What do you mean?"

"When we return, I'll talk to your father."

"My father won't listen to you."

"Why not?" He waggled his eyebrows at her. "You don't believe in my powers of persuasion?"

She rolled her eyes. "My father is the most stubborn man alive. He usually gets what he wants."

"Have a little faith in me." He grinned at her. "I am your future King."

She smiled faintly. She knew he was joking with her, but the thought of the future was sobering. Tali and Pol, both dead, and now Shae hovering on the edge. She said quietly, "I hope Shae will be all right."

Con stiffened; his grin vanished. "Shae is going to be fine," he insisted. He picked up a stick and began to poke at the fire.

"Of course she is," Kaede agreed. Con's brows were knitted with worry again, and she was sorry she had brought it up. If she had doubted his feelings for Shae before, she no longer did.

She watched Con run a hand through his hair; it had grown at least an inch since they had left Cathair, and now it stuck out everywhere, as if he were a porcupine. Kaede noticed he had grown a beard, too, and she wondered when he had stopped shaving. It had been some time, she guessed. Wearing dirty, bloodstained clothes, he looked more like a highway bandit than a prince. But when they returned—*when*, she told herself, not *if*—he would also return to his obligations, and they did not include falling in love with a guard.

Kaede asked, "Has your father spoken to you about marriage?"

"No." Sparks flew up as Con broke apart one of the burning pieces of wood. "He has been busy with his new bride," he said bitterly. "And by the time we return, I suspect I'll have a new half brother or half sister." He stared at the fire with a dour expression. "I'm guessing it'll be at least another year before my father realizes he could use me that way."

At that moment, the cottage door opened, and Taisin came outside. "We're finished," she said. She looked exhausted, with purple smudges beneath her eyes and yellow and red stains on the front of her tunic.

Con stood up and asked immediately, "How is she?"

Taisin sat down on the log, rubbing at her tired eyes. "She is as well as she can be, given the circumstances."

"Is she in pain?" Con asked.

"She is sleeping. Now all we can do is wait."

❧

They slept away the afternoon, curled up around the fire pit, and even Con dozed a little. When Taisin awoke, evening was falling in lush, soft shadows around them, and Mona was pulling an iron teapot out of the fire.

Taisin pushed herself up, blinking in the firelight. "How is Shae?" she asked, her voice thick with sleep.

"She's resting," Mona answered.

Con was holding a small iron cup of tea. "She looks a little better," he said. He had gone inside the cottage as soon as Mona came out, and he had been relieved to see some improvement. Shae's fever had cooled somewhat, although she was still hot to the touch.

Mona poured another cup and handed it to Taisin. "Be careful. It's hot."

Taisin took it gingerly, holding it by the rim. The fragrance of summer flowers wafted up at her. "Where's Kaede?" she asked.

"She'll be back soon. Ah! There she is now."

Kaede came from the lean-to behind the cottage carrying an earthenware jar. "Is this what you were looking for?" she asked, handing it to Mona.

"Oh, yes," the woman said. Her smile spread wrinkles across her whole face. With a deft twist, she opened the jar. "I haven't had visitors in so long." She sounded both eager and a bit uncertain. "The occasion deserves something special, doesn't it?" She handed the jar back to Kaede, who sniffed it: honey. Her mouth watered instantly; it had been so long since she had tasted something sweet that she wanted to upend the entire jar into her mouth. Mona laughed at her. "Use this, my dear," she said, and handed her a wooden spoon and a steaming cup of tea. Then she turned to Con and added, "Although I'm afraid I can't offer you anything to compete with the King's table."

He paused, teacup half-raised to his mouth. He hadn't told her who he was. "How did—do you know who I am?"

"I have seen your face before, Your Highness," she said.

"Where?"

She shook her head, clucking her tongue. "I cannot reveal my secrets. I know you and your companions are embarked on a very important journey, and I am so pleased that I have been able to do my part in it."

"Did you know to expect us?" Kaede asked.

"Expect?" Mona repeated. "I don't think that is the right word, exactly. Although I have been seeing pieces of you all for years, you know."

Kaede considered the old woman's impish expression. "Do you have the Sight?"

"It is not what you would call the Sight," Mona said, clucking her tongue again. "No, not what you would know. Young Taisin here may have an idea...she has visions I would never dream of having." Mona gave Taisin a smile that was almost proud, and Taisin looked nervous. "Do not be afraid of your visions," Mona said to Taisin, speaking as if she were addressing a small child. "You must be open to them—open to everything under the sun and the moon, though these are both obscured to us now...sadly."

Con set his teacup gently on the ground and said, "Madam, you are undoubtedly a wise woman. May I ask how many years you have lived here in the Great Wood?"

She turned her head toward him almost coquettishly. "I am not averse to some flattery, indeed I am not, young prince. I have lived beneath these trees for longer than you have been alive, certainly."

He smiled at her. "Then you must surely know much about this Wood that I—that *we* do not. Will you look at our maps and share your knowledge about the land here?"

"Oh, maps," Mona said, her voice lilting. "What have maps to do with anything? They do not show the true path." She sighed. "But of course I will look at them, though I assure you they are useless."

Puzzled, Con went and retrieved the maps from their long carrying case. He spread them out on the ground near Mona, taking care to avoid the fire. The light flickered over the paper as the old woman crouched down and stared at the lines demarcating the Great Wood, the river Nir, the Kell. Con pointed at a spot south of the intersection of the two rivers and said, "Is this where we are?"

Mona squinted down at the map and said, "That may be. Yes, that may be." She gestured broadly at the northern portion of the map, which was largely unmarked forest. "All of that is wrong. All wrong."

"Have you been north of the Kell?" Con asked.

"No, not I," Mona objected, as if affronted. "I stay to my side of the boundary."

"So there is still an agreed-upon boundary?" Con said.

"Well, *I* have agreed to my own boundary." Mona laughed as if she had told a joke. Then her face grew serious, and she pointed at the line of the Kell. "This," she said. "This is the boundary I have agreed upon. I stay on my side, and they don't bother me."

"Who?" Con asked.

"The fay, of course," Mona said.

"You mean the Xi?" Kaede said.

"The Xi are only one of many races of fay peoples," Mona said. She added with an arch smile, "Perhaps the most arrogant ones. The Fairy Queen, of course, purports to rule them all."

Kaede asked curiously, "What other fay races are there?"

Mona shook her head. "It is not so simple, young one. Many of them have died out. There were wars between many races; few survived." But then she seemed truly delighted as she added, "And yet life moves in its cycles, doesn't it? I believe some fairies survived after all. I saw the loveliest little sprite the other day—moving just like a hummingbird. Do you know those? So pretty."

A thrill ran through Taisin as she heard Mona describe the sprite. Was that the name of the creature she saw in her visions? She burned with questions, but Mona picked up her staff and levered herself to her feet. "Nonetheless, it makes no difference to you," she said. "You won't see anything that doesn't want to be seen."

Con said, "Madam, we must travel north of the Kell. We'll surely encounter the Xi, won't we?"

She gave him a measuring look and answered, "It is unwise of you to cross the river."

"We have an invitation from the Fairy Queen," Con said.

"An invitation?" Mona said, her white eyebrows rising. "A true invitation?"

"Yes," Con said.

Mona shrugged. "Then perhaps all will be well."

"Do you know where we should cross the river?" he asked. "Is there a bridge?"

"I have been to the river, but never forded it. You will be safe enough on this side if you keep quiet about your destination—the Wood listens, you know. But on the other side, it is not a place for humans." She paused for a moment as if considering whether or not to tell them something. At last she said, "When I visited the Kell some years ago, I saw the Xi. They guard the border, I think. A great phalanx of them, hunters all. With bows and swords and grand horses. They kindly allowed me to leave without an arrow in my back."

And then Mona looked up at the darkening sky and seemed to remember something. "Oh, my, it is growing late! Taisin, you had better come with me; I'll need your assistance sitting up with our invalid tonight."

Chapter XXV

By now, Taisin recognized parts of the fortress—the long, sloping corridor; the cavernous ceiling hung with icicles sharp as swords; the endless ranks of golden cages. And then there were the creatures she had seen, each one equally strange and beautiful. Some had scales like fish, and they slipped beneath still pools. Others, with fingers as gnarled as tree roots, nevertheless moved with the grace of leaves in a summer breeze. But the only creature she had seen whole was the winged fairy, who repeatedly flew down that corridor as if she were doomed to traverse the same small space for eternity.

It wasn't until late at night in Mona's cottage, when Shae was finally resting peacefully, that Taisin saw the other woman. Mona was asleep in her chair by the fire, and perhaps it was the greenwitch's presence that made it possible for Taisin to finally see her. One moment Taisin was lying on the pallet she had made on the floor next to the bed, and the next she was moving swiftly down the same corridor she had floated through countless times before—but this time, she was walking.

She could feel the contours of her body—this woman's body—and she wore a gown of some kind of heavy fabric. A cloak of ermine was draped around her shoulders. The floor was cold beneath the thin soles of her shoes, but she was used to the cold; it no longer bothered her. Taisin felt a fierce protectiveness for the ice, and it surprised her. This woman was in love with the mountain she had raised, block by block, from the frozen northern sea. She was no one to be toyed with, for she could shape icebergs into towers so high they scratched the sky. Taisin felt the power in the woman's veins, and she was awed by the strength of it. The way Taisin herself had felt when she had ripped into the fabric of the world to kill those wolves—that was only the beginning of what this woman could do.

She walked briskly to the end of the corridor, and Taisin saw her hand pushing open a door. The sight that greeted her made the woman swell with pride and determination. It was a nursery. On a dais, as if it were a throne, was a cradle made of crystal. Small hands reached up from within, and the woman went to the cradle and lifted out a baby. It was a perfect child in many ways. It had soft, sweet skin, and tiny fingers and dimpled knuckles. Verdant green eyes looked up at her from beneath long black lashes. Then the child opened its mouth and turned its head, and sank a row of pearly little fangs into the woman's arm.

Taisin felt the pain herself; it was as though she had been stabbed by a half-dozen little needles, each one poison-tipped. She jerked on the floor of Mona's cottage, and in the fortress the woman snarled at the baby and threw it, hard, against the edge of the cradle.

Blood smeared against the crystal, and Taisin was stunned by the strength of the woman's rage. It boiled out of her: pain and anger and choking, bitter disappointment.

And then, in a jarring, disorienting lurch, Taisin felt Mona's hand on her, shaking her, calling her name, and she awoke on the floor of the cottage.

The old woman was standing over her, that one milky eye fixed on her as though it could see into her mind. "Where did you go?" Mona muttered, prodding at her with the end of her staff. "No use in flying off to unsafe places. Keep your wits about you."

Taisin pushed her hair away from her eyes; her hand came away damp with sweat. "I will," she said. "I do."

Mona gave her a skeptical look. "You are walking a fine line."

Taisin was confused. The vision of the ice fortress still clung to her, making this world seem hazy, unreal. "What do you mean?"

Mona shook her head as if Taisin were a rebellious child. "What you did yesterday to those wolves—I haven't felt anything like that since...well, not since I was a very young girl. You had better keep an eye on yourself. These things have a way of turning."

Taisin went cold all over. Mona's blue eye was icy as she gazed at her, unblinking, and Taisin felt utterly exposed, as though Mona were peeling back layer upon layer of her defenses and examining each one. Taisin remembered how it felt to bend the meridians of energy to her will: like she was invincible. She realized—half ashamed, half defiant—that she yearned to feel that way again. To hold the webbing of the world in her hands, and to use it.

Mona bent down and clutched Taisin's chin in her bony hand and nearly spit in her face as she said, "You listen to me, young Taisin. You have a strong heart, but even the strongest heart can be tempted."

Taisin tried to pull back, but Mona's iron grip was bruising in its strength. It seemed to reach through her—within her—and smothered the flame of that desire until all that remained was a hard, hot little ember.

Mona let go, and Taisin fell back, gasping and weak. The old woman gestured toward Shae, pushing up her sleeves. "She's ready for her next infusion. Will you bring the herbs?"

Taisin was transfixed by the sight of Mona's bare forearm: There was a mark there, but though it was roughly the same size and shape as a sage's mark, it was a solid black circle, not the symbols that Taisin had seen before. It was as though Mona had once been marked, but had since chosen to efface the symbol—or to erase it. Mona saw her eyeing the mark, and she said shortly, "We don't all make the right choices when we're young."

"What do you mean? Are you a marked sage?"

"No."

"But what is that—"

"I might have once been marked, but I am no longer."

Taisin was incredulous. "How could you reject your station like that? It is an honor to be marked." Another possibility came to her, and the idea that the Council might have stripped Mona of her marking made her look at the greenwitch uneasily. It could only be a horrible thing that would cause the Council to revoke a sage's status.

Mona's eyes narrowed and she leaned down so that she was peering directly into Taisin's eyes with her single good one. "Not everything they teach you is true. I have chosen my own path. So must you." She backed away and returned to Shae's bedside. "Now will you bring me those herbs?"

჻

Later that night, Mona slept again in her rocking chair, gently snoring. But Taisin couldn't sleep anymore; her thoughts circled endlessly around Mona's strange words, the awful vision, and the black mark.

Shivering, she wrapped her blanket tighter around herself and crawled over to the hearth to stir the coals. The flaring light illuminated the books stacked around the trunk nearby, and as the shadows leapt over the bindings, she began to wonder what was in them. She glanced at Mona, who was still asleep, and then reached for the closest volume, pulling it down as quietly as possible and opening it in her lap. It was a journal of some sort containing long lists of what looked like herbs or plants. The last quarter of the pages were blank, and she realized they must be Mona's own records. She closed the book and pulled out another, and another, motivated by a rising compulsion she did not understand. She felt as if she were searching for something. But book after book disappointed her—they all seemed to be journals of plant life, notations about tonics or medicines. In every one, the handwriting was the same: tiny, precise, taking up no more room than was necessary. Taisin assumed it was Mona's work, and it made sense, for she had known precisely what to do for Shae's injuries. Mona had spent her whole life, apparently, studying the medicinal properties of herbs.

The last book on the stack nearest to Taisin was the largest yet, and Taisin opened it expecting more of the same. But this time, there were illustrations, too, and they were not illustrations of plants. The drawings—sometimes crude, but always lifelike—depicted creatures like the ones she saw in her visions. Holding her breath in excitement, she stopped at a picture of a being with wings just like a hummingbird's. There were notes there, too, in Mona's handwriting. *Sprite*, Taisin read. She turned the page. A slender woman with hair like sea kelp: *asrai. Found in the icy waters of the north.* A dwarflike being with legs as thick as tree trunks: *knocker.* And another creature that looked as if it had been sprung from the limbs of an oak tree: *wood nymph.* Taisin stared at it, her mouth open, remembering the body they had buried outside of Jilin.

"Find something interesting?" Mona said.

Taisin started, looking up at the greenwitch. "Are these creatures…are these all fairies?" Taisin asked, her heart racing.

Mona cocked her head, reminding Taisin of a bird with a very sharp beak. For a moment Mona's shadow seemed to arch overhead malevolently, but then Mona settled back into her chair, and she was just an old woman again. "What a silly question," Mona finally said, though there was no sting in her voice. "What else could they be?"

Taisin looked back at the drawing of the wood nymph.

Notes were scrawled around the picture. "Is this your handwriting?"

"Some of it is. Some of that book was wrong. I had to correct it."

"You mean this book was..." Taisin trailed off, thinking. "Where did this book come from?"

"I rescued it from the Academy," Mona said, and she sounded almost cheerful about it.

"You *rescued* it?"

Mona leaned down, the birdlike look back in her eye. "You trust your teachers, do you?"

"Yes," Taisin said, feeling defensive. "Why shouldn't I?"

"Did they teach you about these fairies?"

Taisin hesitated. "No, but—"

"But what, my dear? They have sent you on this journey through the Great Wood without even telling you about the creatures you might encounter?" Mona put her bony hand on her chest, a look of sorrow sweeping over her face. "I wouldn't trust anyone who did that to me. Why should you?"

Taisin was disconcerted. Was Mona right? She thought of Sister Ailan, who had always seemed to be so honorable and honest. She thought of Maire Morighan and the other teachers, who had all been generous and kind to her, and answered every question she posed, no matter what it was. Had she been asking the wrong questions?

Mona seemed to see the confusion in her face, for the old woman said, "You read that book tonight. And when you return to the Academy, perhaps *you* will have something to teach your teachers."

Chapter XXVI

hey spent two nights at Mona's cottage. Taisin showed Con and Kaede the book of fairies, and they pored over its yellowed pages for hours. By the second night, Shae's fever was gone, but she was still too weak to travel. When Mona offered to shelter Shae until she was recovered enough to return to Jilin, they knew they had to move on. Midsummer—and their appointment with the Fairy Queen—was less than a fortnight away, and they had no idea if they would arrive in time.

Con lingered by Shae's bedside on the morning of their departure. She drifted in and out of a drugged sleep, and all he could do was hold her hand. "We're coming back," he whispered, as much for himself as for her. His eyes were hot with suppressed tears. "I promise you."

They left Shae's horse behind, along with her gear and a tent, but they took all the remaining food supplies. There wasn't much, and Kaede began to wonder if she would have to attempt to hunt on her own. She felt extremely vulnerable now, traveling only with Taisin and Con. The two days at Mona's cottage had been a reprieve from cold reality, but now, as they made their way down an overgrown trail that surely hadn't seen human traffic in generations, that reality returned. They had lost their leader in Tali. They had lost Pol and Shae, who knew how to survive in the wilderness. Now they were only three, and Kaede was terrified that the Wood might demand another sacrifice. They took care to stay within sight of each other at all times, and Kaede carried Pol's bow across her lap.

She watched Taisin's back as they rode, wondering what she was thinking. She had been a little distant since the wolf attack, and it made Kaede anxious. What if the things that Taisin had done to those wolves had changed her? There were warnings, rules against using the energies to harm any living being. But had she done anything worse than what Kaede had also done, using Pol's bow?

When the time came for Taisin to perform the protection ritual around their camp, Kaede was tense, wondering if there would be something different in Taisin tonight. And when Taisin's fingers pressed firmly against Kaede's chest, something *had* changed. But it was not what Kaede expected. There was a new strength to her; there were no hesitations in her movements. And the connection that had grown between them was still there. It had slackened a bit in last few days, but now it tightened again. Perhaps because of Taisin's new confidence, today the connection opened up, and for the first time, each could see a tiny part of the other.

In the breathless moment before Taisin realized what she

had done, Kaede saw some of the truth that Taisin was hiding from her. Taisin was falling in love with her—the emotions were as clear and hot as a summer sky. But beneath them was the bitter tang of fear.

When Taisin broke the connection, Kaede staggered. She was overjoyed, but she was also confused. She reached out for Taisin's hand, but she had already turned away to finish the ritual. When it was done, her face was a carefully controlled mask; she would not meet Kaede's eyes.

Con saw the tension between them, and he came to Kaede as Taisin put away her supplies and asked, "What happened?"

Kaede looked up at him, dazed. She couldn't tell him. She wasn't even sure what it meant. And had Taisin seen her own feelings as well? She reddened to think of it.

"Kaede?"

"It's nothing," she said. But her heart hammered in her chest, and she trembled as she went to light the campfire.

❧

In the middle of the night, Taisin woke Kaede to take over the watch, shaking her shoulder gently. Kaede pushed herself up, and Taisin pulled back. Con was asleep in his bedroll on the other side of the low-burning fire, and the trees arched above in a rib cage of bare branches.

Kaede fumbled for words. Her mouth was clumsy, fogged with uneasy sleep. "What did—tell me—"

She half expected Taisin to flee from her, but when Taisin remained where she was, her face pale and tense, Kaede tried again.

"Why—why are you afraid of your feelings?" she whispered.

Taisin bit her lip. She looked away from Kaede; she looked down at her hands; they twisted together as if she were trying to weave a rope around her wrists. She said something so softly that Kaede could not hear it.

Kaede pushed aside her blankets, leaning toward Taisin. "You can tell me."

Taisin touched Kaede's cheek very gently. Her fingers were cold. Kaede reached for her, but Taisin drew back, flushing. Kaede waited. Taisin's eyes, reflecting the firelight, looked like tiny burning stars. Finally she said in a low voice, "I'm going to be a sage."

"I know that."

"I can't—I can't be with anyone." Her words were full of regret. "I'm sorry. I'm so sorry."

The misery in her voice made Kaede ache. She wanted to ease Taisin's pain, but she had no idea how.

Taisin turned away, wrapping her blankets around herself, and then lay down with her back to Kaede. The distance between them, though it was only a few feet, had never seemed so great.

༄

The third day after leaving Shae behind, they came to the river Kell. It was a grand sight to behold. The Nir and the Kell branched off from a wide, tumbling rush of water coming from the north, the Nir continuing south and the Kell running east. Both rivers were swollen with rainfall and thick with boulders that created dozens of small, swift waterfalls. The rains that had doused the travelers repeatedly on their journey had fed into the rivers, making them particularly treacherous to cross.

They agreed to travel east to search for a better place to ford the Kell, and when they came to a shallow beach in the early afternoon, Con stopped. "Perhaps we should just cross here. There are fewer boulders in the river, and who knows how far we'd have to go to find a calmer spot."

Taisin looked out at the river. He seemed to be right— the way was mostly clear. On the far side, the trees looked just like they did on this side. There was no sign of the Xi. "It will be cold," Taisin said.

"We'd better cross soon, then," Kaede said, "or wait until morning. It'll be difficult to dry off after night falls."

Con squinted up at the hard, bright gray sky. "We have time. I don't think we should wait."

They unwound the longest coil of rope they had, tying each horse to it. They secured their bedrolls and supplies as well as they could.

"Hold on to your horse if you lose your footing," Con advised, trying to remember what Tali had taught him. "They will swim." As soon as he was ready, before he could second-guess himself, he led his horse into the river. The packhorse went next, followed by Taisin and her horse, and finally Kaede stepped into the water, leading Maila.

At first, it was just cold. Kaede shivered when the water rose above her boots and began to seep through the fabric of her trousers, but she was not prepared for the icy wash of it when she was chest-deep in the river. They were barely twenty feet from the bank at that point, and there was more than three quarters of the way to go. She began to wonder if this had been a wise choice, but Con was already too far ahead to turn back. She gritted her teeth and plunged deeper into the Kell.

She quickly realized that though the river had appeared to be unobstructed here, the boulders were merely under-water, and the river itself was deeper than it seemed. The closer she swam toward the center of the Kell, the colder it became and the swifter it flowed. Her knee smashed into a submerged boulder and she cried out at the impact. River water gushed into her mouth, nearly choking her. She felt like she was struggling in the embrace of a slippery, suffo-cating beast, and for a moment it pulled her down below. When she fought her way back to the surface, her eyes stung and everything was askew. She saw the trees on the far bank at a strange angle; she saw the gray sky lurching above; she saw Maila battling against the current. Kaede lunged toward her horse, grabbing onto the stirrups beneath the water and kicking back with her legs.

This was not like swimming in the ocean by Seatown. The water there would rise up and buoy her before the waves crested over her head. She knew how to float on those waves, how to close her eyes and pinch her nose shut when the wave came toward her. She knew that those waves would push her inexorably toward the beach, and she and her brothers used to laughingly skim along their crests until they were spit out on the sand. But here the river was pulling her downstream, and she was trying desperately to elude its powerful grip. Ahead of her she saw Con approaching the opposite bank, and Taisin was almost through the wide, fast center. Kaede kept her eyes on them, and she had just crossed the halfway point when Taisin's head went underneath and did not come up again.

It happened so swiftly—as if she had simply been swallowed. Kaede felt as though she had been punched in the gut.

"Taisin!" she screamed, and freezing water went down her throat. She spit out, coughing, floundering, the entire world heaving with the rush of the river.

Kaede sucked in as much air as she could and dived down after her. The water was clear, but there was very little light beneath the surface; all she could see of Taisin was a murky fluttering ahead of her, as if someone were spinning, struggling to escape a trap. She kicked forward, her lungs beginning to burn, and miraculously, she found Taisin's hand. She gripped her fingers as firmly as she could and lunged up toward the light. When she broke through she gasped, desperate for air, and yanked again at Taisin.

She bobbed up to the surface, limp, her body still pulled downstream, her face pale and her eyes closed.

Con had already climbed out of the river, and two of the horses stood shivering on the bank, but now he saw Kaede and Taisin struggling. He pulled out another rope, tying one end to his horse's saddle and then wrapping it around his waist before he began wading back into the water. Kaede tried to sling Taisin's arm around her, but the river was too strong. All she could do was drag her while keeping Taisin's head above water. When Con was waist-deep in the river he threw the rope in Kaede's direction. At first it missed them entirely, and Kaede just stubbornly pushed on toward the bank. She no longer felt the cold; it was as if all the blood in her body had turned to ice. Now there was only one thing to do: overcome the river, and she had no intention of giving up.

The second time Con threw the rope Kaede caught it, rough and wet, in her right hand. She struggled to wrap it around Taisin's waist, and several desperate minutes later, after they had been dragged another twenty feet downstream, she succeeded, and Con began to pull them onto the bank. When her feet touched the riverbed again, Kaede put her arms around Taisin's motionless body and picked her up, the weight of her partially supported by the water, and carried her until Con met her and helped lay Taisin down on the riverbank. They pushed at Taisin's chest, hard, until water bubbled out of her mouth and her eyes opened. She coughed, rolling over, and Kaede helped her up onto her hands and knees, her body convulsing as she spit the water out of her lungs. Taisin began to shake with cold, and Kaede said to Con, "We need to build a fire."

He pulled a mostly dry bedroll out from within the gear packed onto his horse and tossed it to Kaede. "I'll find firewood," he said. "You need to get her out of those wet clothes." He had stripped off his own shirt and was pulling on another, drier one, but he did not bother to change out of his wet trousers before heading off into the trees.

Kaede began to unbutton Taisin's tunic, pulling the heavy, wet cloth away from her chilled skin. Goose bumps rose on Taisin's shoulders when she felt the air, and she shivered more violently. Kaede pulled the blanket toward them and draped it over Taisin, who attempted to unlace her boots with numb fingers. "Just sit there," Kaede ordered, throwing the wet tunic aside. "I'll do that." She listened to Taisin's chattering teeth as she worked the wet laces, wanting to curse at the knots Taisin had tied. But at last she had them undone and pulled the soaked leather off, and as she reached for the clasps that fastened Taisin's trousers, Taisin put her hands on Kaede's to stop her.

"Thank you," Taisin said. Her lips were bluish-purple, her fingers like icicles.

All of a sudden, Kaede realized she was she was staring at Taisin, stripped to the waist, the medallion like a black eye hanging around her neck. Her face was white as snow but for rough red spots burning on her cheeks, and Kaede felt herself flush in response.

They heard Con returning, his footsteps seeming inordinately loud. Taisin pulled the blanket around her bare shoulders, covering herself, and Kaede backed away, sitting on her heels. "You don't have to thank me," she said awkwardly. She looked away; she looked at the river that had almost taken Taisin away from them. From her.

It was deceptively beautiful, for being such a monstrous thing.

They staked out the horses close to the fire, where Taisin sat huddled in the blanket. Kaede hung the kettle over the flames, and before night fell she had brewed tea for them all to sip, crouching close to the blaze.

"Everything's going to be wet for days unless we stay here tomorrow," Con said. "We'll have to lay everything out on the riverbank and hope they dry."

"Is it safe to stay here?" Kaede asked. "What was it like in the Wood?" She glanced at the trees nearby; the low light turned all colors into shadows upon shadows.

"It looked no different than the Wood south of the river. It might be a good idea to stay here and scout around a bit—see if there is a trail. We can leave our things here to dry while we explore this bank."

"Tonight, at least, all we have to do is eat and sleep," Kaede said. "That was not an easy crossing." She put down her cup and went to retrieve supplies for supper. But just at the edge of the camp she saw something that made her halt. There was a horse and rider, nearly obscured by the twilight. And then she saw another beside him. "Taisin," Kaede said in a low voice. "Con. Look."

Taisin and Con scrambled to their feet. Con's sword rang as he pulled it out of its scabbard.

More riders emerged out of the dusk, ghostlike, until they had surrounded the camp. As they came closer they seemed to take on something of a glow. They were tall and pale, with white clothing and eerie, sparkling eyes. Some of them wore swords on their belts; others had quivers of arrows strapped to their backs. There were men and women both, but they all shared the same otherworldly beauty: hard and cold and perfect.

One of the riders pushed his horse a few steps closer to the three humans. He asked in a peculiar accent: "Who are you, and why have you crossed over into our lands?"

PART IV

Some seek to act upon the world,
But success will not follow.
The world is inviolable:
It has no beginning and no end.
Those who seek to change it will be changed;
Those who grasp onto stones will find water.

—*Book of Changes*

Chapter XXVII

aede couldn't tear her eyes away from the riders. They were the most foreign-looking people she had ever seen, and she didn't feel fear so much as curiosity and a rising excitement. Were these the Xi at last?

In answer to their question, Con stepped forward, squaring his shoulders. "I am Con Isae Tan, prince of the Kingdom. Are you representatives of the Xi?"

The rider who had spoken inclined his head. "We are. Why are you here?"

"I have come at the invitation of your queen. Will you allow me to show you the invitation?"

"Show us, then."

Con went to his saddlebags to retrieve the invitation, still ensconced in its intricately carved box. He handed it to the rider, who opened it and unrolled the scroll. "This is an invitation for King Cai, not you."

"I am his only son," Con said. "He has sent me in his stead."

The rider gazed at him, expressionless, and Con felt perspiration rising on his forehead. The man's blue eyes were so penetrating that Con had difficulty maintaining his composure. Finally the rider said, "Come closer, princeling."

Con moved toward him, and to his surprise, the rider dismounted. Con halted, unsure of what to do, and the rider walked slowly around him, examining him as if he were a new dog, acquired for a particular purpose. Con had the disconcerting feeling that the man might pry open his mouth and examine his teeth, but then the rider only asked, "Who are your companions?"

Con let out his breath in relief. He had apparently passed some kind of test. "They are representatives from the Council of Sages."

"The Council of Sages," he said. "I have not heard of them in...many of your generations."

All the riders' eyes flickered to Taisin and Kaede, and Kaede felt as though she had just been buffeted by a strong wind. She stepped back, startled by the force of their gaze. Their leader came to look at her, circling her as he had done to Con. His eyes narrowed on her as if he saw something odd, and for a long moment they locked on hers. She stared back, fascinated—she had never seen eyes of such deep blue—and just as she began to wonder why he was so interested in her, he turned away and moved on to Taisin.

Taisin had watched with growing anxiety as he examined Con and Kaede as if they were fantastical creatures. When he approached her, she felt his curiosity ripple through the meridians between them, and then it sharpened, his eyes focusing on her. He came closer and extended a hand until his fingertips nearly touched her chest. She felt the medallion, hidden beneath her tunic, suddenly burning against her skin. "What do you have there?" he asked.

Wordlessly, her skin buzzing where the medallion radiated heat, she pulled the chain over her head and held it out to him. In his hand, the stone took on a dull light as if it were awakening at his touch. He gazed at it, and she saw him clench his jaw just slightly. "This is not yours to keep," he said. "But you shall wear it until our queen tells you otherwise." He placed it over her head so quickly she barely had time to notice how close he was—a glimpse of the paleness of his throat—and then he moved away and the chain was warm around her neck again.

Behind him several of the riders dismounted and moved toward their belongings as if to take them. "What are you doing?" Con asked, startled.

The man turned toward him and said, "You and your companions will come with us."

"Where?" Con demanded.

"We will take you to your meeting with our queen."

"Right now? It is nearly full night."

The man gave him a tiny smile. "Your meeting is scheduled for Midsummer, and that is scarcely one week from now. We've no time to waste."

"Wait," Taisin said.

The leader turned. "Yes?"

"Who are you?"

He did not answer at first, and even looked back at the

other riders as though they were sharing a secret. At last he said, "We are the Fairy Hunt. You may call me the Huntsman."

⁓

They set off as soon as the horses were saddled, with the Huntsman riding in the lead. Though the Wood was pitch-black all around them, the riders of the Fairy Hunt stood out against the dark. Kaede thought that it wasn't exactly as if they glowed, but rather there was a lightness about them. Their skin was almost translucent, and she could swear she saw the texture of their muscles moving beneath it. She wondered if their blood was red like hers, or if it was some other queer color. Did it flow as thickly as mercury, or was it thin as water? She had never felt so different from someone in her life.

The Xi stopped only to allow their human charges to relieve themselves, and they would have continued without further pause until Con insisted that they be allowed to rest their horses and to eat. Dawn was breaking by then, and the Wood was slowly coming into light. Kaede was exhausted and her stomach growled, and she felt almost too tired and light-headed to find her way from her horse to their supplies. The Hunt had dismounted, too, and the riders were ranged around the three of them in a loose ring, as if to prevent them from running away. Kaede did her best to ignore them as she pulled out their food. They were down to eating biscuits, now, dried hard and nearly tasteless. She took one and handed the tin to Con and Taisin, who looked as tired as she felt. "Tea," Kaede muttered to them. "I'll start the fire."

The Xi watched her curiously as she began to gather wood, but as she approached the edge of their ring, one of them stopped her and asked, "Where are you going?"

"I need to find more wood to build a fire," she said, raising her eyes to the slender man's blue ones. She shivered.

The rider looked behind her and said something to one of the others in a language she did not understand, then turned back to Kaede. "Fire is all you need?" he said, his eyebrows raised as if he were amused. He opened his hand and there, in his palm, a flame danced for her.

She backed away. "I—I want to boil water."

He cocked his head at her. He was younger than the one who led them, she noticed. His face was smooth as a baby's; his hair like white silk capped over his shapely head. His full, pale pink lips curved upward in a smile, and she felt distinctly uncomfortable. He extended his arm, holding out the burning golden flame, and went toward the small pile of wood she had left on the forest floor, and set the pile alight.

Swallowing, Kaede set up the iron tripod and hung the kettle over the fire. It was as hot as any natural fire, but it did not eat away at the wood; instead, it licked at the fallen branches, almost caressing them. But it still caused the water to boil—perhaps more quickly, even— and the tea tasted no different than it had the day before. Con, Taisin, and Kaede squatted on the ground around the fire, for it was good to feel its warmth, and Kaede tried to soften her biscuit in the tea before she ate the rest of it.

Some of the Xi came a bit closer to observe them, but most seemed to rapidly lose interest in their activities and began to pace back and forth, eager to move on. The young one who had started the fire came close enough to lean over Kaede's shoulder and look at the biscuit in her hand. He asked, "What is that called?"

There was a disconcerting gleam in his eye, as if he wanted to have a bite of her rather than the biscuit. Before she could answer, the Huntsman called to him in a sharp tone of voice, and the young one looked briefly petulant before he withdrew, going back to the edge of the circle of riders.

When they finished eating, they packed their cups and kettle back into their saddlebags, and the Huntsman snuffed out the fire. He passed his hands over the flames once, and then the woodpile was bare and cold, not burned at all. Kaede wondered if it would even be warm if she touched it. "It is time to leave," he said, and though his voice was barely louder than a whisper, all of the Hunt turned in unison to their horses, prepared to go.

They rode steadily that day, stopping only when Con or Kaede or Taisin requested it. The Xi did not seem to eat; nor did their horses seem to need any rest. Kaede felt Maila tire as the day progressed, but she continued on as if compelled. The trees around them began to change as they left the river behind. Oak trees gradually gave way to evergreens. The evergreens grew taller and taller. By late afternoon, they were riding through a forest of trees with trunks wider than the length of the wagon they had left behind in Jilin. The branches drooped down at them, heavy with soft, dark green needles. The colors here were richer than they had been south of the river, where half the trees had turned brown from lack of sunlight. The sky was still gray here, but there was something different about the quality of the air. It was warmer, for one thing, almost as warm as it should be at midsummer. But there was something else, too, and it visibly affected the members of the Fairy Hunt. The farther they rode from the Kell, the more the Xi seemed to shine. They were coming home.

⤳

At nightfall, worn to the bone and feeling as though she might fall asleep in the saddle, Kaede was relieved when the Huntsman stopped and told them they could set up camp. He had chosen a clearing near a brook that ran over a rocky streambed, and when Kaede knelt by its side to refill her water skin, the liquid was shockingly cold on her hands. The icy taste of it made her throat momentarily numb. She came fully awake and saw Con and Taisin, too, reeling from the water's chill.

"We should drink *that* in the morning," Con said, and Kaede laughed. Even Taisin, who was so tired she felt like her body had been dragged across that rocky streambed, couldn't help but smile. The three of them looked at one another, and for a moment they felt entirely human again. Weary, hungry, and cold, but human. Kaede felt her muscles begin to relax. For all the strangeness of their escort, she had Con and Taisin with her, and they would do all right.

They slept soundly that night, curled up in their blankets near the Xi's magical fire, the ghostly riders spread around them, again, in a ring. When she woke the next morning, Kaede lay there in silence for a while, blinking her eyes at the early light. Some of the riders were gone. Those who remained did not look like they had slept at all, but nor did they look tired. One of them saw that Kaede had awoken, and he nodded to her almost pleasantly—as if this were an entirely normal thing, for him to be guarding a group of sleeping, worn-out humans in the middle of the Great Wood. And she realized that yes, that was what they were doing—these Xi were *guarding* them. She and Taisin and Con were not prisoners. They were being protected.

The idea startled her. She rolled over onto her back, looking up at the sky cupped by the circle of trees around their camp. She thought there was something wrong with her eyes at first, and she blinked several times, but it was still there: On the edges of the bowl of sky, there was the faintest trace of blue.

Chapter XXVIII

hey traveled for a week in the company of the Fairy Hunt. Kaede often watched the riders surreptitiously, marveling at the grace of their movements. They were like dancers, sinuous and light on their feet, yet there was always something about them that marked them as plainly inhuman. There was a curious play of light and shadow in their faces that made it difficult to understand their expressions. And when one of them looked at her, Kaede found it almost impossible to look away. It was disturbing.

One evening the Huntsman came and sat with them, and at first Taisin, Con, and Kaede simply stared at him, for none of the riders ever joined them at the fire. Finally Kaede, who had just finished eating her tasteless biscuit, blurted out, "Do you ever eat?" Immediately she colored, and Con and Taisin tensed.

But the Huntsman only raised his eyebrows, and Kaede thought she recognized his expression. He was amused. "We eat," he said. "But not while we are on duty."

"Duty?" she repeated, her mouth dry.

"We eat when you sleep," he explained.

"Oh."

They all sat in silence for several more minutes, and then the Huntsman stood and walked away. Con, Taisin, and Kaede looked at one another in confusion.

"Why did you say that?" Con whispered.

"I don't know," Kaede whispered back. "Aren't you curious?"

He gave her an exasperated look, and then Taisin reached out and put a hand on Kaede's arm. Her skin tingled at Taisin's touch. The Huntsman was returning, and he had something in his hand.

He held it out to them with something of a flourish. "Would you like to try some of our food?" he asked. Lying on an unfolded cloth was a square of something that was yellowish-white in color. To Kaede, it looked like a white bean cake, but there was something different about its texture.

"What is it?" Kaede asked. Taisin's hand fell away, leaving a palpable sense of absence behind.

"Cheese," he answered. With a bone-handled knife, he sliced off a small piece and offered it to her.

It tasted nothing like what she expected. It was savory rather than bland; it was chewy rather than soft. The sharp flavor lingered on her tongue after she swallowed it. She wasn't sure if she liked it or not, but she tried to smile at the Huntsman and said, "Thank you."

The corners of his mouth twitched.

As they traveled north, the trees became taller, greener, stronger. And the quality of the light changed. It was as though all those layers of cloud were gradually being peeled away until, at last, on the sixth day they rode with the Xi, they saw the sun.

It had been so long since Kaede had felt its warmth that its first touch brought tears to her eyes; she wanted to strip off all her clothes and stand naked in the light. Taisin had forgotten the way it infused every leaf with vibrant color, causing the veins to stand out in sharp relief against the tender green. And Con could not remember if he had ever seen a sky so blue: robin's egg blue, smooth as glossy porcelain, untouched by clouds.

That same day, they came to a long row of trees planted on either side of the path. In the morning, the path had been only dirt covered in fallen pine needles, but by midmorning, the pine needles were swept away, and by noon the horses stepped onto pavement. It was not like the pavement used in any human city; this was white stone, perfectly cut in long rectangles. At intervals, diamonds of black stone were inlaid in the road, polished until they sparkled in the sunlight. The road became as broad as the largest square in Cathair, with elegant, gold-leafed trees marching down the center. In the distance the Xi city, Taninli, glimmered.

When at last they saw the crystal gates ahead of them, the Huntsman pulled his horse to a halt and turned back to look at his human charges. "We will ride directly to the palace," he told them. "Some of our people may turn out to look at you, but do not be alarmed."

Kaede glanced at Taisin, who seemed slightly ill. As the Huntsman rode ahead, Kaede pushed her horse toward Taisin's and asked, "Are you all right?"

"I'm fine," she said, but she sounded hesitant. Taisin had felt the city coming as early as two days ago; it was an unmistakable knot of energies coalescing together all at once. The closer they came, the more light-headed she felt, and she only hoped that she would be able to adjust to it quickly. So far, though, it was making her feel queasy.

Kaede wasn't affected the same way that Taisin was, but she, too, felt a bit out of sorts as they rode through the gates. The world seemed askew somehow; the shadows fell in the wrong places here, or perhaps her eyes simply weren't accustomed to the angles in the buildings and streets. And the buildings themselves were so strange and exotic. The stone was too smooth to be carved from a mountain, the glass too clear to come from an ordinary forge. The walls were perfectly straight or miraculously curved. Giant windows, cut into facets that held the light like prisms, climbed up the tallest towers. And every structure seemed to fit into the one beside it like a puzzle piece; the only spaces must have been deliberately left open.

In those spaces, the Xi waited and watched. They peered out from balconies, or from beneath archways between houses, or from meticulously landscaped parks that opened onto the white stone boulevard. At first Kaede gazed back at them. In the sunlight, their skin was no longer deathly pale; it was like new-fallen snow, bright and pristine. Their hair, she realized, was a thousand different shades between white and silver; their eyes were sharp, glowing jewels. The pressure of so many eyes on her made her a bit breathless, and after several minutes, she had to look down at her hands, fingers tightly gripping her reins, so that she no longer saw them.

That was when she realized that all the sounds she normally associated with a city—the noise of wagon wheels and beggars and merchants hawking their wares—were absent here. There was only the rise and fall of whispering in the language of the Xi, a kind of hypnotic music. The more she listened to it, the more it made her feel disconnected from her body. But gradually the boulevard climbed out of the heart of the city, and as they left the crowds behind, the whispering faded. At last Kaede allowed herself to look up again, and she saw that they were nearing the glittering crest of Taninli, and before them was the palace of the Fairy Queen.

When they reached the palace gates, the sun hung straight overhead, beaming down hot on their heads. They rode into a grand, circular courtyard, over paving stones set with a mosaic of gold and green in a pattern of swirls. Their horses, lulled into a half doze by the very air around them, were led away by silent-footed Xi clad in tunics the color of fallen autumn leaves. The Huntsman led them inside the palace through doors as tall as a three-story building, and inside it was cool and comfortable beneath ceilings so high Kaede was sure she saw birds flying above her. The Huntsman took them down wide, empty halls filled with light, and Kaede wondered where everyone was. Was the

Huntsman taking care to avoid the inhabitants of the palace, or were the inhabitants avoiding them? A bead of sweat trickled down her forehead. It was warm as midsummer, and she realized with a jolt that it *was* midsummer. Tonight was Midsummer's Eve, and tomorrow would be her eighteenth birthday.

They arrived at a set of smaller doors made of a fine-grained white wood, and the Huntsman turned the round crystal handles and said, "You will be very comfortable here."

Inside there was an apartment of many rooms furnished with chairs carved out of polished tree trunks, with cushions of rose and gold and green silk. The floor was covered in soft carpets, and at the far end of the room tall glass doors opened onto a broad balcony. Sunlight streamed through the windows, filling the room with a lovely midday glow. Con turned to the Huntsman and asked, "When will we see the Fairy Queen?"

"Tomorrow. Tonight is Midsummer's Eve, and we have other matters to attend to." He paused in the doorway and added, "It would be best if you remain here tonight."

"Why?" Con asked.

"It is a night of great celebration for my people. It would be unfortunate if anything were to befall you on the night before your audience with my queen." He looked at each of them to make his point clear. "I ask you to stay here." And then he left them alone, closing the door behind him. Though he had phrased his words as a request, Kaede had a feeling that they would not be able to open that door until he let them out.

Chapter XXIX

aede chose a round room with walls lined with windows. The vista of the city below was astounding—hill upon hill of buildings formed out of the same white stone that built this palace, every window sparkling. Far below she saw the Wood, a sea of trees all around Taninli. Though it was bright as midday inside, she lay down on the round bed in the middle of the round room, and as soon as her head fell upon the silken pillow, she was asleep.

Con took a square room with a balcony running along two entire walls. He opened the doors, letting the filmy white curtains flutter out into the afternoon. The breezes smelled of jasmine. He stood outside for some time, gazing down at the city, and his eyes were dazzled. The longer he looked, the more his mind became filled with a delicious fog. All the pain of the journey could be erased if he just gave in to this extraordinary place. But he felt a persistent, nagging worry in the back of his mind, and as he leaned forward into the sunlight, he closed his eyes. He saw his red-veined eyelids, the colors of countless ordinary human campfires that had warmed his hands night after night. He remembered Tali, and Pol, and Shae, who had looked at him out of pain-filled brown eyes in Mona's cottage. He had promised her he would come back for her. The worry turned to impatient determination; his hands clenched into fists. He turned his back on the glamour of the city and went back inside, where he began to pace.

Taisin's room was filled with trees; they seemed to grow out of the very floor, with smooth, polished bark the color of rust. Glossy leaves, amber on one side and bright green on the other, shaded her bed from the sun that poured in through windows in the ceiling. Tall glass doors opened onto a little round balcony, and when she stepped outside she looked out over a lush, wild garden. In the midst of all the sculptured buildings, the sight of trees and stones and running water was surprising, but as she looked closer, she could see that even this garden had been cultivated with the utmost care. She yawned, and raising a hand to her mouth she went back into the room, stretching. The bed was inviting. After weeks of sleeping on the ground, the feather bed beneath her back was like clouds. She sank into it and slept so soundly that for the first time in weeks, she did not dream of the fortress.

ॐ

Kaede awoke after dark, and when she opened her eyes there were lights dancing on the ceiling, reflected from the city below. She pushed herself up, feeling groggy, and went to the closest window. Down below, Taninli was ablaze with fairy lights: thousands upon thousands of them, winking like fireflies in a summer evening.

She left her room, walking down the short, curved corridor that led to the sitting room, and found Con at a table that had been laid with enough food for twenty. He looked up at her with glazed eyes. "Welcome," he said in a thick voice, "to our banquet."

She sat down across from him, gaping at the spread before her. She could not identify most of what she saw. There was a silver tureen of some kind of fragrant soup; plates piled high with colorful fruits; breads that were round and baked with golden-brown crusts. "What is this?" she asked, picking up an oblong fruit, its bright pink skin shading into orange.

"I don't know, but I recommend it," Con said, and handed her a wooden-handled knife with a blade made of thin, strong stone.

She tested the edge with her finger; it was sharp. When she peeled the skin of the fruit she held in her hand, the flesh that emerged was soft, juicy, and golden. She bit into it and the sweetness startled her; it was like liquid sugar with a tart, lingering tang. She discovered that there were several different kinds of cheese, and she especially liked the soft white one that crumbled in her fingers. She ate until her stomach was full, and then Con poured something from a decanter shaped like a bird into the crystal goblet at her elbow. "I have never tasted anything like this," he said.

She looked at him dubiously. "What is it?"

"I think it's wine."

It smelled like newly budding roses. The fragrance itself was intoxicating enough, and she put it down and looked at Con. "Is there water?" she asked.

He laughed at her, and she realized that he had drunk the wine—perhaps he had drunk too much of it. He had shaved off the beard he had grown during their journey, and it made him look younger and more vulnerable. "There," he said, pointing to a crystal pitcher down the table. "I think that is water."

She stood up to fetch it as Taisin came in from the balcony. The sound of celebration followed her through the open doors—music and voices, all mingled together in a joyous crescendo. "It's midnight," Taisin said, joining them at the table. She picked up a chunk of bread, but like Kaede, she avoided the wine.

Kaede poured water into two goblets, handing one to Taisin. "How do you know?"

"The celebration," Taisin said, gesturing toward the balcony. "It's turned a corner. It must be Midsummer Day now."

Kaede took her goblet of water out to the balcony. Below, among the winking fairy lights, she thought she could see the Xi themselves flooding through the streets. She rubbed her eyes, not sure if they were playing tricks on her. Everything here—Taninli, the palace, the food they ate—seemed obscured by a thin but persistent fog. It was as though some of her senses had been dulled, but others had been sharpened. She was more conscious than ever of the rhythm of the blood in her veins, but she felt oddly disengaged from her breath. Every now and then snatches of music floated up to her, played on instruments she had never heard before. It was so beautiful that it made Kaede's heart ache. She longed to be a part of it, to dance among the Xi, and she realized she was gripping the balustrade with white fingers, her goblet tipping precariously until water splashed down on the white stone. She righted it, stepping back, and blinked, pressing her fingers to her temples.

The door behind her opened with a scrape. It was an unexpectedly ordinary sound for Taninli. She looked over her shoulder and saw Taisin coming to join her. "Happy birthday," Taisin said.

"Thank you." Kaede had not expected Taisin to remember, and she felt inordinately pleased about it.

Taisin stood beside her, looking down at the sea of celebrants. The lights glowed on her skin, making her seem gilded. Kaede could not stop staring at her, and she wondered if even the water in those pitchers was somehow thickened with magic, for nothing seemed usual tonight. The Huntsman might have warned them to stay in these rooms, but he could not prevent the air from carrying the scent of their celebrations up to them, a potent, alluring perfume. Taisin turned to look at her, and her lips parted.

Kaede straightened, taking one step forward, and Taisin seemed to lean toward her just enough—and Kaede saw, then, that what she had hoped for could come true. If she wished it, if she reached out and touched her, Taisin would come to her easily; she only wanted a bit of suggestion. The space between them hummed. It was the most natural thing in the world to slide her finger beneath the strand of hair that fell across Taisin's eyes and tuck it behind her ear. Heat suffused Taisin's cheeks, and Kaede drew her closer, her breath a soft tickle across Taisin's lips, and kissed her.

Everything focused.

Taisin felt every place their bodies touched, and she felt every place they did not. Kaede slid her hands down Taisin's back. Taisin felt the blood singing in her veins; all of her was surging up to meet Kaede, who pressed her closer. They moved, clumsy with desire, and one of them bumped against the crystal goblet, knocking it off the balustrade to shatter, loudly, at their feet.

They broke apart, staring dazedly at the fragments of crystal. The lights below were sharp as diamonds.

Taisin recovered first. "I'll get a cloth," she said, her voice husky, and departed abruptly.

Kaede squatted down and picked up the stem, taking care to not cut herself on the jagged edge. Her breath was ragged in her throat; her limbs felt weak, as though she had just climbed a thousand steps; her hand holding the broken stem shook. A shadow fell over her, and when she looked up, it was not Taisin but Con who handed her a cloth.

"What happened? Taisin told me you needed this, and then ran off."

Below them they heard the roar of the crowd in celebration. Her heart was pounding as loudly as the crowd. "I dropped—I dropped the goblet," she muttered. She took the cloth from him and began to sweep up the broken shards. They glinted in the light spilling out from the sitting room.

"Be careful. You'll cut yourself."

"I'll be fine," she said, but she felt the beginnings of panic whirling in her stomach—*why had Taisin left?*—and she swept up a piece of glass that nicked her thumb. A small drop of blood welled up through her skin. She pressed the white cloth to it, the red blooming like a rose, and her finger smarted from the cut.

 ⌒

Taisin shut herself in her room and sat on the edge of her bed, and all she could think of was how much she wanted to go back to Kaede. Her whole body quivered from wanting it.

Nothing had prepared her for this. None of her books, none of her teachers had said a single thing about what to do with this wild energy pouring through her. She had no idea how to deal with it. She took a deep, trembling breath, trying to moderate the pulsing of her blood. She could still taste Kaede's lips. She pressed her hands to her eyes, but all she could see was Kaede's face.

She curled up on the bed, clutching a pillow to her chest, and gradually the beating of her heart slowed. She counted her breaths, hoping that it would calm her down. One, ten, one hundred breaths. Again and again, until she could push away the lingering sensation of Kaede's hands on her back.

But what if she couldn't fight this anymore? Had she been a fool to even try?

She stubbornly tried to recall every detail of that first vision she had when she was still at the Academy. The beach, the boat, Kaede's face when she pushed away from the shore. The feeling that the most precious thing in her world was leaving her, and it might never return.

Sister Ailan had told her that her vision was a vision of the truth. But what was the truth? Was it that Kaede would leave her behind? Or was it that she loved her?

She heard the whistle of the wind in her ear, singing across the ice. She could no longer feel the softness of the bed beneath her. Cold seeped through her clothing, into her skin, until she felt the icy floor of the fortress beneath her feet.

Now that she had seen the way that glass could be manipulated in Taninli, she knew that the ice was only a cold imitation. She stood in the ice fortress, her fingers curled into fists, and gazed out the window—yes, this was real glass, hard and unyielding—at the landscape before her. The walls of the fortress descended like a mountainside to the ice fields below. In the distance the ocean was azure blue beneath the ice floes, reflecting the great arc of the sky above. Behind her there was motion: the fluttering of wings, the darting shape of another creature. The sprite. It had a message for her, and when she had heard it she reached out and plucked the fairy from the air, pinning its wings back. She watched the sprite's face stretch out in fear, and she whispered to it, soothing it, stroking its hair. An imperfect thing, this one.

But it would be a pity to blame the messenger.

She let it go, feeling its wings brush against her fingers before it bobbed away. She felt its fear, and it both saddened and exhilarated her. She turned back to the frozen vistas outside the window. Soon, she thought, and it sent a thrill through her. Soon her visitors would arrive.

Taisin sensed the woman's anticipation with a clarity she had never experienced before. Beneath that, she felt the heady rush of the woman's power, as if her veins ran with fire. It filled her body, lying on that soft bed in the Fairy Queen's palace, the same way Kaede had filled all of her senses when they kissed.

Chapter XXX

aede did not know what to do. She went to Taisin's room and stood outside the door, but she could not bring herself to knock. She could barely believe what had just happened—it was all so surreal, this place with its impossibly smooth walls and intoxicating lights. Perhaps they hadn't really kissed at all; perhaps it was all just an illusion. But she could still feel Taisin's mouth against hers, the bones of her spine beneath her fingers. Kaede's entire body burned at the memory. But Taisin had fled from her. Kaede remembered their whispered conversation in the middle of the night after leaving Mona's cottage. Taisin was promised elsewhere. What had made Kaede think Taisin had changed her mind? Kaede's heart sank. She turned away from the closed door and went back to her own room.

She spent a restless night in bed, dreaming of walking down the corridor between her room and Taisin's. Each time she knocked on the door, and each time she woke up just before it opened, every muscle tense.

When dawn came, she dressed and went into the sitting room. No one was there, but the table was already laden with fresh fruit and warm bread. There was even a strange object that she eventually recognized as a teapot, and when she lifted the hinged lid, a rich aroma was released. She poured a small amount into one of the delicate porcelain cups and sipped it cautiously. It had an unusual, roasted flavor that she immediately liked.

She finished two cups of it before Taisin appeared. Though she made no sound, Kaede noticed her immediately, standing hesitantly in the doorway. When their eyes met, Taisin blushed, and the sight of her flaming cheeks gave Kaede some courage. She would have gone to her at once, but then Con brushed past Taisin, entering the room with a yawn.

"Are you sure we're not all dreaming?" Con said in a voice still laced with sleep. He picked up an orange fruit and began to peel it, revealing a light pink interior. He pulled off a segment and sighed with pleasure. "This is much better than camping."

Kaede choked on a laugh, and he smiled at her. She wondered if he had said that on purpose, for she felt the tension in the room dissipate—at least a little.

Taisin sat down and took a piece of bread, stealing a glance at Kaede as she said, "I have to agree with you." Kaede caught the end of her look, and all of her came alive with awareness. She thought: Maybe she has changed her mind after all.

❧

That morning, they each made use of the bathing chamber adjacent to the sitting room; they each dressed in the cleanest of their clothes; and then there was nothing to do but pace the stone floor and wait for the Huntsman to arrive.

After so many weeks on the road, the last hour was the hardest to bear. Kaede surreptitiously watched Taisin, who had braided her wet hair and fixed it with a black comb on her head. Her neck was exposed, scrubbed clean and pink, and every time Kaede glanced at her, the pink crept a little farther up until Taisin turned away and went, trembling, to stand by the window, her back to the room. Kaede sat in a chair and looked down at her hands; she could still feel the small of Taisin's back beneath them. Her heart fluttered in her throat. She didn't know how long she could stand this queer pretense that nothing had happened between them. But when she thought of what she might say to Taisin, the words would not come. Her mouth was dry; her palms were clammy. It was like an illness, she thought, or an enchantment: these feelings that cloaked everything in a fog of desire. Here she was in the Fairy Queen's palace at last, after a journey that had killed two men who did not deserve to die; after her hands had been bloodied more than once; and she could barely even remember why she was here. All she wanted was to kiss Taisin again.

Con, who normally would have been sensitive to the strained silence that gripped Kaede and Taisin, was consumed by his own anxieties. Before leaving Cathair, he had discussed the Kingdom's position on the Borderlands Treaty with his father and Lord Raiden, but now that he was here in Taninli, he realized that all the advice they had given him was worthless. King Cai and Lord Raiden knew every detail of the political machinations that were about to erupt in civil war in the southern provinces, but they had no idea what was going on in the Wood. He wondered if they even truly believed that the Fairy Queen existed. She was a figure lost to the mists of history, and though the Council of Sages took her invitation seriously, Con knew that his father only submitted to the Council because of tradition. His father was a man of action; he did his best to ignore the unseen world that the sages worked in. If the Council ever made a demand on him that challenged his power, Con was sure that his father would deny it.

King Cai had told him to play the diplomat; to flatter the Queen yet promise nothing. Con knew that he would not be able to do this. He had seen too much on the way to Taninli to doubt the significance of the Queen's invitation. This was no mere social call, and he was almost sick from nerves. He had visited governors of distant provinces before; he had attended state banquets and done his best to charm those his father asked him to charm. But he was certain that those experiences had been nothing compared to this. He suspected that the Queen had more in mind than a simple renewal of that ancient treaty, and he did not know if he had the power to give it to her—or the judgment to decide if he could.

When the Huntsman came to the door at last, Con sprang up, agitation vying with relief on his face. "Finally," he said. "It's been a long morning."

The Huntsman gave him a sympathetic look. "Shall we go?"

He led them down long corridors of gray-veined marble, past banks of sunny windows, and through a rotunda in which a statue of a unicorn lifted its head toward the arched ceiling. At its feet a stone phoenix spread its wings. They passed Xi dressed in every shade between white and pale blue, who seemed to melt out of sight as soon as Kaede noticed them. The effect was disquieting; it made her wonder if the whole palace was just an extraordinary illusion.

The throne room was reached by climbing one last wide flight of stairs that culminated in grand redwood doors. They reminded Kaede of the doors to the Council chambers; they even had similar handles set in the very center. They opened into a long, broad hall; windows along one wall overlooked a garden sculpted into a perfect wilderness. At the far end of the room, a low dais supported a crystal throne cushioned in green silk. Seated there was the Fairy Queen. When she saw them enter, she leaned forward slightly, laying her right hand on the armrest.

It was a long walk to the dais, and their footsteps echoed in the high-ceilinged room. The Huntsman reached the Queen first and bowed deeply before introducing the humans. He spoke in his own language, but Con recognized their names, and when the Queen's eyes flicked over him, he shivered. The Queen's face was glowing, ageless; her eyes were the color of gold. She was beautiful, but it was a fearsome kind of beauty, like the mirrored edge of a finely crafted blade.

Con swallowed; his mouth was so dry. He stepped forward and bowed to the Queen. "Your Majesty," he said formally, "I come as a representative of my father, King Cai Simin Tan. He regrets that he is personally unable to respond to your invitation."

The Queen spoke in his language: "Why have you come in his place?"

"Our kingdom is suffering through a difficult time, and my father could not be spared."

"Tell me about this difficulty," the Queen said. She studied him intently, and Con had to look away to avoid her eyes. He realized that there was no furniture in the entire room except for her throne; all visitors had to either stand or kneel before her. It was an old trick; his father employed the same strategy. The thought galvanized him. But he allowed himself to look slightly past the Queen as he spoke, so that he would not have to withstand the full force of her gaze.

"For the last several years, Your Majesty, our winters have been…extremely hard. Many of our provinces have experienced storms that have been extraordinarily fierce. Livestock have died; food stores have been destroyed unexpectedly. We have survived these winters, but each summer the harvests have been increasingly poor. This year, summer has not come. My people are starving. Several of the provinces are on the verge of insurrection. This is why my father could not be here." He paused, taking a deep breath. "And there have been other things. There have been sightings of strange creatures near the border of the Wood. Creatures that are not human. We have encountered them ourselves on our journey here."

"What have you seen?"

He told her about the reports his father had received about creatures, possibly fay, entering the Kingdom in the north. He told her about the creature in Ento, and the body that had been found outside of Jilin. The Queen's face remained impassive as he spoke, and when he finished she asked, "Is that all?"

Con bristled. She sounded as if she thought what he had told her was of no consequence. "No, that is not all, Your Majesty. We came here at your invitation, but along the way we lost two of our party. One—Tali, who was a guard to me since I was a boy—he was killed by whatever tortured spirits are haunting the Great Wood that separates your land from mine. And another guard, Pol, was mauled to death by wolves who attacked our entire party. A third, Shae—" Here his voice almost broke, but he continued on with a fresh burst of anger. "Shae was nearly killed as well, and we were forced to leave her behind to make sure we arrived here as you asked, because my people have heard nothing from your kind in generations, and to receive such an invitation during a time of catastrophe—it—" He broke off, trying to compose himself. He looked straight at the Queen. "It could not be a coincidence. We are here, Your Majesty. Why have you asked us to come?"

The Queen swept her eyes over him from head to toe; he felt the hairs on the back of his neck rise. Finally she said, "I am sorry to hear about your companions. And you are correct. My invitation to your king was not a coincidence. But the answer to your question is somewhat…involved." She settled back in her throne and turned her eyes to the long windows.

"Our ties with your people have been mostly severed,

but once, it was different. Once, our lands were more closely entwined. Once, our people mingled with each other. But it was not an entirely peaceful commingling. We live so many generations longer than your people do. Some things that we remember, you forget. We could not coexist without misunderstanding each other.

"So, in time, there was war. A long, bloody war. It destroyed countless numbers of my people as well as yours. At the end of it, the survivors on both sides drew up a treaty to prevent such destruction from ever happening again. Afterward, the remaining fay scattered. The Xi remained here in Taninli, but the lesser fay retreated to their own hollows and mountains and forests. And gradually, your people forgot about us. We both kept to our sides of the bargain. Even if there has been isolation, there has also been peace.

"All this happened before I was born. Few of my people were alive when the treaty was signed. And in the intervening years, some of my people have become curious about your kind. You live such short lives compared to ours; we wonder what makes them worth living."

The Queen looked at Con with a trace of regret on her face, and for the first time that day, the glamour she wore cracked. She did not look old in a human sense, but there were centuries in her, and there had been pain.

She continued: "One Xi woman lived near the border between our land and yours. She encountered a human man one summer, and she took him as a lover. She became pregnant. She was terrified, for she knew her halfling child might not be welcome in either of our lands. She came to

Taninli and begged for my mercy. I gave her shelter here while she labored, but she did not survive childbirth. The halfling did survive. It was a girl. I raised her as my own daughter."

The Queen's face hardened, and once again she gazed out the windows. "She was given everything, this girl—every delicacy, every bauble, every privilege I could give her—but she always wanted more. She was stubborn. She would never acknowledge that she was not truly Xi. She demanded to be named my heir, but it was impossible. The time has not yet come for me to name an heir, and when it does, I will not choose a halfling."

The words were spoken coldly, but it seemed as if the Queen were holding her emotions tightly in check. A blue vein in her right temple throbbed. Taisin began to tense up; she had a dreadful fear that she knew what the Queen was about to say.

"When she realized I would not change my mind—that she would never rule the fay as she desired—she left Taninli. It has been a dozen years since she walked out of this city's gates. In that time, I have sensed her power growing. I believe she is drinking up the energies of the fay and discarding them when they become too weak to benefit her. The ones who survive have come to me seeking help, but I can do nothing for them. She takes their lives; she becomes stronger with each fairy who dies."

Taisin felt sick. All the cages she had seen in her visions; the glimpses of the fay trapped within them—she knew now that they had been imprisoned there by this woman.

The Queen said, "I believe she has built a fortress for herself in the north."

Taisin's skin prickled. She could see that fortress of ice in her mind's eye as clearly as if she stood before it in the snow.

"The meridians of the world are tangled up there, forced into some kind of knot that she has created. She has gathered winter all around her; I can feel the cold from here. Her actions have altered the seasons elsewhere. I have tried to bring the seasons into alignment here in Taninli, but the chaos you describe in your kingdom—it can only be a symptom of what she has done."

The Queen leaned forward and looked at each of them in turn. "I have called you here because she must be stopped before she does more harm to this world. She has been playing with terrible powers, and soon she will destroy more than can be saved."

Con asked: "How can she be stopped?"

"She must die," the Queen said. "That is the only way the energies she has taken can be returned to the world." A tiny, grim smile twisted her lips. "And only a human can kill her."

The Queen's words rang in Con's ears, and he felt a chill spreading over his skin. "But if she is so powerful, how could any human succeed?" he asked. "Surely this is a task meant for one of your own."

"My people are peaceful," the Queen said curtly. "We cannot take the life of our own kind."

"But she is only half Xi—"

"She is one of us, even if she could never be Queen. That is the truth she has always refused to see. Our blood, just as much as yours, runs in her veins. And there is only one weapon that can kill one of the Xi."

"What weapon?" Con asked. "Why would we have such a weapon?"

"One of you already has this weapon. It is a simple one. You have brought it with you." The Fairy Queen turned her golden eyes to Kaede, who felt a shock run through herself. She remembered Fin handing the iron dagger to her, hilt first. *The Xi don't like iron*, Fin had told her.

A heavy certainty settled over her, and Kaede said to the Fairy Queen, "You would have us be murderers."

Taisin stepped forward. "I will do it," she said, her heart pounding. She refused to send Kaede to face this woman.

"No," Con objected. "Taisin—"

"You are the Council's girl, aren't you?" the Queen said, looking at Taisin.

She flushed. "How did you know?"

"Everything they know, and many things they have forgotten, I know." The Queen examined Taisin's determined face intently. "But you have seen things even I haven't seen."

"I have seen the fortress of ice," Taisin admitted. Kaede and Con swiveled to stare at her.

"You never said anything about that," Kaede said, stunned.

Taisin's face paled, and she couldn't meet Kaede's eyes. The things she had seen—the cages, the ice, the sea—should she have told Kaede and the others about them? The visions had been so strange; she hadn't understood them.

The Queen asked, "Have you seen *her*?"

Taisin twisted her hands together. She felt guilty and frightened. "Yes. I've seen her."

The Queen's eyes narrowed. "Do not let her deceive you."

"She is so strong," Taisin said.

"I will give you her name," the Queen said, "so that you may see her for who she truly is."

"Her name?" Taisin was confused. "But how—"

"I named her when she was born. Her name is Elowen."

As she said the name, Taisin felt something inside her shift—as if a bolt had been thrown back from a door, and now all she had to do was nudge it open.

"There is power in naming," the Queen said. "And now you have an advantage, however small, against her."

Con asked: "If we do not kill her—if Elowen remains alive—what will happen?"

"She is like a rising storm. She must be stopped soon." The Queen turned to Kaede again. "You have the weapon. You must do this."

Kaede's fingers curled into fists. All of her balked at the Queen's demand. "I am no assassin."

The Queen gave her a measuring look. "I am not seeking an assassin. I am seeking a hunter."

૮ᴏ

In their sitting room, Con paced back and forth in front of the balcony doors. The Fairy Queen had asked for their decision by end of the day, and Con felt trapped. If what she said was true—and Taisin seemed to believe her—then how could they refuse? Yet Con believed the Queen was asking them to undertake a suicide mission, though Kaede argued that he couldn't predict the outcome. As the hours passed, they talked in circles until Kaede abruptly asked Taisin, "Why haven't you told us about your visions?"

Startled, Taisin responded, "I didn't know what they meant. What use would it have been for me to tell you?"

Kaede looked hurt. "We might have helped you figure them out."

Taisin reddened, feeling chagrined. "I'm sorry. I just— Sister Ailan—" She sat down in one of the armchairs, a miserable expression on her face.

Con stopped pacing and turned to her. "What have you seen?" he asked gently.

She closed her eyes and pinched the bridge of her nose as if her head ached. "I see the fortress, repeatedly. It is made of ice, like a mountain floating on the sea. I see the fay in cages. They can't stand being imprisoned; I think some of them are dying from it. I see her—Elowen. She has a nursery. There was a baby there, like the one we saw in Ento. I don't know what she's trying to do, but it's—" A wave of revulsion swept through Taisin as she recalled the sight of the infant monster smashed against the floor. "She is cruel. She is more powerful than anyone I have ever encountered, except for the Fairy Queen herself."

"Is the fortress guarded?" Con asked.

"I don't think so."

"Then we might have the advantage of surprise," Con suggested.

Taisin frowned. "The fortress is surrounded by open sea. I think we would be visible from quite a far distance."

"Then she could kill us before we even step foot in her fortress," Kaede said. She leaned against the table, her arms crossed.

"True, but..." Taisin trailed off, biting her lip.

"What is it?" Kaede asked. "What are you not saying?"

"I think...I think she will allow us to come." Taisin seemed hopeful and frightened all at once.

"Why?"

"Because she will not think we are a threat. We are three humans with a tiny little dagger."

Con rubbed at his chin, considering Taisin's words. He wondered what Tali would do, and a pang went through him. He looked at Taisin, pale-faced and stiff in her chair carved out of a tree trunk, and then at Kaede, who had dark shadows beneath her eyes. He had known Kaede since they were children; he could remember her in pigtails, chasing him and her brother across the broad palace courtyards. He remembered that her eighteenth birthday was today; she was of age now. But he could not shake the feeling that all of this had come too soon for her, and Taisin was just as young. Tali would never let them take the risk of going after Elowen. Tali would have done it himself.

"Elowen has to be stopped," Con said, "but I will do it."

"What do you mean?" Kaede asked. "The Queen said—"

"I don't care what the Queen said. You've been carrying that dagger, but I can't let you kill her, Kaede. I'll do it."

"Con—"

"You're not going to do it," Taisin protested. "You can't face her. She is very powerful. She'll destroy you."

"If she's so powerful, she can destroy you, too," Con argued.

"I've felt her," Taisin objected. "I'm the only one who has a chance against her. You can't do it." She clenched her hands in her lap stubbornly, but inside, doubt swirled. Elowen was so strong; Taisin had no idea if she could actually defeat her. She only knew that Con—or Kaede—would be defenseless against her.

Kaede was watching Taisin closely. She pulled a chair out from the table and set it in front of Taisin. She sat down, her elbows resting on her knees, and leaned toward Taisin as she looked her in the eye. "You seem to want to do this yourself," Kaede said, "but I don't think that's a good idea." There were only a couple of feet separating them now, and Kaede felt as if that space was pulsing with the beat of her heart. Taisin's cheeks turned pink, but she did not look away. Kaede almost forgot what she was going to say. She took a shallow breath. "If we go, we go together. You and me and Con. We've made it this far; we have to stay together." She looked up at Con. "Do you agree?"

He crossed his arms. "Only if you both promise that neither of you will attempt to face her alone."

"I promise," Kaede said. "Taisin, do you?"

Taisin's stomach quivered. She closed her eyes, rubbing her hand over her face as she remembered the vision of Kaede leaving the shore. Con had stayed on the beach with her. She hoped they would be able to change that future. "Yes," she said at last, reluctantly. "I promise."

"Then we'll go to this fortress," Con said, "and we'll do this together."

When the Huntsman came to their door later, he did not seem surprised by their decision. "I will put things in order," he told them. "We will leave in the morning."

Chapter XXXI

t had not taken long for Taisin to pack up her belongings. Her knapsack waited by the door, and she lay in bed unable to sleep. Supper had been subdued, and Taisin had fled to her room afterward to avoid Kaede. But now, lying here in the dark, Kaede's face was all she could see.

If she had to describe it to someone else, she would dutifully relate the obvious details: light brown eyes, a pleasant nose and chin, and a mouth that smiled easily. But such a description omitted all of what made Kaede's face so extraordinary to Taisin. The mischievous gleam in Kaede's eyes when she saw something funny; the way her eyebrows arched in exaggerated reaction to Con's jokes; the shape of her lips, and the warm, firm texture of them.

Taisin approached the memory of their kiss gingerly, as though it were a wild beast that might knock her down, and yet part of her hoped it would do just that. If she was to be a sage, she would have to turn away from that beast forever.

She would never be able to marry; she would not even be allowed to take a lover. And though she had only had the briefest taste of what she would have to give up, she understood now why sages made that vow. The desire that had awakened within her was like a fog descending on a mountain valley, filling every hollow, slipping between tree limbs, tickling every leaf with its seductive breath. It left no room for the calm contemplation necessary to do a sage's work. And though Taisin had only ever wanted to be a sage, now she wondered how she could possibly deny this feeling inside her.

She splayed her fingers across her heart; she felt the rhythmic beat there, the rise and fall of her lungs beneath. Her body was like a new thing to her; she had never known this ache before. It made her skin flush and her eyes dilate, and some part of her marveled at the focus of the energy that ran through her. All it wanted was one thing: to consume her entirely. To drive her up out of bed in the dark of midnight, to slip barefoot into the corridor between their rooms, and to deliver her, trembling, to Kaede.

⁊

Kaede was asleep, dreaming of a hunter running lightly through the Wood, a quiver on her back. She would sight her quarry and draw the arrow as smoothly as if her body were made of quicksilver. The arrowhead was cold as iron. It was Fin's dagger, protruding from the graceful wooden shaft like an eyesore—and then the shaft turned into her hand.

There was a sound that Kaede later recognized as a door closing, and she awoke to find Taisin standing beside her bed.

Confused, her body tingling into awareness, Kaede whispered, "Is something wrong?"

"No," Taisin said, her voice barely audible.

Kaede pushed herself up, heat coursing through her. "Do you need something?" Kaede asked, flustered.

Taisin's hands flew up to cover her mouth, whether to hide embarrassment or laughter Kaede wasn't sure, but a sort of half-choked sound emerged from her, and Kaede said, "Is it about…last night?" It wasn't until the words were out that she realized what they were, and perhaps if she had been awake when Taisin arrived instead of deep in a dream, she might have never had the courage to continue. But now, still shaking off the musty fog of sleep, she said all in a rush, "I didn't mean to upset you, Taisin. I know you'll be a sage, and I'm sorry I kissed you—if I could take it back—"

"Oh, no," Taisin said quickly, firmly. "No." She came to the bed and sat down on the edge of it, and Kaede felt everything sink toward her. "Don't ever say that," Taisin whispered, a catch in her throat, and now Kaede was more awake than she could ever remember. She heard Taisin's breath quickening, and as they leaned toward each other she could smell the scent of her skin. She wanted to put her nose against Taisin's throat and inhale all of it, all of her. She bent her head toward the shadow of Taisin's neck; her mouth brushed over the fluttering of her pulse.

Taisin was wearing an old tunic, the cloth soft with use. Some of the buttons were coming loose, and when she unbuttoned the first one, it hung down on a single thread. She took Kaede's hand in hers and put it on her skin, and gooseflesh rose at the touch of her fingers. Kaede moved her hand, tracing the shape of Taisin's collarbone. She pushed the tunic back, and Taisin's long black hair brushed over her bare shoulders. And then Kaede leaned toward her and they kissed again. Her mouth opened; she breathed her in.

Taisin remembered the way it had felt when she pulled life into that tiny purple blossom, the torrent of energy through her body. She remembered the way that power rippled through Elowen like molten ore, hot and precious. This was even more exquisitely immediate; there was nothing between her and dizzying sensation. Here was the touch of Kaede's fingers on her skin, and there the soft insistence of her mouth. Taisin felt as though there were a thousand purple flowers blooming inside her, a sea of them, each opening her black eye to the sun, trembling to see the wide-open sky.

∽

Taisin slid into sleep so easily; her body was at ease, vulnerable.

The ice fortress swam into focus almost immediately—she was there again, standing at the window overlooking the beach. This time she felt as though she were merging into the body of the woman who stood there. *Elowen.* She formed the name on her lips, asleep in the tower room with Kaede beside her, and she felt the woman in the fortress come alive. Elowen turned her head just slightly, as though she sensed a presence nearby. She left the window and walked toward white velvet curtains hanging against the icy wall. There was a silver cord dangling from the ceiling, and as she pulled it, the curtains parted and revealed a mirror. It was made of glass like all mirrors, but there was something different about this one, though Taisin could not at first discern the difference. All she knew was that she was gazing at the reflection through Elowen's eyes, and she saw a beautiful woman there.

She was tall, willowy, with long, golden-white hair that swept to her waist. She had yellow-brown eyes and sharp cheekbones, and her lips were the color of a bruised pink rose. Her skin was milky white and smooth as a newborn's. She wore a gown of white silk belted with a gold chain, and her fingers were covered with jeweled rings. When she moved her hands, they flashed in the brilliant sunlight: diamonds, rubies, sapphires.

She smiled at herself in the mirror, and Taisin felt her own lips turning up at the corners. Elowen said to her: "You know my name, but I do not know yours." Taisin heard the words as though she were standing in that frozen palace with Elowen; she heard them as though she had spoken them herself. Fear flooded through her as she realized that Elowen could see her, too. As Elowen sensed her agitation, she threw back her head and laughed. The sound echoed.

Taisin did not at first realize that Elowen had begun to push into her consciousness. They were already so close. They were breathing the same breath; their veins ran with the same blood. Taisin felt disoriented; she felt doubled. She couldn't tell where Elowen ended and she began. But in that round tower room in Taninli, her shoulder bumped against

Kaede, and Taisin drew a breath all on her own, and she remembered who she was. She nearly awoke, but Elowen reached through that mirror and held her there, transfixed, half asleep, half aware, as she demanded, *Who are you?*

Taisin pushed back. It was like running in quicksand, trying to extricate herself from Elowen's power. It was like struggling against a cold, fierce current, and she was afraid she would drown. But she fought her way up, remembering the grip of the freezing river Kell, and when she came to the surface, just as before, Kaede had her arms around her.

She gasped, drawing breath after greedy breath in the dark of Kaede's tower room.

Kaede was whispering to her, stroking her hair back from her damp forehead.

Her blood was roaring, her heart pounding.

Kaede gathered her close and held her until her lungs felt like they were her own again.

～

"It was her," Taisin whispered.

"Who?" Kaede asked.

"The Fairy Queen's daughter." She would not say her name.

"What do you mean?"

"I saw her," Taisin said, and she knew that Elowen was angry.

Dawn was breaking, spreading soft pink light across the eastern sky above the city. Kaede propped her head up on her hand, looking down at Taisin's pale and tired face. She ran a finger over the line of Taisin's mouth.

"She knows who I am," Taisin said.

Kaede's hand stilled. "What does that mean?"

"I don't know," Taisin whispered, but fear filled her. She felt tears pricking at the corners of her eyes. She reached up and pulled Kaede down, pressing her face into her neck. She could not forget the way that Elowen had engulfed her, all power and might, and she had no idea how they could possibly kill her.

Chapter XXXII

hey breakfasted together, sitting at one corner of the table with their knees touching. Despite the shadow of Taisin's vision, they felt enveloped in an enchantment: one in which even the drinking of tea was as magical as any fairy glamour.

When Con came out to join them, Taisin and Kaede hastily scooted apart, but the expressions on their faces were so plain that he laughed out loud. "I see that things have changed," he observed, and Kaede flushed so deeply she couldn't look at him.

The Huntsman came to collect them shortly after breakfast. He told them that the Fairy Hunt would accompany them to the northern edge of the Wood, and then they would have to continue on without their Xi escort. "We will not travel through the lands that she has taken for her own," he explained as he led them through the palace to the outer courtyard.

"But how will we find her?" Taisin asked, hurrying to catch up with his long strides.

"You have a token of hers," he said.

"I do?" Apprehension quivered in her as she tried to think of what she could be carrying that had been Elowen's, and then her stomach dropped. "The medallion," she said, and the alarm in her voice caused the Huntsman to stop and turn back to her. "Is that how—why I have seen so much of her fortress?" she demanded.

The Huntsman regarded her pale cheeks and wide, dark eyes, and said as kindly as he could, "If you were already sensitive, then yes, her medallion may have enabled you to see more of her."

Taisin felt for the chain around her neck and pulled the medallion out. It was black and opaque, as usual, but she felt newly aware of it, and now she wondered how she had ever not known that it once belonged to Elowen. "How did she lose it?" she asked.

Sadness washed over the Huntsman's face. "She left it behind when she left Taninli. It was a gift from the Fairy Queen."

He came toward her and touched the black stone with a gentle finger. A tiny glow burned in the stone for a moment. "It wants to be reunited with her. It will show you the way."

Taisin closed her hand around the medallion, intending to take it off; she wouldn't wear Elowen's chain around her neck. But at the last minute, struggling against an equally powerful desire to keep it, she slid it back beneath her tunic. When she felt the stone pressing coldly against her skin, she was disconcerted by the sense of relief that flooded through her. The Huntsman nodded at her as if she had made the right decision. "The longer you wear it," he said, "the more it also becomes yours."

⁓

In the courtyard, half a dozen riders of the Fairy Hunt awaited them, along with riding horses and packhorses loaded with canvas-covered gear. Con did not see their own, ordinary steeds, and he asked, "Where are our horses?"

"They are resting for your return journey back to your kingdom," said the Huntsman. "You shall ride our horses as far as you can. The dogs will take your supplies the rest of the way."

Eight dogs, each with thick gray coats shading into white bellies and paws, had been led into the courtyard by a thin, spry Xi woman. She spoke to the Huntsman in their language, and her green eyes glanced quickly over the humans. She said nothing to them before she left, but she bent down to her dogs and each met her nose to nose in a solemn farewell.

They left Taninli by the same route they had taken through the city when they arrived. At first the few Xi they saw were simply going about their business as usual, but as they descended into the streets, more and more Xi emerged from their homes to watch them ride past. Once again, Kaede had to look down to avoid their eyes. She couldn't bear to see the doubt in their faces—or, even worse, the hope.

Outside the city gates they turned north, leaving the

boulevard almost immediately and riding straight into the Wood. The manicured trees quickly turned wild, and within an hour of leaving Taninli and its pocket of summer behind, the air began to carry the bite of cold. The horses and dogs moved swiftly—more swiftly than horses or dogs should move, Kaede thought. When she looked ahead of them the trees were a bit blurry, and the dogs blended into the landscape, running silently over fallen leaves. She felt increasingly detached from her body as the day progressed, and it would have disturbed her if her senses had been more alert, but instead, she felt a kind of haze that prevented her from doing anything but staying in the saddle.

At night they stopped beside a bubbling stream to water the animals, and the Xi set up small, strange tents in the spaces between trees. They were round, like bubbles made of canvas, stretched tight over ingeniously bent poles. Kaede crawled into the one the Huntsman told her was hers, and she slept as soon as she lay down on the fur-covered pallet.

The next morning she emerged from her solitary tent, and one of the riders gave her a horn cup full of a hot, bitter drink. It was shocking on her tongue, and when she looked up she saw a barren landscape around her. Tree branches that should have been heavy with green needles were stripped clean, as if a giant had come and swept them bare with his fingers.

A dog butted against her leg, and she bent down to stroke him. His brown eyes regarded her with gentle curiosity, and then she saw Taisin come out from a nearby tent, and soon Con emerged from another. There was no time to do more than wish one another a good morning, for the

Fairy Hunt was readying to go, and they thrust cups of the hot drink into Con's and Taisin's hands and told them to hurry.

They rode again.

᳅

Midmorning on the third day after leaving Taninli, the trees abruptly ended. Kaede twisted back in her saddle and stared at the bare trees behind her, trunks the color of ash. Her breath made clouds in the air. The Huntsman was dismounting from his horse, and his boots touched down in snow. She looked north, away from the Wood, and the land was a broad expanse of white stretching toward a faraway horizon. The blue sky arched there in the distance, but above her head the sun was blocked by clouds.

The Huntsman and the other riders were taking bundles down from their horses, and Kaede watched them in confusion, for it was too early in the day to set up camp. They were unpacking long, slim pieces of wood that folded and unfolded in strange ways, and when they put them together, they formed a strong sledge. Stacks of firewood were then lashed onto the sledge, and most of the provisions that had been carried by the packhorses were transferred there as well. The dogs submitted to being harnessed to it, and before she knew what was happening—there was still something wrong with her sense of time—the Huntsman was asking her to dismount from her horse.

"What's going on?" she asked, trying to inhale the chilly air to wake herself up. Con and Taisin seemed as muddled as she was.

"We must leave you here," the Huntsman said. "Your way lies over the ice field."

Kaede shook her head; it felt woolly.

Taisin said, "We are close."

"Yes," the Huntsman said. "I would suggest you put on your warmer clothing."

One of the Xi came to take Kaede's horse away, and she felt the lick of winter against her skin as she looked out over the glacier.

"We have given you everything we can," the Huntsman was saying. He explained how to use the round oil lamps; how to strap the broad snowshoes onto their feet; how to command the dogs.

Kaede blinked again. The light was so odd here. She turned to the Huntsman, willing herself to focus on him. He seemed just slightly worried. "Tell your queen," she said, "that we will do the best we can."

He looked at her gravely and, for the first time, came to her and squeezed her shoulder in the way her father had done once, when she was a little girl and had been knocked down in a fight with her brother Tanis. She had not cried, even though her nose was bleeding, and her father had crouched down to her eye level, his large, warm hand engulfing her shoulder and upper arm, and said somberly, "My little hellion." But she had known that he was proud of her in that moment, and the memory of him suddenly made a lump rise in her throat, and she had to turn away from the Huntsman to stare at the ice.

Chapter XXXIII

aisin and Kaede walked ahead of the sledge, leading the dogs north, while Con followed behind in their tracks to make sure the load remained stable. Every step across the snow sloughed off a bit of the fog that had clung to them as they traveled with the Hunt, and by midafternoon the vista ahead shone with a clarity that was startling to eyes recently glamoured by Xi magic. The sun was bright overhead; the ice field was broad and unbroken; the air stung their skin with its briskness.

Taisin and Kaede did not speak, for they were wrapped from head to foot in furs, and it was hard going. But more than once they glanced at each other, and each was surprised by the pool of happiness that spread through herself even as she trudged through the falling temperatures and growing dusk.

Their first night on the ice field, they built a small, hot fire in the lee of the sledge, and boiled water for their first hot drinks since morning. The wind had risen and was whipping up the snow in frozen imitations of dust devils, but the night sky was clear and black, with thousands of stars spread in unfamiliar constellations overhead. They crouched as close to the fire as they could, eating a supper of dried fruit and hard, round crackers that tasted, ingeniously, of cheese.

Afterward, as Kaede fed the dogs, Con and Taisin pitched the two tents and unpacked their sleeping furs. Con took five of the dogs into his tent, and Taisin and Kaede took the other three. With the dogs curled up around them, their nest was cozy enough. Kaede slid her arm across Taisin's stomach and nestled her nose into the crook of her neck, and sleep overcame her moments after she lay down. Taisin was awake for only a few minutes more, long enough to wonder if Elowen would come to her tonight, but she was so tired that she couldn't even be properly anxious about it.

Sometime in the hours before dawn, Kaede awoke to hear Taisin speaking. They had shifted apart; Taisin was turned away from her, one arm flung out over the furs. One of the dogs let out a low growl, and Taisin's voice changed, deepening. Kaede could not understand what she was saying, for the words made no sense. The dog beside her tensed up. When she reached out to calm him, she felt his fur rising stiffly down his back.

Kaede shook Taisin's shoulder. "Taisin," she whispered. One of the dogs barked.

Taisin jerked awake, letting out a half-strangled moan. "What? Who is there?"

"It's me," Kaede said.

Taisin pushed herself up. It was too dark to see, but she

felt the dogs creeping back to her, their hackles lowered now, and one rubbed his head against her arm.

"Why did you wake me?" Taisin asked, her voice rough. It didn't sound quite like her own.

"You were talking in your sleep."

"What did I say?"

Kaede thought she sounded nervous. "I couldn't understand you. It wasn't...it was not our language." A beat later, Taisin lay down again, and Kaede asked, "Did you see *her* again?"

"I can't remember," Taisin answered. It was unsettling; her mind was so fuzzy. She lay awake for some time, trying to sort through the hazy memories that kept slipping away from her. But it was no use, and now she could not sleep, and the wind was buffeting the walls of their tent, keening like an army of ghosts.

"Kaede," she whispered, wondering if she had fallen asleep.

She had not. "Yes?" Kaede murmured, and she shifted closer. She heard Taisin's breath grow short; she felt her own skin suffused all over with heat.

Taisin turned to her. How strange and wonderful, she thought, that in the middle of this bizarre journey, there should be this: Kaede, who kissed her.

After a few moments, the dogs slunk off to the foot of the tent, affronted. Kaede stifled a laugh, her hands sliding around Taisin's waist, and later, they slept again.

In the morning, Taisin drew out the medallion and cupped it in her hands. She thought of the fortress of ice; she could imagine the walls of it so clearly, the windows bright in the sunlight, the sea all around it deep sapphire blue. The stone became warm; it pulsed like a tiny heart. Taisin felt it tugging at her until she faced northeast. On the horizon, the blue sky faded into the field of ice, making the land seem endless. "We go there," Taisin said, her voice small, swallowed up by the world of the glacier.

The dogs barked as if in affirmation.

Kaede woke again on the second night to the sound of Taisin's voice. This time she lay still and listened. It might have been the language of the Xi, but Kaede could not make out the different words. They flowed into one another in a singsong pattern that reminded her of chanting, but she had never heard any chanting like this. And then Taisin arched her back and laughed out loud, and the voice that came out of her body sounded nothing like her. The dogs, who had already been stirring awake, backed away and began to growl low in their throats.

"Taisin!" Kaede called, reaching out to touch Taisin's arm.

Suddenly Taisin's body went limp, her eyes blinking open in the darkness of the tent. She let out a weak sigh. "Am I dreaming?" she whispered.

One of the dogs whined and went to lick her face with his rough, wet tongue.

"Am I dreaming?" she asked again, more loudly.

"I don't know," Kaede said, disturbed by the confusion in Taisin's voice.

"I don't want to dream anymore." Taisin sounded as if she were on the verge of tears.

"What were you dreaming of?"

"Elowen," Taisin answered, and the dogs barked. She gave a panicked laugh and added, "She wants to know who you are."

Kaede felt drenched in cold. "What? Why does she want—"

"I don't know. I don't know what she's doing to me," Taisin said, her voice rising.

Kaede pulled her close, pressing her lips to Taisin's hair. "You shouldn't say her name again." She felt useless, and it frustrated her.

Taisin was groggy. She knew that Elowen had been inside her again, but things were different now that Elowen was aware of her. In the past, Taisin had seen the fortress clearly; when she awoke, she remembered. Now she had the feeling that Elowen had been erasing her memory somehow. Her mind felt rubbed clean in some places, and in others it felt like it had been scratched raw. It frightened her.

Kaede fell asleep again; the dogs stretched out, content, on either side of them; but Taisin lay awake thinking for a long time. She could not allow Elowen to take over her mind, and she began to formulate a plan to prevent it from happening.

On the third day, Taisin crumpled in midstep, and when Con and Kaede ran to help her up, she snarled at them. Elowen's voice came spitting out of her: *"Fools."*

They halted, shocked, their hands outstretched to Taisin, lying on the snow. Her face was twisted into a grimace; her eyes were glazed. She began to mutter to herself in the same strange language that Kaede had heard at night. "What is wrong with her?" Con demanded.

"She has been like this before," Kaede said. "The Fairy Queen's daughter visits her when she's asleep." The fact that Elowen seemed to be visiting Taisin now while she was awake was extremely disturbing.

Taisin's eyes were half shut, and her face was so pale it was almost white. Con asked, "What can we do?"

They ended up carrying her to the sledge, making room for her among their tents and blankets. She struggled a bit at first, and Con had to pin her arms to her side while Kaede held her legs. She wondered whether they would have to tie her down, but when they settled her onto the sledge, Taisin's body relaxed. She looked up at them with dreamy eyes and said in Elowen's voice, silky and cold, "It is such a pleasure to meet you both, at last." She laughed, her whole body shaking with mirth while Kaede and Con watched her, horrified.

But as quickly as it had begun, the laughter choked off, and Taisin let out a moan as if she were in pain. She curled up, holding her head in her hands. Kaede stroked Taisin's feverish forehead and asked, "Taisin, what can we do?"

Taisin jerked away from her touch as though it hurt her, and for the first time, Kaede truly wanted to kill Elowen. The anger filled her unexpectedly; her fingers curled into fists.

Taisin, her eyes squeezed shut, said in a shaking voice, "I'll be all right. We just need to go."

So they continued on.

That afternoon they came to a cliff. When Con and Kaede walked to the edge, they saw that the ice field ended in what seemed to be a sheer wall of white. It plunged down a hundred feet to a beach. In the distance, they could see the ocean: intense, cold blue dotted with ice floes.

Con looked in either direction and pointed south. "There. It looks like the cliff is lower there."

Kaede nodded. "All right. Let's go."

After walking for two hours, they found that the ice field did slope down to the beach, but it was a steep descent. "We could continue on," Con said, "and see if there is an easier way down. But we're going farther and farther away from the direction Taisin told us to go."

"We might be able to climb down," Kaede said. "Some areas are not as steep as others. We'll have to be careful, though."

"What about the sledge?" Con asked.

"We can leave the sledge up here. We'll leave half the firewood for the return journey, and the dogs will have no problem."

"And Taisin?"

She glanced back at Taisin, who was sitting on the sledge with a dazed look on her face. The sight of her twisted Kaede's stomach into knots. The closer they drew to Elowen's fortress, the more Kaede wanted to finish this— and finish it quickly. She felt a hard determination growing in her, and though the feeling was new, it was not unwelcome. It gave her courage, and she knew she would need that soon, for she had every intention of making Elowen pay for what she was doing to Taisin.

Kaede met Con's worried gaze and said, "We'll tie her to us. We have rope, don't we?"

He considered it for a moment. "I suppose we have no other choice," he said reluctantly.

Kaede unhitched the dogs, who seemed both surprised and excited at being allowed to roam free at this time of day. Some of them ran along the edge of the cliff, but two sat down behind her as she grimly approached Taisin with the rope. She wasn't sure how Taisin would react to being tied to them; all day she had been slipping further away, and it wasn't clear if she was actually aware of what was going on. But she did not fight when Kaede came with the rope, and just as Kaede knotted it tight beneath her armpits, she gripped Kaede's hand and said fiercely, "I am still here. I am still here. Don't let her tell you otherwise."

Kaede looked into Taisin's dark brown eyes; the sun was reflected in them in bright white spots, and she knew it was Taisin speaking, not Elowen. "I won't," Kaede assured her. "You will have to climb down after Con. Can you do it? I'll stay beside you."

Taisin nodded, though her face was pallid and drawn. "I can do it."

Con descended over the edge first, his belly flat against the snow, and a few of the dogs followed him. They had already bundled their supplies together and pushed them over the cliff, where they slid down the slope until the bundles lodged against an outcropping of ice. Con began to make his way carefully toward the supplies as Kaede helped

Taisin begin her descent. From her vantage point on top of the cliff, Kaede kept an eye on Con as he shoved one of the larger packs along. She was reaching for her gloves, which she had removed to tighten the knots in the rope linking them together, when he slipped.

The rope jerked, and Taisin screamed as she was pulled down the cliff face. Kaede reached for Taisin's hand but was just a moment too late, and the rope tightened around Kaede's waist and yanked her toward the edge.

She fell to her knees and dug her fingers into the ice, but the rope dragged her painfully over the lip of the cliff until her legs were dangling over the precipice, her chest flat on the ground, her chin scraped raw against the snow.

Her heartbeat thundered in her ears; panic rushed through her body. She could not see Con or Taisin. The pack leader came and snuffed at her head. She called out, "Con!"

But he did not respond. And the rope continued to pull at her. Dead weights. Fear threatened to overwhelm her.

She let out her breath in a sob. She began to swing her right leg out, searching for footing—searching for anything. She kicked the glacier wall; small pellets of ice and snow rained down the cliffside, but there was nothing to break her fall.

Her fingers were freezing. Her hands began to slip. The ice would cut into her palms any minute now, and she would die leaving bloody handprints in the snow.

Chapter XXXIV

er cheek was pressed against the ground. She gritted her teeth. Seen up close, the hard-packed snow became glittering ice crystals, sharp as a thousand tiny blades. Her breath steamed out of her; she watched the ice crystals melting. Her hands and arms and back screamed with the strain of clinging to the cliff's edge, but she wasn't about to give up.

And then she slipped again, sliding down a few more inches. Her stomach lurched; sweat broke out on her skin. Her boots scraped against the cliff wall until suddenly— finally—her toe found a tiny outcropping in the glacier wall, no wider than a hand span.

She could hardly believe it. She was breathless with relief. And then she began to drag herself toward the ledge.

It was brutal work. She felt as though her arms might rip themselves out of her body before she was done, and she might even welcome it.

But the ledge was just wide enough to support some of

her weight, and when at last both of her feet were dug into it, she allowed herself to rest for a count of five, her face pressed against her arm, still clinging to the top of the glacier. Then she steeled herself and turned just slightly—just enough—and looked down.

The edge of the ice sheet was particularly steep where she had fallen, but just below her, it banked at a shallower angle. Taisin's body was sprawled there, and a splash of red marked the snow near her head. The sight filled Kaede with dread, and she had to force herself to look past Taisin, where the ground plummeted down again. The slope was not as precipitous there as it was near Kaede, but it was steep enough that she couldn't see what had happened to Con, for the rope attaching them together had disappeared into a crevice.

Looking around her, she realized that Con's fall had dragged her over the edge of the glacier at a particularly bad place. He had begun his descent several feet to her left, where the incline was less hazardous. Something had made him slip, yanking him—and Taisin and Kaede in turn—down to the right, where the cliff wall was nearly vertical.

As she pondered how she was going to climb down from her precarious perch, she suddenly felt the rope around her waist slacken. She looked down; Taisin was still motionless on the snow. But the rope that had gone into the crevice was loose now. Con must have cut himself free. Relief flooded through her. She hadn't known how she could continue on with both him and Taisin weighing her down.

"Con!" she shouted.

There was a long silence. But at last she heard his ragged voice below. "I'm here," he called faintly.

"Are you all right?" she yelled.

Again, a pause. There was a scrabbling noise. His voice came again, thick with effort: "I'm climbing out."

"I'm coming down," Kaede called. She took a deep breath and flexed her fingers, for they were chilled to the bone. But there was no other way: She had to climb down, inch by inch.

It was even slower going than before. She had to search out small toeholds in the glacier wall, and then she had to find places to grip in the ice. Below her, Con still hadn't reappeared, but they called to each other regularly, and she had no time to worry about him. Her shoulders burned, and all she could do was focus on each handhold, each step.

At last she came to the place where Taisin had fallen, and the ground was less steep here, so Kaede turned over onto her backside and carefully scooted down to her. Some of her anxiety ebbed when she saw that Taisin still breathed; the snow beneath her nose was slightly melted. The blood seemed to have come from a long, shallow scrape on her chin. Kaede reached out and touched her shoulder. "Taisin," she said. When there was no response, she shook her lightly, and then said her name more loudly. She was about to consider taking more serious action—though she didn't know what that would be—when she felt Taisin stir beneath her hand. And then she let out a low moan, and her eyes fluttered open.

Kaede was elated. "Are you all right?" she asked, and Taisin pushed herself up, putting a hand to her face where the cut on her chin was bleeding. Her fingers came away wet. "It's just a cut," Kaede said, attempting to reassure her. "Is anything else hurt?"

Taisin felt her head gently. "I think...I think I hit my head." Her tongue seemed to have trouble forming words, but oddly, she felt more like herself than she had for days. Perhaps the fall had somehow dislodged Elowen's grip on her. She began to move, and before Kaede could stop her she slipped on the ice, sliding down several inches, and she gasped, scrabbling for hold on the slick surface.

"Slowly!" Kaede called. "Don't move too quickly." Below them there was a crashing sound, and a cloud of snow flew up from the beach. "Con!" Kaede crawled down a few feet, but she could not see him.

"It's just the—the supplies," his voice came back to them. "I'm all right."

Kaede looked at Taisin, who was gradually realizing the severity of the situation, and said, "We must go very carefully, on our hands and knees. Don't try to rush it."

Taisin nodded just slightly. "I'll follow you."

Kaede began to creep down the slope, the rope snaking between them like an umbilical cord.

༄

It was late in the day before they reached the bottom, and it felt as though every last inch of their bodies had been pricked by ice crystals. They were cold and stiff and hot and sweaty all at once, and Kaede would have done anything at that moment for a fire and a bath and a soft bed to collapse into. But there was only the frozen, sandy beach stretching as far as the eye could see, and Con, sitting on the ground propped up against the packs they had pushed over the edge. The bundle that had been packed with firewood had burst open when it hit the ground, and pieces of wood were scattered all over the snow. The dogs, who had climbed down on their own, waited nearby, their breath steaming out in the air.

At first Kaede couldn't understand why Con's left leg was bent at such a strange angle, but as she walked the last few feet to him, she realized that his face was white with pain. He was pressing his hand to his knee, and it was bloody.

"What happened?" she asked, halting.

"My leg," he said hoarsely. "I think it's broken."

Taisin knelt down beside him, holding her shoulder back a little, as if it had been twisted. Kaede rubbed a hand over her tired eyes, leaving streaks of blood across her face. She winced; her fingers were raw and bleeding from the ice.

Taisin bent over Con's leg, and she said hesitantly, "I can set it."

"You don't sound too sure of that," he said, and there was yet a note of grim humor in his voice.

"I saw Mona do it with Shae's leg."

"But you are not Mona."

"I'm as good as you're going to get."

Kaede looked back at the way they had come. The edge of the glacier was jagged, a series of huge steps torn from the earth. She saw that the crevice he had fallen into was a slim slash in the ground—little more than a couple of feet across. There was a smear of blood across the mouth of it. It must have taken a prodigious effort for Con to pull himself out of there. She said to Taisin, "What can I do to help?"

They broke down one of the tent poles and ripped apart the canvas, using it to bind the pole to Con's leg. Kaede had to hold him down as Taisin worked. By the end of it, he had nearly fainted, and Kaede wished she had thought to bring Shae's flask with them.

The dogs were arrayed in a half circle around them, watching attentively. The sky was darkening. Kaede said, "We'll just have to camp here tonight."

Taisin helped her stake out the remaining tent. There wasn't enough room inside for the three of them and all the dogs, but at least the glacier wall created a sort of windbreak. Kaede collected the pieces of wood and built a fire, and Taisin brewed the same tea for Con that she had made for Shae when she was injured. After they ate their cold supper, several of the dogs curled up together, huddling against their packs, and Taisin and Kaede helped Con crawl into the tent. A few of the dogs followed, whining pathetically as the tent flap closed, and Kaede said, "Oh, let them in. We'll be warmer with them inside."

Taisin had been quiet for most of the evening, but now as her two companions readied for sleep and the dogs nosed their way under the furs, she said, "I'll stay up and keep watch."

"Watch for what?" Con asked, grunting as he lay down, trying to prop his leg up at a more comfortable angle.

"I can't go to sleep, Con," Taisin said, though her face was drawn with weariness.

"But you're exhausted," Kaede said. Taisin was still favoring her shoulder, but she hadn't allowed anyone to examine it.

"Yes. But we're too close to…to her. Today—maybe because I was unconscious after that fall—she seems to have left me. At least temporarily. But if I sleep, it would be like opening the door to her again."

"Are you sure you can stay awake? Do you want me to sit up with you?" Kaede asked.

"No. I'll be fine. It's been a long time since I've had the luxury of stillness." She folded her legs beneath her and pulled the furs around her shoulders so that she wouldn't freeze, and as Con and Kaede slept, she sat, her eyes half open, watching the dark.

❧

It took the better part of the morning for them to fashion a sort of sled for Con, for he could not walk long distances, and Kaede refused to leave him behind. They lashed together the remaining canvas from the tent they had torn up to create a sling, and tied it to the dogs' harness. As long as Con held on, he could be dragged, albeit roughly, across the ground. They set off again after a quick noon meal that Taisin ate only because Kaede forced her to; she had sunk into a daze and had begun to murmur to herself. Kaede realized that she was reciting the Thirty Blessings repeatedly from memory, as though that would keep Elowen at bay.

As the day drew to a close and the stars began to shine in the dark blue sky, Taisin was determined to keep going. Kaede suggested that they stop, but Taisin refused. "Just a little farther," she insisted, and she did not wait to see if her companions followed. She knew they would. Elowen was so close to her now; it was like they were in the same room, divided only by a painted screen.

It was pitch-black before Taisin consented to stop. There was a new moon that night, and even the stars seemed to be dimmed. The small fire they lit only served to make everything outside its circle of light seem darker. After they had pitched their tent, fed the dogs, and passed around their own rations for the night, Kaede was so tired she only wanted to crawl into her furs and sleep. But as she burrowed into the warmth of her bedroll, a curious sound began to knock at the edges of her consciousness. In the distance there was a gentle ringing, like two pieces of metal rubbing against each other. She wondered irritably what was making the noise, and why it was bothering her. But the dogs were so warm against her flank and she was so tired that it didn't bother her for long, and soon she was fast asleep.

It wasn't until morning that she learned what had been the source of the ringing sound. As soon as she stepped out of the tent onto the frozen shore, she saw a small dock scarcely twenty feet from where they had set up camp. At the end of the dock was a rowboat tethered with a sparkling silver chain. The boat bobbed gently on the ocean waves curling onto the shore. And there in the distance, like a snow-covered mountain erupting from the sea, she saw the fortress of ice, its windows glinting in the light of the rising sun.

Chapter XXXV

aisin told them her plan while they ate their morning meal. Though she hadn't slept in days, she felt unnaturally aware, as if all her senses were on high alert. The air here was frigid, but peculiarly exhilarating. "Elowen knows me," she began. "She has been inside me; she has seen through my eyes. I think she expects me to come for her; she's even a little curious."

"You can't go," Kaede said, shaking her head. "You're not well."

"I agree."

Kaede's brows rose. "What?" She had not expected Taisin to give in so easily.

"If I go, I think it will be too dangerous. She could use me." All night, Taisin had agonized over this, initially not wanting to admit it to herself. But Mona's warning echoed in her head: *You have a strong heart, but even the strongest heart can be tempted.* And she had felt the temptation already. Experiencing Elowen's power in her visions had awakened a disturbing hunger to have that power herself. Part of her yearned to go to Elowen immediately; she sensed that Elowen would welcome her as a disciple. Yet everything she had learned at the Academy told her that Elowen's power was a gross perversion of natural law; and even if her teachers had kept some things from her, Taisin believed there had been a reason. She wanted to return to the iron-bound fortress and ask her teachers, directly, for the truth.

Last night, sitting awake in the dark tent, everything became crystal clear. If she went to Elowen, she would be tempted to join her and become as corrupt with power as Elowen herself. As much as Taisin wanted to believe she would be able to resist Elowen, she knew she could not take the risk. When she looked hard at herself, examined her deepmost desires, she realized that she did not entirely trust herself. The realization burned at first, but then it made the decision easy. There was one person whom she trusted completely. Someone Taisin knew would do the right thing. She looked at Kaede. "She could use me," Taisin said, "but I don't think she could use you."

"Why not?"

"You're by nature much more closed off to the energies than I am."

Kaede gave a short laugh. "This is why I've never been able to pass the Academy exams."

Taisin smiled faintly. "Yes, well, in this case, I think it will be an advantage. Because even though you are closed off, you've spent many years studying the practice, and I think it has made you quite self-contained. It's like you've built a little wall around yourself."

"Good. Then I'll go."

Con, who had been listening to the two of them silently until now, interrupted: "You can't go alone. I'm coming with you."

Kaede protested, "Con, your leg—"

"Damn my leg," he said, frustrated. "You can't go alone."

"She's not going alone," Taisin interjected. "I'm going with her."

Kaede's forehead wrinkled. "You just said—"

"Listen," Taisin said fiercely. "Elowen has been inside me. But I haven't just been helplessly letting her in. I've learned some things from her."

Con was uneasy. "What have you learned?"

"I can do it, too." She turned to Kaede. "I can be inside you, to help you fight her."

"Inside my mind?" Kaede said uncertainly.

"Yes."

Con said: "Taisin, I'm sure you're capable of a great many things, but this—this doesn't sound safe. Look at what she has done to you."

"It will be different," Taisin insisted, keeping her eyes on Kaede. Kaede grounded her. "If we are together; if you are willing; it will be different."

Kaede asked, "But if she can't use me because I'm so... self-contained, why can you do it?

Taisin's cheeks burned. "Because you have already opened yourself to me." There was an upwelling emotion in Taisin's face that reached straight into Kaede's belly and tugged at her. Her own face colored. Taisin said hurriedly, "I tried it very quickly last night, when you were asleep. I can do it."

"All right," Kaede said, feeling awkward. She took a breath. "So, let's say your theory holds: She can't use me the way she might use you."

"Then you will go to the fortress," Taisin said, "and I will stay here with Con. And when you need my help, I will be there with you."

"How will you know when I need your help?"

"She has put so much energy into this place that it's practically glowing with it. It magnifies everything that's alive. I think I'll be able to feel when you need me."

"What if you can't?"

"I know I can. I can already sense your feelings, even now." Kaede's stomach gave a little lurch, and Taisin had the grace to look embarrassed. She continued, "And when the time comes, I'll help you."

Kaede said, "You'll help me kill her."

The words hung heavily in the air.

Taisin said, "Yes."

❧

They decided that Kaede would leave that very morning. There was no reason to wait any longer.

She decided to bring nothing but the clothes on her back and the iron dagger that Fin had given her. She unsheathed it and looked at it again. Its blade was dark, inelegant; the textured skin that covered the hilt was nearly black, as though many hands had held it over the decades. It was cold and heavy and sharp, and it had been made for killing. Though she had carried it at her side ever since she had left the Academy, it seemed oddly unfamiliar to her, as if she had never truly looked at it before. She thought she could smell the tang of iron in the air. She wanted for this to be finished.

She moved to resheathe the dagger, but Con said, "Wait." He was sitting by the fire, his broken leg covered with a blanket. "You shouldn't wear it at your waist."

"Why?"

He held out his hand. "Let me see it." She gave it to him and then squatted down nearby. Taisin watched them both curiously. Con ran his hand over the edge of the blade, turning the dagger around. "It's a solid knife," he said. "This is what the Fairy Queen was talking about? Your weapon?"

"I think so. It is made of iron."

"The Xi can't tolerate iron," Taisin said.

He was silent for a few minutes, thinking. Finally he looked at Kaede seriously and said, "I am not a guard, but I have spent my life in the company of them, and I hope you'll take my advice."

"Please," Kaede said, "tell me."

"You should conceal this dagger. If you wear it openly, she'll see it; from what Taisin has said of this woman's power, I believe she could easily disarm you. Your only advantage—besides Taisin—will be surprise. And you've seen how open the land is here. We can't surprise her with our approach—surely she knows we're here already—but you can keep this weapon a secret until you need to use it."

"Where should I conceal it?"

She was dressed in the clothing the Fairy Hunt had given them all: fur-lined boots, warm woolen leggings beneath supple leather leg guards, tunic and fur vest and cloak. Con tapped at her boots. "You can slide it in here. Give me your scabbard and I can fit it into your boot." She took it off, and while he worked out a way to tie it to her leg, he said, "Don't forget your goal. You're not there to negotiate; you're there to kill. Take every advantage you can, Kaede. I don't think it's going to be a fair fight."

After he had lashed the scabbard onto her shin, she fitted her boot over it. The dagger was like a hard splint against her leg, but the boot concealed it neatly, and she could reach in and pull it out without much effort. When she was ready to go, Taisin offered to help with the boat and began to walk toward the dock, leaving Kaede with Con as he inspected the boot and the dagger one last time.

"I wish I could go with you," he muttered.

"You have to watch over Taisin," she told him. "She does things in her sleep sometimes, when she is being visited. She'll talk, or start shaking. You have to make sure she's all right."

"I will." He smiled faintly. "You watch out for yourself. I mean to bring you back to Cathair after this, you know, and make sure you don't have to marry that Lord Win."

She surprised herself by laughing. "I can't wait to have that conversation with my father. Thanks for giving me something to live for, Con."

The corners of his mouth lifted, but his eyes were sad.

At the dock, Kaede surveyed the rowboat. It was small; it looked as though it had never been used before. Elowen had made it especially for them.

Taisin stood beside her. "Are you ready?" she asked.

"As ready as I'm going to be."

"I will be with you." Taisin bit her lip and then asked hesitantly, "Do you trust me?"

"Trust you," Kaede repeated, as if it were an odd thought. "I love you."

Taisin's face twisted with sorrow and fear. This was the moment she had seen in that vision, and she felt it anew, and it was so much worse than she had ever anticipated. Yet she was the one who was sending Kaede to do this terrible thing. Had she always known it? Had part of the dread always been because she knew, somehow, that she was the reason Kaede left?

She cupped Kaede's face in her hands and pressed a hard kiss to her mouth. She whispered: "And I love you."

Kaede wanted to put her arms around Taisin, but she forced herself to step away. It would be easier, she told herself, if she didn't linger.

Her boots scratched against the wooden dock, and she lowered herself into the boat.

Chapter XXXVI

he tried to not look back as she rowed. She didn't know if she would have the courage to keep going if she saw Taisin and Con on the beach behind her. So she lifted and lowered the oar, watching the icy water fall in clear droplets from the blade, and soon the fortress loomed large ahead of her.

When the bottom of the boat scraped onto the icy beach, she jumped out, her boots splashing into the shallow water as she dragged the boat onto the shore. There was no dock on this side, only the fortress. It was like an iceberg—if an iceberg could form in such a way that towers erupted from it. All around the island the ocean was a deep azure blue, and the colors here were so bright and crisp that Kaede had to squint. There was a causeway leading from the shore into the fortress, and at the end of it she could see doors. The island seemed deserted; the snowy ground was scrubbed clean by the wind. There was no sign of activity, human or fay. She moved toward the causeway, her feet scarring the snow for the first time.

The doors to the fortress were made of some kind of white stone, and in the center of each was a round silver ring hanging from a gleaming hinge. Kaede reached out and wrapped her fingers around one of the rings—it was as thick as her own wrist—and when she lifted it, the door swung open. Inside, sunlight spilled through windows set high in walls so tall that Kaede could barely make out the ceiling far above. The hall she stood in was bare of ornamentation but for a pattern inlaid in the floor. Giant diamonds of glass marked out an impressive star. Opposite the doors, a flight of stairs that seemed to be built of blocks of ice curved up out of sight. There was no other exit from the hall, so Kaede crossed the cold floor and began to climb the stairs. With each step she felt the dagger nestled hard against her leg, nudging the muscles of her calf, reminding her of her purpose.

The stairs ended in a long chamber lined with uncurtained windows. Everywhere she looked, the fortress had the faint blue tinge of ice; even the sunlight seemed less golden than white. She stepped into a slanting square of light coming through one of the windows, and though she felt its warmth on her face, it had no effect on the ice all around her. She went to look out the window and saw the sloping shoulder of the fortress, dusted with snow. Far below was the beach, and there was the boat she had rowed, a dark mark against the white. There was certainly no chance she had arrived unnoticed. Where was Elowen?

She heard a faint sound behind her—like the flapping of delicate wings—but when she spun around, her heartbeat quickening, there was nothing there, only a faint shadow disappearing through a doorway she had not noticed before. She forced herself to walk toward it, even though every nerve in her body was telling her to run away from this place. A cold sweat broke out on her forehead.

The corridor she entered curved upward. At first the walls were square with the floor, but as she continued on, they began to curve, too, until the corridor was more like a tunnel carved out of the interior of a mountain. There were still windows in the thick walls, but now they were irregularly cut in the ceiling or at floor level. Tunnels branched off to the sides; some of them slanted down; others had steps carved into them leading up. Once she passed a huge archway, and the sight beyond it caused her to stop and look again. There was a crystal cradle there, and a rocking chair, and on the floor a smear of what looked like blood. It was a nursery. She was drawn inside almost against her will, her curiosity vying against the desire to flee. The hairs on the back of her neck rose as she approached the cradle, but it was empty, and the blood was long dried.

Somewhat relieved—for the memory of the Ento creature had reared up fresh in her mind—she went back out into the corridor, and the shadow fluttered in the distance again. She followed it with renewed determination, but she only ever saw the shadow out of the corner of her eye. The tunnel was so interminable that she was unprepared when it abruptly ended in a vast chamber as large as a cavern. Far above, icicles hung from the rough ceiling. Round windows scattered high in the walls revealed the blue sky, and sunlight streamed in over a sight that caused Kaede to catch her breath. The cavernous room was filled with golden cages, round and square and rectangular, some stacked on top of each other, others standing alone. Inside the cages were the fay she had seen in Mona's book. Some of them looked at her, and their eyes were pinpoints of light: gold and silver and emerald green. The ones closest to her crept to the bars of their cages, and a few extended their arms, reaching for her. One, an excited creature with wings, began to throw itself against the bars, creating a ringing noise. That sound attracted the attention of its neighbors, and a whisper began to spread throughout the chamber, a moving wave of voices that Kaede realized, with a sinking feeling, she had heard before. These were the sounds that Taisin had made at night in her dreams: the eerie, half-senseless murmurings of beings trapped behind bars.

On the far side of the cavern was a door, and Kaede knew, as soon as she glimpsed it, that this was her destination. Her stomach heaved, for this meant that she had to walk through the cavern, past all the cages and all those strange creatures with their sad, brilliant eyes. She took a deep breath and stepped into the prison.

As she walked, she saw that some of the cages were empty, and some of the fay looked almost human. Some were very small—barely the size of her hand, tiny humanoid beings with butterfly-like wings in riotous shades of gold and orange. Several were hunched over in their cages, paying no attention to her as she passed. There were some who looked like human women, but had skin the color of moss and lips like bark; they moved with a lissome grace, treading circles in their cages. One of them reached out to her, and her fingers resembled roots twisting up from the ground. There were cages large enough to contain pools built into the floor, and beings with silvery scales instead of skin swam beneath the surface. Some of the imprisoned fay looked like harmless children, and these horrified her the most, for she wondered if any of them had ever been sheltered in that nursery.

By the time she reached the other side of the cavern, the whispering words had ceased. She glanced back, and the fay in her vicinity were watching her with expectant eyes. In one motion, as if pulled by a greater force, they looked behind her, and a shiver ran down her spine. She turned around slowly, half expecting a monster to rise up and consume her—but there was nothing but the door. An ordinary, human-sized door, with an ordinary, human-sized handle. She walked to it, and when she put her hand on the doorknob, a sigh ran through all the creatures in the hall. She squared her shoulders, nervous sweat dampening her skin, and opened the door.

The first thing she saw was a long expanse of shining ice—the floor was like a frozen lake in midwinter—and at the far end was a dais and a throne that looked just like the Fairy Queen's. But on this throne, Elowen waited. She had golden hair and eyes, high cheekbones, and her mouth was a red slash across white skin. She was clothed from head to toe in white fur, and at her right hand a fairy no more than a foot tall hovered in midair, her wings fluttering like a hummingbird's. A sprite, Kaede remembered.

"Welcome," Elowen said. "Please come closer; it is so rare that I have visitors." She spoke in Kaede's language with the same accent the Fairy Queen had.

Kaede was moving before she knew what she was doing. The floor was slick and cold; she could feel it seeping through the soles of her boots as she walked toward the throne. She also felt the unexpected, dizzying sensation of someone pushing into her mind. Everything suddenly tipped off-balance; the icy floor and walls and windows spun around her; she fell to her knees.

Her vision went black.

There was a deep, insistent tugging, as though someone were trying to pull the very core of her out through her mouth. She moaned, her fingernails scraping against the ice.

Just as suddenly, the pressure eased, and the blackness exploded into blinding white light. She blinked and blinked; the light became white walls and floor and windows—and a throne.

She was twenty feet away from Elowen, and the dagger was pressing against her calf. Her breath steamed out of her.

"That's a surprise," Elowen said. "You're not the one I expected. Who are you?"

"My name is Kaede," she said before she could stop herself.

"Kaede," Elowen said, her tongue caressing the sounds as though they were made of the sweetest honey. Kaede felt her entire body quiver, and for a moment she thought she might do anything at all for Elowen—anything. Still on her knees, she gazed up at Elowen, who seemed to glow with a radiant light.

"What brings you to my fortress?" Elowen asked.

"I have come to kill you," Kaede said, the words pouring out of her, and Elowen laughed.

"Is that so? Wonderful. I hope you will allow me to offer you some refreshment before you undertake your task." From nowhere, a chair appeared in the middle of the floor, and when Elowen said, "Sit down," Kaede obeyed her.

A little round table was drawn up nearby, and on that table stood a crystal goblet filled with golden liquid. "Drink," Elowen said. The word was freighted with such seductiveness that Kaede picked up the goblet without hesitation. She could smell the fragrance wafting up from the wine: honey, peaches, flowers in midsummer, as intoxicating as first love. Kaede's eyelids fluttered as the scent of it wrapped around her.

She raised it to her lips, and just as she was about to take a sip, Taisin flooded into her as though a dam had broken. Kaede couldn't breathe; Taisin was breathing for her. She felt oddly doubled, as if she could see everything twice as clearly. The goblet—the wine—she knew instantly that she must not drink it. With shaking hands, she set it roughly back down on the table. Some of the wine splashed over the rim, spilling onto her hand. She rubbed the sticky liquid onto the edge of her cloak. She could feel Taisin's heart beating in time with her own, and it made her light-headed. To have Taisin so close to her—inside her—and yet not physically present—it was an extraordinarily strange experience. She looked at her hands; they were her own hands, and yet it was like seeing them for the first time. The palms were torn up from the descent down the glacier wall, the skin scabbed over where the ice had cut her. She felt as though Taisin were sliding her own hands into hers, like gloves—but Kaede was the glove. She was the armor that Taisin had put on, here, to face Elowen.

Elowen looked at Kaede with narrowed eyes, unable to discern exactly what had happened, but certain that something had changed. Earlier, Kaede's mind had been a closed box; that was not unexpected for an ordinary human, but no ordinary human should be able to resist the wine. The girl should have drunk it and fallen into a delirium; that was what happened when Elowen issued a command: It was obeyed. Who was this girl? Elowen decided to change her strategy.

She said, "I see my mother has sent someone to challenge me." She twisted the word *mother* in her mouth as if it tasted bitter. She saw the shock on Kaede's face, and a smile pulled at her lips. "Does that come as a surprise to you? No wonder—my mother was always so ashamed of her own weakness for *humans*. She tried to make sure that no one knew I was her true daughter. Not even, it seems, the human she sent to kill me." The sprite floated down to alight on the armrest of the throne, and Elowen stroked her yellow hair, making her shiver. "I suppose she thinks it's some kind of poetic justice: sending a human to do the job. But I think it's more like cowardice. She didn't have the nerve to do it herself. What do you think?"

"I—I don't know," Kaede said. Taisin was fully within her; Kaede couldn't discern which of them was speaking.

Elowen pulled a disappointed face. "Oh, come now. I have so few visitors. You must indulge me with a little conversation. Tell me: What did my mother do to convince you to become a murderer?"

Kaede felt Taisin tense with fear inside her, and the fear spread into her own body as she faced Elowen's catlike golden eyes. Neither of them knew what to say.

Elowen was impatient. "I suppose she told you that I am selfish; that I hunger for power that should never be mine. Did she tell you that? She is wrong, Kaede. She knows nothing of what I want—she has never known. But she can be very convincing, it is true. I believe she has convinced you, even though she did it with lies."

Taisin rejected Elowen's words, but Kaede wanted to know: "What lies?"

"Ah," Elowen said, as though pleased to be asked. "Did she tell you that she raised me with every luxury? That I had everything a girl could wish for? She lied. A thousand baubles are nothing when you are raised to know that you were a mistake—the result of a tragic accident. She told me that my human half meant that I would never be as powerful as an ordinary Xi; that I would be doomed to live a short life and die decades before she would need to name her heir." Elowen's face filled with anger. "I was such a disappointment to her. Do you know what it is like to grow up under that shadow? To have your only parent look at you with disgust?"

Even though Kaede recoiled from the golden-eyed woman in front of her, part of her recognized that Elowen's bitterness disguised a deeper hurt, and Kaede's sympathy showed on her face.

"You understand," Elowen said, her voice turning soft and gentle. "How hard it is, to be rejected by one's own flesh and blood. I see that you have experienced this, too."

Kaede wanted to object, but she felt Taisin pulling her back. Taisin's thoughts came through as clearly as if she had spoken them out loud: *She is trying to manipulate you.* Kaede stayed silent, and Elowen went on.

"How could I endure it? I couldn't. I had to leave. I traveled to your kingdom, though I kept myself cloaked and concealed. I knew that I would never be able to find my father—my mother would never even tell me his name—but I wanted to see what sort of people he came from. I soon learned that my mother, for all her secret weakness for humans, knows nothing about them. She couldn't see, as I did, that the shortness of your life makes you work so much harder than any Xi. It's the fear of death that does it, I think. Don't you agree?"

Taisin and Kaede said together: "Yes."

Elowen smiled. "Yes. And when I learned this, I came north to this place. It called to me; the meridians seemed to speak my name. I knew what I had to do. I raised this fortress, and I called the fay here, to help me. They feed me willingly; they have made me so strong." Her face was suffused with pleasure in her own power, and she leaned forward, asking in a coquettish tone, "Can you guess what I'm doing, Kaede?"

Kaede swallowed. "No."

"I am creating a new race of beings—one that has all the relentless determination of a human and all the power of the fay." Her smile faltered a bit. "It isn't easy, but I've learned from my human side. I'm close to success. And when my people are ready, my mother will have no choice but to submit to me, for I will be so much more powerful than her. She will give up her throne to me. I will rule all the Xi and all the fay, and one day, perhaps, I will go to your kingdom and rule that, too. Who could be a better choice than me? I am both fay and human; I understand both worlds."

Elowen sat back in her throne, a serene look on her face as she folded her ringed hands in her lap. "Now," she continued pleasantly, "you said that you came here to kill me. But I am willing to forget that, Kaede, because I see that my mother has lied to you. And because I do not reject my human half the way that she does, I will extend an invitation to you. It is quite admirable that you have come all this way to me. Of course, I thought it would be someone else—your companion, perhaps?—but you are the one who took the last few steps. And to reward you, I will offer you the chance to serve me. You will live a long life, and your parents will see how wrong they were about you, just as my mother was wrong about me. They will have to bow down to you, as my representative. So, I ask you: Will you join me?"

Elowen's words had been spoken in such a calm, measured tone of voice that it seemed almost irrational to disagree with her. Taisin was frantic, fearing that Kaede would give in to Elowen. And Kaede did feel a certain amount of compassion for the Fairy Queen's daughter, but she could never say yes. She thought of her father, who had his own expectations for her. She had chafed under his demands before, but he had never treated her in the way that Elowen assumed. Kaede knew that he loved her. Perhaps the Fairy Queen loved her daughter, too, but Elowen had never been able to see it.

Kaede said: "I'm sorry. I can't join you."

Elowen's face flushed; her mouth twisted. "That was an unwise decision," she said, and she stood up. "You know that I can't allow you to leave this place alive."

She stretched her right hand toward Kaede, her fingers curling. It was as if she was drawing the air toward her;

Kaede could feel the currents in the room bending to her will. And then, to her horror, the air turned and rushed at her; it swirled around her throat like a thousand scarves, tightening until she had lost all her breath. Elowen was regarding her coolly, as if she were merely an unpleasant task to take care of, little larger than an insect she could crush beneath her shoe. Kaede reached her hands up to her throat, her eyes blinking as she began to faint. She could not breathe; her fingers scrabbled at her skin, but there was nothing there to grab onto.

Taisin, she thought dimly. But she felt no response, and everything began to shatter into spots of white upon black.

Chapter XXXVII

iny sparks danced before her eyes; they were as beautiful as fireflies in a purple twilight. And then the sparks multiplied until they were all she could see, and she wondered if she was flying up into the night sky, coming closer and closer to that giant cloud of stars she had seen above the ice field.

She was no longer in her body; she felt free. She was as small as a drop of dew quivering on a spider's web; she was a minute in an hour in a day in a million years. So much had passed to bring her to this moment: births, deaths, countless insignificant decisions that made her who she had become. All of that—all of her—could end now. She could return to the limitless state that every living creature once was in and will be again.

But she was not ready. Not yet.

And not without regret, she turned away from the pull of the starry sky, and far below her, she saw the fortress, a mountain of white snow. She saw the azure sea broken with ice floes. She saw the beach. She saw Con kneeling on the cold ground gripping Taisin's hands in his. She saw Taisin, her eyes wide open and looking directly at her. Her gaze was magnetic; it pulled her down, down, until she was plummeting toward the earth, toward Taisin and through her. Now, with a stunning clarity, she could feel every fiber of Taisin's being. She could feel her pain, her excitement, her fear. There was the clenching and release of the muscle of her heart. And there was the love between them: a revelation. A way in.

In those brief moments when she was floating free, Kaede had almost forgotten what it was like to be corporeal. Then, she was being channeled through Taisin back into her own flesh and bones again, as if she were being squeezed into clothes that were much too small. Her body was so limited, so attached to the ground. She couldn't, at first, remember how to move, but Taisin did, and she was still within her. Kaede watched her own hand fly up; it grasped the currents of air that Elowen had wrapped around her throat and tore through them. It was like ripping a great bolt of silk, and the air fell in ragged ribbons away from her.

Elowen stood in front of her throne with her arm still outstretched. She looked as shocked as Kaede felt. In that heartbeat, they were equals, and Kaede knew she had to act before Elowen regained her wits. She reached down to her boot, feeling her blood rushing into her fingertips, and drew out the dagger and threw it at her.

But there was no time to even hope it would reach its mark, for Elowen flung it aside with a fistful of energy. The dagger clattered to the floor and slid until it lodged itself in the wall beneath the windows, and then Elowen began to advance on her.

Kaede ran for the dagger, but her boots slipped. The icy floor came rushing up to slam into her hands and knees. She slid; she scrambled on all fours toward the wall. Taisin was gathering up the energy she would need for one more assault, and Kaede felt Taisin's strength rising inside her like a fever.

Elowen came after her, vowing that she would put her own hands around this human's throat. But at the last moment, Kaede's fingers found the dagger, and as she whirled around, Taisin spoke through her.

"Elowen!"

The woman stopped, startled by the sound of her name on someone else's lips.

Kaede swung her hand and slashed through Elowen's gown, cutting into her leg. Elowen let out a scream; she looked down at the blood that dripped onto the floor. A curious steam rose from the wound, and the fabric around it curled back as if it were burning away.

"What have you done?" Elowen shrieked. The skin of her face was nearly translucent; her veins were black rivers beneath her temples.

Kaede pushed herself to her feet. The handle of the dagger fitted into her palm like an old friend. She felt Taisin readying herself. "Elowen," they said together, and Kaede charged at the Fairy Queen's daughter and plunged the dagger into her heart.

Elowen's eyes widened; her mouth parted. Her blood streamed over Kaede's hand. She fell, looking as frightened as a child facing the dark.

Kaede stared at Elowen's body, stunned. The moment the blade made contact with Elowen's heart, all the power that had surged between her and Taisin drained away, and now she felt emptied, unsteady. Her hands were shaking; they were wet with blood. Without thinking, she smeared them over her thighs. When she looked back, the same scene awaited her: Elowen lay there with her eyes half-open, the dagger fixed in her chest, blood pooling down on the floor. It was indeed made of ice, and it was melting.

She forced herself to kneel down and pull the dagger out. The wound itself was burned black as if the iron had scorched Elowen's flesh, and Kaede had to swallow her nausea as she wiped the blade on the very edge of Elowen's ermine cloak.

As she resheathed the dagger in her boot and stood up, the sprite who had fluttered near Elowen's throne bobbed into sight. She was a girl, or she looked like one, except she had little wings growing from her shoulder blades. Her skin was as golden as her hair, and she looked up at Kaede with wide blue eyes that were both sad and triumphant. Then she fluttered down to Elowen's waist, where she pushed aside the folds of the fur robe to reveal a silver key ring. She picked up the ring in her little hands and struggled to fly up to Kaede's eye level, where she said something that Kaede did not understand.

Frustrated, the girl gestured to the open door at the end of the throne room. Kaede heard a rising cacophony coming from the cavern beyond. The girl was shaking the keys, causing them to clink together like bells, and Kaede realized they were the keys to the cages. The fay wanted to be set free.

"Of course," Kaede said out loud. "You should free them." When the girl gave her a puzzled look, Kaede pointed to the door, gesturing the act of turning a key in its lock. The girl understood, and a brilliant smile spread over her delicate features. She even bounced a little in the air before flying speedily down the length of the throne room toward the door.

Kaede looked back at Elowen. The weight of what she had done settled over her again. She took a ragged breath.

She could not leave the body there. It felt wrong.

She glanced around the room for something to use as a shroud, but there was nothing. Finally she settled for folding Elowen's cloak more securely around her. Her flesh was still warm, and it seemed unreal that she was truly dead. Taking a deep breath, Kaede dragged Elowen up and over her shoulder. Her body was surprisingly light, and though it was not a comfortable position, Kaede thought she could manage to carry her some distance this way. She trudged down the length of the throne room and through the door to the prison.

Every last one of the fay came to watch her pass this time. Some appeared sad; others eager; but none seemed interested in avenging Elowen's death. The sprite had already begun to unlock some of the cages, and those who had been set free started to follow Kaede and her burden out of the cavern.

It was a long, hard walk through the many tunnels of the

fortress, and several times Kaede thought she might have lost her way. Elowen's body, which had once seemed light, soon felt so heavy that Kaede wanted to weep with the strain of it, but she would not let herself stop, and she would not accept the help of the fay who followed her. She had killed Elowen, and she had a superstitious feeling that it was her task to bring this to its proper conclusion.

At last she arrived at the entry hall, and she went through the great doors and outside into the sunlit afternoon. She was almost surprised that the sun had not already set, for it felt as though she had been inside that fortress for a lifetime. And then she wondered if carrying Elowen outside had been pointless, for she had been intending to build a funeral pyre, but there was no wood on the beach—not even a single spare piece of driftwood. She laid Elowen's body on a stretch of icy sand and sat near Elowen's head, her eyes squinted against the setting sun. She wanted to give up.

The sprite emerged from the fortress first, followed by one of the lithe, willowy nymphs with fingers like small branches. More and more of them came outside, blinking up at the blue sky, and many of them were carrying torches as though they had known what Kaede was preparing to do. They came toward her, and the first one set her torch down upon Elowen's body, the flames flaring up as they touched the fur cloak that served as her shroud. One by one, they set her afire, and in this way, Elowen's prisoners built her funeral pyre.

Kaede sat still on the beach, watching the flames grow, and she felt a thick, ashen despair settle over her. She had come to this island in the far north with the goal of murder, and she had done her job, but now she only felt like a killer. There was no glory in this. She had seen Elowen's face as she died, and she knew the memory of it would haunt her for the rest of her life. Kaede put her head in her hands and wanted to weep, but tears would not come. She felt split apart, broken, as frozen as the island that bore the weight of Elowen's ambition.

Kaede looked into the flames late into the night, and forced herself to watch as the cloth curled back from Elowen's face, as it ate through her furred mantle and burned away her flesh, until all that was left to see was an empty skull, blackened and charred.

Chapter XXXVIII

aisin heard the voice from very far off, dim and faint. It was comfortable where she was: Everything was dark and soft. Her mind was empty, quiet. She felt free for the first time in weeks, and she just wanted to linger there. A cushion of nothing at all. Blankness.

But the voice would not stop.

Gradually the sounds formed syllables. The syllables formed a word. Her name.

"Taisin."

She recognized that voice.

"Taisin! *Come back.*" It was a demand. There was dust in her mouth, the taste of ashes, gritty and dry. Her tongue was thick and swollen. Her head throbbed. Her shoulder ached—and that was what pulled her back into her body at last. The stabbing, twisting pain in her muscles, where she had wrenched her arm climbing down the glacier wall.

She gasped, her eyes opening to a star-strewn sky.

"Taisin," said the voice again. It was Con. He was holding

her head in his lap, and she looked at his face upside down above her, filling with relief as she blinked. "Taisin, what happened?"

The air was freezing, and it carried the smell of burning. The waxing moon was a sliver in the east. She said: "Elowen is dead."

༄

When dawn broke, Kaede rowed the little boat back to the mainland. A small wind had risen with the sun, blowing drifting snow over the smoking ashes. Elowen would never leave her island.

Taisin and Con had the camp half-packed by the time Kaede set foot on the dock. The dogs came running to greet her, barking loudly in the early morning stillness. Taisin met her halfway and put her arms around her, holding her tight. Kaede wanted to stay there forever, with her face buried in Taisin's hair, but she could still smell the scent of Elowen's funeral pyre, and she wondered if it would always be with her.

When they parted at last, she saw Con hobbling toward them. She embraced him, and he said gruffly, "Welcome back."

She gave him a weak smile, then glanced at their camp. The provisions were already packed up; they only had to strip down the tent, and they could go. She said: "We must leave this place."

Con nodded. "We're almost ready."

They reached the point where they had descended from the glacier by early afternoon, and though they were all exhausted, they had no intention of waiting another minute. It took several hours to make the climb back up. Con was wet with sweat by the time he reached the top, and for long minutes he simply lay there on the snow, looking up at the sky, his breath misting out above him as his leg throbbed.

The sledge was where they had left it, perched alone in a vast white landscape. There was no sign of storm clouds in the sky. The weather, in fact, had been still all day, as though it were waiting, testing out the new balance of power in the world. It put Kaede on edge. It felt like something was unfinished. Elowen was dead, but nothing had been made right.

Their journey across the ice field took less time than their journey out to the fortress, for the weather remained calm and the sledge was lighter now. They left the broken tent behind, and their supplies were mostly gone. Both Kaede and Taisin walked with a kind of dull determination across the snow. Taisin was so exhausted from their battle with Elowen that it was all she could do to put one foot in front of the other. Con watched them with an alert eye, for he was worried about them. At night he gave them more than their fair share of the rations, but they did not notice. They only ate what he handed over and slept so deeply he was afraid, in the morning, that they might never awaken.

They did not know that in the distance behind them, the fay had begun their own journeys home. The knockers—hardy mountain dwellers accustomed to the cold—carried those who would have otherwise frozen: some of the dryads, or the winged sylphs, whose bodies were limp in the wintry air. The asrai and the undines had slipped into the icy northern sea to head south for the mouth of the Kell, where they would swim upstream to their cool lakes and rocky rivers. The sprite who had attended Elowen that last day remembered the name of the one who had saved them, and she repeated it to every fairy she set free with those keys: *Kaede*. So the story of the girl who had defeated their tormentor was passed from one to another in languages that had gone generations without once uttering the word *human*.

Had Kaede known this, she would have told them that she had not acted alone, that both Taisin and Con had helped her. But she did not know the fay were speaking her name, so she was spared the burden of becoming their hero, when in fact she still felt like a murderer.

When they saw the ragged line of the Wood in the distance, Con felt like a sailor long at sea, finally sighting land. Relief surged through him; he hadn't realized how much he had feared that they would never leave that frozen wasteland behind. They quickened their pace that afternoon, the dogs running faster as though they, too, were eager to seek the shelter of the trees. Waiting at the edge of the Wood was the Fairy Hunt: the same riders who had sent them off across the ice field so many days before.

The Huntsman took stock of their bedraggled appearance and ordered someone to care for Con's leg and Taisin's shoulder, and then he came to Kaede and regarded her gravely. "You have done a good deed for us all."

She said dispiritedly, "Have I?"

"You have," he said, but she was not convinced.

The journey back to Taninli took several days. The farther they rode into the Wood, the warmer it became, until at last it was summer again, and they could strip off their furs and pack them away. But despite the warmth, a pall hung over them, and the sun remained hidden behind clouds. Kaede remembered how the Xi had seemed to glow the first time she had entered Taninli, but this time the whole world was muted. She wondered if there was something wrong with herself, for ever since leaving the fortress of ice, she saw everything through a film of ashes.

But as they rode through the streets of the Xi city, it became clear that the same miasma was affecting everyone. Few of the Xi came out to watch them pass, and the ones who did looked haunted. At the palace, a thin layer of dust drifted over the white stone. Their horses kicked it up when they rode into the courtyard, and it floated into Kaede's nose and throat and made her cough.

The Huntsman did not allow them to rest. He took them directly through the quiet, dim halls to the Fairy Queen's throne room. Kaede was shocked to see the Fairy Queen slumped over in her throne, her face as gray as the dust that drifted in ashy piles around their feet. The Huntsman seemed terribly affected by this; he went to her side and knelt down to take her hand, and Kaede realized by the way he touched her that he loved the Queen. When he turned back to them, his face was drawn with grief.

"What is wrong?" Kaede asked, stepping forward. She

put one foot on the first step at the bottom of the dais but hesitated to go farther.

"She is not well," the Huntsman said.

"Should we return at a later time?" Kaede asked.

The Queen stirred. "No." She pushed herself upright and looked at the three humans. "Which one of you killed Elowen?"

The question sent a chill through Kaede. Before she could speak, Con answered, "We acted together, Your Majesty."

"Which of you held the knife?" the Queen demanded, and Kaede flinched, for she sounded like Elowen. "Which one of you?"

Kaede bowed her head. "It was me, Your Majesty. I held the knife."

The Queen sighed. "Come here."

Dread filling her, Kaede climbed the low steps of the dais. The Queen extended her hand, and when Kaede took it, the skin was dry as paper. The Queen pulled her closer so that she had to kneel before the throne. The edge of the seat cut into her belly, and the hard stone floor bit into her knees. The Queen's cheeks were marked with unnaturally bright red spots; her burning golden eyes had the same fierceness Kaede had seen in Elowen. Her hair was white and brittle. She looked defeated; she looked ancient.

"This is what has become of me," the Queen whispered, "for ordering the murder of my own child."

Kaede heard the anguish in the Queen's voice, and guilt burned through her. She was the Queen's accomplice in this murder.

"You are not surprised," the Queen murmured. "Did she tell you that I was her mother?"

Kaede lowered her eyes to where their hands were clasped together, remembering the curl of Elowen's lip as she said the word *mother*. "Yes. She told me."

"I thought that removing her from this world would set things right, but I find that I was wrong. Her death has killed part of me, as well."

A droplet of liquid splashed down on their hands, and Kaede realized that the Queen was crying. Every drop was cold as ice: hard little shards pricking at her skin. Kaede watched numbly as tiny red marks erupted on her hands where the Queen's tears struck. She did not know how long the two of them remained there, the floor bruising her knees as the Queen wept. But at last the Queen drew her hand away and lifted Kaede's chin so that she had to look into the Queen's golden eyes.

She saw the world in them. The Wood around Taninli, the trees bowed down with the weight of the Queen's sorrow. The wind sighing over brown, broken grasses. The glacier, dry and frigid, spread all over with funeral ashes. She couldn't look away, even though the sight of it made her wither inside. Had she done this to the Queen? Was it all her doing—because she had killed Elowen? Kaede drew in a shaking breath. She deserved to feel all the misery the Queen was feeling. She wanted to taste the dust that coated the palace. She wanted to drown in the deepness of the Northern Sea, feel its gelid water seeping into her.

The Queen's fingers pressed against her cheeks. Her

nails scraped against Kaede's skin. "Listen to me," the Queen whispered, her voice rough with pain. "You can save me. You can save all of us."

The words floated into Kaede's mind as if from a great distance. She heard them, but she did not understand. She was engulfed in the enormity of the Queen's grief.

Taisin's voice was thin and sharp behind them. "How?" she asked. She took three quick steps toward Kaede and put her hand on Kaede's shoulder.

Kaede twitched. She felt Taisin's fingers, firm and warm; she drew another uneven breath. The Queen's face wavered before her, coalesced into the image of an old woman, lines cracking from the corners of her eyes and spreading down her cheeks.

"How?" Taisin asked again, her fingers digging into Kaede's shoulder bone, prodding her back to the reality of the throne room. The Queen's hands fell away from her face, and Kaede swayed. Taisin held her arm; helped her to her feet.

"There is only one cure for me," said the Queen.

"What is it?" Taisin put her arm around Kaede, steadying her.

The Queen ached with regret. She felt her energy leaking out of her. Her heart was punctured; she would become a hollow shell. "The water of life," she answered. "I must drink it."

"Where is it found?" Taisin asked.

"It is far from here. Through the darkest Wood and across the three rivers; beyond the red hills and within the trees of gold."

Con had been standing silent nearby, watching Kaede kneeling before the Fairy Queen as if entranced, and a sense of disquiet filled him. "What will happen if you don't drink this water of life?" he asked.

The Queen closed her eyes. "I will die," she said, her voice light as a dry wind. "And my land will die with me."

"Your land," Con said. "What do you mean?"

Kaede understood, now, what the Queen had wanted her to see in her bright yellow eyes. "She means that Taninli will crumble," Kaede said. "She means that the fay will die. And she means that the Wood itself will perish. The trees will fall; the rivers will dry up; the earth will become nothing but ash." As she spoke, the words uncoiling through her, she felt her heartbeat quickening. What would the world come to? It would surely spread to the Kingdom. The border between their lands was porous; the Queen's death would hover over their cities and villages, too. She had a terrifying vision of Cathair drenched in ash-gray rain, covering the red roofs of her parents' home in a choking sludge.

Taisin put a hand on Kaede's cheek. "Kaede," Taisin said. "Open your eyes."

Kaede blinked them open. She hadn't realized they were closed. She saw Taisin's worry-filled face.

"Are you all right?" Taisin asked.

Kaede rubbed at her forehead. She felt unbalanced, disoriented. "I don't know. I saw—I saw Cathair. It was dying, too."

Taisin looked the Fairy Queen. "Are you putting these visions in her mind?"

"She must see what will happen if I die," the Queen said.

"Why?" Kaede and Taisin asked together.

"You, Kaede, are the only one who can save me," the Queen said. "So you must know what will happen if you choose not to."

"Why only Kaede?" Taisin demanded.

The Huntsman said, "The hand that took Elowen's life is the only hand that can bring life to our queen."

Kaede was hot and cold at the same time. Visions, apparently, disagreed with her. "What do I have to do?" she asked. "How do I find the spring where this water comes from?"

"It is not a spring," the Queen said.

Taisin stiffened. She remembered, suddenly, Mona and that little sharp knife drawn along her skin.

"The water of life is the blood of the unicorn," the Huntsman explained.

Kaede stared at him. "The unicorn?"

He nodded. "You must seek out the unicorn and submit to its judgment. If it finds you innocent, then it will sacrifice itself to you and give you its lifeblood. You will bring it back to the Queen."

Kaede remembered the stories, of course. Everyone told them. But this was akin to asking her to hunt down a dragon, and though she had seen enough wonders for an entire lifetime in the short period she had been in Elowen's fortress, this was too much to take in. Besides, in those tales, no one ever survived the judgment of a unicorn. "What if it finds that I'm...not innocent?" she asked, and once again she felt the weight of guilt pulling her down. Her hand had been smeared with Elowen's blood. She had done it, had taken the Fairy Queen's daughter's life. She had seen it pouring out of her onto the ice.

The Huntsman said somberly, "If it judges you guilty, then it will kill you."

A thick silence blanketed the throne room. Kaede felt feverish. Everything seemed unreal. She wiped her hand across her brow, leaving a streak of dust over her skin.

Con's voice cut through everything. "This is mad," he objected. "Kaede, you can't go alone."

"We were there with her in the fortress," Taisin insisted. "Your Majesty, I helped Kaede kill Elowen. I share the burden with her."

The Huntsman looked terribly sad. "Your friends do you much honor, but in the end, it is your choice alone."

Kaede looked at the Queen, frail and aged. She looked at Taisin and Con, whom she might never see again if she did as the Queen asked. But the Queen's grief—and her own guilt—pulled her in the only direction she could go. She turned to the Huntsman and said, "I will do it."

He bowed deeply to her in thanks. "We will leave as soon as possible."

PART V

Those who love are clouds floating side by side:
Dewdrops bending blades of grass at sunrise.
Yet love is the rhythm of nature;
Love is oneness with beauty;
Love is the joyful revelation of the way.

—The Thirty Blessings

Chapter XXXIX

aede rode with the Huntsman out of Taninli later that day. He would not allow anyone else to accompany them. They traveled so quickly that the Wood became a blur of green and brown, moss and bark, but their horses did not tire. She ate the food that the Huntsman gave her, and she drank from the water skin he handed to her without question. The liquid burned down her throat, making her eyes open wide in momentary shock, and then they were riding again.

When they stopped to sleep, she dreamed of ashes, drifts upon drifts of them, covering the Wood in a stale scent of burning. She heard the Queen's voice: *Please hurry.* All around them, the trees were dying. She could feel it so clearly, though she did not understand how or why. Something had changed within her when she looked into the Queen's eyes; now there was a bond between them, Fairy Queen and human girl. Sometimes she would reach out along the length of that bond, and at the very end, she could just sense the quiver of the Queen's heartbeat. She still waited in her throne room.

Kaede and the Huntsman passed through a forest of giant trees, their trunks black with age, the sun obscured by thick, tangled vines. They crossed a narrow wooden bridge over a rushing river, and a bridge that swayed over a gorge carved out of a granite mountainside. Kaede held her breath as her horse picked his way across, seemingly oblivious to the precipitous drop beneath them. Far below another river churned, and above them birds with vast wingspans shrieked, their calls echoing down the rocky canyon.

On the other side, the trees were so densely packed together that their horses had to slow to a walk. From time to time sunlight shone in tall shafts through the foliage, and then there were stretches of shadow, or brief squalls of rain and mist. She saw deer in flight, white tails like flags. She saw crows with their darting black eyes, perched on branches above. Eventually they came to a river that ran sweetly over rounded boulders, and the Huntsman told her it flowed south to meet the Nir. There was no bridge here, and they waded across, for the water was barely higher than her knees. On the opposite bank, the trees began to thin out, and the next time they camped, the earth was the color of ocher and smelled of metal.

They climbed one hill, and then another, and the red soil covered everything until even her hands were tinged a rusty brown. At last they came to a spring that bubbled out of a tiny little cleft in the rocky red hillside, and the Huntsman dismounted and knelt down to it, cupping up a handful of water. When he had tasted it, he said, "We are near. We'll camp here tonight, and tomorrow you'll continue on your own."

"You're staying here?"

He nodded. "The rest of the journey is for you alone."

"But...how will I know where to go?"

He pointed up the hillside. In the distance she saw trees, their leaves as gold as the Queen's eyes. "You'll go that way. Through the trees."

She dismounted and watched as her horse drank from the spring. Her head felt fuzzy. The Queen's presence was much more distant now, and she felt almost unmoored. She wondered how far they were from Taninli. "The unicorn—will it be waiting for me?"

The Huntsman shook his head. "You must seek it out. It does not show itself to everyone."

"Is there only one?"

"I don't know. Once, there were many. But those days are gone."

"How do I seek it out?"

He bent down to unbuckle the saddle from his horse. "That is for you to discover."

"What if I can't?" she asked, and a bubble of panic rose in her stomach. "What if I fail?"

He set the saddle down on the ground and looked at her with a grave expression. "I hope that you won't."

෨

That night she slept poorly. She fell in and out of the same dream she always had: ashes falling over the land, settling into the crevices between tree roots, dusting over every unfurled bud, smothering each hint of life. She allowed herself to get up as soon as dawn broke, and she knelt beside the spring and splashed the freezing cold water on her face, gasping at the chill.

The Huntsman brewed a bitter, dark tea that morning that she had never tasted before. "It will give you strength," he said, noticing her grimace. "You should drink it all."

As the sun rose, she sipped the tea, feeling her body slowly coming to life. The daze that had cloaked her during their journey was lifting, like cobwebs being brushed aside. She looked over the red hillside, at the rocks and the soil and the scrub grass, and then at the arch of the sky, pink and gold in the east. A question that had been forming in her ever since they left Taninli finally found its way to her tongue: "Why is the Queen so tied to these lands? Why does the land fall sick when she does?"

The Huntsman considered her question for some time before he answered. "Our queen is the embodiment of our land. It has been this way since the dawn of time, and it will be so until our last queen dies."

"There have been many queens?"

"Yes."

"Then when one queen dies, why does the land not die with her?"

"She is not like your king. She is not born into her station. Each queen chooses her successor, and each chosen successor must undergo many rituals to prepare for her duties. It may take decades. When the chosen one is ready, her predecessor goes willingly to her death."

"But this queen is not ready to die."

"No. She is not ready. She has not yet chosen a successor, and without one..." He could not finish the sentence. His heart constricted at the thought of his queen being taken before her time.

Kaede dug her fingers into the ground, trapping the soil beneath her nails. It was already turning to dust.

❧

The Huntsman gave her a horn cup with a leather strap affixed to it. The cup had an ingenious cap, carved also of horn, and it latched into place with silver hinges. It was made from the horn of a unicorn.

"After the judgment," he told her, "you must fill this cup with blood, and bring it back." He did not mention the possibility that the judgment might render her incapable of returning. "I will be waiting for you here."

She took the horn from him, feeling oddly calm. She thought she ought to be afraid—terrified, even, for she might be riding to her death. But instead she only felt ready. She had come so far, and in a way she felt as though she had been preparing for this her whole life. She buckled the iron dagger onto her belt and mounted her horse.

She rode toward the golden trees as quickly as she could, but it was noon before she felt the shade of the first tree on her back, and she paused beneath its limbs to eat a dry biscuit and get her bearings. She had never seen trees like this before: white bark and branches so delicate she could not understand how they supported the weight of those leaves.

They looked like gold coins, and when the wind blew through them, she heard a thousand tiny chimes. The trees sang.

She continued on, and the trees began to grow more thickly, until all around her were slim white trunks. Sunlight dappled the ground; afternoon slid into dusk; and shadows spread purple and blue across the golden forest. The wind grew cooler. As far as she could see were these golden trees. There was no end to this forest, and she did not know which direction to go. She dismounted from her horse and decided to make camp for the night.

Her horse was unusually skittish. She felt his muscles trembling as she unsaddled him, and he pranced as if he wanted to leave. "What is it?" she asked, her voice sounding strange in this wilderness. She tried to calm him down, but he continued to be nervous, and at last she had to tie him to a tree, afraid that he would bolt.

She tried to sleep, but the horse's anxiety and the keening of the trees kept her awake. She finally dozed off a little before dawn, only to wake up when she heard the horse whinny loudly. She scrambled to her feet, still half asleep, and saw the tail end of her horse disappearing through the trees.

"Stop!" she yelled, but the horse did not halt. She looked at the tree where she had tied it, and the rope was still knotted around the trunk. The end that had been tied to her horse's halter flapped loose in a slight breeze.

Cold slid down her spine, and her heart pounded. She bent over, hands on her knees, trying to calm herself. She was suddenly aware of how alone she was in this queer place, and she had the uncanny sensation that the singing trees had been singing about *her*. It was a chilly morning, but she felt perspiration rise on her skin. The direction of the wind abruptly shifted, and the melody that had been running through the leaves changed.

Something—or someone—was nearby.

She could not sense people's energies the way that a sage could, but this spirit or consciousness was so focused, so brilliant, that anyone would know it was there.

She straightened, glancing around, but she saw only trees. She tried to swallow her fear; tried to ignore the prickles of panic that raced along her skin. She told herself she was there for a reason, and it was an honorable reason. She clenched her hands into fists and turned into the wind, letting it stream over her head, loosening her hair. The sun was rising, shedding gray light over the golden forest, and in the shadows she thought she saw something moving in the distance.

"I am here for your judgment," she whispered. The shadows moved again, but they did not come closer. She raised her voice, bracing herself. "I am here for your judgment!"

She felt suspended in the wind. The music of the trees rang in her ears. She wondered how long she would have to stand there, waiting. The leaves shook like tambourines.

The unicorn seemed to step out of nowhere. It was a male. His head was small and perfectly formed, shaped like that of a deer, but with a gray beard growing from his chin. The horn, a speckled, ivory spiral, protruded from between black eyes that were undeniably intelligent. He was about the size of a mature buck, with fur that contained all the colors of the rainbow. From one angle, he might look like lichen or moss; but from another, he was as stunning as a phoenix, his coat sliding from gold to silver to fire.

She knelt down before him, her whole body tense, and asked for the judgment.

∽

Though she had felt Taisin enter her mind in Elowen's fortress, this was entirely different. As his consciousness filled her, there was a sensation of perfect openness. All of her, heart and soul, was spread out before this creature, and he examined every last detail of her life.

He saw her memories of childhood—roughhousing with her brothers, running around their courtyard home, begging their mother for rock sugar. There was her first trip to the Academy; the time she had upset Fin by leaving the workshop a mess; the warm saltiness of the sea on a summer day. The moment, that morning in the Council chambers, when she truly noticed Taisin for the first time.

She felt the sway of the King's ship as she left the Academy behind. Shock as she watched the King's guards execute the bandit on the highway.

In Ento: the black eyes of the monstrous child as she plunged the knife into its belly. The horror that gripped her as she watched its funeral pyre.

The split second of sheer panic as the wolves came at her. The stretch of the bowstring as she shot arrow after arrow into their bodies, her stomach tight as a fist.

Taisin: the warmth and the smell of her skin; the pleasure of her kisses. Love, new and fierce.

And then there was Elowen, reaching for her throat. Blackness; everything snuffed out. She floated free, like a seed on the wind. Kaede wondered: Had she died? There had been a moment—she was sure now—when she had ceased to exist as a living human being.

She remembered opening her eyes to see Elowen's snarling face. Her knees skidding across the floor, her hand reaching for her weapon. The iron dagger, buried in Elowen's heart. Blood on her hands.

If she had killed someone who already killed her, did that still make her a murderer?

Her eyes flew open. The unicorn lowered his head. She looked into his black eyes, and though he did not speak in words, she understood him.

Harmony: This was the heart of nature. Every living being—plant, animal, human, fay—had its place in the cycle of life and death. In this cycle, countless creatures worked in tandem as well as against one another. All of these beings formed a complicated whole that shifted and changed in order to maintain that harmony.

Elowen had taken many lives in order to extend her own. Her stockpiling of power had wreaked havoc on nature. Her death was justified. But that did not mean that harmony was restored, for harmony is never achieved through murder.

And Kaede had to accept her part in that. Tears slid down her face. The experience of killing Elowen—of death on her hands—would be imprinted on her always. She had been given an extraordinary gift in Elowen's fortress: a second life. She understood that now, and she knew she had a responsibility to live up to it—if the unicorn allowed her to.

He lowered his horn until the point came to rest lightly against her chest. The touch of it sent a shock through her. All he had to do was push forward, and she would be dead. But he remained still. He was not finished with her.

He showed her that although she may have held the knife, it was the Fairy Queen who put it there, and the Queen had acted out of desperation and self-hatred. She did not want to accept her own responsibility for the tragedy of Elowen's life. Now the Queen was paying her own price: She was dying, and so were her land and her people.

If the Queen died without an heir, the ash that had blanketed Taninli would spread, sifting into the cracks and corners of the Wood, sinking into the Nir until the river became thick and slow. There would be no summer; there would be no autumn or winter or spring—only this never-ending grayness, as if all the color had been leached from the world.

This could not be allowed to pass. The Fairy Queen must live, so that her land could heal. Kaede knew that the Queen would never be the same again. Her time to die would come soon. But she needed to live—for now.

The unicorn lifted his head and gave Kaede permission to draw his blood with her knife, the same one that had killed Elowen.

With shaking hands, she slid the blade across his throat, holding the horn cup beneath it, and drop by drop, his life fell into her hands.

The Huntsman looked as if he had aged a decade when she returned to his camp. Her horse had found his way back on his own, looking none the worse for his experience in the unicorn's grove.

"Is it done?" the Huntsman asked.

She held up the horn. "Yes." She was drained, exhausted.

Relief flooded into the Huntsman's face, making him look almost human. "Then we must return," he said, and called their horses.

He pushed them hard on the journey back to Taninli. Every day that passed brought the Queen one step closer to her premature death, and he could sense the Wood already beginning to wither. The sun, now, was always covered by cloud.

When they returned to Taninli, they found the city much changed. The layer of dust that had fallen over the palace had spread to the streets. The scent of burning hung heavily in the air.

At the palace courtyard, they dismounted quickly. Kaede had slung the horn over her shoulder, and the knife slapped against her hip as she hurried after the Huntsman. In the throne room, the Queen still lay in her crystal chair, and Taisin and Con paced near the windows as if they had never left. But Kaede could not spare more than a glance for them, for the Queen was on the verge of death.

Kaede climbed the steps to the dais and knelt before the Queen as she had knelt before the unicorn. She unlatched the cap and dipped her fingers into the blood, which was as warm as it had been when it dripped from the creature's throat. She smeared it in long strokes over the Fairy Queen's sunken cheeks, and words came to her mouth as though the unicorn were speaking through her: "As life is in the blood, so you shall receive it, for it is blood that brings life." She lifted the horn cup to the Queen's mouth, and a great shudder ran through the Queen's body.

As the blood spilled over the Queen's tongue, Kaede's world lurched. The floor seemed to shake beneath her, and she clutched the horn cup, feeling dizzy. The Queen leaned toward her, and she was so close now that Kaede could see the Queen's pupils dilating. The Queen's mouth opened in a gasp. Kaede saw the smear of blood on her lips, and somehow Kaede, too, could taste it, metallic and bitter. She felt it traveling through her body as if she had drunk from the cup herself. She realized that iron was burning through the Queen—iron from the unicorn's blood—and it would kill her just like Kaede's dagger had killed Elowen.

The Queen's eyes were almost entirely black now; only a thin rim of gold encircled her pupils, and a chill was spreading over her skin like frost. She was dying. Kaede wanted to sob: This was not what she had intended. The Queen was supposed to live!

She closed her eyes; she did not want to see the Queen die. A memory rose like a ghost between them, and Kaede could see it just as the Queen did: a birth. A night of pain, horrible pain, followed by the sweetest dawn of the Queen's life. A baby girl with eyes of gold and hair the color of sunlight. Elowen.

Another ghost of a memory appeared: A hot summer afternoon in the Great Wood. A man alone, lost. There was something beautiful about him: the openness of his face, the strength of his hands. The Queen had no intention of keeping him for long, but he was so different from her many courtiers, with their elegant clothes and cool, appraising blue eyes. This man's eyes were the color of the earth, and his mouth was warm.

Kaede felt the Queen's heart pounding. Moments before she had felt the chill of death on the Queen's skin, but now there was a rising heat. Kaede opened her eyes and saw the Queen's face glowing as if she were lit by a fire within. The light grew until the Queen was bright as a star; she was the brightest, strongest star in a constellation, and every living creature was in orbit around her. But even the Fairy Queen was not invulnerable, for even she could be wholly changed by the smile of a handsome young man on a hot summer day.

The Queen was alive; she was reborn. Joy and relief swept through Kaede, and she took the Queen's hands in her own, discovering that the Queen was clutching Elowen's medallion in her fingers. The chain rustled as it slid between their hands; the stone warmed as the Queen's papery skin became strong and smooth, and her cheeks bloomed pink as a rose.

She smiled at Kaede, a smile that sloughed off Kaede's lingering doubts and sadnesses, and she said, "My huntress: You shall have your reward for what you have given me." She leaned close to her so that she spoke in Kaede's ear, and no one but she could hear.

"My name," she whispered, "is Ealasaid."

When she drew back, Kaede saw her for who she truly was, and she wept to see the Queen's love for her dead daughter, and what difference there was between fay and human was erased, for both understood the sorrow of loss.

Chapter XL

fterward there was a great celebration, and Kaede, Taisin, and Con were granted free reign to go where they pleased within all of Taninli. Con spent many hours with the Fairy Queen, discussing the terms of a new treaty between their lands, for they both agreed that the time of isolation should end. He planned to present the treaty to his father as soon as he was back in Cathair, and if possible, he would bring the King himself to Taninli the next year.

Kaede and Taisin spent their last night in Taninli in the rooms they had been given during their first visit. Though they could have joined the revelry in the streets below, they were content to simply be near each other, for they both sensed that something precious was coming to an end.

It was Kaede who finally said the words, for she could not bear to pretend. "You're going back to the Academy, aren't you?"

Taisin looked away, but she could not deny it.

"I understand, you know," Kaede said resolutely, though it felt like her heart might break.

Tears trickled from Taisin's eyes. She covered her mouth with her hands as if that would hold the emotion inside.

Kaede got up and walked the few steps to where Taisin was seated nearby, and pulled her close. Taisin's shoulders shook as she cried, her face pressed against Kaede's stomach, her arms wrapped around her waist. It was a long time before she could speak, and Kaede knelt down and held her hands while she listened to her.

"It's the only thing I've ever wanted my entire life," Taisin said, her voice breaking. "I've dreamed of becoming a sage since I knew what a sage was, and I've always known what sacrifices it would require. There is still so much for me to learn, and I have so many questions to ask my teachers. But I love you so much. How can I give you up?"

"You're not giving me up," Kaede said, and she kissed her hands. "You'll always have me."

Taisin's eyes welled up with tears again. She dragged one hand free and wiped them away, drawing a ragged breath. "Kaede," she said, and she had never before realized how much she loved the sound of her name, the way it felt to say it, the look on Kaede's face when she heard Taisin call her. "Kaede, if I become a sage, you know what that means. I have to take a vow of celibacy. I will be with no one."

Kaede had planned to tell her that she should not give up her lifelong dream for her; that she had proven herself too gifted in her power to not continue her training at the Academy. But she also ached deeply to think that she might never hold her again. It was like someone was digging a hole in her and dragging out her heart, and she didn't know if she could bear the pain. "It's a ridiculous rule," she said bitterly, startling a laugh out of Taisin.

"There is a reason for it," Taisin said gently.

"What reason?" Kaede demanded.

Taisin stroked Kaede's hair back from her face, her fingers tangling in the black strands. "Every time I look at you, Kaede, I—" She stopped, breathless, her cheeks reddening.

"What?" Kaede said, the core of her quickening.

"Every time I—I—you know I can't think, Kaede. You make me stop thinking." She gave a brief laugh, and when Kaede's hand ran over her thigh, she shivered.

"You think too much," Kaede murmured, and she pulled Taisin's hand from her hair and kissed her bare wrist, pushing back the sleeve of her tunic. Her skin was warm and golden and unmarked.

Taisin sighed, her whole body coming alive. "I'm not a sage yet," she whispered, and they kissed, and kissed, and a few minutes later, they left the sitting room and went to the round chamber overlooking all the city lights, and they closed the door.

∽

It was easier to say some things in the dark.

"When we leave here—"

"—things will change."

"It's better this way," Taisin said. "We'll have to get used to—to the way things are going to be." She felt as though she were kicking herself in the gut.

"You should change the rule."

Taisin smiled. "No matter what happens, I'll always love you."

"Taisin—"

"Wait," Taisin said, putting her finger over Kaede's lips. "Let me say this. I'll always love you, but I make no claim on you. You aren't bound the way I'll be. I know that. There's no reason for you to be alone—"

"Taisin," Kaede said, raising herself up on her elbows and looking down at her. "Stop it. I love you, and right now, that's all there is."

Chapter XLI

he Huntsman and several of his riders escorted them through the Wood as far south as the river Kell.

One morning, Kaede emerged from her tent to find a wreath woven from new leaves and perfect pink and white flowers. She stared at it, confused, until the Huntsman told her it was a gift from the wood nymphs, who had visited during the night.

"A gift? Why?"

"Because you saved them, and you saved their queen."

She blinked at the wreath; it was so lovely, a crown fit for a woodland princess. She gave it to Taisin, who blushed to receive it, and thanked her with words so formal that Kaede's heart ached. They did not know how to tread this new path they had chosen, and sometimes it hurt so much that Kaede had to turn her back on Taisin. When she stared out at the Wood, at the trees and the sunlight and the pattern of oak leaves against the sky, it helped, if only a little.

One night, Con asked her why things had changed between her and Taisin, and when she told him, he was saddened. "Are you sure?" he asked softly. Taisin had already gone to sleep, burying herself in her blankets so that she might not have to stay awake beside the person she had decided to be parted from.

"No," Kaede said, "and yes. How can I ask her to give up what she wants most?"

"She wants you."

"Not only me, and that's as it should be." Though it pained her to say it, she was beginning to discover that she believed it. "Her path is different from mine."

"And what do you think your path is?" he asked.

She looked at the Huntsman, who was standing with his riders some distance away. "I think...I think my path lies with them."

Con glanced over his shoulder at the Xi. "With the Fairy Hunt?" He was surprised.

"With the Xi. And with you." She looked at Con. "When you bring that treaty to your father, I want to be there."

He nodded. "The Queen asked me to bring you next year, when I come back with my father."

"Did she?" Kaede said, and she found she was pleased to hear it.

"Yes. So: Will you come back with me?"

"I will," she said immediately.

"We'll have to give you some sort of title," he mused. "We can't keep calling you the Chancellor's daughter."

She smiled. "A title. I'll think about it."

When they came to the river Kell, Kaede could hardly believe her eyes, for there was a bridge. It was obviously old, and barely wide enough for one rider, but it seemed sturdy enough.

The Huntsman walked to her side and said, amused, "Did you think there was no crossing?"

She glared at him. "You saw us that day—of course we had no idea! Where are we? Are we south of where you found us?"

He glanced up at the blue sky. "South, yes, I think a little bit. If only you had gone a bit farther."

"How would we know?" she cried, exasperated. "All the maps are inaccurate."

"Then it's certainly time to correct them," he said, and gave her a warm smile.

She was overcome with bittersweet emotion. "Thank you," she said, "for everything."

He bowed his head to her. "We are grateful to you. And you—and Con and Taisin, too—will always be welcome in our lands. Perhaps your kingdom has a need for a huntress, to tend the Wood south of this river. You might ride with us one day, and we could teach you."

"You are very generous," she said, and tears came to her eyes.

He seemed to struggle with some emotion of his own, and Kaede wondered if he had ever had a daughter, for she thought he would make a good father.

South of the Kell, the Wood was awakening from its long slumber. Sunlight streamed through the branches overhead, each one heavy with green buds. Flowers bloomed along the edges of the trail, pink and purple and white, and birdsong filled the air every morning. It was like an entirely different forest than the one they had traveled through on their way north. There seemed to be no sign of the malignant Wood that had taken their friends Tali and Pol, and nearly taken Shae, as well.

Con intended to stop first at Mona's cottage, in case she was still waiting for them, and the closer they came to it, the more quickly he wanted to ride. Kaede and Taisin understood his eagerness, and the three of them pushed their horses hard on the first day without the Xi. On the third day, they were startled when Con left them behind in a cloud of dust, galloping down the trail toward a horse they could not quite make out in the distance. As they drew nearer, Kaede recognized it, and she said to Taisin, "It's Shae." She and Taisin halted their horses some distance back, not wanting to intrude on their reunion.

Con pulled his horse to a stop and slid out of the saddle, but when his feet touched the ground he felt unexpectedly shy. Shae dismounted from her horse, but she left one hand on the saddle to steady her, for her leg was still not entirely healed. Her hair had grown so that it fell softly around her face, and though she was thinner than she had been before the journey, Con was glad to see that she had color in her cheeks, and some of that color, he hoped, was due to seeing him.

"Con," she said, and gave him a tentative smile. "Well met."

"Shae," he said, and before he could lose his nerve, he went to her and kissed her, cupping her face in his hands. She let out a little sob, reaching up to put her arms around his neck.

Kaede turned slightly away, not wanting to stare. She had worried that the sight of them might make her mourn what she couldn't have with Taisin, but instead, it awakened something warm and alive inside herself. She was only happy for them, and when she glanced at Taisin, she was glad to see that Taisin felt the same way.

"Do you think it will make a good story?" Taisin asked. "The prince and the guard, who fell in love on a journey to the Fairy Queen's city." The sun seemed to shine especially brightly on this part of the trail. It gave Taisin's hair a halo of deep, dark red; it made her face glow.

Kaede smiled, and though her heart still ached, the love she felt was stronger than the pain. "It will make an excellent story," she agreed. And after they had given the prince and the guard another few moments to themselves, Kaede and Taisin rode down the trail to meet them.

ACKNOWLEDGMENTS

Even though a writer sits at her desk alone, there are many people who stand behind her. Thanks to my wonderful agent, Laura Langlie. Thanks to my awesome editor, Kate Sullivan, who shares my storytelling vision. Thanks to my early readers, Sarah Pecora, Lesly Blanton, and Cindy Pon, for your feedback. Thanks to the whole team at Little, Brown Books for Young Readers who helped to bring *Huntress* into the world: Barbara Bakowski, Kristin Dulaney, Alison Impey, Zoe Luderitz, Stephanie O'Cain, Ames O'Neill, Jen Ruggiero, Victoria Stapleton, and Amy Verardo. And last but not least, thanks to my partner, Amy Lovell, who witnesses good writing days and bad, and loves me anyway. This book is for you.

INTRODUCTION TO
"THE FOX"

By Malinda Lo

The world of *Huntress* is inspired, in many aspects, by Chinese and Japanese traditions. The magic that Taisin practices is based on Taoism and qigong; the archery that Kaede learns is based on kyudo. I also intended to include magical creatures from Asian cultures in the novel, but during the writing process I realized there simply wasn't room to go into detail about them. One chapter that I wrote but ultimately discarded involved Kaede encountering a fox spirit, which is a supernatural being known in Chinese folktales as *huli jing*, and in Japanese stories as *kitsune*. The fox spirit is a shapeshifter, and in many tales it transforms into a beautiful woman who can trick or seduce a human victim.

After I finished *Huntress*, I found that I missed the characters terribly—something that I think a lot of authors experience when they connect deeply with their fictional creations! And I kept remembering the abandoned chapter about the fox spirit. When I was invited to submit a story to the online edition of *Subterranean* magazine for their special young adult issue, I knew instantly that I wanted to turn that chapter into a short story about Kaede. "The Fox" is that story, and it was originally published online in April 2011. It is set about two years after the end of *Huntress*, when Kaede is already working as the King's Huntress. I hope you enjoy it.

"THE FOX"

THE WAY THE WIND BLEW, KAEDE KNEW IT
was going to rain soon. The grasses were laid flat to the
hillside; the trees shook in the gusting air.

She was five days northeast of the village of Anshu,
forty-six days into her first circuit as King's Huntress of the
northernmost province in the Kingdom. Forty-eight days
since she had last seen her: the person she had traveled so
far to forget. Now she was scarcely a week's ride from the
mountains marking the Kingdom's border, but she was no
closer to forgetting.

For several days, she had been following a dry streambed
through the foothills, but today she urged her horse uphill.
If the storm was bad, the stream would flood. She headed
for a rocky outcropping partially hidden behind two giant
oak trees. As she approached, she saw the skeleton of a

fallen oak on the ground, its bark encrusted with white lichen. A narrow but well-worn trail led around the tree, where the rocky hillside opened up in a narrow, dark crack just wide enough for a horse to pass through. She dismounted, looping her horse's reins over one of the branches jutting from the oak, and went inside.

The light from the entrance did not shine far; darkness pooled only a few feet from where she stood. But in the distance, she saw the faint glow of daylight. "Is anyone there?" she called out. Her voice echoed slightly.

There was no answer; the cave felt empty.

She went back outside as thunder rumbled. Her horse stamped, and Kaede put her hand briefly on the mare's neck. "We'll be under cover soon," she said. She untied the bedroll from her saddle and unhooked the lantern, then unbuckled the saddlebags, carrying everything into the cave. She knelt down in the entrance and lit the lantern, and when she shone the light into the cave, she saw a wide open space with a hard-packed dirt floor. The rock walls arched overhead in a ceiling two or three times her height, then sloped down to a lower opening, shaped like a narrow little door, about twenty feet away. This was the source of that dim light.

Holding the lantern, she crossed to the opening and crouched down to peer through. On the other side was a roughly oval space, and on the far side the ceiling went up and up until it abruptly narrowed into a tunnel that ended in a small opening. She saw the sky there like a blue-gray eye. A breath of cool air twisted down from the opening, and below were the ashes of a fire pit.

Someone had stayed here before.

Of course, she should have expected it. She recalled the trail leading around the fallen oak to the entrance of the cave. She shook off the whisper of apprehension that slid down her spine and ducked through the opening into the interior chamber. As she straightened, lifting the lantern in her left hand, black shapes shivered over the walls.

She started, and the hand that held the lantern jerked. The light jumped, and the shapes seemed to jump as well. Her right hand moved automatically to the dagger on her belt, and just as her fingers closed over the hilt she realized what she was seeing. Pictures were painted on the walls: dozens, perhaps hundreds, of sinuous, curving animals, some moving among trees, others running together in packs. She recognized some of the shapes: a deer with branching antlers, a hawk, a wolf, many foxes. As she shone the light over the paintings, the lines seemed to move. She could have sworn that the foxes twisted their ink-black heads to look at her. But when she blinked and looked back, they were only dark strokes on the stone.

She took a step closer to the wall and reached out to touch the nearest image: a fox with its brushlike tail held high as it ran on elegant, delicately rendered paws. It looked like it might leap off the wall straight at her, but the black ink was dry and cool beneath her fingers. She wondered who had known these creatures well enough to paint them with such liveliness.

Thunder cracked again, so loud this time that it felt as though the earth itself had rumbled in response. A gust of wind sang over the chimney hole, sounding a deep, ringing note, as if the hill itself were an instrument. She looked up to see purple clouds scudding over the opening. The rain was coming.

⤳

It took some coaxing to convince the mare to enter the outer cave, but once inside, she settled down fairly quickly. Kaede unpacked her hatchet and went back out to the dead tree, hacking off firewood as fast as she could, racing against the coming storm. Just as she carried the last armful of wood into the cave, the first raindrops fell, heavy and cold.

She built a fire over the ashes in the interior chamber. She boiled water for tea. She cooked rice and ate it with some dried pork. She could hear the rain pounding on the hill above, and from time to time, drops hissed into the fire from the chimney hole, but mostly the cave was warm and dry, and she was glad she had found it.

The firelight sent leaping shadows over the painted walls, making the foxes seem to dance, nose to tail, in one long, sweeping motion across the stone. Leaning against her bedroll, Kaede watched the movement of the light, her eyelids growing heavy, her stomach full. Sometimes, in the evenings, after too many days of riding alone, she allowed herself to remember her: the one she could not forget. The one she tried to leave behind. The one she loved.

Tonight, she drifted on threads of memory until one drew tight: midnight in the palace in Cathair, two days before she was due to depart on her northern circuit. She stood before the moon-shaped gates to the little courtyard guesthouse, her hand on the polished iron knocker.

When the door opened, Kaede saw a woman holding an oil lamp in one hand, her eyes cast into shadow as the light illuminated the tense line of her jaw, her lips parting to say, "Kaede."

"I am leaving," Kaede said, her voice so low it was almost a whisper. "I will be gone for several months."

A pause. "I know."

Kaede looked at her, hoping to find some trace of regret, some shred of sadness. But her face was obscured, and the only sign Kaede saw was the slightest quiver of her mouth. If this had been a dream, perhaps what happened would be different—if Kaede could change it, she would—but it was a memory, and in her memory, she stepped back from the door, turning her face away to hide her own sorrow.

"I only came to say good-bye," Kaede said.

A log crashed in the fire, and Kaede blinked her eyes open. The shapes on the walls twisted as the flames flared, and she rubbed a hand over her face, drawing in a shaking breath.

She wanted to blot out this memory and forget it forever, but it rose up again and again until all she heard was the word *good-bye*, echoing like a curse inside her.

She hated the word. She hated the way it made her feel: desolate, lost.

Angry with herself for sliding into those feelings again, she sat up and yanked at one of the saddlebags, jerking it open and pulling out a battered, leather-bound book. Her pen and ink rolled out, the little black bottle spinning across the ground until she lunged after it and clapped her hand down, striking the dirt with a sound like a slap. She set the bottle upright and uncorked it, her hand shaking only slightly as she dipped the quill into the black ink.

She had begun to keep a record of her journey because she realized soon after she left Cathair that she would never be able to remember everything she encountered, and the King would want a report upon her return. It had become a nightly ritual that soothed her: an accounting of the day's events, carefully trimmed to the barest facts, devoid of emotion.

Day 46: No settlement. The foothills continue, and I can see the red mountains coming. A storm, the first I have encountered in a fortnight, has broken. I am sheltering in a cave behind a stand of oak trees, uphill from the dry streambed. The walls are painted with numerous animals, and the cave has clearly been occupied before. The Kingdom's border is approximately one week distant from here. Then I will enter the Fairy Queen's lands.

Kaede's official title, now, was King's Huntress, but she felt less loyalty to the human King than to the Fairy Queen. On her left hand, she still wore the ring the Queen had given her: a moonstone, simple and round, set flat in a band of hammered silver. In the light of the fire, the stone looked almost pink. Like a sweet spring bud. While she wore the ring, she was under the Queen's protection, but she had never had to call on that privilege. Wherever she went, the fay knew her. There was only one human who went where she did with impunity. But she tried to respect fairy lands and to leave the fay to their own business. Her duties, if not her loyalties, were clear: survey the border and its inhabitants; return to Cathair; report to the King.

By then, two entire seasons would have passed. After so long in the wilderness, the city would be a new thing to her. And her memories, she told herself, would be like dust—easily swept away.

She finished her notes for the day and unrolled her blankets. She was tired, and the cave was as warm and secure as a womb. She fell asleep moments after she lay down.

When she opened her eyes, she knew she must be dreaming, for she saw a woman leaning over her. She had russet-colored hair and a pale face with angular green eyes and a thin nose. Foxlike and lithe, she bent down, and when her lips parted Kaede saw the pointed teeth of a predator.

A sliver of fear ran through her, but she reminded herself that this was a dream—this was not real.

The woman's breath was warm on Kaede's face, and it smelled of something she could not quite place. She had smelled it before. What was it? This little mystery consumed her; it was all she could think of as the woman came closer. It reminded her of an afternoon in the Wood in early winter. A memory of autumn leaves packed on the damp ground, the air carrying the threat of snow—

The woman kissed her, and Kaede felt the prick of sharp teeth on her lips. Her skin parted; blood seeped up to the surface. And like a fist stuffed down her throat, the kiss reached deep into her and pulled at the knot of longing buried there. Her back arched; her mouth opened in a gasp as all those tightly wound emotions came loose. Anguish, dragging roughly through her; suffocating heartache; absence, deep and vast. Yet beneath it all was a thin but strong hum of pleasure, as if she had been born to nurture this grief, and now she was finally free to drink from this bittersweet well until she was intoxicated by it.

She wanted to stop. She was desperate to stop—but she was afraid of what would happen if she did. Would she be hollow afterward? Like a shell discarded on the sand, filled only briefly by the restless lick of the salty sea, and then emptied again.

Kaede felt weighted down by despair, as if someone or something was pinning her down, pressing against her lungs so that she could barely breathe. Hot tears blurred her eyes, and they felt so real running down her cheeks that she began to wonder if she was still dreaming or if in fact she was awake. She blinked slowly, heavily, and as her vision cleared, she did not see the same woman above her. She saw a girl. A girl she knew.

She knew those eyes, the brown irises flecked with shards of black. She knew the smooth curve of those cheekbones. She knew the shape of that mouth and the way it smiled. The way it was smiling now. Kaede could not quite believe it. She thought the face above her must be a mirage. She reached up to touch the girl's long black hair and whispered, "Is that you?"

The girl did not answer, but she tilted her head slightly and shifted her body until she was pressed close to Kaede. She was naked. Kaede could feel the heat emanating from her pale skin, and her own body flushed in response. Her disbelief melted into desire. She wanted to believe it was her.

Kaede ran her fingers along the girl's cheek, traced the line of her jaw. She caressed the girl's throat, her thumb resting on the pulse that beat there. Everything about her was just as Kaede remembered. Her warm skin, the muscles of her back, the weight of her breasts. When Kaede kissed her, she tasted her own longing: a memory of sunlight shining through glass, the fall of her hair in a black fan across the pillow. She wanted to fold all of her into her arms and never let her go again.

But the scent that clung to her was unusual. It was not the same scent of flushed skin and sweat, just slightly metallic—the scent that made Kaede's heart leap. This was different. She remembered, again, that early winter afternoon in the Wood, the scent of fallen leaves crushed underfoot as she ran after the buck. She remembered him stumbling, the arrow lodged in his chest, his antlers dripping with velvet as his head sank to the ground. The smell of blood as she slit his throat. The smell of blood.

This girl smelled, subtly but surely, of blood.

This girl was not who she seemed.

The instant that Kaede realized this, she tasted her own blood on her tongue, hot and bitter. The girl's face wavered; her hair was red again, and then black. Kaede reached up with her left hand and clutched at the girl's bare arm. The moonstone ring glowed white with fairy light when it touched her skin, bright as a beacon. As it spread over them both, the girl let out a sharp, inhuman cry. Kaede stared, transfixed, as the girl's body changed in the light, morphing before her eyes. Her shining black hair thickened into a coarse red; her brown eyes narrowed into sharp emeralds; her face lengthened, developing a pointed chin. She opened her mouth in a snarl, and blood stained the tips of her pointed teeth.

The woman tried to twist out of Kaede's grasp, and the startling quickness of her movements finally shook Kaede fully awake. She realized she was pinned on the ground beneath a woman whose skin was covered with a fine, ruddy down, whose body was taut with muscle. The face she had been wearing was nothing more than a glamour. Kaede had heard stories about this woman—this creature— in many of the northern villages she had visited during her circuit. None of the tales were clear on whether the woman came first, or the fox did, but they all agreed that she could take on the face of any woman, and anyone who succumbed to her charms was sure to die, for she drank all of a person's spirit, leaving only a shattered husk behind.

Now, feeling the lithe weight of this woman-who-was-not-a-woman pressing down upon her, Kaede had no doubt she was real. Her sharp green eyes were heavy with hunger, giving her a kind of rough, bloodthirsty beauty.

Kaede braced herself, sliding her feet up so that her knees were bent, and in one swift motion she flipped her onto her back. Kaede yanked the woman's wrists up with her left hand, pinning her arms on the ground above her head, and with one knee on the woman's belly, she unsheathed her iron dagger with her right hand and pressed it to the woman's throat. She was strong but light, and without her glamour to dull Kaede's senses, she was easily overpowered.

"You are *not* her," Kaede said in a harsh voice. A droplet of blood fell from her own mouth, striking the woman's cheek.

The woman opened her bloodstained lips and said, "I could be her." She had the accent of the fay—a kind of lilting tone, as if she were singing.

"No," Kaede said. "You could never be her."

The woman gave her a frightening smile and said, "If you desire it, I could be."

"No," Kaede said again. She pushed away the weakness in her that made her yearn to give in. "No." She pressed her dagger against the woman's throat until the skin broke, and the scent of burning rippled up from the cut: iron against fay skin.

Pain lit the woman's green eyes. Pain and fury. Her whole body rippled, stretched, as lithe as a snake, as quick as a fox. The downy red hairs on her skin became fur; the joints of her limbs turned. Her nose and mouth became a snout that snapped at Kaede's arm. Kaede recoiled, stunned. A heartbeat later the woman was gone, and the fox she had become had fled from the cave.

The air seemed to reverberate in her wake.

Driven by something she did not understand, Kaede scrambled to her feet. She stumbled through the outer cave and plunged outside into the storm. The rain pounded like a drum on the hollow hill behind her, soaking through her clothes. Rain slid down length of her black braid, pouring like tears over her face. She could barely see five feet in front of her, but she thought she saw a shape rising up just beyond the remains of the fallen tree.

"Stop," she gasped.

The shape lengthened, became a female form again, and looked back.

"Stop," Kaede cried. She could not resist. She wanted to see her again.

The woman stayed where she was, drawing back when Kaede approached so that she remained shrouded by the dark, just out of reach of the glow from the Fairy Queen's ring. But Kaede knew the woman had put on the other face again. The one that Kaede wanted more than anything else in the world to see.

"If you want to see her again," the woman said, "then you must take off your ring."

"If I take it off, you'll kill me. I won't give up my life so easily," Kaede said, though her hand twitched. Would it be worth it? The thought chilled her more than the rain.

"You are already giving up your life, with every day that you long for her."

Kaede flinched at the easy condemnation in the woman's words—and at the uncomfortable truth of them. "You're wrong," she said, but even she heard the lack of conviction in her voice.

The woman came one step closer. The light of the ring, which had faded somewhat, flared up again and exposed the delicate, sharp points of her nails. "Why do you deny yourself?"

"I don't—"

"You could have me," the woman said simply.

The rain slid in cold rivulets down Kaede's back. She said, "But I would still not have her."

The woman asked, "Will you ever have her?"

Without waiting for Kaede to answer, she turned away, her body shifting again, and in the blink of an eye the fox was gone and Kaede was standing alone in the dark, in the rain, with the Fairy Queen's ring cold on her hand.

૭ઙ

She was packed up and ready to go well before dawn. When the first light brightened the sky, she smothered the fire and pulled on her oil-slicked cloak, preparing to go out into the dull gray drizzle. She had changed into dry clothes and tied her wet ones into a knot, which she hung from her saddle. She had not slept at all.

At first she had been afraid that the fox-woman would return, but as the night slowly passed with no sign of her, that fear subsided and was replaced by a persistent, familiar ache. All she could see, in her mind's eye, was that face looming over her. She had thought she was long finished with crying over this, but as she sat slumped by the fire, tears coursed down her cheeks until her body began to shake, and then she was rocking back and forth, clutching her knees to her chest like a little girl. When no more tears came, she sat in silence, drained of her sorrow. A peace seemed to steal over her, quiet and unassuming.

When she went outside, the morning light was soft on her face, and the rain was gentle, too, like a fine mist that cloaked the world in an ethereal tracery of tiny droplets. She inhaled the damp, late summer air, and she was suddenly buoyed by it. All the earth around her was drinking it in—a wash of water, slicking down the blades of grass, clinging to the oak leaves and softening the bark. The ground was wet, too, but she saw no footprints from the night before. There were only the marks she made this morning as she led her mare down the hill toward the newly swollen stream to drink. When she reached the bank and her horse lowered her head to the rushing water, Kaede looked back toward the oak grove and the black crease in the hillside where she had spent the night.

Sitting there on the ground beside the fallen tree was a fox. Its red tail waved briefly, then wrapped around its delicate paws.

Startled, Kaede let go of her horse's reins. She took a step, two steps, back up the hill before she stopped, her eyes fixed on the fox looking back at her.

"Good-bye," she said, tasting the misty air on her tongue, delicate and new.

Turn the page for

an exclusive peek at

ADAPTATION

the first book in Malinda Lo's

new sci-fi duology.

coming September 2012

CHAPTER 1

The birds plummeted to the tarmac, wings loose and limp. They struck the ground with such force that their bodies smashed into dark slicks on the concrete.

"What the—" Reese Holloway pushed herself out of the hard plastic seat facing the floor-to-ceiling windows. Outside, heat waves rippled over the oil-stained runway. She glanced back at David, her forehead wrinkled. "Did you see that?"

David Li looked up from his book. "See what?" His dark brown eyes reflected the hard, bright daylight in tiny dots of white.

Reese tried to swallow the flutter of self-consciousness that rose within her as David met her gaze. She pointed at the windows. "These birds just fell dead from the sky."

David's eyebrows rose. "No way."

"Yeah."

David closed the book over his right index finger and stood. "Where?"

His shoulder brushed against her as he joined her at the windows. She took a tiny step away and said, "Over there—by those two workers." A man in a blue jumpsuit pulled up in a baggage cart while another man, in an orange vest, ran toward him.

"You mean that dark stuff on the ground? Those are birds?"

"*Were* birds."

"Damn."

Blue Jumpsuit was gesticulating at the sky and the remains on the ground, apparently explaining the birds' fatal descent to Orange Vest.

"That was bizarre," Reese said. The unforgiving glare of the sun on the neon-orange vest and the glistening lumps on the concrete gave the scene a surreal cast—like overexposed film. "Have you ever seen birds just crash to the ground like that?"

"No," David said.

Reese watched Blue Jumpsuit pull a plastic bag from a container on the baggage cart. He stuck his hand in the bag and squatted down to pick up the remains as if he were cleaning up after a dog. David went back to his seat, but Reese remained standing until the birds were removed, leaving only a smudge on the pavement: the stamp of their final moments. When she sat down again she felt unsettled, as if the ordinary world had been knocked off-balance and everything was now listing slightly to one side.

Beside her, David had returned to his book, and she saw the title angling across the cover in a retro-futuristic font: *The Left Hand of Darkness*. She glanced at her watch. Their plane to San

Francisco had been delayed, but it was due to take off, finally, in an hour. The waiting had made her twitchy, and her leg bounced with nervous energy. She bent down to pull out her iPod from her backpack, and as she fitted the headphones into her ears she surreptitiously watched David turn a page. He was wearing a short-sleeved shirt, and the skin of his arm had a golden tone like sunlight during Indian summer. She took a shallow breath and forced herself to look at her iPod, scrolling through her music. But as the song titles rolled past, she wasn't paying attention.

David was her debate partner. They had both joined the debate team at Kennedy High School their freshman year, but it wasn't until junior year last fall that their coach, Joe Chapman, suggested they might work well together. And they did. They worked so well together that they qualified for nationals. When Reese's mom found out, she was ecstatic. She even wanted to fly to Phoenix with them for the tournament, but her case ended up going to court during nationals—she was an assistant district attorney in San Francisco—so only Mr. Chapman had come with them.

Now, in the airport as she sat beside David, the memory of that day—was it only yesterday?—and all its disappointments surged up again, slamming into the off-kilter tension that gripped her after witnessing the demise of those birds. *Get a grip on yourself,* she thought.

"I'm going to walk around," Reese said abruptly to David. "Will you watch my stuff?"

David nodded, and she stood, dropping her iPod back into her backpack on the floor. She saw Mr. Chapman threading his way through the seats toward them, carrying two bottles of water. He waved at her, and she waved back as she walked toward the center of the concourse. This trip could not be over soon enough. There were only a few weeks before school ended for the year, and thankfully no more debate practice. All of this weird crap with David would be done with, and she doubted they would be partners again next fall. *That'll be a relief,* she thought, ignoring the twinge in her chest that told her she was lying to herself.

Reese passed the podium, where a blue-and-white-uniformed flight attendant was dealing with a line of five or six travelers. A harassed-looking mother herded two toddlers forward while dragging a suitcase and pushing a stroller. Reese was trying to avoid the stroller, her sneakers squeaking across the glossy floor, when she heard someone scream, "Oh my God!"

She turned to see a woman standing up, hands over her mouth and staring at the flat-screen TV hanging from the ceiling. The news was on as usual, and the Asian American anchorwoman had a hand pressed to her ear as if she were listening to a feed. Her face was grim. Reese took a few steps closer until she could read the headline at the bottom of the screen: *PLANE CRASH IN NEW JERSEY KILLS ALL PASSENGERS.*

Reese gasped.

The anchorwoman lowered her hand from her ear and said: "We have confirmed reports that an Airbus A320 has crashed outside Newark Airport. The cause of the crash has not yet been determined, but eyewitnesses have reported that the plane collided with a flock of Canada geese during takeoff. While airplanes are designed to withstand isolated bird strikes, apparently this was an entire flock—more than a dozen birds in all."

A jolt went through Reese. *Birds?* In her mind's eye she saw the birds plunge to the tarmac again.

Other travelers began to gather beneath the TV screen while the anchorwoman repeated the bare facts. The plane had burst into flames when its fuel tanks exploded upon impact. One hundred forty-six passengers were presumed dead. Emergency crew on the scene were hoping to salvage some clues from the burning mess.

"This is crazy," said a middle-aged woman standing near Reese. "Those poor people!"

"What is this about birds?" said a man in a Red Sox cap. "How could birds do this?"

The anchorwoman interrupted her own report, saying, "We have news of a second crash, this time in the Pacific Northwest. A Boeing 747 has crashed onto the coast near Seattle." The anchorwoman pressed her hand to her ear again. "Information is still coming in. We do not know if there are any survivors of this second plane crash." Her face stiffened, and she stopped speaking for a moment. Finally she lowered her hand and looked into the camera. "Early reports indicate that this plane was struck by birds."

Reese gaped at the television as a collective gasp arose from the travelers around her.

"We have Lamont Bell on the line from the Federal Aviation Administration," the anchorwoman said. "Mr. Bell, what is the chance of two planes being downed by bird strikes within an hour?"

The man's voice sounded scratchy over the audio transmission, but it was clear that he was unnerved. "It's not—it's very unusual. I've never in my entire career encountered two plane crashes of such magnitude due to bird strikes."

"Are you saying that you believe the planes crashed due to a different, unnatural cause?"

"I—no, I'm not saying that. I don't know what caused the crashes. We shouldn't speculate."

"Eyewitness accounts indicate the presence of large flocks of birds. Is it impossible that the plane crashes were due to bird strikes?"

"No, it's not impossible, but it's unlikely."

"Then you do think something else is part of the equation?"

"I don't know," Bell said, sounding exasperated. "Look, I don't want to speculate."

"Mr. Bell, I'm afraid I have to interrupt you again," the anchorwoman said. "I've just received news that there has been a third crash, this time in Texas. Once again, reports do indicate that bird strikes may have been the cause of the crash. And—" She stopped speaking, turning to look off camera. Someone off-screen handed her a sheet of paper, and when she faced the camera again, she read directly from it. "I've been informed that the FAA has grounded all aircraft in the United States while officials assess the threat level posed by these accidents." She looked into the camera. "I'm afraid we have some bad news for travelers today. I repeat: The Federal Aviation Administration has grounded all aircraft in the United States."

Reese's stomach dropped, and the crowd around the TV monitor erupted with questions.

"What do you mean? Is my flight canceled?"

"This is bullshit!"

"What is going on? How could birds possibly do this?"

"It can't be birds—it must be terrorists."

"That's insane. Terrorists can control birds now?"

As the questions piled one on top of another, louder and louder,

Reese's heart began to race. The birds that had smashed onto the runway. Three plane crashes. *Three.* One is unusual; two is a coincidence; but three...how could it be an accident?

People were bumping into her, craning their necks at the TV, talking over the anchorwoman. Reese shoved her way out of the crowd, her skin crawling as disbelief warred with growing panic inside her. *What is going on?* She halted in front of a bank of monitors displaying the flight departure times. One by one, those times blinked out and were replaced by a single word, repeated over and over: CANCELED.

✦ ✦ ✦

Reese couldn't get through to her mom; the call went straight to voice mail. She checked her watch; it was 3:38 in San Francisco. She knew her mom was probably still in court, but Reese was stiff with anxiety. If terrorists were behind these plane crashes, how safe was her mom in a courthouse? David paced nearby, talking to his parents on his phone in Chinese.

Mr. Chapman lowered himself into the seat beside Reese, frowning, and pushed up his black-framed glasses. "This is a mess," he said. Behind them, dozens of travelers were clustered around the podium, trying to rebook their plane tickets. CNN was still droning in the background, but Reese had stopped watching after the fourth plane crash in Colorado. She was filled with a kind of paranoid helplessness, and she kept glancing out the windows as if she were waiting for more birds to plunge from the sky.

"What are we going to do?" she asked, sounding more frightened than she intended.

Mr. Chapman gave her a thin smile. She thought he was trying to be reassuring, but he didn't quite succeed. "We just have to wait. You're too young to remember 9/11, but at first it was just a bunch of waiting. Waiting to hear from the president, waiting to find out who was behind it." He shook his head and pushed up his glasses again, a nervous tick that betrayed his own tension. "Hopefully, there will be some news soon."

+ + +

The line at the Wendy's counter snaked back and forth unevenly across the polished concrete floor of the concourse. Reese guessed there were about twenty-five people ahead of her, which put her right at the edge of the seating area next to the overflowing trash bin. An abandoned Frosty was perched on its side and dripping onto the floor, forming a pool of beige liquid. Reese looked away from the mess, her gaze sweeping up toward the windows set high against the ceiling. The sky outside was dusky blue. She had been stuck in this airport since eleven o'clock that morning—almost nine hours.

Earlier, she had called her best friend, Julian Arens, to tell him she was stuck in Phoenix. He told her that all major airports in the United States were full of stranded passengers, and already some people were concerned the airports might run out of food. If the planes couldn't fly, they couldn't bring in supplies either.

"You're freaking me out," Reese said, only half joking. "Are you saying I should start hoarding those disgusting airport sandwiches?"

"They're probably gone by now," he answered. By the time she went to search out dinner, Julian was right. The deli cases that had once been full of sandwiches and salads were picked clean, and the only food left was the square-shaped burgers at Wendy's.

Her phone buzzed as she was scrolling through the feeds on the Hub; Julian had just texted her.

> Stuff is getting crazy out there.
U have 2 check this out:
www.short.349sy

She clicked on the link, which took her to a blog post on a website called Bin 42. The headline made her eyebrows rise: *Government cover-up of plane crashes continues with media blackout.*

If you've been on the Hub today, you probably noticed that everyone around the world is freaked out about one thing: these bizarre plane crashes. But you might also have noticed that your feeds about them keep mysteriously disappearing. We've uncovered evidence that every 15 minutes, feeds relating to plane crashes, bird strikes, and the causes of such are routinely wiped.

Who has the power to do this? Only one entity: the US government.

Sharona Jacobs

MALINDA LO

is the critically acclaimed author of *Ash, Huntress, Adaptation, Inheritance,* and *A Line in the Dark. Ash,* a lesbian retelling of "Cinderella," was a finalist for the William C. Morris YA Debut Award, the Andre Norton Award for Young Adult Science Fiction and Fantasy, and the Mythopoeic Fantasy Award, and was a *Kirkus Reviews* Best Book for Children and Teens. She has been a three-time finalist for the Lambda Literary Award. Malinda's nonfiction has been published by *The New York Times Book Review,* NPR, the Huffington Post, the Toast, *The Horn Book,* and AfterEllen. She lives with her partner in Massachusetts. She invites you to visit her online at malindalo.com.

THE DIVIDED WELFARE STATE

At a time of fierce conflict over U.S. social policy, Americans are considering whether the public sector should do less and the private sector more. In this pioneering book, Jacob Hacker shows that this battle is as old as the American welfare state itself – and that unearthing its sources and legacies is crucial to understanding America's strikingly unusual social welfare system. What is truly distinctive about American social provision, Hacker argues, is not the level of U.S. spending, but that so many social welfare duties are handled by the private sector, rather than by government. Alongside America's public social programs lies a submerged network of employer-sponsored social benefits, which are heavily subsidized and regulated by government, yet distributed much less evenly than public protections. Examining the twentieth-century development of health insurance and retirement pensions, Hacker unveils the political roots and effects of America's hybrid system and explains why the role of private benefits differs so sharply across the health and pension areas. To do so, he develops a model of path dependence that demonstrates how political choices of the past created interests and organizations dedicated to preserving the private tilt of U.S. social policy. With sweeping history, topical commentary, and a wealth of statistical and cross-national evidence, *The Divided Welfare State* demonstrates that private social benefits not only are a critical element of U.S. social policy, but also have deeply influenced the politics of public social programs – to produce a social policy framework whose full dimensions have yet to be fully debated.

Jacob S. Hacker is Peter Strauss Family Assistant Professor of Political Science at Yale University. He was previously a Junior Fellow of the Harvard Society of Fellows, a Fellow at the New America Foundation, and a Research Fellow at the Brookings Institution. He is the author of *The Road to Nowhere: The Genesis of President Clinton's Plan for Health Security*, which co-won the 1997 Louis Brownlow Book Award of the National Academy of Public Administration. This book is based on his dissertation, which garnered prizes from the American Political Science Association, the Association of Public Policy Analysis and Management, and the National Academy of Social Insurance.

To Oona and Ava

THE DIVIDED WELFARE STATE

The Battle over Public and Private Social Benefits
in the United States

JACOB S. HACKER

Yale University

CAMBRIDGE
UNIVERSITY PRESS

FLIP

PUBLISHED BY THE PRESS SYNDICATE OF THE UNIVERSITY OF CAMBRIDGE
The Pitt Building, Trumpington Street, Cambridge, United Kingdom

CAMBRIDGE UNIVERSITY PRESS
The Edinburgh Building, Cambridge CB2 2RU, UK
40 West 20th Street, New York, NY 10011-4211, USA
477 Williamstown Road, Port Melbourne, VIC 3207, Australia
Ruiz de Alarcón 13, 28014 Madrid, Spain
Dock House, The Waterfront, Cape Town 8001, South Africa

http://www.cambridge.org

First published 2002

Printed in the United States of America

Typeface Sabon 10/12 pt.   *System* QuarkXPress [BTS]

A catalog record for this book is available from the British Library.

Library of Congress Cataloging in Publication Data
Hacker, Jacob S.
The divided welfare state : the battle over public and private social benefits in the
United States / Jacob S. Hacker.
p. cm.
Includes bibliographical references and index.
ISBN 0-521-81288-7 – ISBN 0-521-01328-3 (pbk.)
1. United States – Social policy. 2. Privatization – United States. 3. Welfare state –
United States. I. Title.

HN59.2 .H33 2002
361.6′1′0973 – dc21

2002067734

ISBN 0 521 81288 7 hardback
ISBN 0 521 01328 3 paperback

Contents

v

Tables

Figures

Preface

Whatever else they are about, debates over social policy concern what government should do to influence the well-being and life chances of citizens. The question does not afford a single answer. Faced with social problems, political leaders might turn to new or expanded public programs, they might try to encourage or rechannel private-sector activities, or they might choose to do nothing at all. Myriad possibilities, of course, lie between these options, each relying on different governing instruments – from spending to tax breaks to regulation – each defining differently the scope of public and private responsibility. Anyone who has followed recent political struggles over social policy in the United States cannot fail to be impressed by the diversity and complexity of the choices on the table or the ferocity of the battles over them. The bitterness of these disagreements is itself a reminder of their importance. How government will pursue social welfare aims, whether protections are provided by government or the private sector, which tools of public policy are used – resolution of these issues fundamentally shapes the character of a nation's social policies and who benefits and loses under those policies. It is little surprise, then, that they have been at the heart of the struggle over U.S. social policy from the dawn of the modern American state.

These issues have not, however, been at the heart of the story most of us have learned about U.S. social policy, whether from the voluminous scholarship on the subject or from the ceaseless popular commentary on our present predicament. In academic circles, the central issue of concern has been the development – or, more accurately, the underdevelopment – of the "American welfare state": the genesis, growth, and enduring limits of America's major programs of public spending and provision, most of which originated during the New Deal of the 1930s and the Great Society of the 1960s. Much of this scholarship has been organized around a simple comparative statistic, no less striking for its familiarity: The United States devotes less, much less, of its economy to government social spending than

xi

do other Western nations. The principal challenge students of U.S. social policy have set for themselves has been to understand why. Why are public social programs in the United States less generous, less complete, and less integrated into national economic policy than those typically found abroad? Why is the United States the only affluent capitalist country that does not guarantee universal or near-universal health insurance? Answers have varied, fingering an array of recurrent suspects: antigovernment values, weak labor unions, fragmented political institutions, the scars of racial conflict. But the guiding problematic has remained the same – to explain the unusual contours of public social programs in the United States. Even revisionists who have challenged dominant narratives, or the teleological conception of welfare state development that, they charge, grounds these narratives, have generally accepted this definition of their mission, while disagreeing strenuously with received accounts.

Outside the academy, commentators have not been so quick to see the American welfare state as incomplete or underdeveloped. To the contrary, the litany of complaints that flood today's headlines and airwaves suggests just the opposite: that government is too big, overbearing, and expensive; that it does too much at too high a cost and does it badly. Yet on one point at least, Main Street and the ivory towers converge: When it comes to U.S. social policy, what should be analyzed, dissected, praised, or criticized is first and foremost public social spending. Jeremiads and impassioned defenses alike overwhelmingly center on Social Security, Medicare, and other major programs, largely skipping over the wider range of public policies that pursue social welfare aims and the wider realm of private social benefits that these policies encourage and shape. None of this is missed entirely, of course. How could it be when Americans depend so heavily on private workplace benefits like health insurance and retirement pensions? For the most part, however, these less prominent aspects of U.S. social policy remain beneath the surface of popular consciousness and political debate.

This book looks beneath the surface and shows that the framework of U.S. social policy appears very different when we do so. My animating claim is that we miss a crucial range of public policies and a massive realm of social protection when our field of view is limited to public social programs. It has long been known, or at least assumed, that Americans are more reliant than are citizens of other nations on private social benefits, and in recent years, valuable historical research has started to trace the origins of this distinctive state of affairs. Nonetheless, this basic observation has had limited impact on the major currents of scholarly and popular discussion that swirl around U.S. social policy. This is in part, we shall see, because the full dimensions of the picture remain unrecognized. At a more fundamental level, however, it reflects the fact that we lack strong rationales for treating these broader policy features and realms of social protection as constituent elements of U.S. social policy and politics. This book makes the case for doing so.

The central argument of the book is that neither the structure nor the politics of America's exceptional policy framework can be understood without consideration of private social benefits and the public policies that subsidize and regulate them. Not only does the landscape of U.S. social policy look quite different when we expand our view in this way, but also, and perhaps more important, the politics of U.S. social policy looks quite different, too. This is most simply because alternative ways of providing social welfare goods and services differ tremendously in their characteristics and social effects and, hence, in who supports them and how political debates over them unfold. The politics of private social benefits, I argue, is "subterranean" politics – far less visible to the broad public, far more favorable to the privileged, far less constrained by the features of American politics that routinely stymie major social reforms, and far more dominated by conservative political actors than the making of public social programs. To broaden our view thus requires a unified conceptual approach that explains how the different characteristics of alternative approaches make for very different politics as well.

Yet there is a second reason for bringing these aspects of U.S. social policy into our conceptions of social welfare politics, one that highlights not the differences between public and private social benefits but a key similarity between the two. Public programs and the submerged realm of private benefits are crucially linked by the common effects that broadly distributed social benefits, public or private, have on unfolding political processes. We all know that public social programs can foster powerful constituencies and popular expectations, transforming political victories of the past into enduring features of the present. The same is true, I argue, of private social benefits and the policies that shape them. Originating in the debates of the past, America's private policy path has not just responded to what government has done or not done. It has also crucially influenced what government *can* do, by creating self-reinforcing expectations and interests dedicated to preserving America's massive private realm of benefits and the policies that support it. If the limits of public social programs fostered the private side of U.S. social policy, America's private path also contributed momentously to the limits of public programs – and, indeed, remains pivotal to the politics and the future of the American welfare state today.

Although a work of political science, this book freely mixes political, historical, and policy analysis. It combines cross-national comparative analysis and quantitative data with in-depth historical analysis, focusing on the two largest areas of U.S. social policy: health care and retirement pensions. It draws widely on classic and recent works in American politics and on research on the politics of the welfare state conducted by comparative theorists. It mines a wealth of secondary writings on U.S. social welfare history and the development of American politics, as well as incorporating substantial new archival and primary-source research that proved necessary to fill the many remaining gaps. If there is a limit to this methodological pluralism, it comes in my conviction that political scientists should be as careful in their use of history as they are in analyzing the statistical data that have become their stock-in-trade. The history that I trace does not simply tell us how we reached where we are today. It is a testing ground for arguments about long-term political processes, arguments that can only be assessed through multiple levels of analysis and over long spans of time. And the history I trace is also, in this precise sense, my *explanation* for the distinctive contours of American social welfare practice. By transforming politics over time, public and private social policies have defined the scope of the possible in U.S. social policy long after the forces that gave rise to them have faded into memory. If we are to understand present debates or influence them for the better, we need to see both the boundaries and the opportunities that the past bestows upon us.

For opening my own eyes, I have a good many friends, colleagues, and loved ones to thank. At the top of the list must go Ted Marmor, David Mayhew, and Paul Pierson. Ted has helped me see things more clearly ever since I began graduate school at Yale, and in the ensuing years, with his fierce intelligence and abiding convictions, he has constantly reminded me why I first chose to study the politics of social policy under his guidance. He is now not just a mentor but a close friend whose lessons have extended far beyond the shared interests that first brought me to him. David also contributed to this book even before I knew I was going to write it. His intellectual openness, impressive theoretical and historical range, and unceasing willingness to offer assistance all made him the ideal doctoral adviser, as his many former students can attest. Paul, too, has been a trusted adviser and friend. He has commented on many drafts of this book, always pushing me toward stronger and more precise formulations, always providing both encouragement and constructive criticism. Yet Paul has also been a unique influence on my thinking about how to bring temporal processes into the study of politics. If "politics and history" becomes more than a place-name for political analysts who study the past, it will be in significant part because of Paul's formidable influence, which is evident in every aspect of this book.

Many others have helped me make this book a reality. Although they bear no responsibility for the faults that remain, they deserve much credit for prodding me to produce a stronger piece of scholarship. For assistance and perceptive comments, I gratefully thank Brian Balogh, Edward Berkowitz, David Cameron, Pepper Culpepper, Lynn Etheredge, Tamar Frankel, Christopher Howard, Shep Melnick, Eric Patashik, Theda Skocpol, Peter Swenson, James Wooten, and Julian Zelizer. For advice about publishing, I am indebted to Michael Aronson, Ira Katznelson, Robert Lieberman, Michael Lind, Martha Minow, Jim Morone, Chuck Myers, Mark Peterson, and Kathy Thelen. I also thank those who offered me feedback in connection with talks I gave at Boston College and Boston University in the spring of 2001, as well as the countless others who discussed this book with me at some stage in its genesis.

I have been fortunate to have considerable institutional support for my research. From Yale, I received a Robert Leylan Fellowship in the Social Sciences and a John F. Enders Dissertation Fellowship. In Washington, D.C., I enjoyed productive sojourns at the Brookings Institution (where I received counsel from Sarah Binder, E. J. Dionne, Jr., Frances Lee, Robert Katzmann, Pietro Nivola, Thomas Mann, and Kent Weaver) and at the New America Foundation. I am grateful that Ted Halstead, President of the Foundation, asked me to be among the first to participate in his flourishing vision of a think tank where big ideas are hatched, and for the continuing assistance granted by him, Michael Calabrese, Steve Clemons, Sherle Schwenninger, and Gordon Silverstein. The Harvard Society of Fellows made completion of this book possible, not only by providing an ideal place to write but also by allowing me to benefit from the advice and friendship of a remarkable community of scholars. The Milton Fund at the Harvard Medical School generously supported the final stages of my research, allowing me to benefit from the valuable research assistance of Gina Kramer, Alexandra Moss, Signe Peterson, and Rania Succar.

Archivists at George Washington University's Gelman Library, the Harvard Law School Library's Special Collections Department, the National Archives, the Social Security Administration, and the Wisconsin Historical Society helped me navigate a complex array of government documents and other primary-source materials with patience and consideration. They include Michael Austin, La Nina M. Clayton, Wayne DeCeaser, David Ferris, Francine Henderson, and Harold Miller. Larry DeWitt and Bob Krebs of the Social Security Administration provided me both guidance and wonderfully extensive access to the broad and carefully selected collection that they manage.

Lew Bateman of Cambridge University Press is an exemplar of that increasingly rare breed of academic press editors who really edit. His big-picture advice was complemented by the careful copyediting of Phyllis L. Berk and the able production editing of Janis Bolster, both of whom guided me through the editorial process with a welcome pairing of warmth and efficiency. Many others at Cambridge University Press, including Lauren Levin and Alia Winters, helped at various stages. The Press also graciously allowed me to adapt, for Chapters 1, 3, and 4, portions of my article "The Historical Logic of National Health Insurance: Structure and Sequence in the Development of British, Canadian, and U.S. Medical Policy," *Studies in American Political Development* 12 (Spring 1998): 57–130.

My parents, my sisters, and my close friends facilitated the completion of this book by taking my mind off it long enough to sustain my energy and interest. I look forward to repaying the debts I owe them all. There is one debt, however, that can be neither measured nor repaid, and that is the one that I owe my wife, Oona Hathaway. Oona read everything I wrote, discussed every argument I wished to make, kept me optimistic through every setback and every wrong turn, even when her own professional obligations were pressing. It would be easy to say that without her wisdom, patience, and unselfishness, this book could not have been written. Yet that is only a small part of the story. The truth is that without her – and without our beautiful daughter, Ava – I would not really know what it means to live or love. I dedicate this book to them, faithful guardians of my social welfare.

Part I

The American Welfare Regime

Hitherto, our techniques of social diagnosis and our conceptual frameworks have been too narrow. We have compartmentalised social welfare as we have compartmentalised the poor. The analytic model of social policy that has been fashioned on only the phenomena that are clearly visible, direct and immediately measurable is an inadequate one. It fails to tell us about the realities of redistribution which are being generated by the processes of technological and social change and by the combined effects of social welfare, fiscal welfare, and occupational welfare.

– Richard M. Titmuss,
"The Role of Redistribution in Social Policy," 1965

Politics is always a matter of making choices from the possibilities offered by a given historical situation and cultural context. From this vantage point, the institutions and procedures of the state to shape the course of economy and society become the equipment provided by a society to its leaders for the solution of public problems. They are the tools of the trade of statecraft.

– Charles W. Anderson,
"Comparative Policy Analysis: The Design of Measures," 1971

Introduction: American
Exceptionalism Revisited

After suffering from debilitating headaches for nearly a year, Keeshun Lurk was diagnosed with cancer in 1999.[1] In a sense, he was lucky. Because he was uninsured, he had bounced from the emergency room to the free clinic and back for months, his life-threatening condition undiagnosed, his only real treatment over-the-counter pain medications. Fortunately, one of his neighbors, a consumer activist, had pressed his case, setting in motion the visits and tests that uncovered his illness. It was an irony of Lurk's plight that he was now so disabled that he qualified for public medical assistance. But that was not the only cruel twist of fate. Lurk was a hospital employee – a temporary "floater" ineligible for health benefits – and the hospital for which he worked was in the heart of the nation's capital. Lurk lived, in fact, just three miles from the domed Capitol building where, in the summer of 1999, Congress was battling over a "Patients' Bill of Rights" for the privately insured, having failed five years earlier to extend coverage to the more than 40 million other Americans who, like Lurk, lack employment-based insurance.

The Patients' Bill of Rights was not the only issue before Congress in 1999. As Lurk began chemotherapy, another worker – older and better off, yet facing his own predicament – explained to a Senate committee how his employer of twenty-eight years had revamped the company retirement plan, depriving him of more than $400,000 in expected benefits.[2] James Bruggeman's testimony was a quiet entry in what had become a surprisingly roiling debate. For the first time in decades, pension law had hit the front-page news, fueled by employee protests, a shareholder challenge against IBM's pension conversion, and nearly a thousand age-discrimination filings. Over the past decade, hundreds of America's largest corporations had switched to so-called cash-balance plans, a sort of halfway house between old-style "defined-benefit" plans and newer "defined-contribution" plans that base benefits on workers' investments. By doing so, they had saved millions, inflated their bottom

5

lines, and made their plans more attractive to younger, mobile workers
– but at the cost, in many cases, of large reductions in the eventual benefits of older workers.[3] Two years after Bruggeman spoke, however, an
attempt to clarify the rules for cash-balance plans failed in the House of
Representatives, which instead overwhelmingly voted to *reduce* federal
restrictions on private pensions.

These two episodes seem at first disconnected. Bruggeman, after all,
had a pension plan, a benefit enjoyed by fewer than half of U.S. workers.
And even if it had vanished, he would still have had Social Security,
the nation's essentially universal public pension program. No similar
umbrella of protection shields Americans without employer-sponsored
health insurance, who must instead meet the strict eligibility requirements of categorical public programs for the aged, poor, and disabled.
Between the experiences of James Bruggeman and Keeshun Lurk,
between universal retirement protection and an incomplete patchwork
of public and private health insurance, lies a major gulf in American
society and in the American framework of social policy.

And yet, on a deeper level, Bruggeman and Lurk shared a common
bond. Both discovered that their life fortunes depended crucially on
social benefits that they received not as citizens or as contributors to
public programs, but as employees of particular firms or organizations.
Nor were they unusual in this regard. More than 170 million Americans,
roughly two-thirds of the population, are covered by employment-based
health plans. Fewer than 70 million have government coverage.[4] Private
health expenditures represent nearly 55 percent of total health spending
in the United States – the highest proportion in the industrialized world.[5]
Although occupational pensions cover less than half the workforce, the
more than $460 billion in benefits that they provided in 2000 signifi-
cantly exceeded the $353 billion in old-age and survivors' benefits
awarded by Social Security.[6] In no other nation do citizens rely so heavily
on private benefits for protection against the fundamental risks of
modern life.

Today, the welfare state is at the center of political debate in the United
States and other nations. Buffeted by economic shocks and political
opposition, by aging populations and increasing social diversity, the
massive frameworks of public social provision constructed in the twentieth century face new challenges and new challengers. In the United
States, however, a second and less visible political struggle is unfolding.
For more than two decades, the private side of America's hybrid system
of social benefits has been eroding as corporations eliminate and restructure benefits to cut costs and encourage self-reliance. Coverage under
workplace plans has dropped, benefits have grown more unequal, and

recipients have faced both more restrictions and more of the risks that plans once covered. At the same time, America's political leaders have increasingly looked to the private sector for the models and means for transforming established *public* social programs. President George W. Bush, for example, has proposed diverting a portion of Social Security payroll taxes into privately managed individual investment accounts, and he has committed himself to increasing the role of private health plans within Medicare, the federal health insurance program for the aged. Even without these dramatic changes, however, the role of the private sector in American social provision is increasing as public budgets stabilize and long-term private benefit commitments come due. Between 1975 and 1994, the proportion of U.S. social spending that came from private sources grew by more than a quarter, even though the United States already had the largest domain of private social benefits in the world.[7]

The American welfare state has long been viewed as a "laggard" in comparative perspective – less expensive and extensive, later to develop and slower to grow, than the public social programs of similarly developed countries. Yet American social provision does not stand out in international relief solely because it is more limited than the efforts of other nations. Indeed, as we shall see, the share of the U.S. economy devoted to social welfare spending is not all that different from the corresponding proportion in even the most generous of European welfare states. What is most distinctive about American social welfare practice is not the *level* of spending but the *source*. In the United States, a large share of the duties that are carried out by government elsewhere are instead left in the hands of private actors, particularly employers. Encouraged to provide benefits by a diverse assortment of subsidies and regulations, these actors account for more than a third of U.S. social welfare expenditures, compared with less than a tenth on average in other industrialized nations. When the impressive scope and dense policy underpinnings of private social benefits are recognized, it becomes impossible to view them merely as a small residual sphere of U.S. social protection or as an inevitable handmaiden of a limited public welfare state. Instead, private social benefits come to appear as an integral part of America's unique "welfare regime" – a complex public–private framework that has been actively constructed through political debate and decision and which, in turn, has distinct implications for social well-being and for the boundaries of policy change.

This is the story of America's public–private welfare regime: what it looks like, how it came about, what its social consequences are, and how it shapes the politics of social policy in the United States. I trace a recurrent debate in the political history of U.S. social policy: What role should the public and private sectors play in the provision of valued social goods like health care and retirement pensions? And I show how this ongoing debate, unfolding in the context of previous policy commitments, has created the distinctive mix of public and private mechanisms that define the American welfare regime today. In the process, I both challenge and add to existing accounts of the welfare state and the politics of social policy. Against a long tradition of inquiry, I argue that students of the welfare state cannot ignore private social benefits and the less visible subsidies and regulations that shape them. Not only does the United States rely more heavily on these alternative forms of intervention than do other advanced industrial nations, but private social benefits have also critically shaped the politics of public social programs, fostering and reinforcing some of the most distinctive features of the American welfare state.

America's vast sphere of private social benefits is neither an autonomous market development nor the natural converse of restricted public programs. Widespread collective benefits do not spontaneously arise through decentralized market processes. To become a significant source of social protection, they have almost always required government intervention and support, whether through tax breaks, regulation, or other means. Equally important, as political leaders have sought to bolster private benefits, they have also attempted to make them serve ends different from those that private actors would otherwise have pursued. Part of what I wish to emphasize, then, is that private benefits, although nominally situated in the private sector, have become an essential adjunct to public social programs in the United States. They are systematically intertwined with public policy. They are molded by government intervention. They are fought over by political leaders. They are championed by groups that wish to preserve and expand them. The rise of private social benefits in the United States, in short, is as much a political story as the rise of public social benefits, and no less defining of America's distinctive path.

The political forces at work, however, are not identical to those that animate the development of public social programs. Because private benefits are distributed quite differently than are public benefits, they activate interests and coalitions that are distinct from those that we usually associate with social policy. In exploring these more hidden interventions, therefore, we must begin by examining how private benefits and policies that shape them differ from public programs in their distribution and policy characteristics, and we must explore the aims of political actors who usually receive second billing in social welfare histories but have been among the strongest defenders of private social benefits – most notably, employers and political conservatives. When we do, it will become clear that leading analyses of the welfare state, most of which are concerned solely with public social protections, require amendment if they are to explain America's broader framework of social provision.

Perhaps the most important amendment concerns the political advantages enjoyed by established public social programs. It is now commonplace to claim that large-scale government programs gain constituencies and condition popular expectations, making them difficult to dismantle or reform. Yet widely distributed private social benefits also enjoy many of these same advantages, especially if they become a primary source of social protection for the working population. Because of the political perils of challenging widespread public or private social benefits, many areas of U.S. social policy are prone to what social scientists call "path dependence." Small initial differences in circumstances may have large eventual effects as self-reinforcing processes encourage continued reliance on established institutions of social provision. Timing and sequence, by influencing whether public or private policy alternatives gain an early foothold, can be as important in determining eventual outcomes as the specific political forces involved. By examining the sources of path dependence, we can better explain why the United States has a comprehensive public pension program yet lacks universal government-sponsored health insurance. We can also better understand the motives of those who support private social provision, for in many cases, political actors fight for the expansion of private benefits in an effort to halt or channel the development of public programs. The success enjoyed by advocates of private social protection in the United States has much to do with such "first-mover" advantages.[8]

In this, defenders of private social provision have been aided by America's fragmented political structure. The creation or expansion of large-scale public programs has required major policy breakthroughs in an institutional environment distinctly hostile to them. The creation or expansion of policies encouraging private benefits, by contrast, has occurred through more subterranean political and judicial processes, with less immediate furor but with effects no less important. The peculiar public–private character of American social welfare practice was not foreordained. It was an active, if not always deliberate, construction, a product of choice as well as of accident and inertia. Other outcomes were possible, and some still are today. But whatever the future direction of U.S. social policy, the rise of private benefits as a preeminent source of social protection is surely one of the most important "unseen revolutions" in American political history.[9]

Private Social Benefits and the Welfare State

All of us have an image in our mind of the welfare state. If we share the perceptions of most Americans, we think first of cash assistance for the poor – which has appropriated the term "welfare" in common parlance. Yet poverty relief constitutes only a small corner of the social policy field. Even if we count noncash benefits like health care and food assistance, targeted antipoverty programs still make up less than a fourth of total social spending by federal, state, and local governments in the United States. The bulk of spending instead goes to such inclusive social insurance programs as Social Security and Medicare, which are not specifically aimed at the poor.

Experts have spent much energy and ink debunking popular misconceptions of this sort.[10] By the welfare state, they generally mean "the use of the power of . . . government to protect people from income losses inherent in an industrial society – especially those arising out of unemployment, accidents and illness, and retirement – and to provide for a minimum standard of economic well-being for all citizens, irrespective of circumstances."[11] In this view, the welfare state consists not solely, or even primarily, of assistance for the poor. Instead, it combines targeted antipoverty measures with broad-based social insurance programs designed to protect against common risks.[12] Indeed, an important aim of students of social policy has been to show how nations moved beyond a narrow "residual" conception of social policy as poverty relief to a broader "institutional" vision that put inclusive government programs at the heart of state efforts.[13]

Notice, however, what is still left out of this familiar portrait: the sizable sphere of social welfare benefits provided by private organizations with the active encouragement of public policy. This may at first seem natural. After all, these benefits are not directly funded or provided by the state, which seems a precondition for considering them part of social policy. On closer inspection, however, this reasoning is flawed. To take a topical example, government may require that all employers provide health insurance to their workers. (This is, in fact, essentially what President Clinton's ill-fated 1993 health plan proposed.) Such a requirement would not entail direct public spending or provision, but it certainly would be a component of social policy. In everyday practice, regulation of employer-provided benefits can – and does – take a myriad of lesser forms. For example, private pensions in the United States are heavily regulated under the terms of the 1974 Employee Retirement Income Security Act, which sets minimum standards for plan funding and coverage and requires that benefits be available after a specified number of years.

Or consider tax policy. Tax specialists have long attempted to focus attention on what they call "tax expenditures," provisions of the tax code that allow special exclusions, deductions, and credits for favored individuals, organizations, and activities.[14] Such tax breaks are equivalent to direct government spending, the main difference being that their cost is measured as tax revenue forgone rather than as a direct government outlay. Although tax expenditures have diverse aims, many of them are meant to fulfill social welfare objectives, either by providing direct cash benefits (as does, for example, the well-known Earned Income Tax Credit for the working poor) or by subsidizing private social welfare activities, particularly those carried out by employers. Indeed, the two largest expenditures in the federal code are the exclusions of employer-sponsored health insurance and employer pension contributions and plan earnings from taxable income – which together reduce annual federal revenues by nearly $200 billion, about what is spent on Medicare.[15] Until recently, however, social policy experts have conducted virtually no research on tax expenditures, and most cross-national analyses still ignore the effects of tax policy in their calculations.[16]

The point is not that direct public spending or provision is unimportant. It is merely that these familiar policy instruments do not exhaust the available strategies for intervention. Governments may provide a good directly, or they may regulate its private provision. They may finance a benefit through direct spending, or they may underwrite it by granting special tax breaks. These alternative approaches are scarcely identical, and in fact, a major argument of this book is that their political and distributional characteristics differ substantially. But the difference is not that one counts as government intervention and the other does not. If the concern is what the state does to advance social welfare aims, it makes little sense to restrict our vision only to certain policy instruments while excluding others that may be integral to a nation's social welfare strategy.

This is not to argue that publicly regulated and subsidized private benefits *are* the welfare state. The welfare state is a contested idea, sometimes used to denote a particular form of state organization, sometimes a convenient shorthand for an assortment of income protection and social service programs that share common purposes. The phrase that I prefer, drawing on the pioneering work of the sociologist Gøsta Esping-Andersen, is "welfare regime."[17] A regime is an enduring configuration of institutions and policies that are closely interconnected, exhibiting shared aims and characteristics and evolving in tandem over long periods of time. So defined, the American welfare regime consists of three linked elements. The first is the network of direct-spending social programs – Medicare, Medicaid, Social Security – typically identified as the core of

U.S. social policy. The second is the constellation of more indirect or "hidden" government interventions – tax breaks, regulations, credit subsidies – that are designed to provide similar social benefits or shape their private provision. The third, and perhaps least appreciated, element of the whole is these private social protections themselves, which are a product both of government policy and of the distinctive organizational and economic imperatives of the institutions that provide them. Whether these publicly regulated and subsidized private benefits are part of the "welfare state" or not, they are an essential aspect of America's public–private welfare regime.

This basic insight is not new. In 1958, it was trenchantly voiced by the British social policy expert Richard Titmuss, who criticized the exclusive focus on public spending and provision – what he called the "Iceberg Phenomena of Social Welfare" – and advocated greater awareness of two other "submerged" categories of social policy: special tax favors and workplace benefits.[18] Largely ignored at the time, Titmuss's agenda has in recent years been taken up by a small but growing number of social theorists, historians, policy experts, and political analysts who have sought to uncover these alternative dimensions of social welfare policy and their interplay with government programs.[19] This valuable work has added immensely to our knowledge of specific episodes and policies, as well as of some of the very broad sociological issues that the fact of public–private interplay raises. Yet none of the existing research has covered enough historical or substantive ground, or carefully enough justified or clarified its focus, to present a relatively comprehensive picture of America's distinctive welfare regime. No less problematic, recent interest in the private side of American social welfare history has not been matched by comparable interest in the *political* genesis or effect of these understudied events and policies, or in their place within the larger politics of the welfare state. Finally, in those rare cases where the policy process has taken center stage, the dominant concern has been the effect of public policies on private benefits – an emphasis that obscures the crucial reciprocal influence of private benefits on the politics of public social programs. As a result, these valuable studies still remain poorly integrated into research on the welfare state, which largely retains the focus on the "Iceberg Phenomena of Social Welfare" that Titmuss criticized more than four decades ago.

American Exceptionalism Revisited

Nowhere is the conventional focus on direct spending and provision more evident than in the long-standing practice of equating the welfare state with the share of the economy devoted to government social expenditures. Comparative statistics on government spending first became widely available after World War II, and analysts soon began to use them to compare and rank welfare states.[20] What these pathbreaking studies showed was that levels of spending differed greatly across countries. Some nations devoted more than a third of national income to social benefits; others, far less. Explanations for these huge disparities varied, with some analysts highlighting the effects of industrialization or economic structure, while others cited demographic factors or partisan competition.[21] But all these inquiries began with the conviction that spending levels captured an essential, if not *the* essential, feature of national frameworks of social provision.

The United States has always appeared anomalous in these comparisons. As a share of the economy, U.S. public social expenditures are much lower than those of other affluent Western democracies. Figure I1.1 displays social expenditures as a share of gross domestic product (GDP) for eleven nations. At 17.1 percent of GDP in 1995, U.S. spending is not just the lowest in the group; it is barely more than half the average level of the other nations. A generation of diligent academics has tackled this stark difference, trying to explain why, in contrast with similarly developed nations, "the United States has never established more than a relatively inexpensive and programmatically incomplete system of public social provision."[22] Whether the favored culprit is antigovernment values or fragmented political institutions, the endurance of racial division or the weakness of labor mobilization, social policy experts agree that the "American welfare state is exceptional precisely because it is so limited in ambition and scope."[23]

A closer look, however, suggests that American social welfare practice is in some respects less exceptional and in others more exceptional than is commonly recognized. Thanks to a series of innovative reports recently completed by the Organization for Economic Cooperation and Development (OECD), it has become possible to recalculate traditional expenditure figures to develop a more accurate picture of national spending on social welfare activities.[24] (The Appendix details the development of these estimates more fully.) These calculations – which account for comparative tax burdens, tax expenditures, and private social benefits that are regulated or subsidized by government – produce striking results, as Figure I1.2 shows. The United States, we have seen, ranks last according to the traditional measure of social welfare effort. But once we adjust for relative tax burdens, tax expenditures, and publicly subsidized private benefits (and eliminate duplication across these categories), the United States rises to the middle of the pack. In fact, its net public and

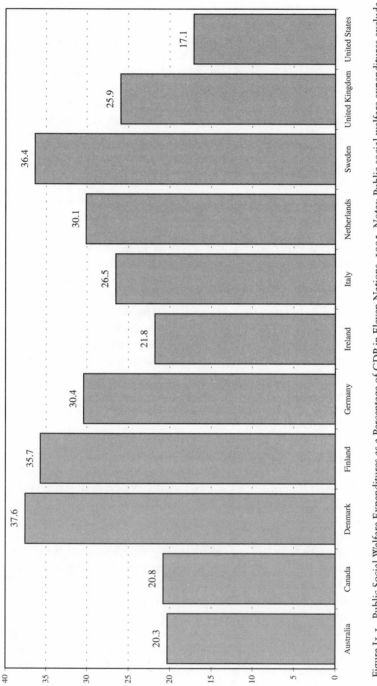

Figure 11.1. Public Social Welfare Expenditures as a Percentage of GDP in Eleven Nations, 1995. *Notes:* Public social welfare expenditures exclude education. They include cash benefits for a wide range of social contingencies – disability, old age, death of a spouse, occupational injuries, disease, sickness, childbirth, unemployment, poverty – as well as spending on housing, health care, services for the elderly and disabled, active labor-market policies, and other similar social benefits. *Source:* Calculated from Willem Adema, "Net Social Expenditure," *Labour Market and Social Policy – Occasional Papers No. 39* (Paris: OECD, August 1999), 30.

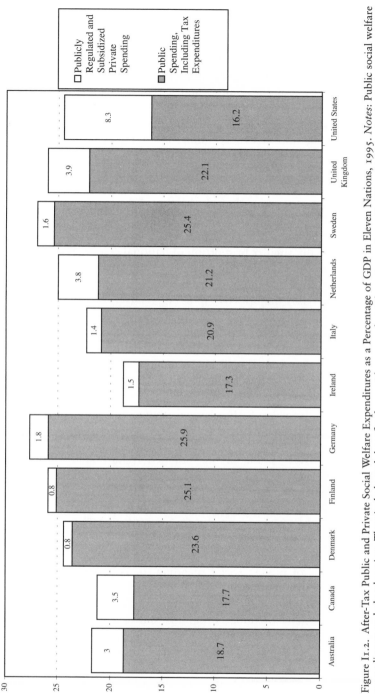
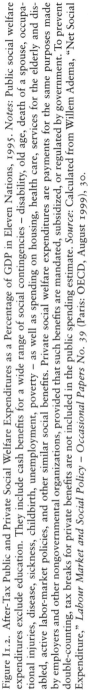

Figure I1.2. After-Tax Public and Private Social Welfare Expenditures as a Percentage of GDP in Eleven Nations, 1995. *Notes*: Public social welfare expenditures exclude education. They include cash benefits for a wide range of social contingencies – disability, old age, death of a spouse, occupational injuries, disease, sickness, childbirth, unemployment, poverty – as well as spending on housing, health care, services for the elderly and disabled, active labor-market policies, and other similar social benefits. Private social welfare expenditures are payments for the same purposes made by employers and other nongovernmental organizations, provided that such benefits are mandated, subsidized, or regulated by government. To prevent double-counting, tax breaks for private benefits are not included in the public spending estimate. *Source*: Calculated from Willem Adema, "Net Social Expenditure," *Labour Market and Social Policy – Occasional Papers No. 39* (Paris: OECD, August 1999), 30.

private spending, at 24.5 percent of GDP, is above the average for all eleven nations (24 percent). Just as striking is how exceptional the American sphere of private social benefits looks in comparative perspective. Private social benefits in the United States represent more than 8.3 percent of GDP, or 34 percent of net public and private spending. In contrast, they represent an average of less than 2.2 percent of GDP, or 9 percent of net public and private spending, in the ten other nations. In none of these nations does private social welfare spending comprise even half as large a share of total social spending as it does in the United States.

All this may seem dry and technical, the minutiae of government statistics and official reports. But its relevance to comparative social policy cannot be overemphasized. Properly measured, the United States does not devote a markedly smaller proportion of national resources to social services and transfers than do other affluent democracies.[25] Not only does the United States tax public benefits more lightly than do other nations, but it also uses the tax code more aggressively to provide benefits and underwrite their private provision. Moreover, the United States hosts a far more sizable sphere of private social benefits than do other nations. American social welfare practice is exceptional, in sum, not because social spending is distinctly low in comparative perspective, but because so much of that spending comes from the private sector.

After viewing Figure I1.2, few will doubt that private social benefits have a substantial presence in the United States. Some may wonder, however, what is so puzzling about this state of affairs. After all, isn't private social provision simply a reflection of low levels of public spending? Don't all relatively small, market-oriented welfare states rely on private social provision to roughly the same extent as the United States does? And isn't the United States – a straggler on the road to the modern welfare state – catching up with other nations as government assumes responsibility for an ever-larger share of social provision? The answer in each case is no.

To begin with, it is simply not true that small welfare states inevitably produce high levels of private social spending (or large public welfare states, low levels). Although meager public programs increase the scope and demand for private benefits, the realization of this potential depends on the specific character of public programs and of policies governing private benefits. Across the eleven nations considered before, as Figure I1.3 shows, public and private expenditures are inversely related. Yet the relationship, while clear, is not overwhelming.[26] Put another way, some nations spend substantially more through the private sector than one would expect on the basis of levels of public spending alone, while other

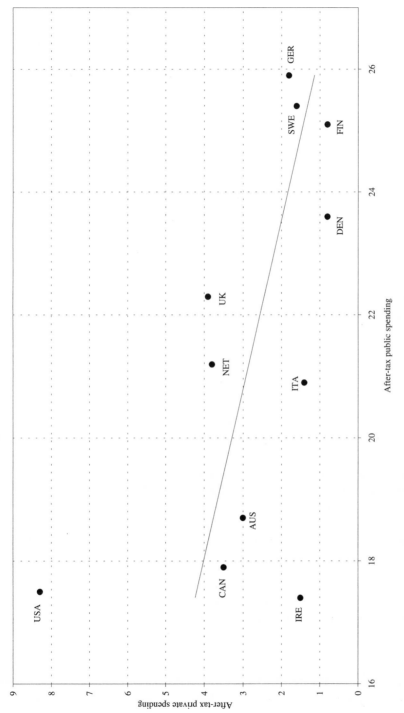

Figure I1.3. After-Tax Public Spending Versus After-Tax Private Spending. *Notes:* Public spending includes tax expenditures with social welfare aims but not mandatory private spending. The Pearson correlation is −0.548. *Source:* Calculated from Willem Adema, "Net Social Expenditure," *Labour Market and Social Policy – Occasional Papers No. 39* (Paris: OECD, August 1999), 30.

countries spend considerably less. The United States falls unquestionably into the former category. A simple model that assumes public spending is the only influence on private spending predicts that the United States spends 4.2 percent of GDP through the private sector – roughly half the actual level.

Even if the trade-off were unambiguous, however, the question would still remain why nations arrive at the particular balance of public and private provision that they do. The frequent neglect of this question seems to reflect the assumption that private social protection is a residual sphere of social provision whose scope is determined solely by the gaps left by government programs. Yet surely the causal arrow runs both ways. Just as the scope of public programs influences the reach of private benefits, the degree to which citizens come to rely on private benefits influences the development of public programs. If so, we cannot treat the development of private benefits as an afterthought. Their reach, their character, the extent to which government encourages them – these may be causes as well as consequences of public-sector developments.

Perhaps, however, the United States is simply emblematic of a larger group of nations united by a shared commitment to individualism, free enterprise, and limited government. In the threefold definition currently popular among comparative analysts, these so-called liberal welfare states stand apart from the large but socially stratified "corporatist" welfare states of continental Europe and the towering "social-democratic" welfare states of Scandinavia.[27] When grouped according to this typology, as is done in Table 11.1, the eleven nations do seem to exhibit consistent differences, with the liberal countries spending less through the public sector and more through the private sector than the others.[28] In the social-democratic nations that are usually considered the quintessence of modern welfare states, private benefits have a very limited presence, which may help explain why they have received little attention in comparative analysis of social policy. Nonetheless – and this is crucial – the United States looks exceptional even when compared with other liberal nations. The average share of social spending devoted to private benefits in the other four liberal countries is 13.4 percent, less than half the level in the United States.

A final possible rejoinder might be that the American welfare state is merely at an earlier point in its development than other welfare states. In this view, private social benefits are social policy holdovers, atavistic remnants of an earlier era that are destined to be slowly eclipsed by government programs. If this were true, we would expect at a minimum that private social spending became less prominent during the "Golden Age" of welfare state expansion after World War II. Yet, in fact, private spend-

Table 11.1. *Welfare-State Types and After-Tax Public and Private Social Spending, 1995*

Welfare-State Type	Gross Public Expenditure as a Proportion of GDP (%)	After-Tax Public Expenditure as a Proportion of GDP (%)	After-Tax Private Expenditure as a Proportion of GDP (%)	Private Share of After-Tax Public and Private Expenditure (%)
Social-Democratic	36.6	24.7	1.1	4.1
Corporatist	29.0	22.7	2.3	9.3
Liberal (excluding U.S.)	22.2	19.1	3.0	13.4
United States	17.1	15.9	8.3	33.9

Notes: The "liberal" welfare states are Australia, Canada, Ireland, and the United Kingdom; the "corporatist" welfare states, Germany, Italy, and the Netherlands; and the "social-democratic" welfare states, Denmark, Finland, and Sweden. The distinctions are drawn from Gøsta Esping-Andersen, *The Three Worlds of Welfare Capitalism* (Princeton, N.J.: Princeton University Press, 1990). *Source:* Calculated from Willem Adema, "Net Social Expenditure," *Labour Market and Social Policy – Occasional Papers No. 39* (Paris: OECD, August 1999), 30.

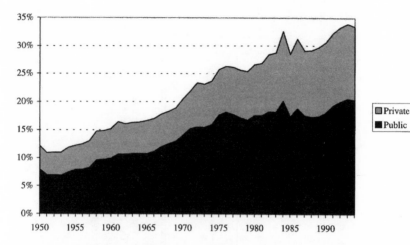

Figure I1.4. Private and Public Social Welfare Expenditures as a Percentage of GDP, 1950–1994. *Source*: Calculated from Social Security Administration (SSA) social welfare expenditures series. Social welfare expenditures encompass public expenditures on social insurance, public assistance, medical care, veterans' programs, education, and housing, along with private expenditures on medical care, welfare services, education, and income maintenance. Unlike the OECD estimates in Figures I1.1 and I1.2, the SSA series includes education and counts as private-spending direct-consumer payments for medical care and education. For additional information, see note 29 to this chapter.

ing in the United States has grown faster than public spending over the postwar period, and substantially faster in the past two decades. Figure I1.4 presents the most comprehensive available series on public and private spending: the Social Security Administration's annual tally of social welfare expenditures, which has included private spending for most years since 1950.[29] Although both public and private social expenditures increased dramatically, private spending actually grew faster, rising from 34 to 39 percent of total spending between 1950 and 1994 (these figures are not exactly comparable to the OECD estimates).[30] America's singular status is certainly not transitory, nor is it markedly eroding. The puzzle of American exceptionalism remains.

The Approach of the Book

If the exceptionalism of the American welfare regime is tied up with the extensive presence of private social provision within it, then the task of the analyst is considerably more difficult than students of U.S. social policy generally acknowledge. Traditionally, accounts of the American welfare state have taken two main forms. The first and most orthodox is a narrative of political failure. The guiding contrast in these accounts is with the more expansive, more generous, more "decommodifying" welfare states of northern Europe.[31] The central plot is of heroic movements and leaders thwarted by America's individualistic political culture, fragmented political institutions, weak labor unions, and enduring racial strife. In contrast, the second narrative highlights distinctive American political successes: the Civil War and mothers' pensions of the late 1900s, America's temporary status as a welfare-state leader during the New Deal, the construction of a capable fiscal state during and immediately after World War II, the GI Bill, the Great Society and War on Poverty, the judicially promoted expansion of antipoverty programs in the 1970s, and the burgeoning of social welfare tax expenditures.[32] Without minimizing the extent to which European-style programs found infertile soil in the United States, these accounts paint a picture of a polity surprisingly receptive to alternative claims for government action.

This book draws to a certain degree on both genres and yet also departs from both. To take the similarities first, no compelling account of U.S. social policy can fail to acknowledge the repeated inability of reformers to win major expansions of the government's role. Before the 1930s, when other nations were moving toward more inclusive social protections, the federal government was hamstrung by a restricted constitutional purview and conservative leadership, and the states were engaged in fierce economic competition that precluded the establishment of costly state-level social programs. Although the New Deal would launch a revolution in the federal role, only one of the permanent social programs to emerge from it, Social Security, would be organized on a purely national basis. And with conservatives able to block most major social legislation from the late 1930s until the early 1960s, it would take another thirty years before the Democratic electoral landslides of the 1960s opened the door for Medicare, Medicaid, and a host of antipoverty initiatives. Other proposed policy departures, notably national health insurance, repeatedly failed. Nothing emerges from the history of U.S. social policy more clearly than the stubborn resistance of American politics to the creation of large-scale national social programs.

Yet the obstacles to social reform in the United States hardly constitute the entire story, as the second, revisionist narrative reminds us. In the first place, major state expansions were won. Compulsory old-age insurance did pass, if belatedly by international standards. So too did unemployment insurance, workers' compensation, public assistance for the elderly, aid to dependent children, Medicare, Medicaid, and a host of other programs. When reformers circumnavigated the multiple roadblocks thrown up by American political institutions and voiced a compelling case for reform, major social programs made it into law and the fabric of U.S. social provision. They may have been enacted episodically, in the "big bangs" of policy change so characteristic of American state-building.[33] They may have been less generous than those found abroad. But they passed, and many of them grew quickly and gained widespread popular support.

Second – and to begin the sketch of my own approach – stalemate in the politics of state expansion did not mean stalemate in the politics of social policy. For much of the twentieth century, indeed, the development of U.S. social policy has followed an identifiable second track of inter-vention, one to which scholars of the welfare state, orthodox or revi-sionist, have paid only limited attention. This second track has embodied the ideal of an "associative state," "an approach that would avoid the 'evils of bureaucracy' by building the needed capacities into the associa-tive life of the private sector or by lodging them in prestigious state-private intersects."[34] The legislative milestones along this track have not been large and highly prominent social programs, but public policies of diverse form – tax breaks, regulations, credit subsidies, government insurance – designed to encourage and shape private responses to public social problems. Unlike the first track of social reform, these less visible interventions have been established amid the calm eddies of U.S. social welfare history as well as during the big bangs of American state-building, in the oft-neglected debates of the immediate post–World War II years and the 1970s, as well as during the New Deal and Great Society. And this second track has, in many ways, benefited from the same insti-tutional and political factors that have retarded movement along the first.

The decentralized and fragmented character of American political institutions, for example, has posed steep barriers to the enactment of national social programs. Yet it has also created rich opportunities for policy entrepreneurs to move smaller-scale changes through the back channels of the legislative, administrative, and judicial processes. Simi-larly, the conservative and moderate politicians who have opposed expansive social legislation have, at the same time, frequently proved quite willing to support government intervention designed to bolster and mold private social provision, as have many of the interest groups arrayed most prominently against public protections. Indeed, once these policies have been put in place, even the most ardent advocates of public social programs have sometimes climbed on board as well, either out of a pragmatic desire to work with what exists or a reluctant recognition that more direct approaches are politically unattainable.

At the very least, it can be said that American politics has created ample room for private social benefits to flourish. Yet the argument I am advancing goes considerably further than this. Private social benefits are central to American social welfare practice and politics. They are not only encouraged by public policy, not only regulated to achieve public ends, not only shaped by the scope and character of public social programs; but they also, in turn, have powerfully influenced the development of U.S. social policy, the preferences and strategies of interest groups and political leaders, and even the public's perceptions of the state's proper role. How this peculiar state of affairs came about and what its political and social consequences are – these are, I am to demonstrate, essential questions for understanding America's exceptional historical path.

At the same time as these questions provide new insights, they also pull us away from the narrow focus on the state and public programs that characterizes much of the research and commentary on the American welfare state. It is not, of course, that government action is immaterial. To the contrary, it has been decisive in shaping the character and course of private social benefits. But to unearth exactly how public policy has been formulated and how it has intersected with private social welfare efforts requires looking more closely than analysts usually do at the interests, demands, and structure of the private organizations that assumed these functions. The story that I tell is not merely of public programs and policies as they shaped private benefits, but of a complex interplay between public and private interventions in which both public and private actors strategically responded to one another over time.

This does not mean that private social benefits should be viewed as equivalent to public social programs, as some critics of the welfare state might have it. Tallying up public and private spending as if it were all of a piece ignores crucial issues of structure and distribution, and in no area is this more true than in the realm of private benefits.[35] Put another way, it matters fundamentally whether a nation's social welfare framework is characterized by low public spending, low taxes, and high private spending, on the one hand, or high public spending, high taxes, and low private spending, on the other; and this is true even if after-tax spending is identical. Nothing can be gained by thinking of private social benefits as a mere substitute means of achieving social welfare aims. They are a different means, with characteristically different ends, and, as a result, they attract different supporters.

Thus, the second step of my argument is to explain how private and public benefits tend to differ and how those differences, in turn, produce contrasting political and social consequences. The crucial differences, I argue in Chapter 1, concern distribution, visibility, and control. Although public programs are less egalitarian than we instinctively believe, they are substantially more risk- and income-redistributive than are private social benefits. Coverage is typically broader under public programs than it is under private auspices, it is more likely to be compulsory, and it is more likely to favor vulnerable and low-income groups. Because most private benefits are provided as an emolument of employment, they are more generous and prevalent among higher-income workers – the very Americans who need them least. Because they divide workers by industry and workplace, they also undercut the ability to pool risks across large numbers of citizens. Moreover, the means by which these benefits tend to be subsidized skews them even more toward the upper end of the income scale. Special tax subsidies for private benefits, for example, generally advantage well-paid workers, not only because they fall into higher tax brackets but also because they are most likely to receive workplace benefits and their benefits are most generous.

The other crucial differences between public and private benefits concern visibility and control. Although many critics decry the unrecognized costs and "uncontrollable" growth of public social programs, these programs appear exceedingly visible and responsive when compared with private social benefits. Most Americans, it is fair to say, do not recognize the extent to which private benefits are encouraged by government, and even many policymakers admit that they have only a sketchy understanding of the subterranean political processes and public policies that shape private social provision. Furthermore, because private benefits emerge from the interplay of public policy and the imperatives of private organizations, they pose greater barriers to political control and to the legislative engineering of outcomes than do most public social programs.

The characteristics of policies are a product of politics. To quote Harold Lasswell's famous definition of politics, they determine "Who gets what, when, how."[36] But these characteristics should also be expected to "produce" politics – to create, that is, recurrent political cleavages and patterns of policy change.[37] This is what I argue private benefits do. They activate a constellation of interests and actors at odds with the constellation usually associated with social policy, and they push toward a "subterranean" form of politics that has favored the demands of these groups and individuals.[38] Conservatives in government, business interests, insurers, medical providers, and other groups generally counted as opponents of expanded social provision have repeatedly sought to enlarge (or prevent the restriction of) the indirect subsidies that underwrite private benefits. Their aims have been both immediate and strategic. In the short term, they have sought government sanction and support for private social welfare activities already performed, justifying such concessions on the grounds that private social benefits serve public ends.

The long-term aim, however, has been to construct a viable private sphere of social provision that can serve as an alternative, or at least a significant counterpart, to public social programs – and, in doing so, to foster a social policy framework modest in its redistributive effect, dependent upon private institutions, and responsive to private interests.

Two examples will serve to illustrate the point and preview the terrain ahead. The New Deal saw the creation of Social Security, the national retirement program that would expand to become the guiding light of U.S. social policy. Yet in the immediate aftermath of Social Security's enactment, it was actually corporate pension plans that flourished most spectacularly, as employers fought for the expansion of tax breaks for private pensions and recast their plans as supplementary benefits for higher-income workers. Mostly behind the scenes, business groups, insurers, pension consultants, and key conservatives in Congress helped establish and codify a favorable set of laws that allowed publicly subsidized private plans to be generously "integrated" with Social Security – which in practice meant that these plans provided little or no benefit to the very workers whom New Deal reformers had sought to help. After the failure of government health insurance during the 1910s and the New Deal, this constellation of actors also joined with the medical profession to demand public support for employer-provided health insurance, arguing in this case that no government protection was needed at all. These demands and their legacies – favorable tax laws, extensive subsidies for private social spending, a massive system of private workplace benefits – eventually forced would-be health reformers to scale back their ambitions and concentrate on Americans left out of the private insurance system, with devastating consequences for reformers' long-term aims.

This brings us to the final, and most crucial, step of my argument: to show how these political struggles over private social provision unfold over time. This is the central aim of Parts II and III, which examine the twentieth-century development of the two largest areas of U.S. social policy: health insurance and retirement pensions. In these parts, I weave together two theoretically guided historical narratives: a story of *parallel development* designed to explain why private social benefits are so prominent in the health and pension areas, and a story of *contrasting development* designed to explain why, despite common cultural and institutional influences, the role of private benefits nonetheless came to differ so sharply across the two domains.

The emphasis of these narratives is on timing, sequence, and the self-reinforcing consequences of early policy decisions – in short, on path dependence. If my initial claim is that private social benefits are central to U.S. social policy and my second is that such benefits are politically distinctive, my final argument is that the specific role that private benefits have come to play in the United States – whom they cover, how and to what extent they are regulated for public ends, and the specific pattern of politics surrounding them – has been decisively shaped by the extent of their development relative to public social programs. The crux of this third claim is that, under certain circumstances, private social benefits have "policy feedback" effects that are not all that different from the policy feedback effects that are created by public social programs.[39] Like public social programs, widely distributed private benefits create embedded institutions, give rise to powerful vested interests, and foster widespread public expectations. And like public social programs, the policies that shape private social benefits (and the benefits themselves) can become extremely resistant to change – especially in a fragmented political system like that of the United States. This does not mean such benefits are "locked in," in the sense that they cannot be altered.[40] For reasons to be discussed, private social benefits are often much more dynamic than public programs, even when the basic policy framework that governs them remains highly stable. But it does mean that the development of widely distributed public and private benefits is likely to be highly path dependent, with early policy choices transforming the menu of future options by pushing policy down self-reinforcing paths from which departure may be difficult.

In path-dependent processes, timing and sequence are crucial. Explanations need to attend not just to *what* happens but also *when* events happen relative to other events or ongoing processes. I argue that when private benefits become deeply embedded in advance of public programs (and, more specifically, when they become what I call a "core," rather than a "supplementary," source of social protection), the prospects for major government incursions into that policy area diminish. More than simply restricting the scope for intervention, such preemption of public alternatives pushes the roster of politically viable options toward *forms* of government intervention that are meant to bolster or work around, rather than to challenge, private social provision. This, in essence, is my explanation for the divergent paths taken by the United States in pension policy, where Social Security became the foundation for supplementary private plans; and in health policy, where private insurance became the core provider of health security while public programs emerged later to serve populations left out of the employment-based system.

The concept of path dependence pushes in two somewhat contradictory directions. The first is toward a greater appreciation of the alternative possibilities that exist in political history. We cease to conceive of policy outcomes as inevitably rooted in enduring characteristics of nations, whether they be institutions or ideas, structure or culture. If timing and sequence matter, then we can often recognize different historical paths leading to very different destinations. The second direction in which we are pushed, however, is toward greater realism about the ability to change institutions once they have become firmly embedded. America's public–private welfare regime will not be transformed into a welfare state of the social-democratic variety, nor will it become the "conservative opportunity society" that some on the right desire. The weight of history guarantees this, as do the dense sinews of state authority and private power that together define America's unusual social policy amalgam. Change will occur, but it will be bounded change – bounded not just by the politics of the day or the vision of leaders and citizens, but also by the division of responsibilities that more than a century of public–private interplay has constructed. I return to these reflections in the chapter that closes this book.

To begin, however, we need a more precise outline of the scope and theoretical foundations of the historical journey to come – the subjects of Chapter 1. This is the most technical section of the book, and some may wish to jump to the historical analysis in Parts II and III rather than forge directly onward, returning to Chapter 1 at the end or when necessary to clarify particular claims. Part IV completes the journey, exploring why the American welfare regime emerged as it did and how this distinctive policy configuration will – and should – evolve in the decades to come.

1

The Politics of Public and Private Social Benefits

Social policies vary in many ways. They are centralized or decentralized, targeted or inclusive, costly or inexpensive. They use different mechanisms, deliver different benefits, address different problems, embody different strategies. Any theory that tried to capture all, or even most, of these differences would prove not just unwieldy but practically useless. In the 1960s, for instance, the economist E. S. Kirschen and his colleagues identified sixty-three distinct policy instruments in their exhaustive (and exhausting) three-volume study, *Economic Policy in Our Time*.[1] Needless to say, as an effort to reduce policy to its essence, this particular exercise left much to be desired.

The intricacies of the terrain should not, however, scare off the aspiring topographer. A map of complex reality, after all, is inevitably a simplified representation that captures only those features of the landscape most relevant to those who will use it as a guide. The goal of this chapter is to present a unified framework for understanding the political development of public and private social benefits in the United States. My aim, therefore, is not to catalog all of the ways in which alternative policy approaches might differ, but to single out a few of the most important differences that both theory and common sense suggest should influence the politics and evolution of social policy.

The exposition proceeds in three stages. First, I step back from the larger issues raised in the last chapter to ask a simple question: In what politically relevant ways do alternative social welfare approaches differ? Answering this question opens the door to a second: How might these differences in turn affect the character of political interaction around these approaches? The third step is to move beyond these static contrasts to show how the historical interplay between critical moments of political opportunity and the path-dependent effects of public and private social benefits provides a crucial explanation for how social policy develops in a particular domain.

Defining Public and Private Social Welfare Approaches

Table 1.1 diagrams the basic conceptual scheme that guides this chapter. In this typology, social policy approaches stretch along a continuum ranging from purely public to purely private action. On one end of the spectrum lies direct government provision; on the other, unfettered private provision; and in between, various hybrid approaches in which government contracts with private actors to provide social welfare benefits or shapes their private provision. As the Introduction noted, most analyses of social policy take the leftmost two categories of intervention as their sole concern. Yet while public spending and provision are undeniably important, government may also influence the availability or delivery of social welfare benefits through other means. These options are admittedly more difficult to measure, involving instruments like regulation that are not easily quantified and requiring attention to both public and private activities. But the evidence in the Introduction makes clear that these hybrid approaches represent a critical sphere of social welfare policy in the United States. We shall see, moreover, that some of the very features that make these approaches difficult to measure – for example, the prominent role that they grant private organizations and the less visible character of the instruments upon which they typically rely – also make them politically distinctive.

Figure 1.1 further clarifies the scope of the analysis, indicating what counts as public and private social spending and providing estimates of the current magnitude of each. As the figure shows, the bulk of private social benefits (accounting for nearly a tenth of the U.S. economy) represents what I term *private social insurance*: health insurance, pensions, and other safeguards of economic security that workers receive through employment.[2] Like public social insurance, private social insurance is "designed to moderate the risks of current income loss or inadequacy by providing secure cash or near-cash entitlements on the occurrence of defined risks."[3] By covering all or most of an employment group, private social insurance spreads risks in a manner similar to public social insurance, although obviously not as broadly. Private social insurance is also heavily subsidized and regulated, in part out of recognition of the public ends it serves. For these reasons, it is substantially different from insurance purchased by individuals or families on their own.

Not everyone, to be sure, will accept these boundaries. Some, for example, may accept my claim that private social benefits are an important part of the American welfare regime, but ask why the analysis stops there. Why not include organized forms of social provision that are *not* substantially shaped by government? Why not analyze informal

Table 1.1. *The Continuum of Social Policy Approaches*

Public →→→→ Private

	Direct provision	Indirect or in-kind provision	Regulation	Subsidies and inducements	Purely private provision
Approach	Direct provision	Indirect or in-kind provision	Regulation	Subsidies and inducements	Purely private provision
Explanation	Provide good directly through either transfer or production	Purchase good from intermediaries or provide vouchers	Regulate the terms of private provision of good	Encourage the private provision or purchase of good	Leave provision of good to market forces or voluntary organizations
Common instruments of governance	Cash payment; government production	Payments to third parties; vouchers	Standards and targets, backed up by sanctions	Tax breaks; subsidized credit; public insurance	In pure form, occurs without intervention
Illustrative social policy example(s)	Social Security, Veterans Health System	Medicare, Food Stamps, housing vouchers	Private pension regulations	Tax exclusion of fringe benefits	Paid sick leave, unsubsidized charitable efforts

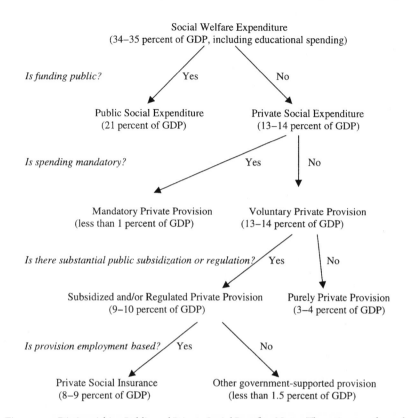

Figure 1.1. Distinguishing Public and Private Social Benefits. *Notes*: The estimates of spending are based on the Social Security Administration's definition of social welfare expenditures, which includes educational spending. These are gross (before-tax) expenditures and are based on various estimates for the years 1993, 1994, and 1995. The public spending estimate includes tax expenditures with social welfare aims and the subsidy costs of federal loans and loan guarantees. Although mandatory private spending is accounted for, the compliance costs of regulation are not, because accurate measures are rare and highly controversial. To avoid double-counting, tax expenditures that subsidize private social spending are not included in the tally of public spending. Although the revenue loss of the home mortgage interest deduction is treated as public spending, private housing expenses are not counted as private social spending on the grounds that they do not constitute organized social insurance or provision. The figures are given as ranges to suggest both the uncertainty of the estimates and their sensitivity to decisions about inclusion. *Source*: Calculated from Willem Adema, "Net Social Expenditure," *Labour Market and Social Policy – Occasional Papers No. 39* (Paris: OECD, 1999), 30; Robert J. Lampman, *Social Welfare Spending: Accounting for the Changes from 1950 to 1978* (Orlando, Fla.: Academic Press, 1984), 71; Social Security Administration (SSA), *Social Security Bulletin Annual Statistical Supplement* (Washington, D.C.: SSA, 1998), 140; Christopher Howard, *The Hidden Welfare State: Tax Expenditures and Social Policy in the United States* (Princeton, N.J.: Princeton University Press, 1997), Table 1.2; Congressional Budget Office, *Credit Reform: Comparable Budget Costs for Cash and Credit* (Washington, D.C.: CBO, 1989), 44–45.

transfers between and within families? Why not consider all government interventions that affect social welfare, from environmental to consumer protection to macroeconomic policies? Once the Pandora's box of non-governmental provision is opened, these critics might suggest, the distinctions drawn between alternative realms of social provision become essentially arbitrary.

This objection invites a pragmatic and a principled response. The pragmatic response is that the farther one moves outside the orbit of the welfare state, the scarcer the data, the weaker the grounds for generalization, and the less meaningful the comparison between public programs and private social provision. These broader features of public policy and social life surely help us understand the overall structure and effect of public social programs. It is far less clear, however, that they have an essential *political* relationship to these programs or that they are the explicit object of government intervention – characteristics that private social benefits unquestionably do exhibit.

The principled response is that this book is not about all social transfers or all government policies with welfare effects. Rather, it concerns organized benefits that share two defining characteristics: They are designed to protect against widely distributed risks to income and well-being inherent in a market economy (or to deliver goods and services related to those risks), and they are substantially colored by public law.[4] Unmediated transfers within and between families, private benefits that operate with little government influence, public and private activities with central purposes other than protection against widespread risks inherent in a market economy – all these are not social welfare benefits as I have defined them, even if they materially affect social welfare. These lines of demarcation are contestable, but not arbitrary. They unite public and private benefits with common characteristics, common purposes, and common roots in public authority. Virtually everything government does affects social welfare.[5] What students of the welfare state aspire to explain are specific aspects of government activity defined by specific characteristics and aims. Far from challenging this aspiration, I am simply arguing that it cannot be achieved without considering the full range of policies that share these essential features and goals.[6]

A second potential set of objections would attack these boundaries from the opposite direction, insisting that private social benefits do not fall within the realm of social welfare policy. Many economists believe, for instance, that employment-based social benefits are merely a form of compensation provided to workers in accordance with their productivity and relative preference for cash and noncash earnings. Much of their theorizing implies that it is foolish to discuss issues of distribution and power, because these benefits are simply the outcome of market processes.[7]

Employer-provided benefits are certainly a form of compensation, but they are not "merely" a form of compensation. They also have a pivotal place in the managerial and political strategies of employers, in the lives of workers, and in the broader universe of American social provision. Employers provide social benefits not just because employees desire them and are sufficiently productive to justify them; they use these benefits for a variety of other ends as well – to structure employment opportunities and advancement, to foster goodwill, to respond to the dictates of collective bargaining, to head off union encroachments. Workers, in turn, depend upon these benefits as an essential source of security. In many areas of social protection, the risk pooling and administrative economies made possible by group insurance are necessary to obtain affordable, comprehensive protection. By no means are these benefits unilateral transfers from employers to workers. Economists rightly argue that, over the long term and as a rule, workers pay for fringe benefits through lower wages. But many of these benefits do encompass special elements of risk sharing and cross-subsidization, and it is partly for this reason that they should be understood as a form of social insurance.

More important, private social benefits are substitutes for and complements to public social programs, and they are actively encouraged and shaped through government subsidies and regulation precisely for this reason. It may be possible to abstract from politics when seeking to explain why a firm provides fringe benefits, though the history traced in the coming chapters strongly suggests otherwise. It is not possible to do so when seeking to understand how these forms of compensation are shaped by government and why the United States has the balance of public and private social benefits that it does.

Finally, a handful of conservatives take issue with the concept of tax expenditures upon which much of federal policy toward private social benefits is premised. The most sweeping version of this complaint is that the equation of tax breaks with spending implies that all income is the government's to collect.[8] This objection, however, misses the force of the tax expenditure concept. Special tax provisions are equivalent to spending not because tax rates could be 100 percent, but because these provisions represent departures from the normal tax treatment of income specifically designed to favor certain individuals, groups, or activities. If politicians decide to provide a special tax break for child care expenses, for example, some families pay less in taxes than they would otherwise (that is, they receive a subsidy), and others pay more in taxes or receive less in government spending – or the government runs a deficit. Just like new spending programs, new tax expenditures must be financed by cuts in other programs, run-up of debt, or tax increases, and this is true regardless of the level of overall taxes. Indeed, Congress explicitly recognized this in 1990 when it made tax expenditures subject to the same rules against deficit spending that apply to other programs.

A concrete example will make the point clear. Older Americans have long received special tax treatment, variously consisting of an expanded standard deduction or personal exemption and some kind of credit against pension or other retirement income. Most notably, the major source of income for most aged Americans – Social Security – has never been fully taxed. This policy, in effect, increases Social Security benefits by about $25 billion a year (in the context of a $400 billion program).[9] Yet this amount is not included in commonly used estimates of social spending, even though the overall effect of the two alternatives – tax forgiveness or spending – is exactly the same, and no consistent definition of social policy would include one and not the other.[10]

Of course, experts can and do disagree about the magnitude of specific tax expenditures. Particularly thorny are issues of valuation (how much noncash benefits are worth) and allocation (who receives how much from company-wide plans). Difficulties also arise in defining the baseline of normal tax treatment.[11] It is essential to keep in mind, however, that these are measurement problems, not challenges to the notion that private benefits are subsidized.[12] Equally important, coming chapters will show that the Treasury Department has repeatedly considered alternative tax approaches *despite* these technical problems and that administrative difficulties were not the primary reason for the endurance of these favorable tax rules. Disagreement about the cost of specific tax breaks cannot be dismissed. For the purposes of political analysis, however, the exact cost is ultimately less important than the more fundamental questions about motive and effect that these provisions raise: Why have public officials crafted tax rules that they recognize as a departure from normal practice, and how, in turn, have these features of the tax code affected the development of U.S. social policy?

Contrasting Public and Private Approaches

The conceptual hurdles behind us, we return to the question that opened this chapter: In what politically relevant ways do alternative social policy approaches differ? The four contrasts highlighted in Figure 1.2 are those with the clearest political implications: the degree of reliance on third parties, the extent of compulsion, the degree of visibility, and the distribution of benefits. Other important differences – for example, the degree

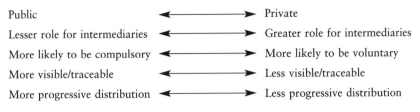

Public   Private

Lesser role for intermediaries   Greater role for intermediaries

More likely to be compulsory   More likely to be voluntary

More visible/traceable   Less visible/traceable

More progressive distribution   Less progressive distribution

Figure 1.2. Four Dimensions of Variation Among Approaches.

of government control over policy outcomes – are the result of the interplay of several features and will be discussed in the next section on political processes.

Degree of Reliance on Third Parties. Approaches differ, most obviously, in the degree to which third parties fund or deliver services. As a rule, more "privatized" approaches place greater responsibility and authority in the hands of nongovernmental actors. Political scientists have paid great attention to delegation of this sort in the context of public contracting.[13] Yet what is true of contracting is also true of most government subsidies. As already noted, two of the largest tax expenditures encourage employers to sponsor benefits; it is these employers that largely decide whether and on what terms to do so. Other subsidies that are targeted principally at individuals – such as the mortgage interest deduction – develop third-party clienteles among the industries that they indirectly benefit. When public authority and resources are shared with private intermediaries, these actors must be seen as powerful claimants and players in their own right.

Extent of Compulsion. More privatized policy approaches are generally less able and likely to compel participation. The hallmark of these approaches, after all, is that they encourage, rather than require, social provision. This difference does not merely have political implications; it also influences the effectiveness of alternative approaches, because compulsory coverage is often necessary to pool risks effectively across sizable and heterogeneous populations.

Degree of Visibility. Generally, the more voluntary a policy and the more it depends on delegation and incentives, the more difficult it is to identify its outcomes and assign blame or credit for them. To begin with, the costs of more privatized approaches are not nearly as visible as the costs of direct spending. Because these approaches compel or encourage private provision, much of the actual expense of benefits is typically assumed by the private sector rather than by government. In fact, even commitments of government resources may be hidden. Until the mid-1970s, for example, there was no federal budget for tax expenditures, and there continues to be debate over the budgetary treatment of government credit, insurance, and regulation. Most important, privatized approaches tend to encourage behavior indirectly and to spread implementation and operation widely. All this makes it difficult to recognize their effects or link those effects to specific government actions or the decisions of particular actors.[14]

Distributional Consequences. The final and perhaps most crucial difference among social policy approaches concerns their distributional effects. As approaches become more private in structure and more voluntary in operation, they tend also to become less able and likely to redistribute income and risk down the income ladder. First, most publicly supported private benefits are provided via employment, where they are awarded in close accordance with total compensation. Second, because social provision in the case of more private approaches is usually voluntary, subsidies go only to citizens whose employers provide benefits or who themselves have the means to undertake the subsidized activities. Third, these approaches tend to foster less comprehensive pooling of risks and often concentrate a greater amount of risk on individual beneficiaries. Fourth, and finally, most subsidies for private benefits take the form of tax forgiveness, which disproportionately benefits higher-income groups.

The skewed distribution of employer-provided benefits is indicated by Table 1.2, which shows the share of private workers receiving health and pension benefits in 1998. The overall pattern is straightforward and predictable: Better-paid employees are much more likely to be covered by the two most common job-related benefits. Not only are coverage rates higher among well-off employees, but the value of private benefits is also heavily skewed toward them, with benefits actually increasing as a share of compensation as one moves up the wage scale. The same is not true of government-mandated benefits like Social Security and Medicare, which reduce inequality across the wage scale.[15] Recent research also suggests that the distribution of fringe benefits is becoming more unequal.[16]

Tax expenditures present a special case. In addition to the factors just presented, their distributional effects are also influenced by the characteristics of tax breaks as a policy instrument. Because most tax expenditures lower taxable income, their value is greatest for upper-income taxpayers in higher tax brackets. Those who do not file tax returns do not receive tax breaks. And, with the exception of the Earned Income Tax Credit, which is refundable and inversely scaled to income, poorer

Table 1.2. *Share of Nonagricultural Private Workers Receiving Health and Pension Benefits, by Earnings, 1998*

Wage Quintile	Pension Benefits (%)	Health Benefits (%)
Lowest	15.7	23.7
Second	34.1	44.5
Third	52.3	59.4
Fourth	63.9	67.3
Highest	72.1	68.8

Source: James Medoff and Michael Calabrese, "The Impact of Labor Market Trends on Health and Pension Benefit Coverage," Preliminary Report of the Center for National Policy, September 2000, Tables H25 and P18. I am grateful to the authors for providing me with this unpublished report, which is based on census data.

Americans who pay no income taxes do not benefit either. Furthermore, some tax expenditures require that tax filers itemize their tax deductions (rather than claim the standard deduction), which is usually only worthwhile for higher-income filers.[17]

The combined effect of these special characteristics of tax expenditures and the skewed distribution of privately provided benefits can be dramatic. Table 1.3 shows the distribution of benefits across income classes of several social welfare tax expenditures for which the Joint Tax Committee of Congress produces estimates. The Joint Committee does not conduct a similar analysis for the special tax treatment of health and pension benefits, but it is possible to obtain comparable estimates. The Treasury Department estimates, for example, that two-thirds of the roughly $100 billion in annual tax subsidies for pensions and individual retirement accounts accrues to the top 20 percent of Americans on the income ladder, while just 12 percent goes to the bottom 60 percent.[18] Table 1.4 provides estimates of the average dollar value of the tax subsidy for workplace health insurance – which cost more than $100 billion in 1998 – for families at different income levels. The tiny benefit received by families in the lowest income category is partially an artifact of their higher rates of coverage through Medicaid and Medicare, but the differences are nonetheless striking. For example, the average annual value of all federal tax benefits for health insurance equaled just $296 for

Table 1.3. *Distribution of Selected Tax Expenditures, 2000*

Tax Expenditure	Total Amount ($B)	Percentage of Total Claimed by Income Class					
		<$10K	$10–30K	$30–50K	$50–100K	>$100 K
Mortgage interest deduction	53.4	0.0	1.3	8.3	38.5	51.9
Untaxed Social Security and railroad retirement benefits	23.5	0.2	28.1	44.4	25.3	2.1
EITC	29.8	25.7	71.9	2.3	0.1	0.0
Charitable giving deduction	26.5	0.0	1.9	6.8	29.2	62.1
Medical deduction	42.5	0.1	6.4	21.6	45.1	26.8
Child care credit	2.2	0.0	18.9	27.3	40.0	13.8

Source: Calculated from Joint Committee on Taxation, *Estimates of Federal Tax Expenditures for Fiscal Years 2000–2004* (Washington, D.C.: U.S. GPO, 1999), Table 3.

Table 1.4. *Average Tax Subsidy for Health Insurance Received by Families, by Income, 1998*

Annual Family Income	Average Subsidy per Family
Less than $15,000	71
$15,000–$19,999	296
$20,000–$29,999	535
$30,000–$39,999	847
$40,000–$49,999	1,195
$50,000–$74,999	1,684
$75,000–$99,999	1,971
$100,000 or more	2,357

Source: Jon Sheils and Paul Hogan, "Cost of Tax-Exempt Health Benefits in 1998," *Health Affairs* 18, no. 2 (1999): 180.

families with incomes of $15,000 to $20,000 but was $2,357 for families with incomes of $100,000 or more.

I have placed special emphasis on distribution for two reasons. First, it is a topic that has received insufficient emphasis in recent research on alternative social policy instruments. The OECD studies that recalculate national social spending argue repeatedly, for example, that international comparisons of the "social effort" of governments that do not make such adjustments miss "institutional differences in the ways in which governments pursue common social objectives."[19] Yet the OECD studies do not investigate, or even mention, the possibility that these alternative strategies might distribute benefits in fundamentally different ways, thus leaving the equally misleading impression that all social spending has similar effects.[20] Similarly, Christopher Howard, in his valuable analysis of tax expenditures with social welfare aims, argues that tax breaks have developed differently than direct-spending social programs mainly because of their ambiguity and the special features of the congressional revenue process. By contrast, he largely confines distributional issues to his descriptive survey of the characteristics of U.S. tax expenditures, discussing such considerations hardly at all in his four lengthy case studies.[21] Yet, as we shall see in the next section and in the chapters to come, the heavy distributional skew of tax breaks for private benefits cannot be treated as an analytic afterthought. It must be placed at the heart of any explanation of the distinctive political dynamics that Howard's study identifies.

Second, distributional considerations have always had a special status in the study of politics, speaking to that famous question of political science: "Who gets what, when, how?"[22] It is a commonplace of political analysis that politicians and parties take disparate stands not merely for technical or ideological reasons, but also because alternative courses of government action have quite different consequences for their constituents and interest-group supporters. Economists and policy analysts sometimes begin with the assumption that government intervention is – or at least should be – a response to identifiable market failures, the correction of which increases total social welfare. Yet, as political scientists never tire of pointing out, the general benefits of a policy do not usually provide a sufficient explanation for its creation. To explain why different approaches are chosen, we also need to know why (and which) political actors see them as in their interest. As the next section makes clear, the answer to that question is, in general, quite different for policies encouraging private social benefits than it is for public social programs.

The Politics of Alternative Approaches

Now that we have explored the variation among alternative policy approaches, the natural inclination is to consider how well they fulfill their goals.[23] This is unquestionably a crucial issue, so crucial, in fact, that I return to it repeatedly. But the question before us now is not about policy performance but about politics: How do the features of approaches matter politically?

This may at first seem an unusual question. We are accustomed to thinking of policy characteristics as a reflection of politics, not of politics as a reflection of policy characteristics. But, in fact, this is a familiar form of argument in political science, dating back at least to E. E. Schattschneider's groundbreaking 1935 study of the tariff revision of 1930.[24] In 1964, Theodore Lowi distinguished *distributive, regulatory,* and *redistributive* policy issues, arguing that each invited a distinct form of political conflict and mobilization.[25] Roughly a decade later, James Q. Wilson proposed a related typology based on the distribution of policy costs and benefits, identifying four basic political patterns in American politics.[26]

Students of social policy occasionally make similar arguments. A ubiquitous claim, for example, is that means-tested programs for the poor are more politically vulnerable than inclusive social insurance programs.[27] Yet much of the writing on the welfare state treats social policy as a package of related interventions that should be aided or hindered by the same influences – labor mobilization, leftist electoral success, collectivist cultural values, the centralization of political institutions, and so on. This may have some truth when the subject is public social programs. It is decidedly not true when the scope of analysis is broadened to include private social benefits.

My goal here is to suggest a few of the most important ways in which political processes should be expected to vary, given the differences among alternative approaches. I identify three main areas of variation: the scope and visibility of conflict, the pattern of policy change, and the character of political division and support. This discussion suggests that it is not possible to speak of a "politics of U.S. social policy." Instead, the interplay between policy characteristics and the basic features of American political institutions create different "politics," which vary consistently but not absolutely along the continuum of approaches. It bears emphasis nonetheless that this form of argument can take us only so far. In the final portion of this chapter, I usefully complicate and amend this static account to bring in the critical role of history, arguing that the sequence and relative development of public and private benefits represent critical independent determinants of political interactions and policy outcomes.

Scope and Visibility of Political Conflict

Two competing visions of American politics have long held sway. The first displays the policy process as a spirited contest among competing political actors in which public demands are a central influence upon policy outcomes. The second sees policymaking as restricted to a relatively narrow circle of participants – "iron triangles," "policy whirlpools," "subgovernments," "policy monopolies" – that exercise decisive control over policy outcomes largely unencumbered by popular influence. During the "community power debate" of the 1960s and 1970s, proponents of each view were quick to embrace it as *the* description of American politics. But today few cling to that notion. Rather, contemporary analysts argue that the character of policymaking varies both over time and across policy issues. It is sometimes characterized by contestation, sometimes by unquestioned agreement, sometimes by popular mobilization, sometimes by a constricted circle of dominant participants.[28] The question is why and when these different images hold true.

One answer that has proved quite popular – and which I shall explore shortly – highlights the contrast between origins and development. Major policy breakthroughs are contentious, but once the basic lines of policy have been established, a restricted universe of mobilized actors controls details within those constraints. Following Lowi and Wilson, however, it is possible to formulate another set of generalizations that concern not the degree to which policies are new or settled, but the incentives for political organization and mobilization that policies with different characteristics create. These generalizations all point to a fairly consistent conclusion: Privatized social welfare approaches are associated with a more subterranean political process than are public social programs, by which I mean both that they are generally less visible and that the scope of conflict surrounding them tends to be more restricted.

The distribution of a policy's costs and benefits critically shapes whether and how interest groups and citizens respond. When benefits are concentrated and costs are widespread, for example, interest groups find it relatively easy to mobilize, while those who pay the costs generally have little stake in a collective response. This is the traditional argument for why trade protectionism, with its diffuse costs to consumers and concentrated benefits for protected industries, has long proved popular in Congress. Yet when it comes to policy costs and benefits, it is perceptions rather than true effects that matter. And perceptions are shaped not just by the rhetoric of political actors but also by the characteristics of policies themselves. Here, the intrinsic visibility of policies and the complexity of the link between policies and effects become crucial.

Tax policy presents a good entry into the subject because nearly all citizens experience its costs. Anyone who has harbored resentment while writing a check to the Treasury Department knows why governments try to take taxes automatically out of paychecks or add them to the price of purchased goods. The less visible and direct taxes are, the more difficult it is for voters to recognize their true magnitude and mobilize against them. Indeed, an irony of the tax revolts that swept the United States in the 1970s and 1980s is that they were only loosely related to overall tax burdens in a jurisdiction. Even if taxes were low, rapid increases in visible taxes, particularly property taxes, prompted public backlash.[29] Harold Wilensky has made a similar claim about tax-based resistance to the welfare state, arguing that indirect taxes (such as sales and value-added taxes) and systems of contributory financing (especially levies on employers rather than workers) "evoke less political resistance to health and welfare spending than systems which rely heavily on direct taxes."[30]

Intrinsic visibility, however, is not the only factor that affects perceptions of costs and benefits. R. Douglas Arnold has introduced the related concept of "traceability," the ability of citizens and groups to link policy decisions to specific outcomes. Traceability is influenced not just by visibility but also by what Arnold calls the "policy effects chain" connecting government actions and the outcomes that result from them.

According to Arnold, effects are most traceable when their magnitude is large, when they follow quickly from government action, and when the causal process producing them is relatively simple. In contrast, policy outcomes that have small or late-order effects or that are the result of complex interactions among multiple actors are much less likely to be recognized or to prompt political mobilization, particularly if affected citizens are not already organized and attentive.[31] A linked body of research has shown that costs are also more likely to mobilize a response than a similar level of benefits, because citizens and interest groups are notoriously "loss-averse," which is to say they are much more likely to respond to the threat of losing existing benefits than to the prospect of receiving the same magnitude of new benefits.[32]

The relevance of this line of argument for understanding the politics of public and private social benefits becomes apparent when we consider that privatized approaches are often characterized by *both* low visibility and low traceability. Not only, that is, do they generally rely on policy instruments that are difficult to quantify or even recognize, but because they induce private activities rather than deliver benefits directly, their effects are also frequently produced through complex interactions among a vast range of actors. This means it is difficult and sometimes virtually impossible to pinpoint the effects of these interventions. Even students of social policy do not know exactly how the tax exemption of employer-provided health insurance or pensions has affected the development of private benefits. If full-time analysts are perplexed, why should we expect citizens to be any more aware of the character or impact of these policies?

By and large, then, more privatized social welfare approaches engender subterranean politics. Public awareness is generally low, and even talented leaders are hard pressed to mobilize the public unless they can demonstrate that immediate and identifiable benefits or costs are at stake. Information about policy effects is both scarce and unevenly distributed, and the incentives to collect information are, for most citizens, meager. Under these circumstances, the political actors who are most actively involved in policy formulation – if there is such active involvement – are those most interested in and aware of its effects. These might be labor groups, business organizations, or third-party providers. But what they share is an interest in the policy under consideration intense enough to prompt mobilization and to warrant the information-gathering and monitoring necessary to understand and contribute to a complex and low-salience policy field. These are conditions under which "subgovernments" should be expected to flourish.

What are the consequences of subterranean politics? In the simplest formulation, these conditions allow policies to pass that would not survive if subjected to the bright light of political scrutiny or the cold calculations of accurate budgeting. Critics of tax expenditures and other forms of "hidden spending" frequently say as much, drawing attention to the scores of special tax breaks for wealthy individuals and corporations – evocatively termed "corporate welfare" – that slip beneath the radar screen of public debate.[33] This argument is not so much wrong as overdrawn. In the social welfare field, most tax expenditures, credit programs, and other less visible expenditures are *not* narrow loopholes solely benefiting business or the very rich. Nevertheless, more privatized social welfare approaches do seem to permit inequities that politicians and the public would be unlikely to tolerate in direct-spending programs, as the distribution of tax benefits reported in Tables 1.3 and 1.4 suggests. It is hard to imagine, for instance, a national leader proposing a retirement program that showers two-thirds of its benefits on the richest 20 percent of Americans, or a new health insurance program that promised $2,357 a year to families with incomes of $100,000 or more, but just $296 to families with incomes of $15,000 to $20,000. And yet, as we have seen, these figures accurately describe the distribution of federal benefits provided by the special tax treatment of health insurance and retirement plans.

But the ramifications of subterranean politics go deeper than this. At the same time as the obscurity and complexity of privatized approaches restrict the universe of active political participants, the decentralized nature of their implementation and operation shifts responsibility away from electoral institutions and toward the more rarified atmosphere of the courts and administrative bodies.[34] At the most fundamental level, privatized social welfare approaches "depoliticize" policy by moving it outside of routine political channels and into the realm of market relations, where it is governed not by collective political decisions but by negotiations between individual workers and employers or by union–management bargaining. Moreover, when such critical social benefits are viewed as the purview of private labor contracts or the workings of autonomous market processes, then the failure to receive benefits is likely to be viewed as an individual, rather than a collective, misfortune. Conversely, when publicly subsidized private benefits *are* received, they are far more likely to be credited to private institutions than to the public policies that encourage and regulate them.

Pattern of Policy Change

Among the most consistent and well-supported claims about American public policy is that major policy innovations follow a pattern of "punctuated equilibria" – long periods of stasis followed by brief periods of rapid and sometimes dramatic change.[35] "The first thing one notices in the historical record," summarizes Hugh Heclo, "is that successful efforts at big, bold policy reforms are rare. Such policy ventures make immense demands on a political environment that is distinctly hostile to the authoritative, coherent use of public power implied by such innovations."[36] In the past century, the largest and most visible public social programs have almost all originated in two "big bangs" of dramatic policymaking – the first during the 1930s, the second during the 1960s and early 1970s. Outside of these "windows of opportunity" for dramatic social reform, the initiation of large-scale public social programs has been rare.[37]

Students of the American welfare state have long debated the reasons for this punctuated path of policy development, but most agree with Heclo that political institutions bear an important part of the credit or blame. Born of a fear of monarchical rule, America's constitutional structure divides political power among the executive, judicial, and legislative branches – and, within the legislature itself, between the House and the Senate. In addition to these horizontal divisions, the American constitutional structure also slices power vertically between the federal government and the states. In the national legislative process, the Constitution and congressional rules provide special procedural rights to the president and Senate minorities through the presidential veto and Senate filibuster, both of which require a supermajority vote if legislation is to become law.[38]

Still, the generic barriers to policy change created by American political institutions do not by themselves explain why new social welfare programs have been so few and far between. What is also critical is that new public social programs have historically invited fierce and open conflict that has sharply divided opponents and advocates along ideological lines. The reasons for this are no doubt legion – the comparative weakness of organized labor in the United States, America's enduring antigovernment tradition, the historical strength of southern opponents of public programs that might interfere with local systems of power – but the essential point is that large-scale public social programs usually entail significant and contested disruptions in regnant policy understandings and existing public–private boundaries. After their enactment, to be sure, this conflict may become muted. (That is what one would expect in a political structure with a substantial status quo bias.) But the initial transformative breakthroughs accompanying the creation of public programs often demand that reformers overcome powerful organized resistance and fierce ideological opposition, and thus place special burdens on a political structure already biased against controversial legislation and slim majorities.

Crucially, however, the same is not generally true of more privatized social welfare approaches. In the first place, as discussed, such approaches generally invite a more restricted scope of political conflict. Moreover, these approaches are usually less costly, or at least perceived as less costly. By encouraging or requiring private expenditures, they shift much of the actual spending on social benefits off the government ledger and onto private actors. As a general rule, more privatized approaches also start as relatively small initiatives, then grow as individuals and organizations recognize and take advantage of them.[39] Finally, because of their greater ambiguity and reliance on private action, these approaches are more likely to be compromise measures, attracting relatively broad support across the political spectrum. In short, they are more likely to overcome the barriers to policy change inherent in American political institutions.

All this suggests three conclusions. First, and most straightforward, privatized social policy approaches should be enacted with greater ease and frequency than public social programs. In contrast with the highly visible conflicts that often precede major programmatic breakthroughs, privatized approaches are likely to be enacted with relatively limited scrutiny and debate. Furthermore, because they have the potential to attract the same moderate and conservative lawmakers who usually oppose public social programs, these approaches can also be enacted even when large, pro-government majorities and supportive presidents are not in power – and may, in fact, be favored in such circumstances because other options are politically unattainable. Howard's study of tax expenditures presents some compelling evidence that the origins of social welfare tax breaks are far more widely scattered across American history than are the origins of public social programs, which are instead concentrated during the two big bangs of welfare state development.[40]

A corollary claim, which has the virtue of allowing cross-national comparison, is that privatized social welfare approaches are advantaged by the fragmentation of political institutions, because fragmentation makes public social programs more difficult to pass but does not necessarily pose the same barriers to policies encouraging private benefits. Ample research suggests that the number of "veto points" in a political system hinders public program adoption and depresses public spending, but comparable analyses of private benefits do not, to my knowledge, exist.[41] Figure 1.3 offers a basic test, showing the relationship between institutional veto points and the private share of social spending in our familiar group of eleven nations. Institutional fragmentation does seem to

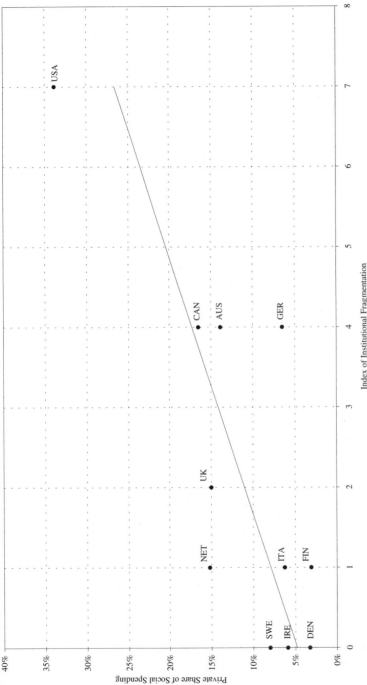

Figure 1.3. Institutional Fragmentation and the Private Share of Social Spending. *Source:* Private share of spending calculated from Willem Adeema, "Net Social Expenditure," *Labour Market and Social Policy – Occasional Papers No. 39* (Paris: OECD, August 1999), 30. Index of fragmentation constructed from Evelyne Huber, Charles Ragin, and John D. Stephens, "Comparative Welfare States Data Set," Northwestern University and University of North Carolina, 1997. The index is the sum of four coded variables: federalism (0 = no, 1 = weak, 2 = strong), presidential system (0 = parliamentary, 1 = presidential or collegial executive), proportional representation (0 = proportional representation, 1 = modified proportional representation, 2 = single-member simple plurality systems), and strength of bicameralism (0 = no second chamber or second chamber with very weak powers, 1 = weak bicameralism, 2 = strong bicameralism). The Pearson correlation is 0.796.

promote private spending, with the United States standing out once again as a distinctive case.

The second broad conclusion relates to political processes *after* policy change. In contrast with public social programs, the origins of which are usually more divisive than their development, privatized social policy approaches are likely to become a source of political conflict – *if* they become a source of political conflict – only after their creation, when their costs and benefits are both larger and potentially more apparent. The reasons for this are exactly the inverse of the reasons that public social programs frequently become settled after enactment. The passage of privatized approaches is generally not a large and visible event that mobilizes large numbers of groups and citizens. This is a benefit for advocates, allowing them to formulate policies beneath the radar screen of debate. But it also means that the passage of a policy provides little prima facie evidence that its aims or potential effects are widely accepted, or that the debates that it raises are already resolved. If challenges emerge, therefore, they typically do so once a policy is in place, when its effects have had time to blossom and critics have had time to recognize and publicize them. Of course, the obscurity of privatized approaches hinders such a response, but challengers may nonetheless be able to raise a policy's profile by publicizing its true costs, negative characteristics, or unanticipated consequences. The very fact that the policy is already in place when this challenge occurs, however, gives its advocates important advantages, as will become clear in the discussion to come.

The third and final conclusion concerns policymakers' control over policy development. Entitlement programs that provide specified benefits to all citizens who qualify under law frequently come under criticism for their uncontrollable character. Yet compared with many privatized social policy approaches, public entitlement programs seem exceedingly well mannered and responsive. Tax subsidies for private benefits are actually identical to entitlement programs in structure. Once the tax treatment of a benefit is decided upon, qualification is automatic, and no additional legislative action or budgetary appropriation is required, regardless of eventual costs. Unlike most entitlements, however, the effects of privatized approaches emerge from the interplay of public policies and a multitude of private decisions by individuals and organizations, making their ultimate outcomes even more unpredictable and unstable.

As Howard rightly argues, this is especially true of tax expenditures, because the value of most tax subsidies is highly responsive to changes in overall tax rates. As rates rise, for instance, the benefits of excluding employer-provided fringe benefits from taxation rise as well, even without any underlying change in the exemption. This allows what Howard calls "growth without advocacy," the ability of policies to expand without political activists laboring on their behalf. One should be careful not to assume, however, that the absence of advocacy means the absence of politics or power. That many of the most important policies encouraging private benefits have persevered even while their costs have exploded is itself a noteworthy outcome, which in turn may reflect their intrinsic appeal or the reluctance of opponents to challenge their potential defenders. "Nondecisions," in short, may be just as deserving of analysis as government actions, and in fact, future chapters will indicate that failure of the government to act was often what champions of private social benefits wanted most.[42] Who those defenders were is the next question before us.

Political Division and Support

A central issue in social policy is risk and income redistribution – how much of it occurs and who benefits and loses from it. The extent and nature of redistribution, however, is generally different for privatized social policy approaches than it is for public social programs. As we have seen, privatized approaches are limited in their ability to alter the distribution of labor market income or spread the risk of costly contingencies. Because, in most cases, their value increases with tax rates and with the generosity of private benefits, these approaches may actually exacerbate disparities in income and exposure to social risks. The argument here is that these effects are not incidental. Many politicians and interest groups advocate such approaches precisely because they redistribute income and risk little, if at all. This means that the base of support for privatized approaches draws from different quarters than those we tend to associate with social policy and, in particular, is far more likely to include conservative politicians and private industry leaders, who in other areas of social policy are staunch opponents of government intervention or spending.

Consider, by way of illustration, the early development of tax subsidies for private pensions. The initial exemption of pensions from taxation does not seem to have been the result of active lobbying, although it was part of a general campaign for business tax relief.[43] But the policy very quickly became a sacred cow among pension consultants, employers, and congressional conservatives who favored industrial pensions over public protections. Beginning in the late 1930s, the Roosevelt administration began a long and almost wholly unsuccessful campaign against the open-ended exemption, the benefits of which were highly concentrated among highly paid personnel, wealthy shareholders, and even company owners. But, with few exceptions, congressional conservatives managed to preserve the exemption, much to the relief of the pension consultants and large companies like AT&T that lobbied against proposed changes. And all this took place at the same time that conservatives in Congress endeavored to keep Social Security a small and underfunded program, and even to allow companies to credit Social Security benefits against the minimal equity requirements that federal tax law incorporated.

The attractions of privatized approaches to conservative interests is not merely a function of their ultimate distribution of benefits. For conservatives, the autonomy and income granted to private organizations by voluntary benefits are at least as valued as the larger societal consequences that these arrangements produce. Employers praise the flexibility of the private benefit system, prizing the goodwill and productivity that employment-based benefits purchase, all the more so because credit for the provision of benefits goes to them rather than to government. It matters little that, in the end, workers pay for private benefits through reduced cash wages; these costs are relatively invisible, and the intrinsic tax and risk-pooling advantages enjoyed by workplace benefits would make them a cause for worker gratitude even if costs were more readily observable. Third-party providers and those who deliver subsidized social services have an even more direct material stake in privatized social welfare approaches. The special tax treatment of home mortgage interest, for example, has helped create a vast real estate juggernaut, while subsidies for private health insurance have fostered a private "medical-industrial complex" unrivaled in size or political influence in any other nation.

Moreover, privatized social policy approaches not only provide direct rewards to conservative interests. They also build up a private sphere of benefits that can stand as an alternative to public programs – an important long-term goal of conservative opponents of expanded government provision. The business-backed National Industrial Conference Board noted in 1925, for example, that "the prevailing opinion among American industrialists favors the voluntary assumption by private industry itself of such responsibility for its personnel and the improvement of industrial relations as it is capable of discharging efficiently. This opinion is supported by the realization that industry's failure to assume such responsibility would almost certainly invite interventions by the state or other outside agency."[44] Immediately after World War II, corporations, insurers, and conservative leaders joined with the medical profession to promote private health insurance as a bulwark against a national health program. "If we can get ten million more people insured in the next year and ten million more in the next year," the architect of the public relations blitz declared, "the threat of socialized medicine in this country will be over."[45] In recent decades, conservatives have successfully pushed for the expansion of tax-favored investment accounts, such as 401(k) plans and individual retirement accounts, which advocates see not only as a direct benefit to the mostly better-off Americans who rely on them, but also as a crucial foundation for the full or partial "privatization" of Social Security.[46]

Conservative promotion of private social benefits has been, in a sense, a counterpart of the well-worn tale about the dogged liberal expansion of public social programs. As social policy historians have meticulously documented, advocates of expanded state responsibility pursued their vision through the careful choice of policy aims and instruments that they believed would increase the probability of future movement in the directions they desired.[47] They tried to create symbolic links between contributions and benefits, to cordon off program finances, to cultivate supportive constituencies, to minimize visible new costs, to bite off smaller pieces of a larger pie – in short, to increase the chance that policies they supported would take root and grow. In this familiar story of policy expansion, liberals are the protagonists, and conservatives the antagonists, holding back the tide the best they can. Yet conservative interests were not just opponents of change. They also sought policies strategically designed to increase the chance that they would achieve *their* goals, and, as coming chapters will show, they were far more successful than is commonly recognized.

To understand *why* they were successful, we need to turn from the relatively static contrasts that we have been exploring and consider processes of historical development – processes shaped by timing, sequence, and the self-reinforcing consequences of public and private social benefits.

Path Dependence, Critical Junctures, and Social Policy Development

The study of political and institutional development has a long and distinguished lineage. Yet the last decade has witnessed a new flowering of interest in the topic. In political science, many of these recent inquiries have marched under the banner of "historical institutionalism," a label evincing a dual concern with political institutions and long-term patterns of historical development. To date, however, these twin subjects have not been equally addressed. While arguments about the effects of institutions have grown ever more sophisticated, the historical side of historical institutionalism has remained considerably less distinct and developed.[48] This is not because scholars working in this tradition have failed to study politics in long-term historical context, but because they have found it difficult to explicate a distinctive understanding of the role and importance of historical analysis, beyond the truism that "history matters." The weakest link in this scholarship "has been the clear articulation of theoretical arguments outlining why the intensive investigation of issues of temporality is critical to an understanding of social processes."[49]

The purpose of this section – the last in my theoretical discussion – is to offer one such argument, bringing together two distinct but related families of claims. The first set of claims revolves around mechanisms of "path dependence" and "policy feedback," processes by which policies and institutions established at one point in time transform politics in the future. The key insight that I introduce here is that many of the features of large-scale public programs that make them self-reinforcing over time are shared broadly by privatized policy approaches. Indeed, some features of privatized approaches already explored – for example, their greater obscurity, the problems of political control they entail, and the vested third-party interests to which they frequently give rise – may actually make them *more* path dependent than comparable public programs.

Having explored path dependence, I extend the scope of the argument to bring in a second set of claims regarding "critical junctures," rare moments of dramatic change that send countries or policies down distinctive tracks. The discussion thus shifts from the long-term political effects of public and private social benefits to the ways in which these effects map onto a punctuated pattern of policy change in which windows of opportunity for major social reform open only rarely and fleetingly. The issue that becomes crucial here is the extent to which private social benefits and policies encouraging them develop in a particular policy area before a window of opportunity for major public social programs opens. How this development occurs can fundamentally affect the preferences of political actors, the strategies they employ, and the prospects for their success.

Path Dependence

One conception of history's role that has been gaining favor among social scientists is contained in the notion of "path dependence" – a term popularized by economists W. Brian Arthur, Paul David, and Douglass North.[50] As these theorists use the term, path dependence is meant to suggest the importance of "temporally remote events, including happenings dominated by chance elements rather than systematic forces."[51] Even seemingly trivial events may have dramatic long-term economic consequences when certain self-reinforcing mechanisms – large set-up or fixed costs, learning effects, coordination effects, adaptive expectations – are present.[52] As a result, gaps may open and persist between the traditional expectations of neoclassical theory and the actual performance of economies or economic organizations.

In political science, the concept of path dependence has taken on a broader meaning and has found increasingly rich expression in writings on state-building and the policy process. Bringing together much of this research, Paul Pierson has identified a number of distinct channels of "policy feedback," through which policies passed at one point in time shape subsequent political dynamics.[53] Policies may alter administrative capacities, create incentives for group formation, teach specific lessons to policymakers, or give rise to widespread public expectations or vast networks of vested interests. Drawing on Arthur, Pierson argues that policies frequently "provide incentives that encourage individuals to act in ways that lock in a particular path of policy development," creating societal commitments that may be quite difficult to reverse.[54] For this reason, the timing and sequence of policies can be extremely important in determining eventual political outcomes. By pushing policy development down a particular historical path, a policy passed at time T_1 may significantly change the range of possible options at time T_2.

Writing more recently, Pierson has elaborated on these arguments to develop a broader and more precise justification for bringing the concept of path dependence into the study of politics.[55] By path dependence, Pierson means social processes characterized by self-reinforcement, in which the cost of reversing an existing course of institutional or policy development increases over time. These processes have a number of distinctive characteristics, but three are particularly crucial.[56] First, in path-dependent processes, timing matters. Early choices and events are far more consequential for ultimate outcomes than latter ones. This implies, conversely, that at early stages of a path-dependent process, several different outcomes – or "multiple equilibria" – are typically possible. What later seems an unavoidable state of affairs may result from small and even happenstance events in the past, the effects of which have compounded over time. Second, path-dependent explanations do not assume that an existing policy or institution is necessarily a reflection of the current constellation of factors surrounding it, much less a functional response to them. To the contrary, because early events are so crucial, current institutions or policies may be a reflection of initial conditions that no longer exist – and, indeed, may actually be inferior to other possible configurations measured against current conditions. Third, and finally, path-dependent processes imply a strong element of institutional inertia. Once past a certain threshold of development, what exists is likely to persist, assuming that the conditions that gave rise to path dependence continue to obtain as well.

Path dependence in Pierson's definition – as in the economics theorizing that inspired it – is driven by *increasing returns*, which means simply that the incentives to remain on a path increase the farther one moves down it. Other theorists have adopted looser definitions of path dependence and pointed to factors besides increasing returns that cause it.[57] Although many of these additions have been valuable, they have also muddied the conceptual waters, making it difficult to specify how claims regarding path dependence are distinct from the truism that the present is influenced by the past. In this book, following Pierson's definition, path dependence refers to *developmental trajectories that are inherently difficult to reverse*. The central argument is that political "actors do not inherit a blank slate that they can remake at will when their preferences change or the balance of power shifts. Instead, they find that the dead weight of previous institutional choices seriously limits their room to maneuver."[58]

Before moving on, it is important to clear away a misconception that treatments of path dependence frequently invite. To say that a process is path dependent is not to say that it is static or that movement off a path is impossible. In some cases, a path may be virtually "locked in" by a massive and irreversible commitment of resources, but most of the mechanisms creating path dependence involve the adaptation and response of individuals and organizations over time to a particular matrix of policies and institutions. This is a deeply dynamic process. Moreover, movement off a policy path is never impossible, only more or less difficult. The difficulty of policy reversal varies with the strength of the factors that create path dependence, and they are likely to differ both across policy areas and over time. The defining feature of path-dependent processes is not that change does not occur but that change is channeled by the self-reinforcing mechanisms that propel the existing path of development. By examining these mechanisms, it is possible to show not only which options are progressively foreclosed, but also which become more attractive to political actors as they work within the constraints of a self-reinforcing developmental path. It also possible to identify the particular forces that might undermine a self-reinforcing trajectory by weakening or overwhelming the mechanisms that encourage continued movement down that path.

What are the features of politics and policy that encourage path dependence? And how do they relate to differences among alternative social policy approaches that we have already discussed?[59] I argue that the possibilities for path dependence are greater to the extent that the following five conditions hold true: *First*, a policy creates or encourages the creation of large-scale organizations with substantial set-up costs; *second*, a policy directly or indirectly benefits sizable organized groups or constituencies; *third*, a policy embodies long-lived commitments upon which beneficiaries and those around them premise crucial life and organizational decisions; *fourth*, the institutions and expectations a policy creates are of necessity densely interwoven with broader features of the economy or society, creating interlocking networks of complementary institutions; and *fifth*, features of the environment within which a policy is formulated and implemented make it harder to recognize or respond to policy outcomes that are unanticipated or undesired. These features, it will become clear, hold for many (but not all) major public social programs. Perhaps more arresting, it will also become clear that they hold for many (but not all) privatized social policy approaches as well. In fact, certain features of privatized approaches may make these policy alternatives even more prone to path dependence than comparable public programs.

Consider Social Security, which represents perhaps the purest case of a policy prone to path dependence. Although Social Security started as a relatively small program by contemporary standards, it nonetheless required a massive initial commitment of financial and administrative resources. Over time, moreover, Social Security created a common rallying point and organizational incentive for what had previously been a scattered potential interest group: the elderly. More important, Social Security's commitments were about as long-lived as any transfer program's could be. Workers who first started paying into the program in their twenties had to premise decisions about retirement four decades hence on its promised benefits. And because the program very quickly became a virtually pure pay-as-you-go system (in which current workers financed the benefits of current retirees), any attempt to eliminate the program or shift its financing into private accounts entailed an increasingly serious "double-payment problem," requiring workers to pay for a previous generation's retirement even while financing their own. It was also unavoidable that Social Security would become densely woven into employment practices and the structure of the labor market. Finally, certain features of Social Security – particularly its pay-as-you-go financing and the fact that recipients in the early years represented a small fraction of covered workers – made it extremely difficult for opponents to draw attention to its ultimate size and cost.[60]

Pay-as-you-go pension programs are an extreme example. They embody notably long-lived commitments, and their very structure facilitates early expansion while maximizing transition costs once they become mature. Nonetheless, other public social programs share many of the same features. Medicare, for example, is only partially financed by earmarked payroll contributions, so the link between contributions and benefits is not as straightforward as in Social Security. Yet the program still creates widespread expectations among workers that insurance will be there when they retire. Moreover, the program not only benefits an organized constituency, the elderly; it also underwrites a vast network of private medical providers, which in recent years has been a major organized force challenging payment reductions. The fact that Medicare purchases medical services in the private sector (and increasingly contracts with private health plans) makes it more vulnerable to internal restructuring than is Social Security, which simply writes checks. Moreover, the program does not embody the same inherent tendencies toward expansion that pay-as-you-go pensions do.[61] But any proposal to eliminate the program or even visibly cut its benefits would face fierce and deeply institutionalized resistance, as congressional Republicans learned when they unsuccessfully tried to restructure the program in 1995.

Now let us consider government-supported private social benefits. To what extent do they embody the characteristics conducive to path dependence highlighted in the context of public programs? The initial inclination is to reply that the possibilities for path dependence are meager, because private social benefits operate in a realm of farsighted economic rationality.[62] Yet this objection misses the reality that private social benefits, as we have examined them, are supported by and densely interwoven with government policies and arise in areas where market failure is endemic. Like public social programs, privatized social policy approaches generally entail the construction of large-scale organizations (private insurance companies, pension management firms, corporate benefit programs); they benefit powerful constituencies and interest groups (from service providers to third-party intermediaries to corporate sponsors); they create enduring societal expectations (leading workers, for example, to see the workplace as the primary source of certain forms of social protection); and they become deeply integrated into economic organization and practice, often requiring interdependent organizational networks to fulfill their ends. Because private social benefits rest on a foundation of government inducements and constraints, finally, they are also prone to the same sort of institutional stickiness that status quo–biased political institutions create in the context of public social programs.

Indeed, in at least two respects that we have examined already, privatized approaches may be relatively more prone to path dependence than public social programs. First, more so than many direct-spending programs, these approaches create resourceful and mobilized vested interests with strong incentive to monitor and respond to threatening policy developments. Because privatized social welfare approaches tend to rely to a substantial degree on third parties, they typically have a base of support not just among beneficiaries but also among private intermediaries who sponsor or deliver benefits. These are political actors who are likely to be already mobilized and organized, to have relatively long time horizons, and to take a continuing interest in policy development. For reasons already discussed, privatized social welfare approaches also attract a greater degree of support from private employers than do public social programs, and as political scientists have long noted, employers are not simply another interest group. Business enjoys a "privileged position" in politics by virtue of its critical role as a provider of jobs and economic growth, a role that electorally sensitive politicians are loath to threaten.[63] To the degree that these economic signals matter, the coalition behind privatized social welfare approaches will be all the more formidable.

Second, the barriers to visibility, traceability, and political control thrown up by privatized approaches may be an additional advantage for their defenders, allowing even paths of policy development that are costly or viewed as undesirable to endure over long periods of time. Critics of path-dependence theory in economics have noted, with some merit, that to the extent that inefficient paths of development can be foreseen, rational economic agents in a competitive market system will have strong incentives to anticipate and avoid them.[64] But such mechanisms of correction are notably weak in politics, and not just because the goals of public policy are generally multiple and contested.[65] The ultimate paths that policies will take are difficult to anticipate, especially when they involve complex interactions among multiple institutions. And once policy paths have been taken, their characteristics and effects may be equally opaque, making it difficult for opponents to transform them into a target of collective political response. As I have argued, all this is likely to be particularly true of privatized social welfare approaches.[66]

In their cultivation of mobilized interests and their general opacity and unpredictability, privatized policy approaches appear to have strong tendencies toward path dependence, even in comparison with public social programs. The *character* of path dependence, however, is likely to differ between privatized approaches and public programs. Because privatized approaches allow much greater discretion on the part of private actors, they are likely to foster a much more dynamic sphere of benefits, allowing substantial changes *within* the confines of existing policy. Most public social programs specify with considerable precision how and to whom benefits should be delivered. The same is not usually true of policy approaches that encourage or regulate private benefits. Furthermore, nongovernmental actors working within these often loose constraints do not have to engage in collective political action to achieve their ends. If they are able to overcome internal resistance, they can adopt changes unilaterally.[67] For this reason, it is important to distinguish between the basic policy framework governing private benefits – which, under appropriate conditions, will be prone to path dependence – and the benefits themselves. The policy framework may be highly change resistant even while the benefits that it shapes are unstable. One implication is that where a large realm of regulated and subsidized benefits arises, there is likely to be a persistent lag between public policy and private practices, as political leaders hamstrung by existing policies find themselves always a step (or more) behind private developments.

The more fundamental conclusion, however, is that privatized approaches may be a source of "policy feedback" no less powerful than public programs, profoundly shaping politics and policy development. This possibility has received virtually no attention in the extensive literature on social policy, but if it is correct, then networks of private social benefits may become just as deeply entrenched as public social programs – and present just as daunting political barriers to would-be reformers. The implications of this conclusion will become clearer once we consider how path-dependent processes intersect with long-term patterns of policy development, particularly with the intermittent "critical junctures" that create opportunities for dramatic policy change.

Critical Junctures

As the concept of path dependence has gained credence, historically minded social scientists have simultaneously gravitated toward a second conception of history's role, contained in the term "critical junctures." Whereas path dependence implies that seemingly small, even happenstance, changes at one point in time may have large eventual consequences through self-reinforcing processes, the literature on critical junctures calls attention to periods of "significant change" that typically occur "in distinct ways in different countries (or in other units of analysis)" and that are "hypothesized to produce distinct legacies."[68] Examples of critical junctures include the establishment of national constitutions, the process of state formation, the development and realignment of party systems, the commercialization of agriculture during modernization, and the process of labor incorporation into politics.[69]

What all these critical moments have in common is their fundamental impact on subsequent historical dynamics. The way in which these crucial periods of transition occurred shaped processes of political and economic development for decades to come. Big historical events have big historical consequences.

Advocates of the concept of critical junctures sometimes link the idea to the notion of path dependence.[70] Yet the two concepts are not identical. Path dependence suggests why the effects of critical junctures may be so profound and enduring. It does not necessarily explain why critical junctures occur, nor does it necessarily imply – as the idea of critical junctures does – that political or economic development is characterized by a series of historical big bangs or "punctuated equilibria" whose legacies persist for long periods of time.[71] In fact, path dependence implies that seemingly "small" events or choices may also have big eventual effects.

In social policy development, critical junctures represent moments of political opportunity when significant new policy departures may be put in place or when the forces for change are strong enough to cut into the ongoing path-dependent development of an existing policy and alter its trajectory. The main cause of such historical turning points identified by students of social policy is major partisan shifts in government, but this is not the only possible cause and, in many cases, such shifts may themselves be a reflection of other factors. Wars, major economic downturns, and other triggering crises are the most notable of these "exogenous" shocks (exogenous in the sense that they are generally not predicted or explained within our theoretical frameworks). What unites these moments is that they create a realignment of political forces substantial enough to overcome the veto points in political institutions and, when relevant, the entrenched path of policy development created by past events and decisions.

The burden of my argument about patterns of policy change is that the barriers to nonincremental change in public policy differ both across political-institutional frameworks (with the United States hosting a particularly "sticky" structure) and across different types of government intervention (with large-scale public social programs facing particularly steep political obstacles). The barriers to major policy change will also depend on the intensity and character of any mechanisms that create path dependence within a particular policy area – which, when increasing returns are at work, become more powerful the farther policy developments move down a particular historical track. Thus, the timing and sequence of policy intervention can be crucial. Early efforts to change a path-dependent process may face significantly lower barriers than later ones. If a policy path is taken before the opportunity to follow another arises, the latter may be all but foreclosed. The temporal location of windows of opportunity for policy change – when they open relative to ongoing path-dependent processes – may be as important for explaining policy outcomes as the strength of the forces behind change at a critical juncture.

Timing in this analysis thus means something very specific – timing relative to ongoing path-dependent processes. Of course, this is not the only sense in which timing is important in politics. Another popular conception of timing refers to the extent to which the broader features of the political environment are conducive to certain types of change at any given moment. An idea's time comes, according to John Kingdon's influential theory of agenda setting, when problems and proposals to address them intersect at a propitious political moment, allowing skillful "policy entrepreneurs" to sell their pet proposals to a receptive audience.[72] Yet illuminating as this perspective has been, theories of agenda setting are better at specifying the conditions that create opportunities for innovation and the forces that drive policy design than they are at explaining the limits on innovation that past patterns of policy create. What too often gets missed in such fluid accounts is the significant constraints created by past institutions and policies that leaders must grapple with even when windows of opportunity for change are open.

This does not mean, however, that path-dependent models of policy development ignore the role of strategic choice and contingency. Quite the opposite: By identifying the conditions under which small events have large consequences, such models offer a clear explanation for why seemingly minor events or choices may have significant and sometimes unintended consequences as their effects ripple outward. As I have argued, moreover, the question of why policies with certain conditions are difficult to change needs to be separated from the question of why windows of opportunity for policy reform emerge. Another potential source of contingency, therefore, is the often unpredictable relationship between path-dependent processes and moments of political opportunity. A final reason that unintended consequences cannot be ignored is that self-correcting mechanisms are weak in politics, especially when public policies are complex or opaque and collective action is difficult to mobilize.

As we shall see, some of the most important policies encouraging private benefits were precisely "accidental" in this sense. For example, the Employee Retirement Security Act of 1974 included a little-noticed clause "preempting" state laws governing health and other benefits that employers funded themselves. Barely understood at the time of its passage, deeply ambiguous with regard to intent, this single provision was interpreted by the courts to mean that self-funded health plans were exempt from state regulation, even though no comparable federal regulations were in place. By the time pro-government liberals realized that the movement toward self-funded insurance would hurt their cause, the movement was largely irreversible and a formidable coalition of defenders had arisen to stymie efforts at reversal.

The insight that emerges from the marriage of path dependence and critical junctures is that the balance of public and private social benefits that develops in a policy domain may be the result not just of the intrinsic characteristics of that area or the particular political and economic forces in play at any point in time, but also the extent to which private or public social benefits gain a significant foothold before opportunities to shift to alternative policy approaches emerge. When either public or private benefits reach a critical threshold of diffusion and size, the political pressures for continued reliance on these networks of provision become very powerful, so powerful in fact that under normal political circumstances, it is highly unlikely that a major departure from the existing path of policy development will occur. As I have emphasized, this does not mean that policy in an area is static or that change is impossible. Yet the constraints on change are such that new policy initiatives in this area are likely to leave undisturbed, build on, or actively attempt to bolster existing networks of social provision, both because these networks generally have organized defenders and because challenges to them entail often massive social dislocations.

What makes this argument more interesting from the standpoint of policy development is that alternative social policy approaches have different characteristics that entail differential barriers to enactment. In American politics, large-scale public social programs necessarily face extremely high barriers, while policies encouraging private social benefits do not. Thus, when public social programs are politically unattainable, the natural tendency is to turn to more privatized social policy approaches. This outcome might be thought of as "satisficing," to use Herbert Simon's famous amalgam of "satisfy" and "suffice" – search behavior induced by a gap between aspirations and reality in which "the level of aspiration begins to adjust itself downward until goals reach levels that are practically attainable."[73] Privatized approaches may not be the best option, on this interpretation, but they are the best that can be achieved. Yet it is crucial to recognize that such policy choices are not neutral with regard to future options. Each intermediate step in favor of privatized social welfare approaches increases the probability that future steps will occur in the same direction. For some political actors, of course, this may be the preferred outcome. Encouraging private benefits now, on this second interpretation, will reduce the scope for public social programs later. The "satisficing" interpretation seems a reasonably good explanation of why labor unions and liberals have embraced privatized social welfare approaches during periods when broader public social programs were unattainable. The second interpretation seems to better describe the reasoning of conservative opponents of government social programs who have sought to encourage the expansion of private benefits.

Looking Ahead

Parts II and III of this book trace a century of political struggle over two areas of U.S. social policy: retirement pensions (Part II) and health insurance (Part III). These two areas represent the largest domains of social spending in the United States (and, in fact, in all affluent nations). Excluding education, roughly two-thirds of public social spending in the United States is devoted to these two areas.[74] The corresponding share for private spending by employment-based benefit plans probably exceeds 90 percent.[75] Equally important, health care and retirement pensions are bedrock foundations of the welfare state, their place within the textbook definition of social policy uncontested. This is important, because my aim is to skirt many of the conceptual fights that have plagued scholarly debates over the welfare state. If the place of these areas of social provision in definitions of the welfare state is secure, it is easier to make the case that private benefits that serve similar purposes and have significant public policy backing should be included in examinations of social policy.

A final crucial justification for choosing these two areas is embodied in a puzzle: Why have U.S. health policy and pension policy followed such divergent paths? In Social Security, the United States has a relatively generous public pension program – not at the top of the international rankings, but not radically out of line with the programs of other advanced industrial nations. Yet proposals for health insurance following the Social Security model repeatedly failed at the same time as Social Security took root and grew, leaving the United States as the only affluent capitalist democracy without a near-universal health program. When we look across nations, major differences can often be traced to major causes. Different political institutions, divergent economic structures, disparate ideals – all could explain why one nation followed one path and another followed another. But when we compare policy areas within a single nation, such holistic explanations are no longer as simple, and we need to look for more subtle variation in policy characteristics or patterns of development. These kinds of internal comparisons – relatively rare in social policy research – draw out in finer detail than cross-national work often does the sources of policy development in a particular area. They also allow more concrete conclusions about the effect of such elusive temporal factors as timing and sequence, which may be obscured in broad international comparisons.

The distinction between health care and pensions is not simply that government dominates the pension field while the private sector dominates health care financing and provision. In fact, celebratory rhetoric about America's "private health system" notwithstanding, nearly half of all health care financing now comes from government sources. Add to this staggering total the indirect policy crutches that prop up this public–private structure – not just the massive subsidies for private insurance but also the government's assumption of risk for the most costly medical groups – and any claim that health care in the United States is laissez-faire or free market is fanciful.

Rather than fixate exclusively on the relative shares of public and private spending, the better approach is to identify the general form and character that government intervention takes. The key distinction is between what I call a "core" and a "supplementary" role for private benefits. In the case of a core role, publicly regulated and subsidized private social benefits are considered the normal line of defense against social contingencies for most workers, with more direct government intervention countenanced primarily for those whom private benefits cannot be expected to help, either because they lack sufficient resources (the poor) or do not have strong ties to the workforce (the elderly, the disabled, and children). Private benefits that play a supplementary role, by contrast, are meant to "top off" public social programs, providing additional protection to those who desire and have the means to afford it. Because such benefits are usually highly concentrated on high-income earners, whose means are greater, they may in the aggregate represent a sizable bloc of spending. But for most workers, supplementary private benefits are simply not a large proportion of the total transfers that they receive.

The coming chapters will explain in far greater depth how this difference in roles matters and, more important, how it originated and endures. But two differences bear mention at the outset. Private social benefits that play a core role are likely to be subject to far more criticism and challenge, precisely because they are expected to provide broad social protection, a goal that publicly regulated and subsidized private benefits have inherent problems achieving. Yet, paradoxically, core benefits are also likely to receive greater deference in public policy, because fears of harming their ability to carry out public ends, however badly they may pursue them, are that much greater. The ironic result – a system of benefits that few seem to like but which nonetheless seems stubbornly resistant to change – is perhaps the strongest illustration of the political limits imposed by path dependence.

Why is it that the specific role – core or supplementary – that private social provision comes to play makes a difference? Drawing on the theoretical perspective outlined in this chapter, I emphasize three main causes. First, private benefits create powerful vested interests and widespread public expectations. Not only do they enrich and strengthen private third-party intermediaries and service providers, but just as important, employers and workers come to depend on private benefits and structure their activities and expectations around their presence. Second, the very division of labor between the public and private sectors in social provision makes public officials extremely sensitive to the potential dislocations that might be caused by major government intervention. Policymakers thus become caught between demands to improve the operation of voluntary private benefits or supplant them altogether and the reality that government actions might harm existing social protections. This suggests that when voluntary private benefits become core providers of social protection, there are real limits to the process of "functional reconversion," whereby existing institutions are reworked to pursue new ends.[76] As the coming chapters will show, the different orientation of public policy toward private pensions and private health insurance illustrates these limits.

Finally, and perhaps most overlooked, the relationship between public and private social benefits shapes the preferences and strategies of actors who seek to influence social policy. A much-debated topic in welfare state research, for example, is the orientation of business toward social policy.[77] Some scholars argue that business has inflexibly opposed virtually all public social programs, while others claim to find substantial evidence of business support for public protections that equalize labor costs across firms, foster human capital, or pool unpredictable risks. But awareness of the relationship between public and private social benefits indicates that these categorical arguments are both equally suspect. *Business responses to the welfare state depend crucially on the character and extensiveness of employment-based private benefits.* It is impossible, we shall see, to explain the far more moderate reaction of the American business community to expansions of Social Security than to proposals for government health insurance without noting the crucial fact that private pensions were built on top of Social Security (and even factored in its benefits), while private health insurance emerged as a wholesale alternative to it.

Similarly, the response of American labor unions to public social programs has been deeply influenced by the growth of private social benefits, which were first pursued by organized labor as a strategic response to the failure of expanded public social protections but then, as they became more generous and widespread, came to shape union perceptions of the desirable mix of public and private protections. Perhaps the most striking example of private benefits shaping political demands, however, occurred among the committed program advocates who pushed for the expansion of government programs from the New Deal into the 1970s. At the same time as these advocates gradually achieved their long-term aims in the field of pensions, they found themselves increasingly hemmed in by the growing sphere of private health benefits and eventually were forced to scale back their ambitions to accommodate the core role of private health insurance. By surveying the long-term development of two policy areas within a single nation – in effect, holding constant many of the large-scale institutional, political, and cultural factors that are typically the focus of welfare state research – we gain a clearer picture of how the different role that private benefits came to play in each area shaped the preferences and strategies of political actors and, in doing so, reinforced the very different trajectories that public and private benefits followed in each.

This method is best termed "comparatively informed historical analysis."[78] It is "historical analysis" because it scrutinizes the chain of causes implied by an explanation over a considerable span of time and at multiple levels of observation – from system-wide interrelationships to the behavior of actors to the beliefs of individuals. Although this approach is avowedly historical, its aim is not to uncover "the past," understood as events leading up to the present, but to explore "particular pasts," understood as "the chain of events that connect putative causal factors with the outcomes we think they explain."[79] Theoretical claims are verified by probing and contrasting extended pathways of policy development to demonstrate that the implications of these arguments hold true. In this method, history is the testing ground for theory and not just the raw material for compelling narrative, though, of course, I hope it is both.

This approach is "comparatively informed" in several respects. Although the focus is a single nation, I do not treat the United States as a self-contained "case" that must be set against other national "cases" to make generalizations. Rather, my method is to disaggregate the U.S. case to compare the distinctive elements of the American welfare regime and their long-term historical evolution and change.[80] The method is explicitly comparative, in short, but the subjects of comparison are change over time and divergent policy paths as much as contrasting national experiences. This approach does not exclude cross-national comparison. Many of the theories that guide my inquiries have arisen in the context of cross-national research, allowing me to juxtapose widely accepted claims about comparative policy formation against the particularities of American developments. At the same time, I draw throughout the analysis on targeted historical comparisons with two countries that share basic similarities with the United States: Britain and Canada. At several points, I also compare policy development across the American states. These "shadow" comparisons – limited but careful comparative inquiries to test particular claims – help me avoid the "just-so" stories of inevitable outcomes that often plague analyses of a single nation.

Another protection against just-so accounts is my reliance at numerous points on counterfactual analysis – hypothetical historical scenarios designed to better pinpoint the effect of particular events or choices.[81] If, as I argue, path-dependent processes have bound policy choice, then it is often necessary to ask counterfactual questions. What options might have been on the table had past decisions been different? What consequences might alternative courses of action have produced? In particular, if leaders had made different strategic choices at critical junctures, would the ultimate outcome have been any different than it was? The answers to these questions are never decisive or self-evident, but when grounded in accepted theories and used alongside cross-national and historical evidence, they provide important insights that are otherwise unavailable.

Evidence for these inquiries comes from a variety of sources, ranging from quantitative data to archival evidence to synthetic use of existing historical, policy-analytic, and journalistic works. Much of the most valuable historical research on private social benefits has been completed in the last decade, and my ability to assemble a comprehensive historical synthesis has been greatly aided by these recent forays into government, labor, and business records. At the same time, the extensive sweep of my analysis and my explicit focus on the politics of policy development have required new archival research, as well as the assimilation of a wide range of public and private statistics and additional secondary sources. Most important, all this evidence is situated within a larger argument about the peculiar path of U.S. social policy – one that not only takes in a century-long sweep of time and two crucial policy areas, but also incorporates important recent currents of thinking about processes of policymaking and political development.

Part II

The Politics of Public and Private Pensions

[Private pension plans] have grown to the point of where they have become a form of social insurance, if you will, in the United States of America. The labor movement would have preferred . . . some other approach to these matters, but this is what has grown up in our society. We would have preferred. . .some outright Government insurance where everything would have been aboveboard and where people could have seen it. That has gone by the board at least for the moment, and we are now operating under these health and welfare and pension plans.

    – Andrew Biemiller, Director, Department of Legislation, AFL-CIO, *Hearings Before House Committee on Education and Labor,* 1957

Congressman Dent: Well, we have to deal with what we have. . . . We have a private pension system in the United States which has accumulated a huge sum of money in reserve. There are many contracts that are consummated between employer and employee. What do we do about it now? . . . Do we give assurance to the employee when he reaches retirement age he will have a stipulated sum of money, or do we eliminate the private pension system altogether?

Nelson McClung, the Urban Institute: I don't think you have the second option. What you are doing is right and good. I guess I am complaining that this second option should be available but it is not. I think it is unfortunate that we let ourselves get into this box. Twenty years ago we could have avoided it. I think now we can probably do nothing but try to improve what we have.

    – *Hearings Before the Subcommittee on Labor,* 1970

Introduction

The United States is currently in the midst of a heated debate over the future of Social Security, the nation's largest and most venerated social program. The urgency and prominence of this dispute inspires memories of the early 1980s, when a bipartisan coalition cobbled together a last-minute deal to restructure the program and head off an imminent funding shortfall.[1] Yet the present debate over Social Security has been sparked not by an immediate fiscal crisis but by a long-term budgetary imbalance posed by the retirement of the baby boom generation in the next century. More portentous still, the agenda for pension reform has shifted substantially since the early 1980s. Then, the focus was on scaling back benefits so that checks could be mailed. Backers of "privatization" enjoyed little fiscal slack to fund the transition to an alternative system, and they had few positive models for a program of private investment accounts.[2] Today, by contrast, Social Security's near-term financial situation is strong, tax-favored retirement accounts are ubiquitous, and leading political figures, including President George W. Bush, openly embrace proposals for the full or partial conversion of Social Security into compulsory individual accounts.[3] Even a limited version of these plans would represent the most fundamental transformation of Social Security – and the balance of public and private retirement provision – since the foundation of Social Security itself.

Though Social Security now faces one of the most serious challenges of its sixty-plus-year history, the debate over its place in American old-age provision is hardly new. Indeed, the role that government should play in securing retirement income has been deeply contested almost from the dawn of the industrial age. America's epochal transformation from localized agricultural and craft production to large-scale corporate capitalism eventually ushered in not one but two vast systems of social provision designed to protect workers' income and well-being during retirement.

71

These were occupational pensions and Social Security, the two collective pillars of U.S. retirement security policy. The proper balance between the two lay at the heart of the initial struggle over Social Security, and it has been a recurrent flash point of conflict as each has dramatically expanded and evolved in the decades since.

And yet, this is a strange sort of conflict – omnipresent but muted, recurrent but often unrecognized, as if Social Security and occupational pensions were wholly separate responses to the needs of the retired. The fluctuating boundary between the two has only occasionally become the object of explicit political debate and decision, and the public–private mix that has come to characterize U.S. retirement security policy is as much a product of the historical accretion of private and public choices as it is of those rare moments of decisive political intervention. Even as Social Security has become the most visible exemplar of the American welfare state, the dense thicket of policies that has come to encourage and regulate private pensions has never received comparable attention – its formation dominated by a narrow circle of interested participants, its study by a relatively small community of legal experts and pension specialists.

Perhaps this is why, despite countless histories of Social Security and many detailed studies of occupational pensions, few observers have charted the political history of their tandem development or described how they were shaped over time by government policy and each other. What exists instead are two distinct histories. The first, steeped in the rhetoric of politics and power, examines the political forces that created the Social Security Act and fueled its subsequent expansion.[4] The second, employing the language of industrial relations and management science, traces the birth of private pensions before the New Deal and their subsequent reincarnation as a major fringe benefit.[5] Rarely acknowledging each other, driven by separate concerns, these two narratives have left largely untold the story of how two such important institutions evolved side by side – and, more importantly, how leaders in business, labor, and government conceived of and tried to influence their contested inter-relationship.[6] Between the welfare state and welfare capitalism lies a largely neglected chapter in the history of U.S. social policy, one that says much about the development of alternative mechanisms of social insurance and the historical and political forces that influence it.

Retirement Security and Market Failure

For all their centrality to modern social policy, retirement pensions were relatively late arrivals on the economic scene. Before the coming of corporate capitalism, Americans continued to labor well into their advanced years and were generally cared for by their families when they could no longer work. What pensions there were came not upon retirement, itself a modern concept, but as payments for service to community, church, or country. Even the massive Civil War pension system, which at its peak delivered benefits to more than a quarter of elderly men in the United States, was based on and consistently justified by this logic of reward for service.[7] In this sense, the pension as we know it today – insurance against the loss of earnings during retirement – is a creature of the modern industrial economy and the transition to wage employment that it wrought.

Because the terminology of pensions is complex, it will help to begin with some definitions. By *pensions*, I mean retirement pensions – organized plans designed to provide income during later years of life spent outside the workforce. Pensions may be either *occupational* (that is, provided by employers to workers) or *governmental* (that is, provided by government to citizens). Pensions may also range from *pay-as-you-go* arrangements, in which benefits are paid out of current contributions, to fully *prefunded* arrangements, in which contributions are put aside to earn interest, with eventual payments made out of the accumulated funds. Most government pension programs are essentially pay-as-you-go (though there are exceptions), and most occupational pension plans are essentially prefunded (though, again, this is not and has not been universally true). Occupational pensions may, in turn, be either public or private, depending on the sector in which those who receive them work. For convenience, I call private occupational pensions "private pensions." When I discuss "public pensions," however, I mean public retirement programs like Social Security, not pensions for public workers, which I generally refer to as "public occupational pensions." I have also adopted the common convention of calling the federal old-age insurance program "Social Security," even though Social Security incorporates other elements, such as survivors' and disability insurance. When I discuss these constituent parts, I mention them by name.

Finally, I use some technical terms specific to private pensions. *Defined-benefit* pensions are pensions that promise a predetermined amount at fixed intervals until the end of life. These pensions usually employ complex formulas linking workers' earnings and length of job tenure to their eventual benefits. A virtually universal element of these formulas are rules governing *vesting*, which concerns the point at which workers retain the promise of pension benefits if they leave the organization that sponsors a plan. Before a pension is vested, which may take a number of years, workers forfeit retirement benefits if they exit a plan.[8] Another extremely common feature of defined-benefit pensions is *integration* with Social Security. In integrated plans, pension benefits are partially or fully reduced by the amount that workers are expected to receive from the federal old-age insurance program. Defined-benefit pensions are similar to retirement *annuities*, a promise to pay a periodic allotment until death (and hence to assume the risk that the purchaser of the annuity will live longer than expected). The difference is that pensions are organized plans into which contributions are periodically made and from which multiple retirees draw benefits, while annuities are usually obtained through a one-time private exchange with an independent risk-bearing party, such as an insurer.

Defined-contribution pensions are pension plans that do not embody the promise of predetermined periodic benefits upon retirement. They are instead a form of organized retirement savings: Eventual benefits are determined by how much is contributed (by employers, workers, or both) and how much interest those contributions earn. As a result, defined-contribution pensions do not promise specified benefits, nor do they assume the risk that workers will outlive their savings. Defined-contribution pensions have become widespread only in recent decades, so discussions of private plans in the historical narrative concern *defined-benefit* pensions unless indicated otherwise.

Retirement pensions can be justified on many grounds: as a means of pulling the elderly out of poverty, as a way to remove older employees from the workplace, as a spur to long and committed service with an employer, or as a mechanism for encouraging long-term savings. In essence, however, the pension is a response to certain problems of foresight and savings capacity that greatly complicate the task of financing retirement income during the working years. Take first the problem of foresight, or what economists call "information failures." Workers are uncertain about how long they – and, indeed, their entire age cohort – will live after retirement. They are uncertain about future economic conditions (especially future inflation), about their lifetime earnings relative to others, and about their likely investment returns. Moreover, there is evidence that workers systematically underestimate the resources they will need to maintain an adequate standard of living in retirement, perhaps because the very idea of retirement seems distant to many of them.[9] Compared with today, such failures of foresight were a far more serious and endemic problem in the early twentieth century, when workers commonly died in middle age and retirement was a relatively novel concept.[10]

The risks and uncertainties of retirement savings provide a powerful justification for some form of pooled retirement protection, but they do not necessarily call for state intervention to provide or mandate such insurance. Other considerations, however, indicate that some degree of government involvement is virtually unavoidable. The most simple is the differential capacity of workers to save and invest during their working lives. For workers with little income, adequate savings may be unattainable and higher-yield investments may be viewed as too risky for what limited savings can be set aside. In retirement, such workers are likely to fall back on communal, familial, and governmental support – a strong motive for mandating that they participate in an inclusive insurance pool through which income and risk redistribution can take place. Individually purchased private annuities, if they exist at all, are not likely to undertake extensive redistribution of this sort. Indeed, annuities markets suffer from a potentially serious type of market failure – namely, the problem of "adverse selection" that results when those who expect to live longer disproportionately purchase private annuities, driving up prices and causing some who might have purchased annuities to go without them. At a minimum, private annuities and pensions seem to require some degree of government regulation to ensure that insurance contracts are sound and honored and that financial reserves are adequate and properly managed.

A combination of these considerations helps explain why governments across the globe are heavily involved in the provision and regulation of pensions. All advanced industrial democracies provide some type of government pension, which frequently consists of several tiers (most often, a first-tier universal pension that provides flat benefits, coupled with a second-tier contributory pension that offers benefits scaled to prior earnings). All these nations also manage occupational pensions for government employees. And all regulate the terms and operations of private occupational pensions, frequently subsidizing them and sometimes even requiring participation in them.

Nonetheless, a glance at the comparative evidence in Table I2.1 suggests that for all these similarities, national pension systems differ greatly in their characteristics, spending levels, and time of origin. Among the nations described in the table, the amount of public spending on old-age programs varies from 11.2 percent of GDP in Germany to 6.1 percent in the United States. Private pension spending ranges by an even greater factor, from .5 percent of GDP in Denmark to 2.4 percent in the United States. And total occupational pension spending (by both the public and private sectors) ranges from less than a fifth of old-age cash benefits in Denmark to almost half of old-age cash benefits in the United States. Here again, as we saw in Part I, the United States stands out as the paradigmatic example of a nation that has encouraged private social benefits as a complement to and substitute for public social programs. Although the Netherlands and the United Kingdom also spend a

Table I2.1. *Public and Private Pensions in Selected Nations, 1993*

	Denmark	Germany	Netherlands	Sweden	U.K.	U.S.
Date of first law	1891	1889	1919	1913	1908	1935
Public "flat-rate" pensions (little or no link between contribution and benefit)?	Yes	No	Yes	Yes	Yes, but contributory (residual pension for nonworkers)	No, but basic pensions given to the indigent elderly
Public earnings-related pensions (link between contribution and benefit)?	Yes	Yes	No	Yes	Yes, but employer and employees may contract out under specified conditions	Yes
Main funding source(s) for contributory pension scheme	Earmarked payroll tax (PT) on employers/ employees	Earmarked PT on employers/ employees, subsidized by general revenues		Earmarked PT on employer, income tax on workers	Earmarked PT on employers/ employees	Earmarked PT on employers/ employees
Government cash benefits for the elderly as a percentage of GDP (including public employee pensions)[a]	6.8	11.2	8.7	10.3	7.3	6.1

Public employee pension benefits as a percentage of GDP[b]	0.8	2.0	1.9	Not available	Not available	1.6
Voluntary private pension benefits as a percentage of GDP[c]	0.5	0.7	2.1	1.6	1.9	2.4
Public and private occupational pensions as a share of all public and private old-age cash benefits[d]	18%	22%	37%	Not available	Not available	47%

[a] Includes contributory and noncontributory pensions and means-tested and non–means-tested benefits.
[b] These are rough estimates based on World Bank data that refer to years ranging from 1984 to 1992.
[c] Excludes mandatory private spending. Includes only private-sector occupational benefits.
[d] Excludes mandatory private spending.

Source: Calculated from Social Security Administration (SSA), *Social Security Systems throughout the World – 1997* (Washington, D.C.: SSA, 1997); Organization for Economic Cooperation and Development (OECD), *Private Pensions and Public Policy* (Paris: OECD, 1992); David W. Kalisch and Tetsya Aman, "Retirement Income Systems: The Reform Process Across OECD Countries," OECD Social Policy Division Working Paper (Paris: OECD, 1998); Willem Adema and Marcel Einerhand, "The Growing Role of Private Social Benefits," Labour Market and Social Policy – Occasional Papers No. 32. (Paris: OECD, 1998); and World Bank, *Averting the Old Age Crisis* (New York: Oxford University Press, 1994), Table A.5.

Figure I2.1. Occupational Pension and Old-Age Insurance Benefits as a Share of Combined Benefits, 1950–1996. *Source:* Private and public occupational plan data calculated from National Income and Product Accounts; Social Security data include only old-age and survivors' insurance benefits and come from Social Security Administration (SSA), *Social Security Bulletin Annual Statistical Supplement* (Washington, D.C.: SSA, 1998), 165.

large share of GDP on private pensions, their public programs rely primarily on flat pensions that do not vary with wages, leaving considerable room for occupational plans. (In the United Kingdom, moreover, the high level of private spending is owed not to voluntary provision but to a clause in the second-tier, earnings-related program that allows individuals and firms to "contract out" for private coverage under strict terms.) As one of a small handful of nations that operate only an earnings-related public program, the United States looks all the more distinctive for its heavy reliance on voluntary private pensions.

What is more, as Figures I2.1 and I2.2 reveal, these current statistics provide only a snapshot of an evolving pension picture. In the United States, the balance between federal old-age insurance and occupational pensions (both public and private) has shifted substantially since World War II, with old-age insurance benefits comprising 41 percent of all pension spending in 1950, hovering near 70 percent in 1960, and then falling to around 47 percent today.[11] Coverage rates, too, have changed. In 1940, Social Security covered just 55 percent of the workforce, and private occupational pensions covered barely 15 percent. In 1988, by contrast, Social Security covered nearly 95 percent of workers, and

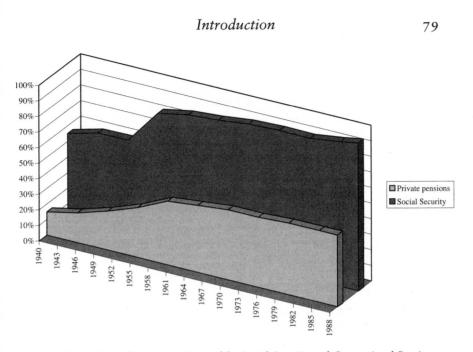

Figure I2.2. Share of Americans Covered by Social Security and Occupational Pensions, 1940–1988. *Note:* The Social Security figure for 1940 is actually from 1939, for 1945 from 1944, and for 1950 from 1949. *Source:* Compiled from House Committee on Ways and Means, *1998 Green Book* (Washington, D.C.: U.S. GPO, 1998), 8; U.S. Department of Labor, Pension and Welfare Benefits Administration, *Trends in Pensions 1992* (Washington, D.C.: U.S. GPO, 1992), 75.

private pensions reached 46 percent. And because pension commitments generally come due years after they are made, many of the most important recent shifts in pension coverage and characteristics have yet to be fully felt.

The particular combination of considerations that predominate in government and private decision making has also shifted over time, undermining any simple appeal to a timeless logic of corporate organization or government intervention. The occupational pension first emerged in the late nineteenth century as an entirely nonbinding token of corporate benevolence, evolved into a sophisticated employer device to influence career patterns, enjoyed special favor for a time as a tax-advantaged mechanism for compensating highly paid employees, and then emerged as a crucial collective-bargaining goal of organized labor, which saw pensions mainly as a welfare arrangement rather than a vehicle for asset accumulation. Depending on whom one asked and when, Social Security was primarily a guarantee of an adequate minimum income in retirement, a device for income redistribution or intergenerational transfers, a mechanism for compelling retirement savings, or a remedy for private market failure.

In the field of occupational pensions, the federal government initially pursued a policy of unconditional subsidization through the tax code beginning in 1914, then began a decades-long process of increased pension regulation that culminated in the passage of the 1974 Employee Retirement Income Security Act (ERISA) – the landmark regulatory law that attempted to transform occupational pensions from a "personnel instrument of private employers" into a quasi-public "instrument of national social welfare."[12] The last two decades have been a period of greater incoherence in government policy toward retirement pensions, with federal law seesawing between restrictive interventions designed to increase equity, on the one hand, and largely distributive interventions aimed at expanding tax-favored investment devices such as IRAs that disproportionately benefit higher-income Americans, on the other.

Some of these shifts in goals have been in response to the failure of previous public or private policies. When Social Security was enacted, the private pension system covered only a small fraction of the working population, and advocates of the program cited the widespread failure of private plans as a justification for a compulsory program. (In fact, the effects of the Great Depression on private pensions were varied, and the total number of plans actually grew in its early years.) ERISA emerged after a series of high-profile, though largely unrepresentative, private plan failures – most notably, the spectacular collapse of the Studebaker auto plant and its 11,000-member pension plan. Yet, in each case, the failure of previous policies was not self-evident but rather an interpretation of inherently ambiguous events. Nor, more important, was failure seen solely or even primarily as an inability to achieve efficient outcomes. Perceptions of failure instead emerged out of an inevitably value-laden process of interpretation in which broad normative concerns about equity, security, liberty, and fairness loomed large.

All this is to say that the failure of the private market to provide satisfactory retirement insurance cannot be the prime reason that government policy has taken the shape that it has. The failure of the market helps explain why government intervention occurred at all, but it does not explain the scope or form that such intervention took or when it occurred. It does not explain why, for example, national leaders did not mandate private pensions, as was proposed at several historical junctures, or why they refused to allow employers who provided pensions to opt out of the Social Security system, as was very nearly done during the final legislative design of the program. It does not explain why Social Security, originally a prefunded and relatively small program covering half the workforce, grew into a massive, pay-as-you-go public system covering nearly all American workers. It does not explain why the regulation and subsidization of private pensions has taken the form that it has, or why the relationship between pensions and Social Security has shifted over time. It does not explain why tax-favored savings plans were created, enlarged, contracted, then expanded yet again.

The Plan of Part II

These are the questions that animate Part II – the first of two parts that deal with the origins and evolution of health and pension policy in the United States. Our initial inquiries about America's distinctive welfare regime in Part I now lead us deeper into the unfolding of public and private pensions in the first half of the twentieth century (Chapter 2) and in the decades after World War II (Chapter 3). We shall discover that a major – indeed, at key moments, *the* major – theme of the twin debates over Social Security and private pensions has been the proper balance between the public and private sectors in the provision of retirement income. We shall find that the course and outcomes of these debates have been shaped not merely by enduring ideological disagreement over the state's proper role, but also by the divergent political and social characteristics of public and private benefits. And we shall see that as America's two-track pension system has matured, the resolution of these debates has increasingly come to be driven by the public and private institutions that already exist – so that political actors have found themselves working to reshape, rather than replace, existing networks of social provision while responding to the logic of policy development set in motion by earlier choices and events.

The development of public and private pensions has, in short, been highly path dependent. This is not surprising given how long-lived pension commitments are. In public pension programs,

> there are often *very* long time lags between the enactment of a policy and the realization of its major public expenditure implications. In the case of contributory pensions, it may be *70 years* – the time it takes for the bulk of the pensioner population to be composed of those who worked a full career under new rules – before policy choices are fully reflected in ongoing expenditures.[13]

But long time lags are not the only reason that the heavy hand of history looms large in the politics of public pensions. Government pension programs are built around *expectations,* particularly the expectations of workers that benefits that they have been promised will indeed be available for them when they retire. In conjunction with the pay-as-you-go structure of most public pension systems, these expectations are a politically powerful force preventing transition away from a mature public pension program. Since current workers fund the system, moving them into an alternative structure or reducing the public role requires either cutting expected benefits or coming up with some other way to pay for them. The mobilization of the elderly that public programs help bring about makes this difficult challenge harder still. Thus, as both critics and defenders of pay-as-you-go pensions have long recognized, public pension laws have built-in features that make them highly politically resilient.

Though less well recognized, private pensions – and the policies that govern them – have similar effects. Just as workers premise crucial decisions about when to retire and how much to save on their expectations about public benefits, they also premise such decisions on promises made by employers to provide private funds when they retire. Just as policy changes that might reduce public benefits mobilize opposition from current and future beneficiaries, policy changes that might threaten private benefits are also likely to invite political challenge, if not from pension beneficiaries themselves, then from the institutions that sponsor and provide pension benefits. And just as the reach and structure of public pensions shape the views of citizens and organized groups, so the scope and character of private pensions influence public and elite conceptions of the government's proper role and the appropriate boundaries of public and private action.

But, of course, private pension plans and the policies that shape them are much less visible and politically salient than is a large-scale public program like Social Security. Writing in the 1970s, the management guru Peter Drucker memorably described the rise of private pensions after World War II as an "unseen revolution," which he saw as "an outstanding example of the efficacy of using the existing private, non-governmental institutions of our 'society of organizations' for the formulation and achievement of social goals and the satisfaction of social needs."[14] This "unseen" character of private pensions cuts in conflicting directions. On the one hand, it has allowed significant changes to occur through stealth and, in this respect, made the private pension system more vulnerable to restructuring (government-initiated or otherwise) than a mature public program. Yet, on the other hand, it has also meant that those who have a large stake in private pensions or wish to encourage them have had a freer hand in shaping public policy. As the history charted in the next two chapters will make clear, the politics of private pensions is subterranean politics, only occasionally involving a broad circle of participants and resisting the scrutiny that public programs typically invite – even when sizable public resources and recognized national policy goals hang in the balance.

What the historical record shows above all is that Drucker was wrong to describe the "unseen revolution" as having occurred "without benefit of government programs or government policy."[15] Quite the opposite: Private pensions have been encouraged by public policy both directly and indirectly – through tax and labor law, through targeted regulatory interventions, and through the structure and reach of Social Security itself. Not only have private pensions been extensively encouraged by public policy; they have also been dramatically reshaped by it, both intentionally and unintentionally. Because Social Security was enacted before private pensions had an extensive presence, it created a floor of retirement security upon which employer-provided pensions built in the years after its passage. Yet as private pensions emerged as supplements to Social Security, they also carved out a prominent place in American social welfare practice that, in later years, proved highly resistant to challenge. Even as the costs of the private pension system to the federal government and to the ultimate aims of Social Security advocates grew more apparent, the two-track system established in the 1940s and 1950s became increasingly embedded. This is reflected in the Employee Retirement Income Security Act of 1974. Although ERISA attempted to reshape the private pension system to make it a more reliable counterpart to Social Security, it also represented an unmistakable affirmation of the integral role that voluntary private pensions had come to play. And because ERISA preserved and ratified the private pension system while at the same time reorganizing it, the law would prove powerless to offset subsequent sweeping changes in private pensions that flew sharply in the face of ERISA's original goals.

Crucial to the way in which this path-dependent process unfolded was the *supplementary* role that pensions came to play in retirement security policy, a position quite different from the *core* role that private health insurance assumed in the health policy domain, where an inclusive public program failed to emerge before the rise of private fringe benefits. Although conservative politicians, business leaders, and commercial insurers worked to make public policy more favorable to an expansive private pension system, they also came to recognize that these efforts depended on a strong public foundation on top of which they could build. Indeed, because most private plans took Social Security payments into account in setting benefit levels, these political actors evinced what would otherwise seem a surprising degree of support for proposals to broaden public coverage and bring public benefits up to basic levels – certainly a greater degree than they offered for even limited proposals for government health insurance.

In similar fashion, the rise of private pensions shaped the interests of American unions, which came to be far more reliant on private social insurance provided via employment than did labor movements in other nations. Workers employed in unionized industries or by large nonunionized employers came to enjoy comprehensive retirement security through a mix of public and private benefits. But the majority of Americans were not so organized or valuable to their firms, and even as pension coverage remained deeply uneven across lines of class, race, and gender, the labor movement's interest in more encompassing protections was increasingly undercut by its victories at the bargaining tables – a feedback effect that, as future chapters will show, was even more profound in the health field.

Finally, because private pensions were adjuncts to a public program that provided a common floor of support for virtually all Americans, federal policymakers proved willing to regulate them to make them a more predictable and sound counterpart to Social Security, even though one result of these rules might be the discontinuance or weakening of a significant number of private schemes. As a result, the structural constraints on policymaking created by private social welfare approaches were not nearly as severe in the area of private pensions as in the health insurance field. Yet these constraints were still powerful and help account for the underlying limits of the dramatic pension reforms of 1974.

The analysis contained in the next two chapters thus challenges the division of scholarly labor that has relegated private pensions to a footnote in most studies of Social Security even as it has encouraged experts on private pensions to treat these benefits as largely independent of the political forces that have driven public programs. Public and private pensions are intertwined not just structurally but also politically, and studies that neglect this interdependence cannot adequately explain the development of either. Neither the growth of Social Security nor the evolution of public policy toward private pensions can be understood without appreciation of the specific role that private benefits came to play alongside America's public pension program.

2

Connected at Birth:
Public and Private Pensions
Before 1945

The development of public and private pensions prior to the close of World War II can be divided into two periods, punctuated by the Great Depression and the New Deal reforms that followed. Before the passage of the Social Security Act, public retirement pensions such as we now know them did not exist. Public pensions were designed to serve "deserving" groups that were not necessarily aged – veterans, widows, the severely disabled – or to provide occupational benefits to government workers. As for private pension plans, pioneering employers in large industries adopted them as early as 1875, but as late as 1929, plans were still relatively scarce, and even for workers ostensibly covered, their benefits were highly uncertain. Although the old-age insurance program contained in the Social Security Act emulated the best private plans in many respects, its broad and compulsory coverage – compromised, but not abandoned, by Congress – cast in stark relief the weaknesses of the fledgling private pension system. It challenged, too, the unfettered management prerogatives of American business, whose most vocal leaders had argued to the end that employers should not have to shoulder new burdens that would imperil profits or gut the existing network of private plans so identified with the pre–New Deal vision of "welfare capitalism."[1]

After the passage of old-age insurance, however, private pension plans began to flourish as never before. The reasons for this were multiple, but ironically, much of the impetus came from Social Security itself. Especially after the Social Security amendments of 1939, old-age insurance benefits were concentrated on middle- and lower-income wage workers, allowing employers to focus their pensioning activities on the white-collar workers whom firms deemed most valuable and encouraging commercial insurers to pitch their products as gap-closing protections especially attractive to the higher paid. The movement of employers to adopt or restructure pension plans on behalf of upper-income workers was further encouraged by what had until then been a little-noticed feature of the tax code that allowed corporate contributions to pensions and the interest income on pension trusts to escape corporate and income taxation. As tax rates rose in the latter years of the 1930s and especially during World War II, employers rushed to exploit this provision, prompting the Roosevelt Administration to demand new restrictions on what it branded a counterproductive federal subsidy. Though never rising to the level of general public consciousness, an important series of legislative and Internal Revenue Service (IRS) decisions in the late 1930s and early 1940s codified the tax advantages of pension plans while imposing very limited new requirements on them – decisions that were largely in line with the demands of the increasing number of employers that operated private plans. At the same time, the distractions of the war and the resistance of the increasingly assertive "conservative coalition" of Republicans and conservative Democrats in Congress kept Social Security taxes and benefits from expanding beyond their modest beginnings. By the end of World War II, old-age insurance was a stagnant and threatened program, increasingly overshadowed by the means-tested payments made to the indigent elderly under state old-age assistance programs, as well as by the growing sphere of private retirement provision.

Nonetheless, the fact that Social Security had entered the scene before the large-scale development of private plans meant that the rapidly emerging private system was building on top of a public foundation. The most visible sign of this was the common practice of "integration," which was sanctioned as a means of meeting the coverage requirements placed on tax-favored private pensions in the 1942 Revenue Act. Integration allowed corporations to factor in Social Security benefits when setting up tax-favored pension plans, even if this meant that lower-wage workers were excluded from private coverage or received meager private benefits upon retirement. Integration was, on one level, deeply at odds with the philosophy of the Social Security Act, because it allowed employers to provide little or no pension benefits to the very workers that old-age insurance aimed to assist. Yet, on another level, integration was premised on the idea that Social Security would be the core provider of retirement income for most Americans. Integration, moreover, gave employers with private plans a reason to support Social Security, for the costs of integrated plans were offset by increases in promised benefits under Social Security. Arriving before the widespread development of private pensions, Social Security thus enjoyed important "first-mover" advantages as it entered the policy space left open by the weaknesses of welfare capitalism – advantages that, as coming chapters will show, accrued to private rather than public social protections in the health policy domain.

Table 2.1. *Time of Adoption of Five Major Welfare Programs (U.S. Rank Among 15 Developed Nations)*

	Initial Adoption	Binding and Extensive
Old Age, Disability, and Survivors	12th	11th
Sickness and Maternity	15th	None
Workers Compensation	15th	10th
Unemployment Compensation	11th	9th
Family Allowances	None	None

Source: Alexander Hicks, Joya Misra, and Tang Nah Ng, "The Programmatic Emergence of the Social Security State," *American Sociological Review* 60 (June 1995): 329–49, 337. The fifteen countries are Australia, Austria, Belgium, Canada, Denmark, France, Germany, Italy, the Netherlands, New Zealand, Norway, Sweden, Switzerland, the United Kingdom, and the United States. The United States is the only country in the group without binding and extensive health care benefits and family allowances.

Discussions of integration and tax law unfolded in the technical digressions of congressional hearings and the rarified atmosphere of federal courts, in the backrooms of Congress and the boardrooms of corporate America. Yet these were crucial discussions, closely monitored and heavily influenced by employers, pension sponsors, life insurers, and congressional defenders of private pensions. Our attention is easily pulled away from these complex and seemingly mundane events. The passage of the Social Security Act stands out as the most dramatic and important milestone in the history of U.S. social policy, and for this reason, scholars have frequently skipped over the decade that followed to jump right into the very prominent and visible expansion of the program after 1950. Yet, as we shall see, we can only comprehend both the impressive reach and the very real limits of old-age insurance by delving into the less visible political developments that shaped the balance of public and private pensions in the years before the end of World War II.

Uncertain Beginnings

The most striking feature of U.S. social policy before the New Deal was the almost complete failure of the broad-based programs for social insurance that were then tentatively taking root in other industrializing nations (see Table 2.1). Although public pension schemes for civil servants and veterans received political favor, compulsory retirement protection for America's wage earners foundered at both the state and federal levels. Instead of public programs, the United States hosted its own indigenous form of organized social protection known as welfare capitalism – a model of social provision based on business benevolence rather than on labor empowerment or coercive state action. In the field of old-age pensions, the reach of welfare capitalism was both limited and uneven, and by the 1930s, reformist critics such as Abraham Epstein dismissed it as a hopelessly utopian vision "strewn with wrecked anticipations" and promising only "more shattered hopes."[2] But private pensions were one of the few large-scale institutions of early welfare capitalism that survived the Great Depression to shape the development of the Social Security Act. And the elusive promise of a private solution to America's social problems remained a regnant idea in elite thinking about social policy, even as its premises were increasingly called into doubt by the developments of the 1920s and 1930s.

The first formal pension plan in the United States was created in 1875 by American Express, a railroad freight forwarder.[3] It was followed by plans in additional companies, first in the railroads, which pioneered the practice, and then in other industries with large managerial labor forces, relatively low labor costs, high profitability, and a strong interest in retiring aged workers – notably, public utilities, iron and steel, oil, and electrical supplies.[4] By 1929, roughly four hundred plans were in operation, and 3.7 million employees worked for firms that provided pensions, although not all were eligible for benefits.[5] In a 1925 survey of employers, the National Industrial Conference Board estimated that 2.8 million workers were covered by private pensions. Because the survey also asked about the date of plan establishment, it is possible to develop rough estimates of coverage for prior years. As Figure 2.1 shows, coverage grew extremely rapidly between 1905 and 1915 and still quite quickly between 1915 and 1925. In no year before the Great Depression, however, did private pensions come close to reaching even a tenth of the private labor force.

Among the pioneering firms that first offered pensions, the reasons for doing so were diverse.[6] In the spirit of welfare capitalism, some of the earliest pension plans were discretionary and ad hoc in character, providing minimal support as an expression of corporate benevolence. But, as firms grew larger and more rationalized, concrete management goals moved to the fore, and pension practices became more formalized. Chief among these goals was the desire to remove elderly workers from the work rolls, particularly in industries, such as the railroads, where age and infirmity posed real threats to increasingly mechanized and bureaucratized production processes. Also crucial, however, was the desire of

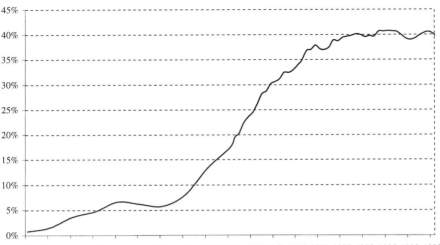

Figure 2.1.   Share of Private Civilian Labor Force Covered by Private Pensions, 1905–1995.
Note: The private civilian labor force is the civilian workforce minus federal, state, and local government workers. *Source*: Pension coverage statistics for 1905 through 1925 are from National Industrial Conference Board, *Industrial Pensions in the United States* (New York: National Industrial Conference Board, Inc., 1925), 5–8; (years prior to 1925 are extrapolated from 1925 estimates); for 1930 to 1940, from American Council of Life Insurance, *Life Insurance Fact Book* (Washington, D.C.: ACLI, 1973) (not strictly comparable to earlier years); for 1940 through 1970, Alfred M. Skolnick, "Private Pension Plans, 1950–74," *Social Security Bulletin* 39 (1976): 4; for 1971 through 1979, Laurence Kotlikoff and Daniel E. Smith, *Pensions in the American Economy* (Chicago: University of Chicago Press, 1983), 28; and for 1980 through 1995, U.S. Census Bureau, *Statistical Abstract of the United States* (Washington, D.C.: U.S. GPO, 1998), 403.

more knowledge-intensive industries to attract and retain highly paid white-collar workers with firm-specific skills. And, of course, many firms that offered pensions were animated by a desire to discourage unionization, with pension plans often stipulating that striking workers forfeited benefits. By providing benefits that were contingent upon long and continuous service and could be received only in retirement, firms hoped to make workers remain loyal during their years of peak productivity and then leave when they hindered efficient operations. Early pensions were thus highly contingent, overwhelmingly "noncontributory" (that is, funded solely by employers), and mostly pay-as-you-go. Even the most generous included lengthy escape clauses stipulating that they were voluntary gifts that implied neither company obligations nor employee rights. Indeed, the best study of early pension plans estimated that fewer than 10 percent of workers enrolled in pension plans would receive any benefits in retirement.[7]

Welfare capitalism was hardly the only obstacle to compulsory public pensions before the 1930s, nor even the most important. The most significant barriers to expanded public protections during this period were instead constitutional and political: the weakness and fragmentation of national political power, the absence of programmatic parties backing reform, the preeminence of the states as the loci of social legislation, and the strength of the opponents of government redistribution. These obstacles were all intimately connected. The constitutional and political constraints on federal legislation pushed reform movements to the state level, where opponents of change were often strongest and where interstate competition enhanced the blocking power of mobile employers by raising the specter of capital flight from activist states.[8] With impressive and consistent ferocity, business organizations and individual employers dismissed old-age programs as costly and dangerous: Programs for the elderly poor would undermine thrift and self-reliance, they charged. Compulsory insurance programs for the working class would supplant nascent private pension plans and undermine business autonomy. And all retirement legislation meant higher state spending and taxes, driving out business and drawing in pension claimants.[9]

This inhospitable institutional and political climate was matched by the weakness of organized pressures for reform. Labor unions were comparatively anemic in the United States (though in many states, no less militant than their European counterparts), and their national leaders were less supportive of government-led reform. Prominent national labor heads, such as American Federation of Labor (AFL) President Samuel Gompers, advocated not compulsory and contributory social insurance programs, but voluntary plans obtained through collective bargaining.[10] Although the AFL did endorse public assistance for the elderly poor, it demanded federal legislation, which had no chance of success. State labor unions, for their part, were far more receptive to all forms of social legislation.[11] But they were consistently hampered in their state legislative efforts by business recalcitrance, by restrictive state constitutions, by the fears of political leaders about capital flight, and, at times, by the opposition of the national AFL leadership as well.

If labor unions were not at the forefront in demanding old-age insurance, neither was America's extensive network of mutual aid societies. In the early twentieth century, fraternal organizations offering various social benefits enrolled an estimated one out of three adult males in the United States, "including a large segment of the working class."[12] In many European nations, similar risk-sharing societies became the foundation for early government interventions to provide sickness and old-age insurance.[13] Yet American fraternal organizations were, on the whole, more culturally fragmented, politically quiescent, and suspicious of the state than their European counterparts.[14] Before the 1920s, the most visible foray of the "fraternals" into the political arena was *against* proposals for government sickness and burial benefits, and in the field of retirement security, they had little political presence until the Fraternal Order of Eagles (FOE) began campaigning for local assistance for the aged during the 1920s.[15] Nor were mutual aid societies major providers of retirement protection: As late as 1930, old-age benefits represented just 2.3 percent of the $153 million in social benefits given out by fraternal organizations each year.[16]

Until the 1920s, moreover, the main organized group demanding social legislation, the American Association for Labor Legislation (AALL), placed other legislative priorities ahead of old-age protection. This strategic choice seems to have been rooted primarily in the philosophy of the AALL's leaders – reform-minded social scientists who stressed prevention against industrial risks, rather than relief of destitution or assistance for those outside the labor force.[17] Fears about runaway patronage spending, made tangible by the dramatic expansion of Civil War pensions, probably also played a role in dulling elite interest in old-age pensions.[18] Nonetheless, fears about corruption cannot explain why pension proposals consistently foundered even after reform-oriented organizations – such as the FOE and Abraham Epstein's American Association for Old Age Security (AAOS) – began to lobby actively for them in the 1920s. Here, business opposition and concerns about interstate competition appear to have been decisive. Despite the considerable efforts of the FOE and AAOS, just six states passed programs before 1929. All took the form of noncontributory assistance. All were granted as charity only to the poorest of the aged, provided at the discretion of counties, and financed at the local level, where funding was stingiest. And all, in practice, were "either inoperative or defective."[19] As Roy Lubove concludes, "The main reason for the failure [of pension reform advocates] was the effective opposition inspired by business organizations."[20]

The absence of broad-based state or federal old-age programs before the New Deal does not imply, however, the absence of government action. There were, to begin with, federal veterans' pensions, the recipients of which represented a staggering 85 percent of total pensioners in the United States in 1928. Then there were municipal, state, and federal occupational pension programs, which covered roughly a quarter of government employees in that same year.[21] A third exception to the general pattern of inaction – one that has received very little attention – was the War Risk Insurance Act of 1918.[22] Though less extensive than Civil War pensions, the War Risk Insurance Act was a major program of compensation and insurance for servicemen and their families passed in the midst of World War I. Its cornerstone – a system of federally administered life insurance underwritten by the government at subsidized rates – would eventually assume a liability of $40 billion, well more than the value of all commercial life insurance then in force in the United States. The program, however, not only was specifically aimed at active servicemen and justified as an extraordinary wartime measure; it also had the support of the commercial insurance industry, the representatives of which argued that they could not assume the unusual risk of combat death.[23] After the war, despite some advocates' hopes for expansion, over three-fourths of policies were allowed to lapse immediately. The War Risk Insurance Act showcased the persistent American desire to turn to programs modeled after private social provision, and in subsequent decades, it would be repeatedly cited as an exemplar of public–private partnership. But it was clearly an exceptional example of pre–New Deal social policy.

As Theda Skocpol has shown, another uniquely favored group during the Progressive Era was women. "Mothers' pensions" provided by the states reached roughly fifty thousand single women with children, most of them widows, in the early 1920s.[24] But although the spread of mothers' pensions showed the impressive influence of women's groups in state politics, actual spending was minuscule. "Unlike much social legislation," Mark Leff notes, "mothers' pension programs were neither expensive nor disruptive to productive efficiency."[25]

Furthermore, none of these varied initiatives – public employee pensions, veterans' pensions and insurance, mothers' pensions – was really public social insurance for the aged. Pensions for public workers were occupational schemes similar in structure to private pensions and motivated by many of the same considerations. For all their differences, mothers' pensions and veterans' programs – as well as pensions for the blind, which were established in roughly twenty states by 1929 – shared the common characteristic that they were designated not for the elderly as a group, but for Americans deemed particularly deserving by virtue of their service to the nation or their special moral or physical status.[26] Nor do Civil War pensions appear to have entailed much redistribution, at least not downward redistribution. The social insurance expert Isaac Max Rubinow concluded in 1916 that "the most singular feature of the American pension system is that it primarily redounds to the advantage of the class least in need of old-age pensions."[27] For American workers before the New Deal, welfare capitalism was the only form of collective retirement provision that at least aspired to more inclusive social protection, however insufficient it was in reality.

Tax Policy and Private Pensions

Government intervention in the private pension field also took more subterranean forms during this period. Yet little of it was directed at promoting old-age security either. State regulation of life insurers to ensure sound reserves and conservative investments was one example.[28] Another that would come to be extremely important was the special tax treatment of private pensions, which emerged out of a series of legislative changes and Treasury rulings between the income tax's origin in 1913 and the Revenue Act of 1926. This favorable tax treatment consisted of – and still consists of – three provisions: corporate deductibility of pension contributions as business expenses; exemption of the value of pensions from workers' income until pensions are received in retirement; and exemption of the interest income of pension "trusts" from taxation. Under this tax structure, corporations that set aside money in pension trusts may deduct their contributions as they do wages and other current expenses, but the workers for whom these payments are made do not have to pay taxes on contributions or trust earnings until they reach retirement, when most face significantly lower tax rates.

The motives behind what would eventually become one of the nation's largest tax expenditures are clouded by the absence of any substantial congressional debate or administrative record that might indicate who exactly supported it and why.[29] Part of the justification was surely technical. The first major Treasury decision, a 1914 ruling allowing corporate deductibility of pension contributions, simply concerned direct employer payments to currently retired employees. The judgment that these benefits should be deductible from corporate taxes seems to have rested on the not unreasonable conclusion that they were a form of compensation, like wages and salaries.[30] As with wages, it made little sense to tax pension payments as corporate income while also taxing them as personal income. A few years later, this policy was extended to employer contributions to pension trusts – investment funds established to stash away savings for future retirees. This posed greater administrative problems because money put in trusts was almost never earmarked for particular employees. Nonetheless, the Treasury Department maintained some consistency by requiring that employer contributions be taxed in the year that they were made, assigning them "to employees, the trust, or to employers, depending on who had control over the funds and on the certainty of obtaining benefits."[31] If employer pension contributions could not be linked to particular employees, then at least they could be taxed at the level of the trust or corporation.

The truly precedent-setting development, then, was the policy – begun in 1921, then codified in the 1926 Revenue Act – to defer all taxation on pension trusts until workers received benefits, allowing tax-free accumulation of trust assets and permitting corporations immediately to deduct contributions that might not be taxed until far into the future, and usually at lower rates. Although this deferral of taxation is the sine qua non of the pension tax expenditure (and the cause of its high price tag), the reasons for its adoption are hazy. Lacking direct evidence, Christopher Howard presents a strong circumstantial case that its creation was a by-product of national partisan struggles over taxation. The victories of pro-business Republicans in the 1918 and 1920 elections led to reductions in taxes on corporations and wealthy individuals, as well as to the creation of new tax breaks, including the special tax treatment of pensions.[32] It is worth noting, however, that tax deferral of pension income is common in industrialized nations, likely because it is quite difficult to know whose income to tax when pensions are not immediately vested in specific employees.[33]

Moreover, according to James Wooten, this universal problem was compounded in pre–New Deal tax policy by the differential taxation of corporate and individual income.[34] Few Americans paid income taxes before World War II, but corporate income taxes were widespread. Thus, if pension trusts were treated as corporations, they would be taxed at higher rates than all but a handful of workers would have been charged on the same amount. Prior to 1926, the IRS tried to finesse this problem by taxing pension trust income as if all of it belonged to a single individual, but this, too, obviously resulted in rates of levy much higher than those individual workers would have faced on their share of the trust income. None of this had proved excessively troublesome when almost all pension plans were pay-as-you-go, since employer payments went directly to workers. But as pioneering firms like Sears, Roebuck & Co. and Eastman Kodak moved to prefund their plans by placing contributions in trusts, the difficulty of assigning trust amounts and interest to individual workers threatened to lead to the *overtaxation* of pensions. The claims of these companies that the tax code was at odds with sound pension practices seems to have carried significant weight with Treasury officials.

Whatever the case, the primary motive for creating this provision was almost certainly not a desire to encourage private pensions on a broad scale. Because tax rates were then low, the benefits of the tax exemption were minimal. Indeed, the slowdown in the adoption of pensions during the 1920s suggests that any stimulating effects were slight. The pension tax expenditure only became critical in conjunction with the expansion of private pensions and the rise of tax rates during the New Deal and World War II. Far more interesting than the question of why these tax provisions were created is the question of why they survived with minimal restrictions even after their costs and the regressive distribution of their benefits became apparent – a question to be taken up shortly.

The common thread connecting the scattered social policy initiatives of the early twentieth century is the consistent inability of reform movements to overcome the institutional and political barriers to more comprehensive social protections. Operating in a decentralized polity in which demands for expanded government action centered on the states, social reformers ran headlong into the opposition of employers and the concerns of state political leaders about the negative effects of social programs on state prosperity and employment. Although a few states created social programs, reforms that threatened to raise costs significantly for a large number of firms that engaged in interstate competition consistently failed to pass.[35] Only private welfare capitalism held out the promise of broader protections, with businessmen, prominent political leaders, and even national union elites claiming that farsighted voluntary action in America's workplaces would eventually solve the problems that other nations had attacked through coercive and costly state interventions. Behind the celebratory rhetoric of welfare capitalism, however, the reach of private pensions was exceedingly limited and uneven, and federal encouragement and regulation of private pensions was as minimal as was government support for all other forms of social protection during this period.

The Road to Social Security

The New Deal changed all that. But it did not, as both conservative and liberal mythology have it, eliminate America's fledgling system of private retirement provision. Rather than supplanting private pensions, New Deal reforms helped reconstruct them, transforming them from employer gratuities that were rarely received into federally subsidized supplements to a national retirement program that, in may ways, emulated the private pension institution. Social Security did what welfare capitalism could not: provide broad retirement protection. At the same time, its limited benefits and slow stagnation during the 1940s provided the impetus for a dramatic expansion and transformation of the very private schemes whose inadequacy had helped prompt its creation.

No account of the social policy breakthroughs of the 1930s can fail to give due credit to the Great Depression. It was not just the economic need that the Depression created, great as it was. The economic catastrophe that worsened throughout the early 1930s also wrought political and institutional upheavals and called into deep question both established political arrangements and the functioning of existing structures of social provision. The election results tell an important part of the story. Thoroughly discredited, the business-backed Republicans overwhelmingly lost the White House, the Senate, and the House to a newly invigorated Democratic Party facing stiff outside pressure from populist social movements. This partisan and ideological reversal was coupled with an institutional transformation no less striking, as the locus of legislative action shifted from the states to the federal government and, within the federal government, from Congress to the presidency. As we shall see, the barriers to public social insurance did not melt away, but they did fall enough to allow reformers to pursue their vision for change.

The 1930s also provided ample evidence of the insufficiency of private retirement provision. Objectively, the flaws of private pensions were scarcely worse than they had been in previous decades. Although many private pensions foundered during the Great Depression, the number of plans (in contrast to the proportion of the population covered) actually rose in the early years of the crisis, and the plans that survived were those most likely to pay benefits, their finances having been placed on firmer footing during the previous decade through contractes with insurers or the creation of adequate reserves.[36] Yet the economic need of the 1930s made the sheer insufficiency of private pensions grossly manifest. Epstein's critical indictment of private pensions as fostering "wrecked anticipations" and "shattered hopes" was only a sharper rendition of the Roosevelt Administration's more measured but no less devastating conclusion that "the very limited coverage and frequent shortcomings of most existing industrial pension programs prevent . . . any reliance upon such programs in meeting the problem of old-age dependency facing the country."[37]

Private pensions were criticized on many grounds: Their coverage was meager, they rarely paid benefits, their finances were often unsound, they discouraged labor mobility, they were designed to thwart unionization. The overarching complaint, however, was not directed at private pensions per se but at the general assumption that private social provision was sufficient in the absence of a government floor of support. New Dealers attacked the ideology of "voluntarism," so associated with the repudiated Hoover presidency, on the general grounds that employers and charities had not and could not assume the burden of providing basic social protection for American workers and their families.[38] As J. Douglas Brown, one of the principal architects of the old-age insurance portions of the bill, recalled: "We figured . . . that not more than 4 percent of people then arriving at 65 were covered adequately under private industrial schemes. . . . [T]he growth in private industrial plans was far too slow, we thought, and the vast range of people would never come under them."[39]

By 1934, when Roosevelt authorized a cabinet-level Committee on Economic Security (CES) to draft legislation, there was little question that Congress would pass some form of expanded public assistance for the elderly poor. Noncontributory old-age pensions for the needy represented an immediate way to relieve economic distress – and to respond to the powerful grassroots movement led by Dr. Francis Townsend, who was demanding a lavish federal pension for every American over 60 years of age. Between 1929 and 1933, nineteen states had passed noncontributory old-age pension laws. Although benefits were low and still rarely received, most of these laws overrode county discretion to mandate that local governments provide some degree of support to the elderly poor.[40] With many of the states in fiscal crisis and public demands for relief mounting, Congress was eager simply to go ahead and provide federal support for the cash-strapped pension programs of the states. Indeed, Roosevelt had to beat back a 1934 congressional proposal for federal subsidization of state programs for fear that it would undercut his ability to package old-age assistance funding with a broader program of social security.

If old-age assistance was gaining momentum, contributory old-age *insurance* was another matter entirely. Popular and congressional demands centered on immediate relief, yet old-age insurance promised no short-term benefits. To the contrary, under the plan eventually presented to Congress, benefits would not be paid until 1942, five years after the first payroll taxes were levied on employers and workers. Moreover, old-age insurance was the only provision of the Social Security Act that members of the CES insisted should be financed and administered entirely by the federal government, rather than jointly with the states. And because Roosevelt and his Treasury secretary wanted the program to be self-financing, the proposal presented to Congress entailed the building up of a massive reserve, with forty-year projections envisioning a fund more than eight times the total amount of money in circulation in 1937.[41] For all these reasons, old-age insurance had little direct political appeal to members of Congress. It survived only because the president and his advisers supported it, and only because Roosevelt intervened at critical points in the legislative process. Even so, it almost did not survive and was the target of repeated hostile amendments – some of which were accepted, some of which were successfully resisted.

Business and the Social Security Act

Given all these political liabilities, why was old-age insurance even included in the Social Security Act? One popular answer sees corporate influence as crucial.[42] According to this view, contributory old-age insurance was little more than an extension of private plans already put in place by leading corporations – conservative in structure, linked to employment, and presenting the powerful advantage of offsetting existing pension liabilities while forcing competing employers without private plans to assume the costs of retirement provision. Old-age insurance, argues Jill Quadagno, "represented the acceptance of approaches to social welfare created by private businessmen."[43] Peter Swenson claims that "Social Security reformers were emboldened to move ahead, knowing that substantial numbers of businessmen would gain competitive advantages from social security taxation in the country's largely domestic competition, even if others might suffer."[44] And Colin Gordon goes so far as to assert that the Social Security Act was "largely an effort (made more urgent by the Depression) to 'even out' the competitive disparities resulting from two decades of private and state-level experimentation with work benefits."[45]

Yet, for all these putative advantages to corporate America, actual business support for old-age insurance – and, indeed, for any portion of the Social Security Act – was extremely limited.[46] What support there was, moreover, was in substantial part a strategic response to the political reality that some form of social legislation was virtually guaranteed to pass, a threat that New Dealers played up at every turn. "Whether business wants it or not," warned Edwin Witte, staff director of the CES, "a federal old age pension bill is certain to be enacted by the present Congress and unemployment insurance is not far off. The real question is whether legislation along these lines shall be constructive or destructive. Through opposing all action business interests are inviting extreme and unsound legislation on these subjects and other aspects of economic security."[47]

Despite Witte's cautions, most business leaders strenuously opposed the Social Security Act. Those who were more sympathetic, such as the handful of progressive businessmen that the Roosevelt Administration recruited for its Advisory Council to the CES, were few and far between, and even their influence has frequently been overstated. Marion Folsom, treasurer of Eastman Kodak and perhaps the most influential business member of the Advisory Council, recalled:

> Back in those days – the thirties – there were very few business people at the time who were informed about Social Security matters. Although they had their own individual employee benefit plans, they were quite skeptical of the federal government getting into this field. They were not very well informed on it, and I would say the great majority were against the federal government getting into old-age insurance and unemployment insurance. . . . [T]here were five of us employers on this original advisory council and we were in a distinct minority because we all felt that something ought to be done and we were willing to help.[48]

In testimony on the bill, sympathetic statements by Folsom and the favorably inclined dry-goods retail industry were drowned out by the cries of business opponents, who, all told, claimed to represent more than fifteen thousand firms.[49] The National Association of Manufacturers criticized the bill's industry-destroying taxes, its grave constitutional defects, its vast administrative machinery, its invitation to "dependency and indigency," and its massive future costs.[50] A representative of the National Publishers' Association presented an informal survey of industry opinion, which showed that "industry and the business [sic] should appreciate very much, very slow action in regard to the bill, particularly old-age pensions and unemployment security."[51] Inside the administration, Witte worried that conservatives "may defeat the entire bill or leave only Federal grants-in-aids to the states for old-age assistance," predicting that "the real fight will probably come over the compulsory old-age insurance system."[52]

Though much of the business hostility to Social Security was general in nature, the development of private pensions before the New Deal helps explain the largely negative reception. In the first place, as we have seen, the proportion of employers that maintained private plans and thus might have theoretically stood to benefit from the equalization or public assumption of pension costs was still fairly small. Although the number of plans may well have reached 750 by 1935, coverage had contracted significantly after 1930 as large companies reduced employment. Almost half the workers with private protections labored in the railroad industry, which was expected to be covered by a federal retirement program separate from old-age insurance. Plan participants outside the railroads probably totaled no more than 2.5 million, or roughly 5 percent of the civilian workforce.[53]

Not only were private pensions relatively rare, but their benefits were in most cases inferior to those promised by Social Security – and their costs accordingly lower. Federal old-age insurance imposed a fixed 2 percent payroll tax divided equally between employers and workers (originally slated to rise to 6 percent in 1948). By contrast, the best early study of private pensions estimated that, in 1927, "pension payments represented less than 1 percent of current payrolls *of the establishments maintaining pension systems.*"[54] Not surprisingly then, a 1939 analysis by the economist Paul Douglas concluded summarily that "the benefits provided by the existing private plans are, in the great majority of instances, inferior rather than superior to those promised under the [Social Security Act]."[55]

Pensions plans were not merely scattered and meager in the 1930s. They also ran largely against the grain of the public old-age insurance program. The private pension was a device of corporate control, its benefits skewed toward managerial and long-service employees, its promises contingent on employer wishes. By contrast, Social Security guaranteed benefits based on service and earnings in any covered firm, and it concentrated benefits on wage earners in the lower half of the income distribution, not on salaried personnel. These requirements limited the extent to which Social Security could offset the existing benefit commitments of private plans. But just as important, they removed employers' *control* over the distribution of a significant portion of pension benefits to a significant proportion of their workers. With this loss of control came a loss of authority over the aspects of pension design, such as length-of-service requirements, that employers had used to make pensions an effective tool of personnel management. Although, as events soon showed, Social Security did not preclude the revision of private pension plans to achieve managerial ends, it was by no means a simple substitute for the private plans that preceded it.

Indeed, an often overlooked sign that the drafters of old-age insurance were skeptical about the potential reach of private retirement plans was the inclusion of a proposal for the sale of voluntary government annuities similar to those issued by commercial carriers. These annuities could serve as a secure primary source of retirement income for persons not included in the compulsory pension program and as a supplement to Social Security for those who were. Besides suggesting a government-administered alternative to private pensions, the proposal envisioned a dramatic preemption of the role of the private insurance industry. But under pressure from the insurance industry, the Senate struck the provision from the legislation during floor debate.[56] A sizable field of voluntary retirement provision was thus spared for private enterprise, yet not before the administration had suggested that government insurance should extend beyond the bounds of compulsory retirement benefits for manual workers.

Even more problematic for the business power hypothesis is the fate of the Clark amendment, named after its Senate sponsor, Bennett "Champ" Clark, a conservative Democrat from Missouri and member of the infamous "conservative coalition" of Republicans and anti–New Deal Democrats.[57] The Clark amendment would have allowed employers that presently operated or later created private plans to opt out of Social Security. At the time of its consideration, leading trade associations and some 145 corporations with pension plans backed the amendment, pressure for which came primarily from the insurance and pension consulting firm Towers, Perrin, Forster, & Crosby.[58] The Clark amendment passed easily in the Senate, with more than half of Democrats and all but three Republicans voting for it. With the Roosevelt Administration insisting that the amendment be excluded from the final legislation, the House–Senate conference was left to wrangle for weeks over the amendment until the deadlock was finally broken by an agreement to set up a special committee to resolve the debate in the next Congress.[59] For reasons to be discussed shortly, this committee eventually gave up trying to reach a compromise when corporate pension sponsors and insurers lost interest, and the issue was never revisited.

Most scholarly studies of the passage of Social Security tend to skip quickly over the Clark amendment, as if it were only a minor unsuccessful challenge to the bill.[60] (This is also the last point at which most studies mention private pension plans.) Yet the amendment not only passed overwhelmingly in the Senate and nearly killed the Social Security Act outright, but it also represents perhaps the clearest case of business and insurance industry intervention aimed at compromising the legislation. The stakes could not have been greater.[61] If the Clark amendment had survived, it would have been nearly impossible for the old-age insurance program to redistribute across income and age groups without prompting an exodus of higher-income and younger employment groups from the public program into private plans. Thus, the amendment went to the heart of the idea of social insurance, the very aim of which was to redistribute across risk and income groups in a way that private insurance under competitive conditions could not. Revealingly, Roosevelt and his supporters steadfastly refused to support the amendment, and it ultimately failed, ensuring that private pensions would supplement Social Security rather than directly compete with it.

In light of all this, it is impossible to argue that Social Security "represented the acceptance of approaches to social welfare created by private businessmen."[62] Though modeled in part on private plans, Social Security embodied a philosophy of social insurance that saw inclusive compulsory protections as essential safeguards against the risks of modern industrial life – preferable both to unassisted private action and to means-tested relief.[63] "Cradle to grave," FDR reportedly declared at cabinet meetings, "from the cradle to the grave [everybody] ought to be in a social insurance system."[64] For all its concessions to political and constitutional reality, for all its conservative and cautious features, the Social Security Act was far more sweeping than most business leaders would have preferred at the time of its passage, much less before the Depression and Roosevelt's election forced social reform onto the political agenda.

This does not mean, however, that the designers of federal old-age insurance were hostile to private pensions. In fact, two of the three major drafters of the program, J. Douglas Brown and Murray Latimer, were intimately involved in the development and study of industrial plans. Acknowledged pension experts who had moved among private, public, and academic positions, they conceived of old-age insurance in part as an extension of the most valuable elements of private plans that would free up jobs for younger workers while preventing the uncontrolled future expansion of gratuitous noncontributory pensions. At the same time, they were quite critical of existing plans and believed them sorely inadequate as a national response to the needs of the aged. Working under Berkeley professor Barbara Armstrong, a leading expert on foreign social insurance, Brown and Latimer melded some of the features of corporate pension plans with the inclusive and compulsory logic of foreign systems – all the while aware, in Brown's words, of "the great pressure of the Townsend movement that the government would have to get into old-age protection one way or another."[65] It was this distinctive combination of foreign and industrial experience, Brown recalled, that "led to the conviction that there must be a constructive, contributory insurance system to meet the mounting cost of old-age dependency."[66]

In the mid-1930s, with private pensions in flux, no one could confidently predict the effects of this new public program on existing private plans. Nonetheless, Brown and Latimer did believe that employers with sound pensions could restructure their plans to accommodate old-age insurance, just as employers in other nations had done when similar programs were established.[67] The progressive business executives recruited for the Advisory Council generally shared this view – or came to share it. Although Folsom testified in favor of the Clark amendment in the Senate, he later reversed himself and advocated that employers simply adjust to the new program.[68]

As the stalemate over the Clark amendment continued, other large employers with private plans followed Folsom's lead. A revealing study of fifty employers conducted for the Social Science Research Council shortly after the bill's passage concluded that while most employers were waiting to act, few with pension plans intended to discontinue them, and nine already planned to change their plans to make them supplementary to the public program.[69] Old-age insurance, it was true, hindered some goals for which pensions had been used, such as resisting unionization. Yet, aside from the new costs it imposed, it presented little threat to corporate plans aimed at the highly paid. Indeed, with its relatively low benefits and progressive benefit structure, Social Security made private pensions *more* attractive to employers as a means of rewarding higher-income workers, allowing them to provide supplementary benefits for these workers at a modest cost. Paradoxically, then, a program that aimed to redistribute income down the wage ladder pushed private plans up several rungs. Employers who restructured or started plans after the enactment of Social Security covered a much smaller portion of their workforce than had previously been the norm, and most "actually excluded wage workers altogether."[70]

Less obvious, but probably no less important in corporate calculations, was the fact that old-age insurance promised to pay out very large "unearned" benefits in its early years. This was virtually unavoidable: Making the oldest generation of workers finance its own protection would mean that benefits would be long delayed and, for many years, tiny. The drafters of Social Security always held that "practically all workers brought under the system initially will receive much larger benefits . . . than could be procured from the combined taxes paid by them and their employers."[71] This conviction, arrived at for independent policy reasons, nonetheless had favorable consequences for employers that operated supplementary plans, because firms could credit prospective old-age insurance benefits against existing pension obligations without paying the full costs in taxation. One estimate prepared by Industrial Relations Counselers (a private consulting firm for which Latimer worked until 1936) showed that "a company would be required to pay 33 to 100 percent more to finance identical old age benefits privately."[72] Given this stark comparison, it was clear that only companies with young employees would find the contracting-out option financially attractive – to the detriment of existing pension sponsors, which generally had older workforces. Between old-age insurance and continued federal delay, most business leaders favored the latter. Between old-age insurance without the Clark amendment and old-age insurance with it, the advantages for pension sponsors generally lay with the former. As one close observer of sponsors' deliberations sarcastically noted, "All employers favor the Clark Amendment; no informed employer favors the Clark Amendment."[73]

In retrospect, too, employers came to realize that exemption from old-age insurance would entail intrusive regulation of private plans, requiring firms not only to provide coverage comparable to Social Security's (which few did), but also to keep adequate records and sufficient reserves to transfer accumulated pension assets when workers changed jobs or corporations failed. Roosevelt's policy advisers skillfully played up this fear, working behind the scenes to make the Clark amendment even more restrictive while their allies took the Senate floor to raise the specter of government intrusion into company plans and even into the process of hiring and firing workers.[74] Although such arguments do not seem to have swayed employers when the amendment was first being considered, they carried greater weight once the Social Security Act passed and firms began to realize that they could retain complete autonomy over their own private plans, even while factoring Social Security benefits into their pension formulas. When the special committee authorized to prepare a revised version of the Clark amendment convened the next year, one of the drafters of the revamped amendment noted that "the letters which have been received from insurance companies and employers have been most discouraging. . . . No solution was received from any company, and replies from several were to the effect that the difficulties presented seemed insurmountable."[75]

In sum, although most employers opposed old-age insurance and many initially supported the idea of contracting out, most also came to accept and even endorse compulsory pensions not long after Social Security's inception. By 1939, according to an impressionistic *Fortune* survey, 82.2 percent of employers favored keeping or changing Social Security, rather than eliminating it, although most (58 percent) believed it required revision.[76] That same year, Folsom stated that Social Security had "been very well accepted both by employers and by employees."[77] Of course, the changing stance of the business community reflected political realism as much as a genuine change of heart. As Social Security became an established program enjoying high levels of public approval, the prospect of repudiating it grew increasingly slim.[78] But employers were, in fact, rapidly accommodating themselves to the new law, and in the process, many were changing their initial perceptions.[79] Because so few corporations had private pension plans before Social Security's passage, the program did not represent an alternative to employer-provided benefits so much as it did a new programmatic reality around which benefit plans had to be structured. And many employers, including those that already operated plans, found that private pensions could be combined with Social Security in ways that allowed them to use corporate plans to influence the career patterns of employees, especially the better paid among them.

Large insurance companies might have been expected to be more vociferous opponents of old-age insurance. Yet insured pension plans never covered more than a sixth of pensioned employees during the 1930s, and pensions were not the major line of business for insurers.[80] By contrast, the Roosevelt Administration's proposal for the sale of voluntary government annuities *was* a major threat to the activities of insurers, and they worked to scuttle the idea. Although the demise of the annuity proposal suggests that the insurance industry remained a powerful voice, the industry had only limited influence on the debate over old-age insurance.[81] Divided by region, size, and specialty, insurers never presented a united front against the Social Security Act. Although few were enthusiastic, some speculated that the program might actually increase employers' need for specialized expertise (because plans would need to be coordinated with Social Security), as well as workers' demand for life insurance (because workers would come to recognize the value of supplementary protection).[82] The president of Equitable Life Assurance argued in 1935: "Just as the business of life insurance received tremendous impetus from the . . . creation and development of the War Risk Bureau, so do I believe that social-insurance agitation forwarded by President Roosevelt and his official associates will result in renewed appreciation and great stimulation of life-insurance activities."[83] The Association of Life Insurance Presidents, a major trade association, did not even take a stand on the Act in 1935.[84]

In the end, the indirect influence of the insurance industry was probably greater than any direct pressure it brought to bear. The core elements of Social Security – its contributory structure, its tight link between contributions and benefits, its conservative financing – all showed the deep imprint of commercial insurance ideals on Roosevelt and his aides.[85] For years, the Metropolitan and other large insurers had propagated the view that "sound" programs required such features, and that departure from them would erode the distinction between public assistance given as charity and social insurance earned as a right. This distinction was inviolate to Roosevelt and the CES, who constructed an old-age program more individualistic and more concerned with fair rates of return than any established abroad. But the ideological imprint of commercial insurers should not be confused with direct lobbying.[86] Much of the CES's case for social insurance consisted of demonstrating the inadequacy of private life insurance as a guarantor of economic security.[87] The Metropolitan, for its part, had been demanding for more than a decade that government intervention, if it were to occur at all, be limited to a state mandate on employers to purchase private pension insurance.[88] Once it became clear that this idea was doomed, insurers argued for a small federal program providing minimal protection and ample room for supplementation. And when the opportunity arose in the form of the Clark amendment, many tried to cripple Social Security outright.[89] After the legislation passed, insurers, like employers, learned not just that they could live with Social Security, but also that it offered important benefits.[90] But, as with employers, that does not mean they supported it before its passage, much less that the program was merely a duplication of private practices on a national scale.

An American Philosophy of Social Insurance

Old-age insurance took the shape that it did largely because of the belief of Roosevelt and his advisers that social insurance against the cost of retirement was needed, and that it should be compulsory, contributory, and national in scope. The motives for this conviction were mixed. One was Roosevelt's deep aversion to relying solely on means-tested relief. A second key motive, as already discussed, was the precedent set by industrial pension plans and foreign social insurance programs. A third and less well recognized motive was the belief of most within the Roosevelt Administration and Congress that retirement of older workers would aid economic recovery by freeing up jobs.[91] In this respect, Social Security dovetailed nicely with the corporate use of pensions as a device for removing older employers from the workforce.[92]

A fourth important motive for a contributory program was political, the recognition that earmarked taxes and a dedicated reserve would be less prone to programmatic retrenchment once the legislative impetus created by the Depression had passed.[93] After Social Security's passage, Roosevelt famously explained to a critic of the Act's payroll contributions that the "taxes were never a problem of economics. They are politics all the way through. We put those payroll contributions there so as to give the contributors a legal, moral, and political right to collect their pensions and their unemployment benefits. With those taxes in there, no damn politician can ever scrap my social security program."[94] As a farsighted political actor hoping to create an enduring program, Roosevelt understood that worker contributions would vastly increase the political cost of departing from the programmatic path that he favored. He would prove correct – but the full effects would not become apparent for almost two decades.

Above all, Social Security embodied the ideal that the government, rather than the private sector, should be responsible for providing basic retirement protection to America's workers.[95] Although private insurance concepts pervaded the thinking of Roosevelt and his aides, the architects of old-age insurance strongly believed that private institutions could not supply true retirement security, both because of the coverage gaps that voluntary provision would create and because scores of private plans would not allow the risk pooling and income redistribution that inclusive social insurance required.[96] A purely self-financing system was also deemed unworkable, but on this point, the CES was overruled by Roosevelt and Treasury Secretary Henry Morgentheau, who together insisted that Congress adopt steeper tax rates to obviate the need for general tax revenues, even if that meant initial benefits had to be small and delayed. Other revisions were also adopted in Congress.[97] The most restrictive was the decision to exclude agricultural workers and domestic servants from participation in the program, which narrowed coverage to barely more than half of the civilian labor force and excluded most blacks.[98] On this and other matters of concern to southern elites, Roosevelt had limited sway, because the bulk of southern Democrats presided over safe one-party districts and enjoyed disproportionate influence in the seniority-based House committee system.

These compromises were significant, but the old-age insurance program eventually enacted still remained remarkably true to the original blueprint. That this blueprint was changed en route to enactment is ultimately far less surprising than its eventual survival. The Social Security Act benefited from extraordinary circumstances: a triggering crisis, widespread recognition of the failure of private organizations to provide retirement security, an overwhelming partisan majority led by a powerful president, and the rise of diffuse but potent social pressures for government action. Despite this, passage of compulsory old-age insurance was never certain. Now considered the principal legacy of the Social Security Act, old-age insurance was in 1935 the Act's most endangered component.[99] Social Security passed not because Congress wanted it but because Roosevelt demanded it and, for institutional and political reasons, was in a position to obtain it.

As we have seen, old-age insurance also benefited from the general weakness of private networks of retirement provision. The spotty and insufficient coverage of private plans not only provided a rationale for government action; it also meant that neither employers nor workers had a large vested interest in the continuance of the existing private system. For some employers, indeed, existing pension liabilities were so poorly funded that old-age insurance provided a much-needed rescue, though few saw it that way at the time of its passage. Moreover, old-age insurance – unlike health insurance – was not yet a field of action in which parties besides employers had much stake. No unified interest comparable to organized medicine stood in the way of old-age insurance's establishment. Though few employers or insurers supported the legislation, neither group mounted as fierce a resistance as they might have. And once Social Security was enacted, both found that they could structure their social welfare activities around, and even benefit from, a program that they had once widely opposed.

The 1939 Amendments

The passage of the Social Security Act was a landmark in the development of the American welfare state, unquestionably the single most important enactment in the history of U.S. social policy. It established the principle that the federal government should play a primary role in providing retirement income and created the framework within which the old-age insurance program would later evolve.[100] Pathbreaking as the Act was, however, old-age insurance was considerably more modest at its inception than is commonly recognized. Not only did the initial program postpone the payment of benefits until 1942, but Roosevelt's commitment to a self-financed program also helped ensure that these initial benefits would be meager. As a contributory program, Social Security limited benefits to workers who had paid taxes. Those who were over 65 when the program was created did not benefit, and those who had paid into the program for only a short period of time received little.[101] Indeed, so committed were Roosevelt and his aides to the contributory ideal that the legislation promised a "money-back" provision that provided a death benefit to the estate of covered workers designed to return what they had paid into the system.

Even before the first payments were made, however, Social Security was substantially changed. The far-reaching 1939 amendments grew out of an odd alliance between liberals who wanted to expand benefits and conservatives who hoped to eliminate the large old-age insurance reserve and thereby ensure that the program remained a modest operation with ample room for private-sector supplementation. Ratifying this alliance was the understandable attraction to Congress of a policy expanding benefits in the short term while postponing tax increases to fund these benefits into the future. The 1939 amendments embodied three major sets of changes. First, they stepped up the payment of benefits by two years to 1940 while postponing planned increases in the payroll tax; second, they changed the benefit formula to substantially increase the awards provided in the early years of the system, to skew them further toward lower-wage workers, and to provide extra support to married beneficiaries; and, third, they replaced the lump-sum death benefit with a survivor's benefit geared toward providing adequate income to widows and dependent children rather than toward returning accumulated contributions. Together, these changes "shifted the whole concept of [old-age insurance] from a hybrid compromise between private savings and social insurance to a clear-cut concept of social insurance. The new focus became *adequacy* and protection of the family unit."[102]

The immediate explanation for the 1939 amendments was the large reserve fund that Roosevelt and his Treasury secretary had insisted upon in 1935. A target of Republican Alf Landon's attacks on Roosevelt in the 1936 presidential campaign, the reserve was alarming to conservatives, not only because it represented a huge accumulation of funds by the federal government, but also because it raised the specter of future expansions of the program unconstrained by the need to impose immediate costs on the taxpaying public.[103] If Social Security were to exist, conservatives wanted it to remain a small program whose societal costs were as visible as possible. For this same reason, many conservatives would later become supportive of an immediate "blanketing-in" of all the elderly, allowing older Americans to receive benefits regardless of whether they had paid taxes into the system – another seemingly expansionary policy that conservatives believed would hem in old-age insurance by revealing program costs and the extent to which current workers paid for current retirees. Ironically in light of present political divisions, therefore, many conservatives argued for pay-as-you-go financing and broader coverage in the late 1930s, while defenders of the existing program called for substantial advance funding and the continued exclusion of most of the elderly.

The 1939 amendments, in short, made liberalizing changes in pursuit of conservative ends. Indeed, if a strong case can be made for the influence of corporate liberals, it is in 1939, not 1935. The 1939 amendments grew out of the recommendations of an advisory council pressed upon the Social Security Board (SSB) by a leading Senate Republican critic of Social Security, Arthur Vandenberg of Michigan. A proponent of private benefit plans, Vandenberg called for the 1937–38 Advisory Council in response to criticism of the reserve by conservative political leaders, employers, and insurers.[104] And unlike the Advisory Council to the CES, this one had decisive impact. Among its members were the usual list of prominent corporate liberals, such as Folsom and General Electric President Gerard Swope. The council also included E. R. Stettinius, Jr., of U.S. Steel and M. Albert Linton, the president of a major life insurance company and perhaps the fiercest critic of the reserve since 1935.[105]

The general philosophy of these industry representatives stressed the constructive relationship between public programs and private social provision, but it also envisioned very definite limits on the bounds of proper state action.[106] Folsom testified to Congress in 1939, for example, that Social Security "should provide basic minimum protection and it should not be intended to cover all the needs of everyone. If you keep it on a minimum protection basis, the individual can supplement it from his own earnings and also from any benefit or pension which he might derive from supplementary plans adopted by his employer."[107] Folsom also promoted the idea of pension integration, whereby private pension plans adjusted their benefits to account for Social Security, thus saving money and skewing private pensions toward higher-income workers. His general belief was that "public benefits had to be kept low and tax incentives . . . needed to be provided for private programs," and he "lobbied tirelessly to these ends."[108]

If the principal fear of the reserve's critics was that the large fund might someday be raided for liberal ends, the concerns of insurers and corporate sponsors of private plans were also more immediate and concrete. Insurers worried, in particular, that the government's accumulation of funds would drive up the costs of investing their own reserves in government bonds. Employers were especially eager to postpone scheduled tax increases. Moreover, it was not lost on either camp that stepping up the benefit schedule and pushing costs onto future generations meant that the unearned benefits paid out in the early years of the program would be even larger than previously contemplated, further reducing employers' obligations under plans integrated with Social Security.[109] By this time an outside expert on the Advisory Council, Edwin Witte fumed privately that these changes were an effort to reduce the burden of promised benefits under company and insurance plans.[110] (He ended up signing on to the Advisory Council report anyway.) Wilbur Cohen, the young assistant to SSB head Arthur Altmeyer, was alarmed enough to pen a confidential memo arguing that "at least subconsciously the representatives of the life insurance companies and the Republicans are fighting the reserve plan on the belief that they can transfer one half of the burden of contibutory old-age pensions (from the employer) to that of the general taxpayer."[111] Altmeyer, however, was untroubled. To him and others inside the SSB, the large reserve was a nuisance that should be jettisoned "to advance a socially desirable program."[112]

Where conflicts might have arisen between left and right, they were muted by the fact that the 1939 amendments were cast as technical changes to an existing program, rather than as an extension of it. Survivors' insurance, for example, might have been expected to invoke powerful opposition from life insurers. But it seems to have received little notice. Perhaps this was because the large reserve was the central concern of the insurance industry, or perhaps it reflected the difficulty of estimating how these new insurance benefits would compare with the death benefit provisions they were designed to replace. Whatever the case, proponents of an expanded program were now able to offer their reforms as modifications of an existing framework, and that seems to have made all the difference.

It is in 1939, then, that we first begin to witness the influence of Social Security itself on the politics of retirement security policy – to see, that is, how "policies produce politics."[113] One path of feedback was administrative. After skillfully managing the Herculean task of registering millions of workers for old-age insurance, the Social Security Board became the leading advocate of an expanded old-age insurance program. Although Altmeyer had resisted the appointment of the 1937–38 Advisory Council, he was able to achieve nearly all his recommendations for old-age insurance expansion through it. Not only did the SSB informally participate in the selection of council members, but it also staffed the council and did all research for it. Folsom later recalled that the council "met with the social security people. They sat in on all our discussions, so everybody came out all together."[114] Control over information and technical expertise – as well as a consistent long-term vision for the program's future – went a long way toward setting the agenda for change when opportunities arose.

Another path of feedback had to do with the features of the program itself. The political logic of the 1939 amendments was irresistible: Congress increased benefits and postponed tax increases, all the while leaving unanswered the question of whether general revenues would be used in the future. What made this possible was the contributory structure of Social Security. It delivered benefits only to past contributors, which ensured that beneficiaries in the early years were far outweighed by active workers paying taxes. (A national population whose age profile was still relatively young helped, too.) Because the ratio of workers to beneficiaries was so favorable, even a small payroll tax could fund benefits far in excess of what early recipients had paid into the program. From a program that promised short-term costs while postponing benefits into the future, Social Security became a program that promised short-term benefits while postponing costs into the future. Each time payroll taxes were scheduled to increase from their original level, Senator Vandenberg demanded that they be frozen, and Congress put off the rise over the SSB's halfhearted objections. Even with the tax rate static, however, Social Security's coffers remained flush as earnings and employment rose during the 1940s.

Congress also steadfastly refused to increase benefits, and benefit levels plummeted in real terms during the 1940s. Given the impeccable political logic of expansion, this erosion of the program comes as something of a surprise. After all, Congress could well have increased benefits or expanded coverage – as Roosevelt and, with even greater force, Truman demanded at numerous points – without raising the tax rate in the short term. Although expanding coverage would, of course, have subjected previously uncovered workers to taxation, it would also have "guaranteed a large net increase in federal revenues, since most of the government's obligations would not be incurred until contributors retired."[115] This at a time when wartime inflation and government deficits both made additional taxation attractive.

Yet neither political self-interest nor reasons of state swayed conservative opposition to Social Security. Although World War II undoubtedly helped push major expansionary reforms off the agenda, the end of the war did little to revive their prospects. It was clear that even without the exigencies of war, the tide had decisively turned against domestic social reform. Between 1936 and 1942, Democratic majorities in the House were reduced from 242 to 10; in the Senate, from 60 to 21.[116] In 1946, Democrats lost control of Congress for the first time since the New Deal, and many who remained were southern conservatives who evinced no interest in expanding Social Security. In this hostile environment, "Social Security remained small, inconsequential, and vulnerable to attack," its diffuse and unorganized clientele representing no more than a quarter of the aged, its benefits on average below the old-age assistance payments of the states.[117] Indeed, were it not for the large projected reserve that helped pave the way for the conservative-backed amendments of 1939, it is questionable whether the program would have been changed at all during its first decade and a half.

The Expansion of Private Pensions

If the story of Social Security's development during the 1940s was one of stagnation, the story of private pensions during these years was one of rapid expansion. The two stories are in fact tightly interwoven. The structure of old-age insurance as solidified in 1939 encouraged the adoption and restructuring of private pensions, and its subsequent failure to expand pushed labor unions and even liberal political leaders to advocate expanded private plans as a temporary substitute for public programs. Rising tax rates during the New Deal and World War II also boosted demand for private pensions, especially among higher-income workers. In the late 1930s, the Roosevelt Administration tried to rein in the pension tax expenditure, but the main policy changes adopted during the 1940s preserved, with some important restrictions, the growing tax subsidies for private social provision, reinforcing the turn toward private pensions that a politically frozen old-age insurance program helped unleash.

By any measure, the growth of private pensions during this period was dramatic. Between 1935 and 1950, as Figure 2.1 shows, coverage under private plans rose from 6 to 20 percent of the nonagricultural workforce. This expansion consisted of two overlapping phases of development. In the first, employers adopted and revamped pensions in response to the Social Security Act and rising tax rates. Pension benefits were directed toward higher-income groups, and the Roosevelt Administration fought to ensure that federal tax favors were contingent upon the achievement of a modicum of distributional fairness. In the second phase, which will be taken up in the next chapter, the stagnation of Social Security, changes in union strategies, and federal encouragement of collective bargaining pushed organized labor to seek valuable social benefits from employers rather than from government. Linking the two phases was a common political thread: the unwillingness of Congress to expand Social Security.

The causes of the growth of private pensions were complex, but three stand out in contemporary accounts and in the careful secondary scholarship on the period.[118] First, Social Security had the effect of encouraging employers to set up pension programs, both because it lowered the amount that employers had to spend to provide adequate retirement income and because, ironically, it allowed employers to target pension benefits more effectively to better-paid employees. Second, tax concessions for private pensions created in the early years of the revenue code became more valuable as tax rates rose during the New Deal and World War II.[119] Precise estimates of the revenue loss incurred by the pension tax exemption are not available for this period, but all evidence indicates that the cost increased rapidly.[120] (Today, as noted in the introduction, the pension tax expenditure is among the largest subsidies in the tax code, costing more than every public social program except Medicare and Social Security.) Third, there were expansionary pressures distinctive to the war years – most notably, the wage freeze of 1942, which exempted pensions and other fringe benefits and thus encouraged employers to offer pensions to attract workers. Although these wartime policies probably "came too late in the war to have caused the rises in pension and health insurance that we see between 1939 and 1946," they added further impetus to an already building expansion.[121]

It is unclear whether the architects of Social Security expected that it would promote the spread of private pensions as dramatically as it did. Edwin Witte, for one, wrote in his memoir of the CES deliberations that "little attention was paid by the Committee on Economic Security to the relation of existing private pension plans to the compulsory old age insurance system."[122] It is clear, however, that very soon after Social Security passed, the Roosevelt Administration recognized that the benefits of private pensions were shifting up the income scale. The occasion for this concern was the realization that private plans were being used as a means of tax avoidance by high-income taxpayers – the target of Roosevelt's attacks on "economic royalists" and of a large tax hike passed the year after Social Security's enactment. In a 1937 letter to Congress, Treasury Secretary Morgenthau complained:

> For 10 years the revenue acts have sought to encourage pension trusts for aged employees by providing corporations with a special deduction on accounts of contributions thereto, and exempting the trust itself from tax. Recently this exemption has been twisted into a means of tax avoidance by the creation of pension trusts which include as beneficiaries only small groups of officers and directors who are in the high income brackets.[123]

Amplifying these points, the undersecretary of the Treasury, Roswell Magill, appeared before a special Joint Committee on Tax Evasion and Avoidance in 1937 to testify that tax breaks for private pensions were increasingly failing to serve their original objective "to encourage a sort of social security on the part of the individual corporations for the benefit of their employees."[124] To bolster his case, Magill drew attention to an article in the insurance industry magazine *The National Underwriter* that highlighted the benefits of pensions for top corporate personnel. Because of the significant tax advantages enjoyed by private plans, the article pointed out, "for each $1 that goes into a pension-trust fund, the actual cost to the employer is only 64 cents." As for Social Security, it "would never do more than provide a small income for the great band of employees. The better paid and more valuable men must be taken care of by private plans."[125]

The reforms initially proposed by the Roosevelt Administration were modest, their centerpiece a requirement that tax favors be contingent on broad participation in corporate plans. With the issue a low priority, Congress enacted merely one of the Treasury Department's proposals, prohibiting employers from dissolving tax-favored pension trusts so that firms could not receive tax breaks for pension contributions that they later simply recaptured. By the early 1940s, however, the cost of the favorable tax treatment of pensions had mounted, and the Treasury Department had grown more alarmed. For the first time, a spirited and far-reaching discussion of the pension tax rules took place within the Department, a discussion that touched upon the most fundamental questions raised by the favorable treatment of private plans. Once seen in almost entirely technical terms, these provisions were now branded by critics within the Department as a "subsidy" that was at odds with accepted income tax practices and good social policy. Under this tax structure, noted one Treasury memo, "the ordinary concept of a public subsidy is reversed since in this case the low-income groups get nothing, the high-income groups a great deal. Furthermore, everyone in the same income class is not given an equal opportunity; the professional man, the farmer, the independent businessman, and uncovered employees receive no chance to benefit."[126] The ideal treatment of pensions, argued experts within the Department's Division of Tax Research, was to make pensions tax deductible by corporations only if workers immediately received a nonforfeitable right to future benefits. Each worker would in turn be taxed on the value of these benefit promises as they were made, as well as on interest income earned by sums put aside, just as would be an employee who received the same amount in the form of direct cash wages.

This was a wholesale repudiation of previous tax policy, and Treasury officials recognized that it was a political minefield. "Serious difficulties must be faced in proposing that interests be vested because fundamental alteration of most existing pension plans would be required," the Division of Tax Research conceded. "To vest rights would involve transformation of the plans into little more than savings accounts. The employer would lose one of the advantages of the plans to him, and the cost of guaranteeing benefits . . . would be increased."[127] Nonetheless, the Department's ambitions did not stop at requiring that corporations grant vested rights to future benefits. In addition, it favored three other major changes in the tax treatment of private pensions: its earlier demand that pension plans not discriminate in favor of highly paid personnel, a limit on the yearly allowance a pension could provide in retirement, and a requirement that pension funding be sound.

As the Treasury Department sought to implement its ambitious agenda, however, corporations and insurance companies with an interest in pensions repeatedly fought the administration in the courts and Congress to preserve the open-ended nature of the tax subsidy. After 1938, with Congress growing more conservative, they won important victories. In 1939, for example, Congress declared that employer payments for private pensions and other fringe benefits would not be considered wages for the purpose of the Social Security payroll tax – a key demand of corporate leaders. This not only encouraged employers to provide pensions but also restricted Social Security's revenues by limiting the definition of payroll subject to taxation. This was a restriction that would prove increasingly consequential as private benefits came to represent a growing share of compensation.

Three years later, in 1942, Congress firmly rebuffed many of the Roosevelt Administration's proposals when it enacted the Revenue Act of 1942. Although Congress adopted vague nondiscrimination requirements and new funding rules, it refused to endorse either mandatory vesting or limits on the amount of pension allowances. It also ratified the already-widespread employer practice of integrating private plans with Social Security by declaring that old-age insurance benefits could be taken into account when determining whether a plan favored the highly paid.

Howard argues that the distribution of pension coverage and benefits was not a major concern of these debates. The "primary objective" of those who wished to restrict the pension tax subsidy was "to reduce tax avoidance among upper-income taxpayers."[128] Although this was certainly a top objective, the goals of reformers were broader and the resistance they faced far more deeply rooted. The Roosevelt Administration's concerns about tax avoidance came to center on private pensions, not so much because of the revenue loss they entailed, or even because this loss was concentrated on the highly paid, but because the administration believed that private pensions, like Social Security, should benefit the average worker. As the Division of Tax Research wrote in an internal report on the pension tax rules, "these provisions could be revised to increase the contribution of the tax subsidy to the welfare of the great body of employees."[129] Morgenthau's special tax adviser, Randolph Paul, explained to Congress that the Department's aim was to suggest "various provisions which would both make the present statute more effective at promoting the welfare of employees through such [pension] trusts and at the same time prevent the utilization of such trusts for tax-avoidance purposes."[130]

The Treasury Department came to Congress armed with evidence that even at the most progressively minded firms, pension plans were heavily skewed toward the upper reaches of the pay scale. Such evidence was not hard to assemble. Although the move toward insured pensions during the 1930s had improved the financial soundness of private plans, firms continued to employ long length of service requirements and to base benefits on final salary – both of which conduced to benefit upper management. The 1939 Social Security amendments, by shifting benefits toward lower-paid employees, further encouraged plans to skew benefits to higher-paid employees and, in many cases, to exclude wage workers altogether. So even as private plans were becoming more numerous, the proportion of a firm's employees that participated in such plans was declining.[131] At the same time, rising tax rates were increasing the value of the pension tax exemption, particularly for upper-income personnel. To the Roosevelt Administration, these growing revenue costs were not only an affront to the wartime principle of shared sacrifice; they also contravened the social purposes of the special tax treatment of pensions.

But resistance to the administration's proposed reforms among insurers, corporations, and congressional conservatives was overwhelming. Even as Treasury insiders formulated their demands, they anticipated that "[s]uch a shift in policy may seem too great."[132] By April 1942, the new Treasury counsel Stanley Surrey (a pivotal player in later tax and pension debates) was reporting "substantial opposition" to the proposed reforms, especially the vesting and maximum benefit provisions. Vesting would raise the cost of existing plans, Surrey pointed out, and the benefit cap "would also be difficult to put into practice because many plans now in existence involve contractual relationships between employer and employee, and revision may be difficult and inequitable."[133] Given that these existing commitments would be adversely affected and that "the opposition would be keen," Surrey recommended that Treasury make no effort to push the proposals that Randolph Paul had advocated in Congress just a few weeks earlier.[134]

As the pension expert Steven Sass points out, the onslaught of opposition was effective precisely because of the increasing reach of private plans – and the increasing support of conservatives in Congress for their continued expansion:

> Although the administration laid a stronger case before Congress in 1942 than it had in 1937, it also met far stiffer resistance. Conservative legislators, including Senator Robert Taft, complained that the administration was inappropriately using the tax code to advance its social program. Practicing pension professionals . . . traveled to Washington to point out difficulties in the Treasury proposal. . . . In addition to these politicians and technical experts, plan sponsors lobbied vigorously against the Treasury proposals. Because of their large numbers of employees and shareholders, these firms carried significant political weight. AT&T, the nation's largest private employer and pension sponsor, indeed led the campaign against the Treasury proposals. The telephone company . . . threatened to terminate [its pension plan] should Congress enact the new proposals. Taking this threat at face value, AT&T's employees and their union officials wrote letters and traveled to Washington to testify in favor of the status quo.[135]

AT&T's effectiveness on Capitol Hill suggested that private pensions had already developed a significant constituency of expectant beneficiaries, one that employers could effectively mobilize with threats of plan termination or revision. According to one contemporary observer, Congress received "an avalanche of protests from older workers who saw their pension prospects endangered."[136]

Although pensions trusts became a leading issue during the formulation of the 1942 Revenue Act, the stakes of the debate were mostly lost amid the jargon of pension finance and tax law. Organized labor and congressional liberals showed scant interest in the deliberations, and only a handful of members of Congress seem to have grasped the details or import of the Treasury proposals. Among them was Senator Taft, the influential Ohio Republican, who argued as he later would of private health plans that special tax treatment was necessary and right to encourage private social provision. According to Taft, government had no interest in pension trusts beyond ensuring basic soundness and preventing flagrant tax avoidance.[137] He objected in particular to rules that would limit the provision of pensions to highly paid employees, arguing that IRS regulations should only be designed to prevent abuse of pension trusts, not to achieve distributional ends.[138]

On the other side, House Ways and Means chair Robert Lee Doughton expressed continuing dismay about the common corporate practice of excluding from private plans the roughly 97 percent of workers covered by old-age insurance who made less than $3,000 per year (the maximum amount of earnings to which Social Security taxes applied, commonly known as the "wage base").[139] Yet the debate over private pensions essentially played out between Treasury officials, on the one hand, and pension consultants, insurers, and large corporations with private plans, on the other – with pension professionals like H. Walter Forster (the animating figure behind the Clark amendment) providing the technical underpinnings for these groups' complaints.[140] Because the Treasury Department would draft and police whatever rules Congress adopted, it had considerable authority. But those who lobbied and testified against its proposals had the ear of Congress, and in the absence of any real congressional or interest-group counterweight, they received much of what they wanted.

The defenders of private retirement protection did not challenge the Roosevelt Administration's assertion that private plans should serve a public purpose. Far from it; in rhetoric freely mixing the old defenses of welfare capitalism with the new language of federal social policy, they spoke of private plans as a form of "private social security" that not only reduced old-age dependency but also lessened the burden on government programs. Testifying before Congress in 1942, for example, the pension consultant Meyer Goldstein extolled the virtues of private plans: "From the standpoint of the social good, we ought to be very grateful in this country that we have the type of tax law that we have had for the past 20 years, because having it we have a more impregnable position for the three or four million people who are now covered by pension plans."[141] A representative of the Industrial Relations Counsel of Chicago carried his praise even further, calling attention to employers' growing recognition of their public responsibilities:

> The moneys contributed by employers...have been of incalculable value in providing both disability and old-age assistance to employees, which assistance would otherwise have had to be furnished by the Government. Management, in other words, capital, has been educated to the point where responsibility for the welfare of employees upon retirement or in case of disability has been accepted as the usual rather than the unusual.[142]

Like the other witnesses who praised pensions, neither acknowledged that few covered workers would actually receive benefits or that the vast bulk of pension spending would go to management and the highly paid. In principle, if not in practice, the defenders of private pensions accepted the view that the legitimacy of private plans, and the tax advantages that they enjoyed, rested in part on their ability to achieve social ends.

If industry interests largely accepted the administration's contention that pensions should pursue public goals, they took issue with its claims regarding the distributional inequities of private plans. It was not discriminatory to skew benefits to the highly paid, industry defenders argued, because such employees contributed more to the productivity of the firm. Moreover, it was natural for private plans to provide little or nothing to wage earners; they, after all, received the most from Social Security. A spokesman for the 37,500 employees-strong National Dairy Products Corporation, for example, noted that after Social Security's passage,

> [t]he first thing that came to our attention was that only 1,200 of our total number of employees received over $3,000. Among those 1,200 were practically every employee that had a real influence on how the company went ahead, how it achieved success over its competitors.... So we decided... we will have nothing paid into the plan by either employer or employee on salaries below $3,000, and we will let the social-security-tax program take care of the salaries under $3,000.[143]

Pension sponsors argued even more vociferously against the proposed limit on yearly pension allowances and the proposal for mandatory vesting, both of which they claimed would undermine the flexibility and productivity-enhancing incentives of a truly voluntary private system. In responding to these arguments, Congress was almost entirely sympathetic. Besides the administration's proposed funding requirements, which were relatively uncontroversial, the only major reform adopted in the Revenue Act of 1942 was a set of participation and nondiscrimination requirements that ostensibly prevented employers from limiting pension benefits to salaried officers and shareholders. Complex and full of loopholes, these rules endorsed the idea that private pensions should benefit rank-and-file workers, but ensured only very limited progress toward that end. The law, for example, required that plans be for the "exclusive benefit of . . . employees or their beneficiaries."[144] This standard could be met, however, by covering little more than half of full-time workers in a firm (part-time workers could be excluded altogether). The regulations also demanded that employers not "discriminate in favor of employees who are officers, shareholders, persons whose principal duties consist in supervising the work of other employees, or highly compensated employees."[145] But not only could private plans grant much larger benefits to higher-paid personnel, so long as they represented no greater a share of total pay; integrated plans could also meet nondiscrimination rules by treating Social Security benefits funded by mandatory taxes as if they were voluntary benefits funded by company contributions.

The eventual integration guidelines, in fact, assumed that a worker's entire Social Security benefit had been paid for by the employer, ignoring the reality that workers also contributed to the program and that an employer's contributions actually paid for only a small share of the benefits enjoyed by its workers. The rules even assumed that employers were paying for the full cost of the spousal and survivors' benefits added in 1939, allowing firms to reduce the pension allowances of workers with incomes below the wage base not simply by 100 percent of the primary social security benefit but by 150 percent. Congress's endorsement of integration meant, in short, that plans could continue to provide little or no benefits to most workers without running afoul of the nondiscrimination restrictions.[146]

Just as important, none of these regulations addressed the problem that the administration had hoped to counter with its abandoned proposal for vesting: the tendency for higher-paid workers to stay long enough at a firm and remain there late enough into their career to earn large pensions. As the pension specialist Rainard Robbins candidly noted in a 1949 monograph published by Industrial Relations Counselors, "It is obvious that, so long as pension credits are forfeitable upon withdrawal from service, pension plans will be of little value to the masses of lower paid workers. Large numbers of these employees will work for many different employers during their active years and yet be with no one of them long enough to acquire the right to substantial company benefits on retirement." If corporations wanted to favor upper management, Robbins concluded, "the present revenue act presents few problems," and "the employer can rest assured that the plan will cost comparatively little except with respect to employees of groups in favor of whom he must not discriminate." Indeed, because most workers would forfeit their benefits by leaving the firm, "contributions made on behalf of employees of other classes will reduce the benefits to be paid employees of the favored group."[147]

The 1942 Revenue Act did set an important precedent. By outlining new participation and nondiscrimination tests, Congress endorsed the principle that pension plans should enhance employee welfare and opened the door to future expansions of the federal government's regulatory role. But because the Revenue Act did little to reduce the tax incentives to use pensions to reward high-income employees, it did little to change the character of the post–New Deal pension institution. By clearing up much of the remaining uncertainty surrounding the relationship between Social Security and private pensions, in fact, the Revenue Act further bolstered the development of corporate plans targeted to the well paid. That, coupled with the high excess profits tax contained in the Act, rising income tax rates, and the War Labor Board's decision to exempt fringe benefits from wartime wage controls, helped spark the most dramatic growth of pensions since the New Deal.[148] The rewards of this growth were not, however, widely shared: Corporations that established plans between 1940 and 1946 covered, on average, less than a quarter of their employees. Plans that integrated their benefits with Social Security also became more prevalent, rising from 65 percent of large plans in 1939 to 80 percent by the end of 1943. And among plans established in early 1944, 90 percent employed integration, were limited to salaried employees, or both.

Thus, while Social Security stagnated in the face of conservative resistance, corporations – spurred on by ballooning tax benefits and Congress's endorsement of integration – continued to expand a sphere of private retirement protection that increasingly excluded Social Security's beneficiaries. The flimsy reforms contained in the Revenue Act of 1942 were hardly a match for the broader forces of change that the Social Security Act and federal tax policy had unleashed.

Conclusion

The New Deal was a critical juncture in the development of the American pension system, one that created, for the first time, a federal program of old-age insurance based on the notion that workers should be protected by a common umbrella of social insurance. Yet the dramatic political opening for old-age insurance was short-lived, and by the 1940s, a more conservative political climate, federal tax laws, and the partially unexpected results of the Social Security Act itself had left the old-age insurance program increasingly overshadowed by the growing role of private pensions. Caught in a holding pattern while an increasingly extensive private system emerged to supplement its meager benefits, Social Security seemed immune to the expansionary tendencies that would mark its later years. By the end of World War II, many of its strongest defenders believed its future was bleak and wondered if it could retain its initial status as the core provider of retirement security in the American social welfare regime.

As we now know, these expectations proved unduly pessimistic. Social Security had inherent advantages born of its pay-as-you-go, contributory structure. Benefits could be raised without new taxes; groups could be brought in without new burdens. As the economy sped up and as more Americans retired with its protections, Social Security would become an ever more popular and politically resilient program. And because the still-modest program formed the foundation of private pension activities – which, after 1939, focused primarily on better-off employees – sentiment for its repeal in the business community was increasingly weak. Indeed, with the building demands of labor for more generous plans for rank-and-file workers, employers with private plans were gaining a new reason to look favorably on Social Security expansion, which would offset the cost of integrated plans and spread pension expenses across all firms.

It was crucial, therefore, that old-age insurance emerged before the widespread development of private pensions – crucial both to its survival during the legislative debate over the Social Security Act and to its expansion in the years after World War II. Yet the subsequent growth of the program should not obscure the rocky initial period after 1939, for it was in these years that the basic division of public and private responsibilities was established and the initial complex of policies governing private pensions arose. This division and these policies were remarkably solicitous toward private pension plans. Largely behind the scenes, a favorable tax regime was codified and defended, one that legitimated private social policies that were at odds with their publicly stated purposes. Federal dollars were used to pay for private plans that excluded from coverage or provided few benefits to the very workers who were the object of federal old-age insurance. Although Social Security and private pensions would both dramatically expand in the postwar era, the notion that the private pension system deserved special tax concessions that were justified by its place in America's broader social welfare strategy would remain a constant. It would, in fact, gain new favor in the 1980s and 1990s as conservatives sought to expand tax-favored retirement plans that would encourage savings, benefit prosperous voters, and perhaps form the basis for a future system of private individual accounts under the public old-age insurance program.

At the same time, however, the debate over the pension tax subsidy carried with it the seeds for future conflicts over the alleged distributional inequities of private plans – and, it turned out, the seeds for future expansions of the state's regulatory presence in the private pension system. Private pensions had come to be defended as a critical constituent element of America's social welfare strategy, a federally subsidized counterpart to the nation's public retirement program. When the promises of private plans came up short, politicians and pensioners would turn to the same battle-tested arguments that employers had made in the 1940s to justify the favored treatment of their plans. Yet this time, these arguments would be used to demand that private pensions be more accountable, more certain, more equitable – in short, more like Social Security. Although the vested interests and policy dilemmas created by the path-dependent development of pensions would set significant and enduring limits on the scope of reform, the Employee Retirement Income Security Act of 1974 would nonetheless clearly indicate that so long as they were understood as supplements to Social Security, private pensions could not escape scrutiny of their coverage, distribution, and predictability.

3

Sibling Rivalry: Public and Private Pensions After 1945

After World War II, private pensions began to enter a new phase of expansion, with labor-oriented plans beginning to appear alongside the company-initiated programs of the past. This development was driven less by tax policy than by the changing strategies of organized labor and the evolving context of collective bargaining. American unions were pulled into conflict over private social protection by the internal exigencies of labor organization, by the continued failure of Congress to expand public programs, by the concerted effort of conservatives to cripple unions' capacity, and, paradoxically, by the actions of liberals in Congress, the White House, and the courts, who found themselves siding with organized labor in defense of private benefits toward which they were otherwise ambivalent or hostile. When the struggle was over, American labor had carved out a new role in the private pension system and, in the process, firmly institutionalized it.

The rise of labor-negotiated plans had two ironic consequences. First, it tied the labor movement closely to the very private system of employment-based benefits that it had once criticized as an inadequate substitute for public social insurance. In doing so, negotiated pensions dampened and redirected, though certainly did not eliminate, the broader demands of the labor movement for public social insurance. Second, and cutting in the other direction, the entry of labor into the pension field made business leaders more willing to support the broadening of Social Security to offset the cost of negotiated plans, most of which were integrated with old-age insurance. Although the Chamber of Commerce briefly tried to rally corporate America behind a proposal to hem in old-age insurance, both strategic realism and self-interest increasingly pressed employers to accept and even support expansions of the old-age insurance program. This intersection of labor and business interests – grounded as if was in the sizable but nonetheless supplementary role that private retirement benefits had come to play – suggested that both private pensions and old-age insurance had gained a secure place in the American social welfare regime, even if the exact balance between the two remained very much up for political debate.

Yet that debate never truly occurred. In the postwar years, public and private retirement provision grew in tandem with little acknowledgement or discussion of the inherent tensions between them. In the 1960s and 1970s, however, these issues briefly rose to the surface of public concern. As Social Security underwent its most dramatic expansion to date, the inadequacies and uncertainties of private pensions looked increasingly glaring. The Employee Retirement Income Security Act of 1974, the nation's first comprehensive law governing private pensions, was the product of this brief moment of ferment. And yet, ultimately, the structure and effects of ERISA can only be understood in the larger context of post–New Deal pension developments. For ERISA was a political breakthrough marked by contradiction – at once a challenge to the autonomous operation of private plans and an affirmation of their central place in the American welfare regime. While the law required that pension plans meet new requirements, it challenged neither the voluntary character of private benefits nor the special dispensation that they enjoyed. And the vision at the core of ERISA looked to the past, to the union-negotiated plans that had arisen in the 1940s and 1950s, even as the private pension system was rapidly moving away from this traditional organization.

The consequences of this contradictory orientation became clear almost immediately after ERISA's passage, as the economy soured and antigovernment forces gained political ground. Even as Social Security was coming under new fiscal strain, ERISA proved largely powerless to resist the shift of private pensions away from the older pension forms that ERISA regulated toward new pension models that were far more individualized and voluntary, and far less interwoven with Social Security. In the 1980s, employers revamped their pension benefits to exploit tax breaks for individualized retirement plans, while conservatives in Washington fought to defend against scattered attempts to revise the favorable provisions of the tax code that were driving corporate activity. Today, almost two decades after the Social Security reforms of the early 1980s, the old-age insurance program is still politically sacrosanct. But it has ceased to command the support it once did, particularly among employers, and benefits under the program represent an ever smaller portion of previous earnings. Perhaps most fateful of all, the program looks increasingly substandard in comparison with the growing complex of tax-favored private accounts, which benefited from the robust stock market of the past decade at the same time as the declining ratio of workers to pension recipients caused Social Security's promised returns to fall. Surely it would be a dramatic reversal of fortune if the private retirement system that was consistently justified as a means to supplement Social Security became the vehicle for replacing the basic social insurance protections of old-age insurance.

Private Pensions and Collective Bargaining

In discussions of the rise of fringe benefits during and after World War II, there is a tendency to see the process as a seamless tapestry and to equate the whole with the gains made by labor in the late 1940s and early 1950s. It is therefore worth reemphasizing the history reviewed in the last chapter. The evolution of private pensions from the late 1930s through the end of World War II proceeded in directions almost wholly inimical to the interests of labor. Organized labor's great drive for private social protection did not begin until after the war, and its gains were distinctly fragile until the very end of the 1940s.

The injection of union-negotiated benefits into national politics reflected the central paradox of postwar labor relations. At the end of World War II, American unions were by many measures stronger than they had ever been, with union density five times greater than before the 1930s.[1] Politically, organized labor had eschewed its earlier voluntarist leanings and was, for the first time, fully committed to public social insurance. Yet, at the same time, organized labor in the United States faced unquestionably the most hostile political environment it had since the New Deal, with congressional conservatives and employers bent on rolling back union influence in national politics and the workplace alike. In this context, bargaining over private social benefits came to serve crucial ends. Negotiated benefits were a means for organizing workers at a time when other tools were under attack. They were a means for raising compensation at a time when wage gains were seen as inflationary. And, perhaps most important, they were a means for obtaining valuable social benefits at a time when unions were unable to obtain federal social legislation. The turn to private social protection thus neatly reflected labor's dual struggle – first, against employers over the proper scope of collective bargaining, and second, against congressional conservatives over the proper scope of the American welfare state.

The forces that pushed unions into conflict with employers over fringe benefits have been well documented both by contemporary observers and by later historians and social scientists, although the interrelationship of these forces and their place within the broader context of U.S. social policy still remain incompletely understood.[2] The initial impetus came from within the labor movement itself. Particularly important was John L. Lewis's ultimately successful 1945–46 campaign for a company-funded pension and welfare fund for the United Mine Workers (UMW).[3] But private social benefits had a prominent place in the thinking of each of the three most powerful labor leaders of the time: Lewis, Walter Reuther of the United Auto Workers (UAW), and Philip Murray of the United Steel Workers (USW). (Murray was also head of the Congress of Industrial Organizations [CIO], which included both the UAW and USW.) By 1949, all three unions had placed private pension and welfare benefits at the center of their bargaining drives. Ironically, the tradition-ally voluntaristic AFL had by this time become the most reluctant to shift attention away from the pursuit of federal legislation, fearing that company plans in the seasonal and high-turnover lines of business rep-resented by AFL unions would be unable to offer true protection. But AFL unions still fought vigorously for pension and health benefits under multiemployer arrangements, and by the early 1950s, the AFL and CIO were united in support of private bargaining, helping to pave the way for their merger in 1955.

To union leaders, labor-negotiated benefits were a valuable resource in battles to organize workers – "a distributive good that union leaders could use to attract followers," "a source of power" for labor chiefs, "a weapon in factional struggles" among unions – all uses of union welfare funds that Congress promptly tried to curb.[4] But above all, private ben-efits served pressing social ends. The meagerness of Social Security ben-efits and the tilt of existing private plans toward salaried personnel meant that aging union members frequently faced bleak prospects in retirement. Far more than employers, then, unions stressed the immediate human distress that negotiated benefits would alleviate, and indeed, most union-backed plans provided greater proportional benefits to low-wage workers, much as Social Security did. Not surprisingly, unions were less concerned about long-term financing, and many negotiated plans accrued significant unfunded liabilities. These financial risks actually tied workers more closely to unions, for the continued strength of union bargainers often became the only guarantee of eventual benefits.

The second set of forces that pushed unions to embrace fringe bene-fits grew out of the fiercely contested relationship between employers and unions.[5] The years after World War II were among the most turbulent in labor history, with spiraling prices and an unprecedented number of strikes fixating the nation. During the war, government intervention and quasi-corporatist institutions such as the War Labor Board had restrained conflict between management and labor, even as union mem-bership had reached record levels. But, with the war over, the conflict reignited, and both unions and employers quickly discovered that fringe benefits were an effective weapon in the battle. Large nonunion employers like Eastman Kodak were particularly adept at using fringe benefits to undermine unionization, closely tracking benefit developments at other firms and in bellwether industries such as steel and autos.[6] Unions, for their part, saw private social benefits as a means of organizing workers, preserving union security, and broadening the range of issues subject to collective bargaining – all of which became acutely pressing after Republicans gained Congress in 1946 for the first time since the New Deal and promptly enacted the antilabor Taft-Hartley Act of 1947.

Pension and other benefit plans divided employers and unions because they raised the thorny question of control – control over plan design, over the terms of coverage, and, even more contentious, over plan assets. Despite the movement of employers toward financially sound pension plans, corporations continued to insist that they retain complete discretion over plan structure and assets. The National Association of Manufacturers (NAM), for instance, argued not merely that it was improper for unions to be involved in plan administration, but that "the entire subject of employee benefit programs must continue to be outside the scope of collective bargaining."[7] Union involvement, according to NAM, was at odds with the voluntary character of private benefits, which "must reflect the conscience and interest of each worker."[8] The Association's appeal to unfettered individual choice was little more than a rhetorical flourish, since employers had long used benefit programs for frankly paternalistic ends. But it underscored the deep hostility and apprehension employers felt about union control. Responding to these concerns, Congress included in the Taft-Hartley Act a requirement that plan funds be placed in trusts and a prohibition on multiemployer plans administered solely by unions.

The third – and, in the end, decisive – set of forces pushing pensions and other fringe benefits onto the bargaining table came from the federal government itself. Congress first failed to respond to labor demands for expanded public social insurance, encouraging a turn to the private sector. Public officials then intervened at crucial moments to require or encourage collective bargaining over fringe benefits, overcoming employer recalcitrance and channeling union energy into benefit negotiations. The motives for these actions were diverse. Conservative resistance to an expansion of public social programs was critical. So, too, was the widespread fear about economic instability that the labor unrest of the late 1940s created. But giving direction and urgency to these concerns was a temporary community of interest among key conservatives and liberals who, for different reasons, wished to encourage the spread of private benefits – conservatives because it lessened dependence on the state, liberals because it compensated for the weakness of public protections. With major expansion of government programs off the table, the battle over public and private social provision was eclipsed by a struggle over the terms on which private benefits would develop. In trying to define those terms, Democrats and labor unions found themselves promoting policy ideas and instruments that they had long viewed with suspicion and concern.

Dilemmas of the Left

By the early 1940s, the continued stagnation of Social Security had become a source of deep frustration for northern Democrats and organized labor. Liberal hopes centered on the Wagner-Murray-Dingell bill, a comprehensive program of social insurance authored in large part by the Social Security Board. Introduced in 1943 and routinely reintroduced thereafter, the bill went nowhere, provoking deep pessimism among its supporters. Meanwhile, Social Security benefits were quickly eroding as a result of high inflation and the congressional freeze on taxes and benefits. A program that had replaced more than 26 percent of preretirement income for the average earner in 1940 replaced less than 20 percent by the end of the decade.[9] Unions could not accept these developments idly. The CIO declared in 1950:

> After a long struggle to obtain comprehensive and reasonably adequate governmental Federal Social Security programs without real success, organized labor stated bluntly, at the onset of bargaining, that to the extent that Congress failed to provide workers' security on a universal basis, long overdue security programs would be sought from the employers across the collective bargaining table. This seemed appropriate because it was primarily the groups representing the employers, with the help of the insurance companies, that believed governmental programs were not necessary and that existing machinery could meet the pressing need.[10]

As the CIO statement suggests, unions justified their campaign for fringe benefits on several grounds, not all of them consistent or equally shared.[11] Fringe benefits were defended, first, as a temporary substitute for public programs that would eventually compel employers to rethink their opposition to government protections. In congressional hearings in 1950, for example, Reuther testified that the UAW had fought "for a noncontributory pension plan in industry because we knew that that was the key to getting action at the federal level."[12] Employers faced with new costs would be more apt to support expansions of Social Security.

Soon, however, this rhetoric of short-run expediency gave way to acknowledgment that private benefits would be needed over the long term. In 1957, Reuther was still condemning the inadequacies of private plans relative to the "economical, efficient, and honest administration of social insurance programs."[13] But he would later speak of private pensions as a "parallel system" or a "dual system" that provided "a broader range of flexibility to innovate ideas and develop programs that more specifically reflect the needs of workers in one kind of industry as contrasted to another kind of industry."[14] For some union leaders, indeed, private benefit plans came to be seen as preferable to public programs.[15] This was the essential dilemma: Private benefits represented an immediate response to the failure of social legislation, yet in the long run, they seemed likely to decrease the support of union members and leaders for the expansion of public programs.

Troubling to labor leaders, this dilemma was even more acute for Social Security administrators and liberal Democrats, who were drawn to the campaign not by any great enthusiasm for private benefits but by a desire to support organized labor and provide immediate social assistance. Within the Federal Security Agency (FSA) – which oversaw old-age insurance from 1939 until the creation of the Department of Health, Education, and Welfare (HEW) in 1953 – program executives found themselves forced to devote increasing energy to private developments even as they feared the long-term consequences for their cause. As much by default as by design, the Agency became a leading source of advice and expertise for labor unions attempting to negotiate private plans, pumping out a stream of research reports and helping the UAW, UMW, and other unions set up their own programs.[16] This unusual advisory role, similar to the function that private consultants had long played in industry circles, was justified on the grounds that the Agency was best poised to consider the effect of private benefit negotiations on unions' broader legislative aspirations and, in particular, to ensure that private benefits would be "supplementary to and interlocked with existing or proposed social security legislation."[17] Involvement in union negotiations occurred on a more individual basis, too. While serving as Social Security Commissioner, Arthur Altmeyer participated in the operation and development of several negotiated plans.[18] During the Korean War, Wilbur Cohen – Altmeyer's right-hand man and future HEW Secretary – chaired a panel that recommended that qualified benefit plans be exempt from wage controls, thus further encouraging and channeling the expansion of private benefits.[19]

At the same time, Social Security program executives recognized that if union-negotiated plans were allowed to move too far into the vacuum created by the stagnation of old-age insurance, they would pose a direct threat to the contributory public program. Altmeyer emphasized in a 1947 statement that the "subject of employee-benefit plans in relation to the basic social security program of the government is of very great interest to us in the Social Security Administration":

> The particular character and force of the current pressure for health and welfare plans is in large measure a result of our failure to complete the structure of our basic social insurance system. . . . It may be suggested that the extensive and widespread development of voluntary employee benefit plans should call for a reexamination of basic concepts. I believe that such a reexamination would bring us again to the conclusion that we need a comprehensive basic social insurance program as a foundation on which to build additional protection. . . . Variations above the basic program provisions in employer contributions and in the benefits available to particular groups of workers can mean desirable flexibility and experimentation. I do not believe, however, that we can much longer afford the complete gaps in coverage and protection which inevitably result from voluntary provisions alone.[20]

Like Altmeyer, President Truman criticized private plans, demanding social provision through "a comprehensive public program of old-age, survivors, and disability insurance, rather than through a multiplicity of unrelated private plans, which would inevitably omit large numbers of the working population and treat others unequally."[21] But Truman ended up supporting union negotiations anyway, and so did leading congressional liberals, few of whom viewed the spread of private social protection any more favorably. The congressional debate over Taft-Hartley thus took a strange twist, as liberal Democrats defended union rights to bargain for private benefits by sounding themes similar to those that conservatives had invoked in defending corporate pension plans in 1942.[22]

Having left the door open for bargaining over fringe benefits in the Taft-Hartley Act, liberal Democrats and their allies endeavored to make the possibility a reality. The first breakthrough was the Truman Administration's 1946 agreement with the UMW mandating an employer-funded plan jointly managed by the union and industry. The second was the famous *Inland Steel* decision of the pro-labor National Labor Relations Board, which declared that collective bargaining over benefits was not merely allowed but mandated by federal law.[23] Even the unequivocal language of *Inland Steel* did not, however, end the conflict. That took the 1949 report of the Steel Industry Board appointed by Truman to resolve the ongoing battle between the steel companies and the USW. The specifics of the Board's recommendations are less important than its resounding endorsement of private benefits. "There was a

time of unenlightened social opinion in this country," explained the
Board, "when it was felt that the needs of workers for insurance against
the insecurities of modern economic life was [*sic*] the concern of nobody
but the worker himself – or of charity. In this generation, that philosophy has been rejected by overwhelming public opinion – and by most of
industry itself." Though it would be preferable if the "Government were
itself to extend the field of security to cover all these . . . hazards," the
Board concluded, "[s]o long as Government does not provide the security at all, we believe that industry should. So long as Government fails
to provide an adequate amount, industry should take up the slack."[24]

The Steel Board report eventually laid the basis for agreement in the
steel industry and opened the floodgates to benefit negotiations in other
industries. The results were dramatic: By 1960, labor-negotiated plans
covered more than 11 million workers, or about half of the total workforce with pension protections. Pension coverage rose from 19 percent
of private workers in 1945 to 40 percent in 1960, a surge that more than
doubled the reach of private plans in the course of less than two
decades.[25] In the process, the character of the private pension system was
transformed. After 1939, private pension plans had all but ignored the
needs of the average worker, a duty that corporate pension sponsors
claimed was Social Security's. In contrast, "[c]ollectively bargained
pension programs were essentially social welfare schemes benefiting a
specific needy class – the elderly union members."[26] Once almost exclusively the province of salaried employees, America's private social welfare
system now became a principal source of support for many wage workers
who had previously fallen back on the meager benefits of Social Security
and their own usually limited resources.

Still, private pensions continued to cover less than half the workforce,
a threshold that proved stubbornly elusive in the coming decades. And
the reach of the new labor-oriented plans, though impressive in historical relief, was nonetheless strictly limited. Although the sharp class bias
of private pensions dulled somewhat, participation in private plans
remained largely confined to employees who were unionized or worked
for large corporations and, within this group, to workers with the most
stable and long-term positions. As a consequence, the principal beneficiaries of the postwar expansion of negotiated benefits were white
men. Although black employment in industry was increasing, African-
Americans were vastly underrepresented within the unionized workforce,
and they were vastly overrepresented in seasonal, episodic, and low-wage
jobs where benefits were rare. Women workers, too, were rarely unionized and remained concentrated in lines of work that offered little direct
access to workplace protections. In neither case was the differential

access to private benefits due primarily to overt discrimination in their provision. Instead, it was mainly the result of job discrimination and broader social inequalities that limited the presence of African-Americans and women in the industries, corporations, and jobs where private benefits were most common.[27]

Gender was, in fact, more deeply embedded in the world of retirement benefits than this. Despite rising levels of female participation in the labor force, private pensions generally reflected a male breadwinner ideal, with eventual benefits based on the assumption that men would support their homemaker wives in retirement. Women, whether working or not, were thus generally expected to receive benefits as their husbands' dependents – an assumption also embodied in the spousal benefit added to Social Security in 1939, though this provision was later made nominally gender neutral.[28] Women found it much harder to earn private retirement benefits on their own, not only because pension plans were generally unavailable where they were most likely to work, but also because features of plans that made them favorable to long-term employees and older unionized workers further served to disadvantage women, who moved in and out of the workforce to raise children and rarely garnered seniority or pay comparable to their male counterparts.

For all the weaknesses and inequalities that remained, however, the explosion of collectively bargained benefits constituted a remarkable breakthrough – an attempt by American labor to achieve through the private sector social insurance protections that it could not extract from government. Yet what was an immediate victory for organized labor had darker implications for the long-term goal of inclusive social insurance. As private benefits spread into some parts of the labor market and not others, they undercut the common constituency for public social insurance and weakened labor support for more expansive government action. Though it is difficult to find outright reversals in the stance of labor leaders, union energy and attention were increasingly devoted to the negotiation and operation of private plans, and national unions emerged at the forefront in defending the favorable regulatory and tax climate for these plans – a cause that brought labor leaders into alliance with the very business groups that had once fought the union role so bitterly.[29]

At the level of the rank and file, the effects were similarly corrosive to the social insurance movement. A revealing study of the steel industry by Lawrence S. Root, for example, found that workers came to see their own benefits not only as superior to government protections but also as a source of advantage relative to other workers.[30] Root discovered "an underlying current in many discussions that if some workers were not adequately covered by employee benefits, it was their own fault for not having successfully organized themselves and pressed their demands."[31] Steelworkers also commonly complained about the new taxes that public programs would impose to fund benefits that they already enjoyed. Subtly but unmistakably, the spread of private plans undermined the notoriously weak solidarity of American workers and undercut support for the expansion or creation of public social programs.

Once again, America's leaders had debated the bounds of public and private social protection. Yet, in the late 1940s, this debate took an unusual turn. If it was mainly conservatives who championed private benefits in the 1930s and early 1940s, it was mainly liberals who did so in the late 1940s and early 1950s. This is only explicable in light of the continued failure of efforts to liberalize Social Security. Michael K. Brown insists that "unions would have made bargaining over corporate welfare programs an issue regardless of the outcome of legislative struggles."[32] But had Congress expanded public social insurance, unions would have had less to bargain over and liberals would likely have been less receptive to their demands. The real question was never whether private plans would exist, but on whose terms they would be designed and, more important, how extensive they would be relative to public programs.

Employers and insurers were complicit in the redefinition of employee benefits that allowed the union breakthroughs of the 1940s and 1950s. Their defense of tax benefits for private pensions in the early 1940s stressed the social contributions that employer programs made. By the late 1940s, caught up in bargaining struggles and facing legal challenges to managerial autonomy, employers were once again retreating to the gratuity conception of pensions that had defined welfare capitalism. But with government playing a greater role in the field, it was harder for employers to defend their programs as purely private and discretionary. Pensions were coming to be understood not as company gifts but as social benefits in which workers, employers, and government all had a stake.

The timing of the explosion in private pensions – after Social Security had been enacted, but at a time when its reach was still limited – was fateful in shaping this conception of the private sector's role. Private plans would not be a substitute for public programs, as in the health insurance field. But they would be a significant and recognized counterpart to public protections. There would be two organized providers of retirement income in the United States, a public program of social insurance and a private pension system encouraged and shaped by federal tax and labor policy.

From Competition to Cooperation

Between 1939 and 1950, private pensions moved into the gap created by the stagnation of Social Security, pushed first by conservative forces bent on preserving the open-ended subsidies for private retirement protection and then by organized labor and Democrats frustrated by their inability to expand public programs. After 1950, however, private pensions and Social Security would expand together, as the nation's public retirement program overcame its initial slow start to become firmly woven into the fabric of U.S. social policy. In 1950, with Democrats back in control of Congress, Social Security coverage was expanded, and real benefits returned to their original levels. The 1950 amendments set in motion a pattern of gradual expansion that lasted for more than a decade, as coverage continue to expand and benefits stayed roughly even with rising prices (though not with wages), thanks to regular election-year increases. The major expansion of Social Security came in the late 1960s and early 1970s, with liberalism momentarily ascendant. Near the high tide of popular support for old-age insurance, Congress enacted a landmark law reforming private pensions to safeguard and broaden the distribution of their benefits – in short, to make them more like Social Security.

Throughout this period, the fierce conflict over the boundaries between public and private pensions that had characterized the early years of Social Security became more muted, as both public and private pensions flourished in a strong economy. The two institutions increasingly moved along separate tracks, both expanding in response to similar forces, but viewed largely in isolation from one another by policymakers. Yet the conflict did not vanish. Efforts to reform private pensions elicited predictable opposition from business groups and insurers, and, on key issues, from labor unions, too. The continued expansion of private pensions similarly created predictable consternation on the part of Social Security's administrators, who acutely feared that private plans would undercut support for further expansion of the program. And when the liberal climate eroded and the economy stagnated in the 1970s, opposition to Social Security once again became manifest among conservatives, who pressed for the expansion of new tax-favored retirement savings vehicles that were attractive to upper-income Americans and could form the basis for a "parallel system" of private retirement benefits.[33]

The concerns felt by Social Security administrators about the stagnation of Social Security reached a crescendo in the late 1940s. By then, Social Security benefits made up less than one-third of total pension payments and, as a share of national income, barely exceeded one-fourth of 1 percent of GDP. Both Social Security taxes and the portion of employee wages subject to taxation also remained low, with the combined employee-employer tax still frozen at 2 percent and the wage base at $3,000. Given inflation, this meant that the portion of covered workers' wages subject to taxation had fallen steadily since the inception of the program – from an initial level of 92 percent to less than 80 percent. Like benefit levels, the level of the wage base shaped the relationship between Social Security and other sources of retirement income, especially at the upper end of the wage scale. As the proportion of earnings taxed by the program fell, an increasing share of workers earned the maximum taxable amount and, thus, received the maximum benefit in retirement. As a result, the program grew more similar to a system of flat-rate assistance rather than to the original vision of universal, earnings-related pensions. To program executives, this flattening of benefits posed a twin threat. For one, it undermined the distinction between Social Security and means-tested old-age assistance payments, which were now higher in many states than average Social Security benefits. For another, it made Social Security less attractive to workers on the higher rungs of the income ladder, who supplemented their increasingly meager benefits with private retirement pensions and personal savings.

The political chances for expansion were greatly improved by the return of Congress to Democratic control in 1948, after Truman had made the alleged social policy inaction of the Republican Congress of the previous two years a major campaign issue. But the 1950 amendments would not have been enacted were it not for the influence of other factors, as the demise of most of Truman's other 1948–49 social legislation, including national health insurance, suggests. One cause was the continuing fear that state old-age assistance programs would swell beyond control. As Martha Derthick argues, Social Security administrators sold the 1950 changes as "a shift in functions from one level of the federal system to another and from one program to another – adjustments within the public sector to which there was no opposition."[34] The question was not how big the public program would be relative to private plans, but whether public funds should be distributed through means-tested state programs or the federal system. On this question, conservatives and business groups were more receptive to a national program than in the past – conservatives because they saw the earmarked payroll tax as a limit on Social Security's expansion (though many still would have preferred immediate coverage of all the aged so that total costs would be transparent), business groups because Social Security benefits now largely offset the costs of integrated private plans (that is, plans with benefit levels inversely related to expected Social Security benefits).

Though corporate leaders opposed many of the administration's social policy initiatives, their overall attitude toward Social Security had moderated considerably since the 1930s and even the early 1940s.[35]

Integration was at the heart of big business's changing stance. As large corporations acceded to labor demands, or preemptively accommodated them, their pension plans began to promise significant benefits to workers beneath the Social Security wage base, benefits that would in most cases be wholly or entirely offset by increases in old-age insurance payments. The implication of this change was not lost on business leaders – or members of Congress. At the Senate Finance Committee hearings on the 1950 amendments, Colorado Republican Eugene Millikin peppered Herschel Atkinson of the Ohio Chamber of Commerce with pointed questions about integrated private plans:

> Senator Millikin: And, of course, those companies that have the provision whereby their pension shall be reduced by the amount of the basic Federal pension – those companies, of course, are rooting and tooting for a better level of Government pensions?
> Atkinson: Yes.
> Senator Millikin: Quite naturally and quite understandably.
> Atkinson: Yes; I think that those feelings are evident.
> Senator Millikin: The system has gained some new and strange adherents in the last year or so.
> Atkinson: I must confess that that is true, sir. . . . Such pressures have been exerted by our Government in labor–management negotiations which involve organized labor's demand for such things as $100-a-month pensions. . . . Now it is perfectly natural that managements [*sic*] which felt compelled to accept, under Government pressure, terms which otherwise might not have been agreed to so precipitously, are not to be found in the van of those resisting material liberalization of OASI [Old-Age and Survivors Insurance] benefit amounts. What else could be expected in a situation of this sort?[36]

Given how intimately Social Security insiders were involved in the development of union-negotiated plans, it would be tempting to see their assistance as a backdoor means of increasing business support for their agenda – as Atkinson's testimony implied it was. Yet the Federal Security Agency had less Machiavellian reasons for steering unions toward integration. To program advocates, it was crucial that organized labor maintain support for the extension of public social insurance and, hence, that private benefits be conceived of either as stopgap measures temporarily filling holes in coverage or as modest supplements to existing benefits. The Agency cautioned the UAW in 1946, for instance, that the union should consider "the probable effect of the adoption of a union security program on future social security legislation," and it urged the union to focus on accident, health, and death coverage rather than retirement benefits. Not only were public protections greater in the pension field, the Agency argued, but in addition, health and accident plans "can be entered into on a year-to-year basis, and can consequently be quickly dropped or modified when social insurance legislation is enacted for the same risks."[37] In light of program insiders' counsel, and faced with corporate unwillingness to accept more generous plans, unions decided that integration was the price that had to be paid for negotiated retirement plans. But after the Social Security liberalization of 1950 wiped out most of the gains made at the bargaining table, unions began to insist on pensions that only partially substituted public for private benefits.[38]

Analyzing the support of the Federal Security Agency for union negotiations, the historian Jennifer Klein argues that Altmeyer, Cohen, and other program activists "regularly advanced the fully articulated basic welfare state/private supplementation position without hesitation."[39] But the vision of supplementation painted by Social Security insiders (and used strategically as much as sincerely) saw private benefits as a means of topping off existing programs or temporarily substituting for those sought but not yet achieved.[40] In stark contrast, most business and insurance defenders of supplementation described Social Security quite differently, as "a basic floor of protection against want," or "a basic minimum layer of protection" designed "to provide merely the bare necessities."[41] "Important as it may be to provide safeguards against the hazards of our economy," NAM emphasized in 1950, "it is even more important that such provision shall not interfere with the incentive to save, and make other voluntary provisions for old age."[42] Between these two views lay a major lingering divide – the contested territory that would continue to spark battles even as the full-scale war receded.

The 1950 reforms also hinged on a reaffirmation by congressional leaders of the sanctity of Social Security's earmarked payroll tax.[43] In taking general tax financing off the table, members of the revenue committees laid out a policy of "self-support" that was inherently expansionary. First, the policy of "self-support" allowed members of Congress to portray Social Security not as a massive transfer system, but merely as means for workers to set aside money for their own retirement, even if current taxes were actually funding current retirees. Second, "self-support" helped justify a broadening of coverage that, while increasing the long-term liability of the program, improved its short-term finances. As new workers were brought into the system, tax receipts immediately increased, while benefits for most of these workers would not be paid for many years. For the same reasons, benefit increases could be financed with very modest increases in the payroll tax. In the short term, only the currently retired would enjoy the new benefits. The total costs would come due much later – and certainly after the next election. Congress had thus turned Social Security's original financing scheme on its head. Abandoning full-reserve financing in 1939, congressional leaders had endorsed a smaller "contingent reserve" while affirming that general revenues would be used if necessary. Now, members of Congress rejected the idea of using general revenues and advocated immediate benefit expansions and gradually raising tax rates in the future. It was a policy choice that would propel the politics of Social Security expansion for the next quarter century.

The political logic of expansion that had failed to materialize in the 1940s thus arrived with a vengeance in the 1950s. The pressures for expansion rolled over what was left of the conservative opposition to Social Security, which grew increasingly disunited and disaffected as the program continued its steady march. When Eisenhower was elected in 1952, for example, conservative opponents hoped briefly that their savior had arrived. But although Eisenhower declared that he supported "the encouragement of privately sponsored pension plans" in his initial legislative declaration on Social Security, he refused to support the leading conservative proposal – a 1953 plan developed by the Chamber of Commerce for the immediate blanketing in of all the aged, financed by earmarked payroll taxes set high enough to pay only for current retirees.[44] Nor did Eisenhower embrace the call of House Republican Thomas B. Curtis to have "private concerns" handle the investment of Social Security funds.[45] In the end, plans for radical reform sank into a void of congressional disinterest, and Eisenhower approved a significant liberalization of Social Security coverage and benefits.

It was not that conservatives had given up on private pension plans or lost all power to repel threats to them. In 1950, they had successfully resisted Truman's proposal for a restoration of the $3,000 wage base to its original inflation-adjusted level – a move universally opposed by conservatives, insurers, and business leaders. As the Republican House report explained the conservative position:

Raising the wage base . . . brings into sharp focus a basic conflict in the conception of the social-insurance system. This conflict is whether the system should serve to afford economic protection at a basic level appropriate for those least able to pay for their own security, or whether it should now be expanded into a national retirement system of high benefits as a relatively complete means of furnishing retirement and survivors' benefits without any need for supplementation by the individual.[46]

During the Eisenhower Administration, the Secretary of HEW was none other than Marion Folsom, the corporate liberal who had long advocated a small welfare state based on a creative tension between public programs and industrial welfare plans. Although Folsom was on the liberal fringe of the business world, his views were not radically out of line with other corporate leaders of the time. Few still clung to the idea of eliminating Social Security, which was fast becoming an entrenched reality of the postwar social welfare landscape. But most wanted the program to remain relatively ungenerous to give private plans ample room for growth.[47]

Not surprisingly, then, Social Security did not dramatically expand during the 1950s and early 1960s, or at least not in terms of benefits. Expansion mainly proceeded outward as coverage under Social Security broadened. The Social Security Act had excluded workers engaged in agriculture and domestic service, the self-employed, and government workers. All these groups, with the exception of certain professionals and public employees, were brought into the program during the 1950s.[48] In contrast with coverage levels, however, benefits did not rise dramatically, nor did the amount of covered earnings subject to taxation return to its initial level. The large benefit increase of 1950 merely undid the benefit erosion of the previous decade, as the comparison of benefit increases with price and wage levels in Table 3.1 indicates. With the exception of a sizable increase in benefits in 1954, benefit levels during the 1950s and early 1960s hardly kept even with rising consumer prices, much less with the growth in wages. The amendments of the 1950s and early 1960s were, in short, a qualified victory for Social Security's defenders. Although they did not radically transform the program, they stabilized it, reaffirmed its purpose, and extended its benefits to groups that, for reasons of political expediency or administrative complexity, had originally been excluded.

By 1960, a two-track system of organized retirement protection had been firmly institutionalized in the United States. Social Security was the core of protection, but for nearly half of American workers, coverage was also provided by occupational plans. The solidification of this public–private framework could be detected in a softening of the contentious rhetoric of the 1940s. Andrew Biemiller of the AFL-CIO captured the sentiment of most labor leaders in his description of private pension plans as "a form of social insurance, if you will, in the United States of America." "The labor movement would have preferred some other approach to these matters," Biemiller conceded, "but this is what has grown up in our society."[49] Business leaders also sounded a more pragmatic note. In the late 1960s, for example, the Chamber of

Table 3.1. *Social Security Benefit Increases Versus Price and Wage Levels, 1950–1974*

Date of Change (and of Enactment, If Different)	Increase in OASI Benefits Since Last Amendment (%)	Increase in CPI Since Last Amendment (%)	Ratio of CPI Increase to Benefit Increase	Increase in Wages Since Last Amendment (%)	Ratio of Wage Increase to Benefit Increase
1950	77	75.5	1.02	148.8	0.52
1952	12.5	9.3	1.34	12.5	1.00
1954	13	0.5	26.00	7.7	1.69
1959 (1958)	7	7.9	0.89	19.4	0.36
1965	7	7.9	0.89	22.3	0.31
1968 (1967)	13	9.3	1.40	18	0.72
1970	15	10.8	1.39	12.2	1.23
1971	10	5.2	1.92	5.3	1.89
1972	20	3.4	5.88	9.8	2.04
1974 (two steps)	11	17.8	0.62	12.6	0.87
1975 (indexation begins)					

Source: For the years 1950–1971, Martha Derthick, *Policymaking for Social Security* (Washington, D.C.: Brookings, 1979), 276. CPI data for later years come from the Bureau of Labor Statistics (http://www.bls.gov) and are not exactly comparable to Derthick's figures. Data on benefit and wage levels after 1971 are from House Committee on Ways and Means, *1998 Green Book* (Washington, D.C.: U.S. GPO, 1998), 38.

Commerce argued that "Social Security should be continued . . . at a reasonable level. Our only fear is that if Social Security grows too large, it will overtake everything else."[50] Business accepted that Social Security would be nearly universal and that it – rather than old-age assistance – would be the primary source of public benefits. Labor accepted that a large sphere of private protection would be left for labor and management to negotiate on their own.

Rare was the acknowledgment of the inherent tensions in this sunny cooperative vision. As the social policy expert Margaret Gordon noted in 1967, maintaining the Social Security system in its current role was, in effect, to express a preference "for a greatly increased role for private and public employee benefit plans although the issue is seldom put this way." The "real question," according to Gordon, was the one being resolutely avoided – namely, the choice "between strengthening the social security system versus permitting private and public [occupational] pension plans to absorb a considerably larger proportion of total contributions to retirement systems than they do at present."[51] Nor was the question merely one of relative size. To allow occupational plans to fill the gap left by what was essentially a holding pattern in Social Security was to maintain the highly uneven coverage and the persistent uncertainties of private plans.

In the 1970s, the management theorist Peter Drucker would describe the rise of private pensions as an "unseen revolution" that had created "pension fund socialism" in the United States – "an outstanding example of the efficacy of using the existing private, non-governmental institutions of our 'society of organizations' for the formulation and achievement of social goals and the satisfaction of social needs."[52] But not only was this "private, non-governmental" system bolstered by largely unrestricted tax subsidies; it also left millions of workers uncovered – the most disadvantaged foremost among them – and millions more uncertain about their benefits. With private pensions deeply interwoven into the tax code and federal old-age insurance, these were now concerns of policymakers as well as of participants in the system.

Social Security's "Quantum Increase"

In the late 1960s and early 1970s, with Social Security coverage nearly universal, the pattern of growth of Social Security shifted from extension of coverage to expansion of benefits. This expansion was dramatic: Benefits rose by 13 percent in 1968, by 15 percent in 1970, by 10 percent in 1971, and by an astounding 20 percent in 1972 – a cumulative real benefit increase of nearly 37 percent (23 percent between 1970 and

Table 3.2. *Social Security Replacement Rates, 1940–2040*

Year of Attaining Age 65	Low Earner	Average Earner	Maximum Earner
1940	39.4	26.2	16.5
1950	33.2	19.7	21.2
1960	49.1	33.3	29.8
1970	48.5	34.3	29.2
1980	68.1	51.1	32.5
1990	58.2	43.2	24.5
2000	57.8	43	25.4
2010	53.1	39.5	25.4
2020	52.5	39	25.8
2030	49.4	36.7	24.2
2040	49.4	36.7	24.2

Note: Replacement rates are calculated by dividing the value of benefits awarded in the year after retirement by income earned in the year prior to retirement. These are hypothetical rates based on the benefits that would be received by a worker who retires at age 65 after a full-time career with steady earnings. The three levels of earnings represent the federal minimum wage (low earner), average earnings in the economy (average earner), and the maximum earnings taxable each year by Social Security (maximum earner).
Source: House Committee on Ways and Means, *1998 Green Book* (Washington, D.C.: U.S. GPO, 1998), 27.

1972). Not only that, but the wage base increased and was pegged to wage levels, benefits were indexed to inflation beginning in 1975, and rising benefit levels along with changes in the benefit structure pushed up replacement rates for low and average earners by roughly twenty percentage points (see Table 3.2). Though not a contributory pension plan, the means-tested Supplemental Security Income program was also established during this period, converting state-based public assistance programs for the aged, blind, and disabled into a standardized federal supplement to Social Security for many of the poorest elderly. When the dust had settled, Social Security commissioner Robert Ball could declare without exaggeration that the nation had "a new social security program."[53]

The "quantum increase" in benefit levels unleashed in the late 1960s was different in both degree and kind from earlier patterns of expansion.[54] Although the benefit increases of these years continued earlier political tendencies – such as the bidding up of benefits in election years – they represented a sharp "departure from established norms of policymaking."[55] The major causes of this departure, according to Derthick, were twofold. The first was the abandonment of the so-called level earnings assumption (in which wages were assumed to remain steady) in favor of dynamic estimates that could, in the short term at least, justify a larger increase in benefits. The second was the leadership of House Ways and Means Chairman Wilbur Mills, whose cautious custodianship of the program had defined its postwar pattern of incremental growth. Mills not only supported the move to dynamic scoring but actually sponsored the 1972 benefit increase, perhaps to help along his own presidential ambitions.[56]

These were indeed important proximate causes of the increase in cash benefits, but the groundwork for such a major shift in policy obviously lay deeper. Perhaps the most important of these underlying causes was also the one most taken for granted at the time: the general liberal climate of the period, which had helped produce huge Democratic majorities in Congress and, between 1960 and 1968, two Democratic presidencies. The mid-1960s had seen the launch of a "War on Poverty" and, more significant for Social Security, the passage of Medicare for the aged and the Older Americans Act, which together declared that the needs of the elderly should be a major national priority. In 1964, Republican candidate Barry Goldwater had broached the subject of restructuring Social Security – and been crushed by Lyndon Johnson. The message was not lost on Republican allies like Richard Nixon, who after his election as president in 1968 staffed his social welfare agencies with moderates and consistently expressed his support for benefit increases in Social Security that would keep the program even with rising prices. For Republicans, in fact, the idea of automatic indexing was fast becoming a *conservative* option, a means of forestalling interparty bidding over Social Security that would expand the program even faster than general price levels.

As an established and popular program with a strong coalition of support, Social Security almost inevitably became the vehicle for addressing a whole series of diffuse concerns about poverty and income inadequacy that, in the absence of the program, might have been handled through different means, or ignored altogether. This was in many ways ironic: Program administrators had long tried to distinguish Social Security from means-tested programs; now they were selling the program to President Johnson and Congress as the nation's leading antipoverty initiative.[57] But, in other respects, it was a logical culmination of Social Security's development. Now nearly universal, Social Security unquestionably provided broader coverage and redistributed income more substantially than did private plans. With rising numbers of Americans benefiting from the program, moreover, Social Security had a large and increasingly well-organized constituency behind it. The plight of the aged had featured hardly at all in the "rediscovery" of poverty that had sparked first Kennedy's and then Johnson's interest in an antipoverty crusade. But because they were an increasingly organized force in American politics and because the administrative means for helping them were already in place, the aged turned out to be one of the new antipoverty agenda's principal beneficiaries.

Finally, the big Social Security benefit increases surely received a boost from the general skepticism toward private plans that set in during this period. By the early 1960s, the basic agenda for pension reform was more than two decades old – an all-but-forgotten legacy of the latter years of the New Deal when Roosevelt had given up on comprehensive reform of the tax-subsidized private pension sector. Although scandals involving the misuse of pension funds by the Teamsters and other unions had prompted congressional investigations in the late 1950s, these investigations had focused narrowly on the misconduct of labor leaders and fund managers. During the Kennedy Administration, however, the broader reform agenda had new life breathed into it with the release of an administration report on private pension funds. The report, authored by a cabinet-level committee chaired by the secretary of labor, declared that "[p]rivate pension plans should continue as a major element in the Nation's total retirement security program."[58] Yet the committee recommended that private pensions be significantly reformed to make them a more effective complement to Social Security, justifying government intervention primarily on the grounds that pensions received special tax treatment. As the 1960s wore on, the pension reform movement picked up political steam and congressional advocates, notably the respected Republican Senate moderate Jacob Javits. Although pension reformers aimed to improve rather than replace private plans, they nonetheless highlighted the weaknesses of existing private arrangements and, in doing so, contributed to the growing interest in expanding Social Security.

The Reform of Private Pensions

In terms of Social Security's relationship to private pensions, the late 1960s and early 1970s marked the high tide of public and political faith in the government's ability to provide retirement income. Although political leaders rarely confronted the potential conflict between public and private pensions head on, the dispute occasionally broke the placid surface of consensus politics. In the late 1960s, Social Security Commissioner Ball himself engaged in a public tug-of-war with the program's actuary, Robert Myers, over the proper role of government relative to private pensions, with Ball arguing that a stagnant old-age insurance program was being overtaken by private plans and Myers claiming that Ball's "expansionist" agenda threatened the vibrancy of private sources of retirement income.[59] Ball's perspective, of course, won out. The large increase in benefits and the wage base – and the requirement that both be automatically raised in the future – undoubtedly "mitigated the need for supplementary benefits from private plans."[60] Moreover, in the inflationary years after 1968, the indexation of Social Security benefits all but guaranteed that the program would grow relative to private plans, which rarely included cost-of-living protections.

The less-visible struggles over pension policy during the late 1960s, however, were more favorable to the private system. Emblematic was a major attempt to revise the tax code's integration guidelines that was launched by the Johnson Administration in the wake of the 1965 Social Security amendments. As discussed in the last chapter, the integration rules allowed private plans to take into account Social Security benefits in determining whether tax-favored plans discriminated in favor of high-income personnel. The rules themselves were numbingly complex, but one feature was absolutely crucial to corporate pensioning: Tax-favored plans could pay benefits to employees with incomes above the wage base even if they paid little or nothing to workers with incomes below the wage base. The exact amount that plans could pay to high-income personnel was determined by an arcane number called the "excess percentage" – essentially, a ratio showing how large a share of prior earnings a pension could pay to high-income employees if it excluded lower-income employees.[61] Closely monitored by employers and insurers, the excess percentage had stood at the extremely generous level of 37.5 percent since 1950, meaning that corporations could replace 37.5 percent of prior earnings for workers with incomes above the wage base even if they provided no benefits to the rest of their workforce.[62] In 1966, however, the Treasury Department attempted to revise this percentage sharply downward to reflect more accurately the return on employer contributions under Social Security. The new limit would be 24 percent – a reduction so large that Treasury officials debated whether it could be achieved at all through the normal regulatory process.[63]

Treasury insiders were right to worry. The opposition was immediate, overwhelming, and effective. For three years, the Department was subject to a withering barrage of complaints from the business community, the central theme of which was that the new regulations would sharply raise the cost of existing plans or require that benefits for upper-income personnel be cut. Of 1,800 comments on the proposed regulations that were received in 1966, for instance, all but one (from a union) were opposed.[64]

Marion Folsom, himself in retirement, wrote to remind the Department that "it has been government policy to encourage these supplementary plans."[65] Wilbur Mills expressed concern about the "drastic changes in regulations pertaining to the integration of pension plans and Social Security."[66] Even Commissioner Ball was skeptical, noting that a better approach was to raise benefits and the wage base so that supplementation was unnecessary for most workers.[67]

In the end, the Treasury Department capitulated. Although it reduced the excess percentage, it devised so many escape hatches for existing plans as to make the new limits virtually meaningless. No change in any plan would be required before 1972, and even at that date, all workers who entered a plan under the old standard would be exempt from the new rules. Most important, employers were allowed "to guarantee an employee that, as a minimum, he will receive a pension no smaller than what he would have received based on the plan's existing benefit formula and his current wage level."[68] *Business Week* crowed that although the 1966 proposal had "threatened to make it dramatically more expensive for companies to maintain generous pensions for their more highly paid employees," the new rules meant that "many plans will not have to be changed at all, and many others can be brought into compliance with the new nondiscriminatory rules at little or no cost to employers."[69] Apparently unsatisfied even by this, the Nixon IRS quietly returned to the 37.5 percent standard after the Social Security Amendments of 1971. If pension reform advocates needed a sign that the private system had become entrenched, that its sponsors and beneficiaries were ready to mobilize against any threat to inherited commitments, that the complexities and obscurities of the law gave the opponents of change overwhelming advantages over the great mass who might have stood to benefit – they could not have chosen a better example than the 1966–69 integration debacle. It would take the marriage of tax policy with public concerns about the security of existing plans to inject political life into the embattled reform movement and pass the Employee Retirement Income Security Act of 1974.

ERISA was meant to address many of the concerns raised by the distribution of private plans. Using the favorable tax treatment of pensions as the entering wedge for enhanced regulation, the architects of ERISA hoped to make pension promises more secure, more portable from job to job, and more equitable in their distribution. The reforms initiated by ERISA fell into three categories. Foremost were a series of participation, vesting, and nondiscrimination requirements designed to broaden and secure pension benefits by ensuring that they did not discriminate in favor of the highly paid or incorporate long length-of-service requirements. Second were funding requirements and fiduciary standards designed to shore up pension finances and make benefit promises more certain. Third was a quasi-governmental insurance program – the Pension Benefit Guaranty Corporation – designed to reduce the risk of pension forfeiture when corporations failed by mandating that all firms participate in a common insurance pool financed by flat premiums. This final provision was sought primarily by organized labor, which wanted a safety net to protect the many underfinanced negotiated plans. In essence a social insurance scheme for workers in declining industries, this governmental underwriting of private pension risk marked a novel departure for the federal government in the pension field.

With the exception of pension insurance, however, the labor movement was largely hostile to ERISA, which it saw as an imposition on private plans. So too were leading business groups, and for much the same reason.[70] President Johnson had shelved pension reform proposals near the end of his administration because of business opposition (his labor secretary, in an act of defiance, sent them on to Congress anyway). Congressional old-timers like Mills pointedly warned Johnson that "they would not touch the issue with a ten-foot pole."[71] Indeed, it was difficult to find any interest representative or pension expert outside of Congress or the White House who wholeheartedly supported the legislation. Reflecting on "the fierce opposition to any Federal legislation by most employer groups and the wavering support by much of organized labor," the *New York Times* described the passage of the bill as a "minor miracle."[72]

Why then did ERISA pass? Part of the reason was that business influence in the legislative process was at a postwar nadir during the period, as business groups fought back similarly far-reaching regulatory proposals in a host of other areas, such as consumer safety and environmental protection.[73] Mobilizing the public through media-savvy campaigns, Ralph Nader and other consumer activists burst into the political spotlight in the late 1960s, allying themselves with a new breed of liberal congressional "entrepreneurs" who were generally disdainful of the oligarchic committee system personified by Mills and his fellow "barons." In many respects, pension reform followed the pattern of other major regulatory laws of the period. It was congressionally centered, with Johnson reluctant to move and Nixon in favor of far more modest legislation. It was pushed along by a high-profile "focusing event," in this case, the spectacular 1964 collapse of the Studebaker auto plant and its 11,000-member pension plan.[74] It benefited from a well-timed book that captured and channeled these concerns, Merton Bernstein's 1964 *The Future of Private Pensions*, which argued that the flaws of private pensions were so endemic that only an expanded Social Security program could redeem them.[75] And it received long-term and committed sponsorship from a crusading congressional entrepreneur, Senator Javits, who articulated the interests of the diffuse and unorganized beneficiaries of pension reform and who built support for his bill largely outside of top congressional circles. In its adherence to the playbook of entrepreneurial politics, ERISA was very much of a piece with other large-scale regulatory initiatives of the early 1970s.[76]

And yet none of this is sufficient to explain ERISA's enactment. Ultimately, the law must be viewed as an outgrowth of the pressures created by federal intervention itself – a legislative response to the forces unleashed by previous public policies. As we have seen, federal law initially took the form of tax relief. Though not the original intent of the law, the effect of the pension tax subsidy was to make pensions an attractive form of compensation, particularly for employees and corporate officers in higher income tax brackets. The Roosevelt Administration proposed comprehensive regulations designed to push pension benefits down the wage ladder, but Congress, with industry behind it, rejected most of the proposals and instead endorsed weak and porous participation and nondiscrimination requirements in the Revenue Act of 1942. These regulations were slightly augmented by the 1958 Federal Welfare and Pension Plans Disclosure Act (WPPDA), which improved plan reporting. In the years prior to the passage of ERISA, however, the regulatory situation essentially stood where it had before the Roosevelt campaign, with the growing tax subsidy a largely hidden nonissue.

Pension tax favors became an issue again in the 1960s, thanks to the tireless efforts of Stanley Surrey, a player in the 1942 debates and assistant Treasury secretary under Presidents Kennedy and Johnson. It was Surrey who popularized the label "tax expenditures" and, along with other Treasury officials, "highlighted the massive size of tax expenditures and underscored the kind of economic inefficiencies, distortions, and unfairness that tax expenditures created."[77] Besides being deeply involved in the debate over the tax code's pension integration rules in the late 1960s, Surrey was the key Treasury official on Kennedy's cabinet-level pension reform committee, which, not surprisingly, concluded that "[t]he basic justification for the indirect public subsidy involved in favored tax treatment lies in the social purposes served by private pension plans."[78] Surrey and his colleagues emphasized that the favorable tax treatment of pensions was costly and avoidable; other possible approaches had been available in 1942 and were, in theory, still available.[79] They also produced and disseminated, for the first time, credible estimates of the forgone tax revenue that resulted from the pension subsidy and other breaks. In doing so, they brought tax expenditures into the open as they had not been before. In 1974, the year of ERISA's passage, Congress responded by requiring that a "tax expenditure budget" be produced as part of the reformed budget process.

By highlighting the real costs of the pension tax subsidy, the new scrutiny of tax expenditures provided a rationale for ERISA's enhanced regulation of private plans. Yet more than that, it helped launch a renewed debate in Congress over the distribution of the pension tax subsidy and of the plans that it encouraged – a debate that formed the basis for the eventual legislative compromise reached. Not since the early 1940s had the pension tax subsidy been openly questioned, but it became a central issue in the floor debate over pension reform.[80] Critics conceded that repealing the tax subsidy was politically impossible. As one Treasury memo put it, "[P]eople and institutions with an entrenched selfish interest in the present [pension and profit sharing] structure are probably too strong politically to permit us to cut it back."[81] Instead, critics proposed various restrictions on the ability to claim pension tax breaks and called for stricter participation requirements and stronger regulations governing the distribution of contributions within plans.

From the other direction, conservatives and the Nixon Administration contended that the benefits of pensions were worth the public cost and, instead of major new restrictions, called for incremental reforms coupled with the creation of tax-favored Individual Retirement Accounts (IRAs) and the expansion of so-called Keogh plans, tax-favored retirement accounts for the self-employed created in 1962 at the instigation of Representative Eugene Keogh of New York. The final bill was a compromise between these conflicting demands. It did little to restrict the value of the tax subsidy, but greatly tightened the regulations surrounding it. It included IRAs, but limited them to workers not currently covered by pensions and set ceilings on the amount that could be put in them. Primarily, however, the architects of ERISA addressed the criticism of the tax subsidy by seeking to require that plans justify their expense by better fulfilling their public purpose of providing secure retirement income.

This was perhaps the most remarkable policy inheritance: the belief that it was the job of the federal government to fulfill private pension expectations. When, in the early 1940s, the Roosevelt Administration had proposed many of the same regulations eventually embodied in ERISA, pension sponsors mobilized workers who had pension coverage *against* the proposal, which was billed as a vast threat to the institution. In the late 1960s and early 1970s, however, ERISA received an unexpected push from pensioners and potential plan recipients, who, at crucial moments, pressed their demands on Congress for protective federal legislation.

Public concerns about pension security – and the growing expectation that government would address them – first became apparent after the passage of the Welfare and Pension Plan Disclosure Act, which "unleashed a nonstop torrent of mail from employees all over the country complaining over their failure to qualify for private pension benefits and mistakenly assuming that the WPPDA provided some remedy in this respect."[82] Public anxiety grew unmistakable, however, during the debate over pension reform. Rather than trying to broadcast the fine points of pension policy, advocates of the Javits bill stoked public outrage with a string of "horror stories" about pensioners who had been denied their promised benefits. When the Senate Finance Committee tried to preempt the debate over ERISA by seizing and dismembering Javits's legislation in 1971, for example, "letters of protest poured into Congress from all over the country," and members of Congress returning home to their districts "discovered a great many disturbed and resentful constituents . . . for whom they had no ready answers."[83] Most Americans now looked to the government for their core retirement income, and most had come to expect that private plans would also be secure. If business or labor could not safeguard such expectations, then government – already a regulator and financier of the private system – would need to step in.

Yet it is important to emphasize what ERISA did not do. As Michael Gordon, Javits's key aide, would later note, "The complaints of participants and beneficiaries could have led to a virtually brand new private benefit system. . . . [S]uch a system might have borne a remarkable resemblance to Social Security itself."[84] Despite the general reformist spirit of the period, however, nothing even remotely close to this was considered. Even the harshest critics of the private pension system acknowledged that it was an entrenched feature of the postwar social welfare landscape, an organized counterpart to Social Security on which millions of workers relied. Significant challenges to the voluntary system – such as major restrictions of the pension tax subsidy or mandates on employers to provide private pension coverage – never received serious attention.[85] Because these were not viewed as realistic options, the fundamental public–private framework that had arisen after World War II was never really up for debate.

To fixate on what the fight over ERISA was about, therefore, is to forget what it was not about and, in doing so, to miss the ways in which the feedback effects of private social provision had narrowed the range of choices before policymakers. ERISA not merely failed to challenge the public–private framework already in place, but in important respects, it was an attempt to strengthen and fortify that framework. Javits declared that the bill's purpose was to "strike a balance between the clearly-demonstrated needs of workers for greater protection and the desirability of avoiding the homogenization of pension plans into a federally-dictated structure that would discourage voluntary initiatives for further expansion and improvement."[86] Signing the bill, President Ford described ERISA as a "model of what can be done by Government to improve the lives of Americans within the private sector without harming the dynamics of our free enterprise system."[87] Far from a repudiation of the strategy of relying on private actors to fulfill national social goals, ERISA represented its explicit affirmation. And because ERISA continued the nation's reliance on the voluntary private benefit system, it would prove largely powerless to buffet the dramatic winds of pension change unleashed after its passage.

In retrospect, 1974 was the last moment when serious reform of private pensions was on the political agenda. In 1981, a presidential commission on pension policy that had been authorized by President Carter proposed requiring that all employers provide a minimum pension to their workers, a policy already in place in other nations.[88] Coming as it did at the height of the Reagan era, this mandatory pension proposal was dismissed even more summarily than the Chamber of Commerce's 1953 plan for restructuring Social Security had been. The 1970s thus passed without a large-scale debate regarding the overall relationship between public and private pensions. Like the large Social Security benefit increases of the period, ERISA was something of an aberration in the history of pension policy – a reflection of a liberal climate and a favorable economic context that evaporated like a mirage in subsequent years. Although retirement income adequacy temporarily emerged as a major issue, public officials failed to reevaluate the basic system for securing retirement income that previous policies had created. It was, in fact, a measure of the embedded character of America's public–private retirement income system – and of the persistence of the faith that private pensions could be made to fulfill public purposes – that many of the same legislators who voted for Social Security expansions that threatened the growth of private plans then immediately turned around and affirmed the need for a larger and more secure voluntary pension institution. Yet this, in a nutshell, was the course of postwar retirement security policy. The political struggle over retirement income arrangements had first centered on the relationship between public and private plans, then on the effects of federal tax policy, then on the character and control of private plans themselves. After ERISA, the overall structure of U.S. retirement security policy – a federal insurance program backed up by private plans that were subsidized and regulated to fulfill similar ends – seemed a vibrant example of public–private partnership. But there were growing cracks in the cooperative façade, as political and economic events would soon starkly reveal.

The Erosion of the Postwar System

The long era of private pension expansion came to a sudden halt in the 1970s, just as ERISA was signed into law. After a century of growth, pension coverage stabilized at its current level of about 40 percent of the private civilian workforce. At the outset of this turbulent era, it was common to blame the troubles facing pensions on the expansion of Social Security or, more often, on ERISA itself. Yet, while ERISA surely contributed to the movement of employers away from defined-benefit plans, the persistence of the pension system's difficulties suggests that deeper economic forces were at play – the stagnation of real wages, the decline of organized labor, the movement of employment from manufacturing to services. As these tectonic shifts in the American economy proceeded, the private pension system over which business, labor, and the state had struggled for more than four decades eroded, challenged by a complex array of alternative plans and a new political enthusiasm for highly individualized tax-favored accounts.

At the time of ERISA's passage, Javits grandly proclaimed that the law was "the greatest development in the life of the American worker since Social Security."[89] "Even a substantially liberalized Social Security," he argued, "could not do the job private pensions can do." Under the legislation, "private plans will develop more rapidly than in the past because the Congress will have assured that pension promises are kept and reasonable expectations built upon those promises are not disappointed."[90] These hopes have not been realized. As Figure 3.1 shows, employer pension contributions have significantly decreased as a share of compensation. (Benefits, however, have continued to rise, as workers covered in the past enter retirement.)

Just as striking is the decline of traditional defined-benefit pensions, under which workers receive fixed retirement allowances based on such factors as past earnings and Social Security benefits, and the rise of defined-contribution plans, under which benefits simply reflect accumulated contributions plus interest. Between 1975 and 1989, the number of Americans in defined-contribution plans ballooned from 11.5 to 36.5 million, while the number in defined-benefit plans inched up from 33 to 40 million (a worker may be covered by both types of plans).[91] Today, virtually all new plans are of the defined-contribution variety, which by

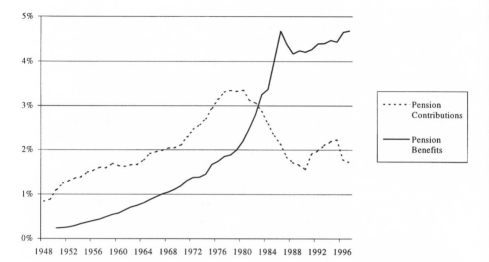

Figure 3.1. Pension Contributions and Benefits as a Share of Total Compensation, 1948–1996. *Source:* Author's calculation from national income and product accounts.

their nature are not integrated with Social Security. Whatever advantages a plan sponsor once gained from Social Security expansion, employers are not receiving them when they operate defined-contribution plans.

In contrast with Social Security, today essentially universal, employer-sponsored pensions continue to be much more prevalent and generous in some sectors of the economy and among some employment groups than others. Coverage is higher in unionized firms than in nonunionized firms, in public employment than in private employment, in larger firms than in smaller firms, and in the manufacturing sector than in the service and retail sector. It is higher among full-time workers than among part-time workers, among men than among women, among older workers than among younger workers, and among workers with longer tenure than among workers with shorter tenure.[92] These differences provide part of the explanation for recent drops in coverage. Since the 1970s, the portion of the workforce employed in manufacturing has fallen, employment in the service and retail sectors of the economy has increased, part-time and short-tenure employment has become more prevalent, and levels of unionization have plummeted – from 27 to 13.9 percent of workers between 1979 and 1998.[93]

More generally, the fall in pension coverage after 1974 was symptomatic of a broader decline in the wages and employment outlook of less-

Table 3.3. *Sources of Income Among Aged Units, 1990*

Source of Income	Share of Aged Units Receiving (%)
Social Security	92
Pensions	44
Asset Income	69
Earnings	22

Note: Aged units are married couples and unmarried individuals aged 65 or older. Pension figure includes private pensions and annuities, regular distributions from individual retirement accounts, government employee pensions, and Railroad Retirement benefits.
Source: John R. Woods, "Pension Benefits Among the Aged: Conflicting Measures, Unequal Distribution," *Social Security Bulletin* 59, no. 3 (1996): 4.

educated workers.[94] The likelihood that a worker's employer will offer a pension plan decreases sharply with income, as does the probability that a worker will actually be included in a plan.[95] And while the overall receipt of benefits is increasing as the pension system matures, the value of pension benefits to currently employed workers is actually growing more unequal. Between the early 1980s and the mid-1990s, the value of pension benefits to current workers dropped in every income group, but by far most rapidly among the lowest-paid workers.[96]

The skewed distribution of private pensions is also reflected in the income of the aged. Substantially fewer elderly Americans receive occupational pensions than receive Social Security benefits, as Tables 3.3 and 3.4 summarize.[97] For Americans in the lowest income category, occupational benefits are extremely rare – a disparity reflected in the benefits that aged Americans receive. If total workplace retirement benefits are arrayed across income levels, as is done in Table 3.5, only 1 percent go to aged Americans in the lowest fifth of the income distribution, while nearly 57 percent go to those in the top fifth. Again, Social Security benefits are distributed far more evenly: 10 percent go to the poorest fifth of aged Americans, while 26 percent go to the richest fifth.[98]

In short, ERISA has achieved one of its central goals: making defined-benefit plans more secure. But it has failed to fulfill its second major aspiration: substantially shifting benefits toward lower-paid employees.

Table 3.4. *Sources of Income Among Aged Units, by Quintile of Income, 1990*

Income Quintile	Social Security (%)	Pensions (%)	Asset Income (%)	Earnings (%)
Lowest	85	8	31	5
Second	96	26	56	9
Third	95	50	75	19
Fourth	95	67	87	29
Highest	88	67	96	46

Source: John R. Woods, "Pension Benefits Among the Aged: Conflicting Measures, Unequal Distribution," *Social Security Bulletin* 59, no. 3 (1996): 5.

Table 3.5. *Distribution of Aggregate Income Among Aged Units, by Source and Quintile of Income, 1990*

Income Quintile	Aggregate Income (in Billions) and Its Distribution Across Income Quintiles			
	Social Security	Pensions	Asset Income	Earnings
	$171.10	$87.60	$117.40	$82.10
Lowest	10%	1%	1%	Less than 1%
Second	18	3	3	1
Third	22	12	8	5
Fourth	25	27	18	15
Highest	26	57	70	78
TOTAL	100	100	100	100

Source: John R. Woods, "Pension Benefits Among the Aged: Conflicting Measures, Unequal Distribution," *Social Security Bulletin* 59, no. 3 (1996): 6. Percentages may not total to 100 percent due to rounding.

Integration rules continue to permit defined-benefit pension formulas to offset expected Social Security benefits. Although defined-benefit plans have lost ground, integration has actually become more common in such plans since the early 1980s.[99] More important, despite the tightening of federal law, it remains the case that the distribution of plan coverage and benefits can be quite unequal and still satisfy federal standards.

Above all, however, the mixed record of federal regulation is rooted in the voluntary character of the private pension system. Employers are not obligated to provide pensions, and many undoubtedly would not, absent favorable tax policies. This brings us to the essential dilemma raised by subsidized private benefits: Any regulation that drives up costs or interferes with corporate goals will undoubtedly reduce the incentive of employers to sponsor benefits in the first place. As Texas Republican Bill Archer argued during the House debate over ERISA:

> This voluntary nature of the system means that employers can either establish a plan or not. They can either end a plan or continue it at reduced or increased benefits. . . . As a result, it is important that . . . we not so increase the costs of these plans . . . that employers will find it financially impossible to continue providing pension plans for their workers or will decide . . . against establishing them in the first place.[100]

Expert disagreement endures, but ERISA does seem to have decreased the attractiveness of defined-benefit plans and may also have contributed to the general fall in pension generosity. At the least, it has done nothing to stem the decline in coverage or the movement away from defined-benefit plans toward less-secure income guarantees.

Finally, whatever ERISA's effects, existing tax breaks for private pensions will always favor better-paid employees, simply because their value is so much greater for workers in higher tax brackets. The fact that pension coverage is distributed so unevenly only magnifies these inherent differentials, creating striking disparities in the distribution of federal tax favors. In 1987, the Congressional Budget Office estimated that "about half of the extra income from the tax advantages of present plans will go to those in the top quartile of the income distribution, and over 70 percent to those in the top half."[101] Current Treasury data show that two-thirds of the nearly $100 billion in tax subsidies for retirement savings (including both private pensions and IRAs) accrue to that the top 20 percent of the population, while only 12 percent accrue to the bottom 60 percent.[102] For most American workers, the promises of the private pension system that ERISA aimed to reshape continue to ring hollow.

The Limits of Reform

If the effects of ERISA have been ambiguous, the direction of political debate in the years after its passage is no less difficult to characterize. The outpouring of pension regulation has not stopped. Nearly every major tax act since ERISA has included new restrictions on the practices of defined-benefit pensions, many aimed at bolstering coverage among lower-wage workers and women and at reducing the degree to which the wealthy benefit from special tax subsidies. In 1983, for example, Democrats and Republicans lined up behind legislation backed by women's groups to make it easier for workers who moved in and out of jobs or took long periods of time off to earn pension benefits. Repeated changes have been made as well in the Pension Benefit Guaranty Corporation to protect the program against huge potential losses and address charges that the scheme favored older unionized industries. Yet alongside this effort to police what remains of the defined-benefit pension system, new pressures to free employers from regulation and provide additional tax-favored savings vehicles for well-off employees have gained force. Public policy toward pensions has also been affected by general changes in tax policy. The Tax Reform Act of 1986 and President Bush's tax cut of 2001, for example, reduced some of the general tax advantages of pensions by lowering marginal tax rates.[103] In contrast, the tax bills of 1990 and 1993, which raised rates to attack the federal budget deficit, moved policy in the opposite direction.

Nonetheless, two overarching trends can be discerned in this complex policy domain. The first is the continued unwillingness or inability of policymakers to reconsider the basic public–private regime established in the immediate postwar era. Despite the evident financial difficulties of both Social Security and occupational pensions, and despite the ongoing shift in the balance between them, policymakers have made only incremental adjustments to the overall framework of U.S. retirement security policy. Although Social Security and private pensions have each separately emerged as topics of debate, they have been considered almost entirely in isolation from each other, and major reforms have been thwarted – whether those reforms would entail major cutbacks in Social Security, on the one hand, or the elimination or substantial restriction of tax breaks for employer-provided pensions, on the other.

The travails of Social Security are best known. As the economy slowed and inflation rose in the 1970s, enthusiasm for the program dimmed. For the first time, the program's finances showed a sizable near-term deficit, and politicians scrambled to place the trust fund on firmer financial footing. The most dramatic reforms occurred in 1983: a bipartisan compromise containing a mix of tax hikes, benefit cuts, and expansion of covered workers that passed just days before the program was projected to run short of funds.[104] One should not overstate the extent to which actual retrenchment of Social Security resulted from these efforts. Indexation of benefits, after all, ensured that they would continue to rise with inflation, and despite conservative talk of radical reform and an ill-fated Reagan proposal for benefit cuts, Congress never considered eliminating or even substantially shrinking the program. Nonetheless, the shift in the politics and perception of Social Security was real, as was the erosion of the program that did occur. Earnings replacement rates dropped ten percentage points between 1980 and 1990 (and will fall to their pre-1970 levels early in this decade). The era of expansion was over. Henceforth, neither employers nor workers would enjoy the windfall gains that had made liberalization of the immature program so irresistible.

On balance, however, the 1983 reforms were a victory for the program's defenders. Although Reagan had carefully avoided Social Security during the campaign, he had spoken out against the program in the past and his administration included "several of the strongest supporters" of radical reform.[105] On Capitol Hill, conservative Democrats seemed willing to join Republicans in demanding major cuts. But in 1981, with a politically maladroit proposal engineered by Budget Director David Stockman, the Reagan administration stumbled badly. Fearing (correctly) that the Reagan budget would lead to huge deficits, Stockman sought $46 billion in savings through cutbacks that would directly affect almost 60 million people.[106] The congressional response was immediate: Democrats savaged the proposal, Republicans disowned it, and the Senate unanimously condemned it. After the fiasco, a more incremental compromise – one that minimized and obscured direct costs while delicately reducing benefits in the future – emerged from a secretive bipartisan commission. The new package was a clear legislative success, giving politicians the cover they needed to endorse painful changes. But it was an equally clear loss for opponents of the program. As Stockman ruefully put it, "The centerpiece of the American welfare state had now been overwhelmingly ratified and affirmed in the white heat of political confrontation."[107]

Though congressional Republicans believed that the Reagan proposal cost them seats in the 1982 midterm elections, the defeat of more far-reaching changes had less to do with the actual mobilization of beneficiaries than with the structure of Social Security itself. With insolvency looming, pay-as-you-go financing turned the conservative dream of a privatized system into a political nightmare. Any attempt to allow people to opt out of the system – whether altogether or into private accounts – posed the insuperable problem of where to come up with the money to pay promised benefits, and in a fiscal context that required painful cuts, not the financing of transition costs. Privatization was thus a prime example of what Arnold, in his study of congressional action, terms "politically infeasible policies" – "policies that would impose large and direct early-order costs on their constituents," which members of Congress "vote against . . . in anticipation of future punishment, not in response to current pressures."[108]

These constraints are better comprehended in comparative perspective. Not all advanced industrial nations have mature pay-as-you-go systems. Indeed, at roughly the same time that Reagan was retreating, the Thatcher government in Britain took advantage of the immaturity of the nation's second-tier pension to create an opt-out provision that has significantly moved the program toward tax-subsidized, government-regulated private accounts.[109] Among mature pay-as-you-go and contributory systems, however, such radical changes are to date unknown, and the dominant pattern has instead "been a series of accommodations to austerity, typically modest in scale for current retirees and those near retirement but often substantial for future generations."[110] A recent comprehensive review of pension reform in industrialized democracies concludes: "When a pension system has been in place for many years, people develop expectations about the level of benefits that they should receive. These expectations are especially powerful in contributory systems, where a sense of 'entitlement' to a given level of 'earned benefits' is likely to arise."[111] As the Reagan administration learned, this is a textbook description of the U.S. old-age insurance program. The 1983 reforms produced significant changes to Social Security that will continue to decrease the generosity of the program over the coming decades. But while the 1983 rescue signaled that Social Security would no longer expand as it once had, it also indicated that it would remain America's core provider of retirement security.

Social Security's status as the untouchable "third rail of American politics" has become the stuff of legend. Far less recognized (but no less impressive) has been the remarkable tenacity of the favorable tax treatment of retirement plans. No episode better illustrates this resilience than the landmark Tax Reform Act of 1986. Although the 1986 rate cuts reduced the value of the pension tax expenditure, it is more notable that the basic tax treatment of pensions – and, indeed, of most other fringe benefits – was left intact in this otherwise extremely comprehensive reform bill. Despite the large amount of revenue that could have been raised, most politicians and policy advisers viewed the idea as either ideologically anathema or political suicide. Strikingly, not one of the major proposals considered in the run-up to the Tax Reform Act eliminated the exclusion of pension contributions and trust income from taxation – not the "pure" tax reform proposals introduced by maverick Democrats and Republicans, not the ambitious initial blueprint by the Reagan Administration known as "Treasury 1," not the legislation actually introduced by Reagan or hammered out by congressional leaders, and certainly not the legislation eventually passed and signed into law.

Some confusion regarding this topic lingers in secondary accounts, so the point deserves emphasis.[112] The 1982 Bradley-Gephardt proposal that helped spark interest in tax reform did propose to limit tax-free employer contributions for health insurance. But with the exception of tighter contribution and benefit limits, pension tax subsidies were left untouched. The Republican-sponsored Kemp-Kasten bill was even more timid, sparing several fringe-benefit exclusions targeted by Democrats Bradley and Gephardt. Neither bill eliminated the special tax treatment of pensions or IRAs. The Treasury I proposal that was secretly developed by the Reagan Treasury – now remembered for its conceptual purity and political naïveté – eliminated many exclusions for fringe benefits and capped the amount of employer-provided health insurance exempt from taxation, but "the tax-preferred status of pension plans was retained and opportunities to save in tax-advantaged individual retirement accounts (IRAs) were substantially increased."[113] Given that the pension tax exemption was the largest social welfare expenditure in the tax code at the time, this was a remarkable concession.

Yet even these reforms were deemed far too politically risky by White House politicos and congressional leaders, who immediately took the tax treatment of all fringe benefits off the bargaining table. The Republican chair of the Senate Finance Committee, Robert Packwood, was perhaps most vehement in opposing the taxation of fringe benefits, making it "clear from the start that his top goal was to save the tax-free status of employee fringes, especially health insurance."[114] Packwood's hard-line stance was backed up by a powerful coalition of insurance companies, business groups, and labor unions bent on preserving the tax-subsidized private welfare system that had become firmly institutionalized in the postwar era.

Equally revealing, the character of tax changes that *did* occur suggests that the potentially enormous political costs of major reform were always the preeminent concern. To be sure, the reduction of tax rates in the legislation reduced the value of the pension tax expenditure, just as the rise in tax rates during and after World War II had increased it. But the very diffuse and indirect nature of the effect made it difficult to pin blame for the change, and even if taxpayers had noticed the shift, they were not likely to be too upset about what was, after all, merely a reflection of the lower marginal tax rates they paid. In stark contrast, eliminating the tax exemption for private benefits would have imposed immediate and traceable costs on all Americans covered by pension plans – effects, moreover, to which scores of pension consultants, business lobbies, and labor organizations were sure to draw immediate and fierce attention. Even in the context of a massive overhaul of the tax code, legislators were not willing to take this step. Instead, as in 1974, regulations were tightened – and the tax treatment of pensions was left untouched. As a legal scholar summarized the situation in 1987, "The massive reexamination of the income tax expenditure in 1974 and again in 1986 imply that, although Congress is willing to go quite far in an effort to ensure some distribution of benefits to low- and moderate-wage earners, tax expenditures to continue the private pension system seem to have become politically untouchable."[115]

The one major exception to this story of political temerity was individual retirement accounts, which were significantly scaled back in 1986 just five years after being dramatically expanded in 1981. IRAs were one of the most divisive subjects in the debate over tax reform. With expansive IRAs supported by Reagan and the majority of the House, the issue was not resolved until the very end. The contentiousness of IRAs – and their eventual vulnerability – had several sources, all of which tellingly distinguished them from corporate pensions. Most obviously, the pool of beneficiaries and third-party defenders was far less extensive with regard to IRAs than with regard to employer-provided pensions: 17 million tax filers claimed IRA deductions, compared with the more than 60 million pension participants.[116] Perhaps more important, IRAs were particularly vulnerable because they were generally acknowledged to benefit upper-income workers even more than employer-sponsored plans. The "fairness" of tax reform was a major concern, and restricting IRAs proved to be one way to balance out the gains upper-income taxpayers enjoyed from the legislation.[117] Perhaps most critical, restricting eligibility for IRAs deprived prospective beneficiaries – an unorganized potential group – far more than it did current account holders. Unlike pensions, which were ongoing employer operations that might be critically affected by tax changes, IRAs were individual accounts that could be added to (or not) at the discretion of eligible taxpayers. And because no one ever considered taking away the special tax status of accounts already established, the question before Congress was always limited to whether *future* IRA tax deductions would be restricted.[118] This was very different from taking away tax favors for employer-provided pensions or imposing taxes on the interest income of existing IRA accounts.

In any case, Congress did not eliminate IRAs, nor did it return them to their limited 1974 status. Instead, the final compromise reached retained IRAs for taxpayers without employer-sponsored plans (the original conception) while restricting IRA eligibility for higher-income workers with employment-based retirement protection. Under this change, 15 percent of taxpayers previously eligible for the IRA deduction lost it entirely, while another 12 percent saw the amount they could deduct cut back.[119] The resulting reduction in IRA deductions was indeed sizable, although the budget savings were more modest and, as we shall see shortly, the cost of IRAs is slated to expand dramatically due to legislative changes in the late 1990s.[120]

The preservation of virtually all of the special tax provisions for private retirement plans offers a fine example of Paul Pierson's claim that "policies may create incentives that encourage the emergence of elaborate social and economic networks, greatly increasing the cost of adopting once-possible alternatives and inhibiting exit from a current policy path."[121] Just as the imperatives of blame avoidance made reform of Social Security perilous, the fear of mobilizing opposition by threatening existing private benefits doomed any interest that tax reformers might have had in challenging the embedded and costly network of subsidies for private retirement benefits in the tax code, even though many believed that these subsidies were inequitable. The most important indicator of path dependence in both cases is not the political struggles that took place, but those that did not – not the alternatives debated, but those that were deemed infeasible even before they reached the level of broad public discussion.

The Privatization of Risk

If the preservation of the essential policy features of the postwar pension system is one important characteristic of recent policy debates, the second major trend cuts in a somewhat different direction. Although Howard argues that "the very incoherence of policy making has been one of the defining features" of pension policy in the last two decades, it is possible to detect a fairly consistent shift in policy, driven by a resurgent conservative strain in American politics, as well as by changes in the economy and the corporate uses of pensions.[122] The tax and deficit battles of the 1980s signaled the beginning of an ongoing tug-of-war over retirement income policy between two increasingly homogenized and polarized parties, with Republicans seeking to create and liberalize individual retirement options and Democrats fighting to place new restrictions on existing pension tax subsidies and limit the top-heavy skew of individual accounts. The overall thrust of policy has nonetheless been in the more conservative direction – toward the expansion of tax-favored retirement plans and toward the loosening of restrictions both on eligibility for them and on the purposes for which they can be used.

The path of IRAs since their inception illustrates the overall pattern. Included in ERISA as a retirement savings device available only to workers without private pension coverage, IRAs were expanded and made available to all workers during the tax-cutting frenzy of the early

1980s. Then, as just discussed, IRAs were saddled with new eligibility restrictions during the loophole-closing efforts of 1986. In 1997, however, IRA participation requirements were liberalized to return them to their pre-1986 levels, permissible uses of the accounts were broadened to include education and housing expenses, and a new plan – called the "Roth IRA" after its chief sponsor Republican Senator William Roth of Delaware – was created that would require account holders to pay taxes up front and then avoid all future taxes on their accounts (including estate taxes). Since, at the time, 70 percent of Americans already had incomes low enough to establish traditional IRAs, the main effect of these changes has been to make tax-favored accounts even more available and attractive to upper-income households. At the same time, the back-loaded structure of their benefits means that they entail very little lost revenue in the short term, postponing their costs to the later years when account holders (and their heirs) are allowed to escape taxation on their investment amounts and interest. Between 1997 and 2002, for example, Roth IRAs are expected to entail just $1.8 billion in lost revenues. Yet the costs will total an estimated $18.4 billion between 2003 and 2007, with $5 billion of the amount coming due in 2007 alone and the expected expense rising by a half billion a year thereafter.[123] This simultaneously facilitates the budgetary acceptability of Roth IRAs in the short term and protects them from revision in the long term, because once taxpayers have paid taxes up front, the political pressures to permit tax-free accrual and withdrawal will be overwhelming.

The story of 401(k) plans is different but similar.[124] The legislative language that would become Section 401(k) of the tax code appears to have been merely intended to clarify the tax status of certain types of profit-sharing plans that had been under Treasury Department scrutiny for some time. In these schemes, employers allowed workers to elect whether to receive compensation in cash, which would of course be taxed as income, or to have the same amount contributed to a profit-sharing plan, which was exempt from taxation. Treasury officials had been struggling with similar sorts of arrangements (known as "cash or deferred arrangements" or CODAs) ever since the mid-1950s, when the IRS had ruled that they could be permitted on a limited basis with stringent requirements. But in the early 1970s, the Treasury Department proposed a new regulation that would have considered these contributions taxable as employee income, on the straightforward grounds that it was workers, not employers, who effectively made the contribution. Responding to employers' complaints, however, Congress temporized, imposing a moratorium on new plans but allowing all existing ones to continue. The 401(k) language finally emerged in the Revenue Act of 1978, a major revenue revision that reflected the growing tax-cutting fervor of the late 1970s. Engineered by Republicans and conservative Democrats over the Carter Administration's protests, the Act cut capital gains taxes and extended or increased scores of tax expenditures.[125] And, in Section 401(k), it swept aside the Treasury objections and cleared the path once again for CODAs.

Section 401(k) passed completely beneath the radar screen of public debate. Certainly no one in Congress recognized how significant it would become. The House and Senate committee reports indicate that members of Congress believed they were merely restoring the status quo ante. "The [401(k)] provision," the Joint Tax Committee estimated, "will have a negligible effect upon budget receipts."[126] Like the pension tax subsidy, the 1978 language only emerged as a critical policy shift in conjunction with the actions of private employers and pension consultants. In 1981, a private benefits expert named Ted Benna saw the potential for such a shift and pressed the IRS to rule that the provision extended to pension arrangements in which workers voluntarily put aside their own wages, much as in an IRA.[127] Benna's conclusion was not self-evident: The early rules had finessed the issue of whether workers truly had control over the elective contributions that employers made, but if workers put aside their own salary, there could be no denying that what was being proposed was to allow firms to set up tax-free plans into which workers directly contributed. The Reagan IRS, however, agreed with Benna, and in the wake of the 1981 ruling, corporate sponsorship of 401(k) plans burgeoned. Responding to concerns about distributional fairness and lost revenue, Congress restricted the amount that could be put into such plans and tried to limit their bias toward upper-income workers. But the limits on contributions remained much larger than those pertaining to IRAs, and the law allowed 401(k) account holders to borrow against their plans and to receive their accumulated contributions as a lump sum if they left their job. In 2001, as part of President Bush's tax reduction plan, congressional Republicans successfully pressed for further dramatic liberalization of 401(k) and IRA rules and the creation of "Roth 401(k)s" similar to Roth IRAs.[128]

In the go-go economy of the 1990s, 401(k)s rose from obscurity to become one of the most celebrated vehicles of private retirement savings. In 1999, *Money* prominently touted their creation in a special section of the magazine devoted to the history of the mutual fund industry. But perhaps equally revealing, the *Money* timeline placed the origins of 401(k)s in 1975, when "ERISA, the law establishing the 401(k) plan, passe[d] after years of advocacy by Ted Benna." [129] This distorted history of pension tax law is notable only in the degree to which it reflects both the hidden origins of 401(k)s and the extent to which private retirement accounts have come to tower over the traditional defined-benefit plans that ERISA was originally meant to bolster. The origins of 401(k)s represents a pure case of subterranean politics – a small provision of a tax code whose massive effects were unforeseen by its founders and whose meteoric growth provoked virtually no political debate. Most Americans with 401(k) plans hardly think of them as a form of public social policy. Most who do not receive them are no doubt unconcerned about the increasing revenue loss that the 401(k) exclusion represents. With any visible social program, such lack of concern would be remarkable. In 1978, Congress had created the opening for a dramatic change in the structure of the private pension institution. Yet, even as the term "401(k)" was transformed from an obscure section of the tax code into a national obsession, few seemed to recognize that government was implicated at all.[130]

The emergence and explosive growth of 401(k) plans and IRAs over the past decade represents one of the most important developments in the history of U.S. pension policy, in part because these tax-favored retirement accounts are the direction in which private retirement benefits, and perhaps even Social Security, are heading. During the 1980s, contributions to IRAs, 401(k)s, and Keogh plans for the self-employed rose from 7 percent of total pension contributions to more than 50 percent.[131] By 1994, contributions to 401(k) plans exceeded contributions to all other types of pension plans combined, and they continue to grow in prominence.[132] Not surprisingly, the assets of 401(k)s and IRAs have expanded at a breathtaking pace, as Figure 3.2 indicates.

Behind this transformation lies a new conception of pensions, for these retirement accounts have few of the characteristics of either Social Security or older defined-benefit plans. Unlike traditional pensions – which are voluntary for firms but not generally for those firms' employees – these accounts are voluntary for individual workers. Participants have a significant degree of control over investment choices, and benefits are often paid as a lump sum upon achievement of a specific age and, increasingly, can be accessed for purposes besides retirement. These provisions raise concerns about the ability of such accounts to provide secure retirement income, particularly for lower-income workers. Because these accounts are voluntary, many younger and poorer employees who are offered them choose not to participate or contribute little. The risk of poor investment decisions or bad financial luck falls entirely on participants – as became painfully clear in 2001, the first year to see an overall negative return on 401(k) plans.[133] And evidence suggests that most lump-sum distributions are not spent on a retirement annuity or rolled over into other retirement savings vehicles.[134]

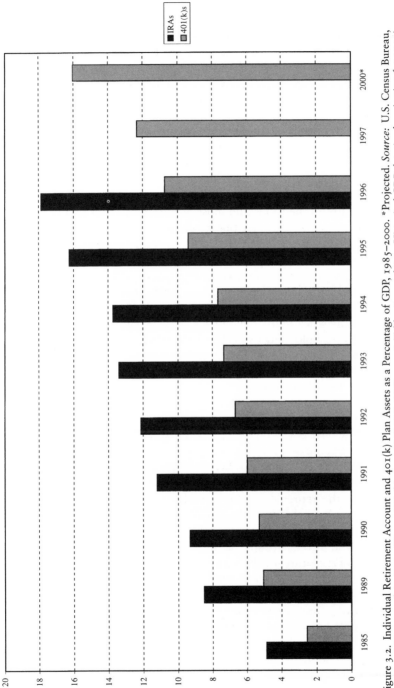

Figure 3.2. Individual Retirement Account and 401(k) Plan Assets as a Percentage of GDP, 1985–2000. *Projected. *Source:* U.S. Census Bureau, *Statistical Abstract of the United States* (Washington, D.C: U.S. GPO, 1999), Tables 851 and 852. Historical GDP data (and projection for 2000) from Congressional Budget Office, *The Economic and Budget Outlook: 2000–2009* (Washington, D.C.: CBO, 2000), Tables F-1 and I-4.

The spectacular collapse of the Enron Corporation in 2001 highlights another risk of individualized retirement plans: the potential for massive income losses that arises when pension accounts are invested too heavily in the stock of the employer sponsoring a plan.[135] On the eve of its bankruptcy, Enron was America's seventh largest corporation, and workers at the company had more than 60 percent of their 401(k) holdings invested in the firm's soaring stock, in part because Enron, like many corporations, matched employee contributions to 401(k) accounts with company shares. Then, Enron's stock price plummeted – from a high of nearly $100 a share to just 28 cents when the pension fund liquidated its holdings in November 2001 – and overnight, thousands of Enron's workers lost both their jobs and most of their retirement savings. These events were a harsh reminder that in defined-contribution plans, losses due to company failure are not federally insured, as is the case with traditional defined-benefit pensions. Nor does federal law place limits on the amount of the sponsoring company's stock a defined-contribution plan can hold (traditional plans cannot hold more than 10 percent of their assets in company stock). Indeed, over half of corporations that have company stock in their employees' 401(k) plans meet or exceed the 10 percent threshold, and 18 percent have more than 50 percent of plan holdings in company stock. This is dangerous investing in any context, but devastating when the investment is in the very company a worker depends on for regular income.

Much as the implosion of Studebaker's pension plan dramatically made the case for government insurance, the Enron experience will likely provoke new restrictions on plan practices regarding company stock. But even fairly draconian limits – which will be fiercely opposed by employers as a threat to the continued health of 401(k) plans – will do nothing to change the broader drawbacks of defined-contribution pensions when it comes to the retirement security of lower-income workers, most of whom do not have the opportunity to invest in a 401(k) plan in the first place. Tables 3.6 and 3.7 summarize the distribution of IRAs and 401(k)s across age and income groups. Because eligibility, participation, and contributions all rise dramatically with income, highly paid workers account for a disproportionate share of total 401(k) contributions. For example, if all workers had been eligible for and contributed equally to 401(k) plans in 1995, employees with annual incomes below $15,000 would have accounted for roughly 15 percent of total contributions, while those with incomes above $75,000 would have accounted for approximately 10 percent. The actual shares, in contrast, were 0.7 percent and 35.3 percent, respectively.[136]

The strength of the stock market in the last decade helps explain the enthusiasm for individualized investment accounts. But the shift must

Table 3.6. *Share of Workers Participating in 401(k) Pension Plans, 1991*

	Age				
Annual Income	25–35 (%)	35–45 (%)	45–55 (%)	55–65 (%)	All (%)
Less than $10,000	4.1	6.5	1.5	6.7	4.5
$10,000–$20,000	9.4	13.7	8.5	9.8	10.5
$20,000–$30,000	21.2	20.7	15.9	10.2	18.3
$30,000–$40,000	29.7	27.3	19.2	26.5	26.2
$40,000–$50,000	28.7	31.6	39.7	25.6	31.9
$50,000–$75,000	39.0	36.2	42.4	43.6	39.4
More than $75,000	44.1	39.5	46.3	31.7	41.3
All	23.1	26.5	26.0	20.9	24.6

Source: James M. Poterba, "The Growth of 401(K) Plans: Evidence and Implications," in *Public Policy toward Pensions*, ed. Sylvester J. Schieber and John B. Shoven (Cambridge, Mass.: The MIT Press, 1997), 182.

Table 3.7. *Individual Retirement Account Participation, by Earnings, 1992: Among Civilian Nonagricultural Wage and Salary Workers Aged 16 and Over*

Annual Earnings	Total Workers (thousands)	Total Contributors (thousands)	Percentage Contributing
Less than $5,000	7,274	167	2.3
$5,000–$9,999	10,419	390	3.7
$10,000–$14,999	15,015	693	4.6
$15,000–$19,999	14,238	777	5.5
$20,000–$24,999	12,408	942	7.6
$25,000–$29,999	9,736	795	8.2
$30,000–$49,999	19,838	2,089	10.5
$50,000 or more	8,566	1,240	14.5

Source: Calculated from Employee Benefit Research Institute, *EBRI Databook of Employee Benefits*, 3d ed. (Washington, D.C.: EBRI, 1995), Table 3.17.

also be seen as rooted in linked economic and political developments of the 1980s and 1990s. By the 1980s, defined-benefit pensions no longer offered the attractions to employers that they had in the more stable employment climate of the 1950s and 1960s, with its strict managerial hierarchies and large unionized manufacturing firms. Nor, as Social Security's tax-to-benefit ratio grew less favorable, did employers have a strong incentive to set up integrated plans whose expense would be partially offset by the federal program. The private pension always had two faces. It was a tax-favored mechanism of personnel control, designed to encourage salaried employees with firm-specific skills to remain with an employer during their most productive years and leave when those years ended. And it was a substitute for public social protections in unionized industries, a nongovernmental means of spreading the risk of old-age dependency among a particularly vulnerable class of workers. In the 1980s and 1990s, with unionization rates stagnating, corporate hierarchies flattening, and manufacturing declining, neither use enjoyed the same relevance it once had. Indeed, 401(k)s and other defined-contribution plans are in essence little more than tax-subsidized wages, stripped of most of the managerial and risk-sharing purposes that pensions once had, not to mention the interlocking ties with Social Security that once made employment-based plans deeply dependent on the health of the public program.

No less important are the underlying political motives behind the expansion of private retirement accounts. After Goldwater's repudiation in 1964, conservatives despaired of ever effectively challenging the expansion of Social Security – and, as indicated by the large benefit increases that soon followed, their despair was well placed. Even in the early 1980s, with new market-based ideas for reform emerging out of neoclassical economics and conservative policy analysis, the push for Social Security reform was quickly crushed by the weight of past programmatic choices, and conservatives ended up bitterly accepting changes *within*, rather than *of*, the basic Social Security framework. The 1983 reforms, however, fostered a new awareness on the part of conservative critics that Social Security could only be fundamentally reformed if there existed a "parallel system" of private individual accounts that could eventually be portrayed as a viable alternative to the public program. Writing in the *Cato Journal* in 1983, the conservative policy analysts Stuart Butler and Peter Germanis advocated a "Leninist strategy" for reforming Social Security based on "a campaign to achieve small legislative changes that embellish the present IRA system, making it in practice a small-scale private Social Security system that can supplement the federal system." Butler and Germanis explained that the conservative challenge was to create a "self-generating process in the private sector . . . identical to the political process that has forced the program in the public sector to grow and serve ever larger constituencies." Expansions of tax-favored accounts would "expand the natural self-interest constituency by making IRAs more attractive to more people," and this constituency in turn "would be better able to achieve further extensions." Alongside this movement to change public policy would be an ongoing process of "education" carried out by conservatives in think tanks, universities, and government.[137]

How widely this strategy has been shared by advocates of expanded tax-favored accounts is difficult to determine. After all, these accounts have considerable appeal to the conservatives who advocate them quite apart from any submerged "Leninist" tactics. They can be sold either as tax cuts or as measures to increase national savings (although there is little evidence that account amounts represent net additions to savings), and their primarily upper-income beneficiaries represent a core voting bloc within the Republican Party.[138] Just as members of Congress who happily expanded Social Security in the postwar years did not need to endorse the grand strategy of program executives, current advocates of tax-favored savings accounts can find reasons to support this "parallel system" in electoral self-interest or philosophical conviction or long-term strategy. Nonetheless, the Butler and Germanis argument is notable for its recognition of the policy characteristics and feedback effects that fostered Social Security's expansion – not just the formation of a capable administrative infrastructure and supportive constituency, but also the features of the program that obscured its immediate costs while highlighting its benefits.

In this, would-be "privatizers" of Social Security are simply grasping the truth that advocates of Social Security learned first: The choice between private and public social policy approaches is never an unfettered one. Even as opponents of public social insurance gained the political upper hand in the 1970s and 1980s, they were unable to achieve their major goal of restructuring Social Security to increase the role of private finance and investment. Although the division over redistribution remained as sharp and enduring as it had in previous decades, the ground on which the political battle was waged shifted as the historical logic of federal policy unfolded. Politicians were fighting over many of the same issues stemming from many of the same fundamental differences between public and private social policy approaches. Yet they were doing so in a radically transformed context, one that featured two giant institutions of public and private social provision that were densely woven into both U.S. public policy and American economic life. Once-viable options had seemingly melted away, or at least become considerably more elusive, while new opportunities for change were emerging that had once been unthinkable. If the failure of committed conservatives to scale back Social Security in the early 1980s illustrated that the pay-as-you-go structure of the program still weighed heavily on the politics of the possible, the weaknesses of ERISA and the limits of tax reform showed that America's public–private framework was at least as resilient when challenged from the other direction.

Conclusion

In the United States, public policy has helped to create a sphere of private social provision that is far larger than in any other nation. Retirement pensions are no exception to this pattern. Despite the centrality of Social Security to U.S. social policy, the federal government has actively encouraged and shaped private retirement provision through a host of measures – from favorable tax treatment to regulations to the specific features of Social Security itself. As a source of retirement benefits, private plans have grown faster than Social Security since the early 1950s and now rival the program in magnitude. And yet the widespread interest in the political development of Social Security has not been matched by similar attention to the political development of private plans. Nor have the connections between these two systems featured prominently in scholarship on the American welfare state, to the detriment of a full understanding of intertwined roles of public and private benefits and the sometimes hidden, sometimes prominent, political struggles that connect them.

Federal old-age insurance benefited from weakness of credible private competitors in the 1930s, a situation solidified by the ultimate failure of the Clark amendment. Yet its slow growth in subsequent decades – coupled with the increasing value of pension tax favors and the ability of conservatives to resist major changes to them – fostered the growth of a private pension system whose distribution was markedly at odds with that of Social Security. With major expansions of Social Security off the political table during this critical period, liberals and organized labor found themselves promoting private retirement provision as a counterpart to Social Security, although along distributional lines different from the ones that business and insurance groups had defended in the years before. America's two-track framework of organized retirement protection is a legacy of these strategic and policy choices.

Conflict over this framework ebbed away after the 1940s. Yet the structure still set the broad boundaries of change. Amid the liberal climate of the 1960s and 1970s, Social Security expanded, but a frontal challenge to the public–private framework never materialized. The period ended, in fact, with the passage of ERISA, a congressional recognition of the public purposes of private pensions. When the political climate shifted in a conservative direction in the late 1970s, Social

Security weathered the storm, too, undergoing a significant but nonetheless incremental revision as politicians sought to avoid blame for unpopular changes. Throughout, the subterranean character of private pension policy and the political advantages enjoyed by tax-favored plans hindered reconsideration of the overall structure of U.S. pension policy.

America's heavy reliance on private retirement provision originated in policy decisions made more than four decades ago, during a period of unusually fierce political debate over the scope of public and private social provision. It was reaffirmed in the early 1970s in an explicit acknowledgment of the nation's two-track system. Today, however, the postwar system of private benefits is eroding without much notice as the conditions that originally gave rise to this extensive framework of private social insurance gradually fade into memory. As employers adapt to new economic realities, they are transforming the private retirement field – or leaving it behind – responding to once-obscure provisions of the tax code and to new ones surreptitiously granted. In the process, they are shifting risks from their balance sheets to workers and divorcing their own benefits from a federal system no longer capable of promising the unbeatable returns of earlier years.

As we have learned, policy commitments of the past can survive even as the forces that created them disappear. Yet the current movement toward private retirement accounts should warn us that the social insurance characteristics of private pensions will continue to grow weaker in the future, with consequences for social welfare and for the continued vibrancy of *public* social insurance that have yet to be fully acknowledged. It is the nature of private social benefits that they fail to elicit the scrutiny or debate that public programs routinely do. But now more than ever, America may need a true political debate about the place of private social provision in U.S. retirement security policy.

Part III

The Politics of Public and Private Health Insurance

I propose . . . the view that when the market fails to achieve an optimal state, society will, to some extent at least, recognize the gap, and nonmarket social institutions will arise attempting to bridge it.

– Kenneth Arrow,
"Uncertainty and Welfare Economics of Medical Care"

The choice is no longer between the traditional type of private practice on the one hand and voluntary health insurance on the other. . . . The alternative in the future is between some form of nonpolitical voluntary insured medical service, such as the state society is sponsoring, and something which will undoubtedly be much worse – state medicine, compulsory health insurance, socialized medicine, or something else.

– Medical Service Association of Pennsylvania, 1939

Instead of turning the current system, which now insures 85 percent of Americans, on its head in order to extend coverage to the rest, the plan I will outline . . . will strengthen existing coverage and focus like a laser on the remaining 15 percent, those without coverage.

– Vice President Al Gore, 2000

Introduction

In September 1993, President Bill Clinton stood before a joint session of Congress, presenting to the assembled representatives and the nation what is now remembered as the most ill-fated proposal of his presidency. Clinton's bold plan for "Health Security" was a sweeping legislative attempt to provide affordable health insurance to all Americans and, in doing so, to complete the long-unfinished business of the Social Security Act of 1935. Within a year of his dramatic speech, however, the president's plan lay in tatters, his presidency in disrepute, and his congressional majority in shambles. Although Clinton would recover from these blows (only to be mired in scandal during his second term), the cause of universal health insurance had encountered another seemingly decisive political defeat – the fifth of the twentieth century. For the foreseeable future, American medical financing would continue along the peculiar path taken in the years after the New Deal, with an incomplete patchwork of private health insurance providing the core of health protection for American workers and their families.

The demise of the Clinton plan offered up a political murder mystery with a virtually inexhaustible supply of suspects and clues. In the years since, no shortage of culprits have been accused.[1] A few appear unquestionably guilty: Clinton had a tenuous electoral mandate, a delicate congressional standing, and a flawed proposal and political strategy. But the most compelling explanation for the messy failure of the Health Security plan – the one overshadowing and underlying all others – is also the one most likely to be taken for granted. Most Americans, between 80 and 85 percent, have health insurance coverage. If they are workers, they are likely to receive insurance as a benefit of employment – an arrangement that, we shall see, has been heavily subsidized through the tax code and extensively encouraged by public policy. If they are older than 65 or very poor, they are covered by public insurance programs that fill the gaps in employment-based coverage. To be sure, private coverage has contracted in recent decades, and many Americans who have insurance are insufficiently protected or risk losing coverage. It remains the case, however, that private health insurance reaches more than two-thirds of nonelderly Americans, overwhelmingly via the employment relationship. And this means, in turn, that proposals for government-sponsored health insurance face singular hurdles – not just the opposition of a huge and resourceful private medical industry, but also the fears of insured Americans about the effect of policy changes on their existing coverage. This is the essential political dilemma faced by health reformers in the United States.

Students of health policy have long been drawn to the puzzle of why the United States is the sole advanced industrial democracy without a national health program.[2] They have paid less attention, however, to the corollary question of why the United States relies so heavily on private employment-based health insurance, assuming, not unreasonably, that this unusual state of affairs is merely the flip side of the absence of a universal government program. The argument of the next two chapters is that this reasonable assumption requires reexamination. Understanding the peculiar character of U.S. health policy requires a political and historical explanation of the rise of employment-based health plans as a regnant alternative to national health insurance – an outcome that was neither foreordained by America's liberal political culture nor an inevitable by-product of early defeats of government insurance. Endemically prone to failure, the market for health insurance had to be actively constructed by private leadership and public policy, which conjoined at critical junctures in the formation of U.S. health policy to create and bolster private institutions as a bulwark against direct state intervention.

Medicine and the Market

Open any introductory textbook on health economics and you will find a long list of reasons that health care is not like other market goods.[3] In the ideal vision of how markets should work, myriad sellers compete to provide homogenous commodities to myriad buyers, who are well informed and pay the full cost of what they consume. Although few markets actually measure up to this demanding yardstick, the health care market falls notably and irreparably short. Sizable public and private payers have concentrated purchasing power that allows them to affect prices. Patients, the "consumers" of medical care, are poorly informed relative to suppliers and insulated from the full cost of their treatment decisions by insurance. Medical providers, for their part, make many of the most expensive clinical choices, opening the door to what economists call "supplier-induced demand." And significant "externalities," both positive (the benefits to society of vaccinations, for example) and negative (the costs to society of charity care, for example), suggest that consumers do not take into account many of the larger societal costs and benefits of their purchasing decisions.

As Kenneth Arrow famously argued nearly four decades ago, the root of market failure in medical financing is uncertainty.[4] More so than perhaps any other field of enterprise, health care is characterized by imperfect information. Patients do not know exactly what services they require; insurers do not know exactly which patients will be sick or which services delivered by providers are legitimate; even medical providers operate with limited certainty that their diagnoses or prescriptions are correct. Moreover, information is not only imperfect; it is unevenly distributed or "asymmetric." Doctors know more than patients about treatment options; patients know more than insurers about their need for care. Because these asymmetries permit the better informed to take advantage of the lesser informed, they also provide incentives to the lesser informed to adopt institutional safeguards against such exploitation. The distribution of information thus influences both power relations and the structure of market institutions.

Indeed, uncertainty is implicated in each of the three central dilemmas of medical finance: *agency, moral hazard,* and *adverse selection.* The agency dilemma arises when one party contracts with another (the "agent") in the expectation that the agent will subsequently choose actions that produce desired outcomes.[5] In medical finance, the classic agency relationship connects patient and physician.[6] Lacking specialized expertise, the patient delegates decision-making power to the physician. Although this is in the patient's interest, it also creates the potential for abuse, precisely because the patient is not in a position to judge fully whether medical services are good or bad, excessive or insufficient. As Carolyn Tuohy has argued, the agency problem has historically been addressed through three archetypal responses: "hierarchy" (government control), "collegiality" (professional self-regulation), and "contract" (detailed purchasing agreements).[7] These responses correspond to the three major loci of allocation and decision making in medical care: the state, the profession, and the market.

If the classic agency problem arises in the context of clinical decision making, moral hazard and adverse selection pertain to the operation of insurance. Because the cost of medical services is high and the need for them is both uncertain and distributed unevenly, it makes sense for risk-averse patients to obtain insurance. Once insured, however, an individual faces a significantly lower price constraint at the time of treatment, creating the potential for excessive risk taking or consumption of services – a possibility referred to as moral hazard. Whether moral hazard is the result of patients seeking more care or providers seeking more income, it lies at the heart of a central paradox of health care finance: The high and uncertain cost of medical care makes insurance desirable, but insurance in turn encourages greater spending by removing some of the price barriers faced by patients and providers. No easy solution to this trade-off exists, and all systems of insurance, private or public, confront it.

Adverse selection also has its roots in the asymmetry of information between insurers and patients. An insurer wishes to offer insurance at a price that earns it profits. But at any price, those most likely to purchase insurance are those most likely to need medical care. And because those who purchase insurance know more than the insurer about their need for care, the insurer ends up with an adverse selection of risks – that is, individuals for whom the premium is low relative to their risk. The rational response for insurers in this situation is to collect as much information as possible about potential subscribers and charge differential rates based on expected risk (or even refuse to insure some people altogether), a process called "experience rating." (The alternative is "community rating," in which premiums are not linked to the characteristics of individual subscribers.) Yet experience rating is expensive, imprecise, and intrusive, and its effect is to segment and shrink insurance risk pools. In turn, the rational response on the part of individuals is to go without insurance if it is too costly given their expected risk. Yet this means that many will fall back on charity care or delay treatment until their conditions become severe and costly. With healthy individuals opting out, moreover, premiums have to be even higher for the insured, further discouraging low-income and low-risk people from purchasing insurance. Adverse selection thus makes it effectively impossible to achieve broad-based coverage through individual private action, and it provides a strong rationale for the pooling of risks through group insurance offered at relatively similar rates to all subscribers.

Common Problems, Divergent Responses

These three dilemmas – agency, moral hazard, and adverse selection – are deeply interrelated, stemming as they do from the common conditions of imperfect and asymmetric information. Together, they define a standard set of problems confronted in all advanced industrial democracies. In this sense, it can be said that there is a distinctive "politics" of health care finance, a politics defined in part by the basic economic exigencies of medical care. In all wealthy nations, rising medical costs and public expectations have created demand for insurance, which in turn has created pressures for control of costs, which in turn has raised the question of who should exert such control in light of the problem of agency: the market, the profession, or the state. In all these nations, private insurance markets have been plagued by adverse selection, which has increased pressures for regulation or socialization of insurance. In all these nations, in sum, citizens and leaders have followed the script laid out in the opening words of Kenneth Arrow, creating nonmarket institutions that, to some extent at least, "bridge the gap" between what the invisible hand of the market produces and social optimality demands.

And yet, not only is this response far from automatic, it has also differed greatly across nations. Insurance programs in rich capitalist democracies range from decentralized voluntary arrangements to mandatory workplace-based schemes to highly centralized compulsory systems of coverage. Consider the alternative models found in Britain, Canada, and the United States – three wealthy democracies closely connected by history, culture, and language. Although Britain initially followed the lead of Germany in creating a national contributory program for manual workers based on existing mutual insurance funds, it had by 1948 abandoned the German model to become the first Western government to adopt a program of free and universal entitlement to publicly provided medical care, the British National Health Service. Canada, by contrast, did not establish a nationwide insurance program until 1957, and then, in keeping with developments in the Canadian provinces, only for hospital care. When Canada finally consolidated its comprehensive insurance program in the early 1970s, it followed neither German nor British precedent but instead allowed the provinces to be the sole insurers for most medical services. The United States, of course, does not have national health insurance despite recurring political debates over the subject. In 1965, President Lyndon Johnson and his allies capped off a long, ideologically charged battle for government health insurance with the passage of Medicare for the elderly (and, later, disabled) and Medicaid for segments of the poor. But all subsequent efforts to extend coverage to the remaining uninsured, including the campaign launched by President Bill Clinton in 1993, ended in failure. Given this diversity, it is implausible to maintain that national health systems are simply a reaction to the common failures of the market. Rather, national responses have been driven by politics as well as economics, by concerns about equality and social justice as well as the efficiency considerations raised by Arrow and others.

In comparative perspective, in fact, the United States is clearly an exceptional case, making tenuous any attempt to use American policy patterns as a guide to the inexorable logic of the market. For all the diversity across advanced industrial democracies – between Britain and Belgium, the Netherlands and Norway, Austria and Australia – the United States is the only nation in which publicly guaranteed health insurance coverage is not universal or close to universal, and it is one of only a few in which the state does not play an active role in controlling national medical costs.[8] It is, in addition, the only nation in which most workers obtain coverage through tax-subsidized voluntary plans sponsored by employers, and the only nation in which public programs are limited to the elderly, disabled, and poor – groups with limited ability to obtain insurance through employment-based insurance. And, not coincidentally, it is also the only nation in which a sizable proportion of the population – in 1998, some 44 million Americans, or more than 16 percent of the population – has no insurance coverage whatsoever and thus must forgo care, pay for it directly, or fall back on charity provision.

Table 13.1 provides a fuller picture of American health policy exceptionalism, comparing spending and coverage across the affluent nations of the OECD. Although American health spending is by far the highest in the world, less than half of that spending comes from public sources, compared with an average of almost three quarters in the other nations. Moreover, well less than half of the population in the United States is eligible for public insurance coverage, compared with an average of 98 percent in the other nations. Given the centrality of public health insurance to the modern welfare state, health policy represents the area of greatest distinctiveness in American social provision, distinguishing the United States not only from the expansive welfare states of northern Europe, but also from other so-called liberal welfare states, such as Britain and Canada. Indeed, if the U.S. public sector paid for a proportion of American medical costs similar to the level found in other nations, aggregate public social spending in the United States would be more than a quarter again as large as it currently is.

The Comparison with Pensions

U.S. health policy is unusual not just in cross-national perspective; it is also distinctive when compared with the other major domain of domestic social legislation most closely associated with the welfare state, retirement security policy. As we have seen in Part I, the New Deal ushered in a contributory federal program of old-age insurance, which

Table I3.I. *Health Spending and Coverage in Selected OECD Countries, 1995*

	Total Health Spending as Percentage of GDP, 1995	Payments by Private Group Insurance, as a Percentage of GDP, 1993	Mean Annual Increase in Share of GDP Devoted to Health Spending, 1980–1995	Public Medical Spending as Percentage of Total Health Spending, 1995	Share of Population Covered by Government Insurance, 1991
Canada	9.7	NA[b]	2	71.4	100%
France	9.9	NA	1.8	80.6	99
Germany	10.4	0.7	1.8	78.4	92
Italy	7.7	NA	0.7	69.6	100
Japan	7.2	NA	0.9	78.4	100
Netherlands	8.8	1.34	0.7	77.1	69
New Zealand	7.1	NA	1.2	76.4	100
Sweden	7.2	0.1	-1.7	81.6	100
United Kingdom	6.9	0.33	1.4	84.3	100
United States	14.2	5.15	3.1	46.2	44
OECD Mean[a]	8.3	NA	1.1	73.7	95

[a] Excluding Turkey and Luxembourg, as well as the five most recent additions to the OECD: Poland, Hungary, Korea, Mexico, and the Czech Republic.
[b] Not available.
Source: Organization for Economic Cooperation and Development, *OECD Health Data 1997* [computer database] (Paris: OECD, 1997); Willem Adema and Marcel Einerhand, "The Growing Role of Private Social Benefits," *Labour Market and Social Policy – Occasional Papers No. 32* (Paris: OECD, 1998), 51; and Organization for Economic Cooperation and Development, *OECD Health Systems: Facts and Trends* (Paris: OECD, 1993), Table 7.2.1. Coverage figure for the Netherlands is for 1990.

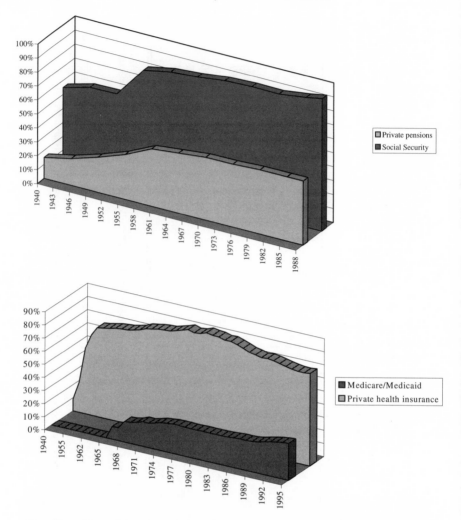

Figure I3.1. Share of Americans Covered by Public and Private Health Insurance and Pensions, 1940–1995. *Note*: The Social Security figure for 1940 is actually from 1939, for 1945 from 1944, and for 1950 from 1949. *Source*: Compiled from House Committee on Ways and Means, *1998 Green Book* (Washington, D.C.: U.S. GPO, 1998), 8; U.S. Department of Labor, Pension, and Welfare Benefits Administration, *Trends in Pensions 1992* (Washington, D.C.: U.S. GPO, 1992), 75; Health Care Financing Administration, "Medicare Enrollment Trends, 1966–1997"; Subcommittee on Health and the Environment of the Committee on Energy and Commerce, *Medicaid Source Book: Background Data and Analysis* (Washington, D.C.: U.S. GPO, 1988), 20; Social Security Administration (SSA), *Annual Statistical Supplement*, 1997 (Washington, D.C.: SSA, 1998), 327; Health Insurance Association of America (HIAA), *Source Book of Health Insurance Data* (Washington, D.C.: HIAA, 1998), 39.

expanded immensely in the decades after World War II to provide relatively comprehensive retirement protection to nearly the entire population. In contrast, proposals for government health insurance were tabled during the New Deal, and postwar American politics proved to be a graveyard for national health insurance, yielding to a large-scale government response only in 1965, three decades after the Social Security Act – and then only to the partial coverage expansions embodied in Medicare and Medicaid. As Figure 13.1 shows, coverage under public and private sources in the health and pension domains represent almost mirror images of each other. In the pension field, public coverage spread wider earlier and remains broader today. In the health field, the exact opposite is true.

This is puzzling, and not just because health insurance was actually higher than pensions on the agenda of many reformers in the early part of the twentieth century. It is also puzzling because health care is arguably plagued by greater failures of the market than is retirement income. If state provision of social goods reflects the market's inability to achieve social optimality, as claims about market failure imply, then it is all the more surprising that the public sector plays the leading role in the pension field, while the private sector dominates medical finance.

The simplest answer to this puzzle would emphasize the unique power of the medical profession. Unlike many social programs, government health insurance involves the purchase of services from a clearly defined and often extremely resourceful profession. As Ellen Immergut argues in her trenchant analysis of the development of national health insurance in Europe, struggles between doctors and the state over health policy reflect a very real conflict of interest between the sellers and buyers of medical services.[9] As the sole sellers of valuable services, doctors are inevitably threatened by the concentration of purchasing power in the hands of one or a few powerful buyers. They therefore have good economic reason to resist universal government health insurance even when its short-term effect may be a rise in their incomes. And, in fact, in no Western nation with national health insurance did physicians unreservedly welcome the extension of state control. This is certainly true of the United States. Although American physicians briefly flirted with compulsory health insurance in the mid-1910s, the medical profession was fiercely opposed to any public scheme by the time the Roosevelt Administration considered including health insurance in the Social Security Act.

Still, it is not true, as Immergut suggests, that doctors in all countries and at all times have been equally hostile to government intervention. In no country has the medical profession wholeheartedly embraced national health insurance. Yet the depth of professional opposition and the alternatives that physicians have supported have varied significantly both over time and across nations.[10] Moreover, these differences appear to reflect not only strategic political considerations but also real variance in doctors' preferences rooted in contrasting market structures. In explaining why physician attitudes differ across time and space, two factors seem to be crucial in all cases: the profession's assessment of its prospects in the political arena and the availability of acceptable private alternatives to government insurance. Throughout the industrialized world, physicians made preemptive concessions when the political deck was stacked against them and fortified their opposition when physician-dominated private insurance emerged as a viable option. Situated at the intersection of a threatening political arena and a sometimes hostile economic market, the medical profession responded differently to proposals for national health insurance according to the threats and opportunities that it faced from each quarter.

To understand why the medical profession succeeded in blocking national health insurance in the United States as it did not in other nations, we therefore need to understand why each of these two crucial factors conduced to its benefit. Why did the medical profession have such marked political success in the American political arena, and how did employment-based private insurance emerge as a viable alternative to a comprehensive government plan? These questions will bring us back to the three recurring themes of this book: the critical role of regulatory, tax, and subsidy policies in bolstering private social provision; the importance of conservatives and moderates in government and the private sector in bringing these policies about; and the influence of the timing and sequence of policy change on the balance of public and private responsibility and, ultimately, on the preferences of political actors themselves.

The comparison between pensions and health care provides crucial analytic leverage for drawing out these themes, demonstrating both the common path-dependent processes at work in the two areas and the specific forces that eventually fostered policy divergence. Despite all the real differences between health and pension policy, the contours of government and private action in the two areas emerged through similar political and historical processes and contained common elements. To be sure, the resistance of the medical profession created a distinct political barrier to public action in health policy, as did the administrative complexity of the field. As previous chapters have shown, Social Security also benefited immensely, and uniquely, from the special expansionary tendencies of pay-as-you-go pensions. Nonetheless, both policy areas witnessed a fierce and ongoing struggle over the respective roles of public and private social insurance. And in that struggle, the division of political actors was similar, though not identical, across the two areas. Conservatives in government, insurers, and business interests were wary of new government social programs, and they worked assiduously to promote private social benefits – a campaign in which they eventually found themselves allied with a labor movement unable to achieve its ends through political channels.

In the health field, however, these efforts took place in a markedly different policy context than they had in the pension field. In particular, the failure of the Roosevelt Administration to squeeze health insurance through the "window of opportunity" created by the New Deal had fateful consequences. During the same period in which Social Security took root and flourished, proposals for expanded government health insurance consistently failed. By the late 1950s, advocates of publicly sponsored insurance had winnowed their aims to the goal of building on private coverage to provide security for groups noticeably left out of the employment-based system – the elderly and the poor. The overall policy pattern was one of generous public assistance for voluntary health insurance and private medical care, with the direct government role restricted to insuring the most costly and vulnerable segments of the population. Moreover, because private health insurance played such a primary function in the health sector, efforts to regulate or reshape it faced overwhelming political resistance, not to mention the staggering fiscal costs of moving the funding stream for a highly subsidized medical-industrial complex from private to public auspices. Indeed, at the same time that the Employee Retirement Income Security Act imposed strict new federal regulations on private pensions, it actually exempted a growing share of private health plans from the state regulations that had traditionally governed health insurance. And from the early 1970s on, nearly all the leading proposals for universal health insurance – whether President Nixon's or President Clinton's – would try to extend the employment-based private insurance system rather than replace it.

Perhaps the most critical and overlooked manifestation of the divergence between the two areas can be seen in the schismatic response of employers. An increasing body of cross-national evidence suggests that employer orientations toward collective social provision are not fixed or universal and that these orientations likely play an important role in shaping a nation's social welfare regime.[11] Virtually all of this research, however, examines variance in employer preferences across nations. What the American case strikingly suggests is that employer preferences may also vary across policy areas within a single country. Over time, employers in the United States adopted nearly opposite stances toward Social Security and government health insurance, precisely because of the different role that each played relative to private benefits. While employers and conservatives came to accept and sometimes even support Social Security as a foundation for tax-favored private pensions, they remained unalterably opposed to national health insurance, which threatened developing private protections. As private insurance spread through the workplace, unions, too, became increasingly less supportive of government insurance for working Americans, which looked less desirable than the generous negotiated benefits that many union members received.

Thus, in both health and pension policy, early policy choices and strategic decisions successively hemmed in proponents of a new policy path, who increasingly came to accommodate rather than challenge existing institutions of social provision. In the same way that many conservatives would concede after World War II that the clock could not be turned back on Social Security, many liberals would conclude, as Edwin Witte expressed it in the early 1950s, that the United States had taken "the voluntary route . . . on health insurance and it's not going to be necessary to cover the working people."[12] The passage of Medicare, often taken as an unqualified repudiation of the voluntary system, was in fact a reluctant concession to Witte's logic. America's biggest government health plan was not only limited to the aged – the only program of its sort in the industrialized world. It not only handed over much of the government's administrative and reimbursement duties to private insurers, particularly Blue Cross/Blue Shield. But it also reinforced the notion that private health insurance could meet the needs of the vast bulk of working Americans. In effect, Medicare and its legislative partner Medicaid removed from the voluntary system the very groups – the elderly, disabled, and indigent – whose plight the private sector unquestionably could not address. And with that plight went much of the pressure for national health insurance.

The historical sequence of policy change was, in short, a decisive factor in circumscribing the options available to health reformers in the post–New Deal decades. With an ongoing flow of largely hidden government support, the private social protections offered by employment-based health insurance became, in many respects, as firmly institutionalized and politically sacrosanct as did the public social protections offered by America's cherished program of old-age insurance.

4

Seeds of Exceptionalism: Public and Private Health Insurance Before 1945

In the United States, neither public nor private health insurance had any substantial presence before the twentieth century. The federal government ran only one true health insurance program: the U.S. Marine Hospital Service, established in 1789.[1] By political default as well as accepted constitutional understanding, state governments were charged with the task of regulating health insurance. But there was little to regulate and even less political inclination to do so. At the dawn of the twentieth century, the principal source of "sickness insurance" was mutual aid organizations, which devoted only a small portion of their modest funds to medical protection. Less cohesive and politically engaged than their European counterparts, U.S. fraternal organizations were also, it appears, less involved in sickness insurance – then the stock-in-trade of European associations, especially Britain's extensive network of friendly societies.[2]

American fraternals were not alone in their reluctance to address medical needs. Among other potential sources of private health security – trade unions, employers, commercial insurers – none provided more than token protection or reached more than isolated pockets of American workers. Instead, it was life insurance and its poorer cousin "industrial insurance" that dominated the American imagination and market.[3] Sold by armies of agents as protection against a pauper's burial, industrial insurance was at once insufficient and inefficient, with less than a third of total receipts paid out as benefits.[4] Yet it was also wildly popular: At the turn of the century, industrial insurance covered more than 13 million workers, financed more than $20 million in burial benefits annually, and required an estimated 416 million home visits a year to collect the small weekly premiums.[5] With more than three-fourths of policies written by America's two life insurance behemoths, Metropolitan and Prudential, industrial insurance's dramatic reach was a reminder of the distinctive prominence of commercial life insurance in fin de siècle

America – and the comparative weakness of sickness and health protections.[6]

The years before World War II, however, unleashed two critical developments that would change the face of health care debates in the United States and elsewhere: the increasingly successful political pressure for government-legislated social insurance and the growing interest of commercial insurance carriers in health and sickness coverage. The second development was in many respects an outgrowth of the first, and in the United States, where agitation for social insurance failed to yield legislative fruit, it paved the way for the initial halting development of private health insurance. But it would take a third critical development to make voluntary insurance a true presence – the intersection of rising medical costs with the calamity of the Great Depression. While national health insurance continued to founder, a network of employment-based hospital insurance plans spread throughout the nation, buoyed by favorable enabling legislation and propelled forward by lingering fear of state control. The political defeats of the early twentieth century were not caused by the widespread presence of private medical protection, but they did contribute mightily to its subsequent emergence.

Sickness Insurance in Europe and America

The general absence of medical insurance in turn-of-the-century America cannot be read simply as a sign of the failure of the market to supply it. Few commercial insurers, it is true, believed the business a viable one, and fraternal societies did, in fact, face serious problems with adverse selection caused by the defection of younger members from mutual risk pools.[7] No less an authority than the president of the Prudential Insurance Company opined that "under present conditions the operations of an industrial company must of necessity be limited to the assurance of a certain sum payable at death."[8] But the primary reason for health insurance's meager presence was that, at the time, medical care cost and did little. The medical risk that workers feared most was not the expense of treatment, but the shock to family income caused by spells of sickness or disability. In most nations, therefore, sickness insurance was just that – a means to replace wages during periods of incapacity. Only later, as medical care's efficacy and costs increased, did the financing of treatment become the central aim of insurance. The United States was thus extreme but not unusual in the extent to which coverage for medical services remained on the fringes of early social welfare activity.

Nonetheless, when social insurance began to spread across Europe at the end of the nineteenth century, sickness protection was among the movement's most prominent examples. It was sickness insurance, after all, that was at the heart of the breakthrough that is usually treated as the founding moment of the welfare state – Germany's 1883 law mandating worker participation in mutual sickness funds and requiring employer contributions.[9] By the outbreak of World War I, most Western European nations had some kind of sickness insurance program.[10] The British National Insurance Act of 1911, for example, featured an insurance plan similar to the German model that required lower-income workers to enroll in friendly societies, with physician services funded through independent government committees. Not all European nations, however, followed the German lead by compelling membership and contributions. The more common first step was to offer direct subsidies to mutual societies in an effort to increase their reach and effect, a move justified by the ideal of "subsidiarity" – the notion that social purposes were best achieved through government assistance of communal institutions.[11] In most nations, however, these initial subsidies deepened into full-fledged mandates or outright government sponsorship.[12]

The United States, by contrast, took a singular path with regard to both social insurance and state subsidization. European governments took existing organizations of communal risk pooling and turned them to state ends. In contrast, American proposals for compulsory coverage encountered repeated legislative defeats, and health insurance emerged from the rubble as a private alternative to both public protections and older informal institutions of mutual aid. America's private health plans were thus not sickness funds of the European variety, with their rhetoric of working-class solidarity and their distrust of medical providers. They were institutions of commerce, protective of the prerogatives of medical providers, and allied in most cases with conservative opponents of national health insurance. Although they enjoyed favorable regulatory treatment and public subsidies, the obligations upon them were minimal. And the special dispensation that they garnered aimed as much to bolster a separate track of voluntary protection as to serve broader state goals. In these contrasts lay the opening gulf between American and European medical finance that would later become a yawning chasm.

To explain the initial breach, however, it is plainly impossible to point to private health protection, scarce, inadequate, and uncertain as it was. Nor can the failure of public social insurance in the United States be simply chalked up to the enduring American suspicion of government and attendant celebration of voluntary social provision. Although the state was vilified and voluntary forms of provision lauded, this was true in other nations that adopted compulsory insurance and does not explain why American proposals – which, in fact, attempted to harness existing mutual societies – failed so consistently and completely. Nor, finally, can these initial defeats be viewed, as commentators have tended to see them, as unambiguous proof of the political strength of physicians, employers, insurers, and labor leaders hostile to state involvement. Interest-group opposition was neither immediate nor universal, and it was effective less because of the intrinsic strength of the involved parties than the massive constraints that reformers faced due to the distinctive constitution of American political power.

The most important cause of legislative inaction, in short, was institutional – the weakness and fragmentation of the federal government and the dispersion of authority across the states, which in turn enhanced the power of mobile business enterprises opposed to new mandates or taxes. The institutional marks on American debates can be seen most clearly in the contrasts among Britain, Canada, and the United States. In the unitary parliamentary system of Britain, leaders of the Liberal Party who were fearful of losing working-class voters to the growing Labour Party were able to press through the National Insurance Act of 1911 over the squabbling opposition of vested groups, though not without making significant concessions to established interests. Although the Canadian federal government acted later, it was able to build on early moves toward public insurance made by provincial governments under the control or influence of leftist third parties. These efforts were assisted by the Canadian federal government's policy of fiscal equalization across the provinces, which attenuated fears of capital flight that might otherwise have prevented provincial leadership.

The United States, however, had neither a strong center of federal power nor subnational governments willing and able to take the lead, neither disciplined parliamentary majorities nor politically effective leftist third parties. Its decentralized federalism, anemic administrative capacity, separation-of-powers structure, powerful conservative judiciary, and winner-take-all electoral rules all conspired to stalemate reformist movements while strengthening the hand of employers. Before the New Deal, progressive reformers had no choice but to push for social insurance programs at the state level, where conditions were far less propitious than they were in Britain, or than they would in the Canadian provinces after World War II. American reformers had to coordinate their efforts across far-flung and diverse states. They had to move their proposals through bicameral legislatures, past independently elected governors, around powerful (and business-friendly) state courts – and, at times, past such roadblocks as state referenda as well. Most important, they had to overcome fears that social policies raising taxes or imposing new mandates on business would lead employers to relocate or precipitate a decline in private investment.[13] The potent dangers that redistributive social reforms posed for state economies and budgets meant that business-opposed policy changes were extremely unlikely to pass.

In the United States, as in Britain, compulsory health insurance first became a prominent political issue during the early 1910s.[14] In 1912, Theodore Roosevelt, running on the plank of the newly formed Progressive Party, campaigned on a platform that endorsed compulsory health insurance. But although Roosevelt's 27.4 percent of the popular vote represented the strongest result by a third-party candidate in U.S. history, Roosevelt's splitting of the Republican vote merely ensured the victory of Democrat Woodrow Wilson, and the Progressive Party wilted from the national scene, an enduring reminder of the dilemmas of third parties in American politics.

After Roosevelt's defeat, the mantle of reform was taken up at the state legislative level by the American Association for Labor Legislation. Supported by many state labor federations, though not the national American Federation of Labor, the AALL pledged in 1916 to lobby for the passage of a health insurance proposal modeled after the German system. Leaders of the AALL believed that health insurance was crucial, not only because it would enhance worker security but also because new levies on employers would encourage preventive measures in the workplace. In its emphasis on prevention, the health insurance campaign was closely patterned after the AALL's successful legislative drives for a federal law prohibiting the use of poisonous phosphorous in the production of matches and for the enactment of workers' compensation laws in numerous states. These early successes left members of the AALL confident that they would have little trouble convincing state leaders to pass health insurance programs, which they believed were much more urgently needed than workers' compensation laws had been.

But the success of workers' compensation was not a good guide to the likely fate of compulsory health insurance. The former had been supported by corporations tired of expensive litigation; the latter was unambiguously opposed by employers and "involved a proud profession, not simply the writing of checks for disability pensions."[15] Although the AALL started its crusade with impressive speed, the momentum of its campaign soon stalled and opponents quickly throttled its proposals in state after state. Leading the fight were employers, commercial insurers, and local medical societies.[16] Allied with them were fraternal organizations fearful that compulsory insurance would displace their role or impose new costs.[17] In California, even Christian Scientists joined the chorus of opposition. After the Russian revolution and America's entrance into World War I, the opposition took to denouncing the AALL bill as "pro-Bolshevik" and "pro-German."[18] In California, a referendum on a constitutional amendment enabling the proposal was crushed amid "wartime hysteria."[19] In New York, the AALL bill managed to gain Senate approval but was then promptly muzzled by the Assembly speaker, a Republican industrialist who swore never to let the bill reach the floor.[20]

Much has been made of the political ineptitude of the AALL and the stridency of the rhetoric surrounding the debate.[21] But it is hard to see how either mattered very much given the institutional constraints the AALL faced. The members of the AALL were not powerful leaders within a centralized national state. They were not representatives of disciplined political parties. Nor were there mechanisms for federal–state cost sharing in the United States similar to those that helped Canada's provincial leaders overcome the constraining effects of federalism. The AALL desperately tried to raise simultaneous interest in its bill in as many states as possible, but in only two – New York and California – did its proposal make any headway. Perhaps if the war had not interceded, the AALL campaign would have fared better. But considering that no other major social programs passed at the state level during this period, this seems highly unlikely.[22]

As intense as the resistance and rhetoric were, then, they were less critical to the defeat of compulsory insurance than the fundamental institutional obstacles that reformers had to surmount.[23] Had it not been that state politicians feared the flight of business from reformist states, the demands of opponents would have had considerably weaker effect. Had it not been that interest groups felt little threat from powerful leaders or disciplined majorities, they might have seen the need to temper their incendiary rhetoric or make the best of legislative inevitabilities. As it was, the AALL was influential enough to set state political agendas, but not to move to enactment proposals that threatened business confidence. With legislation caught in limbo, opposition had time to build, critics to refine their arguments, and interest-group opponents to sense their common cause. If the ideal of voluntarism played an important role, it was mainly to solidify the goals and strategic alliances that were adopted by the foes of compulsory insurance in the face of the AALL's institutionally grounded vulnerability. Voluntarism was an attractive symbol and effective rallying cry precisely because of the weakness of the American state.

Origins of the Voluntary Insurance Movement

The inglorious demise of the first campaign for compulsory health insurance did not leave the terrain unchanged for future legislative efforts. By trying and failing to enact public protections, the AALL predictably soured reformers on the prospect of touching the hornet's nests of organized interests again. Immensely more important, the debate over the AALL proposal helped unite and define the interests of a constellation of groups that might otherwise have found themselves in conflict. Employers, insurers, and doctors did not, after all, always see eye to eye. Organized medicine viewed with deep concern any medical plan operated by companies, and it was only slightly less troubled by the movement of private insurers into the field. These splits had led AALL leaders to believe that they could gain physicians' support for a proposal that excluded commercial insurance plans, much as the British Liberals had managed to buy off doctors by funding physicians through independent government committees. But as it became clear that government action was not in the cards, the diverse elements of the opposition submerged their differences to embrace a vague but unifying principle: Health insurance, if it were to exist, must be kept voluntary and nongovernmental. Whatever divided insurers, employers, and doctors was overshadowed by this simple negative goal – during the debate over compulsory insurance and after.

The most well organized of these groups was unquestionably the medical profession, which emerged from debate over compulsory health insurance bristling with political confidence and vigilant against future threats. American doctors, it now seems clear, were ripe for the sharp turn against government that occurred in their ranks during this period. Of all Western countries in the early twentieth century, the United States had perhaps the most underdeveloped government presence in medical care.[24] What experience doctors had with government was almost invariably negative. During World War I, for example, many states expanded workers' compensation laws to include medical benefits, and doctors complained that the rates were inadequate.[25] More important, American doctors did not face the great problem that British doctors did of having to struggle against widespread lay-controlled purchasers like friendly societies.[26] Instead, doctors generally set their own fees, adjusting them to reflect the income of their patients.

The campaign against the AALL proposal was a turning point in the development of the American medical profession and its leading representative organization, the American Medical Association (AMA). During and after the war, "physicians' incomes grew sharply; and, their prestige, aided by the successes of medical science, became securely established in American culture."[27] Membership in the AMA rose from about 7 percent of physicians in 1901 to more than 50 percent in 1915 to 65 percent in 1930.[28] As a national representative organization, the AMA was based on local and state medical societies, membership in which automatically conferred membership in the national organiza- tion.[29] This "widespread federated" structure, coupled with physicians' considerable resources and capacity for mobilization, gave the AMA unusually extensive leverage in the regionally elected and organized U.S. Congress.[30] This leverage helped the AMA convince Congress in 1927 to discontinue the Sheppard-Towner Infancy and Maternity Protection Act of 1921 – "one of the few government programs enacted over the AMA's protests."[31] And it would become crucial to the AMA's political prospects when American governmental power was nationalized during the Great Depression.

In 1920, the AMA set out its famous official policy declaring the medical profession unalterably opposed "to the institution of any plan embodying the system of compulsory contribution insurance against illness, or any other plan of compulsory insurance which provided for the medical services to be rendered contributors or their dependents, provided, controlled, or regulated by any state or the Federal Government."[32] Yet, fearing private as well as public incursions, the AMA largely sat on the sidelines of the small but emerging field of private coverage. What alarmed leaders of the profession about voluntary insur- ance was not insurance payment per se, but the loss of physician control over fees and treatment that third-party involvement might entail. Accordingly, organized medicine reserved its greatest ire for plans in which doctors accepted a set fee for patients or, worse, became salaried employees of lay organizations – as in the "lodge practice" of fraternal organizations or the "company medicine" of employers' in-house medical facilities. The profession leadership was less concerned about, yet still opposed to, plans that fell short of this "direct-service" model but paid providers on a fee-for-service basis. It tolerated the indirect pay- ments made by insurance policies under the "indemnity" model, in which insurers simply provided cash payments to patients to help them with their bills.[33]

Even so, the leaders of organized medicine were probably out of touch with much of the profession. Under economic strain, doctors often had little choice but to accept whatever payment they could find, whether from industry plans, commercial insurers, or fraternal societies. In state after state, the AMA worked successfully to limit the reach of direct- service plans and prevent new entrants into the field, fighting the plans in courts and legislatures and sanctioning doctors who signed up with them. Yet it became increasingly clear that organized medicine would need to offer and support private alternatives, if not to head off government insurance, then at least to ensure that voluntary health insurance developed along lines friendly to the profession. By 1920, county medical societies in the Pacific Northwest had chartered "industrial service bureaus" to compete for employer and state contracts, and in the 1930s, local medical societies elsewhere began setting up their own nonprofit plans to cover physician charges on a fee-for-service basis with free choice of doctors.[34] By 1935, the AMA's Bureau of Medical Economics was reporting that "nearly 200 different [health insurance] experiments are being conducted or considered by county medical societies in the United States."[35] Faced with new government challenges from above and gathering revolts from below, the AMA subsequently dropped its blanket resistance to voluntary health insurance and replaced it instead with a set of strict guidelines that private health plans were required to meet. Still, until the late 1930s, the medical profession remained a reactive and cautious force regarding voluntary insurance, rarely venturing to the forefront of private developments.

Insurers and employers were not so wary. Ironically, if the AALL had succeeded in demonstrating anything during its futile march, it was the growing need for insurance against the costs of sickness. As David Moss notes, "[M]any insurance executives quickly recognized when confronted with the prospect of compulsory health insurance that they had failed to appreciate the potential of private sickness insurance, which constituted an enormously profitable field into which they could expand."[36] During the debate over the AALL proposal, the large commercial carriers had argued that private insurance alone could adequately address workers' demands for health security. Now, with the specter of compulsory insurance at bay, they set about to show that the voluntary way was not merely consistent with American traditions but feasible and effective as well.

The reason for hope was the innovation of group insurance. Beginning around 1910, carriers had started to write life insurance policies not on an individual basis, as had been the exclusive practice before, but rather by contracting with large groups of employees within a single firm or industry.[37] The advantages of group underwriting were profound. In the first place, insuring large groups greatly reduced the possibility of adverse selection. By spreading costs across myriad workers, group insurance allowed carriers to offer coverage at reasonable rates and without inquiring into the health status of every subscriber or arbitrarily restricting benefits. This method worked well, however, only to the extent that worker participation was broad, and thus, group policies usually went hand in hand with substantial contributions from employers that made the cost of coverage appear low to individual workers ("appear," because employer contributions obviously left less to pay in cash). The employment group became a site for the pooling of risks and the subsidization of coverage, actions on a miniature scale that the AALL had advocated for all wage workers.

The employment group became, in addition, a locus of administration – the second major advantage of group policies. The embarrassingly low payout rate of commercial policies was due to many factors, but chief among them was the tremendous expense of the scores of agents and millions of individual visits necessary to market and administer insurance on an individual basis. Moreover, without a stable administrative base for maintaining enrollment, even scrupulous agents found it difficult to keep individual policies from lapsing. The employment group represented an effective response to these difficulties. Although policies still had to be sold and administered, the cost of doing so dropped as the covered workforce grew. (To this day, administrative expenses comprise a significantly higher share of premium costs for small firms than for large ones.) Insofar as workers remained on the job, they remained in the common risk pool, too. And in large groups, the movement of workers in and out of employment did not much affect the overall distribution of risk.

Thus, the employment group came to be the cornerstone of the new structure of commercial insurance – a position freighted with future significance. In the philosophy of group insurance, American employers were to be the repositories of tiny social insurance systems that spread risks and benefits within, and only within, the universe of their workers. In other nations, the state recognized and encouraged voluntary organizations involved in social welfare provision, but in few did the employment group take on such a prominent role.[38] In part, this was a legacy of corporate America's long, if spotty, commitment to welfare capitalism. In part, it was a response to the AMA's bitter crusade against other potential loci of risk pooling, such as fraternal societies. Above all, however, it reflected the absence in the United States of any other viable private alternative to the employment group as a solution to the dilemmas of medical financing. If health insurance were to remain in private hands, health insurance would have to be employment based.

Progress, however, was slow. True, "beginning in 1915, the companies ... wrote an increasing number of disability claims and accident and health policies."[39] As late as 1926, however, the eight largest group insurers were still concentrated almost exclusively in life insurance, with only 1 percent of their premium income derived from other products.[40] Although group insurance solved many problems, it did not settle the thorny question of how medical services would be paid for by insurers – directly or through indemnity payment – especially since the commercial insurers remained reluctant to finance medical services, as opposed to sickness pay. Nor was it clear that employers were willing to adopt group insurance plans. During the early 1920s, employers were as likely to create company-wide mutual benefit associations or provide medical care through corporate facilities as to contract with an insurer for insurance coverage. Indeed, in the complex assortment of private alternatives that emerged in the 1920s, the option most notable for its weakness was group health insurance, the form of coverage that would eventually become the dominant model in American medical finance.[41]

Then, quite suddenly, the momentum shifted. Between 1929 and 1931, the number of companies writing health and accident polices rose by 20 percent, and the portion of premium income represented by products besides life insurance increased to one-third. Business surveys conducted at the time show dramatic increases in the proportion of large employers providing health insurance, with the share rising from 16 to 34 percent between 1928 and 1935, matching, for the first time, the portion operating mutual benefit associations and nearly equaling the 40 percent offering some kind of retirement pension.[42]

The proximate cause of this reversal, paradoxically, was the Great Depression. Although the economic collapse placed new pressures on informal company arrangements, it also led to "substantial increases in group insurance plans for employees," so much so that insurance assets actually grew between 1929 and 1935.[43] As the economy contracted and increasingly cash-strapped workers sought to protect their dependents, life insurance receipts rose from less than 6 percent of national income in 1929 to almost 12 percent in 1932.[44] Employers were urged to shore up existing arrangements by shifting risk to outside companies, and insurance carriers increasingly offered group pension and health benefits in package deals along with the group life insurance that was their core business.

For employers, the motives for installing group health plans went beyond concerns about the stability of benefits to include the less lofty goal of resisting union encroachments. As with welfare capitalism as a whole, the principal reason that firms initiated health benefits was to foster worker allegiance and retard union organization – aims that became more pressing with the labor upswing of the 1930s. Not surprisingly, then, "industries that faced the most active union organizing efforts – autos, paper, and rubber – show remarkable rates of private health coverage."[45] Except in those few industries where injury and illness were so costly that health coverage provided firms with direct economic reward, health insurance entered the arsenal of welfare capitalism principally as an inducement to worker loyalty. This distinguished it from pensions, an earlier business innovation designed to manage the careers of skilled workers and move unproductive employees out of the workforce, as well as to foster worker allegiance.

Health insurance also differed from pensions in other respects. In the first place, it was a more categorical commitment for employers than cash benefits. Private pensions could coexist with many other sources of retirement income, including – it soon became clear – an encompassing government program. But as firms moved to guarantee a range of medical services, they were carving out an area of employer responsibility that was much more self-contained. Inherent in coverage for medical care was the idea of a primary source of payment for certain defined services, a concept less amenable to overlapping sources of security. In addition, health insurance raised even more starkly than did pensions the question of cross-subsidization. Across industry, nearly all workers eventually retired, though some lived longer than others afterward. But health and accident risks varied substantially across workplaces, creating very different cost experiences. Although this distinctive aspect of health insurance played only a limited role in the early years of the voluntary movement, it would later become a crucial force shaping employee benefit practices and business's public policy orientation.

If the response of employers and commercial insurers to the Great Depression helped set the stage for the rise of group health insurance, the spur that would ultimately become most critical originated elsewhere – in the intersection of business and benevolence at Baylor University Hospital in Dallas, Texas. There, in 1929, the model of hospital coverage that would evolve into the mighty Blue Cross empire was born, earning a modest hospital plan for public school teachers a permanent place in the annals of private social welfare leadership.

Hospitals and their patients demanded such leadership out of simple economic necessity. Like American medical care in general, hospital services were increasingly efficacious, increasingly popular, and increasingly lucrative – until the economic tidal wave of 1929. Hospitals were crushed, their receipts per patient plummeting from $236 to $59 in a single year.[46] Hospital prepayment plans, later labeled Blue Cross, emerged from the crisis as a device to stabilize hospital revenues and allow families to budget in advance for care. First in Dallas, then in a growing constellation of urban centers, business and community leaders assembled the Blue Cross network with the backing of the American Hospital Association (AHA) and seed money from the Julius Rosenwald Fund, a Chicago-based philanthropy founded by a partner in Sears Roebuck & Co. In the process, the concept of Blue Cross mutated from its humble origins, expanding from single-hospital plans to community-wide arrangements. But the new plans all retained two central elements of the founding design: first, the provision of direct payments to medical providers rather than the indemnity model of retrospective reimbursement; and, second, the limitation of coverage to hospital care, which targeted assistance to hospitals and minimized physician resistance.

From the beginning, Blue Cross was an unusual amalgam of civic and business principles – an institution situated in both the commercial sector and "civil society," that domain of social life governed neither by the coercive power of the state nor the profit motive of the market. The early Blue Cross plans were founded by community notables and progressive businessmen who aimed to deliver broad social rewards as well as immediate economic benefits.[47] The strict standards for approval of the plans required that they be nonprofit corporations run by a board of directors representing hospitals, doctors, and the community; and that their employees be paid by salary and not receive commissions for selling policies.

Crucially, the Blue Cross leadership also demanded – and, in state after state, received – special enabling legislation that exempted plans from taxation while giving them special operating charters. These enabling acts were often treated simply as an extension of the favorable tax treatment that hospitals had long received as nonprofit institutions.[48] Yet the rationale for exempting nonprofit hospitals from taxes was that they provided care to all patients regardless of ability to pay. The Blue Cross plans, their social character notwithstanding, only promised to provide benefits to subscribers. Moreover, the state enabling acts not only exempted the plans from taxation but also freed them from many of the restrictions under which other insurers had to operate. These special state charters

> were originally conceived and passed specifically because of the non-profit and social character of the plans. This social characteristic anticipated the enrollment of low-income members of the community and their being provided with protection equal to that received by the more affluent community members at a lower cost. The implication, if not the stated goal, of this element . . . was that Blue Cross would serve as an income redistribution device, a role customarily reserved for governmental action.[49]

Not instruments of government, the plans were thus not wholly private either, embodying in their "philosophy and methodology a mixture of characteristics representative of both social and commercial insurance while continuing to do business in the private sector of the economy."[50]

Compared with existing private insurers, the Blue Cross plans were similarly distinctive. To avoid adverse selection, they were sold almost entirely to employment groups, leaving individual insurance to the commercial carriers. And although limited to hospital coverage, their benefits were otherwise unusually broad. Rather than promise a fixed amount of cash reimbursement (the indemnity model), the Blue Cross plans guaranteed a specific number of days of service during which all charges would be met. Some plans even paid for maternity care and covered dependents, practices avoided entirely by the commercial carriers. The plans' founding principles also prohibited direct competition among plans. Each plan would contract on equal terms with all or most hospitals within a region, and most of the plans offered insurance to all subscriber groups at the same basic community rate – a practice sharply at odds with the experience rating employed by the commercial carriers. Along with nonprofit status, community rating was a crucial reason for the plans' unique legislative status. "The hospital service plans," declared the AHA in 1939, "are a form of social insurance under nongovernment auspices, not merely a form of private insurance under non-profit auspices."[51]

For all the special features of the Blues, however, the plans were still in the business of selling insurance – a fact that would become painfully apparent as they progressively compromised their principles to compete with commercial carriers. And for all the idealism of their founders, the plans would not have expanded so rapidly without the ongoing support of the AHA or the still-brimming reservoir of opposition to government insurance.[52] This was forthrightly acknowledged by C. Rufus Rorem, the AHA leader most responsible for bringing the Blue Cross concept to fruition. "The voluntary plans," he explained, "were an attempt to organize the public buying power on a voluntary basis, without the disadvantage of political control. . . . They were dealing with a practical problem in a practical way."[53] And in a nongovernmental way, as Blue Cross pioneers never tired of emphasizing.

In time, Rorem would leave the AHA trailed by accusations. Critics within the organization charged that he was less vigilant against government incursions than other Blue Cross leaders (which was probably true) and even that he was a communist (which was certainly not). But Rorem, in fact, exemplified the moderate, pragmatic, but generally antigovernment outlook of the Blue Cross pioneers – men who recognized that social problems existed but wished to solve them through private efforts, bolstered if necessary by active but indirect government support.[54]

Skillful and farsighted as they were, the promoters of Blue Cross were ultimately successful because their goals came to mesh neatly with the aims of the three key groups involved in medical finance: hospitals, employers, and doctors. The hospitals enjoyed the closest ties – and reaped the largest rewards. In communities where plans operated, hospitals were assured of regular payments and insulated from cutthroat competition. In return, the AHA provided seed money and administrative support. Furthermore, by promising a specified level of services, the hospitals assumed the risk of unexpectedly high utilization, which, under the indemnity model, had to be budgeted for with cash reserves that made start-up costs daunting. The hospitals thereby greatly contributed to the Blue Cross plans' early competitive advantage.

Employers also played an important role, particularly in communities where a single large corporation dominated. In Rochester, for example, Eastman Kodak enrolled five thousand of its employees even before the local Blue Cross plan began operations. In Detroit, Ford Motor Company and the department store J. L. Hudson helped initiate Michigan's Blue Cross plan.[55] Corporations needed Blue Cross if they were to provide hospital service benefits, and Blue Cross needed employers if they were to enroll large groups. Because of the plans' local character, however, firms with interstate operations found it difficult to arrange group contracts – a drawback that would prove a significant competitive hindrance.

Finally, there were the doctors. Although the AMA railed against hospital prepayment through the early 1930s, local medical societies were often more supportive. Doctors prized Blue Cross's strict noninterference with physician privileges; its focus on moderate-income workers, who were unlikely to seek hospital care without insurance; and its nonprofit, voluntary ethos, which assuaged concerns about the "commercialization" of medicine. Tellingly, when doctors began to set up their own plans in the 1930s, they emulated the Blue Cross structure, giving their plans the label "Blue Shield."

In the years after the abortive AALL campaign, therefore, the placid surface of American politics hid important changes in U.S. medical finance. Thanks to the AHA and AMA, voluntary health insurance would be friendly to the needs and demands of hospitals and physicians. Voluntary health insurance would also be grounded in favorable tax laws and state charters designed to encourage private social benefits. And voluntary health insurance would be based on the risk-pooling advantages of group underwriting, placing employers at the center of the emerging private insurance system. These were individually small developments that set the United States apart from most industrializing nations and defined its distinctive public–private framework of medical finance. But in the aftermath of the New Deal, these small differences would grow very large indeed. For when proposals for public health insurance died once again in the 1930s, private health insurance was poised to expand, the threat of national health insurance never absent from its promoters' consciousness. If the failure of compulsory health insurance during the Progressive era cleared the way for the emergence of voluntary health insurance, the failure of compulsory insurance during the New Deal would open the door for voluntary insurance to become the core source of health security in the American social welfare regime.

The New Deal

As we saw in Part II, the Great Depression transformed the balance of partisan power in American politics and shifted the institutional locus of U.S. social policymaking from the states to the federal government. As dramatic as the upheaval was, however, the opportunities it created were not unlimited. Although Democrats decisively controlled Congress, the party was split between its northern and southern wings. Within Congress, southern Democrats benefited the most from their party's gains in the 1930s. Most came from safe one-party states and districts, and the seniority system in Congress ensured that they would occupy powerful positions within the congressional hierarchy. The regional structure of Congress and the weakness of incentives for party cohesion activated legislators' territorial interests, particularly the distinctive interests of southern politicians, who feared any challenge to the white power structure and low-wage economy of the South. Most of Roosevelt's actions after 1932 can be understood as an effort to build up the presidency and pursue his aims while at the same time attempting to prevent defections within his party's conservative southern wing and to forestall a backlash in Congress or the Supreme Court against the expansion of executive authority.[56]

The members of the Committee on Economic Security were well aware of these constraints. Although they studied the feasibility of including compulsory health insurance in the Social Security Act, they ultimately decided against it. Even an offhand call for a study of health insurance in the bill drew a firestorm of protest from the AMA, which convened an extraordinary emergency meeting of its delegates and mobilized local societies – and, through them, members of Congress – against the legislation.[57] According to Edwin Witte, the opposition of doctors, "plus the fears which this opposition aroused in Congress, doomed all hopes for early enactment of health insurance legislation." The House Ways and Means Committee unanimously struck the reference to health insurance from the bill and "time and again thereafter members of Congress received protests from medical associations and individual physicians against the economic security bill, all based on the [mistaken] assumption that this bill provided for health insurance." Witte and other key committee members – including the head of the CES, Labor Secretary Frances Perkins – came to be convinced that any mention of health insurance in the final legislation "would spell defeat for the entire bill."[58]

Most analyses of the abandonment of health insurance during the New Deal conclude, in essence, that the opposition of the AMA made the administration's decision inevitable.[59] Yet this interpretation fails to explain why compulsory health insurance was not presented to Congress *despite* external opposition, as were other important aspects of the Social Security Act. As we saw in Part II, every one of the social insurance initiatives formulated by the CES – not just health insurance but also old-age and unemployment insurance – faced significant resistance in Congress and within the business community. Although the Social Security Act is now remembered as the crowning social policy achievement of the New Deal, far more government spending and popular attention were showered on direct relief and public employment at the time.[60] Within the Act itself, it was public assistance for the elderly poor rather than old-age insurance that was the subject of the most agitation and demand. "Social insurance," notes Daniel Rodgers bluntly, "came into the Depression United States trailing twenty years of failed importation efforts. It had no powerful political lobby, grassroots movement, or interest group behind it. Many of its early supporters were tired and discouraged."[61] If health insurance lacked strong popular or congressional support, if its enemies were many and powerful, if it offered little in the way of immediate assistance to the impoverished or out of work, this hardly distinguished it from old-age insurance, which made its way into law on the shoulders of the more popular old-age assistance provisions and the more widely demanded unemployment insurance sections.

Nor was health insurance included in the CES's initial ambit merely as an afterthought. In outlining the work of the committee, Witte placed "provisions for medical care" on a par with old-age insurance and unemployment insurance – a judgment backed up by the technical board of the Committee, which agreed in September 1934 that "the problem of medical care should not be regarded as being a third or fourth item in a general program for economic security. . . . [T]his part of the program is equally important . . . and equally feasible."[62] Even after the extent of AMA opposition became clear, there remained those who strongly believed that health insurance had a place in the bill. These dissenters were led by Edgar Sydenstricker and I. S. Falk, the two principal architects of the aborted health insurance provisions, but their ranks also reportedly included the administration's relief administrator, Harry Hopkins, who believed health insurance would be the Social Security bill's crowning achievement.[63]

Until the moment of the bill's introduction, the CES nervously wavered back and forth on health insurance, refusing to concede that it would be left by the wayside. Witte had distinct moments of hope, writing to Perkins in late 1934, for example, that "we cannot dismiss health insurance at this time without being entirely satisfied that it cannot be put into operation on a compulsory basis in the near future."[64] In December, the CES's executive committee approved the recommendations of the medical staff and endorsed in principle the report they had prepared.[65] But while the leaders of the CES generally supported health insurance, their support was not deep or wide enough to warrant a frontal assault on the AMA. In the end, health insurance was simply not a high enough priority to bet the entire legislation on it, and Perkins, Witte, and eventually the president advocated that health insurance be put aside, with the promise that it would be the next issue taken up by the administration. Sydenstricker fumed to Witte that the president was letting himself be "licked by a group of doctors."[66] Falk lamented that Perkins and the others were "unduly timid," as "there wasn't . . . the slightest chance that a controversy over any particular aspect was going to keep the Ways and Means Committee and the Finance Committee from bringing out a substantial program."[67] But Roosevelt's decision stood, and Sydenstricker and Falk's proposal never saw the light of day.

This timidity – or sagacity, depending on one's assessment – is what must be explained. Why did health insurance end up lower on the social reform agenda than other controversial proposals for social insurance, and than it had been in the 1910s? And why did the opposition of doctors carry such political weight? Certainly, health insurance was not postponed because the New Dealers believed that private alternatives were sufficient. The 1935 Report of the CES stated categorically (and wrongly, it turned out) that "voluntary insurance holds no promise of being much more effective in the near future than it has been in the past."[68] Although some opponents of government involvement were touting voluntary health insurance, Falk recalled that "[t]his was pipsqueak stuff. . . . That argument was advanced, but there was no substantial supporting ground for it in going operations."[69] The best estimates of private coverage during the early 1930s indicate that no more than 2 to 3 million workers and their dependents enjoyed any health insurance protection.[70] Moreover, rising medical costs and utilization meant that health care was a significantly greater burden on middle-class budgets than it had been during the Progressive era. Neither the reach of private alternatives nor the objective severity of the problem can explain why compulsory insurance dropped from the priorities of reformers just when the opportunity for change seemed greatest.

Instead, three principal factors – one philosophical, one political, and one historical – underlay the diminished prominence of health insurance as a reform imperative. Philosophically, the New Dealers involved with the health provisions were less enamored than had been the AALL with the concept of prevention, the idea that forcing employers to confront the cost of ill health and accidents would impel business to reduce disease and encourage public health. This shift robbed health insurance of much of the ideological cachet it had once enjoyed, especially among the Wisconsin reformers who dominated the CES and remained strongly committed to the prevention ideal in unemployment insurance. Far more critical, however, health insurance lacked any natural connection to the demands of mobilized political forces like the Townsend movement or organized labor. On other fronts, diffuse social demands for policy change could be credibly invoked as action-forcing mechanisms and counterweights to the organized resistance that social insurance faced. No such obvious social pressures existed with regard to health insurance, however real the problems it addressed.

To this, finally, one must add the lessons and legacies of the first campaign for compulsory health insurance less than two decades before. In the wake of the AALL's defeat, health insurance had faded from the wish list of progressive reformers, who ceded the initiative to groups pushing for old-age and unemployment measures. At the same time, the health insurance campaign mobilized a formidable core of interest-group resistance that new reform efforts would have to overcome. The combined result of these effects was to forestall the same state-level legislative percolation and grassroots coalition building that spilled over into New Deal debates about unemployment and old-age insurance. Though many New Dealers had been recently involved in state debates over old-age and unemployment legislation, for example, none of the top figures in the CES had been active in the AALL health insurance campaign, although many had witnessed firsthand its painful demise fifteen years before.[71] Ironically, then, health insurance faltered during the New Deal not because it had arrived too late as a compelling issue but because it had arrived too early. If it had percolated upward from continuing state-level agitation without the baggage of prior defeat, perhaps there would have been greater social pressure and elite-level commitment in favor of action – and a less cohesive and resourceful opposition lying in wait.

Internal dissension sealed health insurance's fate. Falk and Sydenstricker argued that any proposal should combine three elements: wage-loss protection, coverage of medical services, and public health activities.[72] Yet many public health and children's advocates were less committed to health insurance than to other measures. (In fact, despite omitting health insurance, the Social Security Act did end up containing modest provisions pertaining to public health and maternal and infant care.) An even more critical division emerged when CES members debated whether the administration should offer a radically scaled-back proposal or retreat altogether. Falk and Sydenstricker tried to rally support for a program of federal subsidies to encourage state insurance programs, but Witte was now certain the quest was hopeless, and he marginalized the increasingly bitter duo.[73] Given that AMA representatives seemed willing to discuss a limited program of catastrophic insurance, the failure to agree on a step-by-step strategy may have been a fateful decision in the history of U.S. health policy.[74]

That AMA insiders broached the subject of compromise undercuts the conventional portrait of the organization as an omnipotent force in New Deal debates. In fact, the best evidence that the AMA's power was not absolute was the AMA's own response to the prospect of federal action. In 1934, in a preemptive move aimed at heading off a CES proposal, the AMA House of Delegates voted for the first time to endorse limited forms of voluntary health insurance, repudiating the stance of the most prominent spokesman of the profession, the acerbic editor of the *Journal of the American Medical Association*, Morris Fishbein. To be sure, the AMA endorsement was hedged with qualifications. "All features of medical service in any method of medical practice should be under the control of the medical profession," read the opening principle, and the nine that followed elaborated on this theme, insisting that third parties not "be permitted to come between the patient and his physician in any medical relation."[75] Yet the explicit approval of voluntary coverage was a significant concession, which reflected real fear that the AMA's failure to offer an alternative to governmental insurance would lead to internal dissension, public backlash, and perhaps legislative defeat.[76] In this respect, the AMA's insistent demand that health insurance be kept voluntary and physician controlled was a sign of potential vulnerability as much as of strength.

All the same, the AMA's influence was unquestionably impressive and surely tipped the scales in favor of caution. That influence rested not merely on membership or resources, but on the profession's privileged place within American medical care and American politics. Unlike old-age pensions, the potential entry of government into the health field did not implicate employers and insurers alone. It also required the procurement of services from a respected profession that had worked for decades to exert decisive control over American medicine. On top of this, the medical profession enjoyed disproportionate political power in Congress – first, by virtue of its widespread federated structure, which allowed it to expend its political energies simultaneously at the national level and in congressional districts; and second, by virtue of the personal nature of physician–patient interactions, which allowed doctors to reach millions of individual patients in intimate face-to-face settings. In contrast with business leaders, moreover, the legitimacy of the medical profession was not compromised by the Depression. Leading physicians remained respected social figures with close ties to national leaders.[77]

Whether the opposition of the AMA precluded the passage of any health insurance legislation remains one of the great unanswered questions of the New Deal. Arthur Altmeyer believed that a limited health program could have made it into the bill. But whether it would have survived on Capitol Hill, he still could not say thirty years later.[78] After fighting in two major postwar battles over national health insurance, Wilbur Cohen remained convinced that 1935 had been the only moment after 1916 "when Congress might have enacted some federal legislation relating to health insurance for the entire population."[79] Against these retrospective assessments, one can easily cite the AMA's apoplectic reaction to the merest hint of future action and Congress's eagerness to respond by removing the offending suggestion from the bill. Yet these events occurred in the absence of even the most feeble push for the recommendation for further study, which in any case had only symbolic import.

The contrast with old-age insurance is more instructive. In that battle, the Roosevelt Administration engaged in extensive horse trading and cajoling, giving ground where necessary but eventually forcing Congress to make the difficult choice of defying a popular president on omnibus legislation viewed by the public and most legislators as central to relief. Indeed, as Witte recounts, when the prospects for old-age insurance looked dimmest in the House, "the President . . . told the Administration leaders of the Ways and Means Committee that he considered every part of the original bill to be essential. This activity in support of the bill came at the most critical time and marked a distinct turning point in the history of the measure."[80] For all the certainty of those who believe that a health insurance plan would have withered under the heat of congressional debate, that debate was never entered by the president whose influence carried old-age insurance through Congress and whose committed advocacy would surely have been necessary for any legislation to pass.

The decision to leave health insurance out of the Social Security Act ensured that it would not pass through the window of opportunity opened by the Great Depression. Although some within the administration believed that health insurance would be the next item on the New Deal agenda, that quickly proved a false hope. In the 1938 congressional elections, New Deal Democrats suffered significant losses, and after the election, southern Democrats and conservative Republicans forged the notorious "conservative coalition" that would stymie Roosevelt's ambitions until his death. The president continued to express the view that health insurance should be enacted, but he did not endorse congressional legislation, nor did he ever return to the issue with sustained enthusiasm again.

The AMA emerged from the battles of the New Deal with an aura of political invincibility, an expanded membership, and an unshakable claim to dominance within the medical sector.[81] The threats of the 1930s had finally impelled AMA leaders to allow local medical societies to develop profession-sponsored prepayment plans as an alternative to either government or lay control. But leaders of the newly created Social Security Board would continue to view government health insurance as the great unfinished business of the New Deal. Allied with labor and a handful of liberals in Congress, they would lead the charge for compulsory health insurance almost from the day Social Security was established. These three forces – the conservative coalition, the growth of private health protection, and the emerging pro-reform alliance – would define the boundaries of American health politics for the next three decades.

The Growth of Private Protection

The New Deal represented a turning point in the fortunes of private health protection. Scattered and still scarce, private health insurance was not a major stumbling block for the Roosevelt Administration when it considered government health insurance. In the wake of the Social Security Act, however, the seeds sown during the 1920s and early 1930s burst into flower. With medical providers, employers, and insurers all pushing for private alternatives, a rapidly increasing proportion of corporations enrolled their workers in group hospital and physician plans.

By the end of World War II, private health insurance would enjoy a formidable presence on the American social welfare landscape, and reformers would be forced to rethink the wisdom of their elusive goal once again. Many of the forces driving up private health coverage were the same as the ones that caused employers to adopt private pension plans: fear of further government expansion; favorable tax policies; demand for employees in an increasingly tight labor market; wage and price controls that exempted fringe benefits; and strident labor demands that, after the war, were channeled by the federal government into the routines of collective bargaining. Yet two key differences separated the health care and pension areas. The first was the attitude of vested interests. In retirement security policy, most original opponents of the Social Security Act did not wish to roll back old-age insurance (though according to the 1939 *Fortune* survey, a large majority of employers did want to "modify" it, no doubt by reducing its scope and its potential for expansion).[82] Not only had the dire predictions of wrecked private pensions failed to materialize, but many corporations and insurers also recognized that a government floor of protection allowed them to concentrate their pensioning on the key management and salaried personnel on which business operations depended. In health policy, however, no large-scale public program existed, and no such acquiescence characterized the interest-group response. Instead, opponents of public social insurance were promoting voluntary insurance, through both private leadership and public policy, as a bulwark against future encroachments into the field.

The attitude of vested interests reflected, in turn, a second key difference between health care and pensions: Health insurance was emerging as the core source of social protection in the American welfare regime, rather than as a supplement to public social insurance. By no means was the growth of private coverage as broadly distributed or as swift as the proponents of voluntary health insurance portrayed it. Gaping holes ran the length of the emerging net of private health security, and the groups who fell through them were usually the ones most in need of assistance. Yet the expansion of private health coverage for American workers was indeed impressive – so impressive that American politicians were forced to take notice; so impressive that its advocates began to believe that government insurance might be defeated; so impressive that labor leaders could not ignore its siren call, despite their increasingly insistent demands for public action. Arthur Altmeyer would later lament that the expansion of private coverage in the 1940s had an "almost hypnotic effect . . . in persuading people in the middle and upper economic and cultural levels that voluntary health insurance was solving the problem – in the face of the evidence . . . that voluntary insurance was reaching a

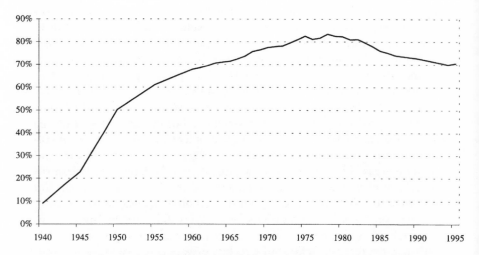

Figure 4.1. Share of U.S. Population with Private Health Insurance, 1940–1995. *Source*: Health Insurance Association of America (HIAA), *Source Book of Health Insurance Data* (Washington, D.C.: HIAA, 1996), 41.

great many people but it wasn't providing effective insurance."[83] Hypnotic or not, private insurance was rapidly filling the void left by the failure of compulsory health legislation and, in the process, becoming the primary mechanism of risk sharing in American medical financing.

As Figure 4.1 demonstrates, the growth of voluntary health insurance in the years after the New Deal was certainly remarkable. In 1937, according to a pioneering study by the Public Health Service, fewer than thirty Blue Cross plans were in operation, with about 600,000 members.[84] Commercial insurers and direct-service plans probably insured 2 to 3 million more Americans, while the physician-controlled plans that would later become the Blue Shield network had virtually no presence at all.[85] By 1940, however, enrollment in some type of private health plan had reached 12 million subscribers – one out of every ten Americans – and roughly half those subscribers were covered by Blue Cross. Enrollment in private health insurance would nearly triple to 32 million by 1945, with well over half those covered enrolled in Blue Cross. (It would then more than double again to 76.6 million in 1950, reaching for the first time a majority of Americans.) When the privately funded Committee on the Costs of Medical Care had surveyed voluntary insurance in 1932, it had barely bothered to mention hospital service plans. A year after the end of World War II, more than eighty Blue Cross plans and forty-four Blue Shield plans were in operation, and commercial insurance companies were in rapid pursuit.

As already noted, Blue Cross's early lead in the rush to enroll new subscribers owed much to special enabling legislation passed in state after state to exempt the plans from traditional insurance requirements and taxes. Like other forms of insurance, health insurance was governed by state, not federal, law.[86] Yet proponents of Blue Cross plans contended that existing state laws should not apply to the plans, and, in nearly all cases, they were successful. By 1945, thirty-five states had granted special legal charters to Blue Cross plans.[87] Typically, these enabling acts placed Blue Cross plans under the authority of state insurance departments but exempted them from state premium and income taxes, general insurance laws, and normal reserve requirements on the grounds that they were "charitable and benevolent organizations." (As nonprofit corporations, the plans were also exempt from federal taxes.) Taken together, these were remarkable concessions whose importance "to the Blue Cross development can hardly be exaggerated."[88]

Blue Shield plans established by physicians also generally enjoyed privileged status in state insurance law. And like Blue Cross, they, too, benefited from their ability to offer service benefits rather than indemnity coverage. Just as the foundation of Blue Cross was the agreement of participating hospitals to provide covered services, Blue Shield plans were the only insurers from which medical societies would allow doctors to accept direct fee-for-service payments. (Commercial insurers, by contrast, had to reimburse *patients*, leaving doctors to collect – and set – fees on their own.) Despite these advantages, however, the Blue Shield plans followed a considerably rockier path than the hospital service plans that they emulated. In addition to the AMA's lingering concerns about prepayment, Blue Shield plans had to confront the resistance of individual doctors to standardization of fees. Many physicians believed that any move in this direction would undercut their income by depriving them of the ability to bill patients as they liked, and for this reason, Blue Shield plans often refused to cover the upper-income patients whom doctors charged most. Even so, the plans would never have made headway were it not for the organizational support of Blue Cross, which was eager to form partnerships that allowed it to offer integrated hospital and physician benefits to compete with commercial carriers.

Another force that had particular impact on the Blue Shield plans was doctors' continuing fear of compulsory health insurance. Indeed, the first medical service plan was created by the California Medical Association in 1939 precisely to head off the threat of a state proposal for compulsory protection. (Despite the governor's support, the plan promptly expired.)[89] In Pennsylvania, where the state medical society developed a physician-controlled plan, the plan's founders made clear to disgruntled physicians what was at stake:

> The choice is no longer between the traditional type of private practice on the one hand and voluntary health insurance on the other. . . . The alternative in the future lies between some form of nonpolitical voluntary insured medical service, such as the state society is sponsoring, and something which will undoubtedly be a great deal worse regardless of the name by which it is known – state medicine, compulsory health insurance, socialized medicine, or something else.[90]

Rhetoric such as this was characteristic of the Blue Shield movement and underscores the extent to which physician-backed plans were driven by political concerns, rather than by the mix of motives that sparked Blue Cross. As Paul Starr explains, "Blue Shield . . . was clearly aimed at preventing a government program from being adopted. While Blue Cross maintained that it was a community-sponsored effort and democratically controlled, the Blue Shield plans had no such pretense."[91] But whatever the differences between Blue Cross and Blue Shield, both were propelled forward by the continuing fear of government health insurance

Though California hosted a brief debate over compulsory health insurance, it was the exception. A thoughtful 1940 review of state legislative activity by the research wing of the Social Security Board concluded that "action of State legislatures [in 1939] was directed primarily toward expansion of voluntary plans and secondarily toward provision of services for indigents. Legislation liberalizing tax-supported hospital and medical care programs or authorizing compulsory health insurance either met open opposition or was allowed to die for lack of support."[92] Of the 200 bills introduced in the states, for example, 62 involved measures to encourage voluntary health plans, 64 proposed some form of medical assistance for the poor, and only 9 had to do with compulsory health insurance. Within these areas, moreover, legislative success differed greatly. Although 43 percent of the proposals to encourage voluntary health insurance were enacted, along with a third of the proposals for medical assistance, only one of the bills dealing with compulsory health insurance made it into law – and it merely recommended further study of the subject. The essential pattern of state legislative activity had thus changed little since the Progressive era. Now, however, fears about state competitiveness were coupled with political pressure for private health security, giving state legislatures the easy road of encouraging voluntary insurance rather than considering tax-financed social protections.

Action at the national level was slightly more promising for reformers, but it, too, went nowhere and served primarily to propel onward the proponents of private coverage. In 1938, a National Health Conference organized with Roosevelt Administration backing briefly revived hope that the president would swing his weight behind national health insurance. The resulting flush of reformist enthusiasm, though fleeting, frightened the AMA into another more expansive statement of support for voluntary health insurance, as well as a behind-the-scenes concession that some federal support for local medical assistance programs for the poor might be necessary. All this, however, was quickly forgotten after the electoral losses of 1938.

Far more consequential in the long term was the introduction the next year of the first of what would be a series of comprehensive social insurance bills backed by organized labor and sponsored by New York Democrat Robert Wagner. The first Wagner bill was a solo venture and contained a modest plan to encourage the creation of public health insurance programs in the states. Beginning in 1943, however, Wagner would raise his sights to demand a national health plan modeled after Social Security, and he would be joined in his crusade by his Senate colleague James Murray of Montana and Representative John Dingell of Michigan. Although it was an open secret that the Wagner-Murray-Dingell bill had been developed by program executives within the Social Security Board, Roosevelt himself never endorsed the measure, which had no chance of passage in an increasingly conservative Congress. But the Wagner-Murray-Dingell bills would set the agenda for reformers for the next decade and, at the same time, keep a steady flame burning under the simmering cauldron of private-sector developments.

This is not to say that federal law was immaterial. Although Congress never addressed the tax treatment of private health insurance before the 1950s, the IRS in effect "treated employers' contributions for the accident and health insurance of their employees as nontaxable fringe benefits from the inception of the income tax in 1913."[93] Yet deep uncertainties about the treatment of health benefits remained, and IRS precedents applied only to group health insurance, not individual union or company plans. A Treasury regulation promulgated in 1919, for example, stated that employers' payments for health insurance should be included in workers' taxable income. Less than a year later, however, the IRS made a special exception for group life insurance, which was extended to health insurance in 1943.[94] Under the 1943 ruling, employer contributions to finance group insurance were treated by the IRS as deductible business expenses, and workers were not required to pay income (or, later, Social Security) taxes on their value – a tax policy similar to that toward pensions.[95] As the next chapter will discuss, this special tax treatment was specifically affirmed and extended in the

Revenue Act of 1954 after several conflicting IRS rulings prompted members of Congress to demand a blanket exemption. As with pensions, the value of the tax-favored status of employer-provided health benefits rose dramatically during the New Deal and World War II as tax rates rose and an increasing proportion of Americans began to pay taxes.

As with private pensions, too, the expansion of private health insurance was further encouraged during the war by the exclusion of fringe benefits from wage and price controls. Given the tight conditions of the labor market, firms were already under heavy pressure to attract and retain workers. But the War Labor Board's decision highlighted the use of fringe benefits as a management tool and gave corporations an additional incentive to adopt them. The fastest growth occurred in Blue Cross plans, the membership of which increased at an average annual rate of 23 percent between 1943 and 1946, when the exclusion was in effect.

It would be a mistake, however, to place too much emphasis on either of these federal policies, if only because the contemporary literature on American health financing has tended to magnify their importance while ignoring the larger motives and forces that animated the development of employer-sponsored coverage. The wage freeze did not, as is often claimed, single-handedly drive up coverage during the war. In fact, Blue Cross enrollment rose faster between 1940 and 1941 than it did during any of the years when the freeze was in effect, and there is some evidence that firms had other means besides fringe benefits to circumvent wage controls if they wished to raise compensation.[96] Although the wage freeze clearly contributed to the expansion of coverage, the rise of private health insurance began well before the war and continued well after it.

A stronger case can be made that the favorable tax treatment of health insurance was a crucial factor in the move to adopt private health plans, but again, its influence should not be exaggerated. Firms began to offer health insurance before taxes were a principal concern of employers and workers, and they did so despite persistent uncertainty about the proper tax treatment of group health insurance, uncertainty that was not resolved until 1954. That tax subsidies were only available to employment-based group coverage is surely one reason that individually purchased health insurance failed to gain much ground, but the more important considerations were the risk-pooling and administrative advantages of group insurance that we have already examined. These points would not need repeating were it not for the inordinate attention that the special tax treatment of employer-provided health insurance has received among health policy specialists.[97] Tax subsidies are a major means by which the federal government underwrites private health security in the United States – a means that, in turn, has distinctive distributional and political effects. But they are not the sole reason that health insurance in the United States is employment based or the sole reason that voluntary health insurance emerged during the 1930s and 1940s as a credible alternative to government health insurance.

The more fundamental reason for the rise of employment-based coverage, as this chapter has made clear, is that a range of groups – doctors, hospitals, insurers, employers – came to see it as a way of achieving not just their own organizational imperatives but also larger political goals. Out of the crucible of the failed reform efforts of the 1910s and 1930s emerged a potential route of escape from the looming threat of government action, one that also delivered important benefits, from employee goodwill to the stabilization of income, to those who adopted and championed it. Provider-friendly voluntary health insurance emerged on a large scale only after a process of organizational selection in which doctors and hospitals restricted the scope of competing alternatives and ensured the preeminence of providers within whatever new forms developed. It emerged only after insurers refined the techniques of group insurance to overcome the inherent difficulties of spreading medical costs and administering benefits. It emerged only after it received the support of favorable public policies that gave it special sanction in tax and regulatory law. And it emerged only after a renewed but aborted push for government health insurance mobilized the opponents of government action to construct a private system of social protection that could stand as an obstacle and alternative to public social insurance. But once private health insurance emerged, it was like dry kindling waiting for a match, ready to ignite in a tight economy in which labor unrest, federal tax laws, and wartime wage regulations all pushed toward expanded coverage.

Conclusion

Private health insurance began as an uncertain commitment viewed with ambivalence by nearly all the actors involved in its creation and growth. By the mid-1940s, however, it was an organizational reality backed by powerful interests and invested with larger strategic aims. This transformation – never smooth, hardly automatic – followed on the heels of two significant political junctures in which compulsory health insurance emerged as a priority for social reformers but failed to gain legislative approval. In the first of these moments, the failed campaign of the AALL, the overwhelming institutional barriers posed by the decentralized organization of the American federal system doomed government action from the start. In the second of these moments, the New Deal, a key strategic decision in the face of uncertain political prospects ensured that reformers would not be able to capitalize on a potential window of opportunity for the enactment of a public program. These events had a dual legacy: They left the field of health insurance open for voluntary initiatives, and they brought into closer alignment a constellation of interests opposed to government action and increasingly in agreement that private group insurance concordant with providers' demands was both intrinsically valuable and the only hope of heading off a program of public health insurance for American workers.

The movement to create and adopt voluntary health plans, in turn, conditioned the aims of the groups with a stake in them. Not only did the defenders of private health insurance argue that public policy should aim to encourage voluntary action, but they also claimed that private initiatives obviated the need for any government program of social insurance in the health care field. Thus, as private health insurance spread into the workplace, it came to assume a place in the practice and ideology of private benefits different from that of employer-provided pensions, which existed alongside the nation's public retirement program, Social Security. Whereas private pensions built on top of the floor of protection provided by Social Security – a floor, employers quickly discovered, that offset much of pensions' cost – private health insurance emerged as the core source of health security for workers and their families. As the next chapter will show, the effects of this contrast would be pronounced: Employers willing to consider expansions of Social Security refused to countenance the passage of national health insurance, and soon, even organized labor saw its enthusiasm for government action to protect working Americans weakened as it successfully obtained private substitutes for the public programs it had so insistently demanded.

These deep differences between health care and pensions hung from real but relatively slender historical threads: the singular opposition of the AMA, the balance of social demands during the 1930s, and the lesser priority placed on health insurance by key New Dealers. But if the decision to leave health insurance out of the Social Security Act was not foreordained, it could not have been more fateful. As private health insurance expanded with the support of powerful groups and favorable public policies, it recast the landscape of postwar health politics. In the years leading up to World War II, private health insurance was shaped by actions in the public sphere. As we shall see, it would soon be shaping them.

5

The Elusive Cure: Public and Private Health Insurance After 1945

The United States emerged from World War II with a growing economy, a strengthened state, and a mobilized national community. It emerged, too, as the undisputed economic and military leader of the Western world. Many on the left believed America's new global responsibilities would unify Americans in support of expanded government programs, much as the Great Depression had before.[1] The war itself led to the passage of government health programs for military personnel and their dependents, and preinduction physicals revealed that a large proportion of young men were not fit for service, raising new concerns about the nation's health.[2] Perhaps most important, public support for national health insurance rose during the war, with the share of Americans expressing support for a health program similar to Social Security reaching 85 percent in 1943.[3]

Yet hopes for national health insurance went unfulfilled, both immediately after the war and in the decades that followed. World War II did not lead to a major new program of government insurance or provision as it did in Britain, nor was it followed by the subnational policy experiments of the sort that bubbled back up into Canadian federal policy.[4] Like Civil War pensions and War Risk Insurance, the special programs extended to soldiers and their families proved to be fleeting experiments or remained the guardians of veterans alone. A quixotic postwar crusade by President Truman to enact national health insurance ended with the repudiation first of his goal and then of his party's presidential candidate. Truman's successor, Dwight Eisenhower, worked to put government squarely behind private health insurance, even as he supported a dramatic expansion of Social Security. In the end, all that survived of the ferment of the late 1940s was a series of federal measures funding medical facilities and research, a massive network of private health insurance encouraged by federal tax and labor policy, and a new commitment on the part of organized labor to achieve at the bargaining table the health security that it could not obtain in the halls of Congress.

The contemporary diagnoses of this persistent stalemate were many: the recalcitrance of the AMA, public fears of "socialized medicine," legislative missteps by reform advocates. But two causes – one obvious at the time, one less so – stand out in broad historical and comparative perspective. The first was the enduring barriers encountered by those seeking to construct pro-reform majorities in America's fragmented political context, where power was divided not only within and between rival branches of government, but also between rival factions within the Democratic Party. As private insurance expanded, however, a second critical constraint came to dominate even this one: the increasingly privileged place of publicly regulated and subsidized private insurance in American medical finance. This distinctive position was sustained not only by powerful vested interests in the employment-based system, and not only by the continued decomposition of the potential constituency for reform. It was also anchored in the American welfare regime's very division of public and private duties, which made public officials acutely sensitive to the effect of government action on private coverage and yet gave them few instruments for controlling spending or expanding public insurance. Much as changes to Social Security entailed massive transition costs and salient losses to mobilized constituencies, changes to the private core of American health insurance posed a test that reformers found themselves repeatedly unable to pass.

The assorted remnants of Truman's ill-fated crusade would therefore vastly complicate the challenge facing future advocates of national health insurance. As employment-based coverage spread through the workplace and the cost of medical care continued to rise, reformers struggled to craft a new reform approach that would work around the burgeoning system of private insurance rather than supplant it. The twin programs that they eventually succeeded in winning in the wake of the landslide Democratic triumph of 1964 would prove to be the first and last major expansions of government health insurance in the twentieth century.

"Out-Dealing the New Deal"

Harry Truman assumed the presidency in a world transformed by war and a nation gripped by doubt. Not only were events on the world stage newly foreboding, but the future of the myriad domestic social reforms that had been postponed during the war also remained uncertain. Near the end of his life, Roosevelt had tantalized advocates of national health insurance by suggesting that he would finally take up their cause, incorporating into his famous Economic Bill of Rights of 1944 "the right to adequate medical care."[5] Yet Roosevelt's authority in Congress had continued to wane, and he never made health insurance a defining issue. By contrast, America's leading ally, Great Britain, emerged from the war with a blueprint for a national health service already drawn up by the wartime coalition government, and the Labour Party promptly proceeded to ram its own version through Parliament after voters swept it into office in 1945.[6] Reformers in the United States knew that such decisive action was unlikely in a nation that had neither parliamentary institutions nor prior experience with compulsory insurance. But many were inspired by Labour's triumph to believe that the "lost reform" of the New Deal could finally be resurrected.[7]

In the United States, however, the war and its aftermath unquestionably hurt the struggle for health reform, and they did so at the very moment that the cause found its first presidential champion. Although World War II strengthened the hand of the president in foreign affairs, control over domestic policy was shifting from the White House to Congress well before it came to a close. And Congress itself was becoming increasingly conservative. In the five years after America's entry into the war, Roosevelt and then Truman suffered a string of policy and electoral reversals, beginning with the jarring midterm defeats of 1942 and culminating in the Democrats' loss of Capitol Hill for the first time in sixteen years in 1946.[8] In Congress, continuing investigations of administration figures attempted to demonstrate the communist underpinnings of the New Deal – charges that would soon be turned against "socialized medicine" and its embattled supporters.[9]

Yet these obstacles seemed only to spur on Truman, who first endorsed national health insurance in a special presidential message in 1945 and then made it the centerpiece of his stunning come-from-behind triumph in the 1948 presidential race.[10] Though Truman never championed a designated administration bill, the legislative ends that he demanded were the same as those contained in the most recent Wagner-Murray-Dingell bill: comprehensive health insurance for nearly all Americans through a federal contributory program modeled after Social Security.[11] Although the bill borrowed Social Security's financing model, therefore, its coverage would in fact have been broader than that of old-age insurance at the time.

Despite Truman's surprise victory, however, national health insurance met the same fate as did most other ambitious social programs he pursued between 1948 and 1950.[12] Although he ostensibly enjoyed a party majority, the president had scant hope of overcoming the cross-party conservative coalition of Republicans and southern Democrats, whose leaders pilloried him for "out-dealing the New Deal."[13] Enraged over Truman's support of civil rights and occupying top positions within the congressional hierarchy, southern Democrats "remained overwhelmingly opposed to his all-inclusive health insurance proposal or to any other major new adventures on behalf of labor-supported, urban-oriented social and economic reform."[14] Hearings on the Wagner-Murray-Dingell bill orchestrated by the bill's supporters only showcased the long list of the bill's opponents, and by 1950, Senator Murray himself had "allowed the bill to languish . . . turning instead to a study of the country's existing voluntary insurance system."[15] It surely did not help that the AMA launched a multimillion dollar lobbying blitz linking the proposal to Cold War fears about socialism. But the reality is that "national health insurance was simply one more Fair Deal program that never came close to passing."[16]

The power of the conservative coalition reflected the distinctive organization of national political institutions in the United States. The separation of executive and legislative elections and the dominance of Democrats in the South weakened any incentives for southern Democrats to go along with presidential initiatives that threatened their interests. Moreover, the oligarchic structure of Congress reinforced legislators' geographic parochialism and gave conservative Democrats from safe one-party regions disproportionate power. President Truman also had the misfortune of pressing for reform at a time when Congress was becoming increasingly institutionalized and slow moving. Congressional turnover was decreasing, seniority was becoming an unbreakable norm of advancement, committees did much of the legislative work and fiercely guarded their jurisdictions, and legislators were running highly localized campaigns.[17] Liberal party leaders and the president simply had few resources to bring recalcitrant Democrats in line. Between 1939 and 1955, the conservative coalition won more than 92 percent of the votes on which the alliance emerged.[18]

All this was no secret to contestants in the health care debate. When the AMA was not tarring national health insurance as "socialized medicine," it poured its energies into preserving the sympathetic mix of representatives on the critical congressional committees. As the AMA's legislative counsel would later recount, the association's lobbyists "had a pretty good idea and understanding that most legislative proposals don't come about by popular demand. . . . They realized that their ultimate fate depended on the composition of Congress and a couple of key committees like the House Ways and Means Committee and the Senate Finance Committee."[19] The AFL-CIO's chief legislative liaison agreed, unhappily, that "the structure of Congress, with the power that rests with committees and . . . the seniority system, means that Congress is very slow to respond to a felt need. . . . [Y]ou almost have to have an overwhelming sweep to get any social legislation through."[20] In a 1963 letter, Wilbur Cohen noted that conservative Democrats "don't need the President – the President needs them." "Our American political system is really unique in the world," he continued. "It is frustrating, exasperating, and complex. It has built in checks to prevent rapid action, dictatorship, and centralization."[21]

Still, not all health legislation was bottled up. Congress eagerly passed the Hospital Survey and Construction Act of 1946 – commonly known as the Hill-Burton Program after its congressional sponsors And beginning in the late 1940s, the federal government poured funds into medical research, training, and science, adding to the indirect support for medical education provided by the GI Bill's educational grants for returning soldiers. These measures were supported by medical interests and conservative legislators, who touted them as alternatives to the more sweeping government action envisioned by Truman.[22] They distributed funds widely as identifiable bundles of "particularized benefits" for which members of Congress could easily "claim credit."[23] And they augmented the already impressive technological arsenal of American medicine, which was fast emerging as the most costly and sophisticated in the world. As Lawrence Jacobs has argued, the United States is one of the few industrialized democracies that heavily funded acute hospital care and medical specialization before it moved to expand financial access to services – a sequence of government intervention that at once funneled new resources to the opponents of national health insurance and greatly raised the potential expense of future expansions of coverage.[24]

The Voluntary Way

In the rosy glow of postwar growth, however, these distant costs hardly seemed to matter. During the health care debate of the late 1940s, the influential consideration was not the expense of expanding coverage but the growing reach of voluntary insurance. Private insurance had not been central in previous battles over government-sponsored coverage, for the simple reason that it had not been central in American medical care. But now it was both, and the opponents of national health insurance called attention to its growth and promise as never before. After the obligatory salvos against socialized medicine had been launched, the critics of government health insurance always turned to the same battle-tested line of defense: Voluntary health insurance was solving whatever problems of financial access there were in America's otherwise idyllic medical system.[25]

It is difficult to overemphasize the degree to which the rapid expansion of private health insurance conditioned the postwar debate over national health insurance or contributed to the lukewarm political support that government insurance enjoyed. Yet later students of the period have tended to downplay these effects, choosing instead to review the rhetorical pyrotechnics of the opposition or reemphasize the legendary power of the AMA.[26] Participants in the debate saw things differently, as their actions and later reflections reveal. I. S. Falk, a prominent figure in the Truman reform campaign as he had been during the New Deal, recalled the trepidation of Social Security administrators regarding the federally encouraged expansion of private coverage:

> We were living day in and day out with the problems of health insurance as a private benefit through the employment relation, and the crises for the future that we thought we were building up through that mechanism. . . . You see, [with] the manpower freeze and the anti-inflation measures, the tax exemption, and the corporate income surcharge taxes, and so on . . . we were in the voluntary health insurance with a bang at that time. We were very well aware of what difficulties we were creating for the future with that.[27]

Marion Folsom, the Eastman Kodak executive who would become Eisenhower's social policy guru, viewed with favor what Falk feared, but he, too, emphasized that "the very fact that these voluntary plans had increased at a rapid rate convinced many people that we didn't need government health insurance for working people."[28]

For moderate conservatives like Folsom, the growing reach of private insurance provided, for the first time, a legitimate alternative to the expansion of Social Security. As early as 1945, the Republican leadership in the Senate prepared for the expected struggle with Truman by examining the development of voluntary plans. A major figure in these efforts was Senator Arthur Vandenberg of Michigan, the man behind the 1940s campaign to freeze old-age insurance taxes. A key member of Senator Taft's Republican Policy Committee, Vandenberg corresponded extensively with his personal physician, who was touting the extensive voluntary plans in Michigan, including the state medical society's own "Michigan Plan." In December 1945, Vandenberg confided that Republicans would "soon be pushed into consideration of the Administration's 'health' plans":

> Our great need, as I have indicated before, is a <u>constructive</u> <u>substitute</u>. The "Michigan Plan" is by far the best thing in sight. . . . We <u>must</u> have some

such alternative, because the appeal of the mass health protection idea is much too powerful to be spurned. . . . If some <u>incentive</u> could be devised to encourage the states to go along on the "Michigan idea" – perhaps modest grants-in-aid of some sort – it would permit us to give Congress a chance to register its preference for this voluntary system.[29]

No specific proposal seems to have emerged out of these contacts, presumably because the threat of national health insurance quickly receded with the 1946 Republican capture of Congress. Yet Vandenberg was merely ahead of his time – and colleagues. By 1949, each of the two credible competitors to the Wagner-Murray-Dingell bill, the bipartisan Hill-Aiken bill and the Republican Flanders-Ives bill, was premised upon the publicly funded expansion of private health insurance. This was a departure for opponents of national health insurance. Before World War II, the only legislative alternative to the Wagner-Murray-Dingell bill agreeable to critics on the right was an extension of federal funds for state medical assistance programs (a policy that, in fact, was quietly included in the 1950 amendments to Social Security). Yet both the Hill-Aiken and Flanders-Ives bills went beyond these minimal proposals to envision a more elaborate scheme of subsidies for low-income individuals who enrolled in private health plans.[30] In the end, these proposals were doomed by the refusal of Truman and organized labor to retreat from a Social Security–type program based on a contributory payroll tax.[31] But they signaled the shift of voluntary plans from a peripheral subject in the debate over health insurance to the center of attempts by conservatives to craft an alternative to government protections.[32]

No better evidence of this shift can be found than the evolving strategy of the AMA, the most visible and vocal foe of national health insurance. From its endorsement of physician-controlled indemnity plans in the early 1930s to its cautious embrace of service benefits later in the decade, the AMA had moderated its stance on private insurance without evincing much enthusiasm for the institutions it newly embraced. During the debate over the Truman plan, however, the AMA made voluntary health insurance the foundation of its bitter assault on government insurance. The most ubiquitous advertisement in the AMA's campaign featured a famous nineteenth-century Fildes painting, *The Doctor*, in which a compassionate physician ministers to a sick child as her grief-stricken parents hover nearby. In the AMA ad, the painting is ringed by the words: "Voluntary Health Insurance – The American Way Will KEEP POLITICS OUT OF THIS PICTURE."[33]

The advertisement, and others like it, were the product of the husband-and-wife public relations firm Whitaker and Baxter, which had earlier orchestrated the California Medical Association's successful battle against a 1945 proposal for public coverage sponsored by Governor Earl Warren. Borrowing a page from that conflict, Whitaker and Baxter emphasized that "[y]ou can't beat something with nothing," and exhorted the AMA to promote private health insurance at the same time as it vilified "socialized medicine."[34] "We want everybody in the health insurance field selling insurance as he never sold it before," declared Whitaker in a speech before the AMA in February 1949. "If we can get ten million more people insured in the next year and ten million more in the next year, the threat of socialized medicine in this country will be over."[35] That month, the AMA announced its intention to promote "further development and wider coverage by voluntary hospital and medical care plans," and in June, it dropped its long-standing opposition to lay-controlled private insurance.[36] Clearly more strategic than sincere, the AMA's new enthusiasm for voluntary coverage nonetheless demonstrated a new faith in the potential of private insurance to forestall a government program.

Although the AMA was the most prominent group touting the virtues and potential of private insurance, it was hardly alone. Commercial insurers and Blue Cross and Blue Shield were obviously on board, and so too was corporate America. All of the major business groups lined up against the Wagner-Murray-Dingell bill as they had against the Social Security Act in 1935.[37] This time, indeed, it was hard to find even corporate liberals sympathetic to the legislation. Folsom was against any federal action that would slow the growth of private plans.[38] (He would later flout business sentiment to support Republican proposals for a limited program of hospital insurance for the aged.)[39] Of the other usual corporate-liberal suspects, Gerard Swope was the only prominent supporter, and he was now retired as president of General Electric.[40] Business leaders let the vitriolic AMA spearhead the opposition to national health insurance. But nearly all were themselves virulently opposed to an expansion of Social Security into the field, preferring employer-controlled private benefits instead.[41]

Whether corporations expanded private health security in the 1940s in the hope of forestalling national health insurance is more difficult to say. "Management may feel that insurance and pension schemes are ransom devices to buy off the Welfare State," the editors of *Life* observed in 1949, echoing similar contemporary statements by benefits managers, insurers, and corporate executives.[42] For most firms, however, private health benefits were adopted for a mix of economic and political reasons, the most important of which were surely the twin pressures to attract workers and respond to (or head off) unions. With organized labor beginning to demand involvement in benefits decisions, corporations could not help but view the rise of private social welfare as a mixed bless-ing – useful for fostering employee goodwill, easy to celebrate in public defense of the free enterprise system, but also a commitment of resources that brought with it significant new corporate responsibilities. Despite these reservations, however, even the staunchly antibargaining National Association of Manufacturers recommended that more firms adopt health plans, while also demanding that all such programs "be based upon the judgment of management and of the owners of the business as to the future of that particular company."[43]

The historian Colin Gordon argues that employers responded to the rise of private health provision with "a short-sighted sense of their goals and concerns." Convinced "that only private provision could stem the greater evil of national health insurance," they found themselves forced to abandon "the prewar pattern of sporadic health provision and managerial discretion" and embrace more formalized and extensive plans, often in response to collective bargaining. Gordon caps his argu-ment with the claim that "given the limited scope and cost of private plans, there was little sense (as there had been in the 1935 Social Security debate) that national legislation might spread the costs of employment-based care more broadly among competitors and regions."[44]

This final contention is problematic – and not only because, as Chapter 2 showed, most employers with pension plans did not push for public programs to spread the cost of benefits in 1935. Private health insurance *was* as extensive in the mid-to-late 1940s as private pensions were in 1935, indeed considerably more so. More than 67 percent of large firms operated health and accident plans in 1946. By contrast, fewer than 4 percent operated group pensions in 1935, and fewer than 16 percent had informal or individual pensions, most of which were modest, discre-tionary, and could not be integrated with Social Security.[45] Among the population as a whole, roughly 3 million Americans actively participated in private pension plans in 1935, while 76.6 million had private health insurance coverage in 1950.[46] Although the divergent postwar response of employers to Social Security and proposals for national health insurance does indeed furnish a crucial point of comparison, it cannot be easily explained by differences in the potential for spreading fringe-benefit expenditures.

The primary reason that employers responded differently to old-age insurance and health insurance, the historical record suggests, was simply that a public program of old-age insurance was already in place in the late 1940s, whereas government health insurance was not. Although most employers opposed old-age insurance when it was first proposed, most had by the late 1940s accommodated themselves to its existence.

Much of this shift in opinion was born of straightforward political realism, a stance of acquiescence rather than enthusiasm based on the assumption that Social Security was an accepted fact of U.S. social policy. As Folsom described the response of Republicans and business leaders: "[T]hey were simply adapting themselves to change. After a system has been in effect for twenty years, the country is pretty well accustomed to it. . . . If they'd come out against Social Security, they'd have had a terrific amount of opposition from a lot of people – not only the older people but everybody else, because the country was pretty well sold on it by that time."[47] Eisenhower's Social Security Commissioner, William Mitchell, echoed these arguments: "[I]t became evident that the Republicans politically could not turn the pages of history back. The Social Security program as a whole, with primary emphasis on old age, survivors', and disability insurance, was a fixture in the American society and the American economy."[48]

Working in favor of Social Security, therefore, was the same factor that was working against national health insurance: the status-quo bias of American political institutions, which made it harder to repudiate an existing program like old-age insurance than to block a prospective one like national health insurance. As Folsom and Mitchell recognized, however, Social Security enjoyed deeper advantages: It served a growing constituency, had become a more visible and popular program, and was interwoven into American labor practice. All this made its elimination or radical retrenchment increasingly improbable.

And yet more than strategic resignation was at work in the shifting reaction of employers to Social Security. As we saw in Part II, many employers had in fact become genuinely supportive of modest increases in old-age insurance benefits and coverage, viewing the program as a floor of retirement protection that created a more level competitive playing field while allowing firms to direct private pensions to the skilled personnel they viewed as most valuable.[49] Indeed, the integration of Social Security and private pensions meant that expansion of old-age insurance offset much of the cost to firms of negotiated private plans. These benefits to employers, I argued in Chapter 2, were not the key motive behind federal old-age insurance, but they were an important consequence of it – one partly anticipated, partly unexpected, and partly the result of business-favorable policies passed in the decade after 1935.

In contrast to company pensions, however, the large-scale emergence of employment-based health insurance occurred in a field lacking a core public program of social insurance. This was a crucial difference. First, and most obviously, the absence of a framework of government health insurance meant that employers *could* adopt private health plans providing basic protection and *could* fight to defeat national health insurance, both of which they vigorously did.

A second result of the absence of a government health program was more subtle. The private benefits that employers adopted in health care were different from those that they adopted in the pension domain. Especially after labor turned to collective bargaining, employer-sponsored health insurance aimed to provide relatively comprehensive protection for most employees within a firm or industry. It was difficult to see how such benefits could coexist with government insurance, and indeed, some employers wrote clauses into their plans stating that they would be discontinued if national health insurance passed.[50] Revealingly, conservatives who defended Social Security as a "minimum basic layer of protection" did not take the same view of public medical insurance. "New problems arise if the government decides to extend social insurance to the field of health benefits," complained the influential Metropolitan actuary Reinhard Hohaus before the 1942 American Life Convention. "These problems would seem to indicate that, in many cases at least, the function of private health insurance and private medical care should be in the nature of an alternative method of providing the *entire* coverage ... rather than just additional coverage to supplement basic minimum protection otherwise offered by social insurance." Of course, Hohaus did not favor public health insurance at all. Like the nation's business and medical leaders, and like the insurance executives to which he spoke, he believed direct government action "appropriate only ... where the choice would seem to lie between a bare minimum governmentally provided, and outright charity or nothing at all."[51]

The Retreat from Universal Insurance

The same was not true of organized labor, which placed national health insurance near the top of its legislative priorities in the late 1940s. Since the failure of the AALL campaign for compulsory insurance, the stance of national labor leaders toward public social insurance had evolved from outright opposition to relatively unenthusiastic support to wholehearted advocacy. With union density greater in the United States than any time before – higher, in fact, than it was at this time in Canada – American unions eschewed the voluntarist outlook that had once characterized their national political activities and now wholeheartedly embraced a reformist political agenda centered around tripartite bargaining, government-guaranteed full employment, and an expansion of public social programs.[52]

The burial of the Truman plan, however, made it clear that unions would either wrest concession from employers or go without health benefits altogether. As early as 1946, United Auto Workers President Walter Reuther had declared: "There is no evidence to encourage the belief that we may look to Congress for relief. In the immediate future, security will be won for our people only to the extent that the union succeeds in obtaining such security through collective bargaining."[53] Reuther's prediction would prove prescient. In the decade after 1945, organized labor negotiated health and pension benefits in industry after industry, which nonunion corporations in turn often matched to forestall or deflect union organizing drives. In 1946, negotiated plans covered fewer than a million workers and their dependents. Between 1948 and 1950, however, the number rose from 2.7 million to more than 7 million, and by 1954, it had reached 27 million – a fourth of all health insurance in the United States.[54]

The rise of collectively bargained health plans closely mirrored the rise of negotiated pensions, but again with a critical difference. Unions treated private pensions as a supplement to Social Security. The vast majority of union-negotiated pensions (some 85 percent in 1950) promised benefits that were either related to or fully inclusive of expected Social Security benefits.[55] By contrast, unions turned to private health insurance as an *alternative* to national health insurance. Following the precedent set in mining, autos, and steel, unions sought "first-dollar" coverage for a broad range of hospital and medical services with few, if any, limits on maximum benefits.[56] Michael K. Brown contends that "labor unions would have made bargaining over corporate welfare programs an issue regardless of the outcome of legislative struggles [in the late 1940s]. . . . Liberalization of social security benefits would not have quelled labor's thirst for private pensions, because they were viewed as a supplement to social security rather than an alternative."[57] The same, however, was not true of health insurance. Had national health insurance or a relatively comprehensive alternative to it passed, the scramble to expand private health plans that began in the late 1940s would have been significantly constrained. As it was, private health plans emerged as the core source of health security, and it was public programs that would emerge later to deal with groups unprotected by the emerging private system.

This had important implications for labor views of national health insurance. For as employee health insurance spread through the workforce, it could not help but reduce the interest of unions and covered workers in a government program of protection.[58] Private health benefits, after all, reduced worker demands for health security while providing unions with an important organizing tool and means of securing member loyalty. Truman Administration officials worried incessantly that private bargaining was eliminating the constituency and rationale for national health insurance – fears that seemed confirmed when John L. Lewis came out against national health insurance after the mine workers negotiated their health and welfare plan.[59] A more ominous portent could be discerned in the contrasting degrees of enthusiasm for national health insurance evinced by the AFL and CIO before their merger in 1955. Traditionally a defender of voluntarism, the craft-based AFL was initially left out of the postwar drive for private health security and thus remained committed to government action, while the industrial unions of the CIO concentrated their energies on winning concessions at the bargaining table.[60] Throughout the Truman battle, however, virtually all national labor leaders continued to voice enthusiasm for national health insurance.

Nonetheless, while the labor movement remained on paper the major organized supporter of national health insurance, its enthusiasm clearly was bleeding away with the emergence of collectively bargained benefits. A confidential memo prepared by the UAW in 1949, for example, strongly emphasized the continuing need for national health insurance but warned that "labor leaders will be forced by their constituents to support collective bargaining programs, rather than government programs, if the proposals for government programs provide for too heavy a levy on earnings."[61] In the early 1950s, the Committee on the Nation's Health, a pro-reform organization with close ties to the Truman Administration, lamented "a tendency on the part of many unions to lose effective interest in national health legislation even thought they may continue to give it verbal support in convention resolutions."[62] Nelson Cruikshank, the AFL-CIO's point man on health insurance from the Truman battle through the passage of Medicare, was considerably more blunt:

> [V]ery frankly ... while there were a lot of labor leaders that still talked about [national health insurance], the steam had gone out of it. You see, if you have it on a contributory health insurance basis, you increase the tax, whereas a lot of the health insurance for union people is paid for by the employer. ... So looking at the choice of a national health insurance scheme in which he would have to support it by a contributor payroll tax as against somewhat adequate protection ... that he could get with the employer footing the bill with the aid of a tax support, he never just turned against it, but the sex appeal went out of it.[63]

The large-scale development of private benefits did not merely decrease the "sex appeal" of tax-financed programs. It also divided workers by sector, region, and union, improving the status of workers in the core of the economy, yet increasing the vulnerabilities of those without insurance by further accelerating medical inflation. And, at the same time, labor-negotiated plans channeled union energies into plan negotiation and administration rather than direct political action on behalf of broader goals. Unions did not cease to act as a force for universal insurance in the decades to come. But their support did grow weaker, their position less unified, and their legislative demands less rooted in rank-and-file agitation. "Provision of health security for some," concludes the historian Alan Derickson, "served to undermine the chances for legislating protection for all."[64]

The major area of exception was retiree health insurance. Although most union-negotiated plans covered dependents, only a small proportion allowed workers to retain employer-based coverage after retirement. Moreover, few employers contributed to the premiums of retirees, which were often several times as great as those for workers. Unions pressed employers to include retirees in negotiated plans and insurers to provide retiree coverage at reasonable rates. Unlike benefits for active workers, however, the needs of retirees remained a responsibility that most labor leaders believed government would have to assume.[65]

If union members were particularly affected by the postwar spread of private benefits, the rise of voluntary protection also appears to have conditioned perceptions of national health insurance among the public more generally, occurring as it did in conjunction with the AMA's postwar public relations blitz. Polls taken during and immediately after the war showed strong majority support for national insurance. Yet public approval declined during the debate over the Truman proposal, and by 1949, support and opposition were almost equal.[66] Of those who expressed familiarity with Truman's plan, support fell thirteen percentage points between 1945 and 1949, while opposition rose sixteen points.

More telling were those few surveys that probed Americans' relative perceptions of public and private insurance. A poll commissioned by the California Medical Association in 1943, for example, found that support for a "socialized government controlled plan" fell from one-half to one-quarter when it was compared with voluntary health insurance.[67] A survey conducted by the AMA asked Americans what might be done to assist with medical bills. The share of those offering a solution who spontaneously mentioned government insurance held steady at 8 percent between 1945 and 1947, while the proportion who mentioned voluntary insurance increased from 39 to 44 percent.[68] A 1949 Gallup poll showed that Americans preferred, by a fourteen-point margin, a national health plan based on employment-based private insurance to the Truman plan.[69]

The president of the Opinion Research Corporation explained to Congress in 1949 that "[a]lthough there is widespread agreement on the need for an easier method of paying for medical care . . . the issue of government versus private sponsorship is still an undecided question in the public mind. . . . [I]t is our considered judgment that that present sentiment favors insurance-company plans over either Government sponsorship or doctor-organization plans."[70]

Yet the clearest sign of the changing fortunes of national health insurance was the changing strategy of its strongest supporters: the Social Security executives who had helped develop the Wagner-Murray-Dingell bill and now realized that its immediate passage was impossible. Even as the Federal Security Agency had become a key player in postwar collective bargaining, it had remained fiercely critical of voluntary health plans, as well as of measures to support them through direct subsidies or additional tax relief.[71] In 1950, however, administration officials bowed to the inevitable and began to search for a more limited legislative alternative that would still retain the contributory social insurance structure of Social Security. Truman initially bridled at the suggestion. Yet the head of the Federal Security Agency, Oscar Ewing, convinced him that a contributory program providing only hospital insurance for the aged could serve as a "pilot plant operation" demonstrating the feasibility of government health insurance.[72] The proposal that was publicly advocated by Ewing in June 1951 and then introduced by pro-administration Democrats in 1952 promised up to sixty days of hospital treatment annually to Social Security recipients, their spouses, and, in the event of death, their survivors.

The new proposal was a major strategic retreat for the advocates of national health insurance, incomprehensible without an appreciation of the constricting legacies of previous policy developments. In contrast to the Wagner-Murray-Dingell bill, which provided near-universal federal insurance against a comprehensive range of medical services, the proposal offered only sixty days of hospital care and extended its protections only to active recipients of Social Security, their spouses, and their survivors. As such, it was a plan without international precedent, for "no other industrial country in the world has begun its government health insurance program with the aged."[73] The proposal looked just as odd when compared with the arguments and commitments of its creators. Not simply limited to the aged and hospital care, the proposal was also restricted to active recipients of Social Security, who in 1952 still represented less than 60 percent of the aged and, on the whole, the better-off among them.[74] Thus, Social Security executives called for federal action by citing old-age poverty and the catastrophic medical expenses faced by elderly Americans as a whole, even while their proposal covered only sixty days of hospital care and excluded the elderly whose plight was greatest.

Only in light of the divergent trajectories of old-age and health insurance can these otherwise perplexing choices be understood. The turn to the aged replicated the successful strategy behind old-age insurance, singling out a segment of the population viewed with sympathy and concern by many. Never mind that Social Security was limited to the aged because it provided retirement income, while health insurance was clearly needed both in retirement and during the working years. The successful expansion of old-age insurance in 1950 made program executives all the more eager to tie health insurance to Social Security's contributory architecture, even if that meant excluding not just active workers but also a significant share of the elderly on whom the case for the program was based.

What cemented these strategic inclinations was the stunning rise of private health security. The elderly were, after all, the most identifiable and clearly "deserving" group left out of employment-based coverage. Poorer and sicker than the rest of the population, they rarely enjoyed health insurance after retirement, and few could obtain affordable insurance because the problem of adverse selection was too great.[75] As just discussed, elderly pensioners were also the one group for which organized labor felt no ambivalence when it came to demanding government insurance. As for the limitation of coverage to hospital care, this was primarily "a response to past AMA hysteria."[76] Yet it was also an attempt to trade on the legitimacy of Blue Cross – a motive that also prompted advocates to incorporate into their reform blueprint a significant administrative role for private plans. As Cohen and others within the administration saw it, "the private sector had sold our case."[77] The proposal would be cast as simply extending accepted insurance practices to the aged. Labor leaders enthusiastically embraced this new attack. According to Cruikshank, hospital insurance for the aged was presented as "a public Blue Cross program. This was our pitch, our strategy: 'Now, we can get this through collective bargaining for our members up to retirement, but we can't do it for the older people.' "[78]

In return for these rhetorical advantages, however, advocates inevitably made significant concessions. Gone from the reformers' rhetorical arsenal was the principled indictment of voluntary insurance that had been so central to their campaign in the late 1940s. Instead, as a 1951 FSA memo instructed, reformers would now argue that their plan "would not adversely affect existing insurance plans," because it "would not invade a field of substantial interest to private insurance, non-profit or commercial."[79] Arthur Hess, a deputy commissioner of Social Security, noted that the argument for government action was increasingly a narrow pragmatic one: "[I]t was just in terms of, 'Everybody accepts the insurance type mechanism as the answer here, and to the extent that it works in voluntary hands and works well, the government can't do it any cheaper. To the extent that it doesn't work in voluntary hands, somebody's got to step in.' "[80] Of course, claiming that private health insurance worked for most Americans weakened the case for the national health program to which Social Security executives were still deeply committed. But it strengthened the case for a hospital program modeled after Blue Cross and made the exclusion of elderly Americans from private health insurance appear all the more pressing.

By the 1950s, therefore, the legacies of past political struggles over health insurance had created a dense thicket of interests and constraints through which any health reform proposal would need to pass. The medical profession had emerged as the dominant actor within American medicine, and its formidable lobbying organization had become the most feared in U.S. politics. Allied with employers, insurers, and the burgeoning medical industry, the AMA and local medical societies were actively promoting private plans that protected the profession's income and prerogatives. They were aided inadvertently by American labor, which had turned away from the political arena in frustration and was concentrating its energies on private-sector negotiations to obtain valuable benefits, such as health insurance. The private-sector welfare system that was being constructed did not, however, resemble the universal welfare states emerging in Europe. Private insurance was reaching the employed, wealthy, and well organized. It was leaving behind the unemployed, poor, and unorganized. In a reluctant recognition of these emerging realities, advocates of government insurance had chosen to limit their initial focus to the most politically appealing of these newly vulnerable groups – the elderly.

Eisenhower and the Triumph of Workplace Insurance

When Republican war hero Dwight Eisenhower entered the White House in 1952, allies and opponents alike expected retrenchment of existing social programs and rejection of new ones. They proved only half right. Although old-age assistance continued to wither and universal health legislation vanished overnight, Social Security expanded significantly and federal social expenditures shifted from veterans and assistance spending to social insurance. These outcomes were not, to be sure, all Eisenhower's doing. But the paradoxical character of the social policy record of his presidency – consolidation and expansion of Social Security, yet few new initiatives, especially in health insurance – does neatly encapsulate the schismatic character of postwar conservative thinking. By the mid-1950s, as we have seen, Social Security enjoyed bipartisan support and general business acceptance. Yet proposals for even modest programs of government health insurance remained a target of bitter opposition and dispute. In this sense, Eisenhower's "middle way" was as much a manifestation of the split personality of conservative sentiment as of his own oft-voiced ambivalence toward the welfare state.

Even this, however, does not capture the most distinctive and interesting aspect of Eisenhower's record: his active leadership in codifying the unique public–private structure of U.S. social policy. For Eisenhower, conservatism meant preserving and strengthening existing social policy approaches.[81] It called for "greater effectiveness in our programs, both public and private, offering safeguards against the privations that too often come with unemployment, old age, illness, and accident." Thus, while Eisenhower believed that "[b]etter health insurance protections for more people can be provided," he insisted that "[g]overnment need not and should not go into the insurance business to furnish the protection which private and non-profit organizations do not now provide . . . [but] should work with them to study and devise better insurance protection to meet the public need."[82] Nowhere was this neglected theme of the Eisenhower presidency on more vivid display than in the three episodes that defined his approach to health insurance: the administration's 1954 reinsurance proposal, the Revenue Act of 1954, and the Federal Employees Health Benefits Program of 1959.[83]

The purest expression of Eisenhower's vision, reinsurance, was also the clearest failure – repudiated by Eisenhower's allies in Congress as well as by the very organizations it was intended to aid. The goal of the proposal was to indemnify private insurers against catastrophic losses to encourage them to sign up high-risk groups like the elderly. According to a drafter of the plan, the proposal would have "put government squarely behind private health insurance" with a modest program that "might have headed off a compulsory plan."[84] But this support was so modest as to be meaningless – a one-time cost of no more than $25 million – and it came with the overwhelming drawback that insurers would need to open their books to the federal government to prove losses. For such minimal assistance, insurers were unwilling to invite federal regulation of an industry long protected from it, and although initially sympathetic, they quickly joined with the AMA to argue that the proposal posed a dangerous precedent. The bill was crushed in the House, with 38 percent of Republicans voting against it.[85]

Yet medical and business groups supported another Eisenhower-initiated effort to bolster private insurance, one that was immensely more significant for the continued expansion of coverage. This was the 1954 clarification of the tax status of employer-sponsored health insurance – which, along with an expansion of the individual medical expense deduction, was a major, if little debated, step in the solidification of America's expanding system of private insurance. The special tax treatment of health insurance did not originate with the Revenue Act of 1954. Even before the Act's passage, as the last chapter pointed out, employer contributions to health plans had generally been treated as nontaxable. But this treatment had been informal, ambiguous, and marked by conflicting precedents. More important, the favorable IRS stance emerged before health insurance was a sizable expense for firms and taxes were a sizable expense for workers – and hence, before the exclusion was a sizable expense for the federal government. By the early 1950s, however, neither the gaping hole in tax receipts nor the evident confusion of present law could be ignored by the IRS. In a series of federal cases, the IRS fought for the principle that special tax benefits should accrue only to conventional insurance, raising new concerns about the taxability not only of self-funded company plans but also of union health and welfare funds.[86] In 1953, the IRS also ruled that, unlike group insurance, "employers' contributions to individual health insurance policies were taxable" as compensation.[87] It was against this backdrop that the 1954 push for a blanket tax exemption occurred, with the goal, as Eisenhower put it, of encouraging "insurance and other plans adopted by employers to protect their employees against the risks of sickness . . . by removing the present uncertainties in the tax law."[88]

The Eisenhower Administration portrayed the tax exclusion of employer contributions and the expansion of the medical expense deduction as obviously beneficial social policies rather than tax measures alone. Treasury Secretary George Humphrey testified before the Senate that the expanded medical expense deduction would assist more than 8 million people, while his undersecretary (none other than Marion Folsom) emphasized that the tax exemption for employer health contributions "would benefit almost all employees at some time or other."[89] Interest groups that had lined up against national health insurance now showed up to sing the administration's praise. Noting that the "rapid growth of voluntary health insurance has made a Federal system of compulsory health insurance unnecessary," the AHA commended the "policy of the present administration to encourage enrollment in voluntary health insurance."[90] The AMA claimed that tax breaks "would encourage people to look after their own health rather than turn to the government for assistance."[91] The *Wall Street Journal* praised the Act as "a part answer to the false lures of socialized medicine," which would not "put the Government in the business of issuing pills or listening through stethoscopes."[92]

Perhaps surprisingly, given labor's stance on national health insurance, union leaders also worked behind the scenes to bring about the 1954 codification. When the Treasury Department announced it was reviewing the tax treatment of fringe benefits, the CIO submitted a frank memorandum to the Department on behalf of "five million wage earners," stating that a "change in the rules of the Bureau of Internal Revenue or a specific amendment to the Internal Revenue Code to define such employer payments as taxable income to . . . employees would be both inequitable and impracticable."[93] The CIO memo pointed out the huge costs and dislocations that would result if employer contributions were taxed and hard-fought contracts had to be reopened. It closed, however, by appealing directly to the Eisenhower Administration's conservative instincts: "One last point – the significance of which cannot be over-emphasized – which must be considered by the Treasury Department, is the harmful effect which a reversal of the present tax ruling would have on the growth of voluntary hospitalization and medical plans."[94] The same CIO that had testified before Congress in 1949 that "[t]he voluntary groups are limited by their very nature from providing comprehensive care to everyone" now criticized any action that would "adversely affect the continued growth of voluntary prepayment plans and their development as a mechanism for providing comprehensive health services to the American people."[95] The unions need not have worried. Although longtime Treasury staff outlined several possible means of taxing benefits, it was a foregone conclusion that Folsom and his seven-member "advisory group" of insurance and industry representatives would recommend expanded tax concessions.[96]

Tax breaks for health care were a form of spending – big spending, it turned out. But they were not treated as such by their advocates, and no one professed to know exactly how much they would cost. This was nicely revealed in a testy exchange between Folsom and Senator Russell Long during the Senate hearings:

> Senator Long: How much will that [tax exemption of health insurance] cost?
> Undersecretary Folsom: We haven't any estimate on that. . . .
> Long: If that is something that you are going to benefit everyone with, why haven't you gone to the trouble of finding what the expense will be?
> Folsom: It is very difficult to estimate it.
> Long: How much do you think it will cost the government?

Folsom: I don't know.
Long: Is it going to be a major loss of revenue?
Folsom: No, but it will be a benefit to the people who get it.
Long: Do you think it will cost as much as $15 million?
Folsom: Oh, probably.
Long: You think it would cost as much as $15 million?
Folsom: We haven't any figures at all on that.
Long: Isn't it your responsibility to advise us how much revenue these benefits would cost?[97]

Nor was there much mention of the distributional consequences of channeling subsidies through the tax code. Walter Reuther of the CIO criticized the medical expense deduction (but not, of course, the tax exclusion of health insurance) on the grounds that its benefits accrued predominantly to higher-income Americans. But his was almost the lone dissent. The Eisenhower Administration, in fact, presented the provisions as a key source of *equality* in the 1954 revision. Nonetheless, the distribution of these health-related tax subsidies comported with no known theory of tax equity, much less any articulated philosophy of social justice. The tax exclusion for employer-provided health insurance benefited only those who had workplace coverage – at this time, roughly half of Americans – and its value was vastly greater for those with higher incomes because they paid taxes at higher marginal rates. Pensions were subject to modest nondiscrimination rules, but health plans were (and would remain) essentially exempt from these requirements. Indeed, although the House version of the legislation had incorporated nondiscrimination language, the Senate bill explicitly designated that the rules that applied to pensions should *not* govern private health plans, and this language was retained in the final legislation.[98]

On the face of it, the medical expense deduction was less skewed, because it exempted medical expenses only if they exceeded a share of income (then 3 percent). Yet the value of the deduction was again much greater for those who faced high rates, and the deduction required that taxpayers itemize their returns, which few lower-income citizens did. Despite this, the major objection to the deduction in Congress came not from liberals concerned about inequities, but from conservatives eager to remove the percentage threshold to offer the greatest possible inducement to private health spending.[99] Save for these occasional conservative complaints, however, the special tax treatment of health insurance and spending went virtually unmentioned during debate over the Revenue Act of 1954. Fundamental policy choices that would cost billions of tax dollars, redistribute benefits and burdens in critical ways, and significantly shape private benefits and the prospects for government insurance were either ignored or treated as salutary modifications worth little comment.

The final initiative that exemplified Eisenhower's approach to health policy was the creation in 1959 of the Federal Employees Health Benefits Program (FEHBP), a plan to purchase private insurance for federal workers. Rather than have government assume the risk of medical costs, the FEHBP contracted with private plans for all insurance functions and simply oversaw enrollment, paying a fixed amount toward private premiums. The vast majority of enrollees chose Blue Cross/Blue Shield coverage – which was not altogether surprising, for the Blues heavily influenced the structure of the legislation.[100] By the early 1970s, the FEHBP accounted for roughly 6 percent of the enrollment and 8 percent of the premium income of Blue Cross. It was, one plan representative declared, "the most spectacular thing that has ever happened in the history of this business."[101]

Though the FEHBP was the "largest voluntary employee group health insurance program in the world," it was not considered a significant event by advocates of national health insurance.[102] In purchasing coverage for federal employees, the government was acting as an employer, not a provider of general social protection. Yet the FEHBP did bring the Blues into a much more intimate and extensive relationship with government than they had previously enjoyed – a new orientation that was mirrored in the increased appreciation of the plans' institutional potential among centrist conservatives in Congress and the White House. After 1959, the FEHBP would be the basis for the key proposals floated by liberal Republicans as alternatives to the Democratic aspiration of federal hospital insurance for the aged. In later years, it would be recast as a market-based approach to national health insurance, then rediscovered as the model for President Clinton's failed Health Security Plan, and finally become the template for restructuring Medicare to increase the role of private health plans.

The birth of the FEHBP at the close of the 1950s was an appropriate counterpoint to the death of national health insurance at the close of the 1940s. In the intervening decade, national health insurance had disappeared from the agenda. Large corporations and labor unions had come to realize, each for different reasons, that private insurance was the best available means of achieving their goals. The medical lobby and political conservatives had embraced private protections as the strongest defense against public incursions. The federal government had entered the field not as a guarantor of social insurance but as a largely passive financier of private industry, providing symbolic affirmation of employment-based insurance by belatedly climbing onto the corporate bandwagon to purchase coverage for its own workers. There was, in short, every sign that private health insurance had won out for employed Americans, just as there was every sign that Social Security would remain the core provider of retirement income.

No votes on this outcome had been taken. No grand alternatives had been put to citizens for a test. Indeed, judging by the debates that did transpire after 1950, there were no real choices to be made. Private insurance received ever more costly subsidies. Yet defenders of the voluntary way denied that government was implicated at all. Some Americans were well served and others left out, but discussion of winners and losers was lost in the celebration of private progress and the complexities of tax tables. Americans had found themselves caught up in a fierce battle over national health insurance, but the increasingly privileged place of private insurance in the American social welfare regime prompted little debate at all.

The Passage of Medicare

The institutionalization of employment-based health insurance set in motion opposed but interwoven forces, cementing the place of private insurance in the workplace yet creating powerful new pressures to assist those left unprotected. This is the fundamental dynamic that lay behind Medicare, explaining both why a government program finally overcame the opposition of its foes and why it was so much more limited than foreign precedents – and than the true aspirations of its supporters. Although the details of the breakthrough were hardly predetermined, the basic structure of Medicare is explicable only in light of the constricting effects that private health insurance had on the agenda of health care reformers. For while Medicare brought the federal government into health care financing on a large scale, it also conformed to the logic of private-sector developments and, as a result, proved an obstacle as well as an aid in the struggle for national health insurance.

If the dramatic postwar expansion of employment-based coverage displaced national health insurance from the political agenda, it also cast in stark relief the growing plight of those who lacked even minimal protection. All told, two-thirds of Americans had some form of coverage in 1958. Yet families with incomes in the highest third of the spectrum were more than twice as likely to be insured as those in the bottom third. Although most families headed by full-time workers had insurance, coverage was much less prevalent among families headed by part-time and temporary workers, women outside the labor force, and the disabled.[103] Only 38 percent of the aged who were no longer working had coverage, with the likelihood of protection inversely related to medical need.[104] Coverage was higher in manufacturing than in other sectors, higher in metropolitan areas than in rural areas, and higher in the Northeast, Midwest, and West than in the South.[105] For those too poor to afford insurance, for those without strong connections to the workforce, for those whose employers did not offer coverage, for those who were old, disabled, or chronically ill, the promises made on behalf of the voluntary way rang hollow.[106]

This was especially true because of a major shift that was occurring in the world of private health insurance: the abandonment of community rating in favor of premium rates tied to the expected health experience of enrollees. Charging similar rates to all subscribers had been a hallmark of the Blue Cross philosophy, as well as a central justification for the plans' special treatment under law. Yet, as commercial carriers moved into the market, offering to lower-risk groups experience-rated premiums that promised substantial savings, the Blue Cross plans found themselves under fierce competitive pressure to abandon this traditional ideal. By 1958, only twenty-two of the seventy-seven Blue Cross plans in operation did not engage in experience rating of some form.[107]

The shift to experience rating had consequences both inimical and conducive to future government action. By favoring large groups across which risks could be safely spread and by rewarding firms and unions with relatively healthy workforces, experience rating immensely strengthened the foundation of large-group coverage while increasing the reluctance of low-risk groups to participate in broader insurance pools.[108] It thus further fragmented and divided the potential constituency for inclusive public social insurance. At the same time, however, the full-scale move to experience rating made it all the more unlikely that private insurance would reach those who were disabled or chronically ill or who lacked strong workforce attachments. Increasingly, insurers argued that any effort to enroll high-risk individuals who were not members of large and healthy groups would lead to massive adverse selection against private plans.

Opponents of national health insurance recognized all too well that the weaknesses of the private system threatened past victories. Moderate conservatives who had worked to encourage private insurance in the early 1950s continued to entreat the private sector to extend coverage on its own. Folsom, for example, tried to attract insurance companies behind a proposal for the relaxation of antitrust laws, which would allow plans to pool risks among themselves, but once again, insurers recoiled at the invitation to federal regulation.[109] Their response exemplified the frustrating progress of middle-way solutions, which were consistently thwarted by the overwhelming barriers to coordinated industry action and the excessive confidence of national health insurance's most persistent foes.

The first obstacle doomed the increasingly desperate private attempts to cover the elderly, whose plight proved stubbornly impervious to the favorable policies and private promotional activities that had helped push coverage to record heights among working Americans. In the early 1960s, a series of coordinated industry approaches were launched with great fanfare: an alliance among the Blues, the AMA, and the AHA; a declaration by Blue Cross and the AHA that it would create a national hospital plan for the aged; a similar declaration by Blue Shield and the AMA; and an ongoing campaign by the Health Insurance Association of America to promote the creation of commercial plans focused on the aged. From the sidelines, congressional conservatives watched and prodded, publicly celebrating the new initiatives while privately reminding the industry of the "urgency of developing a weapon with which to fight the imminent threat of medical aid tied to the Social Security system."[110]

Yet all these efforts came to naught. Commercial insurers continued to poach low-risk groups, driving the Blues away from community rating just as their national leaders demanded the opposite. Plans that enrolled the aged at community rates were unable to compete for regular subscribers, while plans that tied rates to health status were forced to charge exorbitant premiums to the high-risk elderly who desired insurance. The scattered success stories were due entirely to the collaboration of private insurers with state programs assisting the elderly poor. For realists within the national Blue Cross organization and the AHA, it became clear that some federal support would be needed to enroll the aged in voluntary plans.[111]

The gradual softening of Blue Cross and AHA opposition to direct federal support, however, ran headlong into the second major obstacle to a conservative-backed compromise: the continued intransigence of the AMA and other hard-core opponents of federal action. The AMA had reluctantly supported the 1960 Kerr-Mills program to fund state programs for the indigent aged and was convinced that no further concessions were needed. Major business groups were also opposed to a federal program, which was seen both as a new expense and as a dangerous precedent.[112] So, too, were commercial insurance companies, and even the more sympathetic Blue Cross association and AHA continued to argue for assistance to private health insurance, rather than a federal program. Although public opinion was increasingly running in favor of action – polls throughout the early 1960s showed consistent two-thirds majorities supporting Democratic proposals – die-hard opponents remained convinced of their continued political ascendancy.[113]

Nonetheless, work continued on measures that threaded between the AMA's recalcitrance and the ambitions of Democratic reformers. These proposals have received little subsequent attention, for the obvious reason that they did not make it into law. Yet had political events taken a different turn, they very well could have become the basis for eventual federal legislation. Just as with Democratic proposals, the roots of these initiatives traced back to the Eisenhower years. In this case, however, they emerged out the strategic thinking of a small group of HEW Republicans who had ongoing communications with insurance leaders and congressional allies like Senator Javits. The basic aim of this group, according to Assistant Secretary Elliot Richardson, was "to use the Social Security system simply to collect money, which would be used to pay for a uniform amount for the cost of health insurance, which would have been provided alternatively under a government-administered fund . . . [or] other approved options, which might be voluntary or commercial."[114] Thus, the moderates rejected means-tested assistance in favor of social insurance, but also rejected direct federal insurance in favor of a contracting program similar to the FEHBP, in which private insurers would be allowed to underwrite risks.

A compromise along these lines came very close to becoming law, closer indeed than is generally appreciated.[115] By 1957, Cohen was telling Altmeyer that

> [i]f we are going to make any headway in the hospitalization or medical care field, I think we have to reluctantly admit that the only way we can get it is by accepting "contracting out." Each month that goes by the voluntary plans expand and proliferate. . . . I think there is no reasonable hope for even such a modest program as hospitalization insurance unless you are willing to, in some way or other, recognize the existence of existing coverage.[116]

Once he became President Kennedy's assistant secretary for legislation at HEW in 1961, Cohen worked feverishly to assemble votes behind various proposals that would allow aged Americans to turn down government health coverage for private insurance or an equivalent cash grant.[117] Although the effort failed, a bipartisan Senate coalition led by Javits managed to win narrow approval for a cash option in 1964, only to see Wilbur Mills assemble the votes to kill it in the House–Senate conference with the promise that federal legislation would be taken up the next year. Mills, however, was not the only obstacle. Most Republicans remained intransigent, insurers were skeptical, and the AFL-CIO opposed allowing private plans to underwrite federally funded benefits.[118] Still, these ideas came remarkably close to fruition. "[W]ith a little bit more Republican support," speculated Social Security official Arthur Hess, "there could have been a distinct turn that would have caused Medicare to turn out much more like the federal employees' health program, with an underwriting or contracting role for private insurance."[119]

As it was, however, Hess did not have a chance to find out. In 1965, a window of opportunity for major reform opened in the wake of President Lyndon B. Johnson's landslide victory. The 1964 elections ushered in a two-to-one Democratic majority in Congress and, for the first time, gave reform-minded northern liberals within the Democratic party a decisive edge.[120] The 1964 sweep meant that some kind of program for the elderly was a "legislative certainty."[121] The question was what form it would take. In keeping with the incremental strategy outlined more than a decade earlier, reformers were still pressing for federal hospital insurance for the aged. But Mills recognized that such a limited program would create unstoppable pressures for programmatic expansion, just as reformers secretly hoped it would.[122] Fearing, in particular, that unchecked public demands could increase the Social Security payroll tax beyond the breaking point, Mills proposed expanding the Democratic proposal for federal hospital insurance to include two additional items: a physicians' insurance plan financed mainly by general income tax revenues and a federal–state program for the poor, modeled after Kerr-Mills (the enlarged program was called "Medicaid"). The Johnson Administration delightedly agreed, and Mills's "three-layer cake" sailed through Congress over lingering Republican opposition.

Medicare was a reflection of the constricted political opening through which it passed. The bill itself promised that "nothing in this title shall be construed to authorize any federal official or employee to exercise any supervision or control over the practice of medicine."[123] While Medicare did not allow private insurers to underwrite risk, it did permit them to act as "fiscal intermediaries" for the program. These intermediaries would pay for services at rates that were "reasonable and customary," meaning, at the outset, essentially whatever providers chose to charge. Not surprisingly, the cost of the program outstripped even the most expansive expectations voiced before passage. In the decade following Medicare's passage, federal health outlays rose from less than $10 billion to more than $40 billion and from 2.6 percent of total federal spending to nearly 9 percent.[124] The federal government had first built up the technological prowess of the medical complex, then become a generous subsidizer of private health insurance, and then finally stepped in as a largely passive financier of private medical care itself. It did not at first challenge the basic medical structure that had arisen in the aftermath of past unsuccessful campaigns for compulsory health insurance.

America's Unusual and Fateful First Step

Medicare's accommodationist stance was not unique in comparative perspective. In Britain, the initial 1911 legislation incorporated rather than displaced existing insurance providers and paid doctors in the fashion they preferred. In Canada – the closest comparison to the United States – provincial and then national health legislation largely took for granted the private system as it had evolved, substituting public for private insurance without attempting to change the physician-centered structure of medicine. Yet in Canada, the postwar growth of private insurance did not prevent the passage first of public hospital insurance and then of comprehensive government protections. Understanding why casts in sharper relief the distinctive features of the American trajectory.

The United States was distinctive, first, in the degree to which employment-based insurance spread during the 1940s and 1950s. Before Canada's federal hospital plan passed in 1957, 43 percent of Canadians had some form of private hospital insurance, compared with approximately two-thirds of Americans. As late as 1966, when comprehensive medical insurance was enacted in Canada, private physicians' insurance still reached a smaller proportion of Canadians than it did Americans – 53 percent versus 70 percent.[125] More important, by this time a strong foundation for government action had been laid by the passage of federal hospital insurance and a number of provincial programs providing physicians' insurance. Rather than adopting the categorical goal of coverage for the aged that was championed in the United States, Canadian reformers instead successfully pointed to these existing federal and provincial plans as precedents for *universal* government insurance.

Canadian and American reformers, in short, pursued very different "incremental" strategies – national hospital insurance followed by full-scale national health insurance in the Canadian case; categorical coverage for the aged and poor (and, later, the disabled and advanced kidney disease patients) in the U.S. case. These disparate approaches reflected not only the differing progress of private health security in the two nations, but also deep contrasts in the locus and character of each nation's initial legislative breakthroughs. In Canada, as in the United States before the 1930s, social policy was firmly a subnational concern. Yet, unlike the American states, the provinces benefited from a federal system of fiscal equalization that mitigated fears of capital flight from reformist provinces. This became crucial after World War II, when social-democratic parties gained power in several provinces and sought to implement ambitious programs of social insurance. Leftist third parties in Canada also benefited from Canada's tradition of parliamentary representation – which permits a wider range of parties than does the American separation-of-powers system – and from the particularly strong position of regional parties within Canadian federal politics. Canadian voters have long seen regionally based parties as guardians of provincial autonomy, in part because Canada lacks a territorial legislative body like the Senate, and the frequent coalition governments of the postwar period routinely depended on these smaller regional parties for survival. As a result, the agenda for reform in Canada was driven primarily by the innovative actions taken by the provinces, rather than by private-sector developments, as in the United States.[126]

The *character* of early Canadian policy breakthroughs was no less critical. Federal hospital insurance was an important stepping stone to national health insurance, establishing the principle of universal coverage and creating political pressures for the expansion of the existing universal legislation to encompass physician services.[127] American reformers, by contrast, had no positive examples of inclusive government action to build on besides the old-age insurance program. Once it became clear that private insurance had spread to cover most working Americans, the focus on the aged inherent in Social Security almost inevitably pushed organized labor and reform advocates to shift their attention to the elderly. This categorical approach was never fundamentally reconsidered, even in the wake of the 1964 landslide, and it would prove incapable of creating the necessary political momentum for significant further moves toward universal public coverage.

The United States thus charted a distinctive course and ended with a distinctive system – an incomplete patchwork of public and private protection that divided Americans into separate groups, missed millions entirely, and left the state bearing the medical costs of the most expensive segments of the population: the elderly, the very poor, and the disabled. (The last group was incorporated into the program as part of the 1972 "quantum expansion" of Social Security.)

This was a distorted picture of reformers' true vision. Like Social Security's architects, Medicare's architects believed deeply in the need for universal social insurance. Unlike Social Security's architects, however, Medicare's architects battled for that goal in a policy environment in which deep roots had already been planted by powerful private interests. Advocates of Medicare repeatedly found themselves pressed to deny any intention of challenging the core position of private health insurance. Presenting the Medicare proposal to Congress in 1961, for example,

HEW Secretary Abraham Ribicoff stressed that federal hospital insurance was designed "only to take care of the aged. It is not my intention to advocate that we take care of the medical needs and hospital needs of our entire population, and the reason is that insurance is available for younger people. Blue Cross is available, and it can be paid for by the working population."[128] Medicare, claimed Ribicoff, would in fact be of tremendous *assistance* to the private sector, freeing voluntary plans of the growing burden of aged subscribers.[129] Similar themes were sounded by UAW chief Walter Reuther: "When the Wagner-Murray-Dingell bill was submitted to Congress . . . we supported it because, at that time, we did not have comprehensive voluntary programs. . . . Since then we have made great progress. Therefore, we believe that we now have a system under which, if the minimums are met by a Government program, we will encourage the expansion of voluntary programs."[130]

Indeed, one reason that Blue Cross and the AHA grew less hostile to Medicare was the realization, born of hard experience, that medical care for the elderly could not be financed entirely by private sources. For all their instinctive distrust of an enlarged federal role, these private interests were sympathetic to the idea of removing the major expenses of the elderly from the insurance system, allowing private insurers to focus on lower-risk supplementary protection. A signal moment in the debate over Medicare – hailed by Cohen as "a strong endorsement of the President's recommendations" – came with the November 1963 report of a privately funded expert committee that had been formed at the suggestion of Javits in 1962.[131] Comprised of three former members of the Eisenhower Administration (Marion Folsom, as always, among them), as well as representatives of Blue Cross, the AHA, and private insurers, the committee called for a "dual insurance program" combining a modest federal hospital plan financed through Social Security with new antitrust and tax exemptions for private insurance agencies.[132] As Folsom outlined the rationale in a 1963 *Atlantic Monthly* article, a limited federal plan "would relieve these agencies of the most burdensome part of covering older people. These agencies could then offer attractive supplementary plans."[133] This prediction turned out to be correct. Private insurers quickly moved in after Medicare's passage to provide supplementary plans for beneficiaries.[134]

Thus, although reformers believed that Medicare would establish the philosophical precedent and institutional means for broader public coverage, Medicare's immediate effect was to strengthen the private system and bolster the case against broader action. Irwin Wolkstein, a key HEW strategist during the Medicare battle, conceded that as a result of Medicare, "the pressure is less to provide a program for working people because you've taken care of the group for which the need is greatest outside of the private area. That is, covering the aged takes out most of the group for which the present system doesn't work well."[135] Nonetheless, advocates of Medicare saw little choice but to follow the course they had plotted during the 1950s, their strategy having been shaped by the simultaneous rise of Social Security and private health insurance. As Altmeyer later explained, reformers had the problem of "dealing with existing institutions and developing a social program that is built upon, takes advantage of, institutions as they have developed, over the 30 years that we have had Social Security."[136] Other potential pathways for the introduction of government-sponsored health insurance in the United States seemed to have disappeared.

America's two largest providers of social protection, Social Security and private health insurance, had finally intersected in the mid-1960s. By tying the campaign for government health insurance to the ever-more-popular Social Security program, reformers in the United States had tapped into the deepest wellspring of legitimacy for public social insurance. But this strategic choice had also progressively narrowed the possibilities available to reformers, just as the most significant window of opportunity for public coverage since the New Deal loomed up before them. Partly for this reason, Medicare would not serve as a stepping-stone to national health insurance, as reformers hoped. Though Cohen immediately tried to raise interest in a Medicare-style plan for children, the huge initial costs of Medicare and the turmoil of the late 1960s pushed expansion of the program off the immediate political agenda.[137] Yet the more significant and enduring barrier to an enlarged government role was the changing economic and political climate for reform. For in the 1970s, the expansion of the medical industry that Medicare had abetted would collide with America's declining economic fortunes and with new political forces determined to roll back the welfare state. Amid the turmoil, America's leaders struggled to reconcile the conflicting demands created by the nation's public–private system – and found once again that they could neither effectively reshape nor bring under public auspices the troubled arrangements that prior polices had helped construct.

The Struggles of the 1970s

The 1970s dawned with the widespread recognition of a "crisis" in American medicine. This was not a crisis of access or quality. It was a crisis of costs – untenable, explosive, unstoppable health care costs. In truth, the underlying rate of medical inflation changed little between

Table 5.1. *Basic Features of the British, Canadian, and U.S. Medical Systems, 1960–1990*

	Britain	Canada	United States
1960			
Per capita spending (in 1990 U.S. dollars)[a]	79	109	143
Percent paid by government	85.2%	42.7%	24.5%
Public spending per capita (in 1990 U.S. dollars)[a]	67	47	35
Percent of population eligible for public benefits[b]	100%	68%	20%
1970			
Per capita spending (in 1990 U.S. dollars)[a]	147	253	346
Percent paid by government	87%	70.2%	37.2%
Public spending per capita (in 1990 U.S. dollars)[a]	128	178	129
Percent of population eligible for public benefits[b]	100%	100%	40%
1980			
Per capita spending (in 1990 U.S. dollars)[a]	458	743	1,063
Percent paid by government	89.6%	74.7%	42%
Public spending per capita (in 1990 U.S. dollars)[a]	410	555	446
Percent of population eligible for public benefits[b]	100%	100%	42%
1990			
Per capita spending (in 1990 U.S. dollars)[a]	985	1,811	2,600
Percent paid by government	83.5%	72.2%	42.2%
Public spending per capita (in 1990 U.S. dollars)[a]	822	1,308	1,097
Percent of population eligible for public benefits[b]	100%	100%	44%

[a] At purchasing power parity.
[b] Percent of population eligible for a public program covering general medical expenses.
Source: Calculated from Organization for Economic Cooperation and Development, *OECD Health Systems: Facts and Trends, 1960–1991* (Paris: OECD, 1993), Tables 7.1.1, 7.2.1, and A2.1.2.

the 1960s and the 1970s.[138] But now a large portion of that inflation was being financed by government, the economy was worsening, and employers and insurers were finally attempting to control costs on their own. As Table 5.1 shows, neither Canada nor Britain entered the 1970s with a large privately financed medical system. They confronted the economic troubles of that decade already having enacted national programs to provide health care to all their citizens. And the medical systems they had frozen into place were relatively simple, involving stable organizational forms and a few central actors. In the United States, however, the pressures of rising costs were transforming the organization of medicine, splintering the interests of medical stakeholders, and, in the process, pushing reform back onto the national agenda.

The loser in this new political and economic climate was the medical profession. The expansion of private insurance and the defeat of national health insurance had been the profession's escape from the penury of government control. But the profligate medical industry that the profession had helped construct was not the profession's alone to manage. Not only government but also business firms and commercial insurers had their own stake in the finance and delivery of medicine, and their interest in controlling costs was not congruent with the profession's interest in maintaining income and autonomy. From government, the major challenge to professional autonomy was the National Health Planning and Resources Development Act of 1974, a new program of regulatory control designed to encourage more efficient use of health resources. From the private sector, the major challenge was prepaid group practice, which doctors had fought bitterly for years. Prepaid group plans integrated the finance and delivery of medical care, organizing panels of doctors and paying them either a salary or a fixed fee per patient treated. Recast by business and insurance leaders as "health maintenance organizations" (HMOs), these plans gained the support of the Nixon Administration in 1970, and a bill to aid their development was passed by Congress in 1973.

While the alarm about costs spurred new departures, it also briefly revived the fortunes of universal health insurance. This time, however, the president advocating reform was a Republican, Richard Nixon, and the plan he was advocating would not have created a universal government program but rather mandated employers to offer private coverage, offering residual public coverage for the remaining uninsured. The proposal reflected Nixon's political instincts, but it also accurately reflected the system of health care finance that had arisen in the absence of national health insurance. Coverage for the employed would come through the private sector; for the rest of Americans, it would come through the public sector. The federal government would institutionalize the bifurcation in American medicine that its failure to act in the immediate postwar era had created.

Yet Nixon's proposal was not greeted warmly by liberal Democrats, most of whom remained committed to a single federally operated insurance system and believed that Nixon would soon be forced from office by the emerging Watergate scandal. Senator Edward Kennedy and Congressman Mills tried to forge a Democratic compromise, and Senate Finance Committee Chair Russell Long pushed his own proposal for government-sponsored "catastrophic" health insurance that would cover very high expenses. But these efforts fell through when Mills declared that the Ways and Means Committee was mired in "hopeless deadlock" and when labor leaders called for delay until after the 1974 midterm elections in the hope of achieving a large enough liberal majority to overcome a presidential veto. Although proposals for reform were revived under Nixon's immediate successors, Gerald Ford and Jimmy Carter, the worsening economic climate and increasingly conservative political context of the late 1970s doomed any chance for reform.[139]

The early 1970s, by contrast, had been a surprisingly auspicious moment for national action. Contrary to the popular perception of Nixon as a tough-minded conservative, his social policy record was one of almost unparalleled willingness to support new federal spending and regulation.[140] Major business and medical groups, meanwhile, were neither as united nor as mobilized as they had once been, and both were under fire from new consumer-oriented activists who sought to restrict their autonomy. The rising expense of medical care had eroded the alliance between the medical profession and corporate America and had shocked business leaders into countenancing greater federal involvement. Some corporate leaders even had an "open mind" about major reforms, reported *Business Week* in 1970, although few were willing to support a national health plan outright.[141]

Yet deep divisions still bedeviled legislative efforts. The fundamental issue was the extent to which a new public program would displace existing private insurance – and it was a debate with massive budgetary implications. The comprehensive Kennedy-Mills plan, for example, would have entailed new federal costs of $40 billion per year (in the context of a $270 billion budget), while Nixon's and Long's plans were estimated to burden the budget by just $6 billion and $9 billion, respectively.[142] Belatedly, Mills recognized that the best chance for compromise was a bill based on the requirement that employers provide insurance, which slashed the cost of the proposal to $6 billion. But showdown votes within the Ways and Means Committee suggested that many conservatives would not support any mandate, demanding instead new tax incentives for voluntary coverage.

Nor were liberal Democrats and organized labor eager to compromise away their long-fought goal of a universal federal program. If the omnipresence of private health insurance made it harder to find common ground on policy design, it also made liberals less willing to back away from their preferred solution. After all, private health insurance was widespread; public programs filled most of the remaining gaps. Why, liberal stalwarts asked, should the nation settle for a program that fell short of a truly inclusive public program that broadly spread risks and effectively controlled costs? Organized labor, in particular, saw little advantage in a watered-down compromise. The AFL-CIO instead demanded the passage of a uniform federal program that required no co-payments by workers and covered a range of benefits more comprehensive than most union-negotiated plans. These demands, of course, had big budgetary implications (the labor-supported bill would have cost the federal government more than $60 billion a year). But organized labor "continually said that it preferred inaction on health care reform to incremental reform, or even to reform along the lines Nixon had proposed."[143] Perhaps if labor leaders had foreseen future declines in the reach and generosity of private health insurance, they would have seen value in universalizing the existing employment-based structure, imperfect as they judged it be. In 1974, however, labor unions insisted that the status quo could only be bettered by a plan that the political opportunities of the day would not permit.

The influence of political institutions on debates about health care was more complex in the 1970s than it had been in previous decades. The liberal landslide of 1964 had brought to a close the era of the conservative coalition, and in the early 1970s, liberal Democrats promulgated a series of institutional reforms that diffused power within Congress and increased the ability of rank-and-file members to develop legislative initiatives and service their constituents.[144]

The catchword for these changes among political scientists was "fragmentation" – and it was a fragmentation that was mirrored in the political turmoil surrounding U.S. health policy.[145] With almost 90 percent of the public covered by private or public health insurance, efforts to assuage public alarm about health care costs or provide universal health insurance had to navigate carefully around existing private and public arrangements, lest proposed changes mobilize interest groups and constituents fearful of federal intervention. Moreover, Medicare and Medicaid had created new groups with a stake in existing policy, the most formidable of which was the emerging interest association representing the elderly, the American Association of Retired Persons. Reconciling these conflicting interests would have been difficult in any polity. It proved too much for the American political system, wracked as it was by the institutional transformations of the 1970s.

The United States might have universal health insurance today if propitious political circumstances and able leadership had come together in the early 1970s, before the stagflation and resurgent conservatism of that decade stalled further progress toward reform. But if a compromise had been reached, it almost certainly would not have resembled the publicly sponsored health insurance systems found elsewhere. By the 1970s, the complex legacy of past political struggles had left the United States with a costly patchwork of public and private health insurance over which no interested party could exert control. This complicated structure divided erstwhile opponents of government action, but it also divided advocates. It created new public demands for government intervention, but it also split Americans into warring factions. It moved medical costs to the center of public debate, but it gave public and private authorities few means to control them. These dilemmas bedeviled America's fragmented polity and stalemated progress toward health care reform for more than two decades. Yet, as new antigovernment winds swept Washington, a little-noticed legislative legacy of a vanishing liberal era was rapidly reshaping the structure of private medical finance.

The Protected Privileges of Employment-Based Insurance

The most enduring departure in U.S. health policy in the 1970s was also the least recognized, contained as it was in a law designed to govern pensions. But the Employee Retirement Income Security Act of 1974 did not restrict its reach to pensions alone. A provision incorporated into ERISA at the last moment, with little fanfare and essentially no debate, stated that *all* employer-provided health and welfare plans – not just private pensions – would be exempt from state laws that "related to" employee benefits. The meaning of "related to" was ambiguous, but other sections of ERISA suggested that the provision was meant to distinguish between health plans operated by private insurers, which would continue to be governed by state law, and "self-insured" benefit plans operated by employers and union–management trusts, which would be subject exclusively to federal regulation. This, at least, was how the courts interpreted ERISA's "preemption clause" in the huge flow of federal cases that followed the law's passage.[146] Preemption thus meant that self-insured health plans were not subject to state laws governing the scope or character of benefits, state premium taxes, state reserve requirements, and, indeed, virtually all the normal legal remedies that state courts provided for aggrieved or injured parties. This was a massive shift in the regulatory environment surrounding health insurance, and its effects on the structure of American medical finance would be both profound and largely unanticipated.

These effects were unanticipated, in part, because ERISA reshaped the landscape of employee benefits in unexpected ways. At the time of its creation, the preemption language applied only to a minority of health plans: large, often union-negotiated funds that paid claims out of their own coffers. Most employers continued to enroll their workers in commercial or nonprofit insurance plans, which in turn bore medical risk. But in the same way that employers responded to the little-noted tax change embodied in Section 401(k), corporations and unions quickly responded to the largely unnoticed preemption clause in ERISA, underwriting workers' medical risks on their own to limit cross-subsidization across employee groups and evade state regulations and taxes. By the mid-1980s, roughly half of corporate health plans were self-insured, and the proportion rose to more than two-thirds by the early 1990s.[147]

ERISA's full effects were also unforeseen because the target of ERISA's was pensions, not health insurance. Given ERISA's new requirements for pensions, preempting state laws was relatively unproblematic. Yet ERISA contained scarcely any new federal rules to regulate employee benefits more generally. It set no funding or backup insurance requirements; specified no standards for coverage or minimum benefits; contained no prohibitions against unilateral reduction or termination of benefits; and established no limits on medical underwriting.[148] The result, in sum, was a "regulatory vacuum" so large and gaping that the courts seemed initially unable to believe that Congress could have created it.[149] ("While Congress occasionally decides to return to the states what it has previously taken away," wrote a puzzled Justice Harry Blackmun in a crucial 1985 case, "it does not normally do both at the same time.")[150] With employers, insurers, and unions allied behind a broad interpretation of the clause, the meaning of the ERISA language was fought out in a huge and complex stream of legal challenges to state laws and insurer practices. This odd coalition of interests also lobbied Congress to preserve the original ERISA language, quashing calls for clarification of the legislation.[151] As a result, Congress exercised virtually no control over the uses to which the ERISA preemption clause was eventually put.

It is difficult to think of a more important social policy innovation that received less attention than the preemption clause, or a better illustration of the subterranean character of policies governing private benefits. Yet the clause was not a random or haphazard addition to the law. The legislation originally passed by both houses of Congress had carefully limited the scope of preemption, but when the conference committee released its report just days before the final vote, this limited language had been replaced by the much more sweeping section that made it into the final law. Though scarcely any mention of the change was made, it appears to have reflected two concerns, one general and one specific.[152] The general concern was the effects of inconsistent state laws on the benefits activities of large multistate employers, which had long complained about the difficulties of complying with conflicting state laws.[153] The more immediate and specific worry was that state meddling in union legal-services plans and large negotiated benefit funds would raise costs or undermine the autonomy of collective bargaining. Here the most energetic champion of preemption was the AFL-CIO, which was both concerned about the independence of unions' legal-services plans and "eager to prevent the states from taxing and regulating the health and pension plans . . . negotiated under the Taft-Hartley Act."[154] By the late 1970s, as the states became by default the major site of health policy activity, corporations and insurers had come to see the potent advantages of preemption as well. Neither insurers nor employers, however, seem to have played a significant part in drafting the preemption provisions that they would later mobilize to preserve and expand.

Since the passage of ERISA, some federal regulations have entered the vacuum that the preemption clause created, though fewer than one might expect given the complaints about private health insurance that have marked the period.[155] The broader pattern, however, is still one of strikingly weak regulation of employer-provided health insurance, especially when compared with the density of federal control over private pension plans. Despite active demands from state governors to amend or repeal the ERISA preemption, a formidable coalition of labor, business, and insurers has beaten back all major attempts at change, its lobbying led by the ERISA Industry Committee, an association of large employers formed in the wake of the law's passage. The most powerful argument against revision is the same one originally used against ERISA's rules regarding pensions: that new federal regulation will raise the cost of providing health insurance and thus encourage employers to cut benefits or drop insurance. Regulation of health insurance has been attractive to state and federal politicians in large part because it represents an off-budget means of addressing concerns about private coverage. The claim that mandates will reduce coverage thus strikes at the very heart of the rationale for regulation of employer-provided insurance.

Self-insured health plans paid no price for their regulatory salvation. Despite the minimal requirements on tax-favored plans, the generosity of federal tax subsidies has continued to grow. (If forgone income and payroll taxes are included, the cost of tax subsidies for health spending now exceeds $110 billion – or more than half the level of Medicare's outlays and almost half of the total amount employers pay for private insurance.)[156] By the late 1970s, most economists, as well as key figures in the Treasury Department, had become sharply critical of the tax treatment of health insurance. Recognizing, however, that "there was no political support for abolishing the tax-free status of fringe benefits," Treasury officials instead included in President Carter's 1978 tax plan broad nondiscrimination requirements that would apply to all fringe benefits, not just pensions.[157] They sweetened the change by coupling these new requirements with statutory permission for so-called cafeteria plans, in which employees could choose either to receive cash compensation or to select from a "menu" of tax-free benefits. Like 401(k) plans, cafeteria plans further restricted the scope of taxable wages, exempting benefits from taxation even when employees could choose whether to receive them or cash and, indeed, even when employees could choose which benefits they received. Moreover, cafeteria plans were clearly most attractive to well-off workers who faced high marginal taxes and were most likely to choose benefits over cash – which was why Treasury officials believed they would pave the way for new nondiscrimination requirements. Congress created cafeteria plans but killed the nondiscrimination rules.

Similarly, in the early years of the Reagan Administration, proposals for "pro-competitive" reform that would have restricted the tax exemption were floated by administration officials and key members of Congress. But business and labor groups mobilized to throttle the proposed change. "Let me be blunt," declared the director of the Washington Business Group on Health in hearings on the proposals, "there is no significant support for federal legislation mandating a competition system. . . . Employers are very reluctant to support any change that would result in imputed income for employees. The objection is less pointed at health than at the broader concern for taxation of all employee benefits and the resulting employer/labor relations problems."[158] Senate Finance Committee Chair Robert Packwood added his own influential voice to the chorus of opposition, declaring that

> the one reason we do not have any significant demand for national health insurance in this country among those who are employed is because their employers are paying for their benefits. . . . I hate to see us nibble at [that system] for fear you are going to have the demand that the Federal Government take over and provide the benefits that would otherwise be lost.[159]

Following the inglorious demise of the pro-competitive push of the early 1980s, tax reformers took up the crusade against the health insurance exemption in the lead-up to the Tax Reform Act of 1986. As mentioned in Chapter 3, the first Treasury proposal for tax reform suggested capping the tax exclusion of health insurance benefits. Yet restrictions on the value of the health insurance subsidy were eventually abandoned as infeasible – in 1986 and later.[160] All this suggests just how entrenched employer-provided health insurance had become by the 1980s, and how difficult it has proved to regulate since. In the postwar years, U.S. health policy took a fateful turn toward private health security, and in the more conflicted social policy climate of the 1970s and 1980s, Americans and their leaders lived with the consequences. As with private pensions, the web of favorable taxes and regulations that supported private health plans proved highly resistant to revision. Yet, as the core provider of social protection in American medical care, private health insurance posed even more perilous barriers to reform or regulatory control than did private pensions. A telling sign of this can be found in the divergent effects of ERISA on traditional defined-benefit pensions and health insurance. The former emerged as a heavily regulated adjunct to Social Security; the latter was given a means to slip the net of state regulation without being required to take on new federal obligations in return.

The ERISA preemption clause had originally been touted as a source of uniformity in employee benefits. Its effect, however, was to further fragment the health insurance risk pool. As employers rushed to self-insure, the insurance market split ever more into self-contained risk groups, each jealously guarded from outside interference or the imposition of new costs. By encouraging self-funding, ERISA also gave corporate purchasers of health insurance new reasons to eschew collective responses and look for their own solutions to rising health care costs. By the 1980s, states had begun to experiment with limited programs designed to pool costs for high-risk populations. Yet ERISA placed self-insured employment groups beyond the reach of state law.[161] Thus, not only had national politicians failed to pass major insurance reforms, but they had also added new hurdles to the already formidable barriers that stood in the way of state leadership. The forces unleashed would eventually push reform back into the spotlight, but only after almost two decades of stalemate had allowed the troubles of American medical finance to grow much more pressing.

The Clinton Reform Initiative

The underlying pressures for reform stemmed from the destructive competitive logic of private insurance. As medical costs continued to rise, business firms sought to minimize the expense of health benefits. One strategy was to move employees into HMOs and other "managed care" plans; another was to require that workers share a greater portion of the costs of their insurance or eliminate coverage for workers' dependents. Many small and new firms chose not to offer health insurance at all. As more firms self-insured, leaving the worst risks behind, insurance companies refined their techniques for weeding out high-risk groups and limiting coverage for costly conditions. Partly as a result, the number of uninsured Americans began to increase around 1980 and continued to grow throughout the decade, reaching 37 million in 1992. (In 1998, the count was 44 million, an increase of about a million a year.) Even insured Americans, however, were more uncertain than ever about the expense and security of private coverage.

The harshest effects were felt by those on the margins of the employment-based system. Since the mid-1970s, economic inequality has grown rapidly, and inequality in the distribution of health benefits even more so.[162] For workers lacking a high school degree, real wages have decreased by 18 percent and the probability of employment-based coverage by almost 35 percent, while workers with a college degree have enjoyed a 17 percent increase in real wages and a small increase in the prevalence of job-based insurance.[163] African-Americans and Hispanics have been hit particularly hard: Among white Americans, the share of the nonelderly with job-based coverage contracted by 8 percent between 1977 and 1996, but it fell by 18 percent among African-Americans and by 28 percent among Hispanics – to 47.9 percent and 42.1 percent, respectively, versus 71.4 percent for whites.[164] These trends reflect multiple factors: falling rates of unionization; rising numbers of self-employed, part-time, and contingent workers; regional and sectoral shifts in employment; and, above all, rising insurance premiums in the context of stagnant median wages.[165] The essential point, however, is that the foundations of the postwar insurance system have steadily eroded, more than offsetting the modest expansions of Medicaid coverage that began in the late 1980s (see Figure 5.1).

Public sector programs also faced new challenges in the 1980s. The ballooning of the federal deficit made Medicare and Medicaid – the fastest-growing components of the budget – obvious targets for fiscal hawks. But although Congress changed Medicare's payment structure twice in the 1980s, political leaders found it difficult to control expenditures because the cost-abetting incentives originated in a private medical sector that lay largely beyond their control. Politicians were also wary of provoking the wrath of the well-organized elderly beneficiaries of Medicare, the wealthiest of whom had precipitated the repeal of a progressive tax passed in 1988 to expand Medicare's benefits.

The immediate catalyst for the return of reform to the national political agenda was the surprise victory of Democrat Harris Wofford in a special 1991 Senate race.[166] Campaigning in support of universal health insurance during an economic recession, Wofford climbed back from a forty-point deficit in the polls to beat a popular former Pennsylvania governor and U.S. attorney general. His victory sent shock waves through Washington and made health care reform a leading issue of the 1992

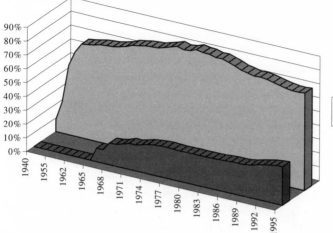

Figure 5.1. Share of Americans Covered by Private Health Insurance and Medicare/ Medicaid, 1940–1995. *Notes:* Medicaid figures start in 1968 and are not reliable until 1973, when states began reporting detailed beneficiary and payment information. Data are unavailable regarding coverage under state programs that existed prior to the passage of Medicare and Medicaid in 1965. *Source:* Compiled from Health Care Financing Administration, "Medicare Enrollment Trends, 1966–1997"; Subcommittee on Health and the Environment of the Committee on Energy and Commerce, *Medicaid Source Book: Background Data and Analysis* (Washington, D.C.: U.S. GPO, 1988), 20; Social Security Administration, *Annual Statistical Supplement, 1997* (Washington, D.C.: SSA, 1998), 327; Health Insurance Association of America, *Source Book of Health Insurance Data* (Washington, D.C.: HIAA, 1988), 39.

presidential campaign. When Democrat Bill Clinton captured the presidency, no one doubted that he would soon introduce a proposal for universal health insurance.

So much has been written about the Clinton reform effort and its fate that a comprehensive summary is unnecessary here.[167] What needs to be emphasized, however, is how deeply the political dilemmas Clinton faced were shaped by the failure of past political efforts to enact national health insurance in the United States. First, the very structure of Clinton's proposal represented a concession to the distinctive structure of medical finance and delivery that had arisen in the United States.[168] The Health Security plan attempted to lock into place a disintegrating private financing system while furthering the movement toward managed care that had been under way for two decades. For most Americans, insurance would be funded largely through employer contributions. Americans would choose among private health plans and be encouraged to select managed care plans. Medicare was explicitly left out of this new system, although much of the funding for the plan came through decreased Medicare payments. Very large employers would be allowed to opt out of the program if they met strict requirements, restrained their own costs, and paid an assessment designed to minimize the dumping of poor risks into the publicly overseen framework.

(Ironically, the failure of the Clinton plan left the field clear for the type of radical market changes that detractors of the proposal had warned would result from its implementation. Partly in anticipation of the Clinton plan, insurers and corporations accelerated their movement toward managed care in the early 1990s, nearly doubling the number of Americans in these more restrictive arrangements between 1992 and 1995.[169] A wave of mergers and acquisitions saw for-profit hospitals and insurers sweep into the field, displacing much of the nonprofit organizational infrastructure upon which the case for public-spirited private medical care had been premised. Although this dramatic transformation did nothing to address the worsening plight of the uninsured, it did slow the rate of medical inflation and lessen cost pressures on employers and public programs. In the rest of the industrialized world, cost containment had been spearheaded by government authorities. In the United States, responsibility for cost control fell by default to the private sector. Indeed, as private actors moved to reshape medicine, government leaders were left scrambling to respond.[170] This reversal of fortune is perhaps the strongest evidence yet that the United States has followed a fundamentally different path of health policy development than have other nations – one that will almost certainly not culminate in the passage of European-style national health insurance.)

A second historically inherited constraint that stood in the way of health care reform was fiscal. Comparative experience suggests that a publicly financed system with clear lines of fiscal responsibility is most able to control medical costs.[171] But adopting such a system in America would require moving a large portion of private medical spending onto the public ledger. This was not considered an option in the United States as it had been in Britain and Canada. Not only was American medicine vastly more complex and vastly more expensive as a share of the economy than British and Canadian medicine had been when national programs were introduced, but it would also have to be underwritten in a much harsher fiscal climate. In response, the Clinton Administration sought to do the opposite of what Britain and Canada had done: keep as much of the cost of medical care as possible in the private sector. To do this and still restrain spending, however, the administration had to propose an elaborate regulatory apparatus centered around a network of new government purchasing agents called "Health Alliances." This regulatory framework became the central focus of the viciously effective attacks on the president's program.

Third, and most important, the Clinton Administration had to navigate around the fragmented collection of private interests activated by current arrangements. These interests included not only countless interest groups that campaigned against the plan but also, and more important, various segments of the American public that differentially benefit from the present structure of medical finance. The thorny challenge Clinton confronted was to move all Americans into a new regulatory framework without appreciably harming the standing of any – a challenge analogous in many ways to the one that opponents of the welfare state face when trying to move citizens out of public programs.[172]

This already daunting task was immensely complicated by three historically inherited constraints. First, most Americans were not aware of the full amount that they paid for health insurance through indirect subsidies, hidden taxes, and (above all) forgone cash wages. Reformers thus had to consider not merely whether Americans would really pay more or less, but whether the new burdens they would bear would be more visible than the hidden costs they already shouldered. Second, the chief beneficiaries of Clinton's proposal – uninsured Americans – were diffuse, protean, and unorganized, while the chief opponents were concentrated and well organized.[173] Finally, budgetary constraints ensured that Clinton would not be able to provide generous "side payments" to affected interests to ease them into the new system. Indeed, the subsidies that he did offer to grease the skids were immediately condemned by opponents as fiscally irresponsible giveaways.

The business response to the Clinton plan was emblematic of the tightwire that the president was forced to walk.[174] Although the nation's major business groups all eventually decried the Clinton plan, this opposition obscured substantial underlying support for some changes in health financing. The problem was that employers were deeply split. Firms with older, unionized workforces or large benefit costs were willing to support fairly expansive proposals that regulated costs and required all firms to provide coverage.[175] Other large firms that provided insurance, however, preferred to encourage large firms to adopt innovative private purchasing strategies, especially after the economy improved and health costs began to abate in 1993 and 1994.[176] A second and even more stark divide separated large and small firms. In the smallest firms, private coverage was rare, and workers were as likely to obtain coverage through a working family member as to receive it from their employers. In larger firms, by contrast, the overwhelming majority of workers had direct coverage.[177] For most large firms, therefore, a mandate on employers to provide insurance would likely lower costs by reducing their spending on family coverage. Quite the opposite was true for most small firms. This division was reflected in the unwavering opposition of the National Federation of Independent Business, a powerful small-business lobby, to any coverage requirement – an idea that many large employers viewed with more sympathy.

These divisions plagued the Clinton administration's policy deliberations. As early as May 1993, the Chamber of Commerce wrote a private letter to the White House that suggested just how difficult it would be to reconcile business demands with inclusive insurance. Criticizing what it saw as a turn toward "a government financed and controlled system, versus one energized by non-government funding, private initiative and competitive delivery system," the Chamber argued that large employers should be allowed to stay outside the Health Alliances and retain maximum control over private benefits: "These companies, most of which are self-insured or experience rated as to their premiums, have driven most of the innovation in cost containment in the country. . . . [E]mployers should not be 'taxed' or surcharged as a penalty for staying out of the [Alliance] pools. They should be encouraged to help contain costs on their own, not penalized!"[178] In early 1994, the Chamber of Commerce, Business Roundtable, and National Association of Manufactures all came out against not only the Clinton plan but also the goal of universal coverage, dooming whatever hope for comprehensive action remained.

Some saw this business abandonment of reform as a reversion to the enduring corporate ideology of antigovernment conservatism. Yet the more important cause was the maddening difficulty of aggregating the diverse interests of corporate America into any statement of positive intent. When health care reform was framed as a means to rein in public spending and make small firms pay a fair share, many large employers went along with the pleas for help of those firms with the most to gain. But when a concrete proposal was on the table, one that of necessity allocated burdens and rewards across business as a whole and challenged the autonomy of corporate benefits, the firms that saw their interests threatened quickly mobilized to bring business associations in line with the lowest common denominator position. After the Clinton plan died, most business organizations continued to do what they had done before – self-insured, moved their employees into low-cost health plans, cut back or dropped coverage – their own conflicting interests once again precluding a collective response.

Whether the American political system is less capable of imposing losses than are parliamentary systems is a subject of some dispute.[179] Although the concentration of legislative powers in parliamentary systems gives governments greater freedom to enact loss-imposing policies, it also makes it easier for citizens to hold them accountable for their actions. On balance, the evidence indicates that the greater discretion governments have outweighs the problem of increased accountability.[180] But the point to be made is that neither Britain nor Canada enacted national health insurance under the stark conditions Clinton confronted. If leaders in those countries had been faced with a medical system as costly and complex as that of the United States, if they had been forced to seamlessly move two-thirds of the public from private and public insurance plans into a common public framework, and if they had faced the challenges that all welfare states faced after the mid-1970s, then perhaps the United States would not be the only advanced industrial democracy without national health insurance.

Contrary to the claim of Sven Steinmo and Jon Watts that "It's the Institutions, Stupid!" sole or even preponderant blame for the defeat of health care reform in 1994 cannot be assigned to U.S. political institutions.[181] American government clearly was not up to the task of passing comprehensive reform, but the immensity of that task reflected the complexity, cost, and fragmentation of the medical system that reformers of the 1990s inherited. Of course, American political institutions were crucial in pushing U.S. health policy down the ill-fated track it took. But the failure of reform in the early 1990s was as much a reflection of the inherited legacies of distant political struggles as it was of the distinctive organization of American political power.

Conclusion

In the wake of the failure of the Clinton plan, incremental reforms have become the order of the day. In 1996, Congress and the president agreed on a package of modest insurance reforms designed to encourage portability of group health coverage across jobs, and in 1997, a new federal Children's Health Insurance Program (CHIP) was created to fund state programs to expand coverage among America's over 10 million uninsured children. Since the mid-1990s, pressure to amend ERISA to allow federal regulation of managed care plans has been building, and Republicans and Democrats alike have called for new tax breaks for private insurance to help the self-employed and those without workplace coverage. These new policies and proposals are all in keeping with past historical patterns. They represent regulatory interventions and largely indirect government supports designed to deal with the most glaring deficiencies of private insurance or to extend protection to Americans who are not expected to be included in employment-based coverage. Indeed, the bipartisan support that these policies have garnered suggests that after the Clinton reform debacle, neither side is eager to refight past battles over the basic division of public and private responsibilities.

It is tempting to see the failure of the Clinton plan as simply another victory for the groups that helped build up America's predominantly private system – for the medical profession, employers, and the insurance industry, and perhaps even for unionized workers who negotiated lavish fringe benefits in the postwar years. Yet the paradox is that many of these groups are genuinely dissatisfied with current arrangements. Doctors bridle at the restrictions imposed by large health plans. Most insurers are facing tough economic times. Employers see health care costs as a continuing economic threat and an often onerous administrative burden (and indeed, some wish to get out of the health insurance business altogether by providing their workers with a fixed payment to purchase insurance individually). The Clinton reform effort failed not because it encountered unified opposition – and certainly not because of the sniping of the once-feared AMA – but because the medical system that arose in the United States created nearly insuperable policy dilemmas while dividing Americans into ever smaller pools of common interest and shared risk. Only this can explain why a medical financing structure so troubled and friendless has so consistently resisted major reform.

In short, the system of private social insurance that emerged in health policy has been as path dependent as the system of public social insurance that emerged in retirement security policy. In the decades after World War II, policy choices were made (or not made) that created dangerous traps for future reformers: a well-subsidized private insurance system based on employment and friendly to the interests of providers, a technologically intensive medical structure so costly as to stymie coverage expansions, and a framework of categorical programs that filled gaps but undermined the case for general protection. These were not accidental developments, but neither were they entirely chosen. They emerged from the sometimes unexpected and often subterranean interaction of public policy with the private benefit activities of employers and unions – and from the concerted attempt by the defenders of private insurance to restrict the scope of shared risk in order to minimize redistribution and retain autonomy over private social benefits.

Two main dynamics have anchored this peculiar historical path. The first concerns the political losses associated with revision of a mature medical-industrial complex structured around employment-based insurance. Americans have come to depend on the private insurance system; powerful vested interests have arisen within and around it. Major legislative changes to that system – even changes that will make Americans as a whole better off – run headlong into the specific dislocations that these reforms will create. The mobilization of those who stand to lose from reform and the asymmetry of response between losses and comparable benefits only compound the problem. As with well-entrenched public programs, retrenchment of established networks of private social provision generates a politics of blame avoidance. In America's fragmented polity, this has proved an extremely tricky and treacherous politics indeed.

But there is a second and deeper reason for the path dependence of American medical financing, one rooted in the distinctive role that employment-based health insurance has come to play. In ceding power and purpose to the employment-based system, policymakers made themselves hostage to the abilities and disabilities of the private sector. Political leaders found not only that the political and economic costs of change were great, but also that the system itself created thorny policy problems that they could not satisfactorily resolve. Helping groups left out of the system also reduced the pressure for more systemic reform. Trying to increase coverage through increased regulation undercut the incentive for firms to provide insurance in the first place. Providing insurance through public programs risked crowding out existing private protections. The division of public and private responsibilities thus conditioned political choices and weakened policy control, placing U.S. health policy in the hands of private actors over which public officials could exercise only limited and blunt authority. Public ends became the responsibility of private institutions, and because they did, public officials became wary of threatening arrangements that they might otherwise have challenged.

Like Social Security, then, employment-based private insurance has become a fixture on the American economic and social policy landscape. Yet in contrast with Social Security, this privileged place has not been kind to the cause of inclusive social insurance. As firms have moved to eliminate and scale back benefits, to segment risk pools and eliminate cross-subsidies, to distinguish ever more ruthlessly among workers on the basis of income and health, public officials have been faced with the challenge of recapturing the elements of social insurance that are leeching out of the American system without jeopardizing the ability of private institutions to carry out the public ends invested in them. The repeated failure of national health insurance, the torturous history of the ERISA preemption clause, and the resilience of the tax subsidy for employer-provided health insurance all suggest that the challenge is monumental. In the years after World War II, the rise of private health insurance made government action seem unnecessary. Now, when it is recognized by many as necessary and indeed essential, government is stalemated by the very private protections in which so much faith was once invested.

Part IV

The Formation and Future of the American Welfare Regime

Today's security-conscious world impedes change. The security lies less in public protections . . . than in the private practices of employers. Big organizations require rules and create customs; the evolving rules and customs form a protective cocoon around many employees, especially those with long tenure.

– Robert J. Samuelson, "Make Room for the Individual," 1981

In a period of financial constraint combined with a continuity of commitment to the ideals of social protection on which the "welfare state" is premised, the one likely outcome will be that the future of the welfare state will be the invention of institutions that are not public and are not private.

– Martin Rein, 1989

The era of big government is over.

– President Bill Clinton, 1995

6

The Formation of the American Welfare Regime

At the dawn of a new century, many of the rallying cries of the last seem no longer to inspire Americans. Although most public social programs have survived the criticisms and strains of the past two decades, the sense once widely shared that government was capable of ameliorating the major risks and dislocations of modern life has long since faded. Faith in government has plummeted; public budgets have stabilized, even fallen; and new social programs have all but disappeared from the political agenda. And yet this "era of permanent austerity" has been accompanied by visible anxiety about evolving economic conditions that have produced both greater prosperity and greater inequality, both new wealth and new risks.[1] For America's leaders, this has been a volatile and confusing new world, equally threatening to those who would cling to the approaches of the past and to those who would deny their continuing relevance.

Amid these uncertainties, pundits and politicians have declared the emergence of a new model of governance: a government that "rows, not steers," that "empowers people to act for themselves," that relies not on "top-down bureaucracies," but on "public–private partnerships" and "market incentives."[2] President Bush has labeled his approach to social policy "compassionate conservatism," vowing that government will enlist "America's armies of compassion" in the private sector to tackle social problems.[3] The Democratic Leadership Council, the organizational arm of conservative Democrats, calls for "an enabling rather than a bureaucratic government, expanding choice for citizens, using market means to achieve public ends and encouraging civic and community institutions to play a larger role in public life."[4] In the 1990s, former President Clinton and British Prime Minister Tony Blair embraced the vague but evocative idea of a "Third Way" that escapes the old orthodoxies of left and right.[5] "We have moved past the sterile debate between those who say government is the enemy and those who say government is the answer," proclaimed Clinton in 1998. "My fellow Americans, we have found a Third Way."[6]

Yet, in the United States, "enabling government" is nothing new.[7] The Third Way is the old way. The dramatic rise of the American state in the twentieth century did not displace the role of the private sector in providing social welfare goods and services. To the contrary: Via regulatory and tax policy, with incentives and restrictions, through the omissions and commissions of public programs, by oversight and by design, American government contributed to the construction of a sphere of private social benefits far larger than in any other affluent democracy. That we too often fail to recognize this is a measure of the distorted picture that most Americans have of the reach and character of state action in the social welfare domain. But if academics are eager to disabuse the public of misperceptions about where its tax dollars go, they have been less quick to move beyond the aggregate measures of social expenditure long at the heart of comparative analysis of the welfare state. Today, even with a salutary new emphasis on the structural mix of activities that characterize "welfare-state regimes," the focus of most research on social policy remains firmly on public spending and provision.[8]

This book has moved beyond this restricted view – not on the grounds that direct public spending is unimportant, but because the conventional view misses much of what is critical about the American historical experience and the dimensions and effects of U.S. social policy. By bringing in less-studied instruments of government intervention, I have sought to demonstrate not only that "welfare is more than what the state provides," but also that what the state does to shape social welfare outcomes extends well beyond direct spending.[9] At the same time, extending our focus highlights the largely hidden politics of the sizable realm of publicly regulated and subsidized private social insurance that has arisen in the United States. Larger than in any other nation, this realm is a defining element of what I have called the "American welfare regime." It has come to represent an increasingly large portion of total social spending in the United States. And it is changing today in form and distribution with effects that the bitter ongoing debate over public social programs has yet to acknowledge.

To extend our view, however, is not to equate public and private social benefits, as if it makes no difference whether social provision ends up in public or private hands. Publicly regulated and subsidized private benefits are properly thought of as part of America's broader social welfare strategy – neither purely private nor purely public, neither an autonomous market development nor solely a result of government policies. Nonetheless, the differences between public and private social benefits are many and deep, and the deepest of these differences relate to the lesser visibility of policies governing private benefits and the limited ability of private social insurance to offer broad protection across both income groups and risk categories. Because of these differences, private social welfare approaches are more likely to develop outside the public eye, to make it into law without momentous political breakthroughs, to start small and grow big, to involve a decentralized assemblage of institutional venues, to depoliticize policy by moving policymaking outside of routine political channels, and to place limits on the control of policymakers over outcomes. Perhaps most important, private social welfare approaches are more likely to attract the support of conservative politicians and groups, both because they confer immediate advantage on private claimants and because, once in place, they hold out the tantalizing promise of putting long-term limits on the direct movement of government into fields of action marked by private social provision.

This last point – about the historical interrelationship between public and private social benefits – provides the entry into my comparative analysis of health care and pension policy. Why is it that the U.S. social policy has come to rely so heavily on publicly regulated and subsidized private social insurance? And why, in particular, does private social insurance play such a core role in U.S. health policy even as *public* social insurance dominates the retirement security domain? The answers hinge on the observation that private social benefits, like public social programs, have policy feedback effects that alter the subsequent landscape of political conflict. Both pension and health policy were characterized by an early and continuing effort to encourage private social benefits, spearheaded primarily by conservative legislators and business groups, but including at times liberal politicians and labor unions frustrated by the absence or slow expansion of public programs. And both pension and health policy were characterized by the emergence of deeply embedded public and private benefits around which powerful interests, expectations, and institutions formed.

Divergence emerged between the two areas, however, because of the relative timing and sequence of public and private developments in the two areas. The passage of Social Security before private plans were widespread structured the environment into which private plans entered. In doing so, it created strong path-dependent processes in favor of the program while softening the opposition of business leaders, who came to see Social Security as the foundation for private pension practices. In contrast, the failure of health insurance during the New Deal and then after World War II created a path of policy development far less conducive to the eventual expansion of public authority. Subsidies for employment-based health benefits and for high-technology medicine created an expensive, fragmented system of health care finance and delivery that undercut the constituency for reform while raising the political and budgetary costs of policy change, eventually pressing reformers to focus on residual populations left out of private coverage. In both cases, challenges to the core provider of social insurance, whether public or private, proved politically perilous.

We return, therefore, to the questions about American exceptionalism that first sparked our journey. What explains the prominence of private social benefits in the American welfare regime? What does this distinctive position tell us about the politics of the welfare state? And what does it say about the future of social policy in the United States? These are the concerns of the final two chapters of this book. This chapter reviews the terrain covered up to now, placing the historical evidence in the context of the theoretical perspective outlined in Part I and using the history in turn to deepen my theoretical arguments. The final chapter looks to the horizon, situating the fierce debates of the present in the broader context of public–private relations and asking what the past development of the American welfare regime foretells for its contested future.

The Development of the American Welfare Regime

No one set out to design the American welfare regime. It does not reflect a single philosophy or the interests of any particular group. It fully pleases neither the left nor the right. Like all multifaceted systems built up over decades, the American welfare regime represents the accumulation of myriad historical episodes, political actors, and policy changes and the complex and sometimes unexpected interaction of these elements over time. It may be possible to identify the progenitors of specific programs and policies, but the whole is the work of many hands and many forces. For the analyst of a regime, the challenge is to tease out patterns within the whole and try to identify their sources and their effects, while at the same time remaining attentive to the complex individual variations over time and across constituent elements.

By targeting my historical inquiries on health and pension policy, I have limited my analysis to a single – yet singular – aspect of the broader universe of organized social provision in the United States: the relationship between public and private social insurance. Research on the interplay of means-tested antipoverty programs and private charitable activities would no doubt emphasize different factors and trends.[10] The twin development of public and private social insurance nonetheless stands out as an inviting window into the politics of the public–private mix in U.S. social policy, both because of the dominant place of health and pension policy within the welfare state and because of the presence of both public and private forms of organized social provision in each policy area. Equally important, the differences across the two areas provide crucial leverage for identifying the causes and consequences of alternative divisions of state and private responsibility in American social insurance. Thus, the story we have traced has woven together two historical narratives: a narrative of *parallel development* aimed at understanding the prominent role of publicly regulated and subsidized private social insurance within the American welfare regime, and a narrative of *contrasting development* designed to explain why private social insurance came to play such different roles in two areas that otherwise share many similarities.

Parallel Development

The tale of parallel development begins with the claim that many of the influences that we might expect to retard the growth of inclusive public social programs – fragmented political institutions, an antistatist political culture, the weakness of labor, nonprogrammatic parties – are either ambiguous with respect to or clearly supportive of the growth of public policies that encourage or shape private social benefits. This is partly because such policies are more likely to gain the support of political actors otherwise opposed to government action in social welfare policy. It is also, however, a reflection of the fact that policies governing private social benefits are generally less visible and less costly than public social programs, at least at the outset. Finally, the same institutional fragmentation that poses significant barriers to the passage of major public programs provides multiple points of access through which these more modest policies can enter public debate and government policy. Along with problems of visibility, moreover, fragmentation makes it more difficult to muster the necessary political will to change these policies once their full effects become transparent. The special tax treatment of employer-provided pensions and health insurance and the preemption of self-insured health plans under the Employee Retirement Income Security Act – now major features of the American regime – all originated with little controversy and only came under challenge once substantial vested interests in their continuance had arisen.

Contrary to the traditional emphasis on the critical breakthroughs of the New Deal and Great Society, the late 1930s through the late 1950s were pivotal years in the establishment of America's public–private welfare regime, just as the 1970s and 1980s were in its entrenchment and consolidation. Against widespread expectations, the Social Security Act contributed to the growing interest of corporate America in private social benefits. The closure of the window of political opportunity opened by the New Deal – coupled with labor mobilization, changes in tax policy, and wage and price controls during the war years – further fostered the rise of fringe benefits. Then, after the war, the overwhelming political resistance to the growth and augmentation of existing public social programs impelled the labor movement to turn to private collective bargaining to seek the expansion and control of private benefits. As scholars of these years have documented well, "The American system of political representation and the composition of political coalitions after the end of the New Deal . . . made it difficult for post-1942 Democratic victories to be translated into majorities that would demand new [public] social benefits."[11] In particular, the split within the Democratic Party between a more liberal northern wing and a more conservative southern wing that enjoyed disproportionate institutional power stymied proposals for the expansion of the public side of the American welfare regime even when Democrats enjoyed power. Until the 1960s, as institutionally minded historians remind us, the United States was still not a fully democratized polity, and the absence of party competition and universal suffrage in the South had telling consequences, both for the fate of social reforms and the political leverage of the labor movement.[12]

The rise of publicly regulated and subsidized private social insurance is not, however, simply the flip side of the familiar story about the failure of public social programs in the United States. The private side of the American welfare regime did not emerge spontaneously because of the failure of more expansive public social programs. Opponents of redistributive public programs had to develop and nurture credible alternatives in areas of the market prone to failure, which they did both through public policy and through private leadership. Their own strategic choices and actions are an important, if often overlooked, part of the explanation for American policy distinctiveness. Nor was it just conservative political actors who were attracted to government intervention to bolster and mold private solutions to public problems. One of the most critical aspects of the historical formation of the American welfare regime was the decision on the part of core supporters of the welfare state, notably organized labor, to compromise their ultimate goals under conditions of strategic disadvantage to embrace policies that they would otherwise have opposed. And once subsidies for private social insurance were in place, many liberals embraced regulatory interventions designed to broaden private benefits with the zeal that many conservatives brought to the tax expenditures to which these regulations were tied.

Most important, private benefits contributed to public-sector failures at the same time as they resulted from them. Carving out areas of private social insurance through favorable state policy also placed real constraints on future political leaders interested in expanding public social insurance – one reason that it contained enduring appeal to those opposed to direct state provision. Just as social reformers sought to build regnant institutions of public social insurance rooted in self-reinforcing policy legacies, opponents of public programs attempted to shore up the foundations of private social insurance so as to limit the potential expansion of public programs.[13] Over time, the *effects* of these conservative-backed interventions – on private practices, on interest-group preferences and strategies, and ultimately on the goals of reformers – became crucial *causes* of the formidable political difficulties that advocates of public programs in the United States faced.[14]

It would be wrong, however, to see these constraints as working in only one direction. The special dispensation obtained at one point typically opened the door to more intrusive government intervention at another. This is why it is not far-fetched to see private social benefits as the American version of programs carried out by government in other nations. For all the inherent weaknesses of the instruments at policy-makers' disposal, there is an unmistakable trend in the historical record toward more active intervention in areas of policy once given over almost entirely to private interests. Subsidies were almost always followed by regulations and then attempts at evasion and then tighter regulations and then litigation and then more regulations. Nothing better illustrates these growing challenges to the autonomy of the corporate sponsors of private benefits than the path of the pension tax subsidy. What had begun as an almost entirely open-ended tax exemption became a contingent reward offered only to private policies deemed to fulfill state purposes. A similar, if less pronounced, movement can be seen in health policy: from unfettered tax subsidies and lavish funding of medical construction and research to government attacks on rising medical costs and an increased federal regulatory presence in health insurance.

Still, what requires emphasis is how porous and ineffective many of these regulations have been. Despite the enormous complexity and extensiveness of the ERISA regulations and the considerable corporate ill will they have caused, they seem to have done surprisingly little to change the distributional profile of private pensions or to broaden their still spotty coverage. Perhaps the economic trends of the past three decades have simply swamped whatever effects ERISA has produced, but it is difficult to come away unimpressed by the failure of federal regulations to even begin to match the dynamic pace of change within the private benefits world. At the same time as public social programs have been frozen in political time, corporations have changed the nature of private health insurance and pensions so fundamentally that the ERISA regulations of 1974 look like relics of a distant era. In health policy, the ERISA preemption clause opened the door to a transformation of American medical care more sweeping than anything Clinton's maligned health care task force could ever have imagined.

Indeed, a defining feature of subsidies and regulations aimed at voluntary private social insurance has been their limited ability to control the outcomes that result from the interplay of public policy with the changing political economy of corporate benefits activities. Richard Rose and Phillip Davies write of the "change without choice" that characterizes modern welfare states, the contours of which are driven by past commitments far more than present decisions.[15] Yet modern public social programs are "uncontrollable" mostly in the sense that they are politically difficult to change, not because policymakers lack the tools to produce intended effects.[16] In the politics of private social insurance, by contrast, there has been choice and change aplenty – almost day to day, the specific rules governing private benefits under ERISA evolve through legislative, regulatory, and judicial amendment – but there has been little control, and what control there has been remains scattered widely across a decentralized assortment of public and private institutions.[17]

The fundamental public policy framework that arose in the postwar years has, however, proved remarkably resistant to change. Much of my argument has stressed the degree to which the political development of private social welfare approaches departs from the well-established generalizations formulated to understand the politics of public social programs.[18] But with regard to the stickiness of public policy governing private benefits – and the embedded role of these benefits themselves – I have emphasized that significant insights can be gleaned from the growing body of research on the sources of resilience enjoyed by public social programs. Central to this research is the notion of blame avoidance, the imperative of diffusing or obscuring responsibility for unpopular policy effects that electorally sensitive politicians must satisfy if they are to threaten widely distributed and institutionally entrenched social benefits. Since the 1970s, blame avoidance has become a more prominent feature of the politics of social policy in all nations as mature public programs have run up against political, economic, and demographic pressures. Expanding public spending generally entails imposing diffuse costs in return for identifiable benefits; cutting it has more frequently involved imposing identifiable losses in return for diffuse gains. This, in turn, has required the turn to diverse strategies of loss imposition – delayed cutbacks, "circle the wagons" coalitions, closed-door policy formulation, omnibus packages, independent commissions – all of which share the aspiration of minimizing visible losses or obscuring responsibility for them.[19] It is no coincidence that the two major retrenchment efforts discussed in previous chapters – the 1983 Social Security reforms and the 1986 Tax Reform Act's restrictions on IRAs – both entailed extensive procedural maneuvering and policy calibration of this exact sort.[20]

To be sure, some features of private social welfare approaches make them more vulnerable to cutbacks, particularly their lesser visibility and the complexity of the connection between policy changes and policy effects. But these features, in fact, push in both directions. Although the lesser visibility of policies governing private benefits means that most citizens are less aware of changes to them, it also reduces the chance that they will be the target of concerted reform efforts. Complexity means that significant changes can be engineered through indirect mechanisms, but the difficulty of establishing what exactly the consequences of subsidies and regulations are also fosters policy ambiguity that allows politicians to embrace these interventions on multiple grounds.[21] And if complexity and lack of visibility militates against the formation of broad coalitions of support, it enhances the influence of the groups most capable of and interested in monitoring policy changes, which are also, in most cases, the groups most supportive of the existing policy framework. Perhaps the best case for the proposition that these features facilitate retrenchment is the 1986 cut in the value of the pension and health insurance tax exemptions. But, as Chapter 3 emphasized, this cutback was the indirect result of a popular policy change, namely, lower marginal tax rates. With the exception of the restriction on IRAs contained in the 1986 tax reform, all proposals for actually taxing private benefits were taken off the table.

It might be argued that the private side of American social provision never became an issue, that its preservation reflects consensual acceptance. Though public policy in this realm has had a low political profile, the claim is undeniably false. Tax subsidies for private benefits faced repeated and direct criticism from the late 1930s on, usually from actors within the state itself. Regulations on private benefits, sometimes tied to tax breaks and sometimes independent of them, prompted political skirmishes throughout these years. As for the benefits themselves, their central place in American social insurance has been the subject of deep and ongoing controversy, as anyone who has followed the history of U.S.

health policy can attest. Whatever the reasons for America's distinctive status, it cannot be said that it occasioned no attention or debate.

What then explains the resilient place of publicly regulated and sub-sidized private benefits in American social welfare practice? One obvious factor has been the natural tendency to build on or try to adapt existing structures of social provision rather than supplant them.[22] Drawing on the language of the "new institutional economics," we might say that policymakers turn to the private sector when the "transaction costs" of directly providing social welfare goods are greater than the costs of encouraging, monitoring, and shaping private social benefits.[23] But the more relevant way of phrasing the problem in the political arena is "tran-sition costs." Moving into an area dominated by publicly subsidized private benefits may be extremely costly – not simply costly in political terms, but costly to public budgets. As the course of U.S. health policy suggests, building up the infrastructure of private social provision raises enormously the expense of any government assumption of financial responsibility in the future. Moreover, because private social benefits meet some of the needs that public social programs might otherwise have addressed, they reduce the political and social gains that weigh against these increased costs.

Fostering private social provision also creates policy "capacity" in the private sector that rivals the capacities of state administrators.[24] Private social insurance has its own administrative and fiscal organization, which state actors may be reluctant to duplicate. (Medicare's reliance on Blue Cross and Blue Shield, though mostly a political concession, is partly understandable in these terms.)[25] And, of course, at the same time as reliance on publicly regulated and subsidized private social insurance builds up the private sector's capacity to administer and finance benefits, it substitutes in whole or in part for the emergence of comparable state capacity, reinforcing reliance on alternative policy instruments such as tax subsidies and regulation.

But no theory of social policy emphasizing technical constraints will take us very far. Immensely more critical has been the *political* costs asso-ciated with shifts of social insurance financing from the private to the public spheres. Just as politicians are loath to take on the clienteles of popular social programs, they are reluctant to impose losses on the beneficiaries of private social benefits. No army of private pension par-ticipants or health insurance subscribers needs to storm Washington for politicians to understand that policy changes seen to undermine signifi-cantly the extensive network of employment-based private benefits will be wildly unpopular, at least in the absence of acceptable substitutes. These are the type of policy changes that are likely to shade into the "politically infeasible" category, rejected not because of the mobilization of potentially affected groups, but out of anticipation of future political fallout.[26] Repeatedly we find that those who considered serious restrictions on subsidies for private social insurance backed away from what they judged a politically infeasible option – and when they did not, almost always found elected officials unwilling to go along.

Perhaps more important, private social benefits cultivate vested interests that are likely to be particularly capable of monitoring policy change and mobilizing against even low-visibility attacks. Chief among these interests are employers, but the list is extensive: insurers, medical professionals, hospitals, pension consultants, investment managers, and, as we have seen, labor unions. These groups may agree on little besides their desire to preserve the favorable treatment of employment-based private social insurance, but no positive agenda is required to play a blocking role in the notoriously status-quo-friendly American political structure. Much has been said about the declining power of labor and the rising influence of corporations in the past few decades.[27] But while the increased power of business may or may not imperil public social programs, it only strengthens the policy foundations of private social insurance.

In seeking to explain "the new politics of the welfare state," Paul Pierson draws a sharp line between the politics of expansion and the politics of retrenchment:

> Welfare state expansion involved the enactment of *popular* policies in a relatively undeveloped interest-group environment. By contrast, welfare state retrenchment generally requires elected officials to pursue *unpopular* policies that must withstand the scrutiny of both voters and well-entrenched networks of interest groups. It is therefore not surprising that variables crucial to understanding the former process are of limited use for analyzing the latter one.[28]

Pierson's claims provide important insights into the political resilience of the welfare state – insights to which my account is obviously indebted. Yet for the United States, and probably for other nations as well, the sharp line of demarcation between expansion and retrenchment needs to be softened.[29] In many cases, welfare state expansion was indeed a popular enterprise that played out in a "relatively undeveloped interest-group environment." But the interest-group environment into which the state attempted to move was not always so undeveloped, and in some cases it was arguably as dense as the network of supporters that grew up around public programs.[30] In these cases, welfare-state building was no less treacherous an exercise in blame avoidance and political maneuvering than welfare-state dismantling. Nowhere is this more clear than in U.S. health policy, where the government-facilitated growth of private benefits helped foster a sharp departure from the path taken in old-age insurance.

Contrasting Development

The story of contrasting development concerns a striking divergence within the universe of American social insurance: the success of Social Security alongside the failure of countless proposals for national health insurance, many of them directly modeled after the old-age insurance program. In cross-national perspective, Social Security has unusual elements (the absence of a universal flat-rate pension, for example), but these pale in comparison to the distinctiveness of the American policy pattern in health insurance. The United States is the only affluent democracy that does not guarantee health insurance to all or nearly all its citizens.[31] It is one of a few that retains any significant role for voluntary private insurance based on employment. "Why no national health insurance in the United States?" is perhaps the most important and enduring in the long list of puzzles about American social policy exceptionalism.

Analysts have tended to assume that a difference this stark, significant, and long-standing must be rooted in some deep and unique feature of the American character or polity: the late and halting development of the administrative state, the "liberal tradition" of individualism and antistatism, the absence of a labor-backed social-democratic party. But while these and other sources of cross-national policy difference undoubtedly help us better comprehend the underlying difficulties that health care reformers in the United States have faced, they do not offer an obvious explanation for why the fates of old-age security and health security diverged so sharply. Forces that are assumed to be at work across national social policy as a whole do not, after all, offer ready explanations for divergence *within* the American framework of social insurance. Nor must it be true that the failure of national health insurance in the United States reflects some master variable whose effects over time have been relatively constant. If path dependence arguments hold true, relatively small but significant differences across nations or policy areas may grow wider over time as self-reinforcing processes magnify early policy divergence – even if the original causes of these processes are no longer the crucial influence that they once were.

The most plausible and frequently cited explanation for why U.S. health policy has followed an exceptional path is the unusually strong position of the American medical profession.[32] Yet this argument is incomplete. Doctors in all nations resisted national health insurance, but the depth of their opposition and their success varied widely.[33] Comparative research suggests that the ability and desire of the medical profession to resist government incursions rest less on the intrinsic resources of the profession or its degree of political organization than they do on the nature of the private alternative available to doctors and the institutional leverage physicians enjoy by virtue of national political structures.[34] What set American doctors apart from those in many nations was the advantages they garnered due to the particular organization of the political environment within which they operated and – less recognized but no less important – the unusual success they had in obtaining private payment from insurance institutions friendly to their prerogatives and interests.[35] To understand both the vehemence and effectiveness of the American medical profession, therefore, requires returning to the question of how public policy and private leadership constructed a private sphere of social insurance that could serve as a substitute for public protections.

The answer cannot be that compulsory health insurance never made it onto the American political agenda. Indeed, health insurance emerged as a political issue before old-age pensions did, and it was the leading item in the Progressive era campaign for state social insurance programs. Crushed by a formidable opposition and the competitive pressures of decentralized federalism, the first campaign for compulsory health insurance set the tone for those to come. During the New Deal, the Roosevelt Administration seriously contemplated including a program of public health insurance in the Social Security Act. But the negative lessons learned from past defeats, the opposition of a medical profession now fully mobilized and alarmed, and the specific action agenda of the Depression all pushed health insurance lower on the list of reform priorities than old-age insurance. Although Roosevelt believed that he would have another opportunity to take up the cause, 1935 proved to be a critical juncture, the last moment for decades to come when new departures in social insurance had a good chance of passage. It was critical, too, because in the aftermath of the Social Security Act, a set of common forces pushed employers to adopt private programs of group insurance for their workers. But while these private social policies built on top of government protections in old-age insurance, they emerged as an alternative to public action in the field of health insurance – and that was a fateful difference.

The American medical profession was not directly responsible for the emergence of private social insurance in American medical care. It initially fought against private plans, embracing them only when their political advantages became transparent. Rather, the initial formation of voluntary insurance required a rich web of private social policy leadership, much of it motivated by true concern about the ability of Americans to afford the increasingly costly fruits of medical science. Public policies at both the state and the federal level also played a critical role in overcoming the inherent tendency of the market toward failure, many of them justified on the grounds that private benefits embodied features of public social insurance, redistributing risk and income in ways that the market would and could not. After World War II, moderates and conservatives in Washington refused to support national health insurance, but they spearheaded efforts to codify and expand the favorable tax treatment of health insurance while actively supporting measures to fund medical research and construction. These policies were justified on the grounds that they would make public health insurance unnecessary, showing the way to a distinctly American response to the dilemmas of modern medical financing. In conjunction with the common pressures driving the adoption of employment-based fringe benefits, this extensive support for private health insurance and medical care fostered a massive and costly framework of private health insurance that increasingly stood as one of the greatest barriers to the passage of a national program based on Social Security.

The effects of the early failure of national health insurance thus became a crucial cause of the political difficulties later faced by American health care reformers. This was perhaps most visible in the evolving positions of organized business and labor. Fierce opponents in general of the Social Security Act, employers grew to accept federal old-age insurance. Although strategic realism was one factor behind the changing business attitude toward the increasingly popular and broad-based program, firms with extensive private pension benefits also genuinely came to see old-age insurance as a necessary floor for corporate plans. Because integrated plans factored in Social Security benefits – which were, in the early years of the program, vastly in excess of worker and employer contributions – they could exclude or provide meager benefits to most workers while supplementing the Social Security benefits of higher-income personnel, all at a relatively modest cost. Not only did old-age insurance generously underwrite the expense of integrated pensions, but it also leveled the competitive playing field by forcing competing employers to provide minimum protection. Yet, at the same time as many employers came to see the benefits in a modest program of Social Security, they remained unalterably opposed to government entry into health insurance, a policy field in which they had carved out an exclusive role. Thus, while the supplementary character of private pensions encouraged employers to accommodate themselves to old-age insurance (and thereby entrenched it further), the core status of employment-based health insurance made employers acutely aware of and resistant to the threat of government action. It was only much later, when rising medical costs became the key concern, that some employers with extensive benefits saw advantage in government efforts to socialize and control medical costs. By then, however, the private track of development had deeply fragmented business interests, created massive networks of vested interests, and raised pressing new problems that thwarted effective action by either government or business.

A similar transformation occurred within the ranks of the labor movement. Frustrated by the slow growth of old-age insurance and the repeated failure of national health insurance, the labor movement turned to private collective bargaining to obtain social insurance, their demands supported by key liberals in Congress and the White House who both sympathized with labor's plight and recognized the importance of defining the terms of postwar collective bargaining. Again, however, the emergence of private health insurance as the core provider of health security gradually changed labor's priorities, pushing unions to focus on health insurance for retirees while reducing their interest in compromise measures for expanded coverage that they deemed inferior to existing private protections. Although most labor leaders remained committed to universal health insurance, they also acknowledged that the interest of the rank and file in the goal had waned with the growth of private protections. In recent decades, even as the elements of risk pooling embodied in private health insurance have unraveled, labor leaders have repeatedly sided with business groups to protect the special subsidies for employment-based insurance and to preserve the destabilizing regulatory vacuum created by the ERISA preemption.[36]

Another legacy of the rise of private health security can be seen in the changing priorities of health care reformers themselves, who discovered that the path of least political resistance led to a carefully chosen strategic retreat rather than a frontal assault on private social benefits and policies encouraging them. By the early 1950s, reformers with close ties to the Social Security Administration had developed an approach that they believed would create an opening wedge for the movement of government into the health insurance field: a proposal for federal hospital insurance for the aged. Tied to Social Security, this approach simultaneously capitalized on the evident strength of the old-age insurance program and the evident weakness of private insurance as a source of protection for vulnerable Americans outside the labor market. This proposal, so unusual in cross-national perspective, can only be understood in the context of the simultaneous expansion of Social Security and the rapid postwar spread of private health insurance among the working population. By focusing on the aged, health care reformers could tie their efforts even more closely to old-age insurance while demanding policy ends that did not frontally challenge the core place of private health insurance in the American welfare regime.

But although reformers hoped that their proposal would be an entering wedge, the Medicare strategy had inherent weaknesses as a foundation for further movement toward universal public insurance, especially after Wilbur Mills craftily foreclosed the step-by-step path that reformers had envisioned by rolling physicians insurance for the aged and means-tested medical assistance into the final legislation. By taking the most costly and difficult-to-insure populations out of the private insurance system, Medicare and Medicaid at once strengthened private insurance and removed much of the remaining political pressure for reform. This was not the only reason that proposals for universal health insurance failed in the 1970s and 1990s, but it did contribute to these political defeats and, more subtly, to a continuing transformation of the goals of reformers.

The divergence between health and old-age insurance manifested itself, therefore, not simply in the vastly disparate political fortunes of public social insurance in pension and health policy, but also in the changing shape of the policy ideas that health care reformers adopted in the years after World War II. By the 1970s, each of the two proposals most likely to gain legislative ratification – a mandate on employers to insure their workers and a proposal for catastrophic insurance to cover very high medical costs – retained a core role for employment-based private health insurance even as they circumscribed it. In the 1990s, President Clinton broke with many of his Democratic allies to embrace a proposal premised on the continuance of financing through employers and the expansion of large managed care health plans. Despite the decline of the conservative wing of the Democratic Party, the divisions among Democrats (and the left in general) over the appropriate model for health insurance reform remained a major barrier to legislative success. And one important reason for this near-fratricidal division was the growing gulf separating those who wished to accommodate existing institutions of private financing and those who wished to supplant them.

Accommodation, however, went beyond judgments about the political feasibility of alternative reform proposals. The nature of regulatory intervention also differed significantly between the health and pension areas. Despite the far greater degree of public and elite dissatisfaction evinced toward private health insurance, private pensions came to be much more heavily regulated than employment-based health insurance under federal law. Even before the 1974 ERISA preemption exempted most large health plans from state regulatory control, the reluctance of federal policymakers to attach conditions to the favorable tax treatment of private health insurance was unmistakable. After the 1974 shift, the efforts of employers and private insurers to take advantage of the resulting regulatory vacuum provoked only a weak and halting federal response. In both pension and health policy, concerns about the effects of regulations on employers' willingness to offer voluntary private benefits were palpable. But politicians proved more willing to impose standards aimed at making private pensions a secure and broadly distributed supplement than to regulate the terms of employer-provided health benefits. This appears to have reflected both the stronger political position of the defenders of private health insurance and the greater concern felt by policymakers about jeopardizing private social insurance in an area lacking a core program of government insurance.[37]

An understanding of path dependence may not be needed to explain why policies that are widely supported and broadly popular continue to survive. But it is essential to resolving the puzzle of why policies that appear widely disliked, even by groups that originally fought for them, endure despite countless efforts to change them. Business and doctors and insurers all, for their own reasons, are dissatisfied with current arrangements. Though often quite happy with their own health care, Americans have expressed ongoing concern about American medical financing as a whole. Scores of political leaders have bemoaned the great national problems of rising medical costs and the growing number of uninsured Americans. But the structure of American health insurance has, for almost four decades now, consistently bedeviled attempts to extend health security to all Americans or to make a serious dent in America's high medical costs. Rising costs have pushed public and private decision makers to contain expenditures within their own restricted universe of control. They have driven insurance underwriters to draw ever finer distinctions among Americans. They have impelled health plans to support ever greater regulation of clinical and patient freedom. They have driven corporate purchasers to bear ever fewer of the cross-subsidies necessary for broad-based insurance to work. The choices and failures that created this distinctly unsatisfactory system grew out of embedded features of American politics and out of strategic choices at critical junctures. But the continued failure of national health insurance in the decades after World War II must also be understood as a reflection of the very policy arrangements that these early decisions and events brought about.[38] Private health insurance, in short, had policy feedback effects every bit as far-reaching and consequential as those unleashed by Social Security, yet these pushed American policymakers away from the goal of comprehensive social insurance rather than toward it.

Private Social Benefits and Theories of the Welfare State

By now it should be clear that any portrait of the American welfare state that does not consider private social benefits or the policies that encourage and shape them is incomplete. These benefits represent a much larger share of social spending in the United States than they do in other nations, their role has increased since World War II, and they are at the heart of some of the fiercest conflicts in American politics today. Moreover, while the United States is exceptional in the degree to which private benefits have grown up alongside public programs, it is not alone. Over the past decade, the proportion of spending channeled through regulated and subsidized private means has risen in most other affluent democracies, too, albeit from a much lower base.[39]

All this suggests that private social benefits will become a more prominent subject of commentary and research in the coming years. Signs of this shift can already be seen, in this book and in other recent studies.[40] Nonetheless, the role of government in shaping private benefits still remains a peripheral topic within the voluminous literature on the welfare state, and attempts to uncover this less-studied realm of social policy have had only limited impact, in part because there has been little effort to fit recent findings within existing research traditions. This is unfortunate, for broadening our focus not only makes the American historical experience more intelligible, but also allows for the amendment and extension of leading claims about the political formation of the welfare state. From the role of political institutions to the influence of employers to the sources and implications of path-dependent processes in political life, novel insights into the politics of social policy emerge when we consider the full range of public policies, social benefits, and political actors that have shaped the American welfare regime.

The Role of Political Institutions

The "new institutionalism" in the social sciences is now over two decades old, its origins dating back to the late 1970s when scholars in a range of fields began to argue for greater emphasis on the rules, procedur and organizations that channel and mold individual and group be ior.[41] If the new institutionalism is no longer new, it is also not a s "institutionalism" but rather a collection of related but distinct sch of thought in political science, sociology, and economics.[42] Beneath this diversity, however, several claims about political institutions find recurrent expression. The most fundamental is that political institutions – the basic organization of a nation's legislative, executive, and judicial organs; the relationship, when applicable, between national and subnational governments; and the laws governing voting and electoral competition – together constitute the "rules of the game" in political life, "creating risks and opportunities for effective policymaking."[43] A second claim is that governments develop capabilities for intervention in the economy and society that make some lines of government action more likely than others, and perhaps even prevent some altogether.[44] A third claim is that public officials enjoy special influence by virtue of their institutional position and thus must be viewed as at least partially "autonomous" from pressures and forces outside government.[45] Institutions, in sum, structure political interaction, foster or retard specific types of government intervention, and empower institutionally advantaged actors with special sovereignty.

Each of these claims has been instrumental in advancing the comparative study of social policy, and each is well illustrated by aspects of my analysis. The multiple "veto points" created by America's fragmented political structure help explain why it is so hard to enact major public social programs in the United States.[46] The historical weakness of the American civil service and federal administrative apparatus, as well as the nonprogrammatic character of American political parties and the halting and limited development of effective mechanisms for revenue extraction, are important to understanding why national social programs developed later and remained fewer in the United States than in European democracies. And one cannot review the history of U.S. social policy without a strong appreciation of the autonomous role played by actors within government – from elected leaders like Roosevelt, Mills, and Javits to executive officials like Altmeyer, Cohen, and Folsom. Even when these actors believed they were responding to the interests of outside groups or the constraints imposed by policies or institutions, it was their initiative, creativity, and acumen that brought together the sometimes diffuse and disorganized demands swirling around them into specific legislative results.

When the broader canvas of public–private relations comes into view, however, it immediately becomes apparent that these three claims are also incomplete. Take first the familiar argument about America's institutional barriers to policy change. The American political structure did not just *constrain* the ambitions of policy advocates; it also created distinctive *opportunities* for political influence and policy change, facilitating the passage of a whole range of public policies designed to shape private social benefits, many quite interventionist and far-reaching. State-building in the United States has not merely been a pale imitation of models found abroad. It has featured the development of truly distinctive governance arrangements, premised much more heavily on private networks of social provision, regulatory and tax law, and judicial policing than is the modal pattern in other Western democracies. Institutionally minded scholars have argued convincingly that "[f]ederalism, bicameralism, and presidentialism constitute potentially important 'institutional' veto points that allow conservative interests the opportunity to oppose welfare policy development and slow policy change."[47] But while political institutions may make policy change more or less difficult across the board, many of their most important effects are mediated by the characteristics of policies themselves – their visibility, their distribution, their implementation requirements, their fiscal needs. As I have argued, the exceptional place of private social benefits in the United States is not simply the product of the failure of public programs, but also a result of characteristics of private social welfare approaches that make them more likely to gain a foothold in an institutional environment hostile to major expansions of public authority.

This points to a larger weakness in reigning conceptions of American policy capacity. Beginning with the distinction between "strong" European states and the "weak" American one, and continuing through the division between the advanced "social-democratic" welfare states of northern Europe and the underdeveloped "liberal" welfare state found in the United States, these arguments have generally betrayed a concern with what the United States did *not* achieve – namely, a universal welfare state along European lines – rather than an interest in the areas of state capacity that did develop and have subsequently encouraged policy down particular tracks.[48]

Tax expenditures stand out in this regard. With a few notable exceptions, taxation has generally been cordoned off from spending, as if fiscal means always sprang forth to meet governing ends and as if the tax structure of a nation was not itself a critical independent shaper of social welfare outcomes.[49] But among the key elements of American exceptionalism, surely one of the most striking is the prominent place of tax expenditures in the provision and subsidization of social benefits.[50] It is striking, in part, because tax expenditures represent an area of state power in which the bureaucratic agency vested with authority, the Treasury Department, has historically been hostile to the basic policy, which simultaneously complicates its duties and contravenes its central mission of raising revenue. Yet, despite repeated attempts, Treasury officials routinely failed to convince members of Congress, and even the presidents that they served, to take the unpopular step of eliminating tax expenditures and jeopardizing private benefits. Income and corporate taxes ratcheted up under presidential leadership during national emergencies were whittled away under congressional leadership during times of peace and prosperity, leaving the United States with very low tax rates in comparative perspective, a massive system of tax breaks for private social benefits, and persistent fiscal hurdles to the passage and expansion of public programs.[51]

Indeed, what comes out most transparently in the history of the tax treatment of private benefits is the extent to which Treasury actions were driven by congressional rather than executive influence. "The Congress," the Constitution declares, "shall have Power to lay and collect Taxes, Duties, Imposts and Excises, to pay the Debts and provide for the common Defence and general Welfare of the United States."[52] And despite massive changes in the standing of the presidency and Congress since 1787, these words retain an essential truth.[53] It should come as little surprise, then, that in contrast with the large public programs so identified with the welfare state, many of which originated during periods of sweeping executive power, policies encouraging and regulating private social benefits have been considerably more congressionally centered, with strategically situated individual members of Congress, rather than parties or presidents, the key instigators of innovation.[54] Arthur Vandenberg, Robert Taft, Wilbur Mills, Jacob Javits, William Roth – congressional denizens like these arguably left as indelible a mark on policies governing private benefits as Roosevelt and Johnson left on American social programs. Looked at from a more institutional perspective, these policies have also comported closely with the basic instincts of members of Congress: their reluctance to impose identifiable losses on organized constituencies; their preference for policies with transparent benefits and diffuse, hard-to-trace costs; their attraction to measures endorsing lofty goals without authorizing the disruptions or resources necessary for their achievement.[55] Congress makes social policy, but it makes it differently than presidents do, and certainly than parliaments in other nations do.

If Congress emerges as crucial in some areas, the courts do so in others. At least since Alexis de Tocqueville famously observed that "[t]here is hardly a political question in the United States which does not sooner or later turn into a judicial one," the commanding place of the courts has been recognized as a defining feature of the American constitutional order.[56] Yet, in research on U.S. social policy, the judiciary has mostly been viewed as a blocking agent whose relevance waned after the Supreme Court upheld the Social Security Act in 1937.[57] Most studies of the history and politics of social policy since the New Deal do not mention the courts at all. If my account is any indication, this is partly a reflection of where scholars have looked. Although court interpretations of statutes have been an important element in the development of some social programs – particularly those in which power is divided between the states and the federal government – the role of the courts in these areas pales in comparison to their influence over the tax and regulatory laws that govern private social benefits.[58] Among the most complex fields in American law today, employee benefits law is "now a dense mixture of private contracting, common law, adjudication, statutory norms, detailed agency regulation, and informal control through legislative oversight."[59] In just the past five years, a dozen Supreme Court cases related to employee benefits and thousands of federal circuit and district court case have been decided, continuing the "tide of litigation" that has long marked the field. The political stalemate fostered by fragmented institutions and ideological disagreement has only heightened the importance of the courts, allowing policy to unfold in directions unanticipated or undesired by its designers.

The litigation surrounding ERISA preemption provides the best example. The sheer number of cases is itself staggering: More than 4,000 opinions dealing with the preemption clause were handed down between 1989 and 1999.[60] (Lawyers in the trenches joke that ERISA stands for "Everything Ridiculous Invented Since Adam.") Yet their substantive policy impact has been no less striking. Federal courts led the way in walling off not just health benefits but a whole range of wage and benefit practices from virtually all state regulation and litigation, allowing, in one of the most notorious cases, an employer to discontinue coverage for AIDS treatment when one of its workers contracted the disease.[61] Although the hard lines initially drawn by the courts have since softened, court interpretations of ERISA nonetheless represent one of the principal reasons that a law heralded as the salvation of the worker has, in practice, bolstered employers' unilateral control over private health benefits and invalidated "scores of progressive state laws."[62] The endless legal debate about the "original intent" of the preemption clause masks the reality that no one involved in the drafting of the legislation anticipated the uses to which the clause would be put or foresaw the near impossibility of fundamentally revising its sweeping language once private interests had moved into the resultant regulatory void. In deciding what preemption meant, the federal courts have been making social policy as much as interpreting it – and making it in forums only weakly capable of grappling with the concerns that prompted ERISA in the first place.

The recourse to the courts is reflective of the special character of private social policy approaches. Tax subsidies and regulation are examples of "third-party" government, in which nongovernmental actors are encouraged and prodded to fulfill governmental ends.[63] "Such arrangements not only invite litigation," observe Harold Seidman and Robert Gilmour, "but since disputes among parties in these relationships cannot be resolved authoritatively within the executive branch, they virtually command a litigation strategy by third parties and their supporting interest associations as a vital means of dealing effectively with federal monitors, rulemakers, and enforcers."[64] Yet the role that the courts have come to play in the benefits field also conforms to the more general American tendency to rely on detailed regulation, backed up by rights of legal action, in lieu of strong spending agencies insulated from outside review.[65] The legalistic character of policies governing private benefits has further hindered their political recognition and control, and made them largely inaccessible to analysts whose substantive interests extend beyond the narrow issues of law that they raise. Future research on the politics of U.S. social policy would do well to consider the wider ramifications of the judicialized nature of these spheres of intervention.

Examining the broader canvas of U.S. social policy points, finally, to some of the very real limits of "state autonomy" in U.S. social policy. Theda Skocpol argues that "[b]ecause states are authoritative and resourceful organizations – collectors of revenue, centers of cultural authority, and hoarders of means of coercion – they are sites of autonomous action, not reducible to the demands or preferences of any social group."[66] What is remarkable about U.S. social policy, however, is the degree to which these sources of autonomy have been parceled out to nongovernmental actors, who are vested by the state with considerable independent power and resources. These arrangements, we have seen, may make it more difficult for public officials to achieve the ends that prompted government intervention in the first place. Yet perhaps more important, they also create a tangible constraint on the freedom of action of public officials, whose policy aims are now substantially dependent upon the health of the private social benefits that public policies seek to encourage and shape.

The deference granted to the sponsors and providers of widespread private benefits represents a form of structural power, "structural" in that it stems from the basic position in the American welfare regime that these organizations occupy rather than from any active effort on the part of these organizations to sway government officials (though, of course, in many cases deference may reflect both).[67] The concept of structural power has fallen on hard times. Sweeping claims about the "imperatives of capitalism" or the "logic of liberal democracies" proved too brittle to accommodate the considerable variation over time and across countries in the political fortunes of allegedly privileged actors. Yet formulated more precisely, and with greater attention to institutional and policy context, this type of explanation has an important place. The fundamental contention is that policy outcomes may reflect not just the resources or influence of competing political actors, but also the underlying relations among them. In the American welfare regime, policy ends of tangible import to politicians – who receives health insurance, how generous retirement benefits will be – are highly dependent upon the continued willingness of private organizations to sponsor voluntary protections. If one wants to know how policy will unfold in these areas, the most revealing question to ask may not be "Who has the most access or resources?" but "How does this division of labor condition the range of options that elected leaders find attractive and feasible?"[68] This is the sort of structural consideration that a regime perspective highlights. And it suggests yet another respect in which the features of policies deeply shape political processes and the power of political actors – most notably, the power of employers.

Business Power and Social Policy

The relationship between employers and the welfare state is an old and enduring issue. Yet, in recent years, this familiar debate has gained fresh life. After a decade in which employers were mostly second-string players in social welfare scholarship, increasingly sophisticated research has emphasized the constructive role of business in the development of social policy, challenging the traditional association of the welfare state with the victory of labor over capital in the political arena.[69] Although these revisionist accounts are diverse, their central argument is that social policies are not simply class struggle by other means, but are positive-sum bargains that reflect the underlying interests of employers (or factions of employers) in certain welfare state programs.[70]

The need to "bring capital back in" is surely pressing.[71] As previous chapters have shown, employers have been crucial actors in the development of U.S. social policy – not just through the well-known blocking role that they have played in conflicts over public programs, but also through their private benefits activities and their influence over policies designed to shape these activities. Ironically, those who emphasize business power have all but ignored these more subterranean policies, fixing their attention instead on public spending programs, where the influence of welfare capitalists is easily overstated. Yet, as my analysis has shown, corporations heavily involved in private social provision closely monitored and repeatedly tried to shape policies governing private benefits – and with considerable success. These, after all, were relatively obscure interventions that invited a restricted scope of political conflict, allowing the most interested parties to have disproportionate influence.[72] In other areas, business faced difficulties forming unified positions and mobilizing to achieve them against other organized forces in a fragmented political environment. The barriers to business participation were not nearly as high and the organized competitors for the ears of politicians not nearly as numerous in the realm of private policy approaches.

Indeed, the historical record suggests that employers exercised their power through a previously little-recognized mechanism: their attempts to preempt fields of social provision that might otherwise have been occupied by government and thereby increase the political and economic costs of government movement into these areas.[73] The rise of employer-sponsored health insurance provides the strongest illustration. Pressed on by doctors and insurers, as well as by the demands of organized labor, employers moved into the field well aware that in the absence of action, the pressures for national health insurance would be overwhelming. At the same time that they adopted private benefits, business leaders and associations (along with conservatives in government, insurers, and medical providers) pointed to corporate action as evidence that government insurance was unnecessary. And they fought bitterly against proposals to displace all or some of this emerging private welfare complex while pushing for policies that underwrote its costs. The increasing reliance of workers on employer-provided health insurance in turn conferred significant new influence on American employers, who claimed that redistributive or highly regulatory policies would imperil their private efforts. Not only that, it gave employers near-unilateral control over social benefits that in other nations were governed by elected leaders rather than by private managers. The rapid swings in the world of private benefits over the past two decades – toward defined-contribution pension plans, toward "managed care," toward restricted benefits coverage, toward individualized concentration of risk – could not have occurred otherwise.

Still, the history of the American welfare regime also challenges the boldest of the business-power claims: that employers are key instigators behind the creation of large-scale social programs. Business leaders have hardly spoken with a single voice, as recent scholarship has usefully emphasized.[74] And while fiercely resistant to new social programs, employers have tended to accommodate themselves to programs after enactment. Nonetheless, the usual stance at the time of initial consideration has been fierce and bitter opposition. Most employers strenuously opposed Social Security and Medicare, keystones of the American welfare state, and even sympathetic employers frequently justified their deviance on the grounds that a constructive position was necessary to head off even less attractive options.[75] Had corporate America consistently gotten its way, the American welfare state would look very different today.

As my discussion of the development of the Social Security Act suggests, those inclined to emphasize business influence have been too quick to assume that the supportive orientation of employers toward the old-age insurance program in the years after 1935 constitutes evidence that the program reflected business interests at the time of its passage.[76] I have argued instead that employers' subsequent reactions to the program are better understood as a combination of political accommodation in the face of an increasingly popular program and managerial accommodation prompted by the partly unexpected positive effects of the program on the development of private pension plans (effects bolstered by rising tax rates, business-supported public policies that encouraged private pensions, and labor pressure for integrated plans). Business firms with private pensions did come to see Social Security as a floor of protection that generously offset the cost of their integrated plans, allowing firms to focus their supplementary pensions on highly skilled workers. But these are best understood as policy feedback *effects* of the legislation and as evidence of the success of employers in shaping federal policies after Social Security's enactment, rather than as crucial motives behind the passage of the program in 1935.[77]

This raises a more general concern. Revisionists are convincing when they argue that many aspects of the welfare state are conducive to overall economic growth or the success of specific business strategies. The evidence that public social programs as a whole are inimical to high levels of economic growth has always been weak.[78] It seems clear, moreover, that different types of capitalist "production regimes" – enduring systems of corporate organization and state–market relations – are associated with different patterns of social policy.[79] But showing that social policies produce positive economic benefits or assist certain production strategies is simply not the same as showing that business influence explains these policies. To begin with, social policies reshape business interests by encouraging specific strategies of domestic and international competition, creating advantages for some firms and disadvantages for others. Thus, over time, national frameworks of social policy should be expected to foster a population of employers capable of thriving within a specified framework of social programs, even if business actors were not important shapers of the original policy structure.

Equally important, employers may oppose government interventions even if they benefit all or part of the business community. In the United States, the reason for this apparent anomaly most often cited is stubborn business distrust of the state. As David Vogel persuasively argues, "The most characteristic, distinctive, and persistent belief of American corporate executives is an underlying suspicion and mistrust of government."[80] This is not merely an ideological resistance: "The criterion by which business evaluates government policy has remained quite firm: does the proposed intervention strengthen or weaken the autonomy of management?"[81] Social policies that offer positive economic benefits by equalizing costs across firms, controlling benefit costs, or removing social responsibilities from corporate balance sheets often involve the sacrifice of managerial control, and this is a concession that American firms have been reluctant to make. At the same time, policies with broad economic benefits generally present corporations with a classic "collective action problem": Diffuse rewards shared in common are unlikely to become the basis for concerted mobilization by organized groups.[82] The structure of American government worsens this inherent problem by making it harder to pass legislation than to block action from taking place. And these institutional obstacles are compounded by the heavily privatized structure of American social provision itself. With involvement in and need for benefits varying greatly across firms, common business interests concerning the equalization, socialization, or control of private benefit costs are extremely hard to come by. The fragmentation of business interests created by experience-rated health insurance and the move to self-funding provides a case in point.

All this indicates that one of the most promising areas of research in the study of business influence may well lie at the intersection of public social programs and employers' private benefit activities. As the contrast between employer views of old-age insurance and national health insurance after the New Deal suggests, the relationship between public programs and private benefits may be an important factor in the formation of employer preferences. Employers grew more favorable toward Social Security as their private benefit activities came to rely on the program's promise of basic retirement security. At the same time, however, they battled against the entry of the federal government into the field of private health insurance, where business and insurers had carved out an exclusive niche. In more recent decades, as growing numbers of retirees and slow wage growth have eliminated the high returns initially offered by Social Security, employers have responded to larger economic forces and new public policies to disconnect private pensions from federal old-age insurance. In the process, they have increasingly lost interest in a program that key employers and business associations once defended and even sought to expand. Social Security still enjoys powerful bases of support, and its massive accumulated commitments will still plague attempts at radical reform. But major changes no longer look as infeasible as they once did, and America's leading corporations can no longer be counted on to back the core role the program once incontestably enjoyed.

No less worthy of analysis than these firm-level effects is the larger place of private benefits within the American political economy. Comparative analysts have recently come to speak of "varieties of capitalism," highlighting the divergent character of even the most fundamental features of capitalist markets in wealthy nations.[83] In the "coordinated" economies of northern Europe, dense organizational ties link firms to one another and to other economic actors. These ties facilitate coordination within and between firms, encouraging skilled production strategies characterized by high wages and extensive investment in the human capital of workers.[84] By contrast, the weakness of business coordination and labor organization in the United States encourages firms to pursue more flexible production approaches based on low labor costs and relatively limited investment in most workers' skills. America's heavy reliance on private benefits is in keeping with this overall picture. Freed from the constraints of high taxes and strong unions, firms in some segments of the U.S. economy have seen continuing advantage in competing on the basis of minimal wages and benefits. The results are apparent not only in levels of income inequality higher than in any other wealthy nation, but also in vast disparities across firms, industries, and regions in private benefit coverage.[85] In the United States, where people live, what industry they work in, and the size of their employer have as much impact on the benefits they enjoy as anything that government does.

The pathway between America's welfare regime and political economy is a two-way street. Anemic public protections and extensive government backing for voluntary benefits foster the low-wage employment sector while encouraging high-wage firms to provide generous benefits to the better paid. And these features of the U.S. labor market, in turn, influence the constellation of political forces that shape social policy, segmenting workers according to their access to private benefits and increasing the voice of low-wage firms, strong historical opponents of public programs. Moreover, powerful competitive pressures discipline firms that deviate from dominant production strategies. As a result of these selection pressures and policy feedback processes, welfare regimes and national economies tend to be self-reinforcing over time, with institutional "complementarities" developing between social policies and prevailing modes of economic organization and behavior. This is an important reason that, as recent scholarship has shown, national economic structures are surprisingly enduring, and it is one more reason that claims about path dependence must be at the center of efforts to understand long-term patterns of social policy development.

The Temporal Dimensions of Politics

In the social sciences, path dependence has increasingly become an organizing concept around which historical and institutional analysis revolves. Yet, in too many cases, the term is little more than a stand-in for the unassailable yet theoretically trivial assertion that "history matters." A central goal of this book is to specify what exactly it means to say that political processes are path dependent and to clarify the essential relationship between path dependence and arguments about timing and sequence. In bringing content to these ideas while using them to understand a critical aspect of U.S. social policy, I have tried to show that path dependence is not merely a fashionable term that social scientists with historical inclinations can use to justify their work, but a powerful set of tools for *explaining* important features of political and social life.

Of course, arguments about timing and sequence are nothing new. Historians and social scientists have long understood, if they have not always had good conceptual tools for demonstrating, that the relative timing and sequence of important historical events may be a crucial determinant of the effects that those events have.[86] What path dependence brings to this long-standing, but largely eclipsed, tradition is an explanation of why the legacies of these "critical junctures" in political development are so long-lived and consequential – why, that is, certain paths of historical development or institutional evolution endure and reinforce themselves over time.[87] More important, scholarship on path dependence has begun to identify the conditions under which, and the mechanisms by which, this process occurs.[88] The dominant thrust of this work is antifunctional.[89] Many institutions or policy configurations cannot simply be understood as optimally tailored to current conditions by political agents. Rather, events and choices of the past, sometimes the distant past, continue to exert influence through the entrenched institutions and self-reinforcing consequences that they create – even if the original forces that gave rise to this path of development no longer hold sway. If path dependence obtains, we need a "genealogical" rather than a "teleological" account, an explanation that points first to moments of formative origin and their enduring effects rather than to present circumstances and their functional requisites.[90]

When paired with an appreciation of historical sequences and critical junctures, the concept of path dependence pushes us toward a "branching tree model" of historical development, in which choices at one point in time reduce the feasibility of other, once-conceivable, options by putting in place enduring institutions or by setting in motion self-reinforcing processes that are difficult to undo.[91] Timing and sequence are at the heart of this conception of historical possibility. When institutions or policies are path dependent, early choices and events play a particularly critical role in shaping the subsequent path of evolution. At different stages in a path-dependent process, the same causes do not produce the same effects. And because each event or choice – each "branch" on the historical tree – significantly changes the context for subsequent decision making, the sequence in which events occur or choices are made may also have a dramatic effect on the eventual outcome. In these cases, we need to attend not just to *what* happens but to *when* it happens, and more specifically, when it happens relative to other events and ongoing processes.[92]

The original body of writings on path dependence emerged in the discipline of economics, where the concept also posed the greatest challenge to existing theoretical approaches (and where it also faces the most serious evidentiary hurdles).[93] Yet to identify and demonstrate path dependence in politics requires both a departure from economic models and a consideration of the special forms of evidence required to show path dependence in the political realm.[94] Markets revolve around exchange, politics around authority. Arguments about the entrenchment of technologies emphasize that even rational and far-sighted actors with fixed preferences may head down suboptimal paths. Arguments about the entrenchment of institutions or policies need also to emphasize the ways in which people's very preferences are reshaped by programmatic and institutional contexts. The standard for judging path dependence in economics is the lodestar of efficiency. In politics, efficiency is not the appropriate metric. Path-dependent processes need to be shown through comparative, historical, or counterfactual analysis that highlights both alternative historical possibilities and the self-reinforcing processes that foreclose them over time.

Drawing on the seminal writings on path dependence in economics, as well as on the recent work of sociologists and political scientists, I have argued that path dependence is most likely when policies lead to the creation of large-scale institutions with substantial set-up costs, when they benefit sizable organized groups, when they embody long-lived commitments, when they are interwoven with broader features of the economy or society, and when there are barriers to the reversal of policy paths that are unanticipated or undesired. These conditions point, in turn, to some of the critical *mechanisms* that create institutional stickiness or self-reinforcing processes. For the purposes of political analysis, the most critical are the risks to elected officials inherent in attempts to significantly alter policies that engender long-term public expectations and have politically effective vested interests in their continuance. But I have argued that other mechanisms may also underpin self-reinforcing processes, emphasizing, most notably, that different divisions of state and private responsibility differently shape the preferences of affected parties and pose distinct challenges for policymakers.[95] These structural effects create characteristic patterns of political development within a policy area that make departure from a path even more difficult than it might otherwise be.

The common sources of path dependence underlie my story of parallel development in health and pension policy. In each of these areas, public social programs and publicly regulated and encouraged private benefits were characterized by features conducive to self-reinforcement. Although students of social policy have increasingly stressed the path-dependent characteristics of large-scale social programs, they have scarcely noted the similar policy feedback processes associated with private social benefits. Yet, in certain key respects, the reasons for believing that policies shaping private benefits are prone to path dependence are as strong or stronger than is the case for public social programs. Chief among these reasons are the lesser visibility and traceability of policies governing private benefits and the greater degree of mobilization and attentiveness of the organized groups that benefit directly or indirectly from them. That the public and private realms of social provision share characteristics conducive to path dependence means neither that they evolve in exactly the same way nor that they are equally immune to change. Indeed, policies governing private benefits typically follow a different trajectory of development than do public social programs and are likely to originate under different conditions. Moreover, in contrast with public social programs, the ambiguity and unpredictability of policies shaping private benefits and the scope that they provide for unilateral private action mean that private benefits can be transformed *despite* relative stability in the framework of policies that govern them. Nonetheless, both public and private realms of social provision have the potential to become entrenched through similar processes of institutionalization and self-reinforcement.

The tax treatment of fringe benefits illustrates the self-reinforcing nature of policy choices regarding private benefits. Like the common law, tax policy has a strongly path-dependent character, with initial precedents becoming the basis for subsequent decisions.[96] Once an area of corporate social policy is granted special tax concessions, there are strong pressures to extend that treatment to similar benefits and similarly situated taxpayers (often justified on the grounds of *horizontal equity*, the idea that like income should be treated alike across tax filers). Early precedents with regard to group life insurance, for example, were gradually extended to other group insurance benefits, such as health insurance. Advocates of the 401(k) provision argued that forbidding new cash or deferred compensation arrangements discriminated against employers who had failed to establish them before the congressional moratorium on such plans. Proponents of tax-favored retirement plans for the self-employed argued that all workers deserved access to a tax-free pension; these plans then became a precedent for extending the privilege to workers without a pension who were not self-employed; and once that was done, "fairness" dictated that these individualized retirement plans be made available to all Americans.

Self-reinforcement also emerged from forces external to the tax policy process. Corporations and workers came to expect as normal the preferential tax status that fringe benefits enjoyed, and embedded systems of benefit provision rose up to take advantage of this new structure of incentives. Finally, tax expenditures fed on themselves because they weakened the fiscal standing of the state. Reductions in the income tax base encourage rate hikes to make up for lost revenue, which in turn further increases the value of tax exemptions. Or they reduce revenue available for direct spending, which in turn increases the propensity to rely on less visible and initially costly tools of intervention, such as tax subsidies and regulation. Paradoxically, then, tax subsidies for private benefits have simultaneously augmented and reduced state capacity, providing an alternative means of pursuing social welfare aims, yet weakening the tools of resource extraction that are a defining element of the modern state.

The two-track structure of American social provision, with its heavy emphasis on publicly regulated and subsidized private social benefits, is an outgrowth of self-reinforcing processes originating in choices and events of the past. To understand this public–private synthesis therefore requires going back to these formative moments to explain both why private benefits emerged in tandem with public programs and why this fundamental division has endured. To understand why this course of development occurred differently in health and pension policy, however, requires turning instead to arguments about timing and sequence – the foundation of my narrative of contrasting development. Although private and public benefits intermingled in both health and pension policy to a far greater extent than in other advanced industrial democracies, they also came to play sharply contrasting roles in each area. In pension policy, private benefits were supplements to an inclusive public program. In health policy, they provided the core of social protection for American workers, with public social programs filling gaps that remained. This striking divergence across two central domains of social policy is puzzling when viewed through the standard lenses used to understand cross-national policy differences. But it becomes more comprehensible when we couple a perspective on path dependence with closer attention to the timing and sequence of government intervention in each area and to the distinctive political dynamics that these temporal factors unleashed.

In examining timing and sequence, two fateful junctures stand out: the New Deal and the years during and immediately after World War II. Weakened by the Depression, challenged by competing political forces, employers and private insurers saw their role substantially displaced by federal old-age insurance. In reaction, they reconfigured private pensions to rest them upon the new public foundation and fought for policies that would sanction and encourage tax-favored plans. In the process, private pensions came to depend crucially on Social Security, softening employer resistance to the program, especially as organized labor began to demand more generous benefits. Simultaneously, however, the decision to leave health insurance out of the Social Security Act created an opening for private benefits to move into the "policy space" that the failure of compulsory insurance in the 1910s had left open. In the wake of the Truman plan's defeat, and in response to private social policy leadership and favorable public policies, private insurance came to be the core source of health security through processes quite similar to those that entrenched the *public* old-age insurance program during the same period.

This process was not automatic. At every consequential step, decisions were made and battles fought. Yet, increasingly, the problems with which America's leaders grappled, the relative power of contending forces, and even the preferences and strategies of political actors bore the imprint of past decisions and events. Policies that helped entrench physician-friendly private health insurance and build up the private medical industry, along with strategic choices by reformers that accommodated rather than challenged the employment-based system for the middle class, created fundamental dilemmas for those who wished to move toward public financing of medical care. Even as the growth of private coverage slowed, then stopped, then reversed, the sequence of past policy threw up thorny problems with which even the most capable political system would have struggled. A scattered framework of employment-based plans, an enormously costly medical-industrial complex, and a patchwork of public and private finance that quelled rather than encouraged collective action – all these shifted the agenda of debate toward regulatory and gap-filling measures and immensely complicated the task of achieving compromise. This policy sequence not only set the United States apart from much of the industrialized world; it also set health insurance apart from pensions, where the core role of old-age insurance fostered expansionary pressures that pushed toward inclusive rather than categorical coverage and toward encompassing rather than fragmented conceptions of interest.

Of course, policy development always follows *some* sequence, and the sequence itself may be a reflection of deeper, less temporally bound forces. At the same time as I wish to emphasize the crucial role that these factors played in propelling the divergent paths of health care and pensions, I want to distance myself from the obviously false claim that there were no other reasons that the two policy areas departed so sharply. The special power of doctors, the administrative and political challenges created by service rather than cash benefits, the priorities of social reformers in the 1930s – these and other factors, I have argued, help explain why compulsory health insurance was left out of the New Deal and why it proved such a distinctly elusive goal before and after. But these differences did not predetermine the choices that political leaders made, nor can they alone explain why the two fields ended up following such dramatically different paths. Instead, their effects must be understood in the context of the self-reinforcing processes unleashed by the initial divisions of state and private responsibility in each policy area, which in turn reshaped the aims and strategies of political actors and the policy boundaries within which they operated. What were, in broader perspective, relatively small differences between the two areas magnified over time, becoming increasingly important shapers of policy outcomes in their own right, even as the forces that had sparked the initial breach diminished in relevance.

In short, arguments about path dependence do not require that paths of development are accidental or contingent. It is certainly true, as proponents of this line of theorizing have emphasized (excessively, perhaps), that the concept of path dependence shows how small or haphazard causes may have large eventual effects.[97] But the concept does not require that the initial selection of paths be wholly open. What it requires, at a minimum, is that an initial set of causes sets in motion a self-reinforcing process that is at least partially independent of the original causes. The initial possibilities do not need to be infinite or equally likely. There may be strong reasons that the path selected is "chosen," as there were in the deliberations over health insurance during the New Deal. When claims about path dependence break down is when the factors that explain the initial choice of path also explain its endurance over time, in which case the path is merely epiphenomenal – a manifestation of some other ultimate set of causes. This is not true, I have stressed, of the contrasting paths of health insurance and pensions. Roosevelt's abandonment of compulsory health insurance had nothing to do with private insurance. His was a strategic choice rooted in reform priorities and fears of the medical profession. Yet as private benefits moved into the resulting policy opening, sustained and encouraged amid the conservative ascendancy of the 1940s and 1950s, it was the private-sector consequences of past choices that increasingly delimited the range of feasible reforms, continuing to do so even after professional power waned and rising medical costs broke the once-cohesive wall of opposition.

Arguments about sequence and timing push us to be more sensitive to the historical context within which politics and policymaking take place. In accounts that invoke temporal factors, the timing and sequence of events make a difference because the same factors operating against different historical backgrounds do not have the same effect.[98] Thus, the seemingly propitious confluence of widespread public dissatisfaction and responsive political leadership failed to produce major health legislation in the early 1990s because of the changed context of American medical care and social policy. Unable to put in place the foundations of universal public insurance before the economic and political troubles of the welfare state worsened, American health care reformers found that even favorable political circumstances were not enough to achieve major reform. Awareness of contextual effects leads to a sensitivity to what Charles Ragin calls "complex conjunctural causation," the notion that some important outcomes are the product of a confluence of conditions in which the individual causal effects of any one factor may be quite different depending on the other factors with which it is coupled.

The rewards of temporal theorizing of this sort can be seen by considering the idea of "first-mover" advantages, an important element of many game-theoretic models of strategic interaction and institutional theories of state-building and party formation.[99] The idea is simple: Under certain conditions of economic or political competition, individuals or organizations that act before others do are placed in a particularly advantageous position.[100] It is surely not the case, however, that first movers in politics always reap such rewards.[101] First movers may actually be worse off, provoking a reaction or revealing crucial information, or the sequence of moves may be irrelevant. Yet this does not mean that all arguments about first movers are invalid. Rather, it underscores the necessity of specifying when and why first-mover advantages prevail. An important conclusion is that first-mover advantages are especially likely when policy or institutional development is highly path dependent, for, in these cases, the tendencies toward irreversibility built into institutions and policies create strong incentives for later entrants to adapt their behavior around these entrenched realities. The reason that private health insurance structured postwar developments is not simply that it gained a formidable presence before public insurance programs were enacted, but that its growing role created identifiable feedback effects that reinforced its position while encouraging public and private actors to coordinate their actions and expectations around it – feedback effects that, in turn, were due to the special features of public and private social insurance that we have examined.[102]

Thinking seriously about the place of time in political analysis also offers new insights into the long-standing debate between structuralist and individualistic accounts. In at least three ways, an approach attentive to path dependence navigates between the twin shoals of institutional determinism and reductive individualism. First, understanding how path dependence unfolds indicates *when* the choices of individual actors are likely to be crucial and when, conversely, they are likely to be overwhelmed by the historical legacies of the past. Although path-dependent processes pose barriers to change once set in motion, the critical moments that create them may be characterized by high levels of strategic uncertainty. They may be moments, in short, when comparatively small strategic choices can make a crucial difference in determining eventual outcomes. Second, scholarship on path dependence has begun to unravel how large-scale structures are rooted in the adaptation and coordination behavior of (boundedly) rational individuals – that is, to suggest some of the individual-level foundations of social phenomena usually captured with catchall terms like "institutionalization."[103] Third, a theoretical perspective in which temporality is front and center brings us back to the enduring questions of political leadership with which political science has long struggled. When our concern is unfolding historical processes, leadership must be understood in part as success in creating policies and institutions with deep temporal moorings, in creating legacies that live on as binding commitments on future political agents.[104] Political leaders who leave an imprint on politics are those who understand the fleeting fragility of victory and try to root their goals in lasting institutional and programmatic structures. To judge leaders by history is to ask first and foremost how well their vision and achievements endure not just in memory but in the lived experiences of citizens.

Finally, although path dependence provides an analytic underpinning for explaining the enduring character of certain institutions and policies, inherent in the concept are the tools for understanding change as well as continuity. By identifying the reproduction mechanisms that anchor paths of development, it is also possible to specify the potential means by which institutions or policies might escape the developmental pathways of the past.[105] If the resistance to change of pay-as-you-go pension programs rests largely on the transition costs and widespread expectations that they engender, for example, then these must also be their key points of vulnerability. To be successful, those who wish to shift public pension schemes to private individual accounts need to raise doubts in the minds of workers that they actually will receive promised benefits and to come up with new sources of funding to pay transition costs – exactly the strategies that opponents of public pensions have adopted.[106] If, to turn to another example, the failure of inclusive proposals for government health insurance rests on the fear of insured Americans that public coverage will be inferior to private protections, then the chances for fundamental reform will increase to the extent that workers come to perceive that their private insurance coverage is threatened or inadequate. Because so much of the contemporary politics of social policy is shaped by the complex of existing public and private social policies, probing the mechanisms of self-reinforcement inherent in existing policies is a valuable method for uncovering both the wellsprings of resilience and the potential sources of change inherent in national frameworks of social provision.

Conclusion

The paths of the past end, ultimately, in the politics of the present. When path dependence reigns, history is not merely a record of what has come before. It is – through the institutions and policies that carry its imprint, through the mechanisms of self-reinforcement that anchor its legacies, through the constellation of constraints and opportunities that constitute its bequest – an active force shaping the debates and dilemmas that we as citizens and leaders must confront. Our challenge, as we cast our eyes toward the future in the final chapter, is to uncover these legacies and explore the directions in which they may yet take us – or in which, through foresight and perseverance, we might yet take them. The paths of the past are rarely, if ever, immutable. Yet neither can they be wished away. Whether the ends that we seek are at hand or in the distance, we must begin by recognizing how profoundly the historical trajectories of the past are embedded in the contemporary politics of the American welfare regime. Only then will we understand the debates of today, and only then can we envision the possibilities of tomorrow.

7

The Future of the American Welfare Regime

The battle over the boundaries between public and private social provision is among the oldest in American political history. Even before the rise of large-scale public and private social policies, Americans debated whether social welfare duties should be carried out by government or instead be left to community, family, or individual. The growth of public social programs and, alongside them, of publicly encouraged private social benefits manifested successive resolutions of this struggle, but it did not settle the dispute. Barriers to public action fell, new roles for the state and private sector came to be accepted, and powerful constituencies and institutions rose up around these roles. But where the lines would be drawn and in what way still prompted simmering conflict, which, repeatedly and sometimes violently, burst into boil.

Still, for much of the postwar period, it seemed that a rapprochement of sorts had been reached. Skirmishes took place on the frontiers of the American welfare regime – over national health insurance most prominently, but also over the scope of Social Security. Yet away from the front, the respective fields of both public and private benefits were secure and relatively accepted. The steady growth of both public and private benefits, the degree to which their development set in motion self-reinforcing political processes, and the extent to which the two spheres were intertwined all encouraged political actors to accommodate themselves to the basic policy framework already in place.

If recent struggles over U.S. social policy indicate anything, it is that the territory once ceded no longer seems so transparently out of reach, the acceptance that these boundaries once enjoyed no longer as comfortably secure. Today, critics of Social Security demand private options within the program, just as they did at Social Security's founding. Today, political leaders fight over the disposition of Social Security's reserves and whether the program should be prefunded, just as they did during the program's formative years. Today, calls abound for a federal health program for the aged based on private health plans, just as they did in the years before Medicare's passage. On nearly every front, the grand new alternatives of the present echo the rejected alternatives of the past.

How can this be? Why have these old debates reopened? As many analysts have pointed out, the economic and fiscal strains on the welfare state and the revival of conservative interests and ideology are a crucial part of the answer.[1] Yet to grasp the turnaround fully, we must also consider how the expectations and institutions that once securely anchored America's two-track system have unraveled, opening the door to new and newly formidable challenges. And even as we recognize these new openings, we must also appreciate how deeply the legacies of the past will shape what can be done within them. If major reform occurs – and in every area its prospects remain profoundly uncertain – one outcome that is clear at this juncture is that it will be deeply channeled by the policy legacies that have brought us to our current moment.

The Welfare State Under Siege

The signs of strain are everywhere, and their sources are no secret. Though propelled forward by war and depression, modern social provision was perhaps most fundamentally a product of affluence. The sustained growth of the postwar years not only funded the expansion of public social programs; it also muted the distributional conflicts that these programs sparked and legitimated the state's burgeoning role. Economic development was less the motor force behind the welfare state than it was an omnipresent feature of the environment within which social policy choices were made. The three decades that followed World War II were, in one evocative description, the "era of easy finance" – years in which robust growth made it possible to finance new spending without painful new taxes.[2] And although easy finance scarcely guaranteed easy enactment or expansion of public programs, it provided a uniquely fertile soil within which both public and private benefits could flourish.

What happened next is well known. Economic growth slowed, and – partly as a result – the fiscal freedom of government contracted. From 1950 through 1973, the American economy grew at a real annual rate of more than 4.2 percent. Since then, despite the boom of the 1990s, it has averaged 3 percent, and in the crucial decade after 1973, it averaged just over 2 percent.[3] Lest these seem like minor differences, had the American economy continued to grow at the same rate after 1973 as it grew in the period before, it would be well more than a third again larger today.

Nonetheless, the economic slowdown is not the only reason for the increased strain on public programs. Equally important is the accumulation of social policy commitments and their increasing costs. Between the 1950s and the early 1980s, public spending on social welfare services more than doubled as a share of the economy.[4] Tax revenues, however, did not keep pace. Although social insurance taxes came to represent a dramatically larger portion of the tax bill, income taxes remained relatively stable as a share of the total, and corporate taxes actually constituted a dwindling share.[5] The tax cuts of the early Reagan years (and the simultaneous indexation of tax rates to inflation) abetted this trend, but they did not cause it. The plain reality is that social spending increased faster than political leaders' willingness to finance it. In the 1980s, this imbalance produced large and recurrent deficits. Its more enduring effect, however, was to pit priority against priority, program against program, new proposals against prior commitments in a fierce Darwinian struggle for fiscal survival.

The effects of this squeeze are unmistakable. Excluding interest payments on the debt, as Figure 7.1 shows, federal expenditures have fallen from a high of roughly 20 percent of GDP in 1975 to less than 17 percent in 2000. (As the figure also shows, this was not due entirely to the defense cuts of the 1990s; nondefense spending fell as well.) The Congressional Budget Office now estimates that the 2002 Bush Administration budget, despite ushering back in federal budget deficits after the fleeting surpluses of the late 1990s, will cause total federal spending (*including* interest payments) to fall to 16.8 percent of GDP by 2012, the lowest level since 1956.[6] In comparative perspective, this is a remarkable degree of expenditure restraint.

The United States is not alone in witnessing a significant change in the climate of budget politics. Across the industrialized world, the expansion of government has slowed, and differences in spending growth between governments of different partisan stripes have narrowed.[7] Government budgets everywhere have been marked by increasing rigidity as the spending commitments of the past run up against economic and political barriers to the tax increases necessary to fund them. With rare exceptions, the fiscal strains that mature welfare states face are due not to new programmatic departures but to the rising costs of existing social programs, driven by indexing provisions, benefits increases already legislated, population aging, automatic stabilizer effects, and high rates of medical inflation.

This new era of austerity has been accompanied by a striking shift in the agenda of social policy. Gone for the most part are the calls for new social programs and incremental expansion of existing ones that marked

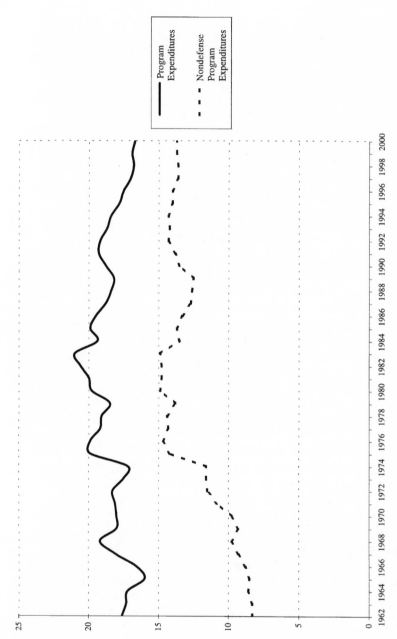

Figure 7.1. U.S. Federal Expenditures as a Percentage of GDP, 1962–2000. *Notes:* Program expenditures are federal expenditures minus interest payments on the national debt. *Source:* Calculations by the Center on Budget and Policy Priorities (http://www.cbpp.org) from data contained in Office of Management and the Budget, *Budget of the United States Government, Fiscal Year 2000* (Washington, D.C.: OMB, 2000); Congressional Budget Office, *The Economic and Budget Outlook: Fiscal Years 2000–2009* (Washington, D.C.: CBO, 2000).

Table 7.1. *Growth of U.S. Private Social Expenditures*
Versus Growth of Public Expenditures, 1950–1994

Years	Ratio
1950–65	1.00
1965–75	0.90
1975–94	1.23

Source: Calculated from Social Security Administration social welfare expenditures series. For additional information about the series, see note 29 of the Introduction to Part I.

the postwar period of welfare state expansion. In their place are demands for cost containment and restructuring within long-standing programs and for the removal of social protections that, critics argue, prevent labor market flexibility and foster dependency. In the few cases where new spending proposals have reached the agenda, they have largely taken the form of tax breaks for private spending on tuition, child care, retirement savings, and health insurance.[8] Perhaps the most dramatic symbol of this new climate is the 1996 welfare reform bill, which revamped the discredited Aid to Families with Dependent Children program (now, Temporary Assistance to Needy Families) to limit the extent and duration of benefits.[9] Yet for all its potent imagery, welfare has always been a financially modest component of U.S. social policy. More indicative of larger trends is the steady wearing away of highly popular existing programs, the political reluctance to discuss new initiatives, and the continued political popularity of tax cuts and new subsidies for private benefits, even in the face of the looming fiscal crunch posed by the retirement of the baby boom generation.

The restraint of expenditures and the movement of new proposals off the agenda have contributed to an ongoing rise in the share of social spending that comes from private sources. Since the mid-1970s, as Table 7.1 shows, private social spending has grown a quarter again as fast as public spending.[10] At the same time, private social benefits are changing. The elements of social insurance that were once integral to these benefits have eroded as firms have moved to contain costs or to eliminate their benefit programs. The fragmentation of health insurance pools, the shift from defined contribution to defined benefit pensions (and from compulsory pensions to ones in which workers voluntarily put aside wages), and the growing inequality of benefits across workers and sectors all suggest that the risk pooling and risk redistribution that once characterized the world of private benefits can no longer be expected.

For a brief moment in the early 1990s, the strains on public programs and the erosion of private benefits shared the spotlight, as President Clinton sought to tackle the problems in American health insurance by putting in place the biggest missing piece of the American welfare state. The resounding failure of the Clinton health plan demonstrated not just the fiscal barriers such efforts face, but also the powerful ongoing hold of antigovernment ideas and interests in American politics – the last of the intertwined pressures that have placed the welfare state under siege. Since the 1970s, the ideological landscape of American politics has undergone tectonic shifts. Increasingly globalized and investor-driven corporations have reasserted themselves as powerful players, after two decades spent fighting to reassert their political advantage.[11] These interests have, in turn, supported and sought guidance from a growing array of conservative think tanks and advocacy groups, which have churned out technically sophisticated prescriptions for major policy reform.[12] Meanwhile, the long-term reshuffling of the American electoral map has weakened moderate forces within both parties, leaving the Republican Party dominated by hard-edged conservative heirs to the southern Democrats of old.[13] The result has been a stunning reversal of political fortune: Where once it was liberals demanding change and backing detailed reform proposals, today it is conservatives who see themselves as the vanguard of the revolution – a revolution to achieve not new public protections but new restrictions on government's scope and role.[14]

This shift has dovetailed with a more general transformation in the world of policy ideas. Since the early 1980s, "privatization" has become a powerful rallying cry in developed and developing nations alike.[15] The word has multiple and contested meanings, but under its banner has marched a recurring collection of initiatives: the selling off of state enterprises, the contracting out of public services, the loosening of command-style market regulations. Governments across the globe have reduced their control over the economy. New schools of thought have emphasized the parasitism and inefficiency of the public sector. Calls for government downsizing and reinvention have resonated widely, not just in antigovernment circles but also within mainstream discussions of government reform. By allowing competition and consumer choice, privatization holds out the promise not simply of smaller government but of more efficient and responsive government – of government that pursues essential ends, but achieves them through improved means.

In social policy, the prescriptions of the privatization credo have always been ambiguous. After all, many public social benefits simply entail the transfer of cash from one pocket to another and thus would seem to pose limited opportunities for streamlining and competition. Moreover, most of the "in kind" (that is, noncash) benefits that remain are already delivered by private providers, though not necessarily through the means that privatization advocates prefer.[16] In practice, therefore, the privatization agenda in social policy encompasses four main priorities. The first is the scaling back of direct government action to encourage thrift, self-reliance, and private provision. The second is the expansion of subsidies for private insurance, savings, and charitable activities. The third is increased government contracting with voluntary organizations and for-profit service providers. The fourth and most ambitious goal is the infusion into established programs of vouchers and other mechanisms that would allow (or require) recipients to opt out of these programs and obtain benefits from private organizations instead. In contrast with radical retrenchment, neither contracting nor opt-out provisions eliminate the government's primary role. Rather, they shift its emphasis from direct state action to the management and oversight of private actors operating within a new framework of regulatory authority.[17]

After two decades of debate, judgments still differ on how far the privatization agenda in social policy has progressed. In most nations with extensive welfare states, it is fair to say, the agenda itself never had much backing. But even in those nations where the ideology of privatization gained committed support, notably Britain and the United States, achievements unquestionably fell short of ambitions.[18] It is revealing that in research on privatization, most of the emphasis is on aspects of economic policy – sales of public companies, deregulation of labor markets, liberalization of services – areas where there has been true change and true global convergence. [19] In contrast, the shared wisdom among comparative students of social policy is that the linked political and economic challenges to the welfare state have failed to significantly reduce the state's size or create marked cross-national convergence in national social policies.[20] Some cutbacks have occurred. Some programs have been eliminated. But if the question is whether major retrenchment has occurred, the answer for most countries is negative.[21]

If the question is how the role of the state is changing, however, it is far less clear that the challenges of the past two decades have had such a modest effect. In the United States, substantial changes *have* taken place in the larger universe of social benefits, and these changes foretell important shifts in the role of government and the composition of social benefits. As the focus of policy debate increasingly shifts from expansion and maintenance of existing programs to their restructuring and even privatization, understanding these effects will become all the more imperative. The United States appears to be approaching a new crossroads in the long debate over public and private benefits, as opponents of existing policies advance new strategies premised on the weakened position of public social programs and the growing role of private social benefits. To see why these challenges loom and what their effect might be, we need to trace how the entrenched realities that mark our current moment intersect with the recurrent public–private conflicts that have marked our past – and which have reemerged at the epicenter of American politics in an era of harsh new challenges to the welfare state as we once knew it.

Revisiting the Boundaries Between Public and Private

During the 2000 presidential campaign, George W. Bush outlined a social policy agenda that was notable mostly for how little it was noted. Burnishing his credentials as a compassionate conservative, Bush called for diverting a portion of Social Security payroll taxes into private investment accounts, for restructuring Medicare to allow private health plans and the traditional Medicare program to compete side by side, and for funding religious organizations to tackle the nation's most persistent problems of poverty and want. These ideas were duly noted by the press, duly sniped at by critics, and duly forgotten after the 2000 election imbroglio and the fight over Bush's signature domestic policy goal, his major tax-cut plan. Since then, they have returned one by one – some imperiled, others still very much in play – to much the same desultory reaction, each criticized or praised in isolation, each a separate "test" of Bush's leadership.

Yet consider this agenda as a whole. What is striking is not the individual items, all of which have been kicking around conservative policy circles for decades. What is striking is that a leading presidential candidate would embrace ideas that, as late as the early Reagan Administration, were viewed as political suicide. What is striking, too, is the extent to which these proposals are themselves an accommodation to present realities, an attempt to push back the boundaries between public and private while acknowledging the central place of public social programs in the popular imagination and American social welfare practice.[22] The paradox of the Bush social policy agenda is that is sells a fundamental break with the past as a natural evolution of long-standing commitments. In invoking the hoary rhetoric of voluntarism in the modern context of the welfare state, Bush promises to take us back to the future.

Social Security's New Insecurity

No aspect of the new political climate is more striking than the recent conservative push to restructure Social Security. America's public retirement program was once considered untouchable. Major proposals for change never moved beyond the fringes of libertarian discourse. Even Reagan, at the height of his influence, steered well clear of them. By the 1990s, however, proposals to incorporate individual accounts into the system had become the moderate reform alternative, backed by many Republicans and conservative Democrats and proposed, in different forms, by two of the three major factions on the deadlocked 1994–95 Social Security Advisory Council.[23] President Bush embraced a vague version during the campaign and, after his inauguration, charged a presidential commission filled with supporters of the idea to prepare a full-scale blueprint (the commission eventually presented three plans for partial privatization of Social Security).[24] Although legislative action is highly unlikely in the near term, especially given the stock-market downturn and the worsening fiscal context precipitated by Bush's tax-cut plan and the economic slowdown of 2001, the president's embrace of partial privatization nonetheless represents a major development. For the first time since the burial of the Clark amendment, the idea of introducing private options into Social Security is under active debate by the nation's political leaders – and this time, it has presidential backing.[25]

The most commonly cited reason for the renewed interest in reform is Social Security's long-term deficit. On its current trajectory, the benefits paid out by the program are expected to exceed payroll taxes around 2016, and these benefits are expected to exhaust the Social Security trust fund and its interest earnings by 2038, at which point incoming receipts will be sufficient to pay for a bit more than two-thirds of promised benefits.[26] Yet, as serious as the fiscal situation is, it does not itself explain why individual account proposals have gained favor. Indeed, to the extent that new private accounts are funded through the redirection of existing payroll taxes, they actually hasten the date at which the exhaustion of the trust fund occurs.[27] This is simply because the funds that go into these private accounts are reserved for account holders until their own retirement and cannot be used to pay for present benefits. The crucial point about the current long-term deficit is therefore that it is *long-term* deficit, caused by the future decline in the ratio of workers to retirees. It is precisely because Social Security is not in deficit presently (and actually has been running surpluses to prepare for the future) that the reform agenda is not dominated by the painful benefit cuts and tax increases that would be necessary to bring the program into short-term balance.

Even more important than the fact of the long-term deficit itself, however, is what it signals about the transformed politics of Social Security. In this regard, the deficit is a marker not of what is going to happen but of what is no longer happening. For decades, the most powerful influence on debates over old-age insurance was the expansionary tendencies of an immature pay-as-you-go system. Social Security was able to provide benefits considerably in excess of workers' contributions simply because so many more Americans paid into the system than drew benefits from it. In current parlance, the "rate of return" was extremely high, and this was true for workers at all income levels. The flip side of this expansionary dynamic, however, is that as the ratio of workers to retirees falls, the deal offered by Social Security grows progressively less favorable, to the point where some younger and higher-income workers may actually earn a negative rate of return. Although there is little sign that Americans have turned against Social Security as a result of this reversal, the case against the program has been greatly advanced by Social Security's increasingly unfavorable balance of payments, which has brought to a close the self-reinforcing pressures for expansion that characterized the program's formative years.

Linked to this well-recognized change is one that is much less appreciated: the transformed character and scope of private retirement plans. After Social Security's creation, corporations, insurance firms, and pension consultants yoked employer-based plans to the public program, initially to save money and concentrate private benefits on the highly paid, but also in later years to respond to labor demands and satisfy the requirements for favored tax treatment. From the standpoint of Social Security's advocates, the supplementary role that private plans came to play had a price: It ensured that private retirement benefits would be skewed in favor of the highly paid, offsetting Social Security's progressive benefits. Yet it carried with it a significant benefit, too: By building their plans on a public foundation, private pension sponsors gained a significant interest in the maintenance and even expansion of the program. Indeed, with public benefits factored into private pension formulas, the same high rates of return enjoyed by early beneficiaries of the program were also indirectly enjoyed by corporations that operated private supplementary plans. This supplementary role was crucial not just to the expansion of Social Security, but also to the decisions of political leaders to regulate private plans to make them more secure and equitable counterparts to the public pension system.

As corporations have shifted to more individualized plans, the explicit links between the public and private systems have steadily eroded, undermining some of the self-reinforcing mechanisms that secured Social Security's privileged position in American retirement provision. Once tightly integrated with a program that offered a tremendous deal to all, private plans now increasingly stand alone – a constant reminder to the well-paid workers most likely to benefit from them that Social Security's weakened fiscal position (and redistributive benefit formula) precludes the high returns that similarly situated workers earned in the past, or that their own private retirement accounts earned during the boom of the 1990s. When Social Security reform was on the agenda in 1983, few Americans knew what a mandatory system of private accounts would look like. With the momentous expansion of tax-favored retirement accounts, the idea is now scarcely so exotic. And American employers, for the most part, have lost their direct stake in the program's health, as corporate plans have broken off from the public pension core around which they previously revolved.

Conservative critics of Social Security actively helped foster this transition. In the wake of the 1983 reforms, they retooled their political approach to accommodate the hard political lessons that they had learned.[28] Their new strategy had two central elements. The first was to continue to encourage private retirement savings through ever-more-flexible and individualized means, acclimating Americans to private accounts and fostering the institutional infrastructure for a full-fledged private system. The second element was to move away from the traditional conservative critique of the program as welfare dressed up as self-help, which counseled benefit cuts and greater resource targeting, to emphasize the positive-sum benefits of a move toward individual retirement accounts. If conservatives had once tried to force bitter medicine down unwilling throats, this new approach capitalized on Social Security's own declining position and the increasing familiarity with private accounts to promise a pain-free transition away from an imperiled and antiquated system.

Private accounts are the heart of this new strategy. Their explicit goal is to encourage stark (and, at bottom, fundamentally misleading) comparisons between the rates of return in Social Security and in the private sector.[29] Carved out from Social Security, private accounts would be vested in particular individuals (and their heirs), freed from the burdens of both income and intergenerational redistribution. In contrast, the traditional program would maintain its essentially pay-as-you-go, progressive, pooled funding structure. As a result, for most workers, especially higher-income workers, private accounts would almost inevitably earn a much higher rate of return than would the traditional program. This is not because the trust fund surplus is held in the form of government bonds, whereas private plans could reap the higher yields (and risks) of the stock market. It is instead overwhelmingly a result of Social Security's pay-as-you-go structure. To the extent that existing benefit commitments are honored, most of Social Security's receipts will be transferred to current beneficiaries, and the program's rate of return will primarily reflect the ratio of workers to retirees. By contrast, a private plan earmarked for a particular individual does not have to bear the cost of these past commitments. Over time, therefore, private accounts will grow faster than the traditional program regardless of how they are invested, and this will be even more true if they are funded by diverting payroll taxes from the Social Security trust fund. Moreover, holders of these accounts will likely come to perceive the traditional program as a relatively poor deal, not recognizing or caring that its lower rate of return is a result of its fulfilling past benefit promises – an attitude reinforced, no doubt, by promotional descriptions of Social Security as little different from a retirement account handled by government.

The second and less explicit political purpose of private accounts is to cast in starker relief the redistributive elements of Social Security.[30] Because accounts would be earmarked for particular individuals, any redistribution would have to be carried out within the traditional program. The larger the private accounts, the more these redistributive aspects of the program would be concentrated within the traditional program and the more visible they would become.[31] Indeed, if Social Security were replaced entirely with mandatory private plans, redistribution would require either a new minimum pension system, which would be open to attack as "welfare," or some measure to transfer funds from personal account to personal account, which would be certain to create resistance among those on the losing end of the transfer. Just as proponents of private accounts expect that side-by-side comparison of the returns of private plans and the traditional program will advantage private accounts, many also believe (though they are understandably more reluctant to proclaim) that accentuating the redistributive elements of Social Security will decrease the widespread support that the program enjoys.

In both these respects, recent proposals for private accounts are strategically adept efforts to capitalize on the weakening of Social Security's core role within U.S. retirement security policy. Whether these proposals can overcome the powerful feedback effects that have blocked change in the past, however, is still a very open question. The distinctive constellation of factors that fostered Social Security's expansion no longer holds sway, but the features of the program that stand in the way of reform, even in its new and more savvy incarnation, remain formidable. The most formidable, of course, is the double-payment problem. Shifting away from a mature pay-as-you-go pension system requires either that past commitments be abrogated or that funds be found to finance the old system while establishing the new. The amount required to fund the transition to even relatively modest individual accounts is staggering, making it unlikely that such financing will materialize, all the more so in the current fiscal climate.[32] The more probable course, then – and the one that President Bush appears to have embraced – is to finance the transition by diverting existing payroll taxes, and this means that benefits must be cut at some point in the future to make up for present losses.

The hope of advocates of this approach is that new private accounts will be popular and lucrative enough that the workers who invest in them will accept significant benefit cuts within traditional Social Security. The size of the projected cuts – 54 percent of benefits for the youngest workers, according to a recent cautious estimate – suggests strong reason for doubt.[33] Moreover, as already noted, diverting payroll taxes into private accounts reduces program revenues, stepping up the date of the program's "bankruptcy," a very visible marker. Ironically, therefore, the fiscal imbalance that helps make the case for dramatic reform also undercuts the rationale for private accounts. As the imbalance worsens in the coming years, it will actually grow more difficult to adopt private accounts, simply because the negative effects on program finances will be that much more immediate and visible.

The double-payment problem expresses a more fundamental quandary for advocates of privatization: the continuing high levels of public support for the program. Social Security now provides less in retirement benefits than private plans, but its centrality to the hopes and expectations of average Americans has scarcely diminished.[34] Americans in the abstract support private retirement accounts, but in the abstract, too, they supported comprehensive restructuring of American health insurance. As President Clinton learned – and as President Bush may yet learn, if he continues to press his case – crafting viable alternatives to existing institutions of social protection is much easier in policy seminars than it is in the messy and dangerous world of politics, when losses are on the table and popular expectations are at stake.

Rethinking Medicare

In contrast with Social Security, it is less surprising that reform of Medicare is near the top of the American political agenda or that the public–private divide has been at the heart of the conflict. Medicare has always been closely intertwined with the private medical sector, and since the early 1990s, proposals for major restructuring have become a perennial subject of debate. Still, with the partial exception of the balanced budget act of 1997, which will be discussed shortly, all of these comprehensive restructuring plans have failed – most spectacularly in 1995, when President Clinton resurrected himself politically by vetoing Republican-backed Medicare legislation. Medicare's payments have been tightened, and the role of private health plans within the program has grown, as a small demonstration initiative introduced in the early 1980s to allow health maintenance organizations to contract with Medicare has expanded to encompass roughly a seventh of Medicare beneficiaries.[35] But the overall character of the Medicare program has remained remarkably stable, especially in light of the turbulent transformations in American health insurance more broadly.

The unsettled character of Medicare's politics and the difficulty that reform efforts have faced have common roots in the program's comparatively peculiar structure. Passed in the 1960s after more than two decades of government measures to expand the capacity of private medicine, Medicare inherited the inflationary tendencies of the medical sector, even as its comparatively limited scope precluded the exercise of decisive authority over medical costs. The predictable result was skyrocketing costs within the program and a steady erosion of the original commitment to noninterference in private medicine. As the fiscal squeeze grew tighter in the 1970s and 1980s, control of Medicare costs became the central imperative. Overwhelmingly, the measures adopted took the form of reductions in the amount paid to hospitals, doctors, and other health care providers – a response that did not impose immediate costs on Medicare enrollees or directly threaten existing benefit promises.

Medicare costs did slow. The program's per capita expenditures have risen slightly more slowly, on average, than private insurance costs since the early 1980s, and dropped sharply below private levels in 1999 and 2000.[36] As large as Medicare is, however, the reach of its cost-containment measures is inherently limited, and its costs are likely to continue to track private levels relatively closely over the long term. This guarantees that controlling Medicare's outlays will remain a burning political issue.

Medicare's restricted scope relative to other national health programs not only limits the program's control over spending. It also distorts the debate over cost containment by magnifying the effect of population aging on the program's finances.[37] In contrast with universal programs, Medicare bears only the cost of specified populations, the largest and most expensive of which is the elderly. When someone turns sixty-five, his or her medical costs suddenly show up in government accounts. For this reason, the fiscal standing of the program is far more sensitive to the age profile of the population than are national health programs in other nations. As the baby boom generation ages, the proportion of Americans older than sixty-five is expected to rise from less than 14 percent in 1995 to 22 percent in 2030.[38] Even if spending is effectively controlled, program costs are certain to increase as the number of enrollees grows.

Here again, however, the undeniable severity of the fiscal pressures on Medicare does not explain the contours of the leading proposals for comprehensive reform, which are better understood as an attempt by critics of the program to overcome the political barriers that have historically blocked retrenchment of public social insurance. The most prominent of these proposals – and the foundation for President Bush's Medicare recommendations – calls for Medicare to adopt a "premium-support" approach, in which beneficiaries of Medicare receive a fixed amount with which to either buy into the traditional program or choose among a roster of private health plans that contract with Medicare.[39] Modeled on the Federal Employees Health Benefits Program, the premium-support approach aims to transform Medicare from a single large insurer that pays health care providers directly into a system of competing health plans. In this system, private plans would assume the risk of enrollee's medical costs, and the public Medicare program would be just another option in the competitive fray. The premium-support approach therefore bears a striking resemblance to the private-plan alternatives to Medicare that moderates like Senator Javits proposed in the lead-up to the program's creation – and raises many of the same concerns.

This approach would depart fundamentally from current practice. Private plans do contract with Medicare in many areas of the country today, but the extent of enrollment in private plans is still relatively modest, and plans are not competitively priced. (Instead, Medicare pays them a rate based on the average amount that the program spends per beneficiary.) More important, beneficiaries who do not enroll in a private health plan – the vast majority – are entitled to the Medicare benefits defined by law for the premium specified in law. Under the premium-support approach, by contrast, the amount beneficiaries pay for Medicare or private health plans would depend on the difference in premiums between these alternatives, and some beneficiaries could end up paying substantially more for their coverage.

If the goal of advocates of restructuring is to rein in Medicare spending, the adoption of a proposal reliant on private health plans seems contradictory.[40] Private health plans have *not* controlled expenditures better than Medicare over the long term. And even within Medicare, contracting with private plans has to date consistently *cost* Medicare money. This is because private plans that contract with Medicare have attracted healthy patients who would have cost the program little, but these plans have received payments from Medicare pegged to average spending levels. This has been a good deal for private plans and for beneficiaries who obtain broader benefits through them. But it has been a bad deal for Medicare, for taxpayers, and for those who remain in the traditional program.

Yet the contradiction vanishes once it is recognized that the rationale behind the premium-support approach is as much political as it is technical. Historically, the main constraint on Medicare restructuring has been the acute sensitivity of its unified constituency to new costs or benefit cuts. Despite severe fiscal pressures, successful changes have virtually all taken the form of cutbacks in provider payments, rather than reductions in benefits or increases in premiums. (Indeed, the Medicare premium has gradually declined as a revenue source for the program.)[41] The one major exception to this story is the premium surcharge imposed by the Medicare Catastrophic Coverage Act of 1997 – which Congress repealed shortly after its passage in the face of fierce protest.

A premium-support approach could weaken the policy features of Medicare that magnify opposition to cost shifting and provide a new mechanism for scaling back the program's commitment. The amount that individual beneficiaries would pay for coverage would depend on the cost of the health plan they enrolled in, which in turn would be influenced by the health characteristics of the patients a plan enrolled, as well as other factors. Different Medicare beneficiaries would thus likely end up paying very different amounts for their Medicare coverage – some more than they do currently, some less. This could fragment the unified constituency that the program currently fosters and, by creating substantial variation in premiums over time, across plans, and across beneficiaries, obscure whatever cost shifting did take place.

At the same time, the premium-support approach would create a new means for scaling back Medicare spending. The essence of the approach, after all, is that beneficiaries receive a fixed amount with which to purchase either public or private coverage. (In current proposals, this amount is a specified share of the average premiums of public and private plans.) This fixed amount can be thought of as the government's defined contribution for Medicare coverage, and how quickly it grows over time will be crucial in determining what proportion of the costs of covered benefits are borne by Medicare and what proportion instead falls on beneficiaries. If the defined contribution is allowed to grow more slowly than the premiums of health plans, then the financial protection offered by

Medicare will progressively constrict, even without changes in the benefit package or explicit decisions to raise beneficiaries' contributions.[42]

Critics have derided the premium-support approach as "privatization," but this is misleading, inasmuch as it implies that Medicare does not incorporate substantial elements of private provision and administration already. Although the premium-support approach would fundamentally transform Medicare, the change has more to do with the distribution of risks than with the delivery services, which is why it cuts so close to the heart of Medicare's social insurance character.

A principal selling point of Medicare in 1965 was that the medical risks that the elderly faced are unusually difficult to insure against, and the current distribution of spending within the program starkly evidences this concern. In 1996, for example, Medicare paid out nearly $32,000 on average on behalf of the 10 percent of beneficiaries with the highest medical costs, but only around $1,700 on average on behalf of the remaining 90 percent.[43] In the context of disparities this large, much of the cost differences between competing plans will unavoidably depend on the mix of patients that they enroll. If private health plans continue to attract healthier patients, then the traditional Medicare program would be left with the most costly patients, who would have to pay sharply higher premiums to retain their traditional coverage. The main safeguard against this outcome that has been proposed is to "risk-adjust" the amount that health plans are paid to account for the types of patients they enroll. But risk adjustment is – and will likely remain – highly imperfect, compensating for only a small portion of the variance in medical risks.[44] And without extremely accurate risk adjustment, a premium-support approach could sharply divide Medicare beneficiaries, leaving traditional Medicare with a dwindling pool of increasingly high-risk enrollees and imposing new costs on those with the highest medical expenditures. Under these circumstances, Medicare might well "wither on the vine," as Speaker of the House Newt Gingrich predicted when the ill-fated Republican Medicare plan was under consideration in 1995.

As with proposals for Social Security privatization, the premium-support approach is best understood as a strategic attempt to overcome the powerful policy-feedback effects that have made retrenchment of the program perilous in the past. Yet, as with proposals for Social Security privatization, the success of this strategy is far from assured. Would-be Medicare reformers do not face one barrier that Social Security reformers do: the double-payment problem. But in other areas, the obstacles to restructuring Medicare are no less daunting than those faced by Social Security's critics. To begin with, the fiscal pressures that Medicare faces are much more serious and immediate than those confronting Social Security. Whereas advocates of Social Security privatization hope to use present trust fund surpluses to finance accounts whose full costs would only be apparent in the future, Medicare reformers lack the short-term fiscal freedom to protect current and near-term beneficiaries from the losses that would accompany the transition to a reformed system. And as with Social Security, insofar as the imperative for change is immediate cost savings, the measures most likely to be adopted are not large-scale restructuring plans but the incremental reforms that have been the hallmark of previous legislative rounds.

This dilemma is well illustrated by the effects of the Medicare reforms adopted as part of the Balanced Budget Act (BBA) of 1997.[45] The most sweeping changes to Medicare adopted since the 1970s, the BBA reforms simultaneously reined in provider payments and created a new program within Medicare called "Medicare+Choice" that was billed as the first step toward full implementation of the competitive reform strategy. At the time of passage, Medicare+Choice was widely expected to increase the share of Medicare beneficiaries that enrolled in private health plans and the range of plans that were offered. Instead, enrollment in private plans has stabilized, new options have not materialized, and plans have pulled out of the program in droves, raised their premiums and cost-sharing requirements, and cut back extra benefits. The principal reason for this ironic result is that the BBA's measures to encourage new private plan options ran headlong into the legislation's overarching aim: to control Medicare expenditures. The BBA reduced the amount paid to private plans in many areas, and it cut provider fees within the traditional portion of the program – which further reduced payments to private plans, because these payments are pegged to the traditional program's per capita spending. Increasingly squeezed, private insurers found themselves barely able to keep above water, much less attract Medicare beneficiaries with extra benefits. Thus, the experience of Medicare+Choice suggests that the same cost-containment imperatives that animate reform efforts also place significant limits on policymakers' ability to expand the role of private health plans.

The experience of Medicare+Choice also underscores a second distinctive problem that Medicare reformers face: the continued weakness of the private insurance market. Over the past decade, supplemental coverage purchased by older Americans or provided to them by their current or former employers has eroded, as have the supplemental benefits provided by health plans that contract with Medicare. The enrollment of healthier Medicare beneficiaries in managed care plans has probably contributed to this erosion, leaving the market for individually purchased supplemental plans with a higher-risk population. The broader cause, however, is more worrisome: As the scope for private protections has increased, the market for insurance among the aged is increasingly resembling that which existed before Medicare's passage. Forced to bear concentrated risks without natural foundations for risk pooling, supplemental insurance plans find it ever harder to offer coverage at rates attractive to lower-risk senior citizens, encouraging further defections from the risk pool and driving up costs for those who remain.[46] This erosion of private coverage is a principal reason that a prescription drug benefit within Medicare has become a leading political issue, even as the larger Medicare debate has been dominated by issues of cost containment.

Nor does the future of private health plans within the program look as bright as it did in the mid-1990s. Older Americans have long been reluctant to enroll in plans that would limit the free choice of provider that Medicare guarantees, especially if they are chronically ill. In recent years, however, unease about HMOs and other managed care plans has permeated American public consciousness more broadly. Scores of state laws have tried to limit the ability of private plans to make medical decisions unilaterally. At the national level, pressure has been building for a Patients' Bill of Rights that would contain similar protections, breaching the wall preventing federal regulation of self-insured health plans set up by the ERISA preemption clause. The effect of a federal patients' rights law would likely be more modest than either critics or defenders suggest. Already, tightly managed health plans have lost ground in the face of public and physician discontent. And although a patients' rights bill would override the very tight restrictions on rights to sue created by ERISA, which were already being softened by the courts, it would do nothing to strengthen the larger regulatory vacuum created by the law, nor would it extend to health benefits any of the broader protections offered to pension participants. Nonetheless, the push for state and federal regulations does powerfully symbolize waning popular confidence in the very types of private health plans that Medicare reformers hope to make the cornerstone of a new system.

Fiscal pressures for reform, renewed conservative opposition, the weakening of self-reinforcing processes in Social Security and Medicare – all these will not automatically translate into major retrenchment. Although the prospects for conservative-backed restructuring are more favorable than they once were, the policy-feedback effects that anchor America's two largest public social programs will still be extremely hard to overcome, however savvy reformers' strategies. But political resistance to conservative-backed reforms will not prevent continued erosion of the scope and generosity of public social insurance. Social Security is expected to replace an ever smaller share of wages in the future even without legislative changes, and its benefits seem certain to fall further behind private retirement accounts even without privatization. Incomplete from the beginning, Medicare's protections have only become more glaringly inadequate over the past thirty-five years. No health plan created today would cover only a limited number of hospital days, leave out prescription drugs, and place no limit on catastrophic costs. The share of income that Medicare beneficiaries spend for medical care is higher now than when Medicare passed, and it will certainly be higher in the future.[47]

A similar path lies ahead for the private side of the American welfare regime. However fast private spending grows, whether coverage levels creep up or down, no matter how many new tax breaks are created or exhortations about corporate responsibility are made, the world of private benefits will not return to the models of old. The harsh truth is that private benefits are likely to become ever more concentrated on the winners in America's postindustrial economy – and ever more elusive and costly for those lower on the economic ladder. For more than two decades now, the shifting tides of private benefits have mirrored the shifting distribution of economic rewards, and for more than two decades now, these rewards have accrued overwhelmingly to the better-off.[48] It is well-off Americans who have benefited most from the expansion of tax-favored investment accounts and flexible benefit options over the past two decades, while it is those who have seen slow (or no) growth in their incomes who have been most likely to lose private coverage. Likewise, the vast bulk of the expanding bevy of tax breaks for private health and retirement plans accrue to those most capable of bearing the risks that these plans cover. Against this tide, the responses under debate – regulation of managed care plans, modest new tax credits for the uninsured, the expansion of gap-filling programs for poor children – stand out only by virtue of their smallness.

But perhaps this should not be surprising. Ever since the welfare state came under strain in the 1970s, the debate over U.S. social policy has been fundamentally bifurcated, fixated on the ills and evils of public social programs, yet largely silent about the myriad ways in which government supports and shapes private benefits. The tax-cut plan enacted in 2001 provided a revealing example of this schismatic perspective. Heavily tilted toward the affluent, the tax cuts contained in the law threaten to increase greatly the fiscal strain that public social programs face in the coming decades.[49] Yet, at the same time as Congress passed legislation virtually certain to dip into Social Security's trust fund, supporters of the bill proudly pointed to changes the legislation made in the tax treatment of private pensions. (The President of the American Council of Life Insurers went so far as to describe the tax-cut plan as "perhaps the most significant retirement security legislation in a generation.")[50] It will at this point hardly come as a surprise that these changes – from a significant increase in the contribution limits for 401(k) plans and IRAs to weaker nondiscrimination rules – will overwhelmingly benefit higher-paid employees and corporate officers.[51]

Taking a wider view may not force us to change our assessment of public social programs. Yet it should impel us to consider the broader range of government activities in the social welfare field and whom they do and do not benefit. Otherwise, we are likely to continue along our present blinkered course, vigorously debating the future of public social programs that primarily benefit middle-class and lower-income Americans while showering ever greater subsidies on private benefits that primarily benefit the highly paid. To hear critics of the welfare state tell it, public social programs have become opulent ocean liners comfortably conveying Americans past the routine eddies of modern life. Surveyed from the longer distance that a wider canvas provides us, they look more like waterlogged lifeboats in a roiling sea of inequality.

Recasting the Debate

The relationship between public and private social benefits is certain to become more politically central in the coming years. Whether this relationship will become more visible, and whether it will be discussed in the informed and broad-ranging manner such a critical topic requires, remain far less certain. Neither students of public affairs nor policymakers have good metaphors or tools for examining the extensive political and social interrelationship of public and private social provision. As Martin Rein and Eskil Wadensjö argue, the relationship between public social programs and employer-provided benefits is usually framed in terms of separate pillars of support, as in the metaphor of the "three-legged stool" of Social Security, private pensions, and personal savings. Yet this image of "solid, autonomous, free standing independent foundations" belies the "fusion, linkage, and interrelations of the elements" – and ignores, in particular, how much the health of private social provision depends on a supportive foundation of public social programs and policies.[52] Without fresh attempts by political leaders to articulate compelling metaphors for the intermingling of public and private, without fresh efforts to spark a true debate about what the government does (and does not do) in the social welfare domain, without fresh challenges to the compartmentalization of policy expertise that has pushed public policy governing private benefits into the shadows of American social welfare practice, the myriad ways in which public power and government policy influence the development of private benefits will remain as they have on the fringes of political discourse.

Historians have begun to chart the dramatic rise of private social benefits in the United States.[53] Sociologists have begun to look at the "welfare mix" across nations, viewing it "in the framework of continuous institutional accommodation to the policy environment in which it is situated."[54] Economists have begun to turn their sights to contracting and bureaucratic organization.[55] What is missing from many of these treatments is any extensive consideration of the political causes and consequences of alternative social policy approaches. As I have tried to show, some of the tools for such a consideration can already be found, but some will need to be developed de novo. Theoretical perspectives on the politics of social policy continue to focus on large-scale programs of spending that emerge out of highly visible and contested political interactions. If debates over social policy do shift increasingly from this familiar territory into the comparatively uncharted realm of privatized social welfare approaches, then it will become all the more important to understand the political roots of these approaches and the effects that they have – both on the structure and standing of national welfare regimes and on the lives of those within them.

It is commonplace for policy specialists today to claim that instruments of governance are interchangeable, that questions of equity or accountability are design issues resolved through the proper calibration of inherently neutral techniques, that the role of the expert is to illuminate the basic workings of alternative options, not to weigh normative issues that are the proper concern of politicians. The need for thoughtful and informed expertise in public policymaking cannot be denied. Yet little progress will be made in understanding and guiding social policy if distributional and political issues are treated as mere afterthoughts in policy analysis and design. In the abstract, policy instruments can be infinitely tailored. In practice, they have characteristic effects that must be recognized and adjusted for. In the abstract, governments can achieve ends through myriad means. In practice, governments do some things well and some things poorly, and the differences are deeply rooted. In the abstract, the working of politics is simply the means by which finely tailored policy blueprints are transformed into realized aspirations. In practice, politics and policy design are inseparable: Politics makes policies; policies make politics. The effects of Social Security privatization or

Medicare restructuring cannot be understood independently of their political effects. How will the creation of private individual accounts affect the coalition of public support behind Social Security? How will the transformation of Medicare into a system of competing private health plans affect the sense of shared fate that its broad risk pool creates? These are difficult questions, but they are no less answerable than the ones to which expert eyes usually turn. And if the forces of privatization continue their steady march, the political questions may turn out to be much the more important.

The welfare state will not wither away. Private social benefits will not take its place. This is true, at a minimum, because the vibrancy of private social provision hinges so centrally on the activist state itself. Yet it also reflects a deeper reality: Americans have never left social insurance to the market, and if they did, true social insurance would not exist. The United States is unique in the extent to which private social insurance has come to play a primary role in protecting citizens against the risks and vicissitudes that a capitalist economy necessarily produces. That role is a product of politics and economics, of choice and accident, of history's heavy hand and the continuing politics of the present. But overarching all is the striving of Americans for both security and opportunity in a land that has always offered both plenty and want. The same will be true of the story of the American welfare regime that has yet to be written.

Appendix

This appendix briefly describes the recent efforts of the Organization for Economic Cooperation and Development to develop a more accurate picture of social welfare spending in advanced industrial nations.[1] The OECD's findings form the basis for Figure I1.1 in the Introduction to Part I, as well as for the cross-national estimates of the private share of social spending referred to throughout the book. Table A.1 summarizes how the OECD statistics were developed.

First, the OECD researchers calculated the extent to which governments claw back public cash transfers through direct and indirect taxation. If social welfare benefits provided on the expenditure side are taxed away on the revenue side, they are not counted as net additions to social spending.[2] This adjustment produces striking results, as line 2 of the table indicates. High-spending nations like Sweden claw back almost a third of gross public expenditure through direct and indirect taxation. In contrast, the United States and other low-spending nations tax away very little of their more modest expenditures. The result is a sizable convergence of spending levels across countries when relative tax burdens are taken into account.

Second, the revised OECD figures include preliminary estimates of tax expenditures with social welfare aims. Such expenditures encompass tax breaks that are tantamount to direct cash benefits (for example, special tax allowances for families with children) and tax subsidies for private social benefits (for example, the tax exemption of employer-provided health insurance).[3] As line 3 of the table indicates, accounting for tax breaks narrows considerably the gaps in spending across nations. High-benefit, high-tax nations provide limited benefits through the tax code, whereas low-benefit, low-tax nations use tax expenditures more liberally (despite having lower overall tax rates, which reduces the value of many special provisions). The United States, in particular, relies heavily on tax

Table A.1. *Public and Private Social Welfare Expenditures as a Percentage of GDP in Eleven Nations, 1995*

	Australia	Canada	Denmark	Finland	Germany	Ireland	Italy	Netherlands	Sweden	U.K.	U.S.
1. Gross public social welfare expenditures (rank in parentheses)	20.3 (10)	20.8 (9)	37.6 (1)	35.7 (3)	30.4 (4)	21.8 (8)	26.5 (6)	30.1 (5)	36.4 (2)	25.9 (7)	17.1 (11)
2. After-tax public social expenditures	18.4	17.3	23.5	25.1	25	17	20.9	21.1	25.4	21.7	15.9
3. Tax expenditures with social welfare aims	0.3	0.6	0.1	0	0.9	0.5		0.1	0	0.6	1.6
4. After-tax private social expenditures (mandatory expenditures in parentheses)	3.0 (0.3)	3.5	0.8 (0.3)	0.8 (0.1)	1.8 (1.0)	1.5	1.4	3.8 (0.5)	1.6 (0.2)	3.9 (0.3)	8.3 (0.5)
5. After-tax public and private social expenditures (line 2 + line 3 + line 4, with adjustments to eliminate duplication) (rank in parentheses)	21.6 (9)	21.2 (10)	24.4 (7)	25.7 (4)	27.7 (1)	18.7 (11)	22.3 (8)	25 (5)	27 (2)	26 (3)	24.5 (6)
6. Private share of after-tax expenditures (line 4 ÷ line 5)	13.9	16.5	3.3	3.1	6.5	8	6.3	15.2	5.9	15	33.9

Notes: Public social welfare expenditures exclude education. They include cash benefits for a wide range of social contingencies – disability, old age, death of a spouse, occupational injuries, disease, sickness, childbirth, unemployment, poverty – as well as spending on housing, health care, services for the elderly and disabled, active labor-market policies, and other similar social benefits. Private social welfare expenditures are payments for the same purposes made by employers and other nongovernmental organizations, provided that such benefits are mandated, subsidized, or regulated by government. Tax expenditures are special provisions of the income-tax code that mimic public social programs, departing from the baseline treatment of income to benefit eligible individuals, groups, institutions, or activities. They are measured as tax revenue forgone. Because of measurement problems, tax expenditures for pensions – which are sizable in several nations, among them the United States – are not included. Any special tax treatment of public benefits is taken into account in the calculation of after-tax public social expenditures, so it is excluded from the calculation of tax expenditures. To prevent double-counting, tax breaks for private benefits are not included in the estimates of after-tax public and private social expenditures. Tax expenditure figures are not available for Italy; estimates of mandatory private expenditures are not available for Canada, Ireland, and Italy.

Source: Calculated from Willem Adema, "Net Social Expenditure," *Labour Market and Social Policy – Occasional Papers No. 39* (Paris: OECD, August 1999), 30.

breaks in comparative perspective, both in absolute terms and as a share of total government expenditures.

Third, and most innovative, the OECD researchers have constructed for these eleven nations a measure of after-tax private social expenditures – that is, after-tax outlays on social benefits made by private organizations rather than by government. The OECD standard for treating private expenditure as social spending is rigorous. It requires not only that such benefits be directed toward social purposes, but also that they be subject to "public intervention by legal or fiscal means that brings these benefits within the social domain."[4] Although data limitations restrict the analysis to only a few benefits, lines 4 and 6 nevertheless suggest how central publicly subsidized and regulated private benefits are in several nations, especially the United States. As line 5 shows, moreover, there is a noteworthy convergence in after-tax spending among nations when private benefits are included in the tally. The United States ranks last according to the traditional measure of social welfare effort, gross public expenditure (line 1). But once we adjust for relative tax burdens, tax expenditures, and publicly subsidized private benefits (and eliminate duplication across these categories), the United States rises to the middle of the pack. Across the eleven nations, the adjustments just described substantially reduce the divergence in total spending levels, decreasing the standard deviation of the eleven nations from 7.1 for gross public expenditures to 2.7 for after-tax public and private expenditures.[5]

Notes

Introduction to Part I: American Exceptionalism Revisited

1. This paragraph draws on the reporting contained in "Second-Class Medicine," *Consumer Reports* 65, no. 9 (Sept. 2000): 42–50.
2. Testimony of James A. Bruggeman to Senate Special Committee on Aging, *The Cash Balance Conundrum: How to Promote Pensions Without Harming Participants*, 106th Cong., 1st sess., 5 June 2000.
3. General Accounting Office (GAO), *Private Pensions: Implications of Conversions to Cash Balance Plans* (Washington, D.C.: GAO, Sept. 2000); GAO, *Cash Balance Plans: Implications for Retirement Income* (Washington, D.C.: GAO, Sept. 2000); David Warsh, "The Pension Game," *Boston Globe*, 24 April 2001, D1; Albert B. Crenshaw, "Pension Trend Painful to Some; Cash-Balance Plans Shift the Risk and Divide the Workforce," *Washington Post*, 15 Oct. 2000, H2; Christine Dugas, "Pension Bill Nears Senate Vote; Critics Say It Hurts Older Workers," *USA Today*, 26 Sept. 2000, 3B; "Votes in Congress," *St. Louis Post-Dispatch*, 6 May 2001, C5; The Associated Press, "Some Older Workers Tell Senate Panel That New Pension Plans Hurt Them; Industry Representatives Deny Plans Discriminate Against Those Workers," *St. Louis Post-Dispatch*, 6 June 2000, A3; Del Jones, "Shareholder Vote Keeps IBM Pension Issues in Play; Cash-Balance Plan Still Controversial," *USA Today*, 26 April 2000, 3B.
4. Calculated from Robert J. Mills, *Health Insurance Coverage: Consumer Income* (Washington, D.C.: United States Census Bureau, Sept. 2000).
5. "Table 3: National Health Expenditures, by Source of Funds and Type of Expenditure: Calendar Years 1994–1999" (Baltimore: Health Care Financing Adminstration).
6. Bureau of Economic Analysis (BEA), U.S. Department of Commerce, *National Income and Product Accounts* (Washington, D.C., 31 July 2001), available from http://www.bea.doc.gov, Table 6.11C; Social Security Administration (SSA), *Annual Statistical Supplement 2002* (Washington, D.C.: SSA, 2002), Table 4.A1.

7. Calculated from the Social Security Administration's series on private social welfare expenditures. See Figure I1.4 and the related discussion later in this Introduction.

8. Discussion of first-mover advantages is a staple of writings on industrial and technological competition, such as Dennis C. Mueller, "First-Mover Advantages and Path Dependence," *International Journal of Industrial Organization* 15, no. 6 (Oct. 1997): 827–50; W. Brian Arthur, "Positive Feedbacks in the Economy," *Scientific American* 262, no. 2 (Feb. 1990): 92–99; and Elhanan Helpman and Paul Krugman, *Market Structure and Foreign Trade* (Cambridge, Mass.: MIT Press, 1985).

9. The phrase is from Peter F. Drucker's classic celebration of private pensions in the United States, *The Unseen Revolution: How Pension Fund Socialism Came to America* (New York: Harper & Row, 1976).

10. See, for example, Theodore R. Marmor, Jerry L. Mashaw, and Philip L. Harvey, *America's Misunderstood Welfare State: Persistent Myths, Enduring Realities* (New York: Basic Books, 1990).

11. Wallace C. Peterson, "The U.S. 'Welfare State' and the Conservative Counterrevolution," *Journal of Economic Issues* 19 (1985): 602.

12. The centrality of risk (rather than income) redistribution to the development of the welfare state is the guiding theme of Peter Baldwin, *The Politics of Social Solidarity: Class Bases of the European Welfare State, 1875–1975* (New York: Cambridge University Press, 1990).

13. The distinction, like so many other features of contemporary scholarship on the welfare state, is owed to Richard M. Titmuss's *Essays on the "Welfare State"* (London: Allen and Unwin, 1958), but it has received its most extensive and thoughtful elaboration in the work of Gøsta Esping-Andersen, especially his *Three Worlds of Welfare Capitalism* (Princeton, N.J.: Princeton University Press, 1990).

14. Stanley S. Surrey and Paul R. McDaniel, *Tax Expenditures* (Cambridge, Mass.: Harvard University Press, 1985).

15. Office of Management and Budget, *Budget of the United States Government Fiscal Year 1999, Analytical Perspectives* (Washington, D.C.: U.S. GPO, 2002), Table 5–3.

16. The most notable exception is Christopher Howard's pioneering *The Hidden Welfare State: Tax Expenditures and Social Policy in the United States* (Princeton, N.J.: Princeton University Press, 1997), which examines tax breaks with social welfare purposes in the American context. A few comparative analyses have been conducted as well, the most comprehensive being a series of OECD reports whose results I shall discuss shortly.

17. "To talk of 'a regime,'" explains Esping-Andersen, "is to denote the fact that in the relation between state and economy a complex of legal and organizational features are systematically interwoven." Esping-Andersen, *Three Worlds of Welfare Capitalism*, 2. Esping-Andersen's term is actually "welfare-state regime," but I wish to emphasize that many of the relevant institutions of social provision are not formally part of the state. For similar reasons, I do not use the popular phrase "private welfare state" in this

book to describe private social benefits. State power and policy may be deeply implicated in the provision of these benefits, but that does not make them part of the state. For additional discussion of the concept of regimes, see Stephen D. Krasner, ed., *International Regimes* (Ithaca, N.Y.: Cornell University Press, 1983); and Karen Orren and Stephen Skowronek, "Regimes and Regime Building in American Government," *Political Science Quarterly* 113 (1998–99): 689–702.

18. Titmuss, *Essays on the "Welfare State."*
19. In addition to Howard's *The Hidden Welfare State*, important contributions to this expanding vein of scholarship include Neil Gilbert and Barbara Gilbert, *The Enabling State: Modern Welfare Capitalism in America* (Oxford: Oxford University Press, 1989); Benjamin Gidron, Ralph M. Kramer, and Lester M. Salamon, *Government and the Third Sector: Emerging Relationships in Welfare States* (San Francisco: Jossey-Bass, 1992); Michael Lipsky and Steven Rathgeb Smith, "Nonprofit Organizations, Government, and the Welfare State," *Political Science Quarterly* 104 (1989–90): 625–48; Beth Stevens, "Blurring the Boundaries: How the Federal Government Has Influenced Welfare Benefits in the Private Sector," *The Politics of Social Policy in the United States*, ed. Margaret Weir, Ann Shola Orloff, and Theda Skocpol (Princeton, N.J.: Princeton University Press, 1988), 123–48; and "Labor Unions, Employee Benefits, and the Privatization of the American Welfare State," *Journal of Policy History* 2 (1990): 233–60; Richard Rose, "Welfare: The Public/Private Mix," *Privatization and the Welfare State*, ed. Sheila B. Kamerman and Alfred J. Kahn (Princeton, N.J.: Princeton University Press, 1991), 73–95; Michael K. Brown, "Bargaining for Social Rights: Unions and the Emergence of Welfare Capitalism, 1945–52," *Political Science Quarterly* 112 (1997–98): 645–74; Michael J. Graetz and Jerry L. Mashaw, *True Security: Rethinking American Social Insurance* (New Haven, Conn.: Yale University Press, 1999); Marie Gottschalk, *The Shadow Welfare State: Labor, Business, and the Politics of Health Care in the United States* (Ithaca, N.Y.: Cornell University Press, 2001); Jennifer Lisa Klein, "Managing Security: The Business of American Social Policy, 1910s–1960" (Ph.D. diss., University of Virginia, May 1999); Andrea Tone, *The Business of Benevolence: Industrial Paternalism in Progressive America* (Ithaca, N.Y.: Cornell University Press, 1997); Michael B. Katz and Christoph Sachsse, eds., *The Mixed Economy of Social Welfare: Public/Private Relations in England, Germany, and the United States, the 1870's to the 1930's* (Baden-Baden: Nomos, 1996); Michael B. Katz, *The Price of Citizenship: Redefining the American Welfare State* (New York: Metropolitan Books, 2001); Steven A. Sass, *The Promise of Private Pensions: The First Hundred Years* (Cambridge, Mass.: Harvard University Press, 1998); and especially the writings of Martin Rein and Lee Rainwater, such as their edited collection *Public-Private Interplay in Social Protection: A Comparative Study* (Armonk, N.Y.: M. E. Sharpe, Inc., 1986) and their essay "From Welfare State to Welfare Society," *Stagnation and Renewal in Social Policy: The Rise and Fall of Policy Regimes,*

ed. Martin Rein, Gøsta Esping-Andersen, and Lee Rainwater (Armonk, N.Y.: M. E. Sharpe, Inc.).

Although these works are primarily concerned with employment-based private social benefits, as this book is, the other principal area of private social expenditure is the charitable activities of nonprofit organizations. Considerable research has been done in this area, much of it showcasing the extensive interconnections between American government at all levels and the so-called voluntary sector. Nonprofit organizations that deliver social and human services are heavily dependent on government for funds, and local, state, and federal governments in turn deliver many essential services through nonprofits. Cross-national research is both rarer than studies of U.S. nonprofits and fraught with greater methodological hurdles, but it does suggest that the United States has a significantly larger voluntary sector than do other nations. Nonetheless, although nonprofits deliver many social services in the United States, their actual social spending is relatively modest compared with the expenditures of either government programs or employer-provided insurance. Estimates by Robert Lampman, for example, show that in 1980, philanthropy accounted for just 2.7 percent of all income transfers made by public and private organizations, down from 4.7 percent in 1950. Robert J. Lampman, *Social Welfare Spending: Accounting for the Changes from 1950 to 1978* (Orlando, Fla.: Academic Press, 1984), 70–71. Valuable recent entries into the large literature on nonprofit organizations and their history include Steven Rathgeb Smith and Michael Lipsky, *Nonprofits for Hire: The Welfare State in the Age of Contracting* (Cambridge, Mass.: Harvard University Press, 1993); Charles T. Clotfelter, ed., *Who Benefits from the Nonprofit Sector?* (Chicago: University of Chicago Press, 1992); Michael Sosin, *Private Benefits: Material Assistance in the Private Sector* (Orlando, Fla.: Academic Press, 1986); Judith Sealander, *Private Wealth and Public Life: Foundation Philanthropy and the Reshaping of American Social Policy from the Progressive Era to the New Deal* (Baltimore: Johns Hopkins University Press, 1997); Kathyrn Edin, "The Private Safety Net: The Role of Charitable Organizations in the Lives of the Poor," *Housing Policy Debate* 9 (1998): 541–73; Bradford H. Gray, *The Profit Motive and Patient Care* (Cambridge, Mass.: Harvard University Press, 1991); Lester M. Salamon, "Government and the Voluntary Sector in an Era of Retrenchment: The American Experience," *Journal of Public Policy* 6 (1985): 1–19; Robert Wuthnow, ed., *Between States and Markets: The Voluntary Sector in Comparative Perspective* (Princeton, N.J.: Princeton University Press, 1991); and Lester M. Salamon and Helmet K. Anheier, *Defining the Nonprofit Sector: A Cross-National Analysis* (New York: St. Martin's, 1997). The role of religious charity has recently gained new attention in response to the "charitable choice" provision of the 1996 welfare reform law, which encourages greater participation by these institutions in the government-funded provision of social and human services. For a fuller review of the social policy (rather than church–state) issues raised by charitable choice, see Jim Castelli and John D. McCarthy, "Religion-Sponsored

Social Services: The Not-So-Independent Sector," Report of the Aspen Institute Nonprofit Sector Research Fund (Washington, D.C.: Aspen Institute, 1998); and Jacob S. Hacker, "Faith Healers: Should Churches Take Over Social Policy?" *New Republic*, 28 June 1999, 16–18. For a valuable general discussion, see Martha Minow, "Partners, Not Rivals? Redrawing the Lines between Public and Private, Non-Profit and Profit, and Secular and Religious," typescript, Harvard University, 2000.

Finally, a separate and larger body of literature looks at indirect policy tools and contracting, although little of it is concerned with social policy. Notable studies in this genre include Paul C. Light, *The True Size of Government* (Washington, D.C.: Brookings Institution, 1999); Lester M. Salamon, ed., *Beyond Privatization: The Tools of Government Action* (Washington, D.C.: Urban Institute, 1989); Donald F. Kettl, *Government by Proxy: (Mis?)Managing Federal Programs* (Washington, D.C.: CQ Press, 1988); and Herman B. Leonard, *Checks Unbalanced: The Quiet Side of Public Spending* (New York: Basic Books, 1986).

20. The quantitative literature on the rise of the welfare state is extensive. The seminal analysis is Harold L. Wilensky, *The Welfare State and Equality: Structural and Ideological Roots of Public Expenditures* (Berkeley: University of California Press, 1975). A good synopsis of recent scholarship can be found in a special symposium, entitled "Two Perspectives on the Welfare State," that appeared in the *American Journal of Sociology* in 1993. See especially the commentary of Edwin Amenta, "The State of the Art in Welfare State Research on Social Spending Efforts in Capitalist Democracies since 1960," 99 (1993): 750–63.

21. The foundational works exploring each of these hypotheses are, respectively, Wilensky, *The Welfare State and Equality*; David R. Cameron, "The Expansion of the Public Economy," *American Political Science Review* 72, no. 4 (December 1978: 1243–61); Fred C. Pampel and John B. Williamson, *Age, Class, Politics, and the Welfare State* (Cambridge: Cambridge University Press, 1989); and Francis G. Castles, ed., *The Impact of Parties: Politics and Policies in Democratic Capitalist States* (Beverly Hills, Calif.: Sage Publications, 1982).

22. Margaret Weir, Ann Shola Orloff, and Theda Skocpol, "Introduction: Understanding American Social Politics," *The Politics of Social Policy in the United States*, ed. Margaret Weir, Ann Shola Orloff, and Theda Skocpol (Princeton, N.J.: Princeton University Press, 1988), 5.

23. Charles Noble, *Welfare As We Knew It* (Oxford: Oxford University Press, 1997), 3.

24. Willem Adema, Marcel Einerhand, Bengt Eklind, Jørgen Lotz, and Mark Pearson, "Net Public Social Expenditure," *Labour Market and Social Policy – Occasional Papers, No. 19* (Paris: OECD, 1996); Adema and Einerhand, "The Growing Role of Private Social Benefits," *Labour Market and Social Policy – Occasional Papers, No. 32* (Paris: OECD, 1998); and Adema, "Net Social Expenditure," *Labour Market and Social Policy – Occasional Papers, No. 39* (Paris: OECD, 1999). A concise description of

the series can be found in Adema, "Uncovering Real Social Spending," *OECD Observer*, no. 211 (April/May 1998): 20–23. The Appendix contains additional information.

25. It is important to distinguish this claim from that of Richard Rose, who argues that the United States spends more on social programs in absolute terms than many OECD nations because it is so much more wealthy. A low-spending nation with a large economy may outspend a high-spending nation with a small economy. Rose, "Welfare: The Public-Private Mix," 80–84. This is something of a debater's point and not the one I am making here. My claim is that even when we adopt the common practice of examining social welfare spending as a share of the economy, the United States does not look radically out of line with other affluent nations.

26. Although the evidence for over-time comparisons is more limited, it does not imply an unambiguous trade-off, either. In the United States, public and private spending have expanded at relatively similar rates since 1940, suggesting that public social provision does not necessarily come at the expense of private social provision. Surveying developments over a shorter time period but in more nations, the OECD reaches much the same conclusion. As a 1998 OECD report notes, "It is difficult to discern a clear relationship between public expenditure *growth* and private expenditure *growth* for the period 1980–1993. An increase in public expenditure does not lead to a decrease in private expenditure, while decreasing or stable public budgets do not automatically lead to increasing private expenditure." Adema and Einherhand, "The Growing Role of Private Social Benefits," 27.

27. Esping-Andersen, *Three Worlds of Welfare Capitalism*.

28. As the table indicates, the typologies cluster more clearly with regard to gross public spending than they do with regard to the other measures. Indeed, only for this measure is the variation within the three welfare-state categories consistently lower than the variation among the eleven nations as a whole. This suggests, ironically, that Esping-Andersen's typology – which aims to move beyond simple indexes of public spending – may capture differences in aggregate public spending better than it does the public–private mix. Furthermore, whatever the measure used, the social-democratic type appears substantially more homogenous than either the corporatist or the liberal type. While the social-democratic welfare states vary only modestly, the liberal and corporatist regimes differ at least as much among themselves as do all eleven nations, and this is true for every measure except gross public spending.

29. *Social welfare expenditures* encompass public expenditures on social insurance, public assistance, medical care, veterans' programs, education, and housing, along with private expenditures on medical care, welfare services, education, and income maintenance. The SSA does not maintain a master file containing the series, nor has it ever published the entire series. The estimates are not available for 1951 to 1954 and 1956 to 1958, and although they are sometimes updated, these updates have been limited to

years at the end and halfway point of each decade. Thus, two criteria were used in assembling the series: first, to use sources that provided the longest continuous string of annual estimates; second, to use the most recent estimates whenever it proved possible to do so and still satisfy the first aim. The figures are drawn from the *Social Security Bulletin's Annual Statistical Supplement* (Washington, D.C.: SSA, 1995, 1996, 1998) and the following issues of the *Bulletin*: November 1960, December 1966, December 1971, December 1972, January 1975, January 1976, January 1977, May 1980, and Spring 1995.

30. The discrepancy between the two reflects differences in the definition of social welfare expenditures and of public and private spending. Unlike the OECD estimates, the SSA series includes educational spending, and it counts as private spending consumer payments for medical care and education. (These differences do not much affect the relative public and private shares.) In addition, the SSA estimates are not adjusted for taxes, although, again, this is likely to affect the absolute values of public and private spending more than the relative shares. Similar long-term historical data are not available for other countries. Very recent trends, however, can be tracked in Britain, Denmark, Germany, and Sweden. In three of these four nations, private benefits gained a larger presence between 1980 and 1993 – the only period for which comparative evidence exists. Yet their overall presence is still so limited compared with their scope in the United States that any talk of relative growth rates is highly misleading. For example, the private share of spending rose by 36 percent in Britain, 46 percent in Sweden, and a massive 266 percent in Denmark (it fell by 10 percent in Germany). Yet these changes represented, on average, an increase of but 1.8 percentage points in the private share of spending – compared with the 7.5 percentage-point increase that occurred during the same period in the United States.

31. Examples, which could be multiplied almost infinitely, are Roy Lubove, *The Struggle for Social Security, 1900–1935* (Pittsburgh, Pa.: University of Pittsburgh Press, 1968); Daniel Levine, *Poverty and Society: The Growth of the American Welfare State in International Comparison* (New Brunswick, N.J.: Rutgers University Press, 1988); Gaston Rimlinger, *Welfare Policy and Industrialization in Europe, America, and Russia* (New York: Wiley, 1971); Raymond Richards, *Closing the Door to Destitution: The Shaping of the Social Security Acts of the United States and New Zealand* (University Park: Pennsylvania State University Press, 1994); and Walter I. Trattner, *From Poor Law to Welfare State: A History of Social Welfare in America,* 4th ed. (New York: Free Press, 1989).

32. The studies I am referring to are, respectively, Theda Skocpol, *Protecting Soldiers and Mothers: The Political Origins of Social Policy in the United States* (Cambridge, Mass.: Harvard University Press, 1992); Edwin Amenta, *Bold Relief: Institutional Politics and the Origins of Modern U.S. Social Policy* (Princeton, N.J.: Princeton University Press, 1998); Julian

E. Zelizer, *Taxing America: Wilbur D. Mills, Congress, and the State, 1945–75* (Cambridge: Cambridge University Press, 1998); Keith W. Olson, *The G. I. Bill, the Veterans, and the Colleges* (Lexington: University Press of Kentucky, 1974); Sar A. Levitan and Robert Taggart, *The Promise of Greatness* (Cambridge, Mass.: Harvard University Press, 1976); R. Shep Melnick, *Between the Lines: Interpreting Welfare Rights* (Washington, D.C.: Brookings, 1994); and Howard, *The Hidden Welfare State.*

33. The metaphor comes from Christopher Leman, "Patterns of Policy Development: Social Security in the United States and Canada," *Public Policy* 25 (1977): 261–91.

34. Ellis W. Hawley, "Social Policy and the Liberal State in Twentieth-Century America," *Federal Social Policy: The Historical Dimension,* ed. Donald T. Critchlow and Ellis W. Hawley (University Park: Pennsylvania State University Press, 1988), 129–30. See also Ellis W. Hawley, "Herbert Hoover, the Commerce Secretariat, and the Vision of an 'Associative State,' 1921–1928," *Journal of American History* 61, no. 1 (June 1974): 116–40; and Robert Griffith, "Dwight D. Eisenhower and the Corporate Commonwealth," *American Historical Review* 87, no. 1 (Feb. 1982): 87–122. Hawley's work was part of the short-lived "organizational synthesis" in American history that grew out of the pioneering scholarship of Alfred D. Chandler and Robert H. Wiebe. Centrally concerned with the rise of bureaucratic organization in corporate America, the organizational synthesis extended its reach into studies of professionalization and American state-building as well. See Louis Galambos, "The Emerging Organizational Synthesis in Modern American History," *Business History Review* 44 (Autumn 1970): 279–90, and "Technology, Political Economy, and Professionalization: Central Themes of the Organizational Synthesis," *Business History Review* 57 (Winter 1983): 471–93, and the valuable attempt to apply this approach to social policy, Edward and Kim McQuaid Berkowitz, *Creating the Welfare State: The Political Economy of Twentieth-Century Reform,* 2d ed. (New York: Praeger, 1988), which emphasizes, indeed overemphasizes, the influence of private-sector managerial elites on American welfare state development.

35. The most recent OECD report on private social spending, for example, notes that "observations on social expenditure levels across countries that do not account for private social benefits and the impact of the tax system are prone to be misleading" (Adema, "Net Social Expenditure," 34). It would be equally misleading, however, to suppose that the composition of social spending does not affect the character of social policy or who benefits from it.

36. Harold Dwight Lasswell, *Politics: Who Gets What, When, How* (Cleveland, Ohio: World Pub. Co., 1958).

37. The original insight that different types of policies produce different modal patterns of politics is owed mainly to Theodore J. Lowi, "American Business, Public Policy, Case-Studies, and Political Theory," *World Politics* 16 (July 1964): 677–715, although it had its roots in E. E. Schattschneider,

Politics, Pressures and the Tariff: A Study of Free Private Enterprise in Pressure Politics, as Shown in the 1929–1930 Revision of the Tariff (New York: Prentice-Hall, 1935), and it received a more systematic and persuasive exposition (and a substantial makeover) in James Q. Wilson, *Political Organizations* (New York: Basic Books, 1973), 327–46.

38. By "subterranean," I mean both less visible and more prone to restricted political participation. This formulation owes much to E. E. Schattschneider's discussion of the "scope of conflict" in *The Semi-Sovereign People: A Realist's View of Democracy* (New York: Holt, Rinehart, and Winston, 1960).

39. Paul Pierson, "When Effect Becomes Cause: Policy Feedback and Political Change," *World Politics* 45 (July 1993): 595–628.

40. The term – a shorthand phrase popularized by the economist Brian Arthur to explain why inferior technological standards might nonetheless be broadly adopted – carries unfortunate connotations, implying that once a particular technology gains a foothold, alternative options cease to become viable at all. Arthur has been widely and justly criticized for overstating the prevalence and extent of technological lock-in. But it is clear that by lock-in, he means not that change is impossible once a given technology gains broad adoption, but rather that change is difficult even when clearly superior technological alternatives exist. W. Brian Arthur, "Competing Technologies, Increasing Returns, and Lock-In by Historical Events," *Economic Journal* 99 (March 1989): 116–31. In any case, I prefer not to use the term, which was first introduced to political scientists by Paul Pierson, *Dismantling the Welfare State: Reagan, Thatcher, and the Politics of Retrenchment* (Cambridge: Cambridge University Press, 1994).

Chapter 1. The Politics of Public and Private Social Benefits

1. E. S. Kirschen, *Economic Policy in Our Time* (Amsterdam: North-Holland Publishing Co., 1964).

2. My use of the term "private social insurance" is unconventional. Typically, "social insurance" is reserved for public programs meeting certain bedrock conditions, such as compulsory participation, contributory financing, and benefits prescribed in law. In my conception, however, social insurance is not an exclusive category defined by a narrow list of criteria that public programs alone can meet. It is a continuum defined by the capability of an insurance system to pool risks widely and cross-subsidize vulnerable groups. Using the term more broadly allows me to emphasize three important points about publicly regulated and subsidized workplace insurance: first, that it departs significantly from conventional private insurance (in which premiums are based, to the fullest extent possible, only on an individual's expected risk); second, that a key aim of government intervention in the realm of workplace insurance is to make private benefits more "social" in character; and, third, that in recent years employment-based benefits have been stripped of many of the social insurance characteristics

that they once often had, such as the broad pooling of risks and the cross-subsidization of lower-income and higher-risk workers.

3. Michael J. Graetz and Jerry L. Mashaw, *True Security: Rethinking American Social Insurance* (New Haven, Conn.: Yale University Press, 1999), 65.

4. For similar conceptions, see Willem Adema and Marcel Einerhand, "The Growing Role of Private Social Benefits," *Labour Market and Social Policy – Occasional Papers No. 32* (Paris: OECD, 1998), 6–13; Graetz and Mashaw, *True Security*, 15–25.

5. It was Karl Polanyi's great insight that political power inhered in even such seemingly self-governing institutions as the laissez-faire economy. Polanyi, *The Great Transformation* (New York: Rinehart, 1944).

6. As Paul Pierson rightly warns, "[A]s the concept of the welfare state, or welfare regime, 'stretches,' it becomes inevitable that quite distinct processes and outcomes will be joined together under the umbrella of a single master variable." "Coping with Permanent Austerity: Welfare State Restructuring in Affluent Democracies," *The New Politics of the Welfare State*, ed. Paul Pierson (Oxford: Oxford University Press, 2001), 420.

7. Robert Hart's comprehensive *The Economics of Non-Wage Labour Costs* (London: George Allen & Unwin, 1984), for example, does not discuss issues of distribution at all. Economists have, however, been among the leading critics of the special tax treatment of employment-based benefits, which they argue distorts the wage-determination process in favor of fringe benefits. See, for example, Mark V. Pauly, "Taxation, Health Insurance, and Market Failure in the Medical Economy," *Journal of Economic Literature* 24 (1986): 629–75.

8. This view gained brief attention in the early 1980s, when Treasury Undersecretary Norman Ture publicly warred with the Reagan White House over plans to close what the Office of Management and Budget deemed tax loopholes. See Lee Walczak, "The Skirmishing Over New Taxes," *Business Week*, 21 December 1981, 117.

9. Joint Committee on Taxation, *Estimates of Federal Tax Expenditures for Fiscal Years 2001–2005* (Washington, D.C.: U.S. GPO, 2001), Table 1; Social Security Admininistration (SSA), *Annual Statistical Supplement, 2001* (Washington, D.C.: SSA, 2001), Table 3.A3.

10. The distribution of benefits is a different story. If Social Security delivered an extra $25 billion in benefits, the progressive structure of the benefit formula would ensure that more would go to the lower-income aged and less to the upper-middle-income elderly who receive much of the present tax break.

11. William Andrews, for example, argues that the medical expense deduction (which allows individuals to deduct very high personal medical costs) is justified because income used to maintain an adequate standard of well-being should not be considered when assessing a taxpayer's ability to pay. William D. Andrews, "Personal Deductions in an Ideal Income Tax," *Harvard Law Review* 86 (1972): 335–36. See also Jay A. Soled, "Taxation

of Employer-Provided Health Coverage: Inclusion, Timing, and Policy Issues," *Virginia Tax Review* 15 (1996): 447–87.

12. The only measurement problem that seriously implicates the tax expenditure concept concerns a single aspect of the tax treatment of private pensions. Neither workers nor employers are required to pay federal taxes on interest earned by retirement plans. In budget estimates, this forgone tax revenue is treated as a permanent loss, rather than as a temporary one that will be partially recouped when workers receive benefits and pay income taxes on them. Technically, these estimates are wrong (although they comport with the budgetary treatment of other spending). Substantively, however, they are probably not far off the mark. There is no question that the tax code enormously favors private pensions. Money that companies put in pension plans is not taxed as employee income, even though companies deduct it from corporate income as they do wages. Because taxes on interest income are deferred, pension plans earn a higher rate of return than they would otherwise. Thanks to compound interest, these relative gains grow geometrically. And because workers are usually in lower tax brackets in retirement, the relative gains are larger still. It is true that many private investments also allow deferral of taxation. The relevant comparison, however, is not between pension plans and other investments, but between pension plans and other labor income. A worker who takes wages and puts them in the stock market pays income taxes on these labor earnings. A worker whose employer siphons exactly the same amount into a pension plan that makes exactly the same investments does not.

13. See, for example, Lester M. Salamon, ed., *Beyond Privatization: The Tools of Government Action* (Washington, D.C.: Urban Institute Press, 1989); Donald F. Kettl, *Government by Proxy: (Mis?)Managing Federal Programs* (Washington, D.C.: CQ Press, 1988); Donald F. Kettl, *Sharing Power: Public Governance and Private Markets* (Washington, D.C.: Brookings Institution, 1993); Harold Seidman and Robert Gilmour, *Politics, Position, and Power*, 4th ed. (Oxford: Oxford University Press, 1986).

14. R. Douglas Arnold, *The Logic of Congressional Action* (New Haven, Conn.: Yale University Press, 1990), 147. See also David R. Mayhew, *Congress: The Electoral Connection* (New Haven: Yale University Press, 1974); and R. Kent Weaver, "The Politics of Blame-Avoidance," *Journal of Public Policy* 6 (1986): 371–98. Of course, visibility is in the eye of the beholder: Policy effects that are unseen by most citizens may be a source of close scrutiny by organized interest groups affected by them.

15. Brooks Pierce, "Compensation Inequality," working paper, Bureau of Labor Statistics, Washington, D.C., 1998.

16. Ibid.; Gregory Acs and C. Eugene Steuerle, *Trends in the Distribution of Non-Wage Benefits and Total Compensation* (Washington, D.C.: The Urban Institute, 1993).

17. Although 29 percent of all taxpayers itemize their deductions, the proportion is 94 percent for households with income above $100,000 and less than 13 percent for those with income below $40,000. The Century

Foundation, *Tax Reform: A Century Foundation Guide to the Issues* (New York: Century Foundation, 1999), 8.

18. Peter R. Orzag, "Raising the Amount That Can Be Contributed to Roth IRAs: The Dangers in the Short Run and the Long Run" (Washington, D.C.: Center for Budget and Policy Priorities, 21 June 2000), 3.

19. Adema and Einerhand, "The Growing Role of Private Social Benefits," 23. Although the most compelling evidence for the distributional differences between public and private benefits derives from comparisons between the two within the United States, it is worth noting that cross-national comparisons also broadly support these generalizations. Across the eleven nations considered in Chapter 1, the correlation between income inequality (using the standard Gini index, a measure of income dispersion) and the private share of social spending is fairly strong ($r = .67$), with the United States leading the other nations on both dimensions. Estimates of the Gini index are available at the Luxembourg Income Study website, http://lissy.ceps.lu/ineq.htm. See also the analysis of Walter Korpi and Joakim Palme, "The Paradox of Redistribution and Strategies of Equality: Welfare State Institutions, Inequality, and Poverty in the Western Countries," *American Sociological Review* 63 (1998): 661–87, which shows a fairly strong correlation between private pension spending and income inequality among the aged. To be sure, many factors besides the character of social spending also affect inequality. U.S. income inequality is comparatively high even before taxes and transfers are taken into account, in part because of its large low-wage employment sector and the absence of centralized wage-bargaining structures like those found in the union-dense nations of northern Europe. Still, the structure of compensation is by no means unrelated to social policy. Indeed, one consequence of the prominent link between employment and benefits in the United States is that social benefits tend to magnify, rather than offset, differences in earnings. Low-wage workers not only earn less than other workers; they are also less likely to receive health insurance, pensions, and other workplace benefits.

20. To the extent that the empirical spotlight shifts from how much governments spend to the structure and mix of social welfare benefits, the need to consider the distributional consequences of alternative approaches becomes all the more pressing. As new cross-national data on income distribution becomes available, much of it produced by the Luxembourg Income Study (LIS), researchers are now for the first time analyzing social policy with a fairly detailed understanding of the distribution of primary income and the way in which it is altered by public policies. For an introduction to the LIS, see Peter Gottschalk, "Changes in Inequality of Family Income in Seven Industrialized Countries," *American Economic Review* 83 (1993): 136–42.

21. This might reflect the tax expenditures that Howard examines. Two of the four – the Earned Income Tax Credit and the Targeted Jobs Tax Credit – are means-tested. In the full roster of tax expenditures, however, these are highly unusual examples. As Howard himself argues, "the public assistance

component [of social welfare tax expenditures] look more like a thin veneer than a full-fledged tier." Christopher Howard, *The Hidden Welfare State: Tax Expenditures and Social Policy in the United States.* (Princeton, N.J.: Princeton University Press, 1997), 34.

22. Harold D. Lasswell, *Politics: Who Gets What, When, How* (New York: McGraw-Hill, 1936).

23. Graetz and Mashaw, *True Security*, 284. See also Lawrence H. Thompson, "The Advantages and Disadvantages of Different Social Welfare Strategies," *Social Security Bulletin* 57, no. 3 (1994): 3–11.

24. E. E. Schattschneider, *Politics, Pressures and the Tariff: A Study of Free Private Enterprise in Pressure Politics, as Shown in the 1929–1930 Revision of the Tariff* (New York: Prentice-Hall, 1935).

25. Theodore J. Lowi, "American Business, Public Policy, Case-Studies, and Political Theory," *World Politics* 16 (1964): 677–715.

26. Policies with widespread costs and widespread benefits, Wilson argued, create a process of "majoritarian politics" in which program expansion occurs without active group mobilization. When costs are widespread but benefits are concentrated, the result is "client politics" – beneficiaries are mobilized but those who foot the bill are not. Policies with widespread benefits and concentrated costs present the opposite model, "entrepreneurial politics," in which organized opponents battle weakly organized beneficiaries, who must be represented by talented political crusaders. Finally, policies that exhibit both concentrated costs and concentrated benefits invite classic "pluralist" conflict among competing groups. James Q. Wilson, *Political Organizations* (New York: Basic Books, 1974), 327–46.

27. This broad assertion does not stand up well to the evidence. Some means-tested programs in the United States have been highly vulnerable. The former Aid to Families with Dependent Children program is a case in point. But others, such as Supplemental Security Income and the Earned Income Tax Credit, have been quite resilient and, indeed, even flourished in times of budgetary austerity. Paul Pierson, *Dismantling the Welfare State? Reagan, Thatcher, and the Politics of Retrenchment* (Cambridge: Cambridge University Press, 1994); R. Shep Melnick, "The Unexpected Resilience of Means-Tested Programs" (paper presented at the annual meeting of the American Political Science Association, Washington, D.C., 1998); Robert Greenstein, "Universal and Targeted Approaches to Relieving Poverty: An Alternative View," in *The Urban Underclass*, ed. Christopher Jencks and Paul E. Peterson (Washington, D.C.: Brookings Institution, 1991), 437–59; Howard, *The Hidden Welfare State*.

28. Christopher J. Bosso, *Pesticides and Politics: The Life Cycle of a Public Issue* (Pittsburgh, Pa.: University of Pittsburgh Press, 1987).

29. David O. Sears and Jack Citrin, *Tax Revolt: Something for Nothing in California* (Cambridge, Mass.: Harvard University Press, 1982), 261–63.

30. Harold L. Wilensky, *The Welfare State and Equality: Structural and Ideological Roots of Public Expenditures* (Berkeley: University of California Press, 1975), 59. See also Douglas A. Hibbs, Jr., and Henrik Jess Madsen,

"Public Reactions to the Growth of Taxation and Government Expenditure," *World Politics* 33 (1981): 413–35.

31. Arnold, *Logic of Congressional Action*, 25–34, 44–51.

32. Amos Tversky and Daniel Kahneman, "The Framing of Decisions and the Psychology of Choice," *Science* 211 (1981): 453–58; Weaver, "The Politics of Blame-Avoidance"; Pierson, *Dismantling the Welfare State? Reagan, Thatcher, and the Politics of Retrenchment.*

33. See, for example, Steve Tidrick, "The Budget Inferno," *The New Republic* 212, no. 22 (1995): 17–23; Dennis S. Ippolito, *Hidden Spending: The Politics of Federal Credit Programs* (Chapel Hill: University of North Carolina Press, 1984); Herman B. Leonard, *Checks Unbalanced: The Quiet Side of Public Spending* (New York: Basic Books, 1986); and Robert S. McIntryre, *The Hidden Entitlements* (Washington, D.C.: Citizens for Tax Justice, 1996).

34. To gain a sense of the complexity of the environment, one need only read an introductory text on employee benefits law, "now a dense mixture of private contracting, common law adjudication, statutory norms, detailed agency regulation, and informal control through legislative oversight." Peter H. Schuck, "Legal Complexity: Some Causes, Consequences, and Cures," *Duke Law Journal* 42 (1992): 13. These are thickets into which the uninitiated fear to tread.

35. Frank R. Baumgartner and Bryan D. Jones, *Agendas and Instability in American Politics* (Chicago: University of Chicago Press, 1993).

36. Hugh Heclo, "Clinton's Health Reform in Historical Perspective," in *The Problem That Won't Go Away: Reforming U.S. Health Care Financing* (Washington, D.C.: The Brookings Institution, 1996), 16.

37. The phrase is John Kingdon's, *Agendas, Alternatives and Public Policies*, 2d ed. (New York: Harper-Collins, 1995), 174–88.

38. David W. Brady and Craig Volden, *Revolving Gridlock* (Boulder, Colo.: Westview Press, 1998); Keith Krehbiel, *Pivotal Politics: A Theory of U.S. Lawmaking* (Chicago: Chicago University Press, 1998).

39. The initial seeds for tax-favored individual retirement accounts, for example, were planted in the early 1960s. The provision was broadened in the late 1970s and early 1980s without full awareness of how quickly investment advisers and banks would encourage individuals to take advantage of it, and by the early 1980s, "Congress had transformed a modest tax preference into the seventh largest revenue loser in the tax code." Arnold, *The Logic of Congressional Action*, 201. Indeed, according to Michael J. Graetz, "The 1981 extension of IRA eligibility produced a revenue loss more than six times greater than that originally estimated." Michael J. Graetz, "Retirement Security Policy: Towards a More Unified View," in *Social Security: Beyond the Rhetoric of Crisis* (Princeton, N.J.: Princeton University Press, 1988), 110.

40. Howard, *The Hidden Welfare State*, 176–77.

41. The literature on institutions and policy change is extensive and growing. See, for example, Ellen M. Immergut, *Health Politics: Interests and Insti-*

tutions in Western Europe (Cambridge: Cambridge University Press, 1992); Antonia Maioni, *Parting at the Crossroads: The Emergence of Health Insurance in the United States and Canada* (Princeton, N.J.: Princeton University Press, 1998); R. Kent Weaver and Bert A. Rockman, *Do Institutions Matter? Government Capabilities in the United States and Abroad* (Washington, D.C.: Brookings Institution, 1993); George Tsebelis, "Decision Making in Political Systems: Veto Players in Presidentialism, Parliamentarism, Multicameralism and Multipartyism," *British Journal of Political Science* 25 (1995): 101–29; Herbert Obinger, "Federalism, Direct Democracy, and Welfare State Development in Switzerland," *Journal of Public Policy* 18 (1998): 241–63; Jacob S. Hacker, "The Historical Logic of National Health Insurance: Structure and Sequence in the Development of British, Canadian, and U.S. Medical Policy," *Studies in American Political Development* 12 (Spring 1998): 57–130; Pierson, *Dismantling the Welfare State? Reagan, Thatcher, and the Politics of Retrenchment*; Sven Steinmo and Jon Watts, "It's the Institutions, Stupid! Why Comprehensive National Health Insurance Always Fails in America," *Journal of Health Politics, Policy, and Law* 20 (1995): 329–72; Sven Steinmo, *Taxation and Democracy: Swedish, British, and American Approaches to Financing the Modern State* (New Haven, Conn.: Yale University Press, 1993); Theda Skocpol, *Protecting Soldiers and Mothers: The Political Origins of Social Policy in the United States* (Cambridge, Mass.: Harvard University Press, Belknap Press, 1992); and the quantitative analyses of Evelyne Huber, Charles Ragin, and John D. Stephens, "Social Democracy, Christian Democracy, Constitutional Structure, and the Welfare State," *American Journal of Sociology* 99 (1993): 711–49; and Duane Swank, "Political Institutions and Welfare-State Restructuring: The Impact of Institutions on Social Policy Change in Developed Democracies," *The New Politics of the Welfare State*, ed. Paul Pierson (Oxford: Oxford University Press, 2001), 197–237.

42. Steven Lukes, *Power: A Radical View* (New York: Macmillan, 1974); Peter Bachrach and Morton S. Baratz, *Power and Poverty; Theory and Practice* (Oxford: Oxford University Press, 1970); Matthew A. Crenson, *The Un-Politics of Air Pollution, a Study of Non-Decisionmaking in the Cities* (Baltimore: Johns Hopkins Press, 1971); John Gaventa, *Power and Powerlessness: Quiescence and Rebellion in an Appalachian Valley* (Urbana: University of Illinois Press, 1980).

43. Howard, *The Hidden Welfare State*, 58–61.

44. National Industrial Conference Board, *Industrial Pensions in the United States* (New York: National Industrial Conference Board, Inc., 1925), 2.

45. Frank D. Campion, *The AMA and U.S. Health Policy Since 1940* (Chicago: Chicago Review Press, 1984), 162.

46. Stuart Butler and Peter Germanis, "Achieving Social Security Reform: A 'Leninist' Strategy," *Cato Journal* 3 (1983): 547–56.

47. Martha Derthick, *Policymaking for Social Security* (Washington, D.C.: Brookings Institution, 1979); Edward D. Berkowitz, *America's Welfare*

State: From Roosevelt to Reagan (Baltimore: Johns Hopkins University Press, 1991); Theodore R. Marmor, *The Politics of Medicare*, 2d ed. (Hawthorne, N.Y.: Aldine de Gruyter, 2000).; Eric M. Patashnik, *Putting Trust in the US Budget: Federal Trust Funds and the Politics of Commitment* (Cambridge: Cambridge University Press, 2000).

48. Of course, *some* justifications have been given for attention to history, but most have been prudential – namely, that institutions develop over long periods of time and that in-depth historical research is the best means by which to assess their effects. Largely absent have been well-grounded *theoretical* justifications for treating historical processes as important analytic subjects in their own right. This point is also made by Paul Pierson's "Increasing Returns, Path Dependence, and the Study of Politics," *American Political Science Review* 94 (2000): 251–67. An admirable attempt to provide such theoretical justifications – though along lines different from those I am pursuing – is Karen Orren and Stephen Skowronek, "Beyond the Iconography of Order: Notes for a New Institutionalism," in *The Dynamics of American Politics: Approaches and Interpretations*, ed. Lawrence C. Dodd and Calvin Jillson (Boulder, Colo.: Westview Press, 1994), 311–30.

49. Paul Pierson, "Not Just What, but *When:* Timing and Sequence in Political Processes," *Studies in American Political Development* 14 (2000): 72.

50. W. Brian Arthur, "Competing Technologies, Increasing Returns, and Lock-in by Historical Events," *Economic Journal* 99 (1989): 116–31; Paul A. David, "Clio and the Economics of Qwerty," *American Economic Review* 75 (1985): 332–37; Douglass C. North, *Institutions, Institutional Change, and Economic Performance* (Cambridge: Cambridge University Press, 1990).

51. David, "Clio and the Economics of Qwerty," 332.

52. W. Brian Arthur, "Self-Reinforcing Mechanisms in Economics," in *The Economy as an Evolving Complex System*, ed. Kenneth J. Arrow and David Pines (Reading, Mass.: Addison-Wesley, 1988), 10.

53. Paul Pierson, "When Effect Becomes Cause: Policy Feedback and Political Change," *World Politics* 45 (1993): 595–628.

54. Ibid., 606.

55. Paul Pierson, "Increasing Returns, Path Dependence, and the Study of Politics."

56. For a fuller exploration, see Paul Pierson, "Not Just What, but *When:* Timing and Sequence in Political Processes"; Paul Pierson, "Increasing Returns, Path Dependence, and the Study of Politics"; Kathleen Thelen, "Historical Institutionalism in Comparative Politics," *Annual Review of Political Science* 2 (1999): 369–404; and James Mahoney, "Path Dependence in Historical Sociology," *Theory and Society* 29 (2000): 507–48.

57. William H. Sewell, "Three Temporalities: Toward an Eventful Sociology," in *The Historic Turn in the Human Sciences*, ed. Terrance J. McDonald (Ann Arbor: University of Michigan Press, 1996); Oona A. Hathaway, "The Path Dependence of the Law: The Course and Pattern of Legal

Change in a Common Law System," *Iowa Law Review* 86 (Jan. 2001): 601–65; Thelen, "Historical Institutionalism in Comparative Politics"; Mahoney, "Uses of Path Dependence in Historical Sociology."

58. Pierson, "Coping with Permanent Austerity," 415.

59. Because most arguments about increasing returns have emerged in the context of economics, considerable translation is required to apply them to politics. The following discussion draws on the seminal writings of Arthur and North; the previously cited work of Pierson, Mahoney, and Thelen; and insights gained from my own analysis.

60. At the outset, Social Security "offered the promise of future benefits to all taxpayers and gave current benefits to several million of the aged in amounts far out of proportion to the . . . taxes they had paid" – all financed by a minimal tax. Martha Derthick, *Policymaking for Social Security*, 248. In later years, of course, the true costs would become apparent, but by then the double-payment problem would make the program even more resistant to wholesale revision.

61. This was in part because Wilbur Mills, Chairman of the House Ways and Means Committee, crafted a deft compromise that rolled together reformers' demands for hospital insurance with competing proposals for physicians' coverage, thus foreclosing the path of incremental expansion by service category that reformers had initially envisioned. Theodore R. Marmor, *The Politics of Medicare*, 52–53.

62. This is the main complaint regarding economic models of path dependence made by S. J. Liebowitz and Stephen E. Margolis, "Path Dependence, Lock-in, and History," *Journal of Law, Economics, and Organization* 11 (1995): 205–26.

63. Charles Edward Lindblom, *Politics and Markets: The World's Political Economic Systems* (New York: Basic Books, 1977); Stephen L. Elkin, "Pluralism in Its Place: State and Regime in Liberal Democracy," in *The Democratic State*, ed. Stephen L. Elkin and Roger Benjamin (Lawrence: University of Kansas Press, 1985): 179–211; Fred Block, *Revising State Theory: Essays on Politics and Postindustrialism* (Philadelphia: Temple University Press, 1987). For a discussion of the ways in which political institutions mediate these signals, see Jacob S. Hacker and Paul Pierson, "Business Power and Social Policy: Employers and the Formation of the American Welfare State" *Politics & Society* (forthcoming).

64. Liebowitz and Margolis, "Path Dependence, Lock-in, and History."

65. Pierson, "Increasing Returns, Path Dependence, and the Study of Politics"; Terry M. Moe, "The New Economics of Organization," *American Journal of Political Science* 28 (1984): 739–77.

66. The home mortgage interest deduction, for example, has been a subterranean policy for most of its almost century-long development, moving into prominence only in recent decades as a result of quixotic crusades against it by tax officials (worried about its huge revenue costs) and proponents of low-income housing (worried about its skewed distribution in favor of the wealthy). Such challenges have, of course, failed to draw much public

attention, and, in any event, they have little prospect of success, given how extensive the benefits of the deduction now are and how organized and powerful the third-party interests supporting it have become. See Howard, *The Hidden Welfare State*, 94.

67. Stewart Wood, "Labour Market Regimes under Threat? Sources of Continuity in Germany, Britain, and Sweden," in *The New Politics of the Welfare State*, ed. Paul Pierson (Oxford: Oxford University Press, 2001), 374.

68. Ruth Berins Collier and David Collier, *Shaping the Political Arena: Critical Junctures, the Labor Movement, and Regime Dynamics in Latin America* (Princeton, N.J.: Princeton University Press, 1991), 27.

69. Classic works dealing with such seminal moments in national development include Seymour Martin Lipset and Stein Rokkan, "Cleavage Structures, Party Systems, and Voter Alignments: An Introduction," *Party Systems and Voter Alignments: Cross-national Perspective*, ed. Seymour M. Lipset and Stein Rokkan (New York: Free Press, 1967), 1–64; Barrington Moore, Jr., *Social Origins of Dictatorship and Democracy: Lord and Peasant in the Making of the Modern World* (Boston: Beacon Press, 1966); and Alexander Gerschenkron, *Economic Backwardness in Historical Perspective: A Book of Essays* (Cambridge, Mass.: Harvard University Press, 1962). See also the perceptive discussion of sequence arguments in modernization theory in Sidney Verba, "Sequences and Development," in *Crises and Sequences in Political Development* (Princeton: Princeton University Press, 1971).

70. Collier and Collier, *Shaping the Political Arena*, 27.

71. The distinction can be clarified by returning to an important argument made by the sociologist Arthur Stinchcombe about "historicist causal imagery." An historicist explanation, according to Stinchcombe, is one in which "an *effect* created by causes at some previous period *becomes a cause* of that same effect in succeeding periods." Some cause x thus creates an effect y; then y reproduces itself in subsequent periods even in the absence of the original cause x. For present purposes, the moment in which the original cause x occurs can be thought of as a critical juncture (with the crucial caveat that such a cause may not be a "big" one), while the self-reproduction of y can be thought of as a process of path dependence. This is also the general character of arguments about "punctuated equilbrium" in biology, in which some original, perhaps even random, event alters the basic stock of genetic material, which then becomes the basis for further functional adaptation through Darwinian natural selection. Arthur L. Stinchcombe, *Constructing Social Theories* (Chicago: University of Chicago Press, 1968), 103. On "punctuated equilibrium," see Niles Eldredge and Stephen Jay Gould, "Punctuated Equilibria: An Alternative to Phyletic Gradualism," in *Models of Paleobiology*, ed. T. J. M. Schopf (San Francisco: Freeman, Cooper & Co., 1972), 82–115.

72. John W. Kingdon, *Agendas, Alternatives, and Public Policies* (Boston: Little Brown, 1984).

73. Herbert A. Simon, "Theories of Decision-Making in Economics and Behavioral Science," *The American Economic Review* 49 (1959): 263.

74. The exact figure is 65.8 percent, which I calculated using the SSA's estimates of state and federal social spending, as outlined in the Administration's *Annual Statistical Supplement 1998* (Washington, D.C.: SSA, 1998), 141. For the purposes of the calculations, Social Security spending was considered pension spending despite Social Security's provision of disability and survivors' insurance, while the means-tested Supplemental Security Income program was considered public aid despite the fact that it serves as a pension program for low-income workers. If state and federal education spending are included in the total, the share of aggregate spending represented by pensions and health care is roughly 50 percent.

75. I say "probably" because the best series of data on total benefit payments, the National Income and Product Accounts (NIPA), does not account for the value of paid leave given to workers upon the occurrence of specified contingencies, such as sickness and pregnancy. Other data sources suggest, however, that paid leave for such purposes represents a small share of employee compensation. See, for example, Employee Benefits Research Institute, *Databook on Employee Benefits* (Washington, D.C.: EBRI, 1992), 29–30. According to the NIPA, private health insurance and retirement plans constituted 91 percent of total benefit payments in 1996 (55 percent and 36 percent, respectively), followed by workers' compensation (6.4 percent), life insurance (2.5 percent), and supplemental unemployment insurance (0.04 percent). *Survey of Current Business*, August 1997, 99.

76. Kathleen Thelen, "How Institutions Evolve: Insights from Comparative-Historical Analysis" (paper prepared for a Workshop on Comparative Political Analysis, Center for European Studies, Harvard University, Nov. 2000).

77. See, in particular, Margarita Esteves-Abe, Torben Iversen, and David Soskice, "Social Protection and the Formation of Skills: A Reinterpretation of the Welfare State" (paper presented at the annual meeting of the American Political Science Association, Atlanta, Georgia, Sept. 1999); Colin Gordon, "New Deal, Old Deck: Business and the Origins of Social Security, 1920–1935," *Politics and Society* 19 (1991): 165–207; Gordon, *New Deals: Business, Labor, and Politics in America, 1920–1935* (Cambridge: Cambridge University Press, 1994), and "Why No National Health Insurance in the United States? The Limits of Social Provision in War and Peace, 1941–1948," *Journal of Policy History* 9 (1997): 277–310; Sanford Jacoby, "Employers and the Welfare State: The Role of Marion B. Folsom," *Journal of American History* 80 (1993): 525–56; and *Modern Manors: Welfare Capitalism Since the New Deal* (Princeton, N.J.: Princeton University Press, 1997); Isabela Mares, "Negotiated Risks: Employers' Role in Social Policy Development" (Ph.D. diss., Harvard University, 1998); Cathie Jo Martin, *Stuck in Neutral* (Princeton: Princeton University Press, 2000); Cathie Jo Martin and Duane Swank, "Employers and the Welfare State" (paper presented at the annual meeting of the American Political Science

Association, Atlanta, Georgia, Sept. 1999); Peter Swenson, "Bringing Capital Back In, or Social Democracy Reconsidered: Employer Power, Cross-Class Alliances, and Centralization of Industrial Relations in Denmark and Sweden," *World Politics* 43 (1991): 513–44; and "Arranged Alliances: Business Interests in the New Deal," *Politics and Society* 25 (1997): 66–116.

78. Alexander George, "Case Studies and Theory: The Method of Structured, Focused Comparison," *Diplomacy: New Approaches to History, Theory, and Policy*, ed. Paul Lauren (New York: Free Press, 1979), 43–68; Ira Katznelson, "Structure and Configuration in Comparative Politics," in *Comparative Politics: Rationality, Culture, and Structure*, ed. Mark Irving Lichbach and Alan S. Zuckerman (Cambridge: Cambridge University Press, 1997), 81–112; Peter A. Hall, "Aligning Ontology and Methodology in Comparative Research" (paper prepared for a Workshop on Comparative Political Analysis, Center for European Studies, Harvard University, Nov. 2000).

79. Hall, "Aligning Ontology and Methodology," 27.

80. This research strategy responds to the recommendation of Gary King, Robert Keohane, and Sidney Verba to make "many observations from few" by expanding the empirical instances in which the observable implications of theories can be tested. *Designing Social Inquiry: Scientific Inference in Qualitative Research* (Princeton, N.J.: Princeton University Press, 1994). It is also indebted to Edwin Amenta, "Making the Most of a Case Study: Theories of the Welfare State and the American Experience," *International Journal of Comparative Sociology* 32 (1991): 172–94.

81. On the analytic use of counterfactuals, see Philip Tetlock and Aaron Belkin, *Counterfactual Thought Experiments in World Politics: Logical, Methodological, and Psychological Perspectives* (Princeton, N.J.: Princeton University Press, 1996); James D. Fearon, "Counterfactuals and Hypothesis Testing in Political Science," *World Politics* 43 (1991): 169–95; and Jacob S. Hacker, "Learning from Defeat: Political Analysis and the Failure of Health Care Reform in the United States," *British Journal of Political Science* 31 (2001): 61–94.

Introduction to Part II

1. Paul Light, *Artful Work: The Politics of Social Security Reform* (New York: Random House, 1985).

2. I use the term "privatization" because it is the most common description given to these proposals. In fact, the proposals that march under this banner do not truly propose to privatize Social Security – that is, eliminate the program and leave workers to provide for their own retirement. Rather, so-called privatization proposals envision a shift from a government-managed program that pays benefits out of pooled tax revenues to a system of mandatory individual accounts in which workers are compelled to put aside retirement savings in government-overseen investment vehicles whose

accumulated assets they alone use in retirement. This is probably better described as "individualization." It would, however, move Social Security in the direction of greater reliance on private savings and investment, which is no doubt why the term privatization is used.

3. For a discussion of these proposals, their advantages and disadvantages, and their likely prospects, see R. Douglas Arnold, "The Politics of Reforming Social Security," *Political Science Quarterly* 113, no. 2 (1998): 213–40; Sylvester J. Scheiber and John B. Shoven, *The Real Deal: The History and Future of Social Security* (New Haven, Conn.: Yale University Press, 1999); Michael J. Graetz and Jerry L. Mashaw, *True Security: Rethinking American Social Insurance* (New Haven: Yale University Press, 1999); and R. Douglas Arnold, Michael J. Graetz, and Alicia H. Munnell, *Framing the Social Security Debate: Values, Politics, and Economics* (Washington, D.C.: National Academy of Social Insurance, 1998).

4. For example, Martha Derthick, *Policymaking for Social Security* (Washington, D.C.: Brookings Institution, 1979); Jerry R. Cates, *Insuring Inequality: Administrative Leadership in Social Security, 1935–54* (Ann Arbor: University of Michigan Press, 1983); John Myles, "Postwar Capitalism and Social Security," in *The Politics of Social Policy in the United States*, ed. Margaret Weir, Ann Shola Orloff, and Theda Skocpol (Princeton, N. J.: Princeton University Press, 1988); and Theda Skocpol with G. John Ikenberry, "The Road to Social Security," in *Social Policy in the United States: Future Possibilities in Historical Perspective*, ed. Theda Skocpol (Princeton: Princeton University Press, 1995), 136–66.

5. For example, Merton C. Bernstein, *The Future of Private Pensions* (New York: The Free Press, 1964); Teresa Ghilarducci, *Labor's Capital: The Economics and Politics of Private Pensions* (Cambridge, Mass.: The MIT Press, 1992); and Dan M. McGill et al., *Fundamentals of Private Pensions*, 7th ed. (Philadelphia: University of Pennsylvania Press, 1996).

6. Two admirable but only partial exceptions are Jennifer Lisa Klein, "Managing Security: The Business of American Social Policy, 1910s–1960" (Ph.D. diss., University of Virginia, May 1999); and Steven A. Sass, *The Promise of Private Pensions: The First Hundred Years* (Cambridge, Mass.: Harvard University Press, 1997). Both are primarily historical analyses, however, and neither traces events of recent decades, with Klein's account ending in 1960 and Sass's with the passage of ERISA. Other scholars have examined particular periods in the development of the private pension system – most notably, the expansion of fringe benefits after World War II. See, for example, Beth Stevens, "Blurring the Boundaries: How the Federal Government Has Encouraged Welfare Benefits in the Private Sector," in *The Politics of Social Policy in the United States*, ed. Margaret Weir, Ann Shola Orloff, and Theda Skocpol (Princeton, N. J.: Princeton University Press, 1988), 123–48; Beth Stevens, "Labor Unions, Employee Benefits, and the Privatization of the American Welfare State," *Journal of Policy History* 2 (1990): 232–60; Frank R. Dobbin, "The Origins of Private Social Insurance: Public Policy and Fringe Benefits in America, 1920–1950,"

American Journal of Sociology 97 (1992): 1416–50; Sanford M. Jacoby, *Modern Manors: Welfare Capitalism since the New Deal* (Princeton: Princeton University Press, 1997); Michael K. Brown, "Bargaining for Social Rights: Unions and the Emergence of Welfare Capitalism, 1945–52," *Political Science Quarterly* 112 (1997–98): 645–74. Howard's innovative 1997 study of tax breaks with social welfare aims, *The Hidden Welfare State: Tax Expenditures and Social Policy in the United States* (Princeton: Princeton University Press, 1997), examines the political dynamics of the tax treatment of pensions plans, while a few other analyses look at the politics of public policy toward private pensions more generally, often from a neo-Marxist perspective – as in Richard Lee Deaton, *The Political Economy of Pensions: Power, Politics, and Social Change in Canada, Britain, and the United States* (Vancouver: University of British Columbia Press, 1989). Finally, Chapter 4 of Gøsta Esping-Andersen's *The Three Worlds of Welfare Capitalism* (Princeton: Princeton University Press, 1990) provides a broad investigation of the public–private mix in pensions in twelve advanced industrial democracies. None of these varied works, however, constitutes a general political analysis of public and private pensions in the United States.

7. Theda Skocpol, *Protecting Soldiers and Mothers: The Political Origins of Social Policy in the United States* (Cambridge, Mass.: Harvard University Press, Belknap Press, 1992), 65.

8. More precisely, they forfeit the portion of retirement benefits due to *employer* contributions. Historically, most defined-benefit plans have required no worker contributions (so-called noncontributory plans) or have been essentially noncontributory, so the definition of vesting offered here is precise enough for present purposes.

9. This discussion is indebted to Graetz and Mashaw, *True Security,* 47–68, and Alan S. Blinder, "Why Is Government in the Pension Business?" in *Social Security and Private Pensions: Providing for Retirement in the Twenty-First Century,* ed. Susan M. Wachter (Lexington, Mass.: Lexington Books, 1988), 17–34.

10. Sass, *The Promise of Private Pensions,* 4–17.

11. These figures are not strictly comparable with those contained in Table I2.1, because only federal old-age insurance and survivors' benefits are included in the denominator, rather than all old-age cash benefits.

12. Sass, *The Promise of Private Pensions,* 221.

13. Paul Pierson, "Big, Slow-Moving, and . . . Invisible: Macro-Social Processes in the Study of Comparative Politics" (paper prepared for the annual meeting of the American Political Science Association, Washington, D.C., Sept. 2000), 13. See also John Myles and Paul Pierson, "The Comparative Political Economy of Pension Reform," *The New Politics of the Welfare State,* ed. Paul Pierson (Oxford: Oxford University Press, 2001), 305–33.

14. Peter F. Drucker, *The Unseen Revolution: How Pension Fund Socialism Came to America* (New York: Harper & Row, 1976), 46.

15. Ibid., 167.

Chapter 2. Connected at Birth: Public and Private Pensions
Before 1945

1. Stuart D. Brandes, *American Welfare Capitalism, 1880–1940* (Chicago: University of Chicago Press, 1970).
2. Abraham Epstein, *Insecurity, a Challenge to America: A Study of Social Insurance in the United States and Abroad* (New York: H. Smith and R. Haas, 1933), 161.
3. Steven A. Sass, *The Promise of Private Pensions: The First Hundred Years* (Cambridge, Mass.: Harvard University Press, 1997), 23.
4. Ibid., 54.
5. Murray W. Latimer, *Industrial Pension Systems in the United States and Canada* (New York: Industrial Relations Counselors, Inc., 1932), 55.
6. In addition to Latimer, the discussion to follow draws on Nancy Altman, "Government Regulation: Enhancing the Equity, Adequacy, and Security of Private Pensions," *Private Pensions and Public Policy* (Paris: OECD, 1992); Merton C. Bernstein, *The Future of Private Pensions* (New York: The Free Press, 1964); Congressional Budget Office (CBO), *Tax Policy for Pensions and Other Retirement Savings* (Washington, D.C.: CBO, 1987); Charles L. Dearing, *Industrial Pensions* (Washington, D.C.: Brookings, 1954); Lizabeth Cohen, *Making a New Deal: Industrial Workers in Chicago, 1919–1939* (Cambridge: Cambridge University Press, 1990); Patricia E. Dilley, "The Evolution of Entitlement: Retirement Income and the Problem of Integrating Private Pensions and Social Security," *Loyola of Los Angeles Law Review* 30 (1997): 1063–198; Teresa Ghilarducci, *Labor's Capital: The Economics and Politics of Private Pensions* (Cambridge, Mass.: The MIT Press, 1992); Dan M. McGill et al., *Fundamentals of Private Pensions*, 7th ed. (Philadelphia: University of Pennsylvania Press, 1996); Alicia H. Munnell, *The Economics of Private Pensions* (Washington, D.C.: Brookings, 1982); National Industrial Conference Board, Inc., *Industrial Pensions in the United States* (New York: National Industrial Conference Board, Inc., 1925); Ann Shola Orloff, *The Politics of Pensions: A Comparative Analysis of Britain, Canada, and the United States, 1880–1940* (Madison: University of Wisconsin Press, 1993); Christopher Howard, *The Hidden Welfare State: Tax Expenditures and Social Policy in the United States* (Princeton, N.J.: Princeton University Press, 1997); and especially Sass, *The Promise of Private Pensions*.
7. Latimer, *Industrial Pension Systems*, 61–101.
8. David Brian Robertson, "The Bias of American Federalism: The Limits of Welfare State Development in the Progressive Era," *Journal of Policy History* 1 (1989): 261–91; David Brian Robertson, *Capital, Labor, and State: The Battle over American Labor Markets from the Civil War to the New Deal* (Lanham, Md.: Rowman & Littlefield, 2000); David A. Moss, *Socializing Security: Progressive-Era Economists and the Origins of American Social Policy* (Cambridge, Mass.: Harvard University Press, 1996); Jacob S. Hacker and Paul Pierson, "Business Power and Social

Policy: Employers and the Formation of the American Welfare State," *Politics & Society* (forthcoming).

9. "The prevailing opinion among American industrialists," explained the National Industrial Conference Board in 1925, "favors the voluntary assumption by private industry itself of such responsibility for the welfare of its personnel and the improvement of industrial relations as it is capable of discharging efficiently. This opinion is supported by the realization that industry's failure to assume such responsibility would almost certainly invite intervention by the state or other outside agency." National Industrial Conference Board, *Industrial Pensions in the United States*, 2. See also Roy Lubove, *The Struggle for Social Security, 1900–1935* (Pittsburgh, Pa.: University of Pittsburgh Press, 1968); Daniel T. Rodgers, *Atlantic Crossings: Social Politics in a Progressive Age* (Cambridge, Mass.: Belknap Press of Harvard University Press, 1998); Theda Skocpol, *Protecting Soldiers and Mothers: The Political Origins of Social Policy in the United States* (Cambridge, Mass.: Harvard University Press, 1992); Moss, *Socializing Security*.

10. Victoria Hattam, *Labor Visions and State Power: The Origins of Business Unionism in the United States* (Princeton, N.J.: Princeton University Press, 1993); William Forbath, *Law and the Shaping of the American Labor Movement* (Cambridge, Mass.: Harvard University Press, 1991); Samuel Gompers, *Seventy Years of Life and Labor: An Autobiography* (New York: E. P. Dutton & Co., 1925).

11. See Christopher Anglim and Brian Gratton, "Organized Labor and Old Age Pensions," *International Journal of Aging and Human Development* 25, no. 2 (1987): 91–107; Skocpol, *Protecting Soldiers and Mothers*, 205–47.

12. David T. Beito, *From Mutual Aid to the Welfare State: Fraternal Societies and Social Services, 1890–1967* (Chapel Hill: University of North Carolina Press, 2000), 2.

13. Peter Flora and Arnold J. Heidenheimer, eds., *The Development of Welfare States in Europe and America* (New Brunswick, N.J.: Transaction Books, 1981), 50–54; Rodgers, *Atlantic Crossings*, 216–35.

14. Ibid., 220.

15. On the generally unappreciated role of the fraternals in fighting proposals for compulsory sickness insurance, see Beito, *From Mutual Aid to the Welfare State*, 144–60, as well as the discussion in Chapter 4.

16. Ibid., 218.

17. Moss, *Socializing Security*, 59–76.

18. Skocpol, *Protecting Soldiers and Mothers*, 272–85.

19. Lubove, *The Struggle for Social Security*, 136.

20. Ibid., 140.

21. Gøsta Esping-Anderson, *The Three Worlds of Welfare Capitalism* (Princeton, N.J.: Princeton University Press, 1990), 95.

22. This description is drawn from James A. Losty, "The Soldiers and Sailors

Insurance Act," (Ph.D. diss., Catholic University of America, 1921); Bureau of War Risk Insurance, *Annual Report of the Director of the Bureau of War Risk Insurance for the Fiscal Year Ended June 30, 1920* (Washington, D.C.: U.S. GPO, 1920); W. F. Gephart, *Preliminary Economic Studies of the War: Effects of the War Upon Insurance, With Special Reference to the Substitution of Insurance for Pensions* (Washington, D.C.: Carnegie Endowment for International Peace, 1918); J. Owen Stalson, *Marketing Life Insurance: Its History in America* (Cambridge, Mass.: Harvard University Press, 1942), 571–73; and Paul H. Douglas, "The War Risk Insurance Act," *Journal of Political Economy* 26, no. 5 (1918): 461–83.

23. At meetings arranged by the Secretary of the Treasury with the hope of convincing insurers to take on this duty themselves, life insurance representatives voted 103 to 4 to support government insurance. Indeed, War Risk Insurance proved to be a tremendous boon for the industry, relieving companies of the risk of wartime death and educating the public about the value of life insurance. The Bureau of War Risk Insurance even paid enlistees' private life insurance premiums while they were in service so that these policies would not lapse.

24. Skocpol, *Protecting Soldiers and Mothers*, 466.

25. Mark Leff, "Consensus for Reform: The Mothers' Pension Movement in the Progressive Era," *Social Service Review* 47 (1973): 404.

26. Lubove, *The Struggle for Social Security*, 124.

27. Isaac Max Rubinow, *Social Insurance: With Special Reference to American Conditions* (New York: Henry Holt and Company, 1916), 408. The Civil War pension system is a special case for another reason, too: It served to siphon off the revenues that resulted from tariffs protecting northern industry, undoubtedly a chief reason for Republican and business acceptance of the program. Richard Franklin Bensel, *Sectionalism and Political Development: 1880–1980* (Madison: University of Wisconsin Press, 1984), 60–103.

28. The politics of government regulation of life insurance has been a neglected topic in the literature on U.S. public policy. Two fine studies, however, are Kenneth J. Meier, *The Political Economy of Regulation* (Albany, N.Y.: State University of New York Press, 1988), and Karen Orren, *Corporate Power and Social Change: The Politics of the Life Insurance Industry* (Baltimore: Johns Hopkins University Press, 1974).

29. As discussed shortly, experts in the Treasury Department later interpreted the decisions that created the pension tax expenditure as expressions of legislative and administrative interest in broadly distributed private relief against destitution in old age – a kind of private social security. This after-the-fact interpretation, so crucial to understanding the tax battles of the 1940s onward, has little evidentiary support. All indications are that these were rules motivated primarily by technical considerations and a desire to lower taxes; their social effects were at most secondary issues.

30. Rainard Benton Robbins, *Impact of Taxes on Industrial Pension Plans* (New York: Industrial Relations Counselors, 1949).

31. Congressional Budget Office (CBO), *Tax Policy for Pensions and Other Retirement Savings* (Washington, D.C.: CBO, 1987), 130.

32. Howard, *The Hidden Welfare State*, 48–63.

33. Andrew Dilnot, "Taxation and Private Pensions: Cost and Consequences," *Private Pensions and Public Policy*, OECD Social Policy Study No. 9 (Paris: OECD, 1992), 66.

34. James A. Wooten, "The 'Original Intent' of the Federal Tax Treatment of Private Pension Plans," *Tax Notes* (6 December 1999), 1305–19. Much of the following paragraph draws on Wooten's valuable in-depth research.

35. Hacker and Pierson, "Business Power and Social Policy."

36. Frank R. Dobbin, "The Origins of Private Social Insurance: Public Policy and Fringe Benefits in America, 1920–1950," *American Journal of Sociology* 97 (1992): 1416–50.

37. Committee on Economic Security, *Social Security in America: The Factual Background of the Social Security Act as Summarized from Staff Reports to the Committee on Economic Security* (Washington, D.C.: CBO, 1937), 199.

38. Robert D. Cuff, "Herbert Hoover: The Ideology of Voluntarism and War Organization During the Great War," *Journal of American History* 64 (1997): 358–72; Lubove, *The Struggle for Social Security*; Carolyn L. Weaver, *The Crisis in Social Security: Economic and Political Origins* (Durham, N.C.: Duke University Press, 1982), 81.

39. James Douglas Brown, *Social Security Administration Project*, Part 3, No. 146, tape-recorded in 1965 (New York: Columbia University Oral History Collection, 1976), p. 44 of typescript.

40. Lubove, *The Struggle for Social Security*, 136–37.

41. Edward D. Berkowitz, *America's Welfare State: From Roosevelt to Reagan* (Baltimore: Johns Hopkins University Press, 1991), 41.

42. See, for example, J. Craig Jenkins and Barbara G. Brents, "Social Protest, Hegemonic Competition, and Social Reform: A Political Struggle Interpretation of the Origins of the American Welfare State," *American Sociological Review* 54 (1989): 891–909; Colin Gordon, "New Deal, Old Deck: Business and the Origins of Social Security, 1920–1935," *Politics and Society* 19 (1991): 165–207; Gordon, *New Deals: Business, Labor, and Politics in America, 1920–1935* (Cambridge: Cambridge University Press, 1994); G. William Domhoff, "Corporate-Liberal Theory and the Social Security Act: A Chapter in the Sociology of Knowledge," *Politics and Society* 15 (1986–87): 297–330; and Jill S. Quadagno, "Welfare Capitalism and the Social Security Act of 1935," *American Sociological Review* 49 (1984): 632–47, as well as the more complex and subtle (but still vulnerable) argument of Peter Swenson, "Arranged Alliances: Business Interests in the New Deal," *Politics and Society* 25 (1997): 66–116; and Swenson, *Capitalists against Markets: The Making of Labor Markets and*

Welfare States in the United States and Sweden (New York: Oxford University Press, forthcoming).

43. Quadango, "Welfare Capitalism and the Social Security Act," 641.

44. Swenson, "Arranged Alliances: Business Interests in the New Deal," 81.

45. Gordon, *New Deals: Business, Labor, and Politics in America, 1920–1935,* 241.

46. Considerable evidence of widespread employer opposition is presented in Edwin Amenta and Sunita Parikh, "Capitalists Did Not Want the Social Security Act: A Critique of the Capitalist Dominance Thesis," *American Sociological Review,* no. 56 (1991): 124–9; and Theda Skocpol and Edwin Amenta, "Did Capitalists Shape Social Security?" *American Sociological Review* 50 (1985): 572–75.

47. Edwin E. Witte, "The Social Security Act and the Business Men" (address to the Minneapolis Civic and Commerce Association, 18 April 1935), 1, General Records of the Executive Director and Staff, CES, Box 3, National Archives and Records Administration (herafter cited as NARA), College Park, Md.

48. Marion B. Folsom, *Social Security Administration Project,* Part 3, No. 158, tape recorded in 1965 (New York: Columbia University Oral History Collections, 1976), 66–67. As Folsom readily admitted, he himself was a recent convert, having opposed government action before the early 1930s. In a 1929 *Atlantic Monthly* article, he opined: "Almost all government schemes are more costly than others because of the inefficiency of operations." Marion B. Folsom, "Old Age on the Balance Sheet," *Atlantic Monthly* (September 1929): 401.

49. House Ways and Means Committee, *Economic Security Act: Hearings Before the Committee on Ways and Means, House of Representatives, Seventy-Fourth Congress, First Session, on H.R. 4120,* 74th Cong., 1st sess., 21 January–12 February 1935; Senate Finance Committee, *Economic Security Act: Hearings before the Committee on Finance on S. 1130, United States Senate,* 74th Cong., 1st sess., 22 January–20 February 1935.

50. Testimony of John C. Gall and Noel Sargent to Senate Finance Committee, *Economic Security Act,* 921–61.

51. Testimony of L. C. Morrow to Senate Finance Committee, *Economic Security Act,* 788. In private, even generally progressive employers generally advocated caution and delay. See "Memorandum: Views of Messrs. Flanders, Leeds, and Julian of the Industrial Relations Committee of the Business Advisory and Planning Council of the Department of Commerce on Economic Security," 24 October 1934, "Memos – Relations with Congress," Materials Related to the CES, Lateral Files, Social Security Administration Historical Archives (hereafter cited as SSAHA), Baltimore, Md.; Business Advisory Council, "Report of the Committee on Social Legislation regarding Old Age Security Sections of the Bill H.R. 7260," 30 April 1935, "Reports," Materials Related to the CES, Lateral Files, SSAHA.

52. Witte to Raymond Moley, 10 May 1935, 1–2, "Witte Correspondence, August 1934-August 1935," Materials Related to the CES, Lateral Files, SSAHA.
53. Murray Latimer, "Industrial Pension Systems," 2–3; Latimer, "Memorandum on Proposed Amendments Permitting Employers with Private Pension Plans to Contract Out of the Government System," 7–8; Joseph P. Harris, "Summary of the Principal Arguments against Permitting Industrial Retirement Systems to Contract Out of the System of State Old Age Benefits," 1, in "Old-Age Security," Unpublished Studies of the CES, vol. 2, Lateral Files, SSAHA. Labor force statistics are from Department of Commerce, *Historical Statistics of the United States, Colonial Times to 1970, Part I* (Washington, D.C.: Department of Commerce, 1975).
54. Latimer, *Industrial Pension Systems*, 231 (emphasis added).
55. Paul H. Douglas, *Social Security in the United States: An Analysis and Appraisal of the Federal Social Security Act* (New York: McGraw-Hill, 1939), 253.
56. Martha Derthick, *Policymaking for Social Security* (Washington, D.C.: Brookings, 1979), 281.
57. James T. Patterson, *Congressional Conservatism and the New Deal: The Growth of the Conservative Coalition in Congress, 1933–1939* (Lexington: University of Kentucky Press, 1967), 759.
58. "Companies Known to Favor Clark Amendment to Social Security Act," in Dr. Rainard B. Robbins, "Confidential Material Collected on Social Security Act and Clark Amendment," 11 July 1935, Murray Latimer Papers, George Washington University. (I am grateful to Professor Edward Berkowitz of George Washington University for providing me a copy of this memorandum.) Senator Clark appointed the general counsel of the Socony-Vacuum oil company to a three-man committee that advised the House–Senate conference on the amendment. Thomas Hopkinson Elliot, *Social Security Administration Project*, Part 3, No. 154, tape-recorded in 1965 (New York: Columbia University Oral History Collections, 1976), 50; Thomas H. Eliot, *Recollections of the New Deal: When People Mattered* (Boston: Northeastern University Press, 1992), 119.
59. Witte, *Development of the Social Security Act*, 157–60.
60. Quadagno, for example, does not mention the amendment at all in analyzing business influence on the legislation in "Welfare Capitalism and the Social Security Act of 1935."
61. Weaver, The Crisis in Social Security, 89–91. See also Douglas, *Social Security in the United States*.
62. Quadagno, "Welfare Capitalism and the Social Security Act of 1935," 641.
63. See Wilbur J. Cohen, "The Meaning of the Term 'Social Insurance,'" 31 August 1934; Barbara N. Armstrong, "Possibilities of a Unified System of Insurance Against Loss of Earnings, n.d.; Armstrong, "Social Insurance: Its Place in a Program of Economic Security and an Outline of the Main Coverage, Benefit, and Administration Provision of an *Ideal* Social Insurance

System," August 1936, in "Social Insurance," Unpublished Studies of the CES, Lateral Files, SSAHA.

64. Frances Perkins, *The Roosevelt I Knew* (New York: Viking, 1946), 283.

65. Armstrong's role as director of the drafting effort has generally been ignored by corporate power theorists. (But see the unconvincing attempt by William Domhoff to dismiss her independent influence in *State Autonomy or Class Dominance* (New York: Aldine de Gruyter, 1996), 51–53.) Yet Armstrong's views on social insurance were both ambitious and deeply rooted in foreign experience, rather than in private developments. In her 1932 book *Insuring the Essentials*, she declares: "Except in the field of industrial accident provision, the United States is in the position of being the most backward of all the nations of commercial importance in insuring the essentials to its workers." She concludes: "The necessity of social organizing to supply the economic security which the wage system denies the individual worker has become incontrovertible." Barbara Nachtrieb Armstrong, *Insuring the Essentials: Minimum Wage, Plus Social Insurance – a Living Wage Program* (New York: Macmillan, 1932), 13, 554.

66. Brown, *Social Security Administration Project*, 107.

67. Brown to Latimer, 2 November 1935, Latimer Papers, Box 1, George Washington University, Washington, D.C.; Latimer, "Memorandum on Proposed Amendments Permitting Employers with Private Pension Plans to Contract Out of the Government System," 8–9.

68. Testimony of Marion B. Folsom to Senate Committee on Finance, *Economic Security Act*, 8 February 1935, 577–78, 588–89; Folsom, "Company Annuity Plans and the Federal Old Age Benefit Plan," *Harvard Business Review* 14 (Summer 1936): 414–24.

69. Rainard B. Robbins, "Preliminary Report on the Status of Industrial Pension Plans as Affected by Old Age Benefits Sections of the Social Security Act to the Committee on Social Security of the Social Science Research Council," Washington, D.C., 21 March 1936, 2, "Industrial Pension Plans Affected by the Social Security Act," Revolving Files, SSAHA.

70. Sass, *The Promise of Private Pensions*, 115

71. Witte to Dr. Walter Hamilton, 13 May 1936, 2, "Witte, Edwin E.," Arthur J. Altmeyer Papers, Lateral Files, SSAHA.

72. Industrial Relations Counselors (IRC), "Memorandum to Clients," No. 15, New York, 23 August 1935, 6, Latimer Papers, Box 10.

73. Quoted in Robbins, "Preliminary Report," 10. A similar conclusion was conveyed to the new Social Security Board by Murray Latimer in a memorandum dated 23 March 1936 ("General Social Security," Altmeyer Papers, Lateral Files, SSAHA).

74. Democratic Senator Alben Barkley of Kentucky charged, for example, that the Clark amendment would require "an army of inspectors and investigators running all over the United States to innumerable places to which they would be called every time a man terminated his employment, either on his own account or on account of his employer, to . . . investigate the

employee's rights under the private plan and under the Federal plan." *Congressional Record*, Senate, 19 June 1935, 9627.

75. Testimony of Thomas H. Elliot to Joint Hearings of the Subcommittee of the Senate Committee on Finance and the Subcommittee of the House Committee on Ways and Means, *Private Pension Systems*, 74th Cong., 2nd sess., Part I, 20 March 1936, 2; Elliot, *Recollections of the New Deal*, 119.

76. "What Business Thinks," *Fortune* (October 1939): 52–53, 90, 92, 95–96, 98. The sampling technique or margin of error of this survey is not included in the article, although *Fortune* states that the survey "is presented here as a laboratory product, the first successful step in the development of something new and unknown. This experiment is based on personal interviews with hand-picked samples of businessmen." Ibid., 52.

77. Testimony of Marion B. Folsom to the House Committee on Ways and Means, *Social Security*, 76th Cong., 1st sess., 2 March 1939, 1130.

78. On the widespread (but poorly informed) popular support for Social Security, see U.S. Department of Health, Education, and Welfare, *Public Attitudes toward Social Security, 1935–1965*, Social Security Administration Office of Research and Statistics, Report No. 33 (Washington, D.C.: U.S. GPO, 1970), chap. 2–3.

79. Sanford M. Jacoby, *Modern Manors: Welfare Capitalism since the New Deal* (Princeton, N.J.: Princeton University Press, 1997), 215–19. See also Irving Ladimer, "Effect of Social Security on Private Pension Plans," *Economic Security Bulletin: An Informative Service for the National Association of Manufacturers* 5, no. 7 (July 1941): 7–9.

80. American Council of Life Insurance, *1973 Life Insurance Fact Book* (Washington, D.C.: ACLI, 1973).

81. The formidable resources and lobbying prowess of the industry are detailed in Raymond Richards, *Closing the Door to Destitution: The Shaping of the Social Security Acts of the United States and New Zealand* (University Park: Pennsylvania State University Press, 1994).

82. Derthick, *Policymaking for Social Security*, 136–37.

83. Statement of Thomas Parkinson, inserted into the record of the Senate Finance Committee, *Economic Security Act*, 206.

84. Derthick, *Policymaking for Social Security*, 136.

85. Mark H. Leff, "Taxing the Forgotten Man: The Politics of Social Security Finance in the New Deal," *Journal of American History* 70, no. 2 (September 1983): 359–81; Richards, *Closing the Door to Destitution*; Rodgers, *Atlantic Crossings*, 444–45.

86. Nor should the importance of business-oriented ideas be overstated. The Social Security Act borrowed widely from domestic and foreign sources, reflecting in particular the "institutionalization of European-acquired social insurance knowledge." Rodgers, *Atlantic Crossings*, 438.

87. Witte to Edward Berman, 7 August 1934, General Records of the Executive Director and Staff, CES, Box 12, NARA; Ralph B. Harris, "To What Extent Does Life Insurance Function as a Savings Institution to Meet Need for Security?" 7 November 1934; Edward Berman, "Report on Life Insur-

ance with Special Reference to Industrial Insurance," University of Illinois, n.d., in "Social Insurance," Unpublished Studies of the CES, Lateral Files, SSAHA.

88. Sass, *The Promise of Private Pensions*, 70–71.

89. According to Robbins, "Companies Known to Favor the Clark Amendment," insurance companies and banks were prominent among the amendment's initial supporters.

90. Thomas Elliot, the Roosevelt Administration's point man on constitutional and drafting matters, recalled that a year after the passage of the Act he told Senator King, a Clark ally, that he would continue to try to craft a compromise version of the Clark amendment. King "laughed and he said, 'Forget it. Mr. Forster [of Towers, Perrin, Forster, & Crosby] was in here only the other day, and he said he never made such a mistake in his life. His business is booming as never before!'" Elliot, *Social Security Administration Project*, 51–52.

91. Exit from the workforce was required to receive benefits in the CES proposal, although this rule was softened in Congress, which allowed beneficiaries to earn small amounts. For the CES position, see "Why Retirement Should be Made a Condition of the Payment of Old-Age Benefits," n.d., "Memos – Relations with Congress," Materials Related to the CES, SSAHA.

92. William Graebner, *A History of Retirement: The Meaning and Function of an American Institution, 1885–1978* (New Haven, Conn.: Yale University Press, 1980), 181–214. Graebner wrongly treats this as the primary motive of the Roosevelt Administration, an inflated charge that the historical record does not support.

93. The argument is strongly made in Wilbur Cohen to Arthur Altmeyer, 10 February 1937, 2, "General Social Security," Altmeyer Papers, Lateral Files, SSAHA.

94. Arthur M. Schlesinger, *The Coming of the New Deal* (Boston: Houghton Mifflin, 1959), 308–9.

95. Roosevelt declared on the Act's third anniversary, "Because it has become increasingly difficult for individuals to build their own security single-handedly, Government must now step in and help them lay the foundation stones, just as Government in the past has helped lay the foundation of business and industry. We must face the fact that in this country we have a rich man's security and a poor man's security and that the Government owes equal obligations to both." *The Social Security Act of 1935: Reflections Fifty Years Later, The Report of the Committee on Economic Security and Other Basic Documents Relating to the Development of the Social Security Act: 50th Anniversary Edition* (Washington, D.C.: National Conference on Social Welfare, 1985), 148.

96. A preliminary attempt at a scheme based on tax incentives and federal subsidies, for example, convinced the drafters that anything short of a fully integrated national system would "have resulted in a monstrous patchwork of coverage, with impossible problems of assuring adequate and equitable

benefits, actuarial and financial stability, or progressive improvement."
James D. Brown, *An American Philosophy of Social Security: Evolution
and Issues* (Princeton, N.J.: Princeton University Press, 1972), 12.

97. Congress abandoned, for example, the CES's proposal for taxing only
workers who made less than $250 a month, leaving high-income workers
out of the system altogether. Instead, all covered workers were taxed, but
the tax applied only to the first $3,000 of wages.

98. Although supported by the Treasury Department on the grounds that taxation of such workers would be infeasible, the amendment found support
in Congress primarily because of southern resistance to the provision of
benefits to agricultural and domestic workers, many of whom were, of
course, black. On the motives behind this decision, compare Robert C.
Lieberman, *Shifting the Color Line: Race and the American Welfare State*
(Cambridge, Mass.: Harvard University Press, 1998), 26–48; and Gareth
Davies and Martha Derthick, "Race and Social Welfare Policy: The Social
Security Act of 1935," *Political Science Quarterly* 112 (Summer 1997):
217–35.

99. Edwin Witte doubted "whether any part of the social security program
other than the old age assistance title would have been enacted into
law but for the fact that the President throughout insisted that the entire
program must be kept together." Edwin E. Witte, *The Development of
the Social Security Act: A Memorandum on the History of the Committee on Economic Security and Drafting and Legislative History of
the Social Security Act* (Madison: University of Wisconsin Press, 1962),
79.

100. In 1937, the last major barrier to its implementation faded away when the
Supreme Court upheld the old-age insurance provisions of the Social
Security Act by a 7–2 margin, basing much of its decision on the conclusion that the states, acting without federal support, could not adequately
pursue national social welfare goals. *Helvering v. Davis*, 24 May 1937,
reprinted in *The Social Security Act of 1935: Reflections Fifty Years Later*,
33–35.

101. The legislation stipulated that such workers should receive an "adequate"
minimum benefit far higher than what they had put into the system. But
the minimum monthly benefit envisioned was still only a tenth of the
average monthly paycheck received by covered employees.

102. Brown, *An American Philosophy of Social Security*, 136. Emphasis in
original.

103. Alfred M. Landon, "I Will Not Promise the Moon: Economic Security Bill,
Administration Bill, Republican Proposal," (speech given in Milwaukee,
Wis., 26 September 1936), reprinted in Donald T. and Ellis W. Hawley
Critchlow, eds., *Poverty and Public Policy in Modern America* (Chicago:
The Dorsey Press, 1989), 156–65. Of course, since Social Security reserves
were held in the form of government bonds, they represented an obliga-
tion that the government owed itself and that it would presumably have
to meet in the future through higher taxes or lower spending. Everyone

recognized, however, that such obligations would be extremely hard to abrogate once they had been assumed.

104. In a 1944 letter to a friend who had mentioned labor unions' concerns about the tax freeze, Vandenberg wrote: "If they [labor unions] can pile up a much larger old-age pension reserve than is needed for the payment of private benefits they will be in a much better position to raise the swollen reserves for increased benefits." Vandenberg to S. R. Banyon, 4 December 1944, *Vandenberg Papers: Correspondence, 1915–51*, Michigan Historical Collections of the University of Michigan, Ann Arbor.

105. M. A. Linton, "The Quest for Security in Old Age: Some Practical Considerations," *Proceedings of the Academy of Political Science*, vol. 16, no. 3 (New York: Academy of Political Science, 1935); Linton, "The Problem of Reserves and a Possible Solution," undated article, "Witte Papers," Altmeyer Papers, Lateral Files, SSAHA. Linton to Altmeyer, 2 December 1937; and Altmeyer to Linton, 4 December 1937, "Letters from Altmeyer," Altmeyer Papers, Lateral Files, SSAHA. Another influential life insurance figure was Reinard A. Houhaus, a Metropolitan actuary who shared Linton's animus toward the projected reserve. See his "Recent Amendments to the Social Security Act," (talk before the Fraternal Actuarial Association, New York, 26 September 1950); and "Social Insurance in a Democracy," *General Proceedings of the Thirty-Seventh Annual Meeting of the American Life Convention*, Chicago, 5–8, October 1942, "Houhaus, Reinhard," Revolving Files, SSAHA.

106. For the general orientation of the life insurance industry, see Social Security Committee of the American Life Convention, Life Insurance Association of America, and the National Association of Life Underwriters, *Social Security: A Statement* (New York: American Life Convention, 1945).

107. Testimony of Folsom to the House Committee on Ways and Means, *Social Security*, 1130. Folsom's later statements on retirement security retain this original emphasis, as is suggested by Marion B. Folsom, "Goals in Governmental and Private Plans for Social Security," (speech delivered on the 25th anniversary of the Social Security Act, Washington, D.C., 15 August 1960).

108. Jacoby, *Modern Manors*, 207.

109. As Murray Latimer and Karl Tufel noted in a 1940 Industrial Relations Counselers publication, "Thus far, at least, the benefits to be distributed by the governmental system have been larger relative to the taxes paid than the normal ratio between costs and benefits under private plans. In other words, the national system, while occasioning the modification of private plans, at the same time has enabled companies to provide more adequate total benefits than was hitherto possible under private plans for the same cost, including old-age insurance taxes." *Trends in Industrial Pensions* (New York: Industrial Relations Counselers, 1940), 43.

110. Theron F. Schlabach, *Edwin E. Witte: Cautious Reformer* (Madison: State Historical Society of Wisconsin, 1969), 177.

111. Cohen to Altmeyer, 10 February 1937, 3–4, "General Social Security," Altmeyer Papers, Lateral Files, SSAHA.

112. The quotation is contained in a letter from Altmeyer to President Roosevelt cited in Edward Berkowitz and Kim McQuaid, *Creating the Welfare State: The Political Economy of Twentieth-Century Reform*, 2d ed. (New York: Praeger, 1988), 132.

113. E. E. Schattschneider, *Politics, Pressures and the Tariff: A Study of Free Private Enterprise in Pressure Politics, as Shown in the 1929–1930 Revision of the Tariff* (New York: Prentice-Hall, 1935), 288.

114. Derthick, *Policymaking for Social Security*, 91.

115. Bartholomew H. Sparrow, *From the Outside In: World War II and the American State* (Princeton, N.J.: Princeton University Press, 1996), 39.

116. Alan Brinkley, *The End of Reform: New Deal Liberalism in Recession and War* (New York: Vintage, 1995), 10.

117. Berkowitz, *America's Welfare State*, 50.

118. See, for example, Robbins, *Impact of Taxes on Industrial Pension Plans*; Dearing, *Industrial Pensions*; Beth Stevens, "Labor Unions, Employee Benefits, and the Privatization of the American Welfare State," *Journal of Policy History* 2 (1990): 233–60; Dobbin, "The Origins of Private Social Insurance"; Howard, *The Hidden Welfare State*; Sass, *The Promise of Private Pensions*; Brown "Bargaining for Social Rights: Unions and the Reemergence of Welfare Capitalism, 1945–1952"; Quadagno, *The Transformation of Old Age Security*, 77–98.

119. This was particularly true of the excess profits tax, which was dramatically increased in 1942 to a marginal rate of 90 percent for affected corporations. Because the tax was widely seen as a temporary war measure, corporations conceived of pension trusts as a mechanism for postponing taxation until tax levels returned to peacetime levels. Many corporations also began putting aside extra funds to pay for past pension credits, thus further reducing their tax burdens. Challis A. Hall, Jr., "Extent and Causes of Recent Growth in Pension and Profit-Sharing Plans Qualified Under Section 165(a), IRC," 7 July 1951, Office of Tax Policy Subject Files, Box 48, NARA.

120. A set of talking points developed for Treasury spokesman Randolph Paul noted that "[t]he amount of the subsidy, i.e., the revenue loss, appears to have reached serious proportions." Shere to Ecker-Racz, 1 April 1942, Office of Tax Policy Subject Files, Box 48.

121. Dobbin, "The Origins of Private Social Insurance," 1437.

122. Witte, *Development of the Social Security Act*, 157. There was no mention whatsoever of private pensions in the copiously documented unpublished CES staff report on old-age security, which instead concentrated on state old-age assistance laws and foreign precedents. Barbara N. Armstrong and Staff, "Old-Age Security Staff Report," Unpublished Studies of the CES, vol. 2, SSAHA.

123. U.S. Congress Joint Committee on Tax Evasion and Avoidance, *Tax Evasion and Avoidance*, 75th Cong., 1st sess., 5 August 1937, House Document No. 337, 4.

124. This was, as I have argued, a questionable interpretation of Congress's earlier motives. But it certainly reflected the Roosevelt Administration's view of the pension tax expenditure.

125. Testimony of Roswell Magill before the Joint Committee on Tax Evasion and Avoidance, *Tax Evasion and Avoidance*, 75th Cong., 1st sess., 2 July 1937, 297, 296.

126. Division of Tax Research, "Summary of the Treasury's Suggestions for Revision of the Tax Treatment of Pension Trusts and Other Deferred Benefit Plans," 23 May 1942, 2, Office of Tax Policy Subject Files, Box 48, NARA.

127. In a bow to political realism, the proposal tread lightly around existing pension commitments, phasing in the vesting provisions and applying them only to older, long-service workers.

128. Howard, *The Hidden Welfare State*, 121. Here Howard draws on the argument of Nancy J. Altman, "Rethinking Retirement Income Policies: Nondiscrimination, Integration, and the Quest for Worker Security," *New York University Tax Law Review* 42 (1987): 485–86.

129. Division of Tax Research, "Summary of the Treasury's Suggestions for Revision of the Tax Treatment of Pension Trusts."

130. Testimony of Randolph Paul before the House Committee on Ways and Means, *Revenue Revision of 1942: Hearings on H.R. 7378*, 77th Cong., 2nd sess., 1942, 2405–6.

131. Sass, *The Promise of Private Pensions*, 115.

132. Division of Tax Research, "Revision of Tax Treatment of Pension Plans," 13 March 1942, 2, Office of Tax Policy Subject Files, Box 48, NARA.

133. Notes from an internal Department discussion among Surrey, Shere, Echholz, Campbell, and Harris, 14 April 1942, Office of Tax Policy Subject Files, Box 48, NARA.

134. Ibid.

135. Sass, *The Promise of Private Pensions*, 106–7.

136. Robbins, *The Impact of Taxes on Industrial Pension Plans*, 15.

137. See Robert A. Taft, "Pension Trusts and Welfare Funds," *Journal of Commerce, New York* (29 May 1946): 3.

138. "Conference Between Senator Taft and Mr. Surrey," 13 May 1944, and "Memorandum on Conference with Senator Taft," 12 June 1944, Records of the Office of the Secretary of the Treasury, Box 187, NARA.

139. On the relation of the base to wage levels, see Derthick, *Policymaking for Social Security*, 285–86.

140. Sass, *Promise of Private Pensions*, 107.

141. Testimony of Meyer Goldstein to Senate Finance Committee, *Revenue Act of 1942*, 77th Cong., 2nd sess., 1942, 508.

142. Testimony of Donald Despain to Senate Finance Committee, *Revenue Act of 1942*, 77th Cong., 2nd sess., 1942, 1954.

143. Testimony of Robert S. Gordon to House Ways and Means Committee, *Revenue Revision of 1942*, 77th Cong., 2nd sess., vol. 3, 1942, 2427.

144. Revenue Act of 1942, 77th Cong., 2nd sess., *United States Statutes at Large*, 56, Part 1 (1942), 862.

145. Ibid.
146. Dilley, "The Evolution of Entitlement: Retirement Income and the Problem of Integrating Private Pensions and Social Security," 1159–65.
147. Robbins, *The Impact of Taxes on Industrial Pension Plans*, 24–25.
148. "In the 27 months between September 1942 and December 1944," writes Sass, "the IRS approved over 4,000 new plans, or eight times the 515 programs in place in 1938. Between 1940 and 1945 the number of insured plans more than quadrupled, to 6,700 from 1,530." Sass, *Promise of Private Pensions*, 118. The figures that follow come from the same source.

Chapter 3. Sibling Rivalry: Public and Private Pensions After 1945

1. Nelson Lichtenstein, "From Corporatism to Collective Bargaining: Organized Labor and the Eclipse of Social Democracy in the Postwar Era," *The Rise and Fall of the New Deal Order*, ed. Steve Fraser and Gary Gerstle (Princeton, N.J.: Princeton University Press, 1989), 123.
2. Beth Stevens, "Labor Unions, Employee Benefits, and the Privatization of the American Welfare State," *Journal of Policy History* 2 (1990): 233–60; Beth Stevens, "Blurring the Boundaries: How the Federal Government Has Encouraged Welfare Benefits in the Private Sector," *The Politics of Social Policy in the United States*, ed. Margaret Weir, Ann Shola Orloff, and Theda Skocpol (Princeton: Princeton University Press, 1988), 123–48; Frank R. Dobbin, "The Origins of Private Social Insurance: Public Policy and Fringe Benefits in America, 1920–1950," *American Journal of Sociology* 97 (1992): 1416–50; Charles L. Dearing, *Industrial Pensions* (Washington, D.C.: Brookings Institution, 1954); Raymond Munts, *Bargaining for Health: Labor Unions, Health Insurance, and Medical Care* (Madison: University of Wisconsin Press, 1967); Jennifer L. Klein, "Managing Security: The Business of American Social Policy, 1910s–1960" (Ph.D. diss., University of Virginia, 1999); Steven A. Sass, *The Promise of Private Pensions: The First Hundred Years* (Cambridge, Mass.: Harvard University Press, 1997); Alan Derickson, "Health Security for All? Social Unionism and Universal Health Insurance, 1935–1958," *Journal of American History* 80 (1994): 1333–56; Michael K. Brown, "Bargaining for Social Rights: Unions and the Emergence of Welfare Capitalism, 1945–52," *Political Science Quarterly* 112 (1997–98): 645–79; Colin Gordon, "Why No National Health Insurance in the United States? The Limits of Social Provision in War and Peace, 1941–1948," *Journal of Policy History* 9 (1997): 277–310.
3. The UMW strike, claimed one union official, "was the single most important force in the negotiated pension movement." Quoted in Sass, *The Promise of Private Pensions*, 129.
4. Brown, "Bargaining for Social Rights," 663.
5. As Brown argues, "[B]argaining over fringes was an issue that touched on the security of union membership.... For labor leaders, fringes were a

device to insure the loyalty of workers; for businessmen, it was a way to undermine unions." Brown, "Bargaining for Social Rights," 650.

6. Sanford M. Jacoby, *Modern Manors: Welfare Capitalism since the New Deal* (Princeton, N.J.: Princeton University Press, 1997).

7. Quoted in Jill F. Bernstein, "Employee Benefits in the Welfare State: Great Britain and the United States since World War II" (Ph.D. diss., Columbia University, 1980), 293.

8. Ibid.

9. House Committee on Ways and Means, *Background Material and Data on Programs within the Jurisdiction of the Committee on Ways and Means* (Washington, D.C.: U.S. GPO, 1989), 14.

10. Quoted in Dearing, *Industrial Pensions*, 47.

11. Stevens, "Labor Unions, Employee Benefits, and the Privatization of the American Welfare State."

12. Quoted in Dearing, *Industrial Pensions*, 47.

13. Testimony of Walter P. Reuther to House Committee on Education and Labor, *Welfare and Pension Fund Legislation*, 85th Cong., 1st sess., 1957, 255.

14. Testimony of Walter P. Reuther to House General Subcommittee on Labor of the Committee on Education and Labor, *Private Welfare and Pension Plan Legislation*, 91st Cong., 1st and 2d sess., 1957, 177. Reuther continued: "[I]t is a very fundamental question of social policy: What is the relative emphasis that we ought to place upon the private and the public, or the public versus the private? We are in favor of a major emphasis upon the public sector, because that is the only instrument through which we can get universal coverage. And we are in favor of that. But you cannot unscramble the omelet." Ibid., 191.

15. After the UMW won its health and welfare fund, for instance, Lewis declared that he would not support national health insurance.

16. I. S. Falk to Arthur J. Altmeyer and Oscar M. Powell, "Suggested Study of Health and Welfare Provisions in Union Contracts," 7 June 1946, Revolving Files, "Source Material and Chronology," Social Security Administration Historical Archives (hereafter SSAHA), Baltimore, Md.; I. S. Falk to Walter P. Reuther, 15 October 1946, Social Security Administration (SSA) Division of Research and Statistics, General Correspondence, Box 13, National Archives and Records Administration (hereafter NARA), College Park, Md.; I. S. Falk, "The UAW Trade Union Social Security Program," 1946, SSA Division of Research and Statistics, Gen. Corr., Box 13, NARA; J. A. Krug to Arthur J. Altmeyer, 4 June 1946, SSA Division of Research and Statistics, Gen. Corr., Box 12, NARA; Altmeyer to Josephine Roche, 18 March 1952, "Mine Worker Pension Fund," Altmeyer Papers, SSAHA.

17. Falk to Altmeyer and Powell, "Suggested Study of Health and Welfare Provisions in Union Contracts," 1.

18. Altmeyer to the Retirement Fund of the Coat and Suit Industry, 8 January 1954, "Retirement Fund Coat and Suit Industry," Altmeyer Papers, SSAHA; Altmeyer to David Dubinsky, 24 March 1969, "International

Ladies Garment Workers Union Retirement Fund," Altmeyer Papers, SSAHA; Altmeyer to A. B. Candido, 7 September 1971, "National Industrial Group Pension Plan," Altmeyer Papers, SSAHA.

19. Wilbur J. Cohen, "Pensions and Welfare Funds Under Wage Stabilization" (paper presented at the fourth annual Conference on Labor, New York University, 16 May 1951), "Wage Stabilization," Wilbur J. Cohen Papers, SSAHA; "Health, Welfare and Pension Programs Under Wage Stabilization," Report to the Wage Stabilization Board by the Tripartite Panel on Health, Welfare and Pension Plans, 22 October 1951, "Wage Stabilization," Cohen Papers, SSAHA.

20. Altmeyer, "Union Health and Welfare Funds," Studies in Business Economics, no. 8 (New York: National Industrial Conference Board, 1947). Reprinted in William Haber and Wilbur J. Cohen, ed. *Readings in Social Security* (New York: Prentice-Hall, Inc., 1948), 132, 134. Similar sentiments are voiced in Wilbur J. Cohen, "Private Pension Plans and the Need for Further Improvements in the Federal Old-Age and Survivors Insurance Program," reprint from Proceedings of the Third Annual Meeting, Industrial Relations Research Association, n.d., Cohen Papers, "Social Security," SSAHA.

The reaction of program excutives to the rise of private benefits calls into question a leading interpretation of the early development of Social Security offered by Jerry Cates's 1983 study *Insuring Inequality: Administrative Leadership in Social Security, 1935–54* (Ann Arbor: University of Michigan Press, 1983). Against the conventional portrait of Social Security as a (qualified) victory for social reformers, Cates argues that the aims of Social Security's early administrators were at base conservative, directed at "blunting . . . the redistributional thrust created by the economic needs of the Depression-era aged." Ibid., 141. To document this fundamental conservatism, Cates cites two main pieces of evidence: the opposition of Social Security administrators to so-called flat-rate plans, which would have provided a flat minimum benefit to all elderly Americans; and their general lack of support for state old-age assistance programs, which provided benefits on the basis of need rather than past contributions. The indigent elderly, according to Cates, were "caught in the pincers movement" created by administrators' deliberate attempts to limit the scope of state public assistance programs while simultaneously resisting proposals for a flat pension benefit or for the "blanketing in" of elderly Americans not yet covered by contributory social insurance. Ibid., 36–153.

The interplay between social insurance and public assistance was not, however, the only arena in which a "pincers movement" took place during this period. For workers higher up the wage scale, program administrators had to worry about another competitor to social insurance – the rapidly expanding field of private pension plans. Strikingly, not once in his detailed study of the 1935–54 period does Cates discuss the expansion of private pensions. If he had, administrative leaders' efforts to maintain the wage-related and contributory character of Social Security would have appeared less sinister, and their commitment to redistribution substantially more robust. Program administrators were committed to a broad basic program because they believed that all but the most highly paid needed social protection. Moving toward a more redistributive flat-rate plan would, they feared, cause middle- and upper-income workers to conclude that they could obtain a better deal through private means, thus undercutting popular support for the Social Security program. The fear that other sources of retirement provision would displace Social Security helps explains why administrators simultaneously worked to retain the wage-relatedness of benefits (which hindered redistribution) and advocated a rise in the wage base to subject more earnings to taxation (which facilitated redistribution). In both cases, the principal aim was to make Social Security the primary source of retirement income for all but the highest earners, thereby protecting the program from political challenges and limiting the reach of private pensions, which were less redistributive than Social Security and distributed quite unevenly across the American workforce.

On the perceived need to make Social Security as attractive as possible for high-wage workers with access to private plans, see Domenico Gagliardo, *American Social Security* (New York: Harper, 1949), 133; Robert J. Lampman, "Should Old Age and Survivors Insurance Be Financed on a Pay-As-You-Go Basis?" *Pacific Northwest Industry*, March 1954, 105.

21. Quoted in Brown, "Bargaining for Social Rights," 666.
22. House Democrat Ray Madden of Indiana complained that Taft-Hartley's restrictions on union activity represented another step "toward increasing the demand for public support when the State refuses to private industry the power and right to help itself." Quoted in Stevens, "Labor Unions, Employee Benefits, and the Privatization of the American Welfare State," 251. The House Minority Report on the legislation declared: "Provisions which deny employers and organizations the opportunity to make voluntary provisions against illness and insecurity can only increase reliance upon the State." Quoted in Brown, "Bargaining for Social Rights," 668. In the Senate, where the House's outright ban on union bargaining over fringe benefits was removed, the rhetoric was no less jarring. New York Senator James Murray – one of the three namesakes of the Wagner-Murray-Dingell bill – argued that public policy should "encourage rather than confine or prohibit voluntary private plans aiding citizens by medical care, hospitalization, or other methods." After all, continued Murray, "these plans decrease the responsibility and burdens of the State. Legal restrictions or prohibitions would, on the other hand, tend to increase the public burden and responsibility and the dependence of the wage earner upon the State." Quoted in Brown, "Bargaining for Social Rights," 647.
23. "The decision was a preemptive strike launched by Paul Herzog, a New York lawyer with solid New Deal credentials and strong labor ties." Brown, "Bargaining for Social Rights," 669. *Inland Steel* was upheld by the

Seventh Circuit Court of Appeals, and the Supreme Court let it stand in *Inland Steel Co. v National Labor Relations Board*, 170 F2d 247 (1948).

24. U.S. Steel Industry Board, *Report to the President of the United States on the Labor Dispute in the Basic Steel Industry* (Washington, D.C.: U.S. GPO, 1949), 60–62.

25. Sass, *The Promise of Private Pensions*, 139.

26. Ibid., 140.

27. Michael K. Brown, *Race, Money, and the American Welfare State* (Ithaca, N.Y.: Cornell University Press, 1999), 184–94.

28. Social Security's broad eligibility and national operation made it much more gender neutral than other social policies. Suzanne Mettler, "The Stratification of Social Citizenship: Gender and Federalism in the Formation of Old Age Insurance and Aid to Dependent Children," *Journal of Policy History* 11, no. 1 (1999): 31–58. For a contrasting discussion that emphasizes how gendered the program nonetheless remained, see Alice Kessler-Harris, *In Pursuit of Equity: Women, Men, and the Quest for Economic Citizenship in 20th Century America* (Oxford: Oxford University Press), 117–69.

29. Derickson, "Health Security for All?" See also Marie Gottschalk, *The Shadow Welfare State: Labor, Business, and the Politics of Health Care in the United States* (Ithaca, N.Y.: Cornell University Press, 2000).

30. Lawrence S. Root, *Fringe Benefits: Social Insurance in the Steel Industry* (Beverly Hills, Calif.: Sage, 1982).

31. Ibid., 201.

32. Brown, "Bargaining for Social Rights," 658–59.

33. Stuart Butler and Peter Germanis, "Achieving Social Security Reform: A 'Leninist' Strategy," *Cato Journal* 3 (1983): 547–56.

34. Martha Derthick, *Policymaking for Social Security* (Washington, D.C.: Brookings Institution, 1979), 274.

35. Jacoby, *Modern Manors*, 268–69; Peter Swenson, "Arranged Alliances: Business Interests in the New Deal," *Politics and Society* 25 (1997): 66–67; Derthick, *Policymaking for Social Security*, 238–51; Marion B. Folsom, interview by Peter Corning, *The Eisenhower Administration Project*, pt. 3, no. 35, tape-recorded in 1968 (New York: Columbia University Oral History Collection, 1976).

36. Testimony of Herschel C. Atkinson to House Committee on Finance, *Social Security Revision Hearings on H.R. 6000*, 81st Cong., 2d sess., 1950, 1493–94.

37. Falk, "The UAW Trade Union Social Security Program."

38. Sass, *The Promise of Private Pensions*, 136–37.

39. Jennifer Lisa Klein, "Managing Security: The Business of American Social Policy, 1910s–1960," 415.

40. As Derthick argues, the appeal of the phrase "a floor of protection" to Social Security advocates was precisely its essential ambiguity, which threw off conservative opponents even as it left the door open for future benefit expansions. "Undoubtedly, its great attractiveness and usefulness,"

Wilburn Cohen claimed, "has been that it can mean different things to different people. Its value is what it conceals rather than what it reveals." Quoted in Derthick, *Policymaking for Social Security*, 271

41. Additional information supplied for the record by the testimony of Pacific Mutual Life Insurance Co. to Senate Committee on Finance, *Social Security Amendments of 1954 on H.R. 9366*, 83d Cong., 2d sess., 1954, 360; Testimony of Ira Mosher to Senate Committee on Finance, *Social Security Revision: Hearings on H.R. 6000*, 81st Cong., 2d sess., 1950, 2003, 2006.

42. Testimony of Ira Mosher to Senate Committee on Finance, *Social Security Revision*, 2004–5.

43. Julian E. Zelizer, "Where Is the Money Coming From? The Reconstruction of Social Security Finance, 1939–1950," *Journal of Policy History* 9 (Fall 1997): 399–424.

44. Dwight D. Eisenhower, *The Public Papers of the Presidents 1953* (Washington, D.C.: U.S. GPO, 1954), 32, item 6, 2 February 1953; Chamber of Commerce of the United States of America, *Improving Social Security* (Washington, D.C.: Chamber of Commerce, 1953).

45. "Private Rule Studied for Social Security," *New York Times*, 23 October 1953, A27.

46. Quoted in Derthick, *Policymaking for Social Security*, 286.

47. Jacoby, *Modern Manors*, 219; Testimony of Folsom to Senate Committee on Finance, *Social Security Revision: Hearings on H.R. 6000*, 81st Cong., 2d sess., 1950, 510–11.

48. Social Security Administration (SSA), *History of the Provisions of Old-Age, Survivors, Disability, and Health Insurance 1935–1996* (Washington, D.C.: SSA, 1997), 28–31; Wilbur J. Cohen and Robert J. Myers, "Social Security Act Amendments of 1950: A Summary and Legislative History," *Social Security Bulletin* (October 1950): 3–13.

49. Testimony of Biemiller to House Committee on Education and Labor, *Welfare and Pension Fund Legislation*, 85th Cong., 1st sess., June 1958, 166.

50. Testimony of E. S. Willis to House General Subcommittee on Labor of the Committee on Education and Labor, *Private Welfare and Pension Plan Legislation: Hearings on H.R. 1045*, 91st Cong., 1st and 2d sess., 1970, 550–51.

51. Quoted in Michael Gordon, "Introduction: The Social Policy Origins of ERISA," *Employee Benefits Law* (Washington, D.C.: Bureau of National Affairs, 1991), lxxi.

52. Peter F. Drucker, *The Unseen Revolution: How Pension Fund Socialism Came to America* (New York: Harper & Row, 1976), 46.

53. Quoted in Derthick, *Policymaking for Social Security*, 339.

54. Ibid., 296.

55. Ibid., 339–68.

56. Julian E. Zelizer, *Taxing America: Wilbur D. Mills, Congress, and the State, 1945–1975* (Cambridge: Cambridge University Press, 1998), 333–37; Derthick, *Policymaking for Social Security*, 358–62.

57. A revealing example is Wilbur Cohen to Richard Goodwin, "The Aboli-
tion of Poverty Among the Aged as Part of the President's Program for the
Aged," 19 June 1964, Cohen Papers, "Department of HEW," SSAHA. "In
this particular phase of the Nation's attack on poverty," Cohen writes, "we
do not need to seek for new approaches; we need only to complete the
job that was begun some 30 years ago and make social security a truly
effective device for the prevention and alleviation of poverty." Ibid., 1.
58. U.S. President's Committee on Corporate Pension Funds and Other Private
Retirement and Welfare Programs, *Public Policy and Private Pension
Programs: A Report to the President on Private Employee Retirement
Plans* (Washington, D.C.: U.S. GPO, 1965), viii.
59. Derthick, *Policymaking for Social Security,* 342; Robert Myers, *Within the
System: My Half Century in Social Security* (Winsted, Conn.: Actex Publi-
cations, 1992), chap. 7; Myers, "Concepts of Balance between OASDI
and Private Pension Benefits: A Partnership or, Instead, the Lion's Share
for OASDI?" *Social Security and Private Pension Plans: Competitive or
Complementary?* (Homewood, Ill.: Richard D. Irwin, Inc., 1977);
Myers to Robert H. Finch, 14 April 1970, "Robert Myers," Altmeyer
Papers, SSAHA; Altmeyer to Myers, 15 November. 1969, "Robert Myers,"
Altmeyer Papers, SSAHA; Myers to Altmeyer, 2 December 1969, "Robert
Myers," Altmeyer Papers, SSAHA.
60. Alicia H. Munnell, *The Economics of Private Pensions* (Washington, D.C.:
Brookings Institution, 1982), 28.
61. Patricia E. Dilley, "The Evolution of Entitlement: Retirement Income and
the Problem of Integrating Private Pensions and Social Security," *Loyola
of Los Angeles Law Review* 30 (1997): 1160–65.
62. If a pension plan did provide benefits to lower-paid workers, of course, the
replacement percentage for the better paid could be proportionately higher.
63. Stone to Gibb, "Summary of Principal Comments Received in Response
to Announcement 65–58," 28 September 1965, Box 106, File 4, "Social
Security – Integration with Pension Plans (2), 1965–66," Stanley S.
Surrey Papers, Harvard Law School, Cambridge, Mass.; "Taking a Cut at
Executive Pensions," *Business Week,* 26 November 1966, 180, 182.
64. Memorandum by Robert Feldergarden to Stuart E. Seigel, 10 November
1966, "Comments upon Announcements 66–58," Box 106, File 4, "Social
Security – Integration with Pension Plans (2), 1965–66," Surrey Papers.
65. Folsom to Henry H. Fowler, 28 November 1966, Box 106, File 4, "Social
Security – Integration with Pension Plans (2), 1965–66," Surrey Papers.
66. Wilbur Mills to Sheldon S. Cohen, 30 November 1966, Box 106, File 4,
"Social Security – Integration with Pension Plans (2), 1965–66," Surrey
Papers.
67. Confidential Memorandum by Robert M. Ball to Stanley Surrey, 31
October 1966, Box 113, File 1, "Social Security, 1962–67," Surrey Papers.
68. "Treasury Announces Final Regulations on Integration of Private Pension
Plans with Social Security Benefits," 12 November 1968, Box 107, File 1,
"Pension Plans – Integration with Social Security (4)," Surrey Papers, 2.

69. "New Rules for Pensions," *Business Week*, 13 July 1968, 39.

70. Memorandum by Gibb to Kurtz, Surrey, Halperin, and Brannon, 18 December 1967, Box 99, File 6, "Pensions 2, 1967–68," Surrey Papers; "NAM Employee Benefits Committee Views on Proposals to Regulate Private Pension Plans," n.d., Box 107, File 2, "Pensions – Cabinet Committee (2), 1964–67," Surrey Papers; "Tax Treatment of Private Pension Plans, a Report to the NAM Taxation Committee of its Subcommittee on General Tax Revision," 17 August 1965, Box 107, File 2, "Pensions – Cabinet Committee (2), 1964–67," Surrey Papers; Gibb to Surrey, "Pensions; reactions to Cabinet Committee Report; Legislative Possibilities," 28 July 1965, Box 107, File 2, "Pensions – Cabinet Committee (2), 1964–67," Surrey Papers; "Public Policy and Private Pension Programs: Controversial Issues and Anticipated Opposition," 9 June 1964, Box 107, File 2, "Pensions – Cabinet committee (2), 1964–67," Surrey Papers.

71. Sass, *The Promise of Private Pensions*, 213.

72. Quoted in James A. Wooten, "Regulating the 'Unseen Revolution': A Political History of the Employee Retirement Income Security Act of 1974," (typescript, State University of New York at Buffalo, School of Law, 2000), 1. I am grateful to Wooten for sharing with me his exhaustive and thoroughly researched manuscript, which represents the first comprehensive history of ERISA.

73. David Vogel, *Fluctuating Fortunes: The Political Power of Business in America* (New York: Basic Books, 1989), 93–112.

74. John W. Kingdon, *Agendas, Alternatives, and Public Policies* (Boston: Little Brown, 1984), 99–108.

75. Merton C. Bernstein, *The Future of Private Pensions* (New York: The Free Press, 1964).

76. James Q. Wilson, *The Politics of Regulation* (New York: Basic Books, 1980).

77. W. Elliot Brownlee, "Reflections on the History of Taxation," *Funding the Modern American State, 1941–1995*, ed. W. Elliot Brownlee (Washington, D.C.: Woodrow Wilson Center Press, 1996), 100.

78. U.S. President's Committee, *Public Policy and Private Pension Programs*, viii.

79. "A Note on the Tax Advantage of a Qualified Pension Plan," 16 March 1970, Office of Tax Policy, Subject Files, Box 47, NARA.

80. Senator Gaylord Nelson of Wisconsin, a Democrat who chaired the Select Committee on Small Business, was perhaps the most outspoken critic, arguing that "[n]o elected representative could successfully defend the proposition that in order to provide some retirement benefit for low income workers it is necessary to provide an unlimited amount of deferred compensation to highly paid executives." U.S. Senate Subcommittee on Labor of the Committee on Labor and Public Welfare, *Legislative History of the Employee Retirement Income Security Act of 1974*, 94th Cong., 2d sess., 1976, 1711. (Since this was essentially the policy before ERISA, apparently most could, at least to themselves.) Democratic Senator William Hathaway

of Maine similarly complained that "the estimated $4.2 billion in lost revenue which we would have under these pension plans . . . could be better spent directly to cover those people in the country who are making, say, up to $10,000 a year." U.S. Senate Subcommittee on Labor, *Legislative History of the Employee Retirement Income Security Act*, 1694.

81. G. Brannon, "Amending the Pension Rules in the Light of Why We Encourage Pensions," 1 February 1971, 9, Office of Tax Policy, Subject Files, Box 47, NARA.

82. Michael S. Gordon, "Overview: Why Was ERISA Enacted?" *The Employee Retirement Income Security Act: The First Decade*, report prepared for the Senate Special Committee on Aging, 98th Cong., 2d sess., 1984, Committee Print, 8.

83. Ibid., 24.

84. Michael Gordon, "Introduction," lxxxviii.

85. The House Labor Subcommittee chaired by Representative John Dent did briefly consider mandating minimum pension coverage, but the idea never made it beyond scattered trial balloons and internal discussions, primarily because it was recognized that the proposal was a political nonstarter. Not only did pension reformers realize that "employer resistance was likely to be fierce," but representatives of the steelworkers' union also pleaded "that it was more important to protect existing expectations than to expand coverage." Wooten, "Regulating the Unseen Revolution," 236–37.

86. Quoted in Michael S. Gordon, "Overview," 25.

87. Senate Subcommittee on Labor, *Legislative History of the Employee Retirement Income Security Act of 1974*, 1085.

88. President's Commission on Pension Policy, *Coming of Age: Toward a National Retirement Income Policy* (Washington, D.C.: U.S. GPO, 1981).

89. U.S. Senate Subcommittee on Labor, *Legislative History of the Employee Retirement Income Security Act of 1974*, 4747.

90. Ibid., 4775.

91. James M. Poterba, "The Growth of 401(K) Plans: Evidence and Implications," in *Public Policy toward Pensions*, ed. Sylvester J. Schieber and John B. Shoven (Cambridge, Mass.: The MIT Press, 1997), 186.

92. Stephen A. Woodbury and Douglas R. Bettinger, "The Decline of Fringe-Benefit Coverage in the 1980s," *Structural Changes in the U.S. Labor Markets: Causes and Consequences*, ed. Randall W. Eberts and Erica L. Groshen (Armonk, N.Y.: M. E. Sharpe, 1991), 105–38.

93. U.S. Department of Labor, Pension and Welfare Benefits Administration, *Trends in Pensions 1992* (Washington, D.C.: U.S. GPO, 1992), 62; Bureau of Labor Statistics, "Union Members in 1998," 25 January 1999, available from http://stats.bls.gov/newsrels.htm.

94. David E. Bloom and Richard B. Freeman, "The Fall in Private Pension Coverage in the U.S.," NBER Working Paper No. 3973 (Cambridge, Mass.: National Bureau of Economic Research, 1992).

95. In 1991, for example, workers with annual earnings below $10,000 had less than a 30 percent chance of working for an employer who sponsored a pension plan, and only a 10 percent chance of being included in an employer-provided plan. In contrast, 80 percent of workers with annual earnings above $50,000 were employed by firms that offered pensions, and more than 75 percent were included in a plan. Celia Silverman and Paul Yakoboski, "Public and Private Pensions Today: An Overview of the System," *Pension Funding and Taxation: Implications for Tomorrow*, ed. Dallas L. Salisbury and Nora Super Jones (Washington, D.C.: Employee Benefits Research Institute, 1994), 8.

96. Brooks Pierce, "Compensation Inequality," working paper, Bureau of Labor Statistics, Washington, D.C., 1998.

97. John R. Woods, "Pension Benefits among the Aged: Conflicting Measures, Unequal Distribution," *Social Security Bulletin* 59, no. 3 (1996): 4. The 1990 figure for occupational pensions actually represents an improvement over previous levels. In 1962, just 14 percent of aged units reported occupational pension income, compared with the 69 percent who received Social Security. U.S. Department of Labor, Pension, and Welfare Benefits Administration, *Trends in Pensions 1992*, 395.

98. Ibid., 6.

99. U.S. Department of Labor, Pension and Welfare Benefits Administration, *Trends in Pensions 1992*, 187.

100. U.S. Senate Subcommittee on Labor, *Legislative History of the Employee Retirement Income Security Act*, 3485.

101. Congressional Budget Office (CBO), *Tax Policy for Pensions and Other Retirement Savings* (Washington, D.C.: CBO, 1987), 109.

102. Peter R. Orzag, "Raising the Amount That Can Be Contributed to Roth IRAs: The Dangers in the Short Run and the Long Run" (Washington, D.C.: Center on Budget and Policy Priorities, 21 June 2000), 3.

103. Howard, *The Hidden Welfare State*, 135.

104. Paul C. Light, *Artful Work: The Politics of Social Security Reform* (New York: Random House, 1985).

105. Ibid., 105; Lou Cannon, *President Reagan: The Role of a Lifetime* (New York: Simon and Schuster, 1991), 245–53.

106. Light, *Artful Work*, 115.

107. David A. Stockman, *The Triumph of Politics: Why the Reagan Revolution Failed* (New York: Harper & Row, 1986), 193.

108. R. Douglas Arnold, *The Logic of Congressional Action* (New Haven, Conn.: Yale University Press, 1990), 73.

109. Paul Pierson, *Dismantling the Welfare State? Reagan, Thatcher, and the Politics of Retrenchment.* (Cambridge: Cambridge University Press, 1994), 53–73.

110. John Myles and Paul Pierson, "The Comparative Political Economy of Pension Reform," *The New Politics of the Welfare State*, ed. Paul Pierson (Oxford: Oxford University Press, 2001), 331.

111. R. Kent Weaver, "The Politics of Pensions: Lessons from Abroad," *Framing the Social Security Debate: Values, Politics, and Economics*, ed. R. Douglas Arnold, Michael J. Graetz, and Alicia H. Munnell (Washington, D.C.: Brookings Institution, 1998), 216.

112. For example, Birnbaum and Murray's well-regarded journalistic account, *Showdown at Gucci Gulch*, leaves the erroneous impression that both the Bradley-Gephardt and Treasury 1 proposals eliminated the special tax treatment of most employer-provided fringe benefits, including pensions. Jeffrey H. Birnbaum and Alan S. Murray, *Showdown at Gucci Gulch: Lawmakers, Lobbyists, and the Unlikely Triumph of Tax Reform* (New York: Random House, 1987), Appendix A, 56. The same problems crop up in political science studies of the 1986 Act, such as Timothy Conlan, Margaret Wrightson, and David Beam's *Taxing Choices*, which fails to mention pensions at all in its discussion of the tax treatment of employer-provided benefits. *Taxing Choices: The Politics of Tax Reform* (Washington, D.C.: CQ Press, 1989), 5, 22, 59–60, 76, 232. Perhaps these misunderstandings should be viewed as an indication of just how little recognized the pension tax expenditure is. Conlan, Wrightson, and Beam, for instance, describe health insurance as "the largest and politically most revered fringe benefit," even though the special tax treatment of qualified pension plans cost the federal government nearly three times as much when the Tax Reform Act was being considered. Conlan, Wrightson, and Beam, *Taxing Choices*, 60. More likely these oversights reflect the reality that policymakers never truly considered eliminating the pension tax exemption, despite its massive size. But this is an important outcome in itself, suggesting just how sacrosanct and taken for granted it had become.

113. The 1984 Treasury Department report stated flatly that the "current exclusions for employer-provided pension and profit-sharing plans are retained." United States Department of the Treasury, *Tax Reform for Fairness, Simplicity, and Economic Growth: The Treasury Department Report to the President* (Washington, D.C.: Office of the Secretary, Dept. of the Treasury, 1984), ix. Treasury 1 did, however, propose to close the door on 401(k) plans – a bold move that was not contained in either the Bradley-Gephardt or Kemp-Kasten proposals (and which did not make it into the final legislation).

114. Jeffrey H. Birnbaum and Alan S. Murray, *Showdown at Gucci Gulch*, 82.

115. Michael J. Graetz, "The Troubled Marriage of Retirement Security and Tax Policies," *University of Pennsylvania Law Review* 135 (Spring 1987): 908.

116. American Council of Life Insurance (ACLI), *Life Insurance Fact Book* (Washington, D.C., ACLI, 1973). U.S. House Committee on Ways and Means, *1998 Green Book* (Washington, D.C., U.S. GPO, 1998).

117. For similar reasons, Congress agreed to impose new restrictions on the total amount that could be put away in tax-favored 401(k) plans – a smaller change that also primarily affected upper-income taxpayers.

118. In fact, taxpayers who were not eligible for IRA deductions under the new rules could still make contributions that were allowed to accrue tax free; they simply lost the initial tax deduction.

119. Jerry A. Hausman and James A. Poterba, "Household Behavior and the Tax Reform Act of 1986," *Journal of Economic Perspectives* 1 (Summer 1987): 113–14.

120. The estimated revenue cost of IRAs fell from $10 billion in 1985 to $9.1 billion in 1990. Joint Committee on Taxation, *Estimates of Federal Tax Expenditures for Fiscal Years 1984–1989* (Washington, D.C.: U.S. GPO, 1984), Table 1; and *Estimates of Federal Tax Expenditures for Fiscal Years 1990–1994* (Washington, D.C.: U.S. GPO, 1989), Table 1.

121. Paul Pierson, "When Effect Becomes Cause: Policy Feedback and Political Change," *World Politics* 45 (1993): 608.

122. Christopher Howard, *The Hidden Welfare State: Tax Expenditures and Social Policy in the United States* (Princeton, N.J.: Princeton University Press, 1997), 132.

123. Iris J. Lav, "The Final Tax Bill: Assessing the Long-Term Costs and the Distribution of Tax Benefits," *A Center on Budget and Policy Priorities Report* (Washington, D.C.: Center on Budget and Policy Priorities, 1997).

124. The following account is drawn from Curtis Vosti, "Happy 10th Anniversary, 401(k)," *Pensions and Investments*, 28 October 1991, 17; James C. Males, "401(k) Plans and the GIC Revolution," *Pension World* 27, no. 4 (April 1991): 45–47; Gary G. Quintiere, "New Rules for Cafeteria Plans and Cash and Deferred Arrangements," *Revenue Act of 1978* (Washington, D.C.: American Law Institute, 1979); and Daniel M. Fox and Daniel C. Schaffer, "Tax Policy as Social Policy: Cafeteria Plans, 1978–1985," *Journal of Health Politics, Policy, and Law* 12 (1987): 609–69.

125. Ibid.

126. Joint Committee on Taxation, *General Explanation of the Revenue Act of 1978*, 95th Cong., 1979, Joint Committee Print, 84.

127. Even Benna later expressed amazement that the 401(k) provision had gone unnoticed: "You'd think something of this magnitude would have a political hero behind it, a champion. It didn't. It wasn't even intended." Albert B. Crenshaw, "401(k) Plans Provide Benefits for Wall Street as Well as Workers," *Washington Post*, 20 March 1999, E1.

128. "Economic Growth and Tax Reconciliation Act of 2001," Public Law No. 107–16, 7 June 2001, Title VI. Among other changes, the Act more than doubles the IRA contribution limits, increases the 401(k) limits significantly, and indexes both to inflation – all revisions of particular benefit to higher-income workers.

129. Jason Zweig, "Look Back and Learn," *Money* 28, no. 4 (1999): 94–95.

130. Criticizing the federal old-age insurance program, for example, Sylvester Schieber and John Shoven argue that "[w]hen workers get a quarterly statement with their 401(k) balance, they know that the money is theirs and protected by law. When, or if, they get a statement from Social Security, it is a promise of a benefit that Congress has specifically reserved the right to modify at any time it pleases." *The Real Deal: The History and Future of Social Security* (New Haven, Conn.: Yale University Press, 1990), 9. But, of course, Congress created 401(k) plans, and it is, in

principle, as free to alter the rules governing them as it is to change Social Security.

131. Stephen F. Venti and David A. Wise, "The Wealth of Cohorts: Retirement Saving and the Changing Assets of older Americans," in *Public Policy Toward Pensions*, ed. Sylvester J. Schieber and John B. Shoven (Cambridge, Mass.: MIT Press, 1997), 85–130.

132. Scheiber and Shoven, *The Real Deal*, 355.

133. Danny Hakim, "401(k) Accounts Are Losing Money for the First Time," *New York Times*, 9 July 2001, A1.

134. William F. Bassett, Michael J. Fleming, and Anthony P. Rodrigues, "How Workers Use 401(k) Plans: Their Participation, Contribution, and Withdrawal Decisions," *National Tax Journal* 51, (1998): 263–89.

135 The following paragraph draws on Steven Greenhouse, "Plan to Put Limits on 401(k) Holdings Draws Fire," *New York Times*, 9 February 2002, C1; and Albert B. Crenshaw, "A 401(k) Post-Mortem; After Enron, Emphasis on Company Stock Draws Scrutiny," 16 December 2001, H1.

136. Bassett, Fleming, and Rodrigues, "How Workers Use 401(k) Plans."

137. Butler and Germanis, "Achieving Social Security Reform: A 'Leninist' Strategy," *Cato Journal* 3 (1983): 551, 553.

138. For a recent overview of the effects of pensions and IRAs on other forms of savings, see William G. Gale, "The Effects of Pensions on Household Wealth: A Reevaluation of Theory and Evidence," *Journal of Political Economy* 106 (1998): 706–23. Gale finds that pensions have a surprisingly limited effect on overall savings.

Introduction to Part III

1. The Clinton reform effort has sparked a cottage industry of retrospective analyses. I have offered a general review and critique of them in "Learning from Defeat? Political Analysis and the Failure of Health Care Reform in the United States," *British Journal of Political Science* 30 (2000): 61–94. See also Nicholas Laham, *A Lost Cause: Bill Clinton's Campaign for National Health Insurance* (Westport, Conn.: Praeger, 1996); Carol S. and William G. Weissert, *Governing Health: The Politics of Health Policy* (Baltimore: Johns Hopkins University Press, 1996); Mark E. Rushefsky, *Politics, Power and Policy Making: The Case of Health Care Reform in the 1990s* (Armonk, N.Y.: M. E. Sharpe, 1998); Jacob S. Hacker, *The Road to Nowhere: The Genesis of President Clinton's Plan for Health Security* (Princeton, N.J.: Princeton University Press, 1997); Hugh Heclo, "Clinton's Health Reform in Historical Perspective," in *The Problem That Won't Go Away: Reforming U.S. Health Care Financing* (Washington, D.C.: The Brookings Institution, 1996); Theda Skocpol, *Boomerang: Clinton's Health Security Effort and the Turn against Government in U.S. Politics* (New York: W. W. Norton & Co., 1996); Haynes Bonner Johnson and David S. Broder, *The System: The American Way of Politics at the Breaking Point* (Boston: Little Brown, 1996); Sherry Glied, *Chronic Condition: Why*

Health Reform Fails (Cambridge, Mass.: Harvard University Press, 1997); Thomas E. Mann and Norman J. Ornstein, ed., *Intensive Care: How Congress Shapes Health Policy* (Washington, D.C.: Brookings Institution, 1995); Joseph White, *Competing Solutions: American Health Care Proposals and International Experience* (Washington, D.C.: Brookings Institution, 1995); and the series of essays collected in a special edition of the *Journal Health Politics, Policy, and Law* 20 (Summer 1995).

2. See, among many, Daniel M. Fox, *Health Policies, Health Politics: The British and American Experience, 1911–1965* (Princeton, N.J.: Princeton University Press, 1986); Colin Gordon, "Why No National Health Insurance in the United States? The Limits of Social Provision in War and Peace, 1941–1948," *Journal of Policy History* 9 (1997): 277–310; Jacob S. Hacker, "The Historical Logic of National Health Insurance: Structure and Sequence in the Development of British, Canadian, and U.S. Medical Policy," *Studies in American Political Development* 12 (Spring 1998): 57–130; Daniel S. Hirshfield, *The Lost Reform: The Campaign for Compulsory Health Insurance in the United States from 1932–1943* (Cambridge, Mass.: Harvard University Press, 1970); Antonia Maioni, *Parting at the Crossroads: The Emergence of Health Insurance in the United States and Canada* (Princeton: Princeton University Press, 1998); Theodore R. Marmor, *The Politics of Medicare*, 2d ed. (London: Routledge & K. Paul, 2000); Ronald L. Numbers, *Almost Persuaded: American Physicians and Compulsory Health Insurance, 1912–1920* (Baltimore: Johns Hopkins University Press, 1978); Monte M. Poen, *Harry S. Truman Versus the Medical Lobby: The Genesis of Medicare* (Columbia: University of Missouri Press, 1979); Michael D. Reagan, *The Accidental System: Health Care Policy in America* (Boulder, Colo.: Westview Press, 1999); Paul Starr, *The Social Transformation of American Medicine* (New York: Basic Books, 1982); Sven Steinmo and Jon Watts, "It's the Institutions, Stupid! Why Comprehensive National Health Insurance Always Fails in America," *Journal of Health Politics, Policy, and Law* 20 (1995): 329–72; and Carolyn J. Tuohy, *Accidental Logics: The Dynamics of Change in the Health Care Arena in the United States, Britain, and Canada* (Oxford: Oxford University Press, 1999).

3. See, for example, Peter Zweifel and Friedrich Breyer, *Health Economics* (Oxford: Oxford University Press, 1997); Cam Donaldson and Karen Gerard, *Economics of Health Care Financing: The Visible Hand* (London: Macmillan, 1993); and the exchange among Thomas Rice, Mark Pauly, Robert Evans, Martin Gaynor, and William Vogt in the *Journal of Health Politics, Policy, and Law* 22 (April 1997): 383–508.

4. Kenneth J. Arrow, "Uncertainty and the Welfare Economics of Medical Care," *American Economic Review* 53 (1963): 941–73.

5. Terry M. Moe, "The New Economics of Organization," *American Journal of Political Science* 28 (1984): 756.

6. With the rise of integrated health insurance arrangements, such as health maintenance organizations, the agent may very well be a health plan or

provider group, rather than an individual doctor (and the principal, an employer or group purchaser).

7. Tuohy, *Accidental Logics*, 11–19.

8. The Netherlands is something of an exception to this generalization. As the table indicates, roughly 30 percent of Dutch citizens obtain private health insurance for acute health care. All citizens, however, are covered against basic health expenses, and the Dutch public insurance system allows only upper-income citizens to opt out, while regulating health insurance to protect high-risk groups.

9. Ellen M. Immergut, *Health Politics: Interests and Institutions in Western Europe* (Cambridge: Cambridge University Press, 1992), 34–37.

10. Hacker, "The Historical Logic of National Health Insurance," 65–67.

11. See, for example, Margarita Esteves-Abe, Torben Iversen, and David Soskice, "Social Protection and the Formation of Skills: A Reinterpretation of the Welfare State" (paper presented at the Annual Meeting of the American Political Science Association, Atlanta, Georgia, September 1999); Isabela Mares, "Negotiated Risks: Employers' Role in Social Policy Development" (Ph.D. diss., Harvard University, 1998); Cathie Jo Martin and Duane Swank, "Employers and the Welfare State" (paper presented at the Annual Meeting of the American Political Science Association, Atlanta, Georgia, September 1999); Peter Swenson, "Arranged Alliances: Business Interests in the New Deal," *Politics and Society* 25 (1997): 66–116; Peter Swenson, "Bringing Capital Back In, or Social Democracy Reconsidered: Employer Power, Cross-Class Alliances, and Centralization of Industrial Relations in Denmark and Sweden," *World Politics* 43 (1991): 513–44.

12. Quoted in Marion B. Folsom, interview, *Social Security Administration Project*, pt. 3, no. 158, tape-recorded 9 June 1965 (New York: Columbia University Oral History Collection, 1976), p. 164 of typescript.

Chapter 4. Seeds of Exceptionalism: Public and Private Health Insurance Before 1945

1. The Marine Hospital Service would later become the U.S. Public Health Service and one of the few federal government sites for reformist agitation in health care in the early twentieth century.

2. Daniel T. Rodgers, *Atlantic Crossings: Social Politics in a Progressive Age* (Cambridge, Mass.: Harvard University Press, Belknap Press, 1998), 219–20; Charles R. Henderson, *Industrial Insurance in the United States* (Chicago: University of Chicago Press, 1911), 41–62. In a 1910 survey of U.S. fraternals, sickness and accident protection comprised less than 2 percent of spending – twenty-three cents a year per member – among the surveyed organizations. David T. Beito, *From Mutual Aid to the Welfare State: Fraternal Societies and Social Services, 1890–1967* (Chapel Hill: University of North Carolina Press, 2000), 218. Even among societies that provided sickness and accident protection, the benefits were extremely low,

averaging $1.34 a member in 1914. American Association for Labor Legislation (AALL), *Brief for Health Insurance* (New York: AALL, 1916), 203.

3. Viviana A. Rotman Zelizer, *Morals and Markets: The Development of Life Insurance in the United States* (New York: Columbia University Press, 1979).

4. Henderson, *Industrial Insurance*, 150.

5. Ibid., 149–51.

6. The three-fourths figure is from Rodgers, *Atlantic Crossings*, 262. In 1910, total life insurance in force amounted to $180 for every person in the United States. Shepard B. Clough, *A Century of American Life Insurance: A History of the Mutual Insurance Company of New York 1843–1943* (New York: Columbia University Press, 1946), 6. By contrast, as late as 1929, federal welfare expenditures had risen no higher than twenty-five cents per person. Edward Berkowitz and Kim McQuaid, *Creating the Welfare State: The Political Economy of Twentieth-Century Reform* (New York: Praeger, 1980), 66.

7. Henderson, *Industrial Insurance*, 116.

8. AALL, *Brief for Health Insurance*, 201.

9. Deltov Zöllner, "Germany," in *The Evolution of Social Insurance, 1881–1981*, ed. Peter A. Köhler, F. Zacher, and Martin Partington (New York: St. Martin's, 1982), 25–26.

10. Peter Flora and Jens Alber, "Modernization, Democratization, and the Development of Welfare States in Western Europe," ed. Peter Flora and Arnold J. Heidenheimer, *The Development of Welfare States in Europe and America* (New Brunswick, N.J.: Transaction Books, 1981), 51–52.

11. Rodgers, *Atlantic Crossings*, 28.

12. Ellen M. Immergut, *Health Politics: Interests and Institutions in Western Europe* (Cambridge: Cambridge University Press, 1992), 59.

13. David Brian Robertson, "The Bias of American Federalism: The Limits of Welfare State Development in the Progressive Era," *Journal of Policy History* 1 (1989): 261–91; David A. Moss, *Socializing Security: Progressive-Era Economists and the Origins of American Social Policy* (Cambridge, Mass.: Harvard University Press, 1996).

14. Indeed, among progressive activists, the passage of the British National Insurance Act of 1911 was watched closely, and in the years after, a number of books extolling the British legislation appeared in the United States – most notably, I. M. Rubinow, *Social Insurance with Special Reference to American Conditions* (New York: Henry Holt & Company, 1916). See also the discussion in Theda Skocpol, *Protecting Soldiers and Mothers: The Political Origins of Social Policy in the United States* (Cambridge, Mass.: Harvard University Press, 1992), 160–204.

15. Odin W. Anderson, *Health Services as a Growth Enterprise in the United States Since 1875* (Ann Arbor, Mich.: Health Administration Press, 1990), 69.

16. According to Lubove, "Employers condemned health insurance as un-American and inequitable, a further imposition on businessmen already

overladen with taxes. The unfair burden it imposed on employers would drive industry from the state." Roy Lubove, *The Struggle for Social Security, 1900–1935* (Pittsburgh, Penn.: University of Pittsburgh Press, 1968), 85.

17. Beito, *From Mutual Aid to the Welfare State*, 144–60.

18. Ibid., 63–86; Ronald L. Numbers, *Almost Persuaded: American Physicians and Compulsory Health Insurance, 1912–1920* (Baltimore: Johns Hopkins University Press, 1978), 75–84.

19. Paul Starr, *The Social Transformation of American Medicine* (New York: Basic Books, 1982), 253.

20. Numbers, *Almost Persuaded*, 91.

21. The American public's culturally grounded opposition to compulsory health insurance during this period has also been emphasized in many accounts, including Daniel S. Hirshfield, *The Lost Reform: The Campaign for Compulsory Health Insurance in the United States from 1932–1943* (Cambridge, Mass.: Harvard University Press, 1970); Daniel Levine, *Poverty and Society: The Growth of the American Welfare State in International Comparison* (New Brunswick, N.J.: Rutgers University Press, 1988), 167–179; and Lubove, *The Struggle for Social Security*. It is true that strong public support for the AALL campaign never existed. But there is no evidence that such support was of crucial importance in the passage of the National Insurance Act in Britain. The difference between Britain and the United States was that, for institutional reasons, the AALL campaign *needed* such support to have any chance of success. As for the results of the California referendum, it should only be noted that the referendum took place at the height of the war amid a fervent propaganda campaign against the bill, that referenda favor the organized over the apathetic, and, most important, that no such referenda were ever held or needed to be held in Britain, Canada, or many other European nations, and that where they were held, as in Switzerland, opponents of reform gained the upper hand. See, for example, Immergut, *Health Politics*, chap. 4; 129–78; Herbert Obinger, "Federalism, Direct Democracy, and Welfare State Development in Switzerland," *Journal of Public Policy* 18 (1998): 241–63.

22. On the fate of other social policy proposals, see I. M. Rubinow, "Public and Private Interests in Social Insurance," *American Labor Legislation Review* 21 (June 1931): 181–91; Skocpol, *Protecting Soldiers and Mothers*; Jacob S. Hacker and Paul Pierson, "Business Power and Social Policy: Employers and the Formation of the American Welfare State," *Politics & Society* (forthcoming); David Brian Robertson, "The Bias of American Federalism"; Moss, *Socializing Security*; Lubove, *The Struggle for Social Security*.

23. It was not then, as Daniel Rodgers supposes, the "field of interests" that principally lay behind the woes of social reformers before the New Deal. The "array of established interests" indeed made the task of the AALL considerably more difficult, but the central difference between the United States and Europe during this period was not the "configuration of interests" but

the constitution of political authority – and, in particular, America's decentralized federalism. Rodgers, *Atlantic Crossings*, 259, 265.

24. Anderson, *Health Services as a Growth Enterprise*, 3–24, 41–50.
25. Numbers, *Almost Persuaded*, 114.
26. Although direct provision of services was common among American fraternal organizations, such "lodge practice" was still far less prevalent than sickness insurance in Britain. Beito, *From Mutual Aid to the Welfare State*, 109–11.
27. Starr, *The Social Transformation of American Medicine*, 260.
28. Ibid., 273; Numbers, *Almost Persuaded*, 27.
29. Numbers, *Almost Persuaded*, 28.
30. Skocpol, *Protecting Soldiers and Mothers*, 55.
31. Starr, *The Social Transformation of American Medicine*, 260.
32. Quoted in Anderson, *Health Services as a Growth Enterprise*, 79.
33. Indeed, when in 1932 the privately funded Committee on the Costs of Medical Care (CCMC) recommended the encouragement of group practice and payment (while rejecting compulsory health insurance), the minority report supported by the AMA targeted its invective on the Committee's advocacy of organized physician groups rather than on its endorsement of voluntary health insurance. The recommendations and principal minority report of the CCMC are reprinted in Lewis E. Weeks and Howard J. Berman, *Shapers of American Health Care Policy: An Oral History* (Ann Arbor, Mich.: Health Administration Press, 1985), 269–76.
34. Helen H. Avnet, *Voluntary Medical Insurance in the United States: Major Trends and Current Problems* (New York: Medical Administration Services, 1944), 34–62; Starr, *The Social Transformation of American Medicine*, 306–9; Louis Schultz Reed, *Blue Cross and Medical Service Plans* (Washington, D.C.: Federal Security Agency, U.S. Public Health Service, 1947), pt. 2.
35. Robert Cunningham, *The Blues: A History of the Blue Cross and Blue Shield System* (DeKalb: Northern Illinois University Press, 1997), 42.
36. Moss, *Socializing Security*, 146.
37. The following discussion of group insurance draws on Avnet, *Voluntary Medical Insurance in the United States*; Starr, *The Social Transformation of American Medicine*; and U.S. Institute of Medicine Committee on Employer-Based Health Benefits, *Employment and Health Benefits: A Connection at Risk*, ed. Marilyn J. Field and Harold T. Shapiro (Washington, D.C.: National Academy Press, 1993).
38. Canada was another nation where employment-based group insurance gained considerable ground, as will be discussed in Chapter 5.
39. Avnet, *Voluntary Medical Insurance in the United States*, 8.
40. Frank R. Dobbin, "The Origins of Private Social Insurance: Public Policy and Fringe Benefits in America, 1920–1950," *American Journal of Sociology* 97 (1992): 1428.
41. Starr, *The Social Transformation of American Medicine*, 295.
42. Dobbin, "The Origins of Private Social Insurance," 1428, Table 1.

43. Ibid., 1428.

44. Edward Berman, "Report on Life Insurance with Special Reference to Industrial Insurance," 5, Unpublished Volumes of the CES, Vol. 6, Lateral Files, Social Security Administration Historical Archives (hereafter SSAHA), Baltimore, Md.

45. Ibid., 1430.

46. Starr, *The Social Transformation of American Medicine*, 295.

47. Indeed, a few key figures in the early years were even sympathetic to national health insurance, believing that widespread voluntary plans might be a first step toward a larger public-private partnership. Odin W. Anderson, *Blue Cross Since 1929: Accountability and the Public Trust* (Cambridge, Mass.: Ballinger Pub. Co., 1975), chap. 5.

48. Although official estimates of federal tax expenditures do not include revenue forgone due to the tax exemption of health care institutions, Pearl Richardson of the Congressional Budget Office estimates that the exemption cost the federal government $3 billion in lost corporate income taxes in 1992. *Health Care Trends and the Tax Treatment of Health Care Institutions* (Washington, D.C.: Congressional Budget Office, October 1994), Box 1.

49. Fredric R. Hedinger, *The Social Role of Blue Cross As a Device for Financing the Costs of Hospital Care: An Evaluation* (Iowa City: Graduate Program in Hospital and Health Administration, University of Iowa, 1966), 52.

50. Ibid., 17.

51. Ibid., 20–21.

52. Students of Blue Cross on both sides of the political spectrum have tended to romanticize the institution's origins – the right to laud the achievements of decentralized voluntary action, the left to tell a fall-from-grace story in which a grassroots communal initiative was subverted by greedy corporate interlopers. The worshipful and regretful interpretations are exemplified, respectively, by Odin W. Anderson, *Blue Cross Since 1929*; and Sylvia A. Law, *Blue Cross: What Went Wrong?* (New Haven, Conn.: Yale University Press, 1974).

53. Cunningham, *The Blues*, 19.

54. Ibid., 32.

55. U.S. Institute of Medicine Committee on Employer-Based Health Benefits, *Employment and Health Benefits*, 67–68; Cunningham, *The Blues*, 26, 98.

56. William E. Leuchtenburg, *Franklin D. Roosevelt and the New Deal, 1932–1940* (Ithaca, N.Y.: Cornell University Press, 1963).

57. Starr, *The Social Transformation of American Medicine*, 269.

58. Edwin E. Witte, *The Development of the Social Security Act* (Madison: University of Wisconsin Press, 1962), 184, 185, 188.

59. See, for example, Antonia Maioni, *Parting at the Crossroads: The Emergence of Health Insurance in the United States and Canada* (Princeton, N.J.: Princeton University Press, 1998), 35–46; Starr, *The Social Transformation of American Medicine*, 266–70; and Daniel S. Hirshfield, *The Lost*

Reform: The Campaign for Compulsory Health Insurance in the United States from 1932–1943 (Cambridge, Mass.: Harvard University Press, 1970), 71–99.

60. Edwin Amenta, *Bold Relief: Institutional Politics and the Origins of Modern American Social Policy* (Princeton, N.J.: Princeton University Press, 1998), 81.

61. Rodgers, *Atlantic Crossings*, 429.

62. Witte, "Report on Progress of Work," 25 September 1934, Materials Related to the CES, "Outlines of Work," Lateral Files, SSAHA; Technical Board on Economic Security, Minutes of the Meeting of the Executive Committee, 27 September 1934, Materials Related to the CES, "Committee Activities," SSAHA. I found these documents thanks to the careful review of the CES materials by Jaap Kooijman, "Condition Critical: The Exclusion of a National Health Insurance Program from the Social Security Act of 1935" (Ph.D. diss., University of Amsterdam, 1994), 33–34.

63. Isidore Sidney Falk, interview, *Social Security Administration Project*, pt. 3, no. 156, tape-recorded in 1965 (New York: Columbia University Oral History Collection, 1976), p. 11 of typescript; Starr, *The Social Transformation of American Medicine*, 267.

64. Quoted in Hirshfield, *The Lost Reform*, 47.

65. Kooijman, "Condition Critical," 36.

66. Sydenstricker to Witte, 21 February 1935, 2, General Records of the Executive Director and Staff, CES, Box 12, National Archives and Records Administration (hereafter NARA), College Park, Md.

67. Falk, interview, 122–23.

68. *Report to the President of the Committee of Economic Security* (Washington, D.C.: U.S. GPO, 1935), 41, reprinted in Alan Pifer and Forrest Chisman, ed., *The Report of the Committee on Economic Security and Other Basic Documents Relating to the Development of the Social Security Act: 50th Anniversary Edition* (Washington D.C.: National Conference on Social Welfare, 1985), 61.

69. Falk, interview, 41.

70. U.S. Institute of Medicine Committee on Employer-Based Health Benefits, *Employment and Health Benefits*, 66.

71. The only possible exception is Barbara Armstrong, who had been active in the campaign for compulsory health insurance in California. She, however, was a staff expert on old-age insurance, and not among the CES's top leadership.

72. The basic approach is outlined in the still-unpublished "Final Report on Risks to Economic Security Arising from Ill Health," 15 July 1935, Unpublished CES Studies, Vol. 7, Lateral Files, SSAHA.

73. Sydenstricker to Witte, 11 February 1935; Witte to Sydenstricker, 19 February 1935; Sydenstricker to Witte, 21 February 1935; Witte to Sydenstricker, 13 March 1935; Sydenstricker to Witte, 18 March 1935; Witte to Sydenstricker, 26 March 1935; General Records of the Executive Director and Staff, CES, Box 12, NARA.

74. Arthur Altmeyer, *Social Security Administration Project*, pt. 3, no. 156, tape-recorded in 1965 (New York: Columbia University Oral History Collection, 1976, 28–31; Falk, interview, 131–32; Altmeyer, "The Development and Status of Social Security in America," *Labor, Management, and Social Policy: Essays in the John R. Commons Tradition* (Madison: University of Wisconsin Press, 1963), 128.

75. Starr, *The Social Transformation of American Medicine*, 299–300.

76. Hirshfield, *The Lost Reform*, 61.

77. Roosevelt's reluctance to take up compulsory health insurance was, in fact, widely reported to have been reinforced by the interventions of noted brain surgeon Harvey Cushing, as well as of his personal physician.

78. Altmeyer, *Social Security Administration Project*, 30–31.

79. Wilbur J. Cohen, "The Social Security Act of 1935: Reflections Fifty Years Later," in Pifer and Chisman, ed., *The Report of the Committee on Economic Security*, 8.

80. Witte, *The Development of the Social Security Act*, 97.

81. Starr, *The Social Transformation of American Medicine*, 273.

82. "What Business Thinks," *Fortune*, October 1939, 52.

83. Altmeyer, *Social Security Administration Project*, 280.

84. Reed, *Blue Cross and Medical Service Plans*, 12.

85. U.S. Institute of Medicine Committee on Employer-Based Health Benefits, *Employment and Health Benefits*, 66.

86. For a moment in 1944, it looked as if this might change. In the precedent-shattering *South-Eastern Underwriter*, the Supreme Court declared that insurance was interstate commerce and thus fell under the regulatory powers of Congress. Congress quickly responded, however, by passing the McCarran-Fergusson Act, which returned to the states their primary regulatory role in the insurance field. This was how the situation stood until the passage of the Employee Retirement Income Security Act, the effects of which will be discussed in the next chapter.

87. Hedinger, *The Social Role of Blue Cross*, 51.

88. Anderson, *Blue Cross Since 1929*, 41. Efforts to encourage voluntary insurance do appear to have been successful at increasing coverage. Controlling for other factors, Melissa Thomasson finds that "insurance companies in states that had enacted enabling legislation . . . sold more health and accident insurance per capita than states that did not." Thomasson, "From Sickness to Health: The Twentieth Century Development of U.S. Health Insurance," Miami University (typescript), March 2000.

89. Cunningham, *The Blues*, 45.

90. Ibid., 52.

91. Starr, *The Social Transformation of American Medicine*, 308.

92. Marjorie Shearon, "A Review of State Legislation Relating to Medical Services and to Cash Payments for Disability, Proposed During 1939," *Social Security Bulletin* 3 (January 1940): 34.

93. Congressional Budget Office (CBO), *The Tax Treatment of Employment-Based Health Insurance* (Washington, D.C.: CBO, 1994), 5.

94. Jay A. Soled, "Taxation of Employer-Provided Health Coverage: Inclusion, Timing, and Policy Issues," *Virginia Tax Review* 15 (1996): 450.
95. "Taxation of Employee Accident and Health Plans Before and Under the 1954 Code," *Yale Law Journal* 64, no. 2 (1954): 222–47. For a statistical analysis of the effect of the 1954 codification that finds a significant positive effect on spending through employer-based coverage, see Melissa A. Thomasson, "The Importance of Group Coverage: How Tax Policy Shaped U.S. Health Insurance," *NBER Working Paper Series*, Working Paper 7543 (Cambridge, Mass.: National Bureau of Economic Research, 2000).
96. Blue Cross coverage calculated from Reed, *Blue Cross and Medical Service Plans*, 12. On the wage freeze, see Dobbin, "The Origins of Private Social Insurance," 1438.
97. Extreme but sadly typical is Regina Herzlinger's anti-insurance commentary: "How did the health care system get into this mess [i.e., insurance rather than direct consumer payment]? Two obscure, seemingly innocuous income tax code provisions have caused it. Eliminating them would eliminate the mess." *Market-Driven Health Care* (Reading, Mass.: Addison-Wesley, 1997), 250.

Chapter 5. The Elusive Cure: Public and Private Health Insurance After 1945

1. Alonzo L. Hamby, *Beyond the New Deal: Harry S. Truman and American Liberalism* (New York: Columbia University Press, 1973), 4.
2. Public hospitals for disabled veterans expanded dramatically during and after the war, and the federally funded Emergency Maternity and Infant Care program financed an impressive 1.3 million hospital cases for the wives and children of low-wage servicemen between 1943 and 1946. Robert Cunningham, *The Blues: A History of the Blue Cross and Blue Shield System* (DeKalb: Northern Illinois University Press, 1997), 61.
3. Hazel Erskine, "The Polls: Health Insurance," *Public Opinion Quarterly* 39 (1975), 135.
4. On the effects of World War II on U.S. social policy, see Bartholomew H. Sparrow, *From the Outside In: World War II and the American State* (Princeton, N.J.: Princeton University Press, 1996); Edwin Amenta and Theda Skocpol, "World War II and Social Provision," in *The Politics of Social Policy in the United States*, ed. Margaret Weir, Ann Shola Orloff, and Theda Skocpol (Princeton: Princeton University Press, 1988), 81–122; and Edwin Amenta, *Bold Relief: Institutional Politics and the Origins of Modern American Social Policy* (Princeton: Princeton University Press, 1998). On World War II's effects on European social policy, see John Dryzek and Robert E. Goodin, "Risk-Sharing and Social Justice: The Motivational Foundations of the Post-War Welfare State," *British Journal of Political Science* 16 (1986): 1–34.
5. Cunningham, *The Blues*, 61.

6. The British National Health Service nationalized the entire voluntary hospital industry, extended free general medical care to the whole of the British population, and set Britain apart as the first nation to create a comprehensive medical system "based not on the insurance principle, with entitlement following contributions, but on the national provision of services available to everyone." Rudolf Klein, *The Politics of the National Health Service*, 2d ed. (New York: Longman, 1989), 1.

7. The phrase is that of Daniel S. Hirshfield, *The Lost Reform: The Campaign for Compulsory Health Insurance in the United States from 1932–1943* (Cambridge, Mass.: Harvard University Press, 1970).

8. See Alan Brinkley, *The End of Reform: New Deal Liberalism in Recession and War* (New York: Vintage, 1995), 137–74.

9. After Republicans took over Congress in 1946, the House Subcommittee on Government Publicity and Propaganda chaired by Indiana Republican Forest A. Harness launched an investigation of the Federal Security Agency, charging that "known Communists and fellow-travelers within Federal agencies are at work with Federal funds in furtherance of the Moscow party line in this regard." Monte M. Poen, *Harry S. Truman Versus the Medical Lobby: The Genesis of Medicare* (Columbia: University of Missouri Press, 1979), 105. Similar claims were also made by Republican Robert Taft in hearings held in the Senate, which featured the Republican's newest "health consultant," Marjorie Shearon. A former Federal Security Agency employee, Shearon became one of the leading propagandists against the FSA and "socialized medicine." See Marjorie Shearon, *Socialized Medicine* (Washington, D.C.: The Shearon Medical Legislative Service, 1947); and the wrenching exchange between Cohen and Shearon in her regular publication *Challenges to Socialism*, 30 March 1960, 1, in which Shearon denounces Cohen for "working to foist upon the United States a program supported by the USSR, the Communist Party, USA, and the Socialist ILO" and criticizes Social Security for conducing "to the dissolution of the home, to immorality, to unethical conduct, to the weakening of family ties, to dependence on public charity, and to the ruination of our free enterprise system."

10. For the reasoning behind this choice, see Jason Solomon, "Fighting for Health Security: An Analysis of the Critical Decisions Presidents Make When Pursuing Legislative Initiatives" (senior thesis, Harvard College, March 1995).

11. In addition, federal grants would be given to the states to provide care to those not reached by the contributory program.

12. Richard E. Neustadt, "Congress and the Fair Deal: A Legislative Balance Sheet," in *Harry S. Truman and the Fair Deal*, ed. Alonzo L. Hamby (Lexington, Mass.: D.C. Heath, 1974), 16–42.

13. Quoted in Ibid., 59.

14. Poen, *Harry S. Truman Versus the Medical Lobby*, 164–65.

15. Ibid., 176; U.S. Senate Committee on Education and Labor, *National Health Program*, 79th Cong., 2d sess., 1946, parts 1–3; U.S. Senate

Subcommittee of the Committee on Labor and Public Welfare, *National Health Program: Hearings on S. 545 and S. 1320*, 80th Cong., 1st sess., 1947, parts 1–2; U.S. Senate Subcommitee of the Committee on Labor and Public Welfare, *National Health Program, 1949*, 81st Cong., 1st sess., 1949, parts 1–2.

16. James A. Morone, *The Democratic Wish: Popular Participation and the Limits of American Government* (New York: Basic Books, 1990), 259.

17. Nelson W. Polsby, "The Institutionalization of the U.S. House of Representatives," *American Political Science Review* 62 (1968): 144–68; Samuel Huntington, "Congressional Responses to the Twentieth Century," in *The Congress and America's Future*, ed. David B. Truman (Englewood Cliffs, N.J.: Prentice-Hall, 1965), 6–38.

18. David R. Mayhew, "Innovative Midterm Elections," Yale University, photocopy, 11.

19. C. Joseph Stetler, interview, *Social Security Administration Project*, tape-recorded 27 January 1966 (New York: Columbia University Oral History Collection, 1976), p. 32 of typescript.

20. Nelson H. Cruikshank, interview, *Social Security Administration Project*, pt. 3, no. 151, tape-recorded 18 November 1965 (New York: Columbia University Oral History Collection, 1976), 200.

21. Wilbur Cohen to Chris Cohen, 6 March 1963. This quotation is from extensive notes on Cohen's papers that were taken by Edward Berkowitz for his book, *Mr. Social Security: The Life of Wilbur Cohen* (Lawrence: University of Kansas Press, 1995). I am grateful to him for leaving them in the Social Security Administration Historical Archives (hereafter SSAHA) for other researchers to use.

22. The Wagner-Murray-Dingell bills contained such assistance, too, but as a constituent part of a larger effort to provide inclusive financial protection against the costs of medical care.

23. David R. Mayhew, *Congress: The Electoral Connection* (New Haven, Conn.: Yale University Press, 1974), 52–61.

24. Lawrence R. Jacobs, "Politics of America's Supply State: Health Reform and Technology," *Health Affairs* 14, no. 2 (Summer 1995): 143–57.

25. Senator Taft, for example, argued in 1949: "I cannot see any reason why with proper encouragement we cannot say that voluntary health insurance is available for anybody who wants it. The people who do not want it do not have to take it." U.S. Senate Subcommittee of the Committee on Labor and Public Welfare, *National Health Program, 1949*, 309.

26. Poen's standard historical account, for example, only devotes a page to the subject. Poen, *Harry S. Truman Versus the Medical Lobby: The Genesis of Medicare*, 67. See also Richard Harris, *A Sacred Trust* (New York: New American Library, 1966).

27. Isidore Sydney Falk, interview, *Social Security Administration Project*, pt. 3, no. 156, tape-recorded 28 July 1965 (New York: Columbia University Oral History Collection, 1976), 240.

28. Marion B. Folsom, interview, *Social Security Administration Project*, pt. 3, no. 158, tape-recorded 9 June 1965 (New York: Columbia University Oral History Collection, 1976), 164.

29. Vandenberg to Abraham Smith, 3 December 1945, *Arthur H. Vandenberg Papers: Correspondence, 1915–51*, Michigan Historical Collections of the University of Michigan, Ann Arbor.

30. The former initiative was sponsored by Alabama Democrat Lister Hill (of Hill-Burton fame) and Vermont Republican George Aiken and had the support of the American Hospital Association, which had helped draft it. Modeled after Hill-Burton, it would have provided federal funding and encouragement to the states to set up programs to pay private health premiums for those unable to afford them. According to Hill, the bill would not rely on "a strange and untried system of compulsion" but would build on "the tried and tested methods of American medical practice and the voluntary prepayment health insurance plans which more than a third of our people have found effective and trustworthy." Moreover, Hill argued that, like the War Risk Insurance Act, the bill would stimulate private purchase of health insurance by demonstrating the need for and effectiveness of private social protection. U.S. Senate Subcommittee of the Committee on Labor and Public Welfare, *National Health Program, 1949*, 141, 144. Surprisingly, the Flanders-Ives bill – prepared by a group of moderate Republicans, including Representative Richard Nixon and Senators Ralph Flanders of Vermont and Irving Ives of New York – went even further toward Truman's position, envisioning a regulated system of private insurance in which premiums would be scaled to income.

31. The logic of this position is outlined in " 'Universal' vs. 'Non-Universal' Coverage Under a National Health Bill – The Commissioner's Position," Social Security Administration (SSA), Division of Research and Statistics, General Correspondence, Box 3, National Archives and Records Administration (hereafter cited as NARA), College Park, Md.

32. Of the two alternatives, Hill-Aiken had the greatest chance of passage, supported as it was by most southern Democrats and the AHA. Yet Hill-Aiken was not only state based but also limited to the poor – two features that made its endorsement by Truman and organized labor inconceivable. The more difficult question is whether Flanders-Ives could have passed. Poen believes not. Poen, *Harry S. Truman Versus the Medical Lobby*, 228. Michael Brown, however, contends that it could have been enacted and that it would have "offered a real possibility for a system of universal health care." Truman's refusal to endorse Flanders-Ives, according to Brown, reflected labor opposition – which, in turn, "had more to do with the gains unions were making at the bargaining table than any hostility to the Flanders-Ives approach." Michael K. Brown, "Bargaining for Social Rights: Unions and the Emergence of Welfare Capitalism, 1945–52," *Political Science Quarterly* 112 (1997–98): 673. This argument faces three complications. First, Truman's refusal to back Flanders-Ives seems to have reflected partisan polarization and opposition to general-revenue financing

more than labor opposition. Poen, *Harry S. Truman Versus the Medical Lobby*, 171. Second, although organized labor was indeed distracted by the struggle over private benefits (as well as the campaign to repeal Taft-Hartley), the fate of collective bargaining over benefits was not secure until after the end of the steel strike in November 1949, and 1949 was the only year in which a legislative compromise had any chance of passage, because 1950 was an election year and because of the outbreak of the Korean War. At this time, American unions were still split over the effectiveness of bargaining, and many (especially within the AFL) still had their sights set on public legislation rather than private bargaining. Alan Derickson, "Health Security for All? Social Unionism and Universal Health Insurance, 1935–58," *Journal of American History* 80 (March 1994): 1352–53. Finally, organized labor's opposition to allowing private health insurance to be at the heart of a public program was principled as well as self-interested – a reflection of labor leaders' deep mistrust of private insurance involvement in public social protection, born both of social insurance philosophy and of the disastrous experience of privately delivered workmen's compensation. See the recollections of Nelson Cruikshank in Cruikshank, interview, 290–91; Lewis E. Weeks and Howard J. Berman, *Shapers of American Health Care Policy: An Oral History* (Ann Arbor, Mich.: Health Administration Press, 1985), 88. Nonetheless, Brown is surely correct that organized labor's failure to lower its sights greatly complicated the already difficult task of reaching compromise. This, as we shall see, would prove even more fateful in the 1970s.

33. The ad is reprinted in Frank D. Campion, *The AMA and U.S. Health Policy since 1940* (Chicago: Chicago Review Press, 1984), 150.

34. Ibid., 162.

35. Ibid., 162.

36. Poen, *Harry S. Truman Versus the Medical Lobby*, 151.

37. Paul Starr, *The Social Transformation of American Medicine* (New York: Basic Books, 1982), 288. See also Joseph G. LaPalombara, "Pressure, Propaganda, and Political Action in the Elections of 1950," *Journal of Politics* 14 (May 1952): 300–25.

38. Marion B. Folsom, interview, *The Eisenhower Administration Project*, pt. 3, no. 35, tape-recorded 10 January 1968 (New York: Columbia University Oral History Collection, 1976), 141–44.

39. Marion B. Folsom, "How to Pay the Hospital," *Atlantic Monthly* (June 1963): 79–82.

40. Poen, *Harry S. Truman Versus the Medical Lobby*, 84.

41. Folsom, interview, *Social Security Administration Project*, 179–85.

42. Quoted in Sheldon Glueck, *The Welfare State and the National Welfare; a Symposium on Some of the Threatening Tendencies of Our Times* (Cambridge, Mass.: Addison-Wesley Press, 1952), 288. An insurance industry executive noted, for example, that "some employers apparently hope to head off the Wagner-Murray-Dingell bill by establishing private health insurance plans now." Quoted in Brown, "Bargaining for Social Rights,"

652. For other similar assessments made at the time, see Colin Gordon, "Why No National Health Insurance in the United States? The Limits of Social Provision in War and Peace, 1941–1948," *Journal of Policy History* 9 (1997): 301.

43. Jill F. Bernstein, "Employee Benefits in the Welfare State: Great Britain and the United States since World War II" (Ph.D. diss., Columbia University, 1980), 293.

44. Gordon, "Why No National Health Insurance in the United States?" 302.

45. Frank R. Dobbin, "The Origins of Private Social Insurance: Public Policy and Fringe Benefits in America, 1920–1950," *American Journal of Sociology* 97 (1992): Table 1.

46. Health Insurance Association of America, *Source Book of Health Insurance Data* (New York: Health Insurance Association of America, 1996), 41; American Council of Life Insurance, *Life Insurance Fact Book* (Washington, D.C.: ACLI, 1996), Table 11.2. Of course, breadth of coverage does not tell us what business expenses were. Unfortunately, National Income and Product Account (NIPA) data on nonwage compensation are not complete before 1950, but in 1976, the SSA estimated employer contributions to private pension and profit-sharing plans for years as early in 1940. Alfred M. Skolnick, "Private Pension Plans, 1950–74," *Social Security Bulletin* 39 (1976): 3–17. In 1940, according to the SSA, employer contributions to private pensions were $180 million and pension benefits were $140 million – or about .34 percent and .25 percent of total compensation, respectively. In comparison, the NIPA data show that in 1950, when the Truman plan succumbed in Congress, employer contributions to health insurance were $745 million and health insurance benefits were $886 million – or about .48 percent and .57 percent of compensation, respectively. So even as late as 1940, employers were spending less on private pensions as a share of compensation than they were spending on health insurance in 1950.

47. Folsom interview, *Social Security Administration Project*, 179–85.

48. William Mitchell, interview, *The Eisenhower Administration Project*, tape-recorded 11 January 1968 (New York: Columbia University Oral History Collection, 1976), 129.

49. Sanford M. Jacoby, "Employers and the Welfare State: The Role of Marion B. Folsom," *Journal of American History* 80 (1993): 218–19; Folsom, interview, *Social Security Administration Project*, 66–74.

50. Brown, "Bargaining for Social Rights," 652; Derickson, "Health Security for All?" 1352.

51. Reinhard A. Hohaus, "Social Insurance in a Democracy," *General Proceedings of the 37th Annual Meeting of the American Life Convention* (Chicago: American Life Convention, 1942), 12, 15.

52. Meltz, "Labor Movements in Canada and the United States," *Challenges and Choices Facing American Labor*, ed. Thomas A. Kochan (Cambridge, Mass.: The MIT Press, 1985), 315–18; Lichenstein, "From Corporatism to Collective Bargaining," 125.

53. Quoted in Brown, "Bargaining for Social Rights," 653.
54. Starr, *The Social Transformation of American Medicine*, 312–13.
55. Calculated from Charles L. Dearing, *Industrial Pensions* (Washington, D.C.: Brookings Institution, 1954), 79.
56. Ibid., 278.
57. Brown, "Bargaining for Social Rights," 658.
58. See Derickson, "Health Security for All?"
59. Edward Berkowitz and Kim McQuaid, *Creating the Welfare State: The Political Economy of Twentieth-Century Reform* (New York: Praeger, 1988), 167.
60. Marie Gottschalk, "The Elusive Goal of Universal Health Care in the U.S.: Organized Labor and the Institutional Straightjacket of the Private Welfare State," *Journal of Policy History* 11 (1999): 372.
61. Harry Becker, "A New Proposal for National Health Insurance," 14 February 1949, 6, Murray Latimer Papers, Box 27, George Washington University, Washington, D.C.
62. Gordon, "Why No National Health Insurance in the United States?" 302.
63. Cruikshank, interview, 28.
64. Derickson, "Health Security for All?" 1355.
65. "[T]he labor movement said, 'Well, politically it is apparently impossible to get the other, but we're going to get what we can for our membership through the collective bargaining route and through nongovernment insurance. But this is going to prove . . . unsound for the older people. They're a high risk, low income group, and the nongovernmental insurance will never cover them.'" Cruikshank, interview, 15.
66. Erskine, "The Polls," 136.
67. Starr, *The Social Transformation of American Medicine*, 282. This, of course, was hardly a neutral description of national health insurance.
68. Campion, *The AMA and U.S. Health Policy since 1940*, 171.
69. Erskine, "The Polls: Health Insurance," 140.
70. Testimony of Claude Robinson to Senate Committee on Education and Labor, *National Health Program*, 73.
71. "Voluntary Prepayment Medical Care in Relation to a National Health Program," SSA, Division of Research and Statistics, Gen. Corr., Box 3, NARA; Arthur J. Altmeyer, "Possible modification of National Health Program (Summary notes on various items)," 16 December 1947, SSA, Division of Research and Statistics, Gen. Corr., Box 2, NARA; I. S. Falk to Mrs. Small, 19 January 1950, SSA, Division of Research and Statistics, Gen. Corr., 1946–50, Box 2, NARA.
72. Poen, *Harry S. Truman Versus the Medical Lobby*, 189–209. Ewing pointed to the head of New York's Blue Cross plan, Louis Pink, as the source of the idea. But while Pink's confession that Blue Cross had "no actuarial experience or data upon which [it] could formulate a program [for the aged]" probably reinforced Ewing's conviction that the elderly could not be effectively served by voluntary insurance, the idea of a limited proposal for the aged had already been seized upon by Altmeyer and

Cohen. Oscar Ross Ewing, interview, *Social Security Administration Project*, pt. 3, no. 155, tape-recorded 26 August 1966 (New York: Columbia University Oral History Collection, 1976), 75–77, quotation on 77.

73. Theodore R. Marmor, *The Politics of Medicare*, 2d ed. (London: Routledge & K. Paul, 2000), 11.

74. Ibid., 10–17, 25–27.

75. Ibid., 12–13.

76. Ibid., 15.

77. Wilbur Cohen, interview, *Social Security Administration Project*, pt. 4, no. 45, tape-recorded 20 July 1966 (New York: Columbia University Oral History Collection, 1976), 19.

78. Cruikshank interview, 71.

79. Wilbur Cohen, "Major Arguments in Favor of Providing Hospitalization Benefits for Old-Age and Survivors Insurance Beneficiaries," 16 August 1951, 1–2, "Health Insurance Considerations (1951–54) (1960–62)," Revolving Files, SSAHA.

80. Arthur Hess, interview, *Social Security Administration Project*, pt. 3, no. 160, tape recorded 22 March 1966 (New York: Columbia University Oral History Collection, 1976), 73.

81. For a more general discussion of Eisenhower's philosophy, see Robert Griffith, "Dwight D. Eisenhower and the Corporate Commonwealth," *American Historical Review* 87 (1982): 87–122.

82. The quotations are from, respectively, Dwight D. Eisenhower, *The Public Papers of the Presidents of the United States* (Washington, D.C.: U.S. GPO, 1954), 32 (Item 6, 2 February 1953), and *The Public Papers of the Presidents of the United States* (Washington, D.C.: U.S. GPO, 1955), 72 (Item 11, 8 January 1954).

83. In histories of U.S. social policy, the Eisenhower years are usually treated as an uneventful prelude to the activism of the 1960s. For example, Bruce Jansson's 371-page *The Reluctant Welfare State*, 2d ed. (Pacific Grove, Calif.: Brooks/Cole Publishing, 1993) – a standard social work text – devotes fewer than two pages to the Eisenhower presidency. See also Walter I. Trattner, *From Poor Law to Welfare State: A History of Social Welfare in America*, 4th ed. (New York: Free Press, 1989), 277–304, which mentions Eisenhower just once in passing.

84. Roswell Perkins, interview, *Social Security Administration Project*, pt. 4, no. 160, tape-recorded 2 April 1966 (New York: Columbia University Oral History Collection, 1976), 37. Another administration insider recalled: "I think there was a general feeling that unless there was substantial stimulation of the private health insurance business, not that carried on by insurance companies but also by Blue Cross, Blue Shield, and group practice prepayment plans, that there would not be the kind of universal coverage which would be necessary if some form of federal insurance wasn't to come into being." Allen Pond, interview, *Social Security Administration Project*, pt. 4, no. 164, tape-recorded 17 February 1966 (New York: Columbia University Oral History Collection, 1976), 2.

85. "The fires of enthusiasm . . . which have been kindled in favor of this bill would probably freeze water, would they not?" one conservative Democrat asked. James L. Sundquist, *Politics and Policy: The Eisenhower, Kennedy, and Johnson Years* (Washington, D.C.: Brookings Institution, 1968), 291–92.

86. "Taxation of Employee Accident and Health Plans Before and Under the 1954 Code," *Yale Law Journal* 64, no. 2 (1954): 222–47; Boris I. Bittker, "The Individual as Wage Earner," New York University Annual Institute on Federal Taxation, Vol. 11 (1952); "The Taxation of Fringe Benefits," Office of Tax Policy, Box 4, NARA.

87. Congressional Budget Office (CBO), *The Tax Treatment of Employment-Based Health Insurance* (Washington, D.C.: CBO, 1994), 5.

88. President's Budget Message of 1954, quoted in Jay A. Soled, "Taxation of Employer-Provided Health Coverage: Inclusion, Timing, and Policy Issues," *University of Virginia School of Law* 15 (1996): 451, fn. 19.

89. House Committee on Ways and Means, *General Revenue Revision*, 83d Cong., 1st sess., 1953, part 1; Testimony of Folsom to U.S. Senate Committee on Finance, *The Internal Revenue Code of 1954*, 83d Cong., 2d sess., 1954, parts 1–2.

90. House Committee on Ways and Means, *General Revenue Revision*, 114.

91. Ibid., 83.

92. "The Tax on Health," *Wall Street Journal*, 3 April 1953, quoted in U.S. Senate Committee on Finance, *The Internal Revenue Code of 1954*, 999.

93. "Memorandum of the Congress of Industrial Organizations in Support of the Principle that Employer Payments for the Cost of Group Hospitalization Medical and Like Benefits are not Taxable Income to the Employee," Office of Tax Policy, Box 4, NARA, 1.

94. Ibid., 19.

95. Ibid., 22; testimony of James B. Carey to Subcommittee on Health of the Committee on Labor and Public Welfare, *National Health Program, 1949*, 421.

96. The Advisory Group consisted of two life insurance representatives, a private benefits consultant, the vice president of Bankers Trust Co., benefits managers from Standard Oil and Armstrong Cork Company, and a lone academic from Yale's Department of Economics. The progress of the Treasury Department's deliberations are outlined in "Report of Meeting of the Advisory Group on Taxation of Retirement Income and Other Fringe Benefits," 9 June 1953, Office of Tax Policy, Box 4, NARA; Dan T. Smith to Mr. Gemmill and Mr. Oakes, 23 September 1953, Office of Tax Policy, Box 4, NARA; J. Pechman to Mr. Gemmill, 29 May 1953, Office of Tax Policy, Box 4, NARA; "Report of Meeting of the Advisory Group on Taxation of Retirement Income and Other Fringe Benefits," 19 May 1953, Office of Tax Policy, Box 4, NARA; "Advisory Group Retirement and Pension Plans and Fringe Benefits," 3 April 1953, Office of Tax Policy, Box 4, NARA; "Memoranda and Comments by Advisory Group," Office of Tax Policy, Subject Files, Box 59, NARA; "Summary of Meeting with the Advisory

Group on Fringe Benefits in Mr. Folsom's office on April 20, 1954," Office of Tax Policy, Subject Files, Box 59, NARA; "Report of Meeting of the Advisory Group on Taxation of Retirement Income and Other Fringe Benefits," 9 June 1953, Office of Tax Policy, Subject Files, Box 59, NARA.

97. Testimony of Folsom to Senate Committee on Finance, *The Internal Revenue Code of 1954*, 83d Cong., 2d sess., 1954, 115.

98. Joint Committee on Internal Revenue Taxation and the Department of the Treasury, *Internal Revenue Code of 1954: Comparison of the Principal Changes Made in the 1939 Code by H.R. 8300 After Action by House, Senate, and Conference*, 83d Cong., 13 August 1954, 8–9. Business leaders made the basis of their opposition to the nondiscrimination rules clear: "Plainly, there is an historical pattern of disparate treatment in this field which is not present for pension plans." Business and Advisory Council Tax Committee, "Comments and Suggestions re. H.R. 8300," Office of Tax Policy, Subject Files, General Records of the Treasury, Box 7, NARA.

99. House Committee on Ways and Means, *General Revenue Revision*, 82.

100. Indeed, the Blue Cross association essentially wrote the legislation in the Senate Committee with jurisdiction and then lobbied for its passage. Not surprisingly, then, the FEHBP required that at least one service-benefit plan be offered, and it included criteria for the service-benefit option that only Blue Cross and Blue Shield plans could meet. The legislation guaranteed that the plans' administrative expenses would be covered; it provided a contingency reserve over which the Blue Cross Association and the National Association of Blue Shield Plans (NABSP) exercised control; and it provided a "risk charge" based on premium income that looked suspiciously like a guaranteed profit on FEHBP enrollees. Cunningham, *The Blues*, 111–14; Sylvia A. Law, *Blue Cross: What Went Wrong?* (New Haven, Conn.: Yale University Press, 1974), 50–58; A. G. Singsen, interview, *Social Security Administration Project*, tape-recorded 15 February 1967 (New York: Columbia University Oral History Collection, 1976); Walter J. McNerney, interview, *Social Security Administration Project*.

101. Cunningham, *The Blues*, 112.

102. Law, *Blue Cross: What Went Wrong?* 50.

103. Odin W. Anderson, *Changes in Family Medical Care Expenditures and Voluntary Health Insurance: A Five-Year Resurvey* (Cambridge, Mass.: Harvard University Press, 1963), 6–11; Starr, *The Social Transformation of American Medicine*, 334.

104. Marmor, *The Politics of Medicare*, 13.

105. Starr, *The Social Transformation of American Medicine*, 334.

106. And because private coverage drove up medical costs and drove out older, informal forms of charity care, those without private coverage were not just relatively disadvantaged but absolutely worse off than they had been before its expansion.

107. Cunningham, *The Blues*, 100.

108. Even organized labor, long supportive of a broad distribution of risks, "increasingly relied on experience rating as a tool to achieve lower

insurance rates for [union] members." Gottschalk, "The Elusive Goal of Universal Health Care in the U.S.," 383.

109. Folsom, interview, *Eisenhower Administration Project*, 141.

110. Cunningham, *The Blues*, 137.

111. Ibid., 134; McNerny, interview, 11–21; Singsen, interview, 9–13.

112. Marmor, *The Politics of Medicare*, 18; Folsom, interview, *Social Security Administration Project*, 182–85; Testimony of Leslie J. Dokovics to House Committee on Ways and Means, *Health Services for the Aged Under the Social Security Insurance System: Hearings on H.R.* 4222, 87th Cong., 1st sess., 1961, 370–73; testimony of John Joanis and Russell Hubbard to House Committee on Ways and Means, *Health Services for the Aged Under the Social Security Insurance System*, 87th Cong., 1st sess., 1961, 624–30; testimony of John E. Carroll to House Committee on Ways and Means, *Health Services for the Aged Under the Social Security Insurance System: Hearings on H.R.* 4222, 87th Cong., 1st sess., 1961, 1785–90.

113. Erskine, "The Polls," 131–33.

114. Elliott L. Richardson, interview, *Social Security Administration Project* (New York: Columbia University Oral History Collection, 1976), 51. Richardson would become HEW Secretary in 1970.

115. Marmor's classic account, *The Politics of Medicare*, for example, does not discuss Cohen's efforts to create an acceptable contracting-out provision or cash option. Nor does he mention the bipartisan Javits-Anderson bill, which was supported by Senator Clinton Anderson of New Mexico (who had introduced Kennedy's Medicare bill), had been drafted for Javits by AFL-CIO representatives hoping to reach a compromise, and was supported by forty-eight votes in the Senate in 1964. The bill would have allowed individuals to retain private group coverage after retirement, with either the sponsoring company or the insurance plan being directly reimbursed by Social Security. These events are also ignored by Martha Derthick's chapter on Medicare in *Policymaking for Social Security* (Washington, D.C.: Brookings Institution, 1979), 316–38. Weeks and Berman, *Shapers of American Health Care Policy*, 87–88; Folsom, "How to Pay the Hospital," 81; Jacob Koppell Javits, interview, *Social Security Administration Project*, pt. 3, no. 163, tape-recorded 16 March 1966 (New York: Columbia University Oral History Collection, 1976), 5–8; Katherine Ellickson, Personal Notes from Conversation with Nelson Rockefeller, in Katherine Ellickson, interview, *Social Security Administration Project*, pt. 4, no. 70, tape-recorded 15 February 1966 (New York: Columbia University Oral History Collection, 1976), M-1; AFL-CIO, "Why Commercial Insurance Carriers Should Not be Used in Insurance Health Benefits for Older People under OASDI," 4 March 1960, typescript, in Ellickson, interview, Z-8. A major barrier to the bill, besides Mill's insistence that any Medicare plan originate in the House, was the continued reluctance of private insurance companies to endorse a federal proposal, despite Javits's entreaties.

116. Cohen to Altmeyer, 9 September 1957, 2, Altmeyer Papers, "Program Proposals," Lateral Files, SSAHA.

117. Memorandum by Cohen to Theodore Sorenson, "Health Insurance Bill – Specifications – Option for Reimbursement to Private Plans," 28 June 1962, "Department of HEW"; Cohen to Sorenson, Memorandum, 29 June 1962, "Department of HEW"; Memorandum by Cohen to Sorenson, "Health Insurance – Option to Beneficiaries to Continue Private Health Insurance Protection," 11 July 1962, "Department of HEW"; "Meeting of Consultative Group on the Administration's Proposed Health Insurance Program for the Aged, 29 October 1962," n.d., "The Fifties"; Memorandum by Robert Ball to Anthony Celebrezze, "A Substitute for the OASDI Benefit Increase in House Bill Which Would Give the Individual a Choice Between Hospital Insurance and the Cash Benefit Increase," 13 July 1964, "Department of Health Education and Welfare"; all in Cohen Papers, Lateral Files, SSAHA.

118. Any insurance underwriting of federal benefits, the AFL-CIO insisted, was "in its essence . . . the use of governmental power to assure compulsory tax income to aid private enterprise, thus placing public power in the hands of private interests." AFL-CIO, "Why Commercial Insurance Carriers Should Not be Used," 2. See also Nelson Cruikshank, "Summary and Analysis of H.R. 11253, Introduced by Congressman Lindsay," 25 April 1962, "Department of HEW," Cohen Papers, Lateral Files, SSAHA. Again, the AFL-CIO position was born, in part, of labor's deep distaste of privately underwitten state workers' compensation programs.

119. Hess, interview, 57.

120. According to David R. Mayhew's study of legislative productivity, the 1965–66 legislative session produced twenty-two important laws, tying for first in the postwar era. *Divided We Govern* (New Haven, Conn.: Yale University Press, 1990). Using a somewhat different method, Sarah Binder finds that this legislative interlude resulted in the passage of more than 70 percent of the major items on the political agenda, the third-highest success rate in the postwar era. "The Dynamics of Legislative Gridlock, 1947–96," *American Political Science Review* 93 (September 1999): 519–34.

121. Marmor, *The Politics of Medicare*, 59.

122. Zelizer, *Taxing America*, 216–18.

123. Quoted in Morone, *The Democratic Wish*, 263.

124. The former figures are from ibid., 266; the latter, from Congressional Budget Office (CBO), *Trends in Health Spending: An Update* (Washington, D.C.: CBO, 1993), 76.

125. Carolyn J. Tuohy, *Accidental Logics: The Dynamics of Change in the Health Care Arena in the United States, Britain, and Canada* (Oxford: Oxford University Press, 1999), 47–50.

126. Malcolm G. Taylor, *Health Insurance and Canadian Public Policy: The Seven Decisions That Created the Canadian Health Insurance System and Their Outcomes*, 2d ed. (Kingston and Montreal: McGill University Press, 1987).

127. In Canada, as Antonia Maioni emphasizes, the 1960s "was a period of consolidating existing federal-provincial arrangements based on universal health insurance principles. The debate centered not on providing health insurance to certain groups, but on the extension of benefits beyond hospital insurance to cover the costs of medical services." Antonia Maioni, *Parting at the Crossroads: The Emergence of Health Insurance in the United States and Canada* (Princeton, N.J.: Princeton University Press, 1998), 119.

128. Quoted in Marmor, *The Politics of Medicare*, 40.

129. Testimony of Honorable Abraham Ribicoff to the House Committee on Ways and Means, *Health Services for the Aged Under the Social Security Insurance System: Hearings on H.R. 4222*, 87th Cong., 1st sess., 1961, 35–36.

130. Quoted in Maioni, *Parting at the Crossroads*, 141.

131. Wilbur J. Cohen, "Memorandum for Honorable Theodore Sorenson," 13 November 1963, "Department of Health, Education, and Welfare," SSA, Cohen Papers, 2; Wilbur J. Cohen, "Memorandum for Honorable Myer Feldman," 29 January 1964, "Department of Health, Education, and Welfare," SSA, Cohen Papers, NARA.

132. Flemming and Folsom, "Financing Health Care of the Aged – Guiding Principles for a National Program of Complementary Public and Private Action," *U.S. Subcommittee on Labor.*

133. Folsom, "Paying the Hospital," 82.

134. In 1999, 63 percent of Medicare beneficiaries had either individual or employer-sponsored supplemental insurance. Another 17 percent received supplemental benefits through private health plans contracting with Medicare, while 11 percent were assisted by Medicaid, leaving less than a tenth without any supplementary protection. The Century Foundation, *Medicare Reform: A Century Foundation Guide to the Issues* (New York: The Century Foundation, 2001), 10.

135. Irwin Wolkenstein, interview, *Social Security Administration Project*, tape-recorded 14 March 1966 (New York: Columbia University Oral History Collection, 1976), 135. The AFL-CIO's Cruikshank saw it as one of the many ironies of the Medicare battle that the AMA had fought Medicare while organized labor had supported it: "Medicare, since it did fill the remaining gap which could not be covered by the . . . non-government plans, meant that all the pressure was removed for national health insurance. Sometimes I used to be kind of amused about this. If we were really . . . basically consistent with our philosophy, the AMA would have wanted to pass Medicare, and I would have wanted to stop it. . . . Now that it's passed, I think all the pressure for national health insurance is removed. You see, it's not just that it fills the gap for the group of the population which non-governmental insurance could not fill, but it removes the intolerable burdens from the non-governmental health insurance. . . . In other words, what we were really doing was making voluntary insurance viable,

for all – shoring it up for almost all of the working population of the country." Cruikshank, interview, 391–92.

136. Arthur Altmeyer, interview, *Social Security Administration Project*, pt. 4, no. 4, tape-recorded 3 September 1965 (New York: Columbia University Oral History Collection, 1976), 19.

137. Memorandum by Cohen to Joseph Califano, "Child Health Insurance Plans," 10 January 1968, "Memoranda," Cohen Papers, Lateral Files, SSAHA.

138. Growth in real health spending per capita was 6.5 percent in the 1960s and 3.8 percent in the 1970s. Joseph Newhouse, "An Iconoclastic View of Health Cost Containment," *Health Affairs* supplement (1993): 156.

139. Starr, *The Social Transformation of American Medicine*, 411–17.

140. Mayhew, *Divided We Govern*, 82–84, 197.

141. One executive told *Business Week*: "If what I've been reading about health care in this country today is true, then standing up against a national health plan would be like arguing against God and motherhood. . . . My snap opinion is that a national plan would involve constantly escalating costs. But more important, a national plan would take away an item worth up to a cent an hour that you can now stack on the bargaining table." Quoted in Linda A. Bergthold, *Purchasing Power in Health: Business, the State, and Health Care Politics* (New Brunswick, N.J.: Rutgers University Press, 1990), 30.

142. Flint J. Wainess, "The Ways and Means of National Health Care Reform, 1974 and Beyond," *Journal of Health Politics, Policy, and Law* 24, no. 2 (April 1999): Table 1. Budget figures from Office of Management and Budget (OMB), *Budget of the United States Government, Fiscal Year 1998, Historical Tables* (Washington, D.C.: U.S. GPO, 1997), Table 3.1.

143. Wainess, "The Ways and Means of National Health Care Reform," 318.

144. Mark A. Peterson, "Congress in the 1990s: From Iron Triangles to Policy Networks," in *The Politics of Health Care Reform: Lessons from the Past, Prospects for the Future*, ed. James A. Morone and Gary S. Belkin (Durham, N.C.: Duke University Press, 1994), 125–31; David W. Rohde, *Parties and Leaders in the Postreform House* (Chicago: University of Chicago Press, 1991).

145. Anthony King, "The American Polity in the Late 1970s: Building Coalitions in the Sand," in *The New American Political System*, ed. Anthony King (Washington, D.C.: American Enterprise Institute, 1978), 287–305; Roger H. Davidson, "The New Centralization on Capitol Hill," *Review of Politics* 50 (1989): 350–51.

146. On the progress of ERISA case law, see Stephen F. Befort and Christopher J. Kopka, "The Sounds of Silence: The Libertarian Ethos of ERISA Preemption," *Florida Law Review* 52 (January 2000): 1–40; Catherine L. Fisk, "The Last Article About the Language of ERISA Preemption? A Case Study of the Failure of Textualism," *Harvard Journal on Legislation* 33 (Winter 1996): 35–103; Jack A. Rovner, "Federal Regulation Comes to Private

Health Care Financing: The Group Health Insurance Provisions of the Health Insurance Portability and Accountability Act of 1996," *Annals of Health Law* 7 (1998): 183–215; Troy Paredes, "Stop-Loss Insurance, State Regulation, and ERISA: Defining the Scope of Federal Preemption," *Harvard Journal on Legislation* 34 (Winter 1997): 239–92; Edward A. Zelinsky, "Travelers, Reasoned Textualism, and the New Jurisprudence of ERISA Preemption," *Cardozo Law Review* 21 (December 1999): 807–70; Dennis K. Schaeffer, "Insuring the Protection of ERISA Plan Participants: ERISA Preemption and the Federal Government's Duty to Regulate Self-Insured Health Plans," *Buffalo Law Review* 47 (Spring 1999): 1085–130; Carl A. Greci, "Use It and Lose It: The Employer's Absolute Right under ERISA Section 510 to Engage in Post-Claim Modifications of Employee Welfare Benefit Plans," *Indiana Law Journal* 68 (Winter 1992): 177–203; William M. Acker, Jr., "Can the Courts Rescue ERISA?" *Cumberland Law Review* 29 (1998–99): 285–300; Deborah Shelby Dees, "Overview of ERISA Provisions and Recent Legislation Governing Group Health Plans," *Mississippi Law Journal* 67 (Spring 1998): 695–757; Jason R. Yungtum, "COBRA and Preexisting Coverage after the Supreme Court's Decision in Geissal v. Moore Medical Corp.," *Creighton Law Review* 32 (June 1999): 1541–84.

147. "ERISA Sets Roadblocks for State Health Reform," *Medicine and Health* (15 June 1992), 3.

148. U.S. Institute of Medicine Committee on Employer-Based Health Benefits, *Employment and Health Benefits: A Connection at Risk*, ed. Marilyn J. Field and Harold T. Shapiro (Washington, D.C.: National Academy Press, 1993), 84.

149. This was how the effects of preemption were described by one of the original drafters of the clause. Daniel M. Fox and Daniel C. Schaffer, "Health Policy and ERISA: Interest Groups and Semipreemption," *Journal of Health Politics, Policy, and Law* 14 (1989): 240.

150. *Metropolitan Life Insurance v Massachusetts* 472 U.S. 724 (1985), 740. A District Court judge later opined: "Occasionally, a statute comes along that is so poorly contemplated by the draftspersons that it cannot be saved by judicial interpretation, innovation, or manipulation." Acker, "Can the Courts Rescue ERISA?" 285.

151. Fox and Schaffer, "Health Policy and ERISA," 247–57.

152. The following discussion of the genesis of the ERISA preemption clause draws on the perceptive interview-based account of Fox and Schaffer, "Tax Policy as Social Policy," as well as U.S. Senate Subcommittee on Labor of the Committee on Labor and Public Welfare, *Legislative History of the Employee Retirement Income Security Act of 1974* (Washington, D.C.: U.S. GPO, April 1976); Fisk, "The Last Article About the Language of Erisa Preemption?"; and Befort and Kopka, "The Sounds of Silence: The Libertarian Ethos of ERISA Preemption."

153. Fox and Schaffer, "Health Policy and ERISA," 241.

154. Ibid., 242.

155. In 1982, employers who offered health plans to their employees were required to cover certain workers who would otherwise be eligible for Medicare. In 1985, a last-minute amendment to the year's Consolidated Omnibus Budget Reconciliation Act required employers to offer, but not subsidize, continuing access to group health plans for workers leaving a job (the restrictions are known as the "COBRA requirements"). And in 1996, the Health Insurance Portability and Accountability Act placed new restrictions on the practices of self-insured plans to encourage portability of benefits across jobs and limit specific exclusions from coverage. At the same time, Congress added two specific benefit mandates – one requiring minimum levels of coverage for maternity care, the other seeking parity of coverage between mental health services and other medical treatment. These were all remarkably complex (and, at times, incoherent) laws filled with glaring loopholes and have provoked a continuing wave of litigation. But they do suggest some federal movement into the ERISA vacuum with the aim of regulating private health plans under federal law.

156. John Sheils and Paul Hogan, "Cost of Tax-Exempt Health Benefits in 1998," *Health Affairs*, 18, no. 2 (1999): 176–81.

157. Fox and Schaffer, "Tax Policy as Social Policy," 612.

158. Willis Goldbeck quoted in Thomas R. Oliver, "Health Care Market Reform in Congress: The Uncertain Path from Proposal to Policy," *Political Science Quarterly* 106 (1991): 465.

159. Cited in Fox and Schaffer, "Health Policy and ERISA," 615.

160. More recently, President Clinton considered taxing a portion of employer-provided health benefits in his failed Health Security plan, but he backed down from the goal of immediately taxing health benefits in the face of resistance from organized labor. Jacob S. Hacker, *The Road to Nowhere: The Genesis of President Clinton's Plan for Health Security* (Princeton, N.J.: Princeton University Press, 1997), 125, 150.

161. With the exception of Hawaii, which obtained a federal waiver from ERISA only because it had instituted a mandated benefits plan before the law took effect, the few states that have considered more ambitious reforms have found themselves unable to reach many of the privately insured within their borders.

162. Paul Ryscavage, *Income Inequality in America: An Analysis of Trends* (Armonk, N.Y.: M. E. Sharpe, 1999); Brooks Pierce, *Compensation Inequality* (Washington, D.C.: Bureau of Labor Statistics, 1998); Gregory Acs and Eugene Steurle, *Trends in the Distribution of Non-Wage Benefits and Total Compensation* (Washington D.C.: The Urban Institute, 1993); Acs and Steurle, "The Corporation as a Dispenser of Welfare and Security," *The American Corporation Today*, ed. Carl Kaysen (Oxford: Oxford University Press, 1996), 360–82.

163. Calculated from Jon R. Gabel, "Job-Based Health Insurance, 1977–1998: The Accidental System Under Scrutiny," *Health Affairs*, 18 (1999): 65, 72.

164. Calculated from ibid., 65.

165. On the last factor, see the persuasive analysis of Richard Kronick and Todd Gilmer, "Explaining The Decline In Health Insurance Coverage, 1979–1995," *Health Affairs*, 18 (1999): 30–47.

166. Jacob S. Hacker, "National Health Care Reform: An Idea Whose Time Came and Went," *Journal of Health Politics, Policy and Law* 21 (1996): 647–96.

167. For that, see Theda Skocpol, *Boomerang: Clinton's Health Security Effort and the Turn Against Government in U.S. Politics* (New York: Norton, 1996); Haynes Johnson and David S. Broder, *The System: The American Way of Politics at the Breaking Point* (New York: Little Brown, 1996).

168. Jacob S. Hacker, *The Road to Nowhere*, 14–15, 58–60, 86–99, 162–70.

169. Mark A. Peterson, "Introduction: Health Care into the Next Century," *Journal of Health Politics, Policy, and Law* 22 (1997): 297.

170. By the late 1990s, most state Medicaid programs had moved their beneficiaries into private health plans, and the proportion of Medicare beneficiaries enrolled in HMOs that contracted with the federal government had reached nearly a fifth, with conservatives calling for even more aggressive contracting out.

171. This is well illustrated by the contrasting records of the United States and Canada after 1971 – the year Canada consolidated its national insurance program. Although Canadian and U.S. levels of health spending followed almost identical paths for much of the twentieth century, they diverged in the early 1970s, and Canada now spends significantly less as a percentage of GDP than does the United States. The limits of Canadian cost control relative to the European experience are often noted. But, acting later, Canada institutionalized a much more costly medical system than did most European nations. The relevant comparison for judging Canadian success at controlling costs is the United States, and by this measure, Canadian national health insurance has had an impressive record.

172. Paul Pierson, *Dismantling the Welfare State? Reagan, Thatcher, and the Politics of Retrenchment* (Cambridge: Cambridge University Press, 1994).

173. On the difficulties of and preconditions for "entrepreneurial politics" of this sort, see James Q. Wilson, *Political Organization* (New York: Basic Books, 1973), 15–16.

174. The following paragraphs draw on John B. Judis, "Abandoned Surgery: Business and the Failure of Health Care Reform," *American Prospect* 6 (Spring 1995): 65–73; and Cathie Jo Martin, "Nature or Nurture? Sources of Firm Preference for National Health Reform," *American Political Science Review* 89 (December 1995): 898–913.

175. These large corporations were the backbone of the National Leadership Coalition for Health Care Reform, a coalition of employers and unions that included Bethlehem Steel, Chrysler, and General Electric.

176. Scott Greer and Peter Swenson, "Foul Weather Friends: Big Business and Health Care Reform in Historical Perspective," IPR Working Paper 00-30, Northwestern University, 2001.

177. Employee Benefits Research Institute, *Databook on Employee Benefits* (Washington, D.C.: EBRI, 1992), Table 6.23.
178. Robert E. Patricelli to Ira Magaziner, 10 May 1993, Ira Magaziner Papers, Records of the Interdepartmental Working Group, NARA.
179. Paul D. Pierson and R. Kent Weaver, "Imposing Losses in Pension Policy," *Do Institutions Matter? Government Capabilities in the United States and Abroad* (Washington, D.C.: Brookings Institution, 1993), 111–12; Duane Swank, "Political Institutions and Welfare Restructuring: The Impact of Institutions on Social Policy Change in Developed Democracies," in *The New Politics of the Welfare State,* ed. Paul Pierson (Oxford: Oxford University Press, 2001), 197–237; Paul Pierson, "Coping with Permanent Austerity: Welfare State Restructuring in Affluent Democracies," in *The New Politics of the Welfare State,* 430.
180. In the case of the Clinton plan at least, advocates of reform found it exceedingly difficult to coordinate their efforts around a single proposal, and legislators backed away from comprehensive measures as the 1994 elections approached for fear of individual electoral reprisals.
181. Sven Steinmo and Jon Watts, "It's the Institutions, Stupid! Why Comprehensive National Health Insurance Always Fails in America," *Journal of Health Politics, Policy and Law* 20 (1995): 329–72.

Chapter 6. The Formation of the American Welfare Regime

1. Paul Pierson, "Coping with Permanent Austerity: Welfare State Restructuring in Affluent Democracies," in *The New Politics of the Welfare State,* ed. Paul Pierson (Oxford: Oxford University Press, 2000), 410–56; Timothy M. Smeeding and Lee Rainwater, "Luxembourg Income Study Working Paper No. 266: Comparing Living Standards Across Nations: Real Incomes at the Top, the Bottom, and the Middle" (Maxwell School of Citizenship and Public Affairs, Syracuse University, 2001); John Stephens, Evelyne Huber, and Leonard Ray, "The Welfare State in Hard Times," in *Continuity and Change in Contemporary Capitalism,* ed. Herbert Kitschelt et al., 164–93; Richard Clayton and Jonas Pontusson, "Welfare-State Retrenchment Revisited: Entitlement Cuts, Public Sector Restructuring, and Inegalitarian Trends in Advanced Capitalist Societies," *World Politics* 51 (1988): 67–98.
2. See, in particular, Will Marshall and Martin Schram, eds., *Mandate for Change* (New York: Berkeley Books, 1993); David E. Osborne and Ted Gaebler, *Reinventing Government: How the Entrepreneurial Spirit Is Transforming the Public Sector* (New York: Plume, 1993); David E. Osborne and Peter Plastrik, *Banishing Bureaucracy: The Five Strategies for Reinventing Government* (Reading, Mass.: Addison Wesley Pub. Co, 1996).
3. Remarks by President George W. Bush to the United States Conference of Mayors, Detroit, Michigan, 25 June 2001 (Washington, D.C.: White House Office of the Press Secretary, 2001).
4. Democratic Leadership Council, "About the Third Way," Fact Sheet (Washington, D.C., 23 June 2000).

5. See Rudolf Klein and Ann Marie Rafferty, "Rorschach Politics: Tony Blair and the Third Way," *American Prospect* 45 (July–August 1999): 44–50; and Anthony Giddens, *The Third Way: The Renewal of Social Democracy* (Cambridge, U.K.: Polity Press, 1988), esp. 99–128.

6. President Bill Clinton, State of the Union Address, 27 January 1998.

7. Neil Gilbert and Barbara Gilbert, *The Enabling State: Modern Welfare Capitalism in America* (Oxford: Oxford University Press, 1989).

8. Gøsta Esping-Andersen, *The Three Worlds of Welfare Capitalism* (Princeton, N.J.: Princeton University Press, 1990). A recent comprehensive review of comparative and historical research on social policy, for example, makes no mention of private social benefits. It describes the goal of the field as "explaining differences in the adoption, the form, the extension and sometimes the retrenchment of major social programs." Edwin Amenta, "What We Know About the Development of Social Policy: Comparative and Historical Research in Comparative and Historical Perspective" (paper presented for the Project on Comparative-Historical Analysis at Brown University, Providence, Rhode Island, 28–29 April 2000), 2.

9. Martin Rein and Eskil Wadensjö, ed., *Enterprise and the Welfare State* (Cheltenham, U.K.: Edward Elgar, 1999), xvi.

10. My research, however, offers two salient cautions to those who would look solely at antipoverty policy to explore the past and future direction of social policy in the United States. Not only do antipoverty programs make up a small part of the American welfare regime, but in addition, the issues of privatization that are discussed in the antipoverty area mainly concern the costs and benefits of government contracting. This is an extremely narrow focus that ignores both the extensive realm of social policy that falls outside the antipoverty ambit and the extensive range of policy instruments besides contracting that bring government into contact and collaboration with private forms of social provision. See my discussion in the notes to the Introduction to Part I, in which I point out that although nonprofits deliver many government-funded social services in the United States, their actual social spending is relatively modest compared with the expenditures of either government programs or employer-provided insurance. See also Steven Rathgeb Smith and Michael Lipsky, *Nonprofits for Hire: The Welfare State in the Age of Contracting* (Cambridge, Mass.: Harvard University Press, 1993); Michael Sosin, *Private Benefits: Material Assistance in the Private Sector* (Orlando, Fla.: Academic Press, 1986); Kathryn Edin, "The Private Safety Net: The Role of Charitable Organizations in the Lives of the Poor," *Housing Policy Debate* 9, no. 3 (1998): 541–73; and Lester M. Salamon, "Government and the Voluntary Sector in an Era of Retrenchment: The American Experience," *Journal of Public Policy* 6 (1985): 1–19.

11. Edwin Amenta and Theda Skocpol, "Redefining the New Deal: World War II and the Development of Social Provision in the United States," in *The Politics of Social Policy in the United States*, ed. Margaret Weir, Ann Shola Orloff, and Theda Skocpol (Princeton, N.J.: Princeton University Press, 1988), 118.

12. Edwin Amenta, *Bold Relief: Institutional Politics and the Origins of Modern American Social Policy* (Princeton, N.J.: Princeton University Press, 1998), chap. 5; Paul Frymer, *Uneasy Alliances: Race and Party Competition in America* (Princeton: Princeton University Press, 1999).

13. Steven M. Teles, *Whose Welfare? AFDC and Elite Politics* (Lawrence: University Press of Kansas, 1998).

14. Paul Pierson, "When Effect Becomes Cause: Policy Feedback and Political Change," *World Politics* 45 (1993): 595–628.

15. Richard Rose and Phillip L. Davies, *Inheritance in Public Policy: Change Without Choice in Britain* (New Haven, Conn.: Yale University Press, 1994).

16. See Paul D. Pierson and R. Kent Weaver, "Imposing Losses in Pension Policy," in *Do Institutions Matter? Government Capabilities in the United States and Abroad*, ed. R. Kent Weaver and Bert A. Rockman (Washington, D.C.: The Brookings Institution, 1993), 110–50.

17. Robert A. Dahl, *Dilemmas of Pluralist Democracy: Autonomy vs. Control* (New Haven, Conn.: Yale University Press, 1982).

18. Here I am indebted to Christopher Howard's *The Hidden Welfare State* (Princeton, N.J.: Princeton University Press, 1997), which emphasizes the unusual political characteristics of tax expenditures.

19. R. Kent Weaver, "The Politics of Blame-Avoidance," *Journal of Public Policy* 6 (1986): 371–98.

20. Paul Light, *Artful Work: The Politics of Social Security Reform* (New York: Random House, 1985); R. Douglas Arnold, *The Logic of Congressional Action* (New Haven, Conn.: Yale University Press, 1990), 210–23.

21. Howard, *The Hidden Welfare State*, 183–85.

22. This is the essential point of the theories of "incrementalism" that have had a prominent place in the study of American politics. See, for example, Charles E. Lindblom, "The Science of Muddling Through," *Public Administration Review* 19 (1959): 79–88; Charles E. Lindblom, *Intelligence of Democracy: Decision-Making Through Mutual Adjustment* (New York: Free Press, 1965); and Aaron Wildavsky, *The Politics of the Budgetary Process* (Boston: Little Brown, 1964).

23. For relatively accessible introductions to the new institutional economics, see Oliver E. Williamson, "Transaction Costs Economics and Organization Theory," *Industrial and Corporate Change* 2 (1993): 107–56; and Terry M. Moe, "The New Economics of Organization," *American Journal of Political Science* 28 (1984): 739–77. A sophisticated application to public bureaucracies is Murray J. Horn, *The Political Economy of Public Administration* (Cambridge: Cambridge University Press, 1995).

24. On state capacity, see Peter B. Evans, Dietrich Rueschemeyer, and Theda Skocpol, eds., *Bringing the State Back In* (Cambridge: Cambridge University Press, 1985).

25. As Social Security Deputy Commissioner Arthur Hess recalled: "[T]he decision to bring the states into the disability picture and the decision to bring

the states and the intermediaries into the Medicare picture were in considerable part motivated by the practicalities of the legislative situation and not entirely because somebody thought as a philosophy of public administration or political science that this was the way to set it up. . . . But on the other hand, many of us felt . . . that the problems that were involved in moving into the health care field or into relations with physicians . . . really involve issues that many existing state or voluntary organizations have faced. Moreover, these are issues they have to continue to face as part of their involvement in the mainstream of health insurance or medical insurance reimbursement and hospital cost reimbursement, and so it was felt that there were some real advantages, at least initial advantages, that come to disability insurance but most emphatically to the health insurance programs by adopting this pattern." Arthur Hess, interview, *Social Security Administration Project*, pt. 3, no. 160, tape-recorded 22 March 1966 (New York: Columbia University Oral History Collection, 1976), pp. 47–48 of typescript.

26. Arnold, *The Logic of Congressional Action*, 73–74.

27. See, for example, Cathie Jo Martin and Duane Swank, "Employers and the Welfare State" (paper presented at the Annual Meeting of the American Political Science Association, Atlanta, Georgia, September 1999); David Vogel, *Fluctuating Fortunes: The Political Power of Business in America* (New York: Basic Books, 1989).

28. Paul Pierson, "The New Politics of the Welfare State," *World Politics* 48 (January 1996): 143–44.

29. Switzerland is another nation where the state had to contend with "interests accumulated around . . . decentralized social security arrangements" and ended up with "a peculiar public-private mix," though one that features more active governmental oversight and control of private social insurance. Not surprisingly, it also has one of the most fragmented political structures in the advanced industrial world, featuring both strong federalism and a much-used popular referendum process that "decisively blocked the early take-off of the Swiss welfare state." Herbert Obinger, "Federalism, Direct Democracy, and Welfare State Development in Switzerland," *Journal of Public Policy* 18 (2000): 248, 259, 243. See also Ellen M. Immergut, *Health Politics: Interests and Institutions in Western Europe* (Cambridge: Cambridge University Press, 1992), 129–78.

30. Nor has *retrenchment* of the welfare state always been unpopular. In the mid-1990s, there was strong public support for welfare reform (though for reforms less punitive and more expansive than those achieved). See R. Kent Weaver, *Ending Welfare As We Know It* (Washington, D.C.: Brookings Institution, 2000); Teles, *Whose Welfare? AFDC and Elite Politics* (Lawrence: University of Kansas Press, 1996).

31. In the Netherlands, it is true, roughly 30 percent of the population obtains private health insurance for acute health care. All citizens, however, are covered against basic health expenses. Moreover, the Dutch system leaves out only upper-income citizens who are fully capable of purchasing

insurance on their own, and it regulates health insurance heavily, requiring, for example, that private insurers provide basic insurance at below-cost premiums to high-risk groups.

32. This has been the dominant approach in journalistic analyses of American health politics, such as Richard Harris, *A Sacred Trust* (New York: New American Library, 1966).

33. Immergut, *Health Politics*.

34. See, in particular, Jacob S. Hacker, "The Historical Logic of National Health Insurance: Structure and Sequence in the Development of British, Canadian, and U.S. Medical Policy," *Studies in American Political Development* 12 (1998): 57-130; Immergut, *Health Politics*; Antonia Maioni, *Parting at the Crossroads: The Emergence of Health Insurance in the United States and Canada* (Princeton, N.J.: Princeton University Press, 1998); Carolyn J. Tuohy, *Accidental Logics: The Dynamics of Change in the Health Care Arena in the United States, Britain, and Canada* (Oxford: Oxford University Press, 1999).

35. Hacker, "The Historical Logic of National Health Insurance." See also Paul Starr, *The Social Transformation of American Medicine: The Rise of a Sovereign Profession and the Making of a Vast Industry* (New York: Basic Books, 1982).

36. Marie Gottschalk, "The Elusive Goal of Universal Health Care in the U.S.: Organized Labor and the Institutional Straightjacket of the Private Welfare State," *Journal of Policy History* 11 (1999): 367-98.

37. It might be argued that the greater propensity to regulate private pensions is a reflection of the more unequal distribution of employer-provided retirement plans. Yet, according to data assembled by Brooks Pierce, private health insurance actually contributes more to inequality of compensation (wages plus benefits) in the bottom half of the wage distribution. (Because health insurance is a relatively fixed cost, it does not add much to compensation inequality at the top of the wage scale – and, indeed, slightly reduces it at the very top.) Moreover, Pierce's data show that the value of health insurance benefits varies much more *within* firms than does the value of retirement benefits. Finally, health insurance is the largest fringe benefit cost to firms, so any inequality in its distribution influences total compensation inequality by a proportionately larger amount. Brooks Pierce, "Compensation Inequality," working paper, Bureau of Labor Statistics, Washington, D.C., 1998, 7, Table 1, Table 6.

38. Hacker, "The Historical Logic of National Health Insurance."

39. Willem Adema and Marcel Einerhand, "The Growing Role of Private Social Benefits," Labour Market and Social Policy – Occasional Papers No. 32 (Paris: Organization for Economic Cooperation and Development, 1998).

40. See note 19 in the Introduction to Part I for an overview of recent scholarship on public–private interplay.

41. General reviews of the new institutionalism include Horn, *The Political Economy of Public Administration*; Peter Hall and Rosemary Taylor,

"Political Science and the Three New Institutionalisms," *Political Studies* 44 (1996): 936–57.

42. Even within political science, two overlapping approaches have coexisted since the late 1970s: "rational-choice institutionalism" and "historical institutionalism." Rational-choice institutionalism has been principally concerned with the ways in which institutions coordinate collective action and structure highly individualized strategic interactions. See, for example, Keith Krehbiel, *Information and Legislative Organization* (Ann Arbor: University of Michigan Press, 1991); Kenneth A. Shepsle and Barry R. Weingast, "The Institutional Foundations of Committee Power," *American Political Science Review* 81 (1987): 85–104; Kenneth A. Shepsle, "Institutional Arrangements and Equilibrium in Multidimensional Voting Models," *American Journal of Political Science* 2 (1979): 27–59; and William Riker, "Implications from the Disequilibrium of Majority Rule for the Study of Institutions," *American Political Science Review* 74 (1980): 432–47. By contrast, historical institutionalism has been principally concerned with the ways in which institutions alter the overall distribution of political power, shape individual and group preferences, and mediate between broad social demands and eventual policy outcomes. In addition to the general surveys cited previously, see Paul Pierson and Theda Skocpol, "Historical Institutionalism in Contemporary Political Science" (paper presented at the Annual Meeting of the American Political Science Association, Washington, D.C., 30 August–2 September 2000); Kathleen Thelen, "Historical Institutionalism in Comparative Politics," *Annual Review of Political Science* 2 (1999): 369–404; Evans, Rueschemeyer, and Skocpol, eds., *Bringing the State Back In*; Peter A. Hall, *Governing the Economy: The Politics of State Intervention in Britain and France* (Cambridge, U.K.: Polity Press, 1986); Sven Steinmo, Kathleen Thelen, and Frank Longstreth, eds., *Structuring Politics: Historical Institutionalism in Comparative Analysis* (Cambridge: Cambridge University Press, 1992).

43. R. Kent Weaver and Bert A. Rockman, "Assessing the Effects of Institutions," in *Do Institutions Matter? Government Capabilities in the United States and Abroad*, 39. For a recent application of the institutional perspective to electoral competition (an application that bridges, to an extent, rational choice and historical work), see Gary Cox, *Making Votes Count: Strategic Coordination in the World's Electoral Systems* (Cambridge: Cambridge University Press, 1997).

44. Margaret Weir, *Politics and Jobs: The Boundaries of Employment Policy in the United States* (Princeton, N.J.: Princeton University Press, 1992); Margaret Weir and Theda Skocpol, "State Structures and the Possibilities for 'Keynesian' Responses to the Great Depression in Sweden, Britain, and the United States," in *Bringing the State Back In*.

45. Theda Skocpol, "Political Response to Capitalist Crisis: Neo-Marxist Theories of the State and the Case of the New Deal," in *The New Deal*, ed. Melvyn Dubofsky and Stephen Burwood (New York: Garland Publishing, Inc., 1990), 238–84. Theda Skocpol, *Protecting Soldiers and Mothers: The*

Political Origins of Social Policy in the United States (Cambridge, Mass.: Harvard University Press, Belknap Press, 1992).

46. The term is that of Immergut, *Health Politics*, 26–29.

47. Duane Swank, "Political Institutions and Welfare State Restructuring: The Impact of Institutions on Social Policy Change in Developed Democracies," in *The New Politics of the Welfare State*, 210. Like other statistical studies, Swank's analysis examines the effect of political institutions only on public social provision.

48. On "strong" and "weak" states, see Peter Katzenstein, ed., *Between Power and Plenty* (Madison: University of Wisconsin Press, 1978); and John Zysman, *Governments, Markets and Growth: Financial Systems and the Politics of Industrial Change* (Ithaca, N.Y.: Cornell University Press, 1983). On social-democratic versus liberal welfare-state regimes, see Esping-Andersen, *The Three Worlds of Welfare Capitalism.*

49. These pioneering studies include Christopher Howard, *The Hidden Welfare State*; Sven Steinmo, *Taxation and Democracy: Swedish, British, and American Approaches to Financing the Modern State* (New Haven, Conn.: Yale University Press, 1993); Julian E. Zelizer, *Taxing America: Wilbur D. Mills, Congress, and the State, 1945–1975* (Cambridge: Cambridge University Press, 1998); Cedric Sandford, Chris Pond, and Robert Walker, eds., *Taxation and Social Policy* (London: Heinemann Educational Books, 1980); Michael K. Brown, *Race, Money, and the American Welfare State* (Ithaca, N.Y.: Cornell University Press, 1999); Paul Pierson, "The Deficit and the Politics of Domestic Reform," in *The Social Divide: Political Parties and the Future of Activist Government*, ed. Margaret Weir (Washington D.C.: Brookings Institution, 1998), 126–78.

50. Howard, *The Hidden Welfare State.*

51. John F. Witte, *The Politics and Development of the Federal Income Tax* (Madison: University of Wisconsin Press, 1985); W. Elliot Brownlee, *Funding the Modern American State, 1941–1995: The Rise and Fall of the Era of Easy Finance* (Washington, D.C.: Woodrow Wilson Center Press, 1996); Arnold, *The Logic of Congressional Action.* Arnold notes (p. 195) that between the origin of the income tax in 1913 and 1981, Congress voted to increase taxes only twice during peacetime.

52. *The Constitution of the United States*, Article II, Section 8.

53. Steinmo, *Taxation and Democracy*, 101

54. This comes out quite clearly in Howard, *The Hidden Welfare State*; and Zelizer, *Taxing America.*

55. Arnold, *The Logic of Congressional Action*; David R. Mayhew, *Congress: The Electoral Connection*, (New Haven, Conn.: Yale University Press, 1974); James T. Patterson, "Congress and the Welfare State," *Social Science History* 24 (2000): 367–78.

56. Alexis de Tocqueville, *Democracy in America*, trans. George Lawrence, ed. J. P. Mayer (Garden City, NY.: Anchor Books, 1969), 270.

57. On the pre–New Deal role of the courts, see, for example, Victoria Hattam, *Labor Visions and State Power: The Origins of Business Unionism in the*

United States (Princeton, N.J.: Princeton University Press, 1993); William Forbath, *Law and the Shaping of the American Labor Movement* (Cambridge, Mass.: Harvard University Press, 1991); and the discussion in Melvin I. Urofsky, "State Courts and Protective Legislation during the Progressive Era: A Reevaluation," *Journal of American History* 72 (June 1985): 63–91.

58. R. Shep Melnick, *Between the Lines: Interpreting Welfare Rights* (Washington, D.C.: Brookings Institution, 1994). See also Donald L. Horowitz, *The Courts and Social Policy* (Washington, D.C.: Brookings Institution, 1977).

59. Peter H. Schuck, "Legal Complexity: Some Causes, Consequences, and Cures," *Duke Law Journal* 42: 13.

60. John H. Langbein and Bruce A. Wolk, *Pension and Employee Benefit Law*, 3d ed. (New York: Foundation Press, 2000), 496.

61. *McGann v. H&H Music Co.*, 946 F.2d 401, 14 EB Cases 1729 (5th Cir. 1991).

62. Catherine L. Fisk, "The Last Article About the Language of ERISA Preemption? A Case Study of the Failure of Textualism," *Harvard Journal on Legislation* 33 (1991): 38.

63. Donald F. Kettl, *Government by Proxy: (Mis?)Managing Federal Programs* (Washington, D.C.: CQ Press, 1988); Kettl, *Sharing Power: Public Governance and Private Markets* (Washington, D.C.: The Brookings Institution, 1993); Lester M. Salamon, ed., *Beyond Privatization: The Tools of Government Action* (Washington, D.C.: Urban Institute Press, 1989); Harold Seidman and Robert Gilmour, *Politics, Position, and Power*, 4th ed. (Oxford: Oxford University Press, 1986).

64. Seidman and Gilmour, *Politics, Position, and Power*, 136.

65. Ibid., 392.

66. Skocpol, *Protecting Soldiers and Mothers*, 42.

67. On the distinction between "structural" and "instrumental" power, see Robert R. Alford and Roger Friedland, "Political Participation and Public Policy," *Annual Review of Sociology* 1 (1975): 429–79; Fred Block, *Revising State Theory: Essays on Politics and Postindustrialism* (Philadelphia: Temple University Press, 1987); Charles E. Lindblom, "The Market as Prison," *Journal of Politics* 44 (1982): 324–36; and *Politics and Markets: The World's Political-Economic Systems* (New York: Basic Books, 1977); and Jacob S. Hacker and Paul Pierson, "Business Power and Social Policy: Employers and the Formation of the American Welfare State," *Politics & Society* (forthcoming).

68. My formulation of this question is indebted to Stephen L. Elkin, "Pluralism in Its Place: State and Regime in Liberal Democracy," *The Democratic State*, ed. Roger Benjamin and Stephen Elkin (Lawrence: University of Kansas Press, 1985), 179–211.

69. See, in particular, Margarita Esteves-Abe, Torben Iversen, and David Soskice, "Social Protection and the Formation of Skills: A Reinterpretation of the Welfare State" (paper presented at the Annual Meeting of the

American Political Science Association, Atlanta, Georgia, September 1999); Colin Gordon, "New Deal, Old Deck: Business and the Origins of Social Security, 1920–1935," *Politics and Society* 19 (1991): 165–207; Gordon, *New Deals: Business, Labor, and Politics in America, 1920–1935* (Cambridge: Cambridge University Press, 1994); and "Why No National Health Insurance in the United States? The Limits of Social Provision in War and Peace, 1941–1948," *Journal of Policy History* 9 (1997): 277–310; Sanford Jacoby, "Employers and the Welfare State: The Role of Marion B. Folsom," *Journal of American History* 80, no. 2 (1993): 525–56; and *Modern Manors: Welfare Capitalism Since the New Deal* (Princeton, N.J.: Princeton University Press, 1997); Isabela Mares, "Negotiated Risks: Employers' Role in Social Policy Development" (Ph.D. diss., Harvard University, 1998); Cathie Jo Martin, *Stuck in Neutral* (Princeton: Princeton University Press, 2000); Cathie Jo Martin and Duane Swank, "Employers and the Welfare State" (paper presented at the Annual Meeting of the American Political Science Association, Atlanta, Georgia, September 1999); Peter Swenson, "Bringing Capital Back In, or Social Democracy Reconsidered: Employer Power, Cross-Class Alliances, and Centralization of Industrial Relations in Denmark and Sweden," *World Politics* 43 (1991): 513–44; and "Arranged Alliances: Business Interests in the New Deal," *Politics and Society* 25 (1997): 66–116. For the more traditional perspective, see, among many, Gøsta Esping-Andersen, *Politics Against Markets: The Social Democratic Road to Power* (Princeton: Princeton University Press, 1985); Walter Korpi, *The Democratic Class Struggle* (London: Routledge, 1983); Esping-Andersen, *The Three Worlds of Welfare Capitalism*; and John Stephens, *The Transition from Capitalism to Socialism* (London: Macmillan, 1979).

70. These accounts differ, however, on the crucial issue of whether employers themselves are responsible for creating this congruence or merely reinforce it once it exists, and they vary in the extent to which they believe that this congruence represents the active political influence of employers or merely the functional dictates of the economy, dictates presumably reflected in policy because elected politicians wish to encourage growth.

71. Peter Swenson, "Bringing Capital Back in, or Social Democracy Reconsidered."

72. The concept of the "scope of conflict" remains the greatest of E. E. Schattschneider's many contributions to American political science. See his *The Semi-Sovereign People* (New York: Holt, Rinehart, & Winston, 1960).

73. On the antistatist impulses of pre–New Deal welfare capitalism, see Andrea Tone, *The Business of Benevolence: Industrial Paternalism in Progressive America* (Ithaca, N.Y.: Cornell University Press, 1997).

74. Swenson, "Bringing Capital Back In, or Social Democracy Reconsidered"; Gordon, "New Deal, Old Deck."

75. As the department store magnate Lincoln Filene, a general supporter of a strong federal response, warned fellow businessmen: "It is a foregone conclusion that this whole question [of unemployment compensation], along

with other allied questions of economic and social security, will be placed before Congress by the President with definite recommendations which will unquestionably result in definite national action." Hearings before the U.S. Senate Committee on Finance, *Economic Security Act*, 74th Cong., 1st sess., 1935, 822.

76. This is particularly true of Peter Swenson, "Arranged Alliances." Although careful not to suggest that employer lobbying was directly responsible for the legislation, Swenson contends that New Dealers crafted their proposals around business interests in response to the "signals" sent by leading capitalists.

77. This points to a more general trap in political analysis: the temptation to read preferences off of outcomes. Sometimes this is warranted, but sometimes it is not. For example, the American Medical Association did not back Medicare even though physicians turned out to be "among Medicare's most prominent beneficiaries." This result was both "unintended" and "largely unanticipated." Theodore R. Marmor, *The Politics of Medicare*, 2d ed. (Chicago: Aldine de Gruyter, 1999), 83–84.

78. Nicholas Barr, "Economic Theory and the Welfare State: A Survey and Interpretation," *Journal of Economic Literature* 30 (1992): 741–803; Rebecca M. Blank, ed., *Social Protection Versus Economic Flexibility* (Chicago: University of Chicago Press, 1994); Geoffrey Garrett, *Partisan Politics in the Global Economy* (Cambridge: Cambridge University Press, 1998).

79. Evelyne Huber and John D. Stephens, "Welfare State and Production Regimes in the Era of Entrenchment," in *The New Politics of the Welfare State*, 107–45; and *Development and Crisis of the Welfare State: Parties and Policies in Global Markets* (Chicago: University of Chicago Press, 2001); Peter A. Hall and David Soskice, "An Introduction to Varieties of Capitalism," in *Varieties of Capitalism: The Institutional Foundations of Comparative Advantage*, ed. Peter A. Hall and David Soskice (Oxford: Oxford University Press, 2001), 1–68.

80. David Vogel, "Why Businessmen Distrust 'Their' State: The Political Consciousness of American Corporate Executives," *British Journal of Political Science* 8 (1978): 45.

81. Ibid., 51.

82. Mancur Olson, *The Logic of Collective Action: Public Goods and the Theory of Groups* (Cambridge, Mass.: Harvard University Press, 1965).

83. Hall and Soskice, "An Introduction to Varieties of Capitalism."

84. At the cost, in some cases, of higher levels of unemployment and steeper barriers to female labor force participation.

85. In the American states, for example, the proportion of employers offering private insurance coverage varies from more than 60 percent of firms in Hawaii (where coverage is mandatory), Rhode Island, Delaware, Pennsylvania, Connecticut, Massachusetts, and Michigan to fewer than 45 percent in South Carolina, Texas, Iowa, Louisiana, Oklahoma, Mississippi, Arkansas, and Montana. Estimates are based on data from the Health Care

Financing Administration, as prepared by the Office of National Health Statistics, Washington, D.C., 2000.

86. Classic works include Alexander Gerschenkron, *Economic Backwardness in Historical Perspective: A Book of Essays* (Cambridge, Mass.: Harvard University Press, Belknap Press, 1962); Barrington Moore, Jr., *Social Origins of Dictatorship and Democracy: Lord and Peasant in the Making of the Modern World* (Boston: Beacon Press, 1966); Samuel P. Huntington, *Political Order in Changing Societies* (New Haven, Conn.: Yale University Press, 1968); and, in a more methodological vein, Sidney Verba, "Sequences and Development," in *Crises and Sequences in Political Development* (Princeton, N.J.: Princeton University Press, 1971), and Arthur L. Stinchcombe, *Constructing Social Theories* (Chicago: University of Chicago Press, 1968).

87. Ruth Berins Collier and David Collier, *Shaping the Political Arena: Critical Junctures, the Labor Movement, and Regime Dynamics in Latin America* (Princeton, N.J.: Princeton University Press, 1991), 29.

88. Paul Pierson, "Increasing Returns, Path Dependence, and the Study of Politics," *American Political Science Review* 94 (2000): 251–67.

89. On functional explanations in the social sciences, see the classic essays of Carl G. Hempel, "The Logic of Functional Analysis"; and Jon Elster, "Functional Explanation: In Social Science;" both are reprinted in Michael Martin and Lee C. McIntryre, ed., *Readings in the Philosophy of Social Science* (Cambridge, Mass.: MIT Press, 1994), 349–75 and 403–14, respectively.

90. The distinction is made by Paul A. David, "Why are Institutions the 'Carriers of History'? Path Dependence and the Evolution of Conventions, Organizations, and Institutions," *Structural Change and Economic Dynamics* 5, no. 2 (1994): 206.

91. Verba, "Sequences and Development;" Margaret Levi, "A Model, a Method, and a Map: Rational Choice in Comparative and Historical Analysis," in *Comparative Politics: Rationality, Culture, and Structure*, ed. Mark Irving Lichbach and Alan S. Zuckerman (Cambridge: Cambridge University Press, 1997), 17–18.

92. Paul Pierson, "Not Just What, but *When*: Timing and Sequence in Political Processes," *Studies in American Political Development* 14 (2000): 72–92.

93. W. Brian Arthur, "Competing Technologies, Increasing Returns, and Lock-in by Historical Events," *Economic Journal* 99 (1989): 116–31; Arthur, "Positive Feedbacks in the Economy," *Scientific American* 262, no. 2 (1990): 92; Arthur, "Self-Reinforcing Mechanisms in Economics," in *The Economy as an Evolving Complex System*, ed. Kenneth J. Arrow and David Pines (Reading, Mass.: Addison-Wesley, 1988), 9–31; Paul A. David, "Clio and the Economics of Qwerty," *American Economic Review* 75 (1985): 332–37; Paul Krugman, "History and Industry Location: The Case of the Manufacturing Belt," *American Economic Review* 81 (May 1996): 80–83; Douglass C. North, *Institutions, Institutional Change, and Economc Performance* (Cambridge: Cambridge University Press, 1990). The major

challenge, centered on Arthur's work on technological standards, is S. J. Leibowitz and Stephen E. Margolis, "Path Dependence, Lock-In, and History," *Journal of Law, Economics, and Organization* 11 (April 1995): 205–26.

94. This is a principal aim of Pierson, "Increasing Returns, Path Dependence, and the Study of Politics."

95. For a trenchant argument along similar lines that emphasizes the logic of interplay between state, market, and the medical profession in health care, see Tuohy, *Accidental Logics*.

96. Oona A. Hathaway, "The Path Dependence of the Law: The Course and Pattern of Legal Change in a Common Law System," *Iowa Law Review* 86 (January 2001): 601–65.

97. James Mahoney, for example, places considerable – to my mind, disproportionate – emphasis on contingency in "Path Dependence in Historical Sociology," *Theory and Society* 29 (2000): 507–48. In fairness, however, his is an expansive definition of contingency, which encompasses events that are fully determined so long as they are not explained by the same theoretical tools used to explain path-dependent processes.

98. In other words, when "windows of opportunity" for policy change open is often a critical determinant of what emerges from them. John W. Kingdon, *Agendas, Alternatives, and Public Policies* (Boston: Little Brown, 1984), 193–200; Collier and Collier, *Shaping the Political Arena*; Pierson, "Not Just What, but *When*: Timing and Sequence in Political Processes"; Tuohy, *Accidental Logics*; Hacker, "The Historical Logic of National Health Insurance."

99. See, for example, Dennis C. Mueller, "First-Mover Advantages and Path Dependence," *International Journal of Industrial Organization* 15 (October 1997): 827–50; W. Brian Arthur, "Positive Feedbacks in the Economy," *Scientific American* (February 1990), 92–99; Elhanan Helpman and Paul Krugman, *Market Structure and Foreign Trade* (Cambridge, Mass.: MIT Press, 1985); Kenneth S. Corts, "Endogenous First-Mover Advantages," Harvard Business School Working Paper No. 99–113 (Cambridge, Mass., 1999); and the discussions in Pierson, "Not Just What, but *When*: Timing and Sequence in Political Processes," and Thelen, "Historical Institutionalism in Comparative Politics" – both of which cite a number of classic and recent works in institutional analysis.

100. This is either because moving first forces other "players" to accept outcomes favorable to the early mover (the game-theoretic formulation) or because first movers enjoy organizational and resource advantages that allow them to achieve a dominant place before other challengers arrive (the institutional formulation).

101. Thelen, "Timing and Temporality in the Analysis of Institutional Evolution and Change," 10.

102. These first-mover advantages can be understood in terms similar to those used to understand "preemption of policy space" in federal political systems, the process whereby "the enactment of policies at a decentralized

level may constrain the options available to authorities in the central tier." Paul Pierson and Stephan Leibfried, "Multitiered Institutions and the Making of Social Policy," in *European Social Policy: Between Fragmentation and Integration*, ed. Stephan Leibfried and Paul Pierson (Washington, D.C.: Brookings Institution, 1995), 22.

103. The most important theoretical thinking in this direction has been that of North, *Institutions, Institutional Change, and Economic Performance*.

104. The concept of "commitment" has received increasing attention in political science, particularly among students of monetary and fiscal policy. For an introduction, see Eric M. Patashnik, "Unfolding Promises: Trust Funds and the Politics of Pre-Commitment," *Political Science Quarterly* 112 (Fall 1997): 431–52.

105. Thelen, "Historical Instutionalism in Comparative Politics," 46–47.

106. Steven M. Teles, "The Dialectics of Trust: Ideas, Finance, and Pension Privatization in the U.S. and U.K.," paper delivered at the Association for public policy Analysis and Management (New York, 1998).

Chapter 7. The Future of the American Welfare Regime

1. Paul Pierson, *Dismantling the Welfare State? Reagan, Thatcher, and the Politics of Retrenchment* (Cambridge: Cambridge University Press, 1994); Fred Block, Richard A. Cloward, Barbara Ehrenreich, and Frances Fox Piven, *The Mean Season: The Attack on the Welfare State* (New York: Pantheon, 1987); Thomas Byrne Edsall with Mary D. Edsall, *Chain Reaction: The Impact of Race, Rights, and Taxes on American Politics* (New York: W. W. Norton, 1991); Paul Pierson, ed., *The New Politics of the Welfare State* (Oxford: Oxford University Press, 2001); Theodore R. Marmor, Jerry L. Mashaw, and Philip L. Harvey, *America's Misunderstood Welfare State: Persistent Myths, Enduring Realities* (New York: Basic Books, 1990).

2. C. Eugene Steurle, "Financing the American State at the Turn of the Century," *Funding the Modern American State, 1941–1995*, ed. W. Elliot Brownlee (Washington, D.C.: Woodrow Wilson Center Press, 1996), 409–44.

3. Author's calculation from National Income and Product Accounts, available online at http://www.bea.doc.gov.

4. Social Security Administration, *Annual Statistical Supplement to the Social Security Bulletin* (Washington D.C.: GPO, 1998), 140–42.

5. House Committee on Ways and Means, *1998 Green Book* (Washington D.C.: GPO, 1998), Tables I-11, I-12.

6. Congressional Budget Office (CBO), *The Budget and Economic Outlook: Fiscal Years 2003–2012* (Washington D.C.: CBO, January 2002), Table 1-2; Office of Management and Budget, *Historical Tables: Budget of the United States Government, Fiscal Year 1998* (Washington D.C.: GPO, 1997), 21.

7. Evelyne Huber and John D. Stephens, "The Politics of the Welfare State after the Golden Age: Quantitative Evidence" (paper presented at the

Annual Meeting of the American Political Science Association, Washington, D.C., 1997).

8. Jacob S. Hacker, "A 'Tax-and-Credit' Budget Shortchanges the Public," *Los Angeles Times*, 13 February 2000, M1, M6.

9. R. Kent Weaver, *Ending Welfare As We Know It* (Washington, D.C.: The Brookings Institution, 2000).

10. Between 1980 and 1993, the overall proportion of gross U.S. social spending that came from private sources rose from 28 percent to 35.5 percent. (These figures are not adjusted for taxes.) Although these trends have been uniquely prominent in the United States, stirrings of similar developments can be detected elsewhere. Willem Adema and Marcel Einerhand, "The Growing Role of Private Social Benefits," Labour Market and Social Policy – Occasional Papers No. 32 (Paris: Organization for Economic Cooperation and Development, 1998); Martin Rein and Eskil Wandensjö, eds., *Enterprise and the Welfare State* (Cheltenham, U.K.: Edward Elgar, 1997).

11. David Vogel, *Fluctuating Fortunes: The Political Power of Business in America* (New York: Basic Books, 1989).

12. David M. Ricci, *The Transformation of American Politics: The New Washington and the Rise of Think Tanks* (New Haven, Conn.: Yale University Press, 1993); David Callahan, *$1 Billion for Ideas: Conservative Think Tanks in the 1990s* (Washington D.C.: National Committee for Responsive Philanthropy, 1999).

13. Edsall and Edsall, *Chain Reaction*; Michael Lind, *Up From Conservatism: Why the Right Is Wrong for America* (New York: Free Press, 1996), chap. 1; Jonathan M. Schoenwald, *A Time for Choosing: The Rise of Modern American Conservatism* (Oxford: Oxford University Press, 2001); David M. Rohde, *Parties and Leaders in the Postreform House* (Chicago: University of Chicago Press, 1991); Gary C. Jacobson, *The Politics of Congressional Elections* (New York: Longman, 2001).

14. See, for example, Marvin N. Olasky, *Compassionate Conservatism: What It Is, What It Does, and How It Can Transform America* (New York: Free Press, 2000); Richard K. Armey, *The Freedom Revolution* (Washington, D.C.: Regnery, 1995); and Jack Kemp and Ken Blackwell, eds., *IRS v. The People: Time for Real Tax Reform* (Washington, D.C.: The Heritage Foundation, 1999).

15. See Daniel Yergin and Joseph Stanislaw, *The Commanding Heights: The Battle Between Government and the Marketplace That Is Remaking the Modern World* (New York: Simon & Schuster, 1998); E. S. Savas, *Privatizing the Public Sector: How to Shrink Government* (Chatham, N.J.: Chatham House Publishers, 1982); Jeffrey R. Henig, "Privatization in the United States: Theory and Practice," *Political Science Quarterly* 104, no. 4 (1989–Winter 1990): 649–70; Peter Self, *Government by the Market? The Politics of Public Choice* (Boulder, Colo.: Westview Press, 1993); Nicolas Spulber, *Redefining the State: Privatization and Welfare Reform in Industrial and Transitional Societies* (Cambridge: Cambridge University Press, 1997); Julian Le Grand, "The Theory of Government Failure,"

British Journal of Political Science 21 (1991): 423–42; and Carol Graham, *Private Markets for Public Goods: Raising the Stakes in Economic Reform* (Washington, D.C.: Brookings, 1998).

16. Lester M. Salamon, ed., *Beyond Privatization: The Tools of Government Action* (Washington, D.C.: Urban Institute Press, 1989).

17. Giandomenico Majone, "From the Positive to the Regulatory State: Causes and Consequences of Changes in the Mode of Governance," *Journal of Public Policy* 17 (1997): 139–67.

18. Pierson, *Dismantling the Welfare State?*

19. Nicolas Spulber, *Redefining the State*; Herman Schwarz, "Round Up the Usual Suspects! Globalization, Domestic Politics, and Welfare State Change," in *The New Politics of the Welfare State*, 17–44; Organization for Economic Cooperation and Development (OECD), *Privatization, Competition, and Regulation* (Paris: OECD, 2000).

20. Huber and Stephens, "The Politics of the Welfare State after the Golden Age"; and *Development and Crisis of the Welfare State: Parties and Policies in Global Markets* (Chicago: University of Chicago Press, 2001); Pierson, *Dismantling the Welfare State?*; Duane Swank, "Political Institutions and Welfare State Restructuring: The Impact of Institutions on Social Policy Change in Developed Democracies," in *The New Politics of the Welfare State*, 197–237.

21. It is generally agreed, however, that major retrenchment did occur in New Zealand and, to a lesser extent, Britain, with significant but smaller cutbacks in some continental European and Scandinavian nations. Paul Pierson, "Coping with Permanent Austerity: Welfare State Restructuring in Affluent Democracies," in *The New Politics of the Welfare State*, 431–56.

22. For a full understanding of the roots, character, and progress of these conservative reform strategies, we await the results of important research being done by Steve Teles of Brandeis University. I am grateful to him for allowing me to review his thoughtful research proposal, "Parallel Paths: The Political Strategy of Conservative Social Policy, 1975–2000," Brandeis University, March 2001.

23. Sylvester J. Schieber and John B. Shoven, *The Real Deal: The History and Future of Social Security* (New Haven, Conn.: Yale University Press, 1999), 263–89.

24. President, Address, "President's Commission to Strengthen Social Security, Establishment," *Weekly Compilation of Presidential Documents* 37, no. 18 (2 May 2001): 691–2; President's Commission to Strengthen Social Security, "Interim Report," Washington, D.C., August 2001; President's Commission to Strengthen Social Security, "Strengthening Social Security and Creating Personal Wealth for All Americans," Washington, D.C., December 2001.

25. Indeed, supporters of privatization sometimes describe their goal as setting old-age insurance back on the "road not taken" when the Clark amendment was defeated. Bruce Bartlett, "The Clark Amendment: What Social Security Might Have Been," National Center for Policy Analysis, 22 August

2001; Carolyne Weaver, *The Crisis in Social Security: Economic and Political Origins* (Durham, N.C.: Duke University Press, 1982).

26. *2001 Annual Report of the Board of Trustees of the Federal Old-Age and Survivors Insurance and Disability Insurance Trust Funds* (Washington D.C.: Social Security Administration, 19 March 2001).

27. Diverting two percentage points of payroll from Social Security into individual accounts would, for example, step up the date of exhaustion by roughly fourteen years under present Board of Trustees' assumptions. Henry J. Aaron, Alan S. Blinder, Alicia H. Munnell, and Peter R. Orszag, "Governor Bush's Individual Account Proposal: Implications for Retirement Benefits" (Washington D.C.: The Century Foundation and the Social Security Network, 6 June 2000).

28. The following paragraphs draw on Martin Feldstein, ed., *Privatizing Social Security* (Chicago: University of Chicago Press, 1998); Karl Borden, "Dismantling the Pyramid: The Why and How of Privatizing Social Security," *The Cato Project on Social Security Privatization*, no. 1, Cato Institute, 14 August 1995; Martin Feldstein, "Privatizing Social Security: The $10 Trillion Dollar Opportunity," *The Cato Project on Social Security Privatization*, no. 7, Cato Institute, 31 January 1997; Henry J. Aaron and Robert D. Reischauer, *Countdown to Reform: The Great Social Security Debate* (New York: Century Foundation Press, 1998); Peter G. Peterson, *Will America Grow Up Before It Grows Old?* (New York: Random House, 1996); Schieber and Shoven, *The Real Deal*; Peter J. Ferrar and Michael D. Tanner, *A New Deal for Social Security* (Washington, D.C.: The Cato Institute, 1998); and Michael B. Katz, *The Price of Citizenship: Redefining the American Welfare State* (New York: Metropolitan Books, 2001), 232–56.

29. On the misleading nature of the comparison, see John Geanakoplos, Olivia S. Mitchell, and Stephen P. Zeldes, "Would a Privatized Social Security System Really Pay a Higher Rate of Return?" *Framing the Social Security Debate: Values, Politics, and Economics*, ed. R. Douglas Arnold, Michael J. Graetz, and Alicia H. Munnell (Washington, D.C.: Brookings Institution, 1998), 137–57; John Geanakoplos, Olivia Mitchell, and Stephen P. Zeldes, "Social Security Money's Worth," *Prospects for Social Security Reform*, ed. Olivia S. Mitchell, Robert J. Myers, and Howard Young (Philadelphia: University of Pennsylvania Press, 1999), 79–151; Hans-Werner Sinn, "Why a Funded Pension System Is Useful and Why It Is Not Useful," NBER Working Paper, no. 7592, Cambridge, Mass., March 2000.

30. Critics of Social Security have at the same time challenged the notion that Social Security *is* income redistributive, pointing to alleged discrimination against minorities and the poor caused by their shorter average life expectancies. President's Commission to Strengthen Social Security, "Interim Report," 23–28. The evidence is overwhelming, however, that Social Security favors lower-income workers even after adjusting for life expectancy and other confounding factors. Although some minority groups do have shorter life expectancies than whites, these groups tend to have

lower average earnings, too, and therefore benefit from Social Security's progressive benefit formula. They also benefit disproportionately from survivors' insurance. Alan Gustman and Thomas Steinmeier, "How Effective Is Redistribution under the Social Security Benefit Formula," (paper presented at the Second Annual Joint Conference of the Retirement Research Consortium, May 2000); Julia Lynn Coronado, Don Fullerton, and Thomas Glass, "The Progressivity of Social Security," *NBER Working Paper*, no. 7520, February 2000; Aaron, Blinder, Munnell, and Orszag, "Perspectives on the Draft Interim Report of the President's Commission to Strengthen Social Security."

31. Making the accounts voluntary, as President Bush proposes, would actually make this problem worse, as private accounts are likely to be most attractive to higher-income workers.

32. Diverting two percentage points of the payroll tax into private accounts would, for example, increase Social Security's long-term liability by roughly $3 trillion – roughly the amount required to bring the system into long-term balance. Schieber and Shoven, *The Real Deal*, 366.

33. Of course, private accounts would compensate for some of these losses. Under assumptions quite generous to private plans, however, real benefit cuts for thirty-year-old workers would still be at least 20 percent. This estimate assumes that total benefits would be cut equally for all workers. Henry J. Aaron, Alan S. Blinder, Alicia H. Munnell, and Peter R. Orszag, "Perspectives on the Draft Interim Report of the President's Commission to Strengthen Social Security," (Washington D.C.: The Century Foundation and the Center on Budget and Policy Priorities, 23 July 2001).

34. Fay Lomax Cook and Lawrence R. Jacobs, "Assessing Assumptions about Americans' Attitudes Toward Social Security: Popular Claims Meet Hard Data" (paper prepared for the 13th Annual Conference of the National Academy of Social Insurance, Washington D.C., 24 January 2001).

35. Richard Kronick and Joy de Beyer, *Medicare HMOs: Making Them Work for the Chronically Ill* (Chicago: Health Administration Press, 1999), 1.

36. Marilyn Moon, *Medicare Now and in the Future* (Washington D.C.: The Urban Institute Press, 1993), 18–20; Annual Report of the Board of Trustees of the Federal Hospital Insurance Trust Fund, available at http://www.hcfa.gov/pubforms/tr/default.htm.

37. Joseph White, *False Alarm: Why the Greatest Threat to Social Security and Medicare Is the Campaign to "Save" Them* (Baltimore: Johns Hopkins University Press, 2001), 103–4.

38. CBO, *Historical Effective Tax Rates, 1979–1997: Preliminary Edition* (Washington D.C.: CBO, May 2001).

39. Henry J. Aaron and Robert D. Reischauer, "The Medicare Reform Debate: What Is the Next Step?" *Health Affairs* 14 (Winter 1995): 8–30; The White House, *A Blueprint for New Beginnings: A Responsible Budget for America's Priorities* (Washington, D.C.: U.S. GPO, 2001), chap. 5; Mark Merlis, *Medicare Restructuring: The FEHBP Model* (Washington, D.C.: The Henry J. Kaiser Family Foundation, 1999).

40. Adam Clymer, "Battle Over the Budget: The Strategy; Of Touching Third Rails and Tackling Medicare," *New York Times,* 27 October 1995, 21.

41. In 1997, to prevent further erosion, Congress stabilized the premium at a quarter of Medicare Part B costs.

42. Indeed, a primary selling point of the defined-contribution model from a budgetary standpoint is that to the extent that the government's contribution rises at some specified rate, it is relatively easy to predict what Medicare spending in the future will be. Joseph White, "Understanding Long-Term Medicare Cost Estimates," (Washington D.C.: The Century Foundation, 1999).

43. Century Foundation, *Medicare Tomorrow: The Report of the Century Foundation Task Force on Medicare Reform* (New York: Century Foundation Press, 2002), 27.

44. Richard Kronick and Joy de Beyer, *Medicare HMOs: Making Them Work for the Chronically Ill* (Chicago: Health Administration Press, 1999).

45. Marsha Gold, "Medicare+Choice: An Interim Report Card," *Health Affairs* 20, no. 4 (July/August 2001): 121–38; Theodore R. Marmor, *The Politics of Medicare,* 2d ed. (Hawthorne, N.Y.: Aldine de Gruyter, 2000): 144–45.

46. Thomas Rice, "Supplemental Insurance and Its Role in Medicare Reform," in *Medicare Tomorrow,* 189–218.

47. Marilyn Moon, *Medicare Now and in the Future,* 10–11.

48. Between 1979 and 1997, the real income of the poorest fifth of American households dropped by 1 percent, while that of the second and middle fifths rose by just 6 percent and 10 percent, respectively. By contrast, the real income of the top fifth of American households rose by half, and that of the top 1 percent by 157 percent. Congressional Budget Office, *Historical Effective Tax Rates: 1979–1997* (Washington D.C.: CBO, May 2001).

49. CBO, *Budget and Economic Outlook;* CBO, *An Analysis of the President's Budgetary Proposals for Fiscal Year 2002* (Washington, D.C.: CBO, May 2001); Joint Committee on Taxation, *Distributional Effects of the Conference Agreement for H.R. 1836* (Washington, D.C.: U.S. GPO, May 2001); Citizens for Tax Justice (CTJ), "Final Version of Bush Tax Plan Keeps High-End Tax Cuts, Adds to Long-Term Cost," Washington, D.C., 26 May 2001, available at http://www.ctj.org/html/gwbfinal.htm. According to the CTJ estimates, which are the only available ones that include the effects of the estate tax's repeal, 37.6 percent of the total tax cut would go to the richest 1 percent of Americans, 56.5 percent to the richest 10 percent, and 14.7 percent to the bottom 60 percent of the income scale.

50. American Council of Life Insurers, "'Most Significant Retirement Security Legislation in a Generation' signed by President Bush Today," 7 June 2001, Washington, D.C., available at http://www.acli.org

51. According to analyses of similar legislation, about 77 percent of the $50-plus billion in pension tax benefits that these provisions would provide over the next ten years would go to the top 20 percent of Americans. Peter R. Orszag, Iris Lav, and Robert Greenstein, "House-Passed Pension Changes

Would Overwhelmingly Benefit Corporate Executives and Owners: Provisions Could Lead to Pension Reductions for Low- and Moderate-Income Workers" (Washington D.C.: Center on Budget and Policy Priorities, 1 August 2000).

52. Rein and Wandensjö, *Enterprise and the Welfare State*, 12.

53. Important recent examples are Michael K. Brown, "Bargaining for Social Rights: Unions and the Reemergence of Welfare Capitalism, 1945–52," *Political Science Quarterly* 112 (1997–98): 645–74; Jennifer Lisa Klein, "Managing Security: The Business of American Social Policy, 1910s–1960" (Ph.D. diss., University of Virginia, May 1999); Tone, *The Business of Benevolence*; Katz, *The Price of Citizenship*; and Steven A. Sass, *The Promise of Private Pensions: The First Hundred Years* (Cambridge, Mass.: Harvard University Press, 1998).

54. Rein and Wandensjö, *Enterprise and the Welfare State*, 2. See also Martin Rein and Lee Rainwater, *Public-Private Interplay in Social Protection: A Comparative Study* (Armonk, N.Y.: M. E. Sharpe, Inc., 1986); and Martin Rein, Gøsta Esping-Andersen, and Lee Rainwater, eds., *Stagnation and Renewal in Social Policy: The Rise and Fall of Policy Regimes* (Armonk, N.Y.: M. E. Sharpe, Inc.).

55. See, for example, Florencio López-de-Silanes, Andrei Shleifer, and Robert W. Vishny, "Privatization in the United States," Harvard Institute of Economic Research Discussion Paper, no. 1723, Cambridge, Massachusetts, May 1995; David E. M. Sappington and Joseph E. Stiglitz, "Privatization, Information, and Incentives," *Journal of Policy Analysis and Management* 6 (1987): 567–82; and Rebecca M. Blank, "When Can Public Policy Makers Rely on Private Markets? The Effective Provision of Social Services," NBER Working Paper, no. W7099, Cambridge, Massachusetts, April 1999.

Appendix

1. Willem Adema, Marcel Einerhand, Bengt Eklind, Jørgen Lotz, and Mark Pearson, "Net Public Social Expenditure," Labour Market and Social Policy–Occasional Papers, No. 19 (Paris: OECD, 1996); Adema and Einerhand, "The Growing Role of Private Social Benefits," Labour Market and Social Policy–Occasional Papers, No. 32 (Paris: OECD, 1998); and Adema, "Net Social Expenditure," Labour Market and Social Policy–Occasional Papers, No. 39 (Paris: OECD, 1999). A concise summary of the preliminary findings can be found in Adema, "Uncovering Real Social Spending," *OECD Observer* (April/May 1998): 20–23.

2. Calculating the degree to which public benefits are subject to direct and indirect taxation is not easy and requires the adoption of sometimes controversial assumptions. The specific methods used by the OECD researchers are explained in Adema, "Net Social Expenditure," 20–26.

3. Tax breaks for private pensions and individual investment accounts – which are large for a number of nations, including the United States, but are

difficult to measure or compare across nations – are not included in the tax expenditure estimates in Table A.1. Because tax breaks for private benefits are excluded from the final tallies of after-tax spending (line 6) to avoid double-counting, this has no effect on the revised rankings. (Double-counting is a problem because these tax subsidies, by design, push up levels of private social spending and therefore show up in both the tax-expenditure estimates and the statistics on private spending.) If included in Table A.1, however, tax breaks for private pensions would substantially increase the value of social welfare tax expenditures for a number of the nations listed, most notably, Canada, the United States, the United Kingdom, and the Netherlands.

4. Adema, "Net Social Expenditure," 9.

5. This probably underestimates the degree of convergence. To avoid the possible double-counting that might result if both private expenditures and tax subsidies for them were included in the total, the U.S. total excludes the billions of dollars in tax expenditures that are lavished on employer-provided benefits, which amounted to 1.3 percent of GDP in 1995 (and more than that if tax expenditures for pensions are included). For lack of good comparative data, it excludes, as well, the substantial benefits provided, with government encouragement, by America's comparatively large "third sector" of nonprofit organizations and charitable service providers. Although the reasons for omitting these expenditures are sound, the effect is to depress the final estimate of U.S. spending and therefore the extent of convergence.

Index

adverse selection
  in annuities, 75
  in Blue Cross, 204
  in health insurance, 199, 236, 244
  in medical finance, 182, 183
AFL-CIO, 140, 224-5, 246-7, 255, 258.
    See also American Federation of
    Labor; Congress of Industrial
    Organizations
African-Americans
  health insurance and, 261
  pension coverage of, 107, 132-3
aged people. *See* elderly people
agency, in medical finance, 181
agricultural workers, 107
Aid to Families with Dependent Children,
    21, 317, 353n26. *See also* welfare
Aiken, George, 400n30
Altmeyer, Arthur, 110, 111, 130, 131,
    138, 211, 213-14, 246, 251
American Association for Labor
    Legislation (AALL), 91, 195-8
American Association for Old Age
    Security (AAOS), 91
American Association of Retired Persons,
    255
American Express, 88
American Federation of Labor (AFL), 90,
    127, 195, 233. *See also* AFL-CIO
American Hospital Association (AHA),
    203, 239, 245, 250, 400n30
American Medical Association (AMA),
    197-9
  federal government action and, 245,
    246
  hospital prepayment and, 205, 215
  Medicare and, 245, 409n135, 423n77
  national health insurance and, 224
  Social Security Act and, 206-7

tax breaks for health insurance and,
    239-40
voluntary health insurance and, 210,
    227-8
  See also medical profession; physicians
Anderson, Clinton, 407n115
Andrews, William, 350n11
annuities, 74, 75, 100, 105
antipoverty programs, 10, 21, 40, 278
  Social Security and, 144
  See also welfare
Archer, Bill, 157
Armstrong, Barbara, 102, 395n71
Arnold, R. Douglas, 42, 159
Arrow, Kenneth, 181
Arthur, W. Brian, 52-3, 349n40
Association of Life Insurance Presidents,
    105
Atkinson, Herschel, 137
AT&T, 117

Balanced Budget Act (BBA), 330
Ball, Robert, 143, 145-6, 147
Barkley, Alden, 369-70n74
Baylor University Hospital, 202
Beam, David, 386n112
Benna, Ted, 165
Bernstein, Merton, 148-9
Biemiller, Andrew, 140
Birnbaum, Jeffrey H., 386n112
Blackmum, Harry, 257
Blair, Tony, 275
blame avoidance, 282
Blue Cross, 202-6, 214-15, 216, 218,
    228, 242, 244, 245, 250, 284
Blue Shield, 205, 214, 215, 216, 228,
    242, 245, 284
Bradley-Gephardt tax reform proposal,
    161